THE COLONY OF GOOD HOPE

Kim Leine is a Danish-Norwegian novelist. His previous novel
to be translated into English, *The Prophets of Eternal Fjord*, was
shortlisted for the 2017 International Dublin Literary Award
and won the Golden Laurel Award, Denmark's leading literary
prize, and the Nordic Council's Literature Prize, awarded for
books published across all the Nordic countries.

Dedicated to Inge Kyst
– friend, first reader, mother-in-law

'And God tempted Abraham and said unto him, Take Isaac, thine only son, whom thou lovest, and get thee into the land of Moriah, and offer him there for a burnt offering upon the mountain which I will show thee.'

Søren Kierkegaard: *Fear and Trembling*

'Luther once read this story for family devotions. When he had finished, Katie said, "I do not believe it. God would not have treated his son like that."

"But, Katie," answered Luther, "he did." '

Roland H. Bainton: *Here I Stand. A Life of Martin Luther*

Contents

PART THREE: FATHERS AND SONS

PROLOGUE

The Skerries, Godthåb

I am Aappaluttoq, the Red One. I can go anywhere, as the priest says, albeit his words are scornfully meant, and yet it is true, as he well knows, though he will never admit it. For I possess a hole, not the farting hole or the eating hole, or any other hole the eye may see, but invisible, and through it I am able to vanish within myself, like an eddy which consumes its own current, and then I am able to release my spirit, my *tarniga*, that it may fly as I lie bound and unconscious on the ground. The body is the human's mortal envelope, but the soul may travel great distances through the air. I can journey to any place I wish. Not that it is easy. On the contrary, to wrench oneself free of the body is as painful as it is difficult and requires the most unflinching contempt for death, but once free there is nothing complicated about it. I can travel to the past, for the time that is gone still exists, in spaces adjacent to what we call the present, and one needs only to learn how to pass through its walls. The future exists too, in a way, though its spaces are as yet empty and therefore of little interest, unless emptiness is what you happen to be looking for. I once sat down in a space in the future and stayed there until the past came washing by, a great, slow wave of time. It was like seeing images cast up onto a wall, images in which I had no part. I can also travel to other worlds, strange places where everything is different. Perhaps God created countless worlds that exist alongside each other? Perhaps there is a world where people have three heads, and feet poking out of their backs so they can lie down when they walk? Who knows. I am not in touch with God, but I know that He is mine at least as much as He is the priest's. I believe in the Lord God, our Father, and I believe in His son Jesus Christ, whom I saw being nailed to the cross with long and crooked nails. I heard the moist sigh of the Saviour's flesh as the iron passed through it. I heard his groans and saw the soldiers draw on the ropes, raising his cross into the upright between the two criminals. I heard the scorn that was poured upon him. I saw the spears that prodded and poked. I have nothing against the Christians having come to this land. It is a good thing, I think, for being a savage is no laughing matter, I can attest to it myself. Something needs to change if we Greenlanders are ever going to enjoy a better life. What I do object to is the way in which they have come, and the way they behave here. We Greenlanders are better Christians than they, though we are not even christened.

///

I stand on the shore and watch the boat approach. A sail, four oarsmen, the priest and his two boys. In my arms I hold a boy child, the only one I have left. I know I must give him up. If I do not, he will die. His mother died a week ago, withered away, refusing to eat or drink, insisting on death, contrary to the last. It was her revenge on me. There was nothing wrong with her, apart from her not wanting to live. At least not with me. I held her, shook her, shouted at her, begged, pleaded and wept. But her mind was made up. All she did was smile. I curse you, you devil, she whispered, and turned her back on me. They were her final words.

But I loved you, I said, though I was speaking to a dead woman.

My boy's name is Paapa. He was ten winters old then. The other children died one by one. The boy and I were the only ones left. I had taken him with me to the small settlement of Danes at the mouth of the fjord. The priest there, Albert Top, Egede's helper at the time, taught us the Scriptures and prepared us for the Baptism. He taught us to read and write. Said the Lord's Prayer with us. But then a problem arose. Egede would not bestow on us the sacrament of Baptism. He thought us unready and believed that no sooner had we been baptized than we would go away and continue living as savages, thereby desecrating the holy sacrament. And so I took the boy, sat him behind me in the kayak and paddled away.

My wife was uninterested in the Christian message. She had not been with me when I was with the Danes, but took another man in my place. I killed that man – caught up with him at sea, dragged him from his kayak and cast him into the depths, so that he drowned. I brought his kayak home with me. It was a good kayak. Of course, it was not a Christian thing to do. Hardly even Greenlandish. But it felt good. Technically, I was not yet a Christian, and I had been a stranger among my own kind ever since my initiation. If the priest had baptized me, I would not have done it. And then I would have escaped the heathen darkness that has been my weakness as it has been my strength.

But no matter, for I fetched my wife and took her back to me, threw her in the dead man's kayak and dragged her to the settlement where my boy had stayed behind. I thought it would be good for us to be alone together, to reacquaint ourselves and forgive. But then she decided to die. And die she did.

I am Aappaluttoq, the Red One. It was the name I took when I came down from the fells with the wisdom within me. It is many years ago now. Before that, I was called something else, something so ordinary I can barely recall it, a name meaning grouse or fox, or something of the sort. But then I was initiated and took, or was given, a new name. I am an *åndemaner*, as the Danes call it. A shaman. To the Greenlanders I am an *angakkok*. What I know is beyond the knowledge of any other. What I know is something no one else even wishes to know. This is a fact. I know, for instance, that the Danes brought with them something greater and better than themselves: the Christian faith. A sorry ship may be laden with precious cargo.

When my wife died, the boy's health deteriorated. He would not eat the food I put in front of him. I despaired.

What is wrong with you? I asked. Why will you not eat?

She told me not to, the boy whispered through dry lips.

Who did?

Mother.

What did she say?

She told me to starve.

She told you that?

Yes.

Pallid, yellow skin. Dark shadows under his eyes. Skin and bone.

I did what I could. I tried to put food in him, but he pressed his lips together. He grew weaker by the day. Eventually he drifted into sleep. But his heart continued to beat, quick and erratic, a tiny thumping under cold skin. And then I saw the boat. An oared vessel with a staysail, the priest standing in the prow in his black cassock, and his two young sons. I went up and fetched the boy.

Egede jumps from the vessel as it scrapes the sand. He turns towards his sons.

Wait here.

He comes to me.

I know you, he says. Top taught you last winter.

I say nothing.

What is wrong with the boy? he asks.

He is sick, I tell him in Danish, which surprises him. I think he is dying. Will you take him?

He ignores the question, but says: The mother?

Dead, I tell him. Can the priest not take him? I know you take sick children and care for them.

Sick heathen children are a penny a pound, he says. A source that never runs dry. It is my wife who takes them in. It is her pleasure and pastime. However, I believe we are full up at present.

I am insistent. I step forward towards him with the boy draped in my arms. I hold him out to the priest.

Take him, in the name of Jesus.

He looks at the boy. I know what he is thinking. He is thinking of the Saviour brought down from the cross, and I can see it annoys him. He sighs.

Very well. In the name of the Lord then.

I lay the boy down carefully in the boat. But as I make to step inside myself, Egede presses the flat of his hand against my chest and pushes me away.

The boy only.

But I cannot be without him.

Egede shakes his head. You can come and see him. You know where we are.

And with that they sail away. I stand watching them until they can be seen no more. I return to the tent. I am alone in the world. Perhaps it is for the best.

A couple of months later when I visit the Danish settlement, I find the boy immediately. He has regained all health. I am overjoyed. But when I approach to embrace him, Egede intervenes.

What do you want? he demands. You've no business here.

I have come to collect my son, I tell him.

He is baptized now. He is a Christian. A good boy at that. He will be useful to me in the mission.

He places a hand on the boy's shoulder, as if to protect him from me. The boy and the priest look at me, and I look at the boy.

Go now, Egede says.

You cannot take my son from me, I tell him.

Frederik Christian, he says, looking my son in the eye. What is your wish? Will you follow your heathen father or stay here with me?

Paapa looks at me. His gaze is dark and solemn. He shakes his head.

There, you see, Egede says with a smile.

Frederik Christian? What name is that? I ask.

His Christian name, Egede replies. He belongs to me now.

I will come back for him, I say.

And I will have your arse riddled with shot, he tells me.

I return to the kayak and paddle home. I return several times in order to claim my son, but Egede remains adamant. I try to wrestle the boy from the man's grasp, but Egede punches me to the ground, and when I get to my feet blood is running from my nose. After that I keep away from the Danes for a long time. I stay at home. I must collect my strength alone.

Later, Paapa is confirmed. He grows up and thrives. I see him now and again, though only after some years have passed. There is no other way. Dear to us is but that which we have lost.

Long before a person dies, we grieve in anticipation. For all that lives must die. We grieve from the moment we are born. Even God must bear eternal grief, having sacrificed Him whom He loved the most. And now He takes it out on us people. Life is God's vengeance for the distress he brought upon Himself.

One might consider that since we grieve in anticipation through most of our lives we are then relieved when calamity eventually strikes. But we have no such luck. We discover that grief is but a prelude to more grief. A beast is born, the beast of Grief, and it writhes and squeals with pain as it is born into the world. For the beast of Grief has lain with itself, procreated with itself, and begotten itself.

When a person dies, we ourselves die too. We split open, and the river of death, whose name is Styx, runs through us like fire and ice. We are divided into two parts that may never be joined. Red Man/ Black Man.

PART ONE

The Grand Design

1

An Encounter in the Deer Park

Carried to the 64th latitude we found there a good and safe haven in what is known as the Baal's River on the western side of Greenland. Before we came to this land, approximately two miles from it, a number of Greenlanders approached us in their small boats. Here I saw the people for whose sake I had taken such hardship upon myself. Their first scrutinies put me in a disconsolate frame of mind, as they too indeed seemed disconsolate and pitiful; for what is more wretched than life without the knowledge of God? I could do nothing but sigh, on their behalves and mine.

FROM HANS EGEDE'S JOURNAL, 1721

On the afternoon of the second Friday after Easter, 16 April 1728, Copenhagen's old palace opens its mouth and shuts it again with a bang. A closed carriage rolls out, drawn by a team of two horses, a carriage without distinguishing marks or monograms of any kind, its curtains drawn. On one window's sill, beneath the curtain, rests a pale and dappled hand bearing a signet ring. On the box next to the driver sits a footman in black livery and hat, while on the small platform at the rear of the carriage stands a young groom, his long hair flowing behind him. The horses, two mares, are white like the palace from which they have just been disgorged. Horse hooves and iron-clad wheels clatter echoingly across the rickety wooden bridge that leads over the moat between the main building and the palace square, becoming a flat metallic thrum upon the cobblestones. The carriage careens through the slush as the driver flicks the whip, directing the horses into a left-hand bend made uncomfortably sharp by the limited leeway between the gate and the Chancellery buildings opposite, as well as by the traffic of coaches, handcarts and Amager wagons that busy about the square. Elegantly, if somewhat hazardously, it beats a narrow path among them, lurching on over the Højbro bridge to the square that is Amager Torv before grinding to a halt amid the general bustle that surrounds the market stalls. The two horses stamp impatiently. The hand in the window is withdrawn.

Did you see that? a young lad asks, dragging a handcart loaded with a pair of barrels towards a farmer, perhaps his father.

No. What? says the father.

It was the King.

You're seeing things, lad.

Didn't you see the ring?

The passenger inside sees and hears the exchange, but then they are gone. He smiles to himself. My subjects, he thinks. How strange they are.

The carriage continues towards the Nørre Port gate, and soon they are out in open country. The passenger with the signet ring draws the curtain to one side with the back of his hand and gazes out.

Spring, he thinks to himself in wonderment. The same miracle every year.

His mind still rings with the tones of the minuet his fool played for him on the clavichord as he changed into his riding dress. Its subtlety and elegance, but also its strict regularity. It is the kind of music that puts him in mind of the new architecture, though he is unsure as to whether he likes either. But still, the music is hard to escape once it has wormed its way into the mind. He moves his lips: *ba-da-dam, bam-bam ba-da-dam*, and then a trill that he imitates with a roll of the tongue. There, now I am smiling, he thinks. Who would have thought?

The winter has been long, a harsh and tedious cold, with much snow. Now the snow is retreating from the fields. Anemones and whatever they are – the names escape him – peep out of the ditches, and the beech is on the brink of coming into leaf. Already, cows and sheep graze at the roadside. The air is mild, though the lingering frost of night nips still. He finds the winters increasingly arduous, and every year when the season is at its darkest he finds himself in doubt as to whether another spring will be granted him at all. The year, or perhaps life itself, is like the hill of Valby Bakke. You haul yourself up it with much difficulty and exertion, eventually reach the top; and there, the light returns, the land lies open before you, and off you hurtle.

His head and body ache after having sat in conference all morning with the Privy Council, putting his name to resolutions, listening to the mind-numbingly meticulous reports of his ministers. Afterwards, the surgeon administered a cupping and an enema for good order, prodding and pressing his abdomen and enquiring about his rheumatism, then attended to his secret ailment, emerods, golden so-called, swabbing them with a pungent and abrasive tincture. Thereafter he was allowed to go. Now, in the Deer Park, his Grand Chancellor and friend, Count Holstein, together with his former page Henrik, stands waiting for him with the horses, ready for the hunt. A small, private occasion, not the public event of later in the year. Just him and his friends. He has looked forward to the day for weeks.

King Frederik is fifty-seven years old. He has survived the pox, wars, bubonic plague and a failed marriage. His face is furrowed, scarred by the pox, but his only real suffering is age, this slumberous state of which seemingly he cannot be rid. He has served his country as absolute monarch for nearly thirty years, exactly half his life. It wears him down. Previous sovereigns had things easier. They weren't as close to the people. He though must wade among his subjects and all their various problems from morning till night. And yet he is not unfond of it. The sense of his finger resting on the people's pulse. His working day is long, he travels the entire land inspecting regiments and construction projects, naming ships, opening institutions, cutting silk ribbons, sending criminals to gaol, pardoning others, wording, as good as single-handedly, the new ordinances that are put up on the gates and walls all about the land. People have no idea of the trouble it is to be absolute. He is his people's servant, a duty he takes seriously and of which, moreover, he is proud. But sometimes one has to get away.

The thing is, one cannot. Not properly. For wherever one goes, one's person is always in attendance, lugging with it its portfolio of problems, its every malaise and noxious effluvium. The self cannot be escaped. His fingers pick out a fan from the pocket of the carriage door. The Queen must have left it there. He flicks it open and fans himself, savouring the waft of scent, cloying and yet piquant. *Engelshjerte*, my angel heart. He loves her still. They have succeeded in maintaining a form of innocence in their love for each other. Whenever he creeps into her bed chamber, he feels he is about something forbidden. The thought excites him. He has barely touched another woman since they married. He married her twice, in fact, first left-handedly while Louise was still alive, then again immediately after her death. Perhaps it was too soon, yet it was important to cement her position. The thought of her still makes him lustful, her magnificent hips and thighs, the golden mound of her pubic hair that seems almost to float above her warm and fragrant sex. He smiles to himself as the carriage rumbles past scatterings of cows and goats. In the matter of children, however, she has been unfortunate, the poor woman. One after another they have died in infancy or early childhood. Louise, at least, left two, including his son Christian, the crown prince, the only person of whom he is truly afraid. Bad-tempered and sullen he is, smug and self-satisfied, always quick to claim the moral high ground. The Crown Prince despises his stepmother, the Queen, and most likely his father too. How will he conduct himself when I am gone? No doubt he will get rid of Anna Sophie at the very first. I must speak to him. Otherwise he will pull everything down that I have built up, and he will piss on my grave.

The carriage rattles and rolls. He must release a belch. His hand grips the windowsill. Now they follow the shore of the Øresund strait. Across the water lies the enemy. Skåne, the lost land. It was not my doing, he ponders. One may inherit land. Yet one may also inherit land that is lost. He sighs. At least Karl is dead. That's always something. The man who fired the bullet that struck the Swede king between the eyes ought to have been rewarded with his own estate. But no one knows his name. Most probably it was one of his own. The treacherous Swedes. They are the yellow of their flag. The blue is their simple-mindedness. A dangerous mixture.

His thoughts wander as the land drifts by. He thinks of the grand new colonization plan in which he has entangled himself. He has met all through the week with the Commandant Landorph and the Baron Pors, whom he has personally appointed governor of the colony, as well as with others who will be going with them. Together with his privy counsellor Hvidtfeldt he has drawn up a list of convicts, soldiers from Bremerholm, considered suitable as crew. He has spoken to several of them personally, probing them about this and that in the company of an officer. Of course, they have not been informed as to the nature of the plans being made for them. But they will be told in good time. If it should come to their ears that they are destined for Greenland, one would surely risk them absconding. That, certainly, would be his own impulse. He well remembers the Pastor Egede, who went there as a missionary some years ago with all his family, a wife and four children, and with whom he has since carried on a regular correspondence. A Norwegian, as unyielding as the rock of the country that bore him. He did not much care for the man, the great hook of his nose, the glare of his gaze, and yet felt him to be of the required substance and equipped for the task. Now all sails are set, and a new colony is being added to the Danish crown. Perhaps, if they are successful in their endeavours, it might make up for the matter of Skåne.

Egede sends him gifts from the place, among them a small figure of bone, a devil of some sort, carved by a savage. For some reason he carries it around in his pocket, often taking it into his hand and turning it absently until it has become quite smooth. It is his talisman. He dares not show it to a soul. It lies in his hand now. Such a hideous grin it has, he thinks to himself with a shudder of discomfort. Such sharp teeth and piercing eyes. It resembles evil itself, and yet is impish and fun. It is God laughing, he thinks to himself. And then, immediately: No, what nonsense. I should say the Lord's Prayer.

Perhaps there is gold there, he muses, stroking the figure with his thumb. Egede seems to suggest so. Perhaps also silver and copper, and iron too. Immeasurable riches. Shipload upon shipload of precious metals. If fortune is with me I shall be remembered as the king who resurrected our economy and restored greatness to Denmark. He must force himself to get a grip before he starts imagining streets paved with gold, processions in homage to him, regattas. We could do with a new palace, he thinks, rather more modestly. Certainly there ought to be money enough for that.

And then there are the heathens. He studies the figure in his hand. The savages. Not only must the economy be saved, there is also the matter of salvation in the life to come. How many Greenlanders must be living in savagery, yet to even hear of Jesus, not to mention be delivered in Him. Surely, if he were to be seen as the man who led an entire heathen population to salvation, his posthumous reputation in the eyes of God and men would be enhanced indeed. He drops the figure back into his pocket.

///

I am Aappaluttoq, the Red One. I am flying. My arms held against my frame, I thunder across the sky, and my hair is a comet's tail in my wake. I am two places at once. Lying in the peat-hut, bound by hand and foot, biting the bitter floor of soil, and nestled snugly in the King's inside pocket.

///

Frederik has always been terrified of hell. Especially when he was young and travelled around southern Europe leading a life of debauchery, his terror was sometimes unbearable. Nights of feasting, drinking and whoring, days of remorse and contrition. Later, after he married and became king, this fear of hell abated. Now it has returned to him as his death day approaches like a dark and relentless wave. And, in the nature of things, a king has much to do penance for, it is something that cannot be helped. The imperative of difficult decisions. Among them the matter of his failing Louise, his manoeuvring her into obscurity. No doubt she resides in her heaven now with no longer a care, rubbing her hands in glee as she awaits her reward, to see him hounded into the flames. He shifts uneasily at the thought and feels the hard nodule of his anus contract in spasm.

Why this tendency of his to think only of the most unpleasant matters? He has long since resolved not to torment himself with what he cannot alter. And yet it comes stealing.

I should have stayed in Italy that time, he tells himself. And married Teresa. It was not a sin, that which took place between us, or only a small sin at most. It was love. Everything else has been but failed attempts to carry out my duty. She committed herself to the nunnery, I to becoming king. It was my father who scuppered it, who destroyed my happiness. But no, I shall think no more about it. His hand reaches into his pocket for the figure again, but he forces himself to refrain.

He stares out at the iron sea, the feathery clouds against their background of blue. The wind has picked up. The chopping waves are tipped with white. The yellow hills of Skåne seem almost to smile at him kindly. Falsely immaculate.

He instructs the driver to turn down to the shore and pull up. He climbs out and pisses into a bush, inhaling the air of spring deep into his lungs. He walks on the beach with the carriage following on at a distance, the liveried footman a few paces behind. He gathers a small handful of the flattest stones and endeavours to skim them across the water, though clearly he has lost the knack, for they leap up as they strike the surface and then vanish immediately with a plop. The footman reminds him not to get his feet wet, for the weather remains chilly at this early time of year, and submissively he withdraws a step or two from the water's edge and walks on, sensing a calmness inside him for being here, between the sky and the sea, where a king is but a man. Reaching the Deer Park he makes sure to halt at the famous spring and swallow a cup of its invigorating waters, breaking the used cup against a tree as is the custom.

Henrik, the king's former page, a tall black man from the West Indies, born a slave though long since a deservedly free man, stands waiting for him at the hunting lodge. They greet each other heartily. Henrik has recently married, and the King jokes about their now infrequent meetings, for not even a king can compete with a woman. Henrik laughs good-naturedly. He is the same age as the King, though looks younger, a stately and elegant man. He wears a powdered wig with a pigtail, a tight-fitting blue coat of elegant cut and gleaming black riding boots with spurs.

Frederik looks at him. You were the finest jewel in my crown, he says. Why on earth did I get rid of you?

His Majesty bestowed upon Henrik the honour of marriage, the blackamoor says.

I should never have allowed it, Frederik replies. The bonds of Hymen must surely be more burdensome than those of the King. And Henrik laughs too, and bows deeply. They are physical in conversation, nudging and back-slapping, occasionally seeming almost on the verge of rough-and-tumble, as when they were children together and would roll about the floor. Now, though, they are too old for such behaviour.

A clamour of braying dogs comes from the kennel.

I hear the hounds are ready.

And hungry beasts they are too, Your Majesty. They have not eaten in two days.

Count Holstein joins them, leading his horse, a great black stallion, by the bit. Holstein was his page too in boyhood. Now he is Grand Chancellor. The dullest of worlds, where boys become grand chancellors and kings. Henrik disappears into the stables to fetch the king's mount.

How fat you've grown, Frederik says.

The word is stout, Your Majesty.

Do you think the horse can carry you?

It could carry a king, Holstein retorts.

I should never have made you Grand Chancellor. Not only are you fat, you are also impudent. How is the Grand Chancellor's wife?

Stouter, the count replies with a grin. And how is my king?

Well, he says.

Henrik appears with his white mare, Celeste. She recognizes him at once, and, knowing what his presence here means, whinnies with delight, tosses her head and rolls her eyes. He takes the reins from Henrik and holds her head in his hands, scratches behind her ear and places a kiss on her forehead. Have you missed your daddy, my girl? He climbs into the saddle and trots a couple of circles, wincing now and then on account of his tender arsehole. Henrik brings him a small silken parcel containing a cutlet of veal. Frederik raises himself and positions the cutlet between his buttocks, seating himself and shuffling it into shape as Holstein respectfully looks the other way.

Ah, that's better. It is a trick he learnt from Tsar Peter, a lump of meat between anus and saddle, to alleviate the discomfort of the haemorrhoids.

Gentlemen. Let the hunt begin.

The gamekeeper appears now with the bloodhound, and his helpers, equipped with convoluted hunting horns, follow on with the pack of hounds as yet leashed. The dogs quiver with excitement and can barely be held back.

Henrik has mounted his stallion. The King and his two former pages proceed towards the woods, side by side at a slow walk, so close together that their knees now and then touch as they follow the gamekeeper and his hound. They enter the trees. The dogs are well trained and know they must not bark. Quietly sniffing the ground, their snouts sweep over the bed of the woods as they pass on, and after a short time they are out of sight. The three men talk of this and that as they ride. An hour passes.

The gamekeeper returns and points. There. A fine stag. A splendid head of antlers.

Frederik waves his hand. Let the dogs loose.

The leashes are released. The hounds have the scent and stand at the ready, a front paw raised here and there in tremulous excitement. The horns are sounded. The dogs hesitate a moment and then tear away. Frederik and his two friends spur their mounts and follow on at a trot.

He has always been fond of riding. He was given his first horse at the age of five and took part in his first hunt aged eight. It was the only time he was ever really together with his father, a man who in all other situations was remote and elevated, and even later, when Frederik grew up, he found him unapproachable and felt he barely knew him, this man, the King, who would not involve his son in the governing of the realm, nor even call upon him to attend a meeting of the Chancellery. The matters of state were a mystery to him until suddenly his father met his death in that fateful encounter with the stag, here in this very park, and he, Frederik, became king from one day to the next, bound to manage all the affairs of the kingdom. A king is a lonely man. The only place in which he may find intimacy and affection is in the marital bed, and here, on the hunting grounds.

He stands with knees bent in the stirrups, anus lifted from the soggy cutlet, leaning forward a measure, careful to avoid the branches that whip back towards them as they ride, following Celeste's rhythm, delighting in the way she steers them so elegantly past all obstacles, and he tightens his knees around her girth as she prepares to jump, and encourages her with little words of love and devotion. The two others are ahead of them now, the path too narrow for three horses abreast. He sees them from the corner of his eye, hunched forward like himself. The deer, a fine specimen indeed, with splendid antlers, runs in great leaps and bounds, changing its direction all the time, the hounds snapping at its heels, though well knowing that they must not bite, but simply run the animal into the ground. Frantically they bay, and he hears how joyful they are in all their ferocity, and he too is heartened now, he feels himself godly and young again, as if not a single winter had been added to his age since he was twenty years old.

Now they emerge from the trees and the entire scenario opens out before him, Holstein at his left, Henrik to his right, the hunt attendants blowing their horns to excite the hounds, no matter that their efforts are clearly superfluous, and there, at the head, alone and condemned, the deer, its graceful movements which at once gladden him and move him to tears. For some obscure reason, the animal reminds him of himself.

///

Johan Hartman is twenty-two years old. He is enlisted in the Fynske Land Regiment but has granted himself leave in order to come to Copenhagen. Some would say he has deserted. It is a serious matter. A man could be sent to Bremerholm to be whipped and toil himself to death. The first two weeks in the city he spent drinking and whored himself senseless, squandering all his money. He then met a girl, Sise, a servant in a drinking house in Vestergade, a sewer of shoes and boots by trade, though circumstances forced her to serve in order to get by. In the daytime she plied her trade, sewing and mending, and in the evenings and nights she swung beer tankards and plates filled with stew across the counters and tables, supplementing her meagre income the way people do in such places. Johan had her now and then in one of the upstairs rooms. She was young and decent, ruddy-cheeked and healthy as a milkmaid, and with all her teeth intact. He liked that. Five marks, she demanded, and he would place the money in a bowl by the bed. The third time he went upstairs with her, he said he had no money left and moreover had no intention of paying her again. She yelled at him and made a commotion, and was about to call the landlady, but he managed to quieten her down and told her of the idea he had.

We'll move in somewhere together and start up on our own.

Why?

Because I like you.

But you don't even know me, and I don't know you.

All in good time.

All right, she said. But I won't lie with you for free. I've never lain with anyone for free. Only if they forced me.

I won't force you to do anything, he said.

And they shook hands.

They found a basement room in the Klædebo quarter and made a cobbler's workshop of it, where she sat between great piles of the stinking footwear people brought them, mending the broken leather she then treated with pig's fat, replacing heels, pulling out twisted tacks and putting in new ones, and when he came in to see her she would turn and smile at him with a row of tacks between her lips. He found her custom, of one sort as well as another. He made sure only men of some decency were allowed the pleasure of lying with her. They earned enough, but they were so young, and neither had ever learned to save and be sensible with money. For every five marks they earned, they spent ten. And thus it was that their debts grew as their income increased. They had to pay for laundry, materials and equipment, food and wine, bribes for the watchman, and of course the rent for the room. The landlord too had to be bribed, but when eventually they found themselves unable to pay two weeks on the run, they fell out with him and he reported them for running a brothel.

I want no more of that ungodly traffic, he told them.

Johan promised to find the money, but the man would hear none of it. The watchman, now in collusion with the landlord, came the same day and took Sise off to the Spinning House, which is to say the women's gaol in Christianshavn. And there she sits now. He dare not write to her, for he has deserted from his regiment on Fyn and risks being sent to Bremerholm.

He has wandered about for some days after Sise was taken from him. The spark he once felt is dampened now, and he cares not what is to become of him. His yearning for her is a physical hurt, and not even at the bottom of the deepest cup of ale is any relief to be found for such a hurt, all that may be found there is more hurt. It feels like the fear of death, mingled with anger. He thinks of her all the time, he sees her radiant and naked in his mind's eye, and he resolves that if ever he is reunited with her, he will never again give her out to unfamiliar men. He will take her with him to Germany, from where he hails, and there they will settle on a farm north of Hamburg.

He wakes up in a tree. The thought of where he is, however, does not present itself to him as he wakes, and although he has wedged himself well into a fork between two branches, the mere motion of waking is sufficient to dislodge him and he falls to the ground, befuddled by sleep, head heavy with drink. The earth is damp and cold. He feels certain he will become ill, perhaps succumb to pneumonia. Yet he remains there upon the mouldy earth, among rotting leaves and branches. The treetops are aflutter with birds. They sing and chirp. He reminds himself that it is the spring. Somewhere, he hears the sound of baying dogs. He is afraid of dogs, and scrambles to his feet, tilting his head to listen. But they seem not to be approaching.

He brushes the dirt from his clothes and pats his pockets. But he has nothing, not even anything to eat, and no longer a penny to his name. Where am I? Ah, the Deer Park. Now he remembers. A soldier friend brought him out here to the nearby pleasure garden, where he spent the rest of the money he had earned with Sise. It doesn't matter now, he tells himself. I am nothing without her. I might just as well go down to the Sound and drown myself.

He staggers on his way. Icy water seeps into his boots. He finds a path and follows it for a while. Hearing the baying hounds again he makes ready to leap into a tree. But then they are gone.

He wanders out onto an open expanse of land which slopes gently away towards the Øresund. He strides over its soggy ground, through the patches of snow that still remain here and there. Eventually he stops and turns. He looks towards the fringe of the woods. Is there a thunderstorm on its way? The sound he hears is indeed like thunder. But in April? No, he must be imagining things. He sniffs the air. Thunder is a thing that may be smelled. A fresh, metallic smell. If it is not thunder, then perhaps it is summer lightning. Or a salute of cannon from a ship. Perhaps the Swedes have invaded again. In which case, armies must be mobilized and he will be sent to the gallows if he fails to turn up. The gallows make a man famous. But the pleasure is brief.

All is quiet again. He walks on, only to hear behind him a sudden flapping in the air, and as he swivels round he sees pigeons alight from the treetops. Something must have alarmed them, for they are a long time grouping together again. Eventually, though, they find each other and angle across the sky to vanish behind the trees across the open land.

And then he hears the dogs again. This time it sounds like they are coming towards him. He stands a moment, his boots sinking into the sodden earth, and tries to work out from which direction they are coming, in which direction he should run. But he cannot move, he is petrified with fear, and all he can do is stand and stare towards the woods.

The first thing he sees is a stag come tearing through the scrub, hurtling towards him, a springing, zigzagging flight. Then come the dogs, a whole pack, snapping at its rear. They have yet to see him. But he realizes it is too late to run. There is nowhere to hide, and his boots are stuck. He doubles up, ready to protect himself with his arms, and then he catches sight of some men emerging from the trees, blowing their horns, and after them three riders side by side, with flowing wigs and gold-braided coats, one a black man of imposing proportion, upright in his stirrups. And now they come, a living nightmare, steering directly towards him, albeit seemingly more interested in the stag than in him. The hunted animal flies past, closely followed by the slobbering hounds, and he drops to his knees, arms above his head, in the midst of rippling canine muscle and fur. But the dogs charge past without noticing him, followed by the tramping hornblowers and, eventually, the three horsemen amid the thud of hooves.

He curls up on the boggy ground and lies there until the hunt has come to a halt, then gets to his feet to see the stag sunk to its knees under buckled legs, the dogs dancing about it, their thin tails thrashing as they bark and snap at the air. The three riders dismount and one of them, he recognizes him now, having seen him several times at the garrison on Fyn, draws his hunting knife, grips the stag by the antlers and cuts its throat. He signals to the dogs and immediately they throw themselves upon the now dead animal, tails whipping the air, tongues licking greedily the gushing blood.

Johan removes his feet from his helplessly entrenched boots and walks barefoot, as if drawn on a lead, towards the three horsemen. The blackamoor is the first to notice him.

Who are you? he says. What are you doing in His Majesty's hunting grounds?

I got stuck, he says, pointing back at the boots which protrude from the ground.

The two other horsemen, one of whom is the King, turn and look at him with curiosity. The King holds his glistening knife in his hand. His face is benevolent, satisfied after the kill.

Bow to His Majesty, says the blackamoor. Say your name, soldier.

He knows how pitiful he looks, barefoot, his clothes little more than rags, smeared with the green mould from the tree in which he slept, and yet he kneels, as proud as he is humble, swipes off his hat and bows to his king.

My name is Johan Hartman, Your Majesty. Enlisted in the Fynske Regiment.

The Fynske? says the King. Then what is he doing here?

Your Majesty, Hartman splutters, abruptly breaking down into a sobbing that feels utterly marvellous. It's a very long story.

///

He skins the stag himself, slicing out the innards and tossing them to the dogs. It is a most splendid bloodbath, a foul and delightful mess. Eventually, he mounts with the others and together they ride back to the hunting lodge where they partake of a good meal. He has invited the soldier to come with them. He has always been fond of such chance encounters with his subjects and finds it amusing to bestow on them unexpected privileges. The man stuffs himself. Clearly, he is hungry indeed. Now and then he lifts his gaze and looks across the table at the King. Frederik smiles back at him, lifts his glass and toasts.

What meat is this? the guest enquires.

Cutlet of veal, Count Holstein replies, fixing his smiling gaze on the man. How does it taste?

Delicious, Your Grace. I've never tasted such a tender cutlet in all my life.

The laughter that erupts around the table is friendly. He finds himself blushing.

A fire burns in the fireplace. The walls around them are decorated with portraits of family members, most of them dead. Frederik converses with his friends, jokes with them, listens to their versions of the hunt, contradicts them, a comradely banter. Their guest sits with a timid smile on his lips, wishing to join in, though lacking the courage. Not until they have finished the meal and he is seated with a glass of sherry does Frederik address him again: Let me hear now what you have to tell.

Afterwards, he allows him a lift into the city on the back of his carriage. He leaves him in the charge of an officer who is instructed on the King's order to accompany him to Bremerholm. Fair is fair. But the King promises to look closer into the matter with a view to finding a solution to Hartman's predicament, perhaps even bringing him together with his sweetheart again. Love is the most beautiful thing of all in life, for a king as well as a soldier. It humbles us all and makes us equal.

Come to think of it I may already have the answer, he says, his hand curling around the bone carving in his pocket. And for your fiancée too. Be patient, my friend, and you will hear of it.

With that, he takes leave of the soldier and drives home to his dearest angel heart. He places the figure on the bedside table, but his queen does not care for it, it frightens her, and she tosses it into the drawer.

So now I lie in darkness. Now I wake.

Where have you been, Red, my fellows wish to know, laughing as they loosen the straps with which they have bound me. Far away, eh?

To the other side of the sea, I mutter. Give me something to eat.

2

Couplings

Of other notable perceptions regarding my discourses with the Greenlanders on matters religious, I found in them a great eagerness to listen and be instructed therein. In particular they found much delight in considering the biblical illustrations I had taken with me in order to explain to them in a rudimentary way what I could not say in words. They declared a complete belief in what I told them about God, taking pleasure above all in hearing of how God's son was to return and resurrect the dead who believed in and loved and feared God, and take them with him into Heaven.

FROM HANS EGEDE'S JOURNAL, 1723

Monday, 19 April, early in the morning, Hyskenstræde, Copenhagen. Claus Enevold Pors, forty-five years old, formerly major with the free company at Trondheim, farm owner from Vendsyssel, who, with immediate effect, and completely out of the blue, has been named Governor of the planned colony in Greenland, lies in his bed, massaging the feet of a young wench he picked up on his way home a couple of hours before. He stares at the rich cunt which seems almost to glow darkly as a lump of coal where her fleshy thighs meet, and approaches it, crawling up the mattress on his stomach. Normally it works. But not today. He groans in despair.

Skård! he calls out. Help me, Skård!

The woman hears this as an exclamation of excitement and says something come-hitherish and wenchlike, which only makes him even more limp.

Pors groans impatiently. Skård, are you there?

But his servant is not there.

He pulls on his member, inhales the sweet, vinegary odour of the woman's feet, bends her legs backwards, she willingly drawing them up underneath her to spread her cunt, which opens to send him a vertical grin, her buttocks parting to reveal her anus. Dark star, he thinks to himself and touches it with the tip of his index finger. No, more pinkish perhaps. An odour of ambergris and musk wafts towards his nostrils. His finger slips inside her and the woman gives herself to him. It ought to help, and yet it does not. Her cunt smells of seaweed, warm and inviting. He grunts ill-temperedly. What's wrong with me? he wonders. I, who am always erect in the mornings, even without a woman. It is, in fact, at this time Skård must come.

On the staircase an elderly man with long white hair and frosty eyebrows is on his way up to the bel étage from the ground floor with a sealed envelope in his trembling hand. The man is the Major's manservant, an Icelander by the name of Skård Grimsson, a servant of the Pors family for some twenty years, firstly to the former gentleman of the house, the now deceased bankrupt, subsequently to his son. He has not heard that his master was out this night and has come home with a wench, and assumes that he is in his bed asleep. Skård is accustomed to assisting the Major with his morning toilet, comprising, besides washing and towelling and the application of ointments, a hasty tossing off. The latter act has been recommended to him by a physician, so Pors has explained, a hygienic precaution in order to avoid confluence and acidification of the fluids, and since masturbation is a sin that may lead to all manner of calamity, including both consumption and melancholy, it has been bestowed upon Skård to ensure his master's relief. He has little against it. Work is work, and achieving excellence in one's chosen field will forever be a matter of part discomfort, part satisfaction. Besides, for this particular service Pors remunerates him with a commission.

But now there is an envelope, sealed with red wax, delivered only shortly before by a messenger from the palace.

Skård reaches the landing and pauses outside the door, gasping slightly for breath, evacuating his nose methodically, index finger against first one nostril, then the other, narrowing his eyes and peering with satisfaction after the globs of mucus that have been expelled to the floor and smearing them into semi-oblivion under the sole of his boot. Then he knocks hard on the door.

A letter for the Major!

Pors groans despairingly from within. Can it not wait?

It's from the King, I reckon, Skård says to the door.

He rolls out of bed, his member at last come to life. Promptly it has reacted to the sound of Skård's voice, like a small dog which hears his master's call and eagerly springs in the air. He crosses the floor with it bobbing in front of him and opens the door.

Skård, long since used to seeing the Major in his present state, is not the slightest bit embarrassed by the sight. He leans forward and peers into the room to see the woman lying naked on her back.

Ah, I see, he says. But there was this letter. He puts out his hand with the sealed envelope balanced on his upturned palm.

He should not have been so frivolous. Pors realizes immediately that the sight of Skård's calloused hand is more than his member can endure, and before he can take the letter he has splashed it with sperm.

///

Skård fetches water and assists him in dressing. Amid his manservant's meticulous attentions, Pors tears open the letter and reads. For the first time, he is addressed in writing as Governor. Splendid! His member almost rises again. The letter summons him to the Garnisonskirke at noon in full uniform. The offenders who are to make up his crew in the colony these next many years are to be brought together in matrimony.

Go in and wake Titia, he says to Skård. He wishes her to go with him to the church.

Skård enters the adjoining room, but returns almost immediately.

The jomfru is risen, he says. However, she seems to be unwell.

Pors's young housekeeper appears in the doorway.

Well, come in, then, he says. No reason to be shy.

The girl enters and sits down on a chair. She looks sideways at the as yet half-naked Pors, then at the woman in his bed.

Good morning, she says.

Slept well, my girl? says Pors.

There's too much noise from the street, says the jomfru Titia. I'm not used to it. The watchman has kept me awake with his hourly verse.

Noise is a part of the city, Pors tells her. Enjoy it while you can. You'll miss it where we're going.

Who's that? Titia asks.

My betrothed, says Pors. What was your name again?

Sise, says Sise from the bed. My father's name was Hans. But they call me Sise Petticoat.

Do they indeed? Well, Sise *Petticoat* Hansdatter, allow me to introduce my housekeeper, Titia. She is from Køge, and before that from darkest Germany. She is new in the city. You could teach her a thing or two, I should imagine.

Nothing that'd do her any good, says Sise.

Pors feels a need to boast of the letter he has received from His Majesty. He waves it in the air. Do the ladies know what this is?

I can't read, says Sise.

Then let me tell you. This, he says, is grand politics. Are you aware of who I am?

Isn't he an admiral or something? Sise ventures in the formal third person, resting her foot on top of her bended knee and scratching her ankle. Titia glares at her but says nothing.

Admiral! he repeats with a good-natured chuckle. The girl is ignorant indeed, Titia. Though not without her charms, certainly. No, my fine friend, this is a letter from the King. He hands it to Titia. It is His Majesty's most gracious wish that I shall be master of a new land. Greenland. Do you know of Greenland, my girl?

I might have heard of it, Sise says obligingly.

You will know of it presently, I assure you. We are writing history today, little Sise. You and I, and Skård, and young Titia here.

Not me, says Sise. I can't read or write.

Then you may tell your grandchildren of it.

He paces back and forth a moment, washed and smelling of ointment. Titia sits poring over the letter. He halts in the middle of the floor.

I am to be a kind of king myself, you see. King of Greenland! A fine thing indeed to tell the grandchildren, that you, Sise, were betrothed to the King of Greenland, and you, Titia, were his housekeeper. Quite something, eh, wouldn't you agree?

Sise sits up on the edge of the bed. I want my five marks.

For what? says Pors. For lying in my bed and doing nothing? No, spare me the looks. He cannot help but laugh at the sight of the sour face she puts on. You shall have your five marks and more besides.

He considers himself in the great mirror. Skård dances about him and hums as he attends. Titia shifts on the chair. The sun of morning falls into the room. It looks like a lovely spring day, the manservant says.

A good day to be married, says Pors.

Are we to be married? Sise says. I tell you I won't.

Not to me, you foolish girl, Pors replies.

My poor old father, bless his soul, always said the best day for a marriage was the thirtieth of February, Skård says.

Ha ha, most amusing, Skård, says Pors.

February hasn't got thirty days, Titia points out.

Exactly, says Skård. To me, every day is the thirtieth of February.

The old man lies down on the bed, Sise rising to make room for him. He lies on top of the covers with his boots on, folds his arms behind his neck and proceeds instantly to snore.

Poor old fella, says Sise. He must be exhausted.

Rather like an old hunting dog with no use left in him, says Pors. One hasn't the heart to put him out of his misery.

I don't think it's allowed, says Titia.

Pors turns to face her. You look like a street girl who's been working all night, he says, discontented. What's the matter with you?

I don't feel well, the jomfru says. I think I'll go to bed again.

You will not, you're going to church, Pors tells her. He looks at Sise and explains to her: the jomfru Titia is a kind of papist, you see. She doesn't much care for the Danish churches.

That's not why, Titia says, staring darkly into the air in front of her.

I see, says Pors curtly. Moral despondency, then?

I really don't feel well. I need to go to bed.

Then get you to bed, Pors snaps, turning away from her. But you, he says, his eyes now on Sise. You are a pretty one this morning. Such delightful colours. He holds her face between his hands and turns it to the window. Apple cheeks, golden hair, and such a fine, red and pouting mouth. In this light I can properly see you now. In fact, I may not be finished with you at all.

Goodnight, says Titia. I'm going for a lie down.

The gentleman can go down the Dragoon and find me when he wants, says Sise. That's where I am.

No, I have other plans for you now. Your presence is called for. Put your clothes on and come with me to the church.

The church? On a Monday?

Have you something more important to be getting on with?

I need to find my fiancé. I've lost him.

You mean someone like you is engaged? To what kind of a fellow, one wonders?

He's a soldier.

Soldiers come by the dozen. We'll find you a new one.

But he's mine. We're getting married. He said so himself.

Come on, Pors says impatiently. Put on your petticoat, Sise, and no more splitting hairs. The King himself has asked me to find you.

The King? she says. I don't know no king.

Well, it seems the King knows you, says Pors. And he wants to see you at the Garnisonskirke in an hour.

///

Sise has been looking for Johan since last Friday when they let her out of the gaol. A couple of days it came to before they threw her out for lack of room. Since then, she's been going about the city asking after him in places she knows he frequents. It's been like chasing a shadow. He was here not long ago, they tell her, he was here last night and was asking after you. But then on the Saturday night she loses the scent. She was scared something had happened to him, and so she went to the Dragoon in Vestergade. Someone came and called her name out, an old man with a mane of white hair. Sise Petticoat! Is there a Sise Petticoat Hansdatter here?

That's me, she said. Am I to be taken to the Spinning House again? Can't they make up their minds?

You're a lucky girl, said the man. You've been chosen.

For what?

You'll find out soon enough. My gentleman wants to speak to you. Come with me.

And so she came here to the house in the Hyskenstræde. She hadn't a clue what was going on. And then all it was was a fine gentleman who wanted to lie with her. But she still hasn't got a clue what's going on. Something's happening that's got something to do with her. And there's nothing she can do about it.

Now she accompanies the fine gentleman through the city. She is clad in a loosely hanging dress. On her head she wears a cap of flax with a brown bonnet tied under her chin. On her feet are a pair of well-worn clogs. The man in front of her is in a golden uniform with braid and a very splendid three-cornered hat from whose top a feather bobs. At his side he wears a sword that drags and hops along the cobbles in his wake. He resembles mostly a king's cavalryman. People turn and stare. Here and there, she is recognized. Has Sise found herself a new sweetheart? they enquire. She picks up her skirts and stumbles on at the man's heels. Occasionally he glances over his shoulder to see if she is still there. She could quite easily slip down a side street and be gone, for finding Johan is still foremost in her mind. Yet she is gripped by a doggish kind of submissiveness that compels her to follow along with this man she barely knows.

Outside the church, an astonishing throng of people and carriages is gathered. Fine carriages, too, among them, and immediately she spots the King and Queen only paces away, walking arm in arm towards the entrance. Someone shoves her forward and all of a sudden she finds herself before the royals. She lowers her eyes to the ground. The King speaks. Ah, a good job we found her, Pors. Otherwise we'd have been forced to take another. Lord knows, there are plenty, but I promised the young man I'd find this Sise, and I should very much like to be a man who kept his promise. She doesn't understand a word of it, and before she can ponder the matter she is nudged inside the church and steered to a seat on the left along with some other women. She recognizes several from the Spinning House. They greet her gladly. So, you're here too? What's happening, do you know? Why have they sent us to church? Are we to repent our sins again? Sunday was yesterday, wasn't it?

I don't know, she says. I don't know any more than you. They forced me here.

To the right sit the men, soldiers all. They seem rather dishevelled. They're from Bremerholm, says the woman on Sise's left. Convicts. Terrible scoundrels. They could certainly do with a sermon.

There is a rustle of skirts all around as the King and his entourage enter the church, the Queen with a long train trailing behind her, the King in uniform. The priest receives them with a deep bow, then kneels to kiss the hand of the Queen. The royal couple seat themselves in front of the altar, and again the skirts rustle among the congregation. A service begins. The organ plays. A hymn is sung. The priest speaks, his voice thin and feeble in the church's great interior. He says a prayer.

Sise sees none of it, and hears nothing, for she has noticed Johan on the other side of the aisle, with the other convicts.

Johan! she exclaims. The men turn and look at her. Desperately, she waves. Johan! His neighbour nudges him, and now he turns and sees her. His jaw drops.

You, here? he mimes.

Someone shushes. She looks at him questioningly. What's going on? He shrugs his shoulders and shakes his head.

She looks up at the altarpiece, where the Saviour is nailed to the cross, knees together as if he needed a pee. She wonders if there is anything under the loincloth. A wooden dick? She shakes her head and feels completely out of sorts. Do the King and Queen do it with each other? She's been with so many men, more than she can count. And she doesn't even like it. To her it's a job. When she lies down to sleep they come somersaulting, one after another. They never leave her alone. In a way it was a relief to be sent to the gaol. There, at least, she can escape having to lie with all these men. But the food is not good. The Dragoon is better on that count, she must concede.

Dear Jesus, she prays. Help me. And she folds her hands together and feels herself crying.

The woman on her left, Maren Black-hat, digs an elbow in her side. Dry your tears, love. We're to be coupled with the scallywags over there. A mass wedding.

Who?

The Bremerholm lot. Didn't you hear what the priest said? They're sending us to the colonies, two by two. Like the animals.

Oh, she says. But I won't.

Try saying no, Maren says with a grin.

Sise presses her face to Maren's shoulder, and Maren pats her cheek. They hold hands. She looks sideways towards the male convicts. Soldiers, all of them, redcoats with whom the city is brimming, many of them regulars at the Dragoon. They glance about and look just as perplexed as the women.

Now it begins. A woman, a lady-in-waiting perhaps, plunges her hand into a leather pouch held out by the verger and pulls up a scrap of paper. She smiles gleefully and calls a name out into the church. One of the men gets to his feet slowly and approaches with hesitant steps. Are you Johan Furst? the priest asks. Yes, mumbles the soldier. The priest takes his arm and stands him with his face to the congregation. A young man of the court dips his hand into another pouch. He shouts out a woman's name: Johanne Nielsdatter. She steps up and is placed next to Furst. The next woman to be called out is Maren Black-hat, to be coupled with one called Franz Glitker, a German. She pulls a grimace and gives Sise a pat of encouragement as she gets up. Jauntily, she strides down the aisle, stands next to her man and places her arm in the crook of his elbow to rapturous shouts from the pews. One couple after another is brought together in the same way. The pews to the left, where Sise sits, become empty. She looks across the aisle and sees that Johan too remains. And now the man and the woman who have been drawing the names seat themselves again. We're not going, she thinks to herself with a mixture of relief and disappointment. But then what are we here for?

The King rises, the Queen also.

Will Sise Hansdatter now approach? he says.

She sits there as if paralysed and gapes at the King.

No, thanks, she croaks, though fortunately no one hears.

Step forward, my child, says the King. He holds out his hand. Someone nudges her from behind and she gets to her feet and walks forward, her clogs clacking against the stone. The King takes her hand.

She is Sise Hansdatter, called Sise Petticoat?

Yeah?

Do you know that your king loves you, Sise?

The King knows me, then?

The King loves all his subjects, even the lowest of the low.

She stands with her head tipped back, staring up at the sovereign who gleams with gold and braid. Behind his shoulder hangs Jesus on his cross.

But there is another who loves you, says the King.

Is there? she says, her head quite empty. Who in the world can it be?

The King turns towards the Queen, who calls out: Approach, Johan Hartman.

Johan springs to his feet and edges his way into the aisle. He comes towards her and she reaches out her hand and holds onto him.

Where have you been, you swine? she whispers. I've been looking for you everywhere.

Shh, he says.

Let the wedding begin! says the King.

The priest commences the ceremony. He addresses each couple in turn. The offenders utter their I do's and one after another are declared man and wife until death them do part. But when he comes to the end of the row, to Johan and Sise, she is no longer sure. She feels all eyes are upon her, even the King's and the Queen's. She feels her legs will give way beneath her. Johan tugs discreetly at the sleeve of her dress. But she cannot speak the words. They're stuck.

Do you not want me? Johan asks.

I don't know, she says. It's all so sudden.

But the priest makes short work of it and declares them married nonetheless, the same as the others. Sise feels relieved that there is something greater than herself which has made the decision on her behalf. But leaving the church, Johan must almost drag her with him. And when the bells begin to peal in the tower, she feels everything go dark.

///

The twelve newly wed couples are driven out of the city by farmer's cart to an inn on Vesterbrogade called the Hope. Places have been set for them at a long table. Busy waiters come in, the steam from their serving dishes and tureens whirling in the air behind them. At the head of the table sits Claus Enevold Pors. His housekeeper, the jomfru Titia, has been collected by carriage and is seated further along. She is bleary-eyed with fatigue, or whatever is the matter with her. As long as she causes no trouble, Pors thinks to himself. I promised the apothecary to take care of her. He brings a toast and surveys the men and women in front of him. Most are only half his age. My God, he thinks. What a rabble.

To his right sits Ole Lange, one of the two missionaries who are to be deployed. He too looks exceedingly young, newly fledged and with blooming cheeks, he looks more like a candidate for the confirmation. To Pors's left sits Jørgen Fleischer, the Paymaster, a man with red hair beneath his wig and oblique, piercing eyes, for which reason he is known as Fox. He looks dishonest, Pors thinks. Look out for him. Diagonally across from Fleischer is Jürgen Kopper. Kopper has been appointed Trader of the new colony. A face like a horse's. Has he got a bad stomach? An abject-looking man, if ever there was one, though at least reliable.

Some soldiers from the garrison are present to keep order among the released offenders. Technically, the King still retains the power of life and death over them and they are to be returned to the garrison and locked in as soon as the feast is over. They sit outside, in a closed courtyard. The sun angles down on the food, on the men and women. Pors holds them in his gaze, studying them one by one and repeating their names. There is Peter Hageman, now married to the one they call Cellar-Katrine; there, Christopher Falck and his new wife, Filthy

Ane; Johan Hintz and his Ane Woollen-sock; Frantz Glitker and Maren Black-hat; Christian Peyn and, what was her name again, Jewish Karen; Hans-Henrik Wiencke and Maren of the Pots; Bernhard Meyer and Screaming Margrete; Georg Weerback and Wispy Kirstine; Johan Furst and Johanne Long-stocking; Johan Bretel and his Ane of the Muck-heap; Peter Mogensen and Stiff Lise; and there, Johan Hartman and the prettiest of all the girls, Sise Petticoat. I am not finished with you, Sise Petticoat, Pors says to himself.

///

Sise still feels weak after her fainting in the church. She wishes she could rest in a bed.

I've not said I do yet, she says.

But the priest wedded us, you heard him, says Johan.

You've got to say I do. To God. It doesn't matter what the priest says. Don't you go believing you've got me just because the priest said so.

Johan shakes his head. I don't understand women. It was all you could talk about for weeks.

Sise looks down the table. Many of the men are already groping their women, who don't seem to be minding much. She glances at Pors at the table end. He sees her, lifts his glass and smiles. She winces, yet lifts her own and toasts. She thinks of the old manservant with the lovely white hair and his eyebrows like the morning frost. What's he doing now, she wonders. Maybe still snoring in the Governor's bed. The lucky devil, she yawns.

Congratulations on your lovely wife, Pors says to Johan. You can hardly be dissatisfied there. Are you not going to kiss her?

He tries to extract a kiss from her, only she twists away from him.

Hard to get, eh? says Pors. Kiss him, for goodness' sake. He's your husband! Otherwise I'll come and do it myself.

She gives in, and Johan's soft, moist mouth touches hers. She bursts into tears and the women from the Spinning House, her friends, cheer.

A long and happy life! Pors declares, getting to his feet.

They repeat the toast all down the line: A long and happy life!

Hurrah for King Frederik the Fourth!
Hurrah for the King!
Hurrah for Greenland!
Skål!

Pors gives a rather lengthy speech of which Sise understands little, only that it concerns them being the first inhabitants of a new country, a splendid country, bigger than Norway, unfathomably large and rich, where there will be garrisons, castles and towns, thousands of people, hundreds of thousands, but we, he reiterates, we are the first, we are the pioneers, argonauts embarking on this very first expedition, and I, Claus Enevold Pors, have been appointed Governor to begin with, though I shall be a father for you all, a loving father, and you shall come to me with your sorrows and joys, as to King Frederik, for indeed I shall be your king, and by my mother's sacred memory I shall be a loving king. Skål!

Skål! And they raise their glasses.

Somewhere, a cow lows.

///

I am Aappaluttoq. I am red as fire, red as blood, red as the iron that glows in the forge, red as the sea when the sun descends, red as death. My name is Red.

It is not easy to be far from home. The body and spirit lose touch with each other. Afterwards they must become acquainted again. It takes time, and will not always succeed. I have known shamans unable to bring themselves together again, who have lain dormant for weeks until dying. Sometimes I meet their homeless, tormented spirits. They float about, confusedly and without purpose. The easiest thing to do when travelling afar is to have a physical object in which to materialize oneself, for example the carved figure of bone carried by the King in his pocket. I can feel his sticky hand about my body. It is a familiar and comforting feeling. When I lie there in his pocket, I know I can always come back to the groaning body in the peat-hut.

Yet sometimes I release myself from that figure of bone and go out into the streets of Copenhagen. I wander about there. I see things I cannot or will not talk of. Crimes, nameless horrors. If you think yourself a bearer of a benevolent and elevated culture, Dane, then you should follow me on one of my wanderings in this royal city between the hours of twelve and six in the morning. I am fond of it. I enjoy being the invisible guest who sees what should never be seen. And I hate myself for liking it.

But I am fond of your king. I understand him. His weaknesses are mine, the weaknesses of us all. He is a man. And I am his subject. This is how it must be.

///

The released inmates have been quartered in a dormitory inside the garrison. Here they will remain until their departure. Sise lies next to Johan, though head to toe so as to find room in the narrow bunk. The light is extinguished. It is dark. She lies listening to the sounds from the other bunks, moaning and sniggering.

Skål, you old slag, says Peter Hageman to his wife, Cellar-Katrine. Theirs is the adjacent bunk.

Skål, and goodnight, says Katrine, planting a sloppy kiss on his mouth.

You've an ugly face, but a lovely arse, says Peter. And a person can't have it all.

You can help yourself, says Katrine. But I'm going to sleep if it's all the same to you. It's been a long day.

Fine by me, Peter says. I'm so horny I could shag a corpse.

Sise shudders. She wonders if it feels different when you're married. Perhaps it's nice, though she finds it hard to imagine. She has never felt anything but discomfort. Fetid smells and discomfort. Perhaps that's something God takes away once you've said your I do. Now she regrets not having spoken the words in the church. In truth she is not yet properly wed. Maybe she can visit the priest, Ole Lange, and ask him to repeat the ritual. But for the time being she's as unmarried as ever. She gave Johan a kick when he tried it on just now. He sighed and turned his back on her. He's asleep now. His feet in their thread-bare socks lie pointing into the air beside her.

She has realized by now that they are to be moved somewhere far away. But where it is she has no idea, nor if it will be hot or cold there.

What if I die on the journey, she wonders. Then I will die without being married. Her bleeding was several days ago. She is clean and ready. She thinks of Pors, the 'admiral', who wanted her last night, but was unable. So much has happened since then. But she has not been wed. She is the only one unwed in the entire dormitory.

A hand touches her in the night. She pushes it away, half in sleep. Yet it returns, and grips her shoulder. She stirs and sees the old man, his long white hair, the frost of his eyebrows, his pale eyes in the light of a lamp. He puts his finger to his lips.

The gentleman wishes to see you, he whispers.

She gets up and follows him out of the dormitory in her stockinged feet. They walk down a long corridor, up a flight of stairs and around several corners before she is shown into a room that smells of bed chamber and leather. The Icelander nudges her forward.

Pors is lying on the bed. He is naked. His long member hangs limply between his thighs, but when the Icelander approaches it begins to swell and rises into an arc that juts from the hair of his pubis.

Come, my girl, says Pors with a smile. Now I shall claim my *jus primae noctis.*

He wants to lie with me, Sise says matter-of-factly.

What, does she understand Latin? Pors replies somewhat surprised.

I understand what I want to understand, says Sise. As my mother always said.

I see, says Pors. But let us now finish what we started last night.

When Pors is finished with her, the Icelander returns her to the dormitory.

Johan is awake as she climbs into the bunk beside him.

Where have you been? he asks.

An errand.

Couldn't you use the night pot?

I'd rather the latrine.

They lie for a while without speaking. She can tell he's awake.

It's not my fault, she says.

What?

That I'm so coy. Only I can't do it unless I'm forced or paid money for it.

Do you want me to force you, is that it?

No, thanks.

Shall I pay you money?

You haven't got any.

Then I don't know what to do.

Tomorrow we'll go to the priest, she says. I'll say I do.

He turns over. He puts his arms around her legs. She can feel his mouth through her stockinged feet.

Thanks, he says, thanks, my darling.

Only I doubt it'll make a difference, she thinks to herself.

3

A Maiden's Voyage

This 2nd of January I went to the neighbours here on the
island and spent the night there in one of the dwellings. The
Greenlanders who had taken to the waters to hunt returned
home in the evening and, like all other days, had caught
nothing, wherefore the state of health among them was already
poor on account of lack of nourishment and livelihood. On
this occasion I reminded them of their great ingratitude and
disdain of God, for never did they thank God for their nour-
ishment, nor did they appeal to him thereof, yet lived as before,
in the manner of unthinking beasts, which behaviour had
provoked God to revoke his blessing of them and allow them
to suffer.

FROM HANS EGEDE'S JOURNAL, 1726

I've never sailed north of the Hebrides. I've ploughed the shallow
and unruly waters of the Baltic, pendulated with the packet service
between Christiania and Copenhagen, and paddled my way up the
slurping rivers of Africa, in places so narrow it was like passing
through a sliver of monkey cries, bird screams and chirping cicadas,
and I've even been caught in the crossfire between two warships in
the English Channel; I've lost my mast at Helgoland and my rudder
at the mouth of the Neva, I've plied the routes with trading ships
between the western ports of Europe, seen more dodgy dockland
alehouses than my memory can or will contain, and drunk even more
kinds of spirits, but I've never tasted the cold waters, not the ones
with salt and ice cubes in them, and neither have my crew, nor the
passengers for that matter, and what a peculiar lot they are; I can't
stand passengers, the sea's for seamen, anyone else ought to stay at

home. My name is Didrik Mühlenfort, I'm the captain of this ship, the good ship *Morian*, a frigate, for frigates normally do have men's names, she's armed and equipped, and reinforced at all ends. We're on our way to Greenland. But what Greenland is, no one's been able to tell me.

I've seen the woman, the young girl, they dragged her on board like she was a drunken delinquent on her way to the gallows, she dropped down on the street, they said, fell down feeling unwell, a housekeeper, they said, for that gold-braided gentleman with the cocked hat and the miserable face, a Major Pors who's to be governor up there, and he had an old manservant with him too, but the girl, she was so young, and I wondered what might be wrong with her, but then they carried her into the major's cabin and for a long time I never heard a peep from her, much less saw anything of her.

I don't want sickness on my ship, I told the major so. But it's not his ship, he jeered at me, it's the King's. But it's me who's in command, I told him, and sick people should stay ashore where they belong, where they can be buried under six feet of soil if needs be, for the sea bed's littered with dead who ought to have stayed at home and had words spoken to them by a priest, only then, with a conjuror's flourish he produced a document with the royal seal on it, monogram and the whole works, and asked me to read it out loud, let me hear the words, he said with pointed sarcasm, and a fine handwriting it was, but illegible all the same, though after a moment I managed to pick my way through as much as to read 'that he convey the Governor Pors and his people etc. to Greenland and abide by his instructions and decisions etc.', and this, clearly, was no good, meaning as it did that this major, or governor, could contend for precedence with me as captain of the *Morian*, and if there's one thing that can cause mischief on a ship and among its crew, it's having two masters rather than one, for a ship has only one rudder and ought rightly to have but one hand to set the course, and that hand sits as yet firmly on my right arm.

A minor convulsion, said Johan Struff, the ship's surgeon, after I sent him in to the young woman, she's improving now, certainly there's nothing mortally wrong with the girl, merely an unrest in the soul, a consternation, I believe; I've cupped her, he said, and her blood is pure and fresh, whereupon he licked his lips as if he had tasted this maiden's blood himself, only then he spat his brown tobacco sauce over the gunwale. Well, let's see what amusement we can contrive from this business, I said. A ship full of horses and women, said Struff, would seem a temptation indeed to our Lord, or rather the Devil, and this indeed was as true as was said, I replied, but the King has resolved it so, and we'd be served to make the best of it.

Indeed, twelve horses in all, good riding horses, girthed up beneath the deck; one of them, a white mare, they said was a gift from the King to the Governor Pors, who clearly must have enjoyed certain royal privileges for there weren't much governor about him, he looked more like a farmer, and the horses, they were already looking poorly, and I guessed we'd be eating horsemeat before we got there, and I was right too.

And the women, a score of them in all; besides the Major's house-keeper, various servants and officers' madams, twelve tarts we had from the women's gaol, the Spinning House as they call it, coupled with twelve spineless scoundrels from Bremerholm, all a part of His Majesty's designs, making the voyage to be the backbone of his planned colony, only the lot of them were looking as poorly as the horses, so no doubt we'd have our troubles with them too, I thought to myself as we came out into the open sea and it began to show its teeth.

I've reached my fortieth year, still a bachelor, married to the sea, I suppose you could say, and a difficult marriage it is too, seeing as I don't care much for sailing at all, but I can't pack it in now, it's what I do, and when the ship was ready to set sail I felt myself gripped as always by a raging impatience to leave, the way I always have.

The boats were going back and forth between the inner harbour and the roadsteads with latecomers and all the paraphernalia they'd suddenly decided at the last minute that they couldn't be without, as well as the hay bales for the livestock, and the hours passed, it was as if the ship were gripped by the same fever as myself as the hour of departure approached, but at the same time as this activity rose to a veritable frenzy, a languor descended, as if the ship, like a woman to the altar, couldn't make up its mind and was stalled by all manner of doubts and kept on finding new things that had to be done so as to put off those fateful words: Let go the moorings! A ship is never ready, one must make short work of it, and early in the afternoon I gave the command, and the last of the passengers almost tumbled aboard with their various cargo, chests and sacks and packages bundled up from the boats to clutter the deck, but it all could be put away later, now we were setting sail, for otherwise we never would. I signalled to the pilot, and he signalled in turn to the tugs, and the boatsmen shouted to the oarsmen, and the oarsmen leaned their backs into it, the ropes tightened and the *Morian* slid creaking and sighing from the snarl of ships at anchor, the sails were set, snapping and flapping as they filled, the first lurch shuddering through the hull; we were on our way up through the Øresund and I took a deep breath of air and let it out again, released.

My mind was for the sea from an early age, the first ship I steered was the crayer the *Hope*, and later I stood on the quarterdeck of several frigates, this was what I put in my application for this berth, I didn't mention that I hated sailing, but I may as well have done, because the very next day there came a message from the palace informing me I was appointed captain of the frigate the *Morian*; clearly they were in need of someone and needed him right away, the letter of my employment was more like a royal command, and I did have my doubts, for while a sea voyage might not look like much on paper, the fact of the matter is a different thing entirely, a knife-edge balance between life and death over an abyss of water eager to swallow a man up, but it was too late for second thoughts, in principle I could have betrothed myself to someone in all haste and used it for an excuse, but that wouldn't have been like me at all, I'm a bachelor and that's the way I'm staying, otherwise it'd feel like having two wives.

I hail from Kristiansund, my father, Christopher Mühlenfort, was a customs officer there, my mother, Elisabeth Munthe, came from a good family in Trondheim where her brother was principal of the Latin school, but they're dead now, all three, they departed this life whilst I was out at sea, that's what sailing's like, everything seems to stand still while you're at sea, but when you come ashore events have jumped ahead and whole lives, whole worlds are gone forever.

We steered towards Elsinore, feasting on the first mouthfuls of fresh sea air, and now I loved it, it's only on land that I hate to sail, the sky was clear, streaked only with lines of white here and there, the air was mild, it was spring, the date was 21 May, the wind was south-westerly, a gentle breeze nudging the *Morian*'s sails, propelling us forward at good speed, so all in all it couldn't have been better, from land we were saluted, first a few white puffs of smoke, then the muffled thunder of the cannon, to which we replied with the six-pounders we'd been armed with, hurrahs were shouted, so the formalities were met and I could enjoy a leisurely jaunt to Elsinore.

At starboard aft we had the one consort, the galliot the *West-Vlieland*, at port the other, the light brigantine the *Fortuna*, all three ships manned by Norwegians like myself, apart from the odd Dane, three foaming fans in our wake we spread, the merchant flag flapped and fluttered, my uniform was freshly laundered, and I thought to myself things don't get better than this, as I stared at the wakes of the three ships mingling into one and vanishing again, indeed, this is what sailing is, I thought to myself, you draw a line on a canvas of water and immediately it's erased again.

I took a few rounds of inspection to make sure the stowage was by the board, spoke with the men I hardly knew, but they were countrymen as mentioned, most of them, and I spoke with some of the passengers too, in particular a clergyman from Frederikshald on his way to teach the savages the Lord's Prayer, we looked at the cannon that had come aboard, light ones of iron, and the muskets in their crates, packed with straw, and I said they looked second-rate, but there was certainly plenty of them, was the King thinking of declaring war on someone, I asked, for there was more than a hundred barrels of pitch and enough black powder and lead to stock a whole garrison with bullets, no, His Majesty wished to tread carefully, said the priest, lifting the corner of a tarpaulin and asking what kind of timber is this, an enormous amount of short planks, coffins, I said, they've made provisions for death, the gentlemen of power, indeed, he said, paling visibly, indeed, let us hope there won't be need for them all, but I was more concerned about all that gunpowder, if a fire breaks out, I said, we'll be blown to kingdom come, and what a bang it would be, Major Pors said, now having joined us, he seemed to think it funny.

Over on the *Fortuna* it was even worse, she too was laden with building materials up to the yard, and Captain Reinecke, who I'd met earlier that morning, had spoken of displacement, if we encountered a high sea, he said, we'd risk having to ditch half of it over the side so as not to capsize, and as if that wasn't enough I've got a whole Noah's Ark of goats and sheep and cows on board, they've taken up the entire between-deck with their braying and lowing, their stamping and their smelling of wool, and the crew are laughing their heads off, those of the other two ships, that is, for mine are cursing it, they say we'll be dragging the stench of the stables after us all through the North Atlantic.

We ourselves were more fortunate, for the fine gentlemen, among them the soon-to-be Governor Pors, naturally required a certain degree of comfort, though I felt certain we would see our share of bother, and even if the voyage did proceed without a hitch, we'd always have the two dozen convicts to shake things up, a wretched flock of drunkards and lascivious tarts, a good number of them never having stood on a ship's deck before and already hanging over the gunwale, feeding the Øresund fish with what was still left of their last meal, and as yet there was hardly a ripple on the sea, so it was going to be a long voyage the sorry fools had ahead of them, but for landlubbers the very sight of a ship can be enough to make them dizzy.

I waylaid the Major Pors on deck, he had a scowling, self-important look on his face, strutting about as if he had a plank down his back, and I predicted there'd be trouble with him, former navy, so I under-stood. Morning, Your Excellency, I said, a bit of deference to soften him up, and he smiled and nodded, his mouth as puckered as pleated fabric, I thought he was about to snarl at me, but all he said was Kronborg Castle already, and pointed in towards the land. We've a good wind today, I said, a south-westerly. Indeed, he said, I'd noticed, though mark me, it'll be a different matter altogether once we're out in the Skagerrak. Let's hope for the best, I said. Certainly, he said in that snide way of his, out of the corner of his mouth, one can always hope. Has he sailed in Greenland before, he asked. No, I said, has Your Excellency? Of course not, he snapped. This is my first voyage there too, I said, endeavouring to lighten the mood. And then I asked him: How's the Governor's jomfru shaping up? I've not seen her since we came aboard. She's sleeping, he told me. I shook my head and said how terrifying it must be for a young girl to embark on such a voyage as this, with no one really knowing what we'll find there. But she's here of her own accord, he said, she wasn't prospering at home. Really, I said, and where does she come from? Køge, he said, the Apothecary family there, Fuchs is the name, relations of mine, albeit distant. Not that she spent much time there, she grew up in a nunnery in Germany, though fled the nuns and ended up with her father's brother, the Apothecary Fuchs. And now she's running away again, I said, to Greenland. Indeed, he said, when a person gets going after a standstill, it can be hard to stop again. Anyway, let's hope the jomfru has a good voyage, I said, and wished him a pleasant day.

We had by then reached Elsinore and I sent a boat ashore with the last of our escorts, the pilot, a priest from the Missionskollegium and a pair of His Majesty's representatives, whereupon salutes were exchanged again and the Governor ordered his manservant, a white-haired fellow as decrepit as his housekeeper is young and fair, to fetch a bottle and some glasses from the cabin, and so we stood there on the deck and toasted, Jørgen Landorph, commandant over the military contingent, joined us too at this point. Salutes were exchanged again from both sides, and Pors commented that we'd soon better get a move on before the Swedes began to bombard us. Weigh anchor! he bellowed, and the men all looked from him to me, and after a moment I told them, you heard what the gentleman said, weigh anchor!

Open sea, the spray and the wind; the rigging sang, and the ropes beat their tattoo as Sjælland dwindled away behind the billowing sails of the *West-Vlieland* and the *Fortuna*. When evening came I dined with the officers and Pors, a number of bottles were drunk, all were in rather high spirits and the Commandant Landorph was somewhat unfortunate with a couple of remarks concerning Pors and his jomfru, at which point the Major got to his feet, leaned over the table and delivered him a stinging flat-hander that sent his wig into the pea soup and Landorph himself to the floor, from where he had to be helped up by the other men, dabbing blood from his nose with a handkerchief. It's only the drink, I told myself, such things happen, it'll all be forgotten by morning, but of course it wasn't.

///

The wind is kind to us. After three days at sea we sight the Norwegian coastline and I plot the course due west towards the Shetland Islands at which we arrive a week later, though the wind is now more contrary. We put into Lerwick, seat of the former Danish crown colony, and remain there a couple of days, letting the livestock ashore so they can stretch their legs and munch some fresh grass. The Major rides off inland on his mare, which seems to have coped well with the voyage, he spoils her with oats and hunks of bread, but the other horses are ailing, they've got diarrhoea from the mouldy hay and lack of exercise, girthed up as they are, the lower deck is a mire of filth and must be hosed meticulously.

Now Pors's young housekeeper shows herself on deck for the first time since her embarkment, she stands at the gunwale one day, this after our setting sail from Lerwick and we're out on the open sea again; her dress flutters in the wind, the same as her dark hair, yet there is something oddly imperturbable about her gaze. Does she spy anything interesting, I ask, whereupon she gives a start, and says that she's never been to sea before, and how deep is it? Some hundred fathoms, I reply, and I see the perspiration beading on her upper lip and forehead. Is the sea-sickness bad, jomfru? It's like a thing alive, she says, her stare still fixed on a point far in the distance, it swells and nauseates, she says, and glances up at me, a fleeting smile passes over her face like moonlight in between clouds. But what is down there? Fish, I say. Whales, and the creatures of the deep, a teeming life, my girl. But ships too, she says. Indeed, shipwrecks too, I tell her, and no small number either. Dead seaman, she continues. Thousands, I say it's like one can almost hear them. They sing, can you not hear? I've dreamt of them, they wander about at the bottom, upright they sway this way and that, and there is a forest there, everything takes place slowly and all is silent, for it is the bottom of the sea; they look up at us, I don't know if they want to return here or if they want us to join them down there, but they are dead, I say, they have no thoughts of us and we ought not to give them any either. Yet she smiles as if she knew something, and her smile feels like a chill in my neck, and she looks at me sideways and mumbles something in a foreign language, nunnery-speak I shouldn't wonder. You shouldn't be afraid of the sea, I tell her, I shall make sure you come safely ashore. Are you master of the sea? she asks. No, but I am master of this ship, I reply, and wish her a pleasant day, I've matters to attend to, if the jomfru will excuse me, but after I leave her she remains for a long time looking out over the waves. No, women and horses have no place at sea, but belong to the land.

///

The wind has picked up and the passengers, in particular the convicts, are seasick and lie vomiting in their bunks. Clearly they bring with them numerous ailments from the land, consumption and poor health altogether, they haven't the strength to drag themselves onto deck or to the latrine hole to empty themselves, and can only let go when they must, and the Governor is mostly three sheets to the wind, he staggers about on deck with a bottle in one hand and his sword in the other, as if it were a walking cane, where's that bloody Commandant! he growls, let me poke a hole in him, and then his manservant comes, an Icelander they say, and drags him back to his bed, though presently to appear again, the Icelander, standing at the gunwale all through the pale night, looking like he's staring a hole in the sky, his long white hair fluttering in the wind as he stares at the dull silver of the firmament, the gulls as they plunge to scoop something up in their beaks, then arrow upwards again, hugging the sails, frolicking in the turbulence they create, then new diagonals in the air, and it seems he will never tire of watching them. I go up to him and ask about the jomfru, is she quite of her right mind, I enquire, but he simply looks at me, a silent, unfathomable gaze beneath his frost-white eyebrows, smoke curling from his pipe, so one can tell he at least breathes like the rest of us who are still among the living, for not a word does he utter, what is he, idiot or sage?

One night I am awakened by a piercing scream. I roll out of the bunk and go out onto the deck, for I always sleep fully clothed and am used to being shaken awake at all hours, yet this scream is like a nightmare, a scream from Hell itself, and I am already on deck before my senses are returned, standing there blinking into the wind, with people all around me in bewilderment, what was that, did someone scream?

It's light as day, though a stormy day of lashing rain, sea and sky as one, and then a new scream sounds through the weather, a sudden tumult and men's voices and I descend to the Major's cabin, snatch open the door and see two men bent over a bunk, the Major and his manservant gripping the jomfru as if in the business of strangling her, she for her part kicking and thrashing, and then another scream that rips through the air and propels me several steps backwards by its sheer might, but then I get a grip, I leap forward and grab the Major by the nightshirt, roaring at him, what in the Devil's name are you doing to the girl? and surely he is aware then of my presence, yet he takes no notice, the cabin is thick with the most unpleasant smells and a sticky dampness, and a moment later the Major clambers onto the bunk, which creaks under his weight, he lies on top of the girl with the whole volume of his frame, the manservant assisting, holding the girl by the legs, his long white hair hanging before his eyes, and while I keep trying to pull the Major away, yelling at him to stop, the manservant turns his furrowed face towards me behind its curtain of hair and says quite coldly and with the rusty voice of the old that the Master Struff has been summoned.

The girl arches her back, she rolls her eyes so only the whites can be seen, the orbs like marbles in her skull and foaming at the mouth, and then she screams once more; ah, I see now, I mutter, and release the Major, stepping back to make room for the ship's surgeon, Johan Struff, who enters now accompanied by a pair of officers and Miltzov the clergyman, elbowing his way to the jomfru and assuming command, ordering the men to hold her steady while he examines her, closing her eyelids, slapping her face and shouting her name, Jomfru Titius! Yet the spasms will not relent.

A convulsion, Struff opines, straightening into the upright again. Is she often afflicted like this? Never before, says Pors, his grip on the girl now released, delivering her into the hands of the officers. Not in such a way. He wipes a blood-trickling scratch on his cheek and studies the red now smeared on his sleeve. She's normally so quiet. Has she been at the aquavit? Struff asks. Not a drop, say Pors.

Now it seems the jomfru has settled, and she gulps in air. Only then her body arches upwards again, new waves of convulsions from the chest down. She wrestles a leg free and kicks one of the officers in the chest; he emits a groan, a laugh of surprise quickly supplanted by a wincing grimace as he clutches his ribs; another officer takes her leg and presses it down into the bedding straw. Hold her tight, Struff instructs, the convulsions make her as strong as a horse, I shall let her blood, he says, and takes out the equipment, unpacking it calmly before making a swift incision at the girl's elbow, her blood instantly leaking into the bedding. He asks the manservant to wring a cloth in cold water and then tears open her nightshirt from the throat down, placing an ear to her chest. A number of bystanders have gathered now, half a dozen men at the bunk, watching the naked girl quiver and tremble, calmer now, and yet her body stiffens several times again in small aftershocks, and she groans, long moaning sighs like a calving cow, her eyes, which formerly rolled in their sockets, become still, and she stares up at the ceiling, but then we hear a cry from the crow's nest and our attentions are turned, several times the call is heard, land ahoy! I dash to the deck, the Icelander following me like an unsettled dog, and together we stand and stare out into the leaden air where a shadow looms and waves crash at a shore. Your fatherland, most like, I say to the Icelander, but when I turn he is gone.

We drop anchor in an inlet. I send the first officer, Peder Dan, ashore in the boat. He returns early next evening and has found a fishing village further north. East Iceland, he says, it seems we've been blown off course.

We sail north to the village and anchor in a natural harbour, and in the time we are there the weather improves, though still a layer of cloud presses down on it all, a score of stone dwellings and a church, and beyond this a dark, open flatland and a row of fells in the west whose peaks are hidden to us. But here we bring the horses ashore and wait for some days for our fellow ships to appear, which they do not; we attend service in the little stone church and the inhabitants are friendly, albeit mute. Pors orders two of the horses slaughtered, for they are badly the worse for wear; the carcasses are hoisted up to the yard, where they hang and drip, and all is peaceful enough, the jomfru remains in her cabin, Miltzov the clergyman is with her.

I go to Pors to speak to him about his housekeeper, but all he says is I can kiss his arse. What the Major does with his staff is his own affair, I tell him, but I'd ask him to do it ashore, because I don't want no lechery on this ship. The captain can shove it, he says, he can mind his own business, then I'll mind mine. Everything that happens on the voyage is written down in the log, I remind him, and it doesn't look good, this business with the jomfru. My dear Captain Mühlenfart, he then says, what exactly does he think he's going to put in his log? Everything that concerns the voyage, I tell him, cold as ice, for I've heard his insult. And what events has Mühlenfart witnessed until now, I wonder, which concern the voyage sufficiently to be written down in his log? That he is turning His Majesty's ship into a den of iniquity, I reply. Ah, a lecher I may well be, he says then, but my jomfru has nothing to do with it, he can ask his Master Struff to examine her, if he wants it confirmed. Then why does she suffer these attacks, I say, something must surely have brought them on? Ask Struff, he says, I'm not a physician.

It's about the jomfru, I say to Struff later on when I approach him on the deck, and he walks back and forth with his hands behind his back and says these convulsions are seen often in girls that age, it's their liquid balance got out of hand, it'll even out again once we're ashore. Has the Major harmed her in any way? I enquire. How should I know? Struff replies. You could examine her, I say, but he scoffs dismissively, I'm not putting my fingers up such a young girl, he says, I'm no beast, and anyway what business is it of ours what the fine gentlemen get up to with their servants? A man's a man, and this voyage is long indeed. It's my business, I tell him, I won't have it going on aboard my ship, the Major can have his fun with the tarts below deck, if he wants, I'm not going to intervene in that, they're already spoiled, but an innocent girl in his care, he can keep his hands off, otherwise I'll go to his superiors as soon as I'm home again. I honestly couldn't care less, he says and yawns in my face, I'm just a physician, and the girls down there aren't exactly mouth-watering, who would want anything to do with them?

So I go to the clergyman Miltzov, though all I get out of him is pious prattle about the trials and tribulations of our earthly life, the grace of our good Lord etc., and besides, he's forbidden to divulge anything told to him by a person in distress who has need of his comfort.

Then to Jørgen Landorph, the Commandant, and this is indeed grist to his mill; the dirty old man, he exclaims, and married too, someone ought to teach him to keep his cock inside his pants, I've half a mind to do so myself, speak to him, I mean, but we've got to work together, so perhaps it's best to stay on his good side, Landorph says with a sigh.

But among the officers there is now regular animosity towards the Major, they believe him to have committed an offence against the girl, this being what has made her ill, and there is much indignant talk around the dinner table, where Pors, galloping about the foggy country on his royal mare, now seldom appears.

The crew, however, seem of a different opinion, some mutter that she is possessed by the Devil, for they've heard she grew up in a nunnery, papist at that, says Jens Smith, she'll have lain with sin itself, it stands to reason; to this some of the men who have sailed in the south say no, the Catholics are Christian people like ourselves, only with more pictures in their churches, they speak the Bible's own language when they pray, there's nothing wrong with them; but Jens Smith says he doesn't trust them, that the jomfru will end up sending the whole ship, man and mouse, to the bottom of the sea, and then Miltzov comes to me.

I can't find the jomfru anywhere, he says. Is she not in her cabin? No, that's what I'm saying, he says, her bunk is empty, I've searched high and low, she can't be just gone, and yet it seems she is, he says, for aboard the ship she is not. And so I go around asking if anyone's seen the girl row ashore, or maybe she swam, says a boatsman, it's only a few ship's lengths to the shore; jumped in the drink, says Jens Smith, good riddance, the Draug's taken her, and now they're getting married in Latin at the bottom of the sea.

But the same day as the jomfru is reported missing, the where-abouts of Pors's manservant Skård are likewise questioned, no one has seen him on board, some claim to have seen him ashore; no doubt he's jumped ship to be with his own people, Jens Smith reckons, and now he'll be sitting chewing sheep's eyes with the rest of them, and he'll be welcome, but then Pors returns from one of his sojourns into the country.

The Major is distraught to hear that both his servants have made themselves scarce and wishes to depart again immediately to search for them, so I borrow one of the horses to ride with him, but after only an hour my arse feels like chopped meat, I'm no practised horseman, and the horses don't much care either for the uneven, stony land, the lava stone, says the Major, expelled hundreds of years before by a volcano, and rushing rivers too that we must cross, with green, ice-cold meltwater that washes over the horses' flanks, soaking us to the skin; but then we encounter some shepherds and ask if they have seen a young girl wandering about, and indeed they have, they found her in the field, quite distressed, crawling on all fours, and brought her to a farm, and they point over towards the fell where the ground rises upwards and where stand a cluster of weatherworn buildings, and there we find her.

It is a poor man's holding, held together by ends of wood, peat and stone, and here lies the jomfru in a bed and is soundly asleep. The people of the farm are alarmed by this guest and wish to be rid of her as soon as possible, so Pors must give them a bottle of aquavit from his inexhaustible reserves; he lifts her up in his arms and will carry her out to the horse, but the girl wishes not to go, she kicks and screams and wrenches herself away, hurling at us cups and plates and other effects of the household, babbling strings of Latin, evoking the Devil, I believe, her countenance is by any account diabolical, and she manages to smash the tiny place to pieces by the time we get her tied up with a length of rope and laid across Pors's horse, all this with the aid of the farmer and his two sons, and then we ride back to the *Morian* with her, and she howls the entire way, and only when the clergyman Miltzov closes the cabin door behind the two of them does she settle.

I've always believed priests to be an impractical lot, says Pors, but sometimes it may indeed be useful to have one nearby.

Now Landorph begins to speak of proceedings, and the officers agree with him that something should be done to help the jomfru in her distress, but all this comes to nothing, for I give the order to cast off and then we all have other things to think about than the demented jomfru; she for her part gives no sign of life, the priest is with her, Pors wanders the deck as befuddled as before, his manservant no longer there to help him into his bed, and often I find him curled up and snoring inside a coil of rope, and otherwise he goes about calling for his valet, Skård! Skård? like a lost child calling for its mother, he's been with the family as long as I recall, he tells me mournfully, he's like a father or a big brother to me, but the general opinion is that the Icelander had had enough of the Major's antics and chose to be reunited with his countrymen, and it serves him right, says Landorph, the man's a lech and a tyrant.

But then one night when I go up onto the deck to have the wind drive away a bad dream I find him standing there, the Icelander, puffing on his pipe and gazing out at the sea as before; he near frightens the life out of me, one of the men says he just appeared all of a sudden and has been standing there an hour at that point, so I go up to him and ask him where on earth he's been all this time, your gentleman's been searching high and low for you, but all he does is look at me with a little smile to curl the corner of his mouth.

///

The sea becomes more troubled, great waves come rolling from the north-west, especially so after we leave Iceland's lee, and it's the horses that come off worst, for horses don't belong on the sea, they're no more comfortable there than ladies and tarts, their legs are too long and thin, they can't find the proper purchase, and what's more, the hay is rotten and the floor down there where they're girthed up is awash with their thin shit and must be hosed and swept several times daily; three horses must be put down, Jens Smith does the job, a swift blow to the forehead with his hammer and their legs splay immediately, eyes rolling in their skulls, and then they are hung up from the yard and the cook slices them open and slings the insides over the gunwale, leaving the carcasses to swing with the swell, spreading sticky fans of blood upon the deck, not a pleasant sight by any means, but horsemeat is at least a welcome change from salted pork, only now we've got problems with the convicts too.

I have them sent up onto deck a few hours every day so they can be freshened up a bit by the sea air, which to me is one of the joys of this world, but I can barely stand to look at the wretched loons, the way they fall over and can only remain lying where they fell, without the strength to lean over the gunwale to empty themselves, though the women seem to do better at this than the men, even if their mouths are as filthy as the rest of them, yelling and bickering the way they do, and fighting too in that peculiar way women have of fighting, pulling each other by the hair, and one of their number, Cellar-Katrine they call her, stands on the bridge and raises her arms like a mad prophet, cackling and cursing diabolically, wishing the ship and its crew to be sent to the bottom of the sea, and indeed I must concede there is much pith in her curses, and quite some humour too, though of course I am obliged to punish her, for no one can go unpunished for cursing a ship; Landorph however believes this to be his jurisdiction, he wants her hanged, but I'll have no hangings on my ship, I tell him, it's quite enough we've got the four horses dangling there from the yard already, and so we argue the matter for some time while the hag herself, the object of our disagreement, stands there gaping at us in turn, looking like she can see both sides of it, but eventually I order that she be tied to the mast, her clothes torn from her back and twenty strokes administered of the ferule, these then delivered with cheerful aplomb by Jens Smith, the rest of the rabble looking on, though without seeming much deterred by the sight, and indeed her spouse, Peter Hageman, mocks and taunts her as she's punished, the others too scoffing and jeering. When eventually the ropes are loosened and two seamen make to help the ragged, half-naked shrew back below, she tears herself away, spits on the deck and expels a new shower of curses, arguably worse even than those for which she was punished in the first place. I am awed indeed by such resolve, yet have no option but to order her tied once more and another twenty strokes administered, these happily shutting her up, and this time when the ropes are untied she flops forward onto the deck, and the men pick her up and bundle her back down the hatch with much commotion.

Pors is his miserable old self, he's left the aquavit on the shelf and begins now to put his nose into my work, we must ahead, directly into it, he says as I stand one day with the old moth-eaten chart and am plotting the course; no, I tell him, we must circumvent the land, and I draw in a circle on the chart. But you don't know where the land is, he says, where it begins and where it ends, so what is it you wish to circumvent? No, ahead, Mühlenfart, and we shall encounter it soon enough. But inshore the storms will be the worse, I tell him, we must keep a distance. To where then will you sail, he says, America perhaps, and be barbered by the redskins? You've already led us astray once, now sail due west, end of argument! And with that he produces the King's instruction from his pocket and waves it under my nose, whereby I've no choice than to plot the course according to his wish.

The ship heels over, I'm worried stiff the cargo's going to shift, so I send some men down below to secure the bulkier items and redistribute the weight, but once there's a displacement it's hard to rectify and you can only hope things don't get worse, the strangest things happen to cargoes, they live their own lives, something comes loose and slides about and it'll soon take other items with it and before you know it you've got a list on your hands and the ship goes down. It's that Cellar-Katrine and her cursing, the men reckon, you should have hanged her from the yard like the Commandant said.

I go down into the shared quarters where the convicts are, and a hideous stench hits me in the face like a blow from a wet towel, their evacuations swill about the floor, following the movements of the ship this way and that, the inmates lie in their hammocks, swaying back and forth beneath a swinging lamp, the ropes by which they are secured creaking like some kind of echo to mock the groans of their sick incumbents who lie cocooned and whimpering, vomiting and cursing; some speak the Lord's Prayer, others, as if to defy all belief, enjoy each other's flesh in this dreadful, squelching squalor, their hammocks shudder and swell like larvae struggling to free themselves; it's the first time since I was a boy that I've felt a hint of the sea-sickness, and then a man comes staggering towards me from his bed, latrine fluids sloshing around his ankles, he grips the door frame, luminous with the sea-sickness's green lustre, and I can see it's the aforementioned Peter Hageman, spouse of the hag who cursed the ship, and he asks me when do we arrive, Captain? In a week's time things will be better, I tell him. A week? My wife will barely survive the next hour. Sea-sickness always feels worse than it is, I tell him, I've never heard of anyone die of it. But still I am relieved to return to the deck and breathe in the fresh air.

All progressing splendidly, Mühlenfart, Pors exclaims, persisting in his use of the insulting perversion of my name, a most splendid passage indeed; the Major is unafflicted by the sea-sickness, and now we shall soon see land, he says. Yes, not many days yet, I reply. He fills himself with the salted pork and pease porridge and drinks wine; I myself drink ale. The Governor will be looking forward to stepping ashore and embarking upon the colonization, I suggest to him. Indeed, he says, 'tis His Majesty's wish to recover the lost land that has lain abandoned these several hundred years, but for me it is a calling, I feel my whole life has been but preparation for this; Denmark will once more be a great nation after the losses we have suffered, the colonization of Greenland will be only the beginning, the foundation stone of the new empire that has shaped itself in the mind of our king, and if the good Lord lets me live long enough I hope to call myself governor of a province in this empire, for after Greenland we shall take back Sweden, and then it will be Germany's turn, that great confusion of princedoms just waiting to be subsumed under the Danish crown, and who knows what it might lead to. You make it sound like the Roman Empire, I said, but Pors declines to take this as a joke, he looks at me sternly and says, *Imperium Daniae*, we're making Denmark mighty again, Denmark will be the Roman Empire of our age. *Bene tibi*, I say. *Bene tibi* to you too, Mühlenfart, he says back, and on that we toast. Skål.

The air is fresher and cleaner tasting, though the weather is very changeable; the light has changed too, and I know it means that we are approaching land. The Major seems to have been right in plotting due west, for the winds are not as fierce as I'd feared and the passengers may now emerge onto the deck again, their hammocks strung up between the masts, and there they hang and sway among the equine carcasses, the ship heeling and lurching, throwing the people into involuntary dance on the deck, or a game of tag, the way they reach out and grab each other so as not to be swept overboard; and clouds drag their rain showers along with them, glittering silver in the sunlight, the light playing its tricks, shimmering mirages in the air, the strangest visions to behold; the ship groans in the heavy waves, and we are well into a southerly current, but I am unable to chart our position, the sun being the only heavenly body to be seen, the sky too light now even at midnight to see a single star; only now there is a coastline in view, emerging and vanishing quite as quickly again; we encounter a belt of drift ice and sail alongside it, making gentle headway, though the ship reels in the current, and the sea foams about the bow, the rudder hardly any use at all. I told you so, Pors boasts. Due west. Had we sailed according to your own half-baked reckonings, we'd have been halfway to America by now, and I can only agree with him. The man in the mast spies a flock of seals on the ice, and shortly afterwards a fox slinking over the floes; the passengers are jubilant, some men of the crew volunteer to go out onto the ice, they are armed with muskets and return with a pair of seals which are then cooked for dinner.

There is great unrest among the inmates, they argue and fight, the women pull tufts of hair from each other's scalps and the Major cheers them on, plying them with aquavit, and knives appear too, flashes of steel, and several are gashed in the arm or leg; in short, their health seems restored. Pors arranges wrestling contests so that they may exhaust themselves without killing each other, and people sit in the rigging and up on the yard cheering on the contestants, wagering money on their favourites, though in truth they are sorry contests indeed, for the combatants are as meagre and feeble as old men, even if at best they are something and twenty; however, with our gentle headway they're looking healthier by the day.

In the mess there is much talk about Pors, some believe him to be a madman, the Paymaster Fleischer, known as 'Fox' on account of his red hair and sly-looking gaze, speaks of delusions of grandeur; the man's a peasant, opines the Trader, Jürgen Kopper, called 'Horse' because of his long face, for all have had their clashes with the Major Pors, and now it all comes pouring out like dregs out of a wine skin, insults, effronteries and the harshest of words, the Governor's drunkenness, the way he treats his poor jomfru; they whisper and mumble, and above their heads the planks creak, for it is the very subject of their talk, the Major Pors, who paces the floor of his cabin.

Is he of noble descent? someone wants to know. I believe so, replies Commandant Landorph, who is familiar with the Major from times previous, but his family fell into debt and the manor was sold off. Pors's own beginnings were more humble, he started out as a non-commissioned officer and worked his way up, though of course not without rubbing just about everyone up the wrong way. Indeed, says 'Fox' Fleischer, to the colonies with him, that's how we get rid of mad dogs of his ilk, but however did he get to be governor, 'Horse' Kopper wonders. You may well ask, says Landorph, but I dare say he cultivates some ally at the court, perhaps even the King himself. And thus goes the talk.

///

The jomfru emerges again. No one has seen so much as her shadow for weeks, now she goes arm in arm with the Major, and behind them lumbers the manservant Skård beclouded by the smoke of the pipe that would seem to be fastened permanently to the corner of his mouth. Pale and sickly she looks, the jomfru, her face contorts into the oddest grimaces, and she halts and stares emptily towards the land, which now is in sight the whole time. Pors points and says something to her, and she looks up at him, that great big gaze of hers, and he in turn looks down at her, and quite as demented as each other they seem, perhaps they are even a good match, I think to myself, two lunatics to help each other along, I'm sure there's a saying in that, but anyway sooner or later they'll both end up in the ditch, and that'll be their problem, for now the passage is soon complete and I have abided by His Majesty's instruction and can deliver them to their own sorry fates, as well as to the contempt and disdain of Landorph and the other officers.

We reach the sixty-fourth latitude, the weather clears up, and I can again chart our position. I sail the ship through skerries and here we encounter a French whaler; visits are exchanged, we toast and salute, first a French toast, *salut*, then a salute with the cannon, and then, only a couple of days later, we are met by a boat from the *West-Vlieland* sent out to look for us, and they pilot us in to the Hope Isle, where the Pastor Egede resides; there we anchor alongside the galliot and the *Fortuna*, much to the relief of those on board the other vessels, who had feared the worst for us; they themselves have suffered a couple of deaths along the way, though otherwise theirs has been a gentler passage than the *Morian*'s.

I shake the hand of Egede himself, he lives with his family and some colony folk in a small dwelling-house, sixteen souls in all in such a little box. The land is dark and sparsely vegetated, and the storm batters in from the sea. So this is where the pastor and his family have lived for seven years, it almost defies belief!

Presently the jomfru comes ashore, arm in arm with Pors, who from now on is to be addressed as 'Governor' or 'Your Grace'; she looks pale and unwell, yet curtsies daintily for the Pastor, the Madame and their two daughters. And then there is enquiry and proceedings against those who in one way or another have offended during the passage, though not Pors, for he is himself lay-judge, and to his credit may be said that he is lenient towards the accused and would preferably give them amnesty one and all and thereby start with a clean sheet now that we are all safely ashore, but Landorph is for punishment, for flogging, Landorph is for the branding iron, the whipping post, the rack, the gallows. Landorph is enraged and vindictive, but I know full well who it is he wishes to punish, yet he knows he cannot touch him and therefore his rage must be taken out on others, for

Pors has his royal order, his appointment to governor, and now the two men must work together in the years to come. I don't know if I'm relieved to be leaving again soon, or disappointed at not having the chance to see how things pan out with these two cockerels.

I go about on the land. The earth makes me heavy as lead, pulling me down. How tired and old I feel! But so it is always. The sea makes me old, but I feel it first on land. I hate sailing. I wish I could walk the whole way back home again, but I fear the distance would be too far for my boots to withstand, and there's that damned sea in between. And, of course, the ship must be sailed, and the hand that steadies the rudder is as yet attached to my right arm.

The next day sees punishment of the convicted men. I write this passage in my journal: 'These floggings and other forms of corporal punishment are thus our, His Majesty's emissaries', first official actions on Greenlandic soil.'

Didrik Mühlenfort, Captain

PART TWO

Imperium Daniae

1

The Guest

To-day the good ship the Kronprinds Christian returned from the north and had plainly done much good trade. The men reported that the Greenlanders up north had complained that some foreign ships which were there for the purpose of trading had robbed them of three whalefish, and having heard that our king was such a mighty gentleman asked that he defend them from the assaults of these foreigners and prevent them from stealing their rightful goods or in any other manner causing them harm. In return they were willing to allow the King's men all the blubber and other goods they might otherwise have lost.

FROM HANS EGEDE'S JOURNAL, JULY 1728

Henrik Balthasar Miltzov steps from the privy and falls flat on his arse. Mud splatters about him, and he grips his wig as if somehow to rescue it from being soiled. He sits for a moment and wonders if he might have injured himself. No, all bones are intact. The earth is a mire and he must first turn onto all fours in order to rise. He scrabbles to his feet and finds himself staring into the eyes of a man who is seated on a rock some few paces away, watching him with interest. A savage. He holds a bone in one hand, a knife in the other. He appears to be carving a figure.

Miltzov bids him a good morning.

Peace of God, says the savage. Did you hurt yourself, priest?

Eh? says Miltzov.

It was a fine spectacle. No injuries, I trust?

Miltzov's colleague, Ole Lange, hurries to his attendance and takes him by the arm.

No, I'm all right. The ground is slippery, I fell. He tries to wipe the thick, slimy mud from his hands onto a rock.

Egede's waiting for us. He wants to give us a tour.

Arm in arm they proceed to the dwelling-house, the one as uncertain on his feet as the other. Reaching the slope, they feel themselves immediately beginning to slide, and without purchase they glide slowly towards the shore, gripping each other for grim death.

Will we be all right, I wonder? Lange says with a laugh.

If you fall, I fall too, Miltzov replies.

Don't I know it.

Egede is standing on a rock, legs slightly apart, leaning his weight on his staff. His eyes follow the two men as sedately they slide by. Their involuntary procession comes to a halt and they clamber up the dry rock on which Egede stands.

I'll have the native women sew you some of their hide boots, says Egede, himself sporting a pair. They're very obliging in the matter as long as they can keep the needle in payment. I've not worn anything else for years, and have not fallen on my arse since.

Who is that man? Miltzov asks, turning in the direction from which he came. But the savage is gone. He bid me good morning with the peace of God.

What did he look like? Egede asks, glancing about.

Miltzov endeavours to describe him. Black shoulder-length hair fastened with a kind of harness. Clothing of skin. He sat carving a bone.

One of their warlocks, Egede says curtly. A sorcerer. They claim they can fly. Beyond the moon. To the bottom of the sea. That sort of thing. Swindlers, the lot of them. This one has been with us for some years. A bad man indeed. I'd thought myself rid of him. If our paths cross again, he'll soon know that I'm not afraid of him.

They look peaceful enough, says Miltzov, his attention now on a group of natives pulling a skin boat onto the shore. The same clothes of skin. Bare chests. Much mirth.

One needn't go into the desert to avoid looking evil in the eye, says Egede.

Miltzov and Lange exchange glances, but say nothing.

Egede turns abruptly and begins to walk. Lange and Miltzov look at each other questioningly. Then they follow the priest.

Does he mean mischief, this sorcerer? Miltzov enquires.

Yes, Egede replies, skipping from rock to rock, the two younger men hesitantly attempting to follow suit. Beware of him. He will not be ashamed to send an arrow into your back if he gets the chance.

Does he hate the Danes that much?

Yes, all Danes, though me in particular. He believes I've taken something that belongs to him.

What would that be?

Egede says nothing.

Can't he be captured and punished?

We've been trying for some years. But he is sly, and as slippery as soap. Many's the time I've had him in the sights of my musket, but lead seems not to bother him, the Lord's Prayer likewise. He has a knack of vanishing without a trace, then appears again when one is least expecting it. He is in league with the Devil himself. He calls himself Aappaluttoq, the Red One.

The Commandant Landorph will surely be willing to track him down and put him in irons, says Lange.

Egede snorts and skips on, turning then to face them. If you're to be any use to me, you must learn to approach the natives with a firm hand. Without fear. Without lenience. Without mercy. They are to be punished. Cold-blooded, they are, as the cockroach. But they're subdued easily enough. Use the whip when necessary. Or simply wave it under their noses. It's often sufficient.

But will they not hear of salvation? Miltzov asks.

Oh, but indeed. They are in fact quite susceptible and easily moved. One can captivate them with tales of the Saviour and other stories from the Bible. And in one way they do wish to be delivered. They are also God's creatures of a sort, and thereby as naturally inclined towards salvation as any other, although their inclination may at times be hidden away in all of Greenland's blubber. And no sooner has one left them than they have forgotten all that one has imparted to them and devote themselves once more to their silliness and lechery.

///

I am Aappaluttoq. I have for a moment since been with the Pope in Rome. I was served tea and biscuits, and spoke to him for an hour or more on the subject of Christianity and how it became divided by 'the great Luther', and moreover how Erasmus was by far the better reformer. He was a kind and reasonable man. His name was Benedict, and there was much to trouble him. The antics of the priests, gambling and other things he was against. In many ways he was unfortunate and was unable to carry into effect what he wanted, cheated and duped by his own men. All this he told me.

I have flown in spirals and figures of eight around the sun and moon. It was a dizzying flight. I pressed my arms close to my body and flew. At one point I lost consciousness, which is dangerous indeed, for if both one's *timi*, which lies bound and croaking on the floor among the blubber lamps, and one's *tarni* fall unconscious, it can be difficult to put them together again. I know of several who have perished during such a flight. I have penetrated to the core of the earth, a glowing mass into which I poked a finger without being burned, and I have of course been to the bottom of the sea, for there sits the woman with the tangled hair, and this is above all what a shaman does, swim down to *Sassuma arnaa*, which is what we call her, to comb and brush her hair, for it is she who gives us the animals we hunt, those that live in the sea, and if her hair is too tangled by the rubbish we people throw into the sea, she will hold back the animals and we must starve in punishment. These things may quite easily exist alongside belief in God and Jesus, our faith in *Sassuma arnaa*, *Tornaarsuk* and *Sila*, and all the others too, which fact I conveyed to Benedict and found him in agreement with me. We Catholics have our saints and guardian spirits too, and pray to them, he said. Basically, it's the same. I could introduce Christianity into this country as effortlessly as anything if I were allowed to do it my way. I think, in fact, that we Greenlanders are a kind of Catholics. Egede, however, cannot fathom this at all. Therefore, we can only be enemies.

///

Egede skips lightly from rock to rock in his soft shoes of hide. He plants his staff and vaults over clefts and chasms without so much as glancing down. Lange and Miltzov must clamber and crawl on all fours like obedient dogs, scrabbling over the rocks where Egede springs like a goat. Now he stops on a pinnacle, stands and balances without a wobble. He rests his staff on his shoulder. The wind tugs at the tails of his long coat and ruffles his wig. He waits until the two young clergymen catch up with him, then jabs his staff in the air as if indicating to them a broom cupboard in which they might store their chattels.

Baal's River. So called after an Englishman.

The two clergymen stand beside him and look at the view.

The fjord and its tributaries reach some fifteen Danish miles into the land, Egede says. After that, the ice means one can proceed no further. Impossible to negotiate.

It's said there are people living on the other side, says Lange. Norsemen?

Perhaps. The old writings refer to it as Østerbygden, the Eastern Settlement. There was a monastery there, and a bishop too. I've done as I've been able in order to relieve them, as was His Majesty's wish. They are his subjects, of course, yet stand in papist aberration, if they are not all dead or mingled with the natives. The Augsburg Confession will be quite unknown to them. It hardly bears thinking about.

Dreadful, indeed, Miltzov mumbles.

Devil worshippers, Egede growls. Perhaps it's for the better if they're all gone. Why no sign of life from them in hundreds of years? Why have they not shown themselves on this side of country? They are known to be excellent seafarers.

A good question, says Miltzov willingly.

They cultivate the Devil, says Egede with a sly grin. For which reason they keep themselves to themselves. I don't know which is worst, these dastardly, cold-blooded natives or those belligerent papists.

Is there a map of the land? Lange asks, though only to distract the affronted priest towards matters less volatile.

Only the occasional Dutch sea chart and a few sketches done by my own hand. Largely, the land is quite unexplored. The Eastern side lies in darkness, naturally. I endeavoured to sail south of the land some years ago, but was forced to turn back because of ice. The Evil One has his little lodge over there, and blocks all passage so that he might keep his worshippers to himself.

Adam of Bremen writes of Greenland in his *Gesta*, says Miltzov.

And then there is the *Speculum Regale*, Lange adds.

Papist upchuck, Egede snaps. Worthless. Shite and phantasms. The earth is divided into rings, of which those in the middle are glowing hot, while those at the outside are ice-cold. The Northern Lights are thereby reflections of the hot rings. And so on. And anyway, the *Speculum Regale* contains little at all about Greenland, so clearly you haven't read it. Read Peder Friis and his description of Norway. Apart from that, let me give you a piece of advice: read as little as possible, the more to observe with unbiased gaze. Besides that, be certain I shall teach you well.

Indeed, Mr Egede, the two men say in unison, like schoolboys.

How old are the candidates? Egede asks.

Thirty-one, Miltzov replies.

Twenty-five, says Lange.

Egede looks from one to the other from the more elevated rock on which he stands. Where is your family from? he asks Lange.

My father, Magister Peder, is minister of the royal chapel at Frederiksborg Castle. My mother's name is Karen Krestensdatter.

Egede shakes his head. Never heard of them. Are they alive?

Yes, both alive.

And you're not betrothed, I hope?

No, certainly not.

Family and other bonds can only be left behind if a man is to come here, says Egede. Love will make him fat of arse and slow of mind.

And yet Mr Egede has brought his own family, says Lange.

That is quite another matter. He looks at Miltzov piercingly. And where might you be from?

Frederikshald, he replies. My first living was there.

But you don't speak Norwegian?

No, I seem to have lost it somewhere during the course of my studies.

Frederikshald, says Egede. That's nearly Swedish, is it not?

Right on the border, says Miltzov. The home guard is everywhere.

I'm from the Lofoten islands myself, says Egede. Further north than here. Longer winters, longer summers, better weather. Here, it's all the same.

Will Mr Egede return to his homeland when his task is completed here? Miltzov enquires.

I doubt it.

Without another word he turns and proceeds by the lightest of springs down the northern side of the rock. Lange and Miltzov remain standing for a moment before commencing their ungainly descent.

///

I am Aappaluttoq. Has anyone seen my son? The priest took him from me when he was a little boy. Now he is half-grown. I see him often, though he knows me no more, or will not acknowledge me. To be a stranger to your own son is a painful thing. I wish not to take him back, only to make myself known to him, so that he may know who I am. They cannot deny me that. A father should know his son, and a son his father. It's the order of nature. I gave him the name of Paapa. Now he answers to a Danish name, is clad in Danish clothing, a cocked hat, he smells like a Dane, speaks like a Dane, and reads the Bible like a priest. I wish to tell him his true name, so that he may know who he is. A person needs to know his name, for in the name is the soul. I wish to tell him who his father is. I am Aappaluttoq, I will say, the great shaman of whom you have surely heard. You need not be ashamed of me. Be proud, my boy. I think it will be good for him to know. At least, it is my hope.

///

Egede and the two young priests descend to an inlet which, as far as Miltzov can judge, would seem to be parallel to that at which Egede's house stands. There are some tents and a number of skin boats, large and small, drawn up onto the shore. A native boy sees them and shouts something. A dozen natives appear and come towards them. They seem good-natured enough. The long hair of the men is gathered by pearl-studded harnesses fastened beneath the chin, the women's hair is worn in a top, which seems almost to pull their faces upwards and lend them a cheerful, rather frivolous appearance. Their breasts are bare and rather flat. One holds a large child which clings to her, its weight resting on her hip as it suckles her milk. Miltzov looks the other way.

Poul! Egede calls out, shouting the name out louder again after a short moment: Po-ul!

A young Dane appears. Egede has no need to present him by name, for they share the same beak of a nose, though the son has a somewhat milder line to his mouth, and kinder eyes.

My son Poul, he says nevertheless in his by now familiar offhand manner, jabbing his staff by way of indication.

The lad bows and presents himself politely.

Poul will be sailing back home with the ship to prepare for the priesthood, Egede tells them.

Are you to follow in your father's footsteps and become a missionary? Lange enquires.

Yes, that is the plan, Poul replies. I wished to become a sea captain, but my father refused. He glances up in his father's direction.

If you are still thinking of becoming a seaman, then I shall find you a gallows on which to hang yourself, says Egede. My son speaks the native tongue fluently, he goes on. We have embarked upon a translation of the New Testament into Greenlandic. The Evangelists.

From the Greek? Miltzov asks.

We're sticking to Luther's splendid German.

I won't be going until the autumn, the lad says. I can take you out in the boat and show you the district.

We would appreciate it, says Lange.

One of the natives says something. Poul translates. He wants to know if the King has sent you.

Yes, says Miltzov. King Frederik has sent us.

We know the King, says the man. My uncle has met him.

Indeed? says Miltzov, his incredulous eyes returning to Poul.

It's true enough, says Poul. A small number of the natives sailed with one of the ships to Denmark so that His Majesty might meet his new subjects. Regrettably they caught the pox and most died, though not before having shaken hands with the King.

Are you to help *palasi* tell us stories? they ask.

Palasi?

Their word for us priests, says Egede. A corruption of the North-Norwegian pronunciation of the word, I should think. *Præst.* With a couple of vowels added and the *t* thrown out.

I'll help you with the language, as much as I can before I leave, the young Egede says. Then Niels can take over.

Niels?

My brother.

Is he not to be a priest too?

No, he's to be a merchant, says Egede. He hasn't the head for the priesthood.

They chat for a while. The natives join in the conversation, freely and without restraint, and Egede and his son switch between Norwegian and Greenlandic. When addressing the two young clergymen, they modify their dialect and employ a slightly more formal Danish. An elderly man, clearly the *oldermand* of the settlement, says something solemn.

He wishes you welcome to his land, says Poul Egede. He permits you to go about peacefully wheresoever you will, and to shoot the game and take a native wife.

I don't think that's allowed, says Miltzov awkwardly.

It may be forbidden, but it's done all the same, says Egede. Such is life here. One has to be pragmatic. The law must follow on the heels of lechery, as it has always done, moderating, though never entirely eradicating. Since we are to colonize the country, we may as well mix with the locals. Besides, it will make our missionary efforts that much easier in the long run. Fornication, however, is most certainly not permitted.

It is said that the native women are hollow-backed, says Lange.

Twaddle, says Egede. They're as good as all other women. Head and arse are where they are in ours too. They're broad below and narrow above, so a man can tell which is the important part.

///

I am Aappaluttoq. I steal into the dwelling-house. It is warm and smells of food, and there are people, all Danes from the ship. They do not see me. I can't see Paapa anywhere. And I cannot call for him. The priest is not there, which is good. He knows me. And he despises me, though I have never done him any wrong. Well, perhaps teased him a bit. He doesn't like that. He thinks I'm the Devil. He would throw me out if he saw me, or else he would beat me. I don't want to fight with the priest today. All I want is to find my son, to say hello to him and then leave. My kayak lies up the shore in an inlet, I will tell him. I frequent the skerries further south, and I will tell him where they are. Come and visit me sometime, if you will. I wish you no harm. All I want is to say hello to you.

///

They enter one of the tents, the oldermand's, and are shown to a large bench. The place is teeming with people, mostly women and children. The women's eyes are lively, Miltzov finds. Those of the children are more reserved. The gaze of the men appears as if through a film, a deathly membrane. He finds them beautiful, and no longer refrains from looking at the women's nudity. But there is a raw stench of urine, untanned hide and boiling flesh that is repulsive to him.

Food is served to them, large lumps of meat on tin plates. Egede and his son immediately pull out their knives and cut off chunks to put in their mouths. The two young priests follow suit. The meat does not taste bad, Miltzov and Lange, seated next to each other, agree. It is very salty, perhaps even boiled in brine. It tastes slightly of whale oil and is delicate on the tongue.

Egede speaks to the natives. He mixes Norwegian and Greenlandic, and his son translates. Apparently, it is the story of the feeding of the five thousand. The natives interrupt him with questions and he ponders over his replies. Now and then his son interjects in order to explain something. It seems they have no conception as to what wine might be. Is it aquavit? Aquavit makes people wild and mad in the head. No, it's not aquavit. Trees are likewise a mystery to them. Egede explains that these conversations are of great use to him in his translation work. For instance, he has chosen to render a line of the Lord's Prayer as *give us this day our daily meat*. Bread is something they know only from the Danes, it is not a natural part of their diet, and thereby the meaning would be lost.

Do they not eat bread? Miltzov asks.

Sometimes they are given it here, but then they complain of stomach aches.

Is there drunkenness among them? Lange wants to know.

No, not that I know of. As such, they are innocent, Egede says. In many ways they are like children, mischievous and inconsiderate as children can be, but also innocent. The fact of the matter is that there is not a scrap of badness in the majority.

But these shamans? Miltzov enquires, unable to dismiss from his mind his earlier encounter with the savage. What about them?

Never a paradise without a serpent, says Egede.

Emerging from the tent, the air, mild but a short time ago, feels icily cold.

///

I am Aappaluttoq. I can make myself invisible. I become as glass or water. Thus I may wander about the rooms of the priest, among all these people who sit and eat and talk, without any of them noticing me. I have been here many times, and never was I seen by a single soul. Only the priest sees me, and his wife, Gertrud. There she is. She sends me a glance and nods. I lose confidence when the priest appears, and lose the ability to remain invisible. Several times he has beaten me, I don't know why. Perhaps he is simply fond of it. We Greenlanders do not hit each other. It never happens. We might kill an enemy if necessary, pierce him with a harpoon or a bird arrow, cut his throat perhaps, though only when he turns his back. We consider it an impoliteness to kill someone face to face. But the Danes are different. They wish to change us and make us believe in Christ. I know Christ. I've got nothing against him. I've even met him. A nice man, and yet commanding, not nearly as mild and gentle as they want him to be. He listened intently to what I had to say. I've read their Bible too. I read Danish better than most Danes. It was the missionary Top who taught me it. I find it to be a good book. I like the story of Job, who loses everything and sits there tossing dust into the air. In the Bible a person may read about themselves, that's the good thing about it. Anyone can find themselves in it. The story of Job is my own story. I should like to have told the priest about it. But he's impossible to talk to.

///

Käthe! Käthe! Egede calls as they enter the house. Ah, there you are. Has he been here? Have you seen him? Have you spoken to him?

Madame Egede, whose proper name is Gertrud Rasch, helps her husband remove his skin shoes and hangs them up on a line.

We've boiled a big pot of barley porridge, she says without answering his questions. The ship has brought oats, and some have escaped the mildew. The girls have made butter of goat's milk cream.

Remember to salt it well, says Egede. I wish to taste salt. He rubs his hands. Salt is a good measure against devilry. Where is the salt?

The bowl is pushed across the table to him. He picks some grains between his fingers and tosses them over his shoulder.

The two Egede girls are at the age of confirmation. They approach bashfully. Their unattractiveness makes them seem all the more touching, Miltzov finds. Their father's beak protrudes from their tender faces, an unsightly detail. God's trembling hand, he thinks to himself. The son Niels has departed on an expedition further north together with a native foster-brother. Lange and Miltzov seat themselves and converse the girls, who have seated themselves on the floor as if they were natives, their feet tucked beneath their narrow behinds. They are shy, stammering and blushing, though soon warm up in conversation with the two young clergymen. The girls ask them about Copenhagen, where their father has been, though they never, about the various quarters of the city, as if they were familiar with them from personal experience: Have they seen that sign in Østergade, that statue on Ulfeldts Plads, this or that building? Have they been to the Palace and met the King and Queen, and are their dogs not wonderfully sweet? The girls become excited, something kittenish and manipulably girlish comes over them. Miltzov sees them from above, the shortened perspective, the soft sweeping line to their hips, their stockinged feet, toes peeping through undarned holes with which they absently fidget. Eventually, their mother tells them to leave the young candidates in peace, they've had a long voyage and there'll be plenty of time to ask their questions later, and so they get to their feet and withdraw obediently.

///

Where is he? Paapa? I cannot see him anywhere.

I steal up the stairs. There are various rooms with beds inside, a stench of old bedding straw, the foul-smelling sleep of the Danes, of piss and sweat, rottenness and exile. Does my son smell like this, now that he has become a Dane? People who are torn up by the root quickly begin to smell, like corpses. Or does he still smell faintly as a Greenlander?

I open the doors and look inside, but Paapa is nowhere. In one of the beds lies a woman. There is something wrong with her. Her nakedness is like wax. She froths at the mouth, her body trembles, arches upwards and collapses limply again. Some women are like that. I have seen it before, in our own women too. It is a kind of moon sickness.

I bend over the bed, hold my hand flat against her stomach and press her down into the straw. Immediately she relaxes, her breathing becomes calm and steady, and she opens her eyes. I know you, she says. I have dreamt about you.

I am Aappaluttoq. Have you seen my son?

She does not reply. Instead she spreads her legs and invites me. Some women are like that. One must certainly feel sympathy for them. She begins to growl and murmur some words. Her eyes are dark as coal. She says something about the Devil. I am not your Devil, I say. I am Aappaluttoq. Try to understand. I am looking for my son. But she continues to growl and mutter about the Devil. She is mad, the poor woman. I lie down with her, nudging her gently aside with my hip to find room. I grip her head and hold her tight. She calms. I make love to her, pressing myself inside her. It is delightful. She is very young, I sense, untouched, filled with sweetness that ruptures about my cock. And then she sleeps. I leave her sleeping. My cock drips blood and semen. My head feels heavy. So it is always. One loses a part of oneself, and leaves it with them. They steal it from you, hiding it away in a compartment inside themselves, guarding it like a treasure, and you are a measure poorer when you leave.

The men look up at me as I pass through the room. And Egede is there. I am invisible no more. I cannot be invisible when he is about, not to everyone. Who are you? the men enquire. What are you doing here? We want no monkeys here.

Egede leaps to his feet. Glasses topple and fall to the floor. He shouts out: There he is, the Devil!

The two new priests jump up too. They stare at me, or stare through me. They cannot see me. So it is. Some can see me, others not.

I am not the Devil. And I am no monkey either. I know of monkeys. I have seen them in a forest a long way away. I am Aappaluttoq.

But I do not say so. I pass calmly through the room and out of the house. I run across the rocks, I return to my kayak, push away from the shore and paddle out into the open sea where I can shout and scream and weep with no one to hear me.

///

My dear Hans, says Madame Rasch, Egede's wife. Whatever is the matter with you? There's nothing there. You're seeing things.

But indeed there is. Did you not see him, Käthe? He was here. Right there. He points. His finger trembles.

A ghost? says one of the men. I saw him too.

You're drunk, says the one next to him. Or else not drunk enough. Have some more.

Sit down, Hans, says the Madame. Remember we have guests. Drink a cup of ale. She stands behind him, grips his shoulders, presses him down onto the chair. He wipes his brow, picks up a random cup from the table and downs its contents.

Mother Käthe is a pillar to me, he says, wiping his mouth with a still trembling hand. I could not manage in this land without her.

Miltzov and Lange glance at each other.

Why does he call her Käthe? Miltzov whispers to Lange.

It was the name of Luther's wife, says Lange. I think he is rather

obsessed with the great reformer. Listen and I think you will find he
quotes him all the time.

When it is time to eat, the sick girl, the jomfru Titius, called Titia,
is brought down from her chamber upstairs. Miltzov goes to her,
takes her moist hand and leads her to the table. She seems unusually
settled and satisfied with all things, speaking coherently and with
reason with the Egede girls. She has brushed her hair and put on a
clean dress, and there is a colour in her cheeks. She eats greedily
and asks for seconds.

It gladdens me to see you feeling better, Titia, says Miltzov.

I am well now, she says. Someone came and did something. And
now I am well.

Pors and some officers arrive in a boat. With them they have
brought some small cannon and several barrels of gunpowder. Salutes
are fired, there are fireworks and speeches, a party lasting well into
the night. Miltzov, who does not drink, drinks. For the first time in
his life he becomes wildly drunk.

///

A meeting of the colony council, the next day in Egede's rooms. They
have been onto the mainland and decided on the placement of the
colony. Landorph, Egede and Pors, this triumvirate of power, sit at
the head of the table. Miltzov and Lange are seated next to each other
further down. Egede harps on about the Mission being the important
thing. The Trade and the military are there to serve it. I have spoken
personally with the King on the matter, he says.

I too have spoken with King Frederik, says Pors, only a couple of
months ago as it happens. He expressed very clearly that he wishes
a healthy and profitable Trade to be established.

Indeed, he is plagued by debt like all kings, says Fleischer, the
Paymaster. Always on the lookout for income.

No, the Mission must come first, Egede protests. There can be no
discussion. The natives are to be Christianized, whereafter the old
Norsemen on the eastern side of the land are to be found and reformed
into the Lutheran faith.

This project is greater than any of you can fathom, says Pors earnestly. It concerns something quite apart from Christianizing a few savages. And without the Trade we cannot achieve any of these matters. The Trade absolutely must come first, just as a man's bodily nourishment must come before all else.

A well-nourished sinner is still a sinner, says Egede. And what goes in through the mouth soon comes out through the arse again. Faith must naturally take priority. What will the Governor do with nourishment and trade if he is to burn in Hell in spite of it all?

Pors's countenance is severe. After a moment he says: First of all we must find a name for the new colony. The choice is ours, gentlemen.

Porsminde? says Landorph.

Oh, but that would be all too kind, my dear Landorph, the Governor replies cloyingly. I was rather thinking along the lines of Frederiksten, perhaps?

Frederikshald? says Miltzov.

Frederiksborg? Lange suggests.

Frederikshåb? the Trader Kopper chips in.

Kronprins Christians Borg? says Fleischer. Or just Christiansborg?

No, the Crown Prince is a miserable sort, says Pors. We do not care for him.

Dronning Anna Sophies Borg? one of the other officers poses.

Women bring bad luck, says Pors. No good. Besides, it's too long. Let's have something short and snappy.

Godborg?

Godsten?

Guldborg?

Gudhavn?

Gudhjem?

Kristborg?

Fredensborg?

Fredensten?

Godthåb, says Egede.

A silence descends. All eyes turn to the priest.

Yes, says Pors. Godthåb. It sits well on the tongue. Why not?

Why not Porshåb? mutters Landorph, who has been drinking. Or Claushavn? he adds, a tad desperately. No one laughs.

Any objections to the name of Godthåb? Pors asks the council. First, second, third time of asking. Then Godthåb it is. Bombardier, a threefold salute for the colony of Good Hope!

///

The next morning. Miltzov emerges from the privy. He has vomited, his guts are inside out. I do not drink, he tells himself. I am not a person who drinks. Never again. A small glass only. Hair of the dog. As of tomorrow I am done with it. He steps forward and almost loses his footing in the sludge. It has snowed. Snow, he wonders. In July? Everything is different here. I am different. The evenings are ruin, the mornings a resurrection. This is the new life.

He crouches down on all fours, picks up a handful of snow and rubs it in his face. When he looks up, the savage is there, barely an arm's length away, a bone in one hand, a knife in the other.

Peace of God, priest.

2

The Best of all Possible Worlds

This day I crossed with the boat to the new colony so that I might see how far they had advanced with the building work, which was yet to be completed, therefore making us anxious indeed that the house would not be sufficiently ready for us to move in before the winter. My family and I now had no other dwelling than an open storage shed which stood out at the old colony.

FROM HANS EGEDE'S JOURNAL, SEPTEMBER 1728

Abyssus abyssum!

How hideous is man. He inhabits a hideous world, the most hideous of all possible worlds. Who was it who said that? And as if to add insult to injury, it is now raining. It has rained and snowed since our arrival here. The ships lie shrouded in fog. The sea sighs heavily. The earth sighs when trodden upon, and the soul sighs when the foot becomes soaked. The rocks trickle with rainwater. The grey sky dips, sated and weary, to the land. The natives are filthy swine. The Danes hardly any better. When I see a man, I see his corpse, the dull, blue-green sheen of the muscles, the rotten belly, the grin of death. I cannot help it. It comes with the profession. The colony is full of corpses, more than a hundred; they dance their bony dance and grin; they drink and fornicate and pretend they are not dead. Man is a maggot-sack hastening towards the grave.

This is the problem of man, the opposite is true of the animals. We are created in God's image. We carry within us the discrepancy between mortal flesh and undying spirit. And so we turn to God, for we cannot grasp our death. Man is too big to die, but too small to fathom his own death. Therefore, God ought surely to be death's opposite, and its remedy? But for the blackcoats, the priests. It has all got out of hand with them. They say to us: Prepare ye for death! In the realm of the priests, God and death have become as one. This is their great mistake.

My name is Christian Kieding, surgeon of the colony. I am thirty-four years of age, born in Jutland. In Bergen I served at the garrison, becoming then barber-surgeon on the pink the *Kronprinds Christian*, which arrived here this spring, a couple of months before the three ships with the turmoil that is to be the King's new colony.

The weather here is most peculiar. I am not even sure one could say it was raining. The moisture seems to hang in the air like wet washing, though without quite approaching what one would refer to as fog. It is the clouds of the sky descended to earth, to go about among men like the Titans of old. And that is on a good day. Often it blows up a storm from the south-west. Then, the rain, or the sleet, is slung sideways and finds its way inside the smallest crack or crevice, into one's clothing, into one's bones, into the crates of provisions, into the building materials, into everywhere. Much has already been discarded, meat unfit to eat, wriggling with maggots, timber gone to rot. The maggots thrive in the damp weather. For the moment they chew on the salted pork in the barrels. Soon they will find other, fresher meat on which to sate themselves. The tents in which the crew sleep are ruined. They have sought shelter in some peat-huts that house the natives in winter. This is worse than Bergen, and Bergen is bad. Yet the people are chased outside, for there is work to be done. At present they are erecting the foundation walls of the governor's residence. *Primum prima*, as the old Romans used to say. The Governor himself keeps to his cabin in the *Morian*, which lies at anchor off the colony. The men are covered from head to toe in thick clay and resemble African slaves. Some jumped in the harbour to wash off the mud, only to clamber back onto land again as dirty as before and a whole lot colder. Now they lie coughing in their miserable beds. I tell them to take off their wet clothes and scrub themselves with flax so as to stimulate the flow of blood in their veins. But they shrink from being naked and would rather have aquavit than good advice from me. They can do as they please. There is no shortage of aquavit, and the quota has been put up in order to ease the mood. Drunkenness is on the rise, not just among the common crew, but also the officers. Occasionally, I will happen to see the Governor standing on the deck of the *Morian* staring in at the land, partly enveloped by fog. After a moment, he retires to his cabin again. He can do as he pleases.

The priest, Egede, seems not to be bothered by the bad weather. Nor has he been afflicted by the spreading consumption, the same being true of his family, his wife and the four youngsters, and the native boy who always follows along on his heels. He tells me the plants of the countryside, scurvy grass and angelica, are good for treating the sickness so many seamen suffer. In the winter it may be dug up from under the snow. And make sure to always be in motion, he says. Move about, work, do not sit still, or else misery and sickness will be upon you. He is forever chewing on some matter from the vegetable kingdom, and I now follow his advice. There are many herbs inside the peninsula. I drink nothing but fresh water and a little ale, and feel myself to be well. Never better, in fact.

His wife is much older than him, well over fifty, while he is around forty. They are dull, but as imperishable as old woodwork. Madame Egede seems stiffened into the mould of the dogged old woman, her face furrowed like a length of driftwood. The girls have their monthly indispositions, always at the same time, an irascible pair who resemble their father in mind and stature. They are of course besotted with the two young magisters and sit at their feet with their legs tucked underneath them, trying to make themselves delectable, which in many ways they are, especially when seen from behind. If they had any sense, they would sit facing away from the young gentlemen and tempt them with their rearmost curves. A girl with long hair, a sweeping loin and a pair of undarned socks poking out from under her backside can only call to a man's aesthetic senses and engender his sympathy. But do not turn around, girls! Strange, how much a nose can ruin a good face, or indeed a whole person. Egede came from the north of Norway. He had made a nuisance of himself, so I hear, got some backs up, the *sognepræst* with whom he shared his fish tithes, the provost, the bishop and the parish officer, and then the thought occurred to him that he might travel to Greenland. I shouldn't wonder they were glad to be rid of him. He had read accounts about the ancient Norsemen who were meant to be living here, but found only these small, dark people who had never heard of Jesus, much less of Luther, who is Egede's house-god. Now he has taken it upon himself to save them instead. Most likely they would be best served living the way they have always done. But Egede still talks of the Norsemen, of them living in isolation with their devil worship and papism on the eastern side of the land. Pors has announced he will make an expedition there, and thinks he will ride over the ice-cap on horseback. I imagine his journey will be short. Or else long, as long as the afterlife.

Naturally, there is a shortage of building materials. Most will be used on the new residence, which will house both governor and priest in their separate wings, and where we, the officers, too will be quartered. No one seems to have given a thought to where the numerous crew are to be put up. They growl and mutter about it, though mostly to pressure the governor into putting up their aquavit ration. And this indeed is done, time and again, by the grace of our own highly esteemed pasteboard admiral. The Governor is straight out of the comedy house in Copenhagen, strutting about in his long wig, red uniform, sword and cocked hat. The officers have no time for him. But the crew love and honour him. And indeed one would do well not to underestimate him. He is a cunning one, shrewd for all his fine new clothes. Now and then, when the rain stops, he is to be seen galloping about on his mare, the water spraying from the animal's hooves. The general dissatisfaction is directed more towards those more immediately in charge, the Paymaster and the Trader, as well as the officers who run the daily work and command them about.

The twenty-four released offenders are a fine illustration of how desperate and ill-conceived the King's colonial fancies are when carried out into the real world. They are the worst rabble a person can imagine. Young people, though hardened and clouded in their deepest souls, where one must suppose a ray of sun has never once shone. Nearly all are ill with the consumption and the effects of the sea voyage. Not that it seems to hold them back. The women sell themselves to the officers and the tradesmen in return for tobacco and aquavit, and their husbands pocket the proceeds. And so it is that our Danish customs have been brought here to be mingled with the native swine. I shall wager that most have kicked the bucket by the time the first winter has gone. They can do as they please.

I don't know why I'm so glad to be here. And yet I am. I wander about the inland landscape, dismissive of the rain, dismissive of the wind, finding grandness in the smallest detail – the tiny flowers that grow among the rocks, the misty, gurgling moors, quite white with cotton-grass, the wild thyme which has such a rich and splendid scent when rolled between the fingers, the stillness, the flitting sparrows, which are not frightened by man at all, but will come and feed from the hand – rather than in the spectacular surroundings, which anyway are shrouded by cloud. I gather herbs and plants, many of which presumably possess medicinal properties. I see hares and grouse, ravens, a fox whose zigzagging course I follow. It looks over its shoulder and keeps an eye on me. I will not harm you. It does not seem afraid of me either, though it has never seen a white man before. We come onto higher ground, behind a fell, to a tarn whose full extent is unclear to me due to the mist. I walk along its shore, and drink some water. It is pure and thirst-quenching. The fox pauses, it has seen a lemming or a mouse and stands for some time with a front paw raised, then steals forward all of a sudden to pounce, and the next moment a wriggling, squeaking rodent is locked in its jaws. It looks at me as if to say: There, you see, that is how it is done.

I carry a musket, of course, on my wanderings. But I do not use it. I have no desire to shoot anything. I am a friend of nature, no roaming murderer.

The whole colony project is rather fascinating. Grand in design, folly in practice, as any enterprise which emanates from the Chancellery. I shouldn't wonder if not a single one of the fine gentlemen in those corridors possessed even a shred of the knowledge required of its human and material resources. Yet there is great dramaturgy in the endeavour, whose servants we all our. The spread of civilization! The conquest and cultivation of the barren land. The stupidity evident in the detail is balanced by the beauty of the whole. It possesses its own relentless momentum and bears with it its own survival, as we men bear with us our death. And thus the march of history and the fate of the individual run parallel in their opposite directions.

The dwelling-house on the Hope Isle, in which the Egede family have lived these past seven years, is being pulled down around its occupants, myself among them, who in the meantime have become more or less homeless. Daily I sail in to the new colony to see how the work is progressing. I cannot suffer the stuffy room. Family life is anathema to me.

I am not married. The salary of a garrison surgeon is modest indeed. Nor have I ever had the wish, not seriously. Of course, I have had my flings. I was in love with a girl once. It was in Bergen. Her name was Sørine Hall, and she was a merchant's daughter. Alas, good Sørine, how sad your fate. A sixteen-year-old girl with spindly legs and thick pigtails, a freckled nose and eyes like a cow. Cows have such lovely eyes. But still they are cows. I was some years her elder, this was a couple of years ago. Her father, the merchant Gottfred Hall, was friendly to me. We smoked many a cigar and drank many a dram together. She was the last of his children to remain unmarried. I visited them often. They lived on their own with their servants. The mother had died some years before. It was clear to me that both she and her father were merely waiting for me to declare my intentions. But the strange thing is that the attraction went away, vanished simply, as the snow vanishes in spring. Suddenly I disliked her. I had kissed her a few times, and had held her to my chest and felt the desire, hers as well as my own. But of course she was coy and reticent, and although I knew full well that this was how it was meant to be, she being a respectable young lady of good family, this nonetheless made me despise her. I could no longer abide the sight of the girl. She was a dalliance, I saw it so clearly then. She knew nothing of housekeeping. Her teeth were slightly protruding. She gave all the impression of someone refusing to take life seriously. I noticed then that her breath smelled, an oddly nause-ating odour, as if she were suffering the consumption. That smell is indeed noticeable and I have myself made the diagnosis on numerous occasions by simply leaning my nose towards a patient's open mouth. It is an interesting bouquet. We all of us go about with a corpse inside us. And such a corpse smells. I terminated our acquaintance by writing her a letter. I do not love you. You are better served with another. Etc. Why not be honest? In the long run it is always the most considerate. I heard that the jomfru was sent to some family in the interior. But whether she lived or died, I have no idea. Most likely she died. It did not concern me. I was free.

The Governor's housekeeper, the jomfru Titius, comes to me, a frail and tender-aged girl with the face of a Nefertiti. She has moved in with the Egedes. I am pregnant, she says, blurting the word.

I press her abdomen, though am unable to determine if she is or not.

My bleeding has not come.

It's probably the voyage. I'm sure it will come again.

I don't think so. I thought I'd tell you.

Have you been with a man?

I don't know. Perhaps, when I was asleep or dead.

I see. It would not surprise me if a man had made free with her while she lay enfeebled by her falling sickness. Let us see in a couple of months. If you are pregnant then, I will be able to feel it. What will you do if you really are?

I'd like to have a child.

A child is not a doll. It needs care and looking after.

I know.

If what you believe turns out to be right, perhaps you would prefer to go home again in the *Morian*?

No, thank you. I like it here.

Then we are two, I say, and smile.

When I was young, I naturally wished to be a poet. I wrote sonnets, hymns, odes and villanelles to my beloved, which is to say, for want of another, my mother. I would sit up in the evenings and nights, writing as if in the grip of a fever. In the daytime, I would mutter out the feet of verses, and my mother was afraid I was going mad, so often did I go about talking to myself. I did not show my poems to anyone. I wished to let them lie and then return to them after a year or two in order to appraise them objectively from that greater distance. And indeed I did so, only to see that all of it was dreadful, banal, shamelessly bad. Whereupon I burned the lot and thereafter felt myself freed. That evening, I drank until drunk with some student friends. You seem so glad, they said. Have you ditched your sweetheart? Something like that, I told them. Since then, I have not felt the inclination to shape a verse. I have no ear for poetry either, and do not read it, preferring the prosaic marble of old Latin verse to the lyrical quagmires of the new Germans.

A number of the convicts have built their own peat-huts and have moved in with their women. Peter Hageman is one, a drunkard and a blighter. His wife is called Cellar-Katrine. Unfortunately, she became sweet with one of the older men, Georg Weerback, whose own very young wife, Wispy Kirstine, was summarily shown the door to live alone with the rest of the crew. This Kirstine is both prettier and more decent than any of the other convict women, so it defies my understanding that she could be ditched for such a haggard and toothless tart as Katrine. But no doubt she plays her instrument that much better than any of the others. In the meantime, Hageman soon tired of living alone and took the young Kirstine to himself. A man of the old school, he beat the girl and pulled her hair if she would not obey him. Black and blue she went about for a while, holding a hand to her ear after her ear-drum seemingly was perforated by a fiercely delivered blow from the hand of her chivalrous beau. However, the said Cellar-Katrine quickly became jealous of the young girl and eventually administered her a beating too, whereafter she took the opportunity to move back in with our Monsieur Peter again. Now once more the couple inhabit their peat-hut in nuptial bliss and harmony. This kind of marital drama is seen most every day. They can do as they please.

The *Morian* has departed, accompanied by ear-splitting cannon-ades from the land. The Governor has moved into Peter Hageman's peat-hut together with Titia, for which reason Hageman himself has been forced to occupy another, poorer dwelling along with his wench.

The eldest Egede son has left with the ship. He is to go into the priesthood and follow in his father's footsteps here in this country. The galliot the *West-Vlieland* lies here still. Perhaps she will remain here over the winter. But even now, after the *Morian*'s departure, we can feel the winter approach, the inklings of what it will be like here when not a ship remains in the roadstead.

A number of crates containing salted meat, which have stood out in all weather since arriving here in July, were today opened. This meat too was of course infested with maggots and had to be ditched in the sea. However, some natives who have settled close to the colony and have already learned, like the crows and the ravens, to scavenge from us, retrieved it from the bottom and then boiled and ate it. Now they have become ill. At Madame Rasch's request I have shown them the kindness of attending to them. They are all quite enfeebled, two of them seriously so, evacuating what is inside them from both ends and most certainly dying. Two children have distended bellies and eyes like fishes of the deepest sea, this from the diarrhoea and vomiting, and the loss of fluids that goes with it. They too will die. I bled a couple of these poor wretches, though found any other procedure futile. Those who are not affected as badly are of course alarmed by the situation and have expressed the wish for all to be baptized before they perish so as to avoid the descent into Hell, whose terrible details Egede has minutely elaborated to them. I pass this on to him. He declines.

I have preached to them for years until blue in the face, he says, and they have been nothing but contrary and inveterate. They are completely ignorant of the Gospel's notion of grace, no matter how much I have endeavoured to make it plain to them. I cannot defend baptizing such people. His native son stands at his side, nodding piously at his father's every word.

But infants receive the gift of grace in the baptism, I object. A person can hardly be more ignorant than a new-born child?

A child is brought to the baptism by a baptized guardian, whether it be the priest himself or a relative of the child. These people are heathens to the depths of their souls. Who should keep them to the Christian faith until the confirmation?

They will die before they get that far.

Then let them die. What do you say, Frederik Christian? He turns to his foster-son.

Yes, let them die, says the boy.

We stand buffeted by the wind, conversing in the open air. My hair, my clothing, my thoughts are wrenched this way and that and brought into disorder. Normally I am not bothered by windy weather. Egede is as little disturbed by it as by anything else. He is a pillar of serenity. But inside he is seething. He glares at me.

That they should be gripped by the fear of Hell in their hour of death and wish therefore to save themselves at the last minute is no concern of mine. Let them go to Hell, yes. They are awaited there.

Let them go to Hell, the boy repeats.

But will they not be consigned to limbo, as persons unbaptized? I ask.

Perhaps. Limbo is a papist invention, the Bible says nothing about it, Luther neither. However, there is a mention of an intermediate state for the unbaptized who are pure of heart, a state of paralysis, neither fire nor salvation. No need to tell them this, though. The fright will do them good.

Two of the sick survive, the rest perish in pain and fear. They can do as they please.

///

Johan Furst is the first of the Danes to die. One of the released offenders. He lies in his bed a week with a rattling cough and bloody sputum. He has been weak since the voyage, his condition gradually worsening. I bled him, applied leeches and cupping-glasses, and paler he grew, though never was he well again. It was a peaceful death. He was given the sacrament and clutched a crucifix in his hand as he passed in sleep. His spouse by lot, Johanne Nielsdatter, called Johanne Long-stocking, sat by him until the last. It seems the women cope much better in the damp weather here than their men.

I am told it has been the wettest and windiest summer in living memory. Everything is sodden, food, clothing, building materials. We are wet to the soul. And there are more deaths: two among the offenders, a couple of tradesmen, a soldier. I should think they burn poorly where they are, though time is on their side.

///

The Egede house is now pulled down and all of us moved into Godthåb. The residence is but half-built. The colony council has decided the house is to be divided into several parts, one for the Governor and one for the Egede family, with a combined school and mission room in between, the first floor given over to the two young clergymen and the officers, myself among them. For the time being we must shelter in the peat-huts and in the few tents that remain serviceable.

Fuel is in short supply. The coal is being saved to make sure we don't run out in the winter. We burn our building materials, which amounts to pissing in our trousers to stay warm. All of us are freezing, cold to the marrow, and all of us coughing and hacking. Some have sought shelter with the savages, whose dwellings are forever boiling hot and where they sit naked, sweating like Jutland carthorses. They burn blubber. We could do the same, if only our stoves were made for it. There is plenty of it. It swims in the fjord.

The Governor and Egede may often be seen walking and speaking together. They seem to have come to some understanding. Happily so, as they are to live door by door when the house is finished. When the council meets, every Saturday, they endeavour as best they can to be in agreement, though often it is hard work, for the one is as singular as the other. It has now been decided that one of the ships, the *West-Vlieland*, will remain at the colony through the winter and serve as quarters for some of the officers as well as a store for various goods that they may be kept dry. The other ship, the *Fortuna*, has sailed.

///

The twenty-ninth of August. For once, there is sunshine today. The good weather prompts a ceremony by which the colony is formally declared. In his speech, Pors makes the prediction that the good weather is a herald of the colony's good fortune. What the past two months of misery might herald is something he does not comment on. His speech is rather hopeful, sanguine almost. He is of course drunk, as most of the others, though not me. I drink seldom, and only in moderation. It is a day off, a day of festivity. Pors concludes with the words, Remember what the philosopher says: we live in the best of all possible worlds!

The sunshine and warm weather seem to agree.

Egede gives his first sermon in front of the residence, regardless that it remains unfinished. He asks the Lord to bless 'Godthåb, the royal Danish colony in Greenland'. All the people of the colony are gathered, those who are well enough. More than three score on the open space in front of the house. How many of us will be left, I wonder, when the first year here is celebrated?

After the Governor has spoken, and the priest has delivered his sermon, a salute is given, a long series of cannonades into the blue sky. We proceed to the Governor's peat-hut for dinner. His old grey eminence, Skård, serves for us. He has prepared the food with the housekeeper, Titia. They make an odd couple. As we begin on the soup, the rain begins to lash against the panes. It is almost as if a sigh of relief is heard around the table. Back to normal again.

Skål, says the Governor. Let us not hold back on the aquavit.

Even Egede is drunk that night. However, his intoxication does not make him cheerful, but seething with anger. He rants on about fire and brimstone, the Devil, the Antichrist in Rome. He can do as he pleases.

///

The following week, four more of the men die, two enlisted soldiers, one among the offenders and a carpenter. Many more lie ill. Yet the Earth still turns. And why should it not? If the Earth felt for those who lived on it, it would forget to revolve on its axis, or else it would spin faster, spiral out of control, shaking off all life that wriggles upon it, to vanish out among the cold and extinguished stars or be burnt up in the sun's embrace. But the Earth does not feel for us. And we should be glad of the fact.

I still stand with my feet planted firmly on this soil. I am going nowhere. I'm fine here. I love this place, and as the English bard writes:

'I must be cruel only to be kind;

thus bad begins and worse remains behind.'

3

Two-Kings

We have for some time neither seen nor heard anything of Apaluttork, nor in any other way perceived his persecutions. Lord, allow him now peace in his soul, if he will not turn to you and seek forgiveness for his malice, that he may find a merciful and proximate end, and we be relieved of him. Amen.

FROM HANS EGEDE'S JOURNAL, OCTOBER 1728

The cannon outside the governor's residence splutter hoarsely. Long live King Frederik the Fourth!

Frederik Christian became ill following a trip with his foster-brother Niels. The two youngsters had been out all day in a boat in rain and sleet and had come home soaked to the skin and shivering with cold. He lay in the parlour in Egede's rooms and lingered between life and death, and in a clear moment he heard Egede say to his wife: I pray each day that the Lord will let him live, for He it was who gave him to me, and so it is my wish that He allow me to keep him. These overheard words of his foster-father gave him strength, and he was able to rise from the straw of his makeshift bed on the floor and drag himself to the table where the family were seated while Egede read to them from his sermons. They stared at him in dismay, as if he were already a ghost. Still, they gave him the plate of porridge he asked for, and he forced himself to eat it. After that, he slowly recovered.

So, you didn't want to miss the King's birthday, Egede had said, looking at him with eyes which glowed with tenderness.

This was the beginning of October. In just over a week the birthday was to be celebrated. They had only recently moved into the great colony house, the Governor at one end, the Egedes at the other.

Between the two dwellings, within the elbow of the two wings, lay the mission room, as if it were a buffer between religious and temporal powers. The house smelled of tarred, moist timber. There was a hammering and a sawing from morning till night, and the mason was still at work slapping mortar into the joins of the outside walls.

Now the cannon sound again. A toast to King Frederik!

He was confirmed in the summer. Fourteen years old. Now he was a man. But what else was he? The small number of other natives who had been baptized were all dead. He did not belong either to the Danish Christians. But he knew that Jesus loved him. Egede kept telling him so. Otherwise, being a Christian, one of the chosen, could be taxing indeed. The past two years he had assisted the priest with his missions, travelling about and reading for the natives, taking part in the services, instructing parents who wished their small children baptized, endeavouring to explain to them about grace, about suffering and guilt, about prayer, forgiveness, and life in Heaven. Most of it was lost on them, he knew. They wanted only what was tangible to them, they wanted rattling good stories, and they wanted everything here and now.

The life of the heathen as he remembered it was full of fear and darkness. Now it was no longer within him, but without. The Devil. Or perhaps more simply his native father.

His father, the shaman and Egede's arch-enemy, always lurking about and wanting him back. He believed Egede had stolen his son away from him. He had threatened Egede with a harpoon, only for the priest to wrench the weapon from his hand and strike him to the ground with his fist. Since then they had seen little of him. But he knew he was there somewhere, that he was watching him. It was worst when he was away on one of his own trips and thus more vulnerable. Egede, with his brute strength and fearlessness, would not be there with him then. Always when he crawled inside the house of a savage he would scan the room to see if he was there. He was afraid of him. Egede had said that the shamans were in the pay of the Devil. They were damned, condemned to Hell, and they knew so too, for which reason they had nothing to lose.

Can they not even be forgiven by the Lord's intercession? he had asked.

Can the Devil find forgiveness? Egede had replied.

He had decided what he would do if his father appeared while he was on his own. He would hold up his crucifix and bid him be gone in the name of Jesus. What would happen then? Would his father fall down dead? Would he go up in smoke?

It was a burden to have a father so condemned.

Jesus was a strong, older brother. He looked after him. He followed him everywhere. Frederik Christian dreamt about him often, as he had nightmares about his father. They would be standing facing each other, flaming both, Jesus in a dazzling white light, his father glowing red. As far as he had understood, Jesus and the Devil were sort of brothers. Archangels, one fallen to the earth where he caused as much nuisance as he could until the final reckoning, the day of judgement, when he knew he would lose. He wanted the Christians to fall with him. He wanted to pull as many as possible down with him. Egede had told him all of this.

I contend with him too, Egede had confided in him. Every day is a fight against evil. We must be wary, never believe ourselves safe, never become complacent. If we do, he will sense it.

What will happen to the Devil on judgement day? Frederik Christian asked.

He will be enchained, my boy. For a thousand years, then to be set free for the final reckoning.

I don't understand, he said. Why set the Devil free?

No one knows, Egede replied. It is a mystery. Perhaps it is because the Devil is God's son and that God loves him despite everything, no matter that he has let him down. But in the end he will of course kill him.

A thousand years, said the boy. That's a long time.

Compared to eternity it is nothing, said Egede. You must learn to think from the perspective of the eternal, my boy. As I have learned. That is why we say: Prepare thyself for death. Death is eternal. Life is but an ill-smelling fart compared to eternity.

But is it not a sin to long for death? Those who commit suicide cannot go to Heaven.

It is a sin to long for death. It is not a sin to long for eternity. This is what we call a paradox.

The cannon rumble, once, twice, thrice. A toast to His Majesty! A drinking bout is going on in the governor's residence. It began this night and will continue for at least another day and night. Everyone is drunk, even Egede. And Frederik Christian too. He has found a medicine to combat his angst. A small glass containing a clear liquid. The Devil cannot be in such a small glass. Surely not?

He had no idea if it were even possible for him to be saved. There was so much he did not understand. Charged with teaching the natives, he found himself compelled to learn more, for they asked him so many questions that left him at a loss. And when they sensed his uncertainty they would exploit it immediately and begin to dig into the matters he had failed to understand. But he could not keep on asking Egede. He was afraid his foster-father would think him stupid. As such, his questions were left unresolved and he felt himself even stupider. It was a vicious circle.

The crew held him in little esteem. They called him 'Two-Kings' on account of his double name. It was not kindly meant. The natives too looked askance at him, to them he was *Qallunaajaraq* – the little Dane. He wore Danish clothing, linen trousers, smock, a long coat and a three-cornered hat of which he was exceptionally fond, given to him by one of the officers.

Egede would often beat his children, including Niels. But he never laid a finger on Frederik Christian.

Why does he punish you and not me? he asked Niels.

He must like you better, his foster-brother replied.

No, said Frederik Christian. That's not it. It is because I am unlike you.

Think yourself lucky.

But I want him to beat me.

God's truth, you are indeed an odd one, said Niels. I can hit you if you want. And he struck him on the cheek with the flat of his hand.

I would prefer him to do it, said Frederik Christian, rubbing the sting.

The cannon expel their fire into the night. Long live the King! Frederik Christian sits on top of the wood box. He has pissed in his trousers. But he doesn't care. He feels himself pervaded by love.

The Governor has ordered salutes to be fired on the hour for the next twenty-four hours. But the bombardiers are drunk too, they lose track of time and no sooner have they fired one salute than they are busy reloading for the next.

It was the late afternoon of the King's birthday. The sun was descending. It looked like it was dissolving, its red disc melting into the boiling sea. It was the maddest of sunsets, and quite unnatural, illuminating the clouds from below with deep and blushing hues that shimmered outwards and upwards, filaments of orange, yellow, green and violet. The colony folk observed it with a blend of awe and terror. Several burst into tears, but most simply stood, silent and stunned. Such a sky was surely an omen, most likely of something bad. When eventually the twilight came and the stars appeared with their cold and dependable twinkling, it seemed like a relief. The people went back inside, to eat and drink some more.

The colony's officers, the three men of the cloth, the Trader, the Paymaster and the colony surgeon Kieding, were seated around the table. Frederik Christian sat by the stove and thought of how long he would be allowed to stay up. Titia gave him a plate of food. He tried to follow the conversation. The sunset was not mentioned.

Another salute rattled the panes.

Those cannon are more surely in the service of Bacchus than Mars, Egede commented.

Gunpowder and spirits are the only things of which we have an abundance, said the Commandant Landorph.

Another salute, the third time in that hour. The three Greenlanders who were seated by the door, helpers in the trading company and invited by Pors, jumped in fright. The Governor instructed Skård to pour them aquavit, which however they declined, preferring to drink water. They guzzled the food and sat there looking out of place.

For goodness' sake, drink a toast to your king! Pors boomed. It is your duty.

Timidly they put the glasses to their lips and sipped, spluttering the contents into the air and convulsing into fits of coughing, much to the merriment of the Danes.

Quite as I remember my own first dram, exclaimed the Paymaster Fleischer, his foxlike face split into a grin.

It's good for the health, Pors explained to the Greenlanders. Good medicine. Drink now, my friends!

He raised his glass towards then, only for them to shake their heads.

Then give them ale instead, said Pors. Skård! Ale for our native friends.

The manservant came shuffling in his slippers with frothing cups he handed to the three men. They eyed the ale suspiciously and hesitantly tasted the froth.

Skål! Pors bellowed. Drink now, dear friends. Do you think I would poison you? I order you to drink the toast of the King.

He got to his feet and stepped over to them, clacked their cups against his own, and now each swallowed a mouthful.

That's more like it, said Pors. But I shall not be satisfied before you have drunk up. Skål!

The cannon thundered a reply.

Look, they drink indeed, said Landorph.

All heads turned to see the Greenlanders reluctantly down their ale.

Indeed, said Fleischer. Now the Greenlanders drink. The Governor has at last loosened them up. About time too.

Skål, O innocent babes of the land, Miltzov slurred, raising his glass. Until recently I was as you and did not drink. Now you are like me and do drink. Skål!

All the men followed the priest's example. Skål, noble children of this splendid land!

I feel confident we shall get on well now, Fleischer commented, his narrow eyes peering at the other men. If there is a single thing I've had against the natives here, it is that they will not share a dram. Once they drink, they are on our side. Nothing is duller than drinking on one's own.

First ale, then the aquavit, says Pors. Let them be drunk. Skård, the bottle!

Skård entered with the bottle and replenished the glasses of the three men by the door. They drank obediently, and without coughing.

There, you see. Now you have learnt an important lesson, said Pors. Already you are half-Danes. When you return home, be sure to take some food back with you so that your people can see how abundantly you have been plied. And here, he continued, take these pocket knives, one each. Yes, go on, take them. They are a gift from the Governor Pors. Give my regards to your families and tell them they are from the Governor. And drink up! Drink up, innocent children of God, and you shall be toasted and saluted on your way!

The cannon sounded again. Shouts went up from the battery, the bombardier and his men calling another toast for the King.

Skål for the colony of Godthåb! said Pors.

Skål! said the men.

Skål for Denmark!

Skål for the King!

And for the Queen!

Which one of them?

The Queen of Sheba!

Skål for us!

///

I am Aappaluttoq, the Red One. I go my own ways. It was me who made the red sunset. It's not difficult. There are many things much more difficult than that. And as the people stood and stared, enthralled and terrified, I stole inside the house of Egede. I lay down in the priest's bed, next to the Madame. Is it you, she said. Such a long time since I saw you last. I've been on a long journey, I told her. I've been with the King, he sends his regards. Listen to the cannon, she said. How they rumble. They're having a party, I said. They're getting my son drunk. The poor boy, she said. What have we done to him? You've ruined him, I said. I am sure we shall pay for our sin, she said.

I lie there for some time, talking with the Madame. She enquires about all manner of things, and I tell her about our land. Later, she writes it down in her secret diary.

But now you must go, she says. Go, before my husband returns. He cannot bear the sight of you, and if he found you here beside me in the bed, he would surely depart his senses.

He has already departed his senses, I say. Perhaps they would be returned to him if he came in and found us. But it is easier to make the sun go down than to bring your husband to reason. So now I shall leave you. Goodbye, Gertrud.

Goodbye, my friend. Kiss me before you go.

And I kiss her dry and wrinkled mouth.

///

But who is that seated on the wood box with nothing to drink? Pors said. Skård, give the young man a cup of ale and then a glass of the aquavit. If we are to carouse, then let us carouse, and all men be equal in it! We shall make no difference between great and small, heathen or Christian.

Frederik Christian was handed a foaming cup of ale. This was the first time, he had never drunk alcohol before, and he glanced at Egede to be certain he had his permission. But Egede sat hunched over the table in deep conversation with the physician. The three natives were already into their second glass of aquavit and looked the merrier for it too. If they can, then I can also, he told himself. And if Egede does not like it, then he can beat me. He guzzled the ale Skård gave him, belched and handed him back the empty cup. A small glass of aquavit was placed in his hand, and he downed that too. It felt like swallowing a glowing ember that slid but slowly down his throat.

His eyes water, but he ignores them. His glass is replenished. A clock ticks, it sounds as if it were muffled. The air thickens around him. He feels like he is submerged under water.

The cannon pound. Or perhaps it is something inside his head that pounds. He drinks. A warmth festers and gurgles inside his stomach like a sulphurous pool. It spreads through his body like ripples from a stone tossed into a pond. Such a heavenly state. He sees his hand as it puts the glass to his lips, he feels the weight of the aquavit inside it, downs its contents and bites off a piece of the bread on his plate, feeling the way it is chewed apart in his mouth, dissolving into a delightful mash. Bread has never tasted as good.

Not to speak of my digestion, he hears Kopper say, tossing his horselike head. It's gone to pot completely.

It is indeed a vast country we have placed under the Crown, says the Commandant Landorph.

Too vast, perhaps, says Fleischer.

I must run to the latrine a dozen times a day.

Though quite how vast we do not know. No one has yet sailed around it.

The crew house is awash with shite.

Then keep away from it, says Fleischer. No one's forcing you.

They are swine indeed, says Miltzov. They empty their bowels on the floor.

I've heard it said it's joined with Spitzbergen.

They can't hold on to it. They've all got the dysentery. Coming out both ends, it is.

And my feet, Kopper complains. My feet are swollen from all the dampness and cold. I need help to pull off my boots in the evening.

Iceland, more likely, says Pors. Spitzbergen's an island.

Iceland? Fleischer says.

Yes, says Pors. I've heard there to be a ribbon of land from Iceland's north-western tip reaching towards Greenland.

The place is filthier than Copenhagen, says Miltzov.

And that's saying something. The Øster quarter is a pigsty these days.

That's where they're from.

Then I'm sure they feel at home.

It is indeed a splendid country once you get to know it, says Egede. Though I concede that first impressions may belie it.

Can't keep a thing inside me, says Kopper. It runs right through.

Those first impressions have now lasted half a year, says Fleischer.

I think we are joined with America, Landorph opines.

Life is but a joke, says Kopper. A poor one at that. I'm certainly not laughing, that's for sure.

A skipper by the name of Jens Munk sailed to the far north, says Egede. He believed there to be a passage between the two lands. But no one has found it yet.

A joke? says Fleischer.

Nearly all of them perished. The scurvy, it was.

They say all these lands are joined at the top, says Lange. What says the Lieutenant to that theory?

Full of ambition and grand designs, says Kopper. And then death comes along and makes a joke of it all. Vanity, as the poet says.

I have no opinion on the matter as long as no one's been up there to see and returned home to tell of it, says Landorph.

You're in good humour today, Kopper, Fleischer says, his foxlike eyes looking askance at him. Normally I'd say you were as sour as vinegar, but today you're grumpy at worst. Let's drink a glass together.

I don't d-drink, Miltzov hiccups. I've g-given it up.

Skål, dear colleague, says Lange.

I intend to cross the land as soon as possible, Pors declares. To explore its nature and geography.

It will be a long expedition, says Egede. The ice stretches to the horizon in the east.

Piss and shit, says Kopper. That is what we leave behind us here.

Enough of such filth, says Egede.

The cannon boom. The Greenlanders cheer.

Besides drunken natives, Fleischer adds. Look at them, they're well away.

And the boy, says Landorph. Your native page seems to be drunk, Egede.

Indeed, look how he grins, says Fleischer.

Egede looks over his shoulder and sends his foster-son a tender smile. Let him enjoy himself, he says.

And now it's raining again, Kopper observes.

All fall silent and listen to the rain lash the panes. A wind is getting up.

Back to normal again, says Fleischer with a sigh. I was getting worried there.

A toast to King Frederik, says Pors. Long live the King!

They rise and lift their glasses. The Greenlanders too leap to their feet. They do as the Danes, bellowing out a skål and sweeping their arms towards the window. At once the cannon pound.

What on earth has happened to the poor lad? says Miltzov.

All eyes turn towards the wood box. Frederik Christian has slid to the floor and has fallen asleep in a pool of urine. Egede staggers towards him and pokes him with the toe of his shoe. He shakes his head regretfully.

That first time, says Pors dreamily. To fall asleep in one's own waste. How sweet the sight. I remember it like it was yesterday.

Yes, his innocence has now been taken, says Miltzov, downing another aquavit. I myself have given it up.

Looks like it and all, says Lange.

You are a one to talk, you d-drunken pig, says Miltzov.

A toast to young Two-Kings, says Fleischer. Long may he live!

The cannon thunder. Frederik Christian sleeps with a smile on his lips. Egede has laid his coat on top of him.

///

He remains in the governor's house for some days and is again deathly ill. But the Governor mocks him. That kind of sickness soon passes over. Do as I do, take a hair of the dog that bit you.

He gives him a cup of strong ale, and it helps. But Titia keeps him beside her. He lies in her bed and snuggles up. She draws him close, strokes his hair, sings for him and murmurs prayers in Latin. He feels safe. Now and again he gets out of bed and wobbles across the floor to in turns relieve himself and fill a cup with ale. But the jomfru calls him back to her and pulls him down into the bed. She is like a sister. She kisses him, but does not interfere with him, unlike the tarts in the crew house who put their hands down his trousers to grip and fondle his cock. She tells him of the Immaculate Virgin, of the nuns who brought her up. Hers is another form of Christianity, an unlawful one, which Egede calls papism. If he only knew that his son lay here, being spoonfed with saints and popes, the Virgin Mary and the seven sacraments, he would perhaps kill him with his bare hands. But the jomfru speaks of other things too. She tells him about the world, about elephants, the planets, the round earth, the moon and sun. These are things she has read about during her time with the nuns who whipped her until she bled.

Why did they whip you?

They whipped themselves too. It is their way of driving out evil.

Are all Christians so? he asks.

God loves you. Therefore he punishes you.

Not me, he says sadly.

You must sin first. Then you shall be beaten.

Can I not be loved without first having sinned?

No, my child, Titia says lovingly.

It sounds demented.

Blessed be the demented, she says. We are all demented, though some more than others.

You must be the most Christian person of all in the colony, Titia.

After some days he is compelled to leave her. Egede has been asking after him. They are to go into the fjord to missionize.

Still in the land of the living, I see, says Egede, and places a tender hand on his shoulder. A little drink once in a while can only gladden the heart, as Luther said. Whoever drinks beer, he is quick to sleep, and whoever sleeps long does not sin. But you must learn to drink in moderation, boy. You will learn it in time.

Egede does not beat him. He is even kinder than normal.

They sail to the various settlements inside the fjord for a week or so. They work together, side by side. Egede preaches, Frederik Christian translates. And he reads for the children. Egede is pleased with him.

They return to the colony. Pors wants him in the house, to be his new manservant. Skård has become strange of late and will only sit in a corner all day puffing on his pipe. He carries water, he cleans and tidies and helps the jomfru keep house. The jomfru is tired. She is pregnant, she tells him. Her body feels heavy.

Who has made you pregnant?

The Devil, she sniggers. But you must tell no one, for they will come and throw me on the bonfire.

He knows the jomfru is not quite right in her head. But she is good to him. They lie curled up together in the night, and she always makes sure he is covered up so as not to shiver in the cold.

Often there is drinking in the Governor's parlour. The colony council meets on Saturdays, and afterwards a number of the men stay behind, eating and drinking into the night. The more they drink, the coarser and more spiteful they become. They tease him about being the jomfru's sweetheart, they get him drunk and make him take off his clothes and lie with her as they stand by the bed cheering and jeering. She opens her legs willingly and allows him inside her.

It doesn't matter, she whispers. Do with me what you want.

But Pors does not care for it. It is filth, what you are making the boy do.

He throws him out and will not have him living there any more. He moves in with the Egedes again. Egede has heard of his escapades. But he does not beat him. He moves in on the first floor, where he lives with the two young clergymen. He instructs them in the Greenlandic language and gives them advice as to how best to speak to the natives about Christianity. They take notes and enquire as to all manner of matters. They are very kind to him. He eats with the family downstairs. Aquavit is not consumed in Egede's end of the house, at least not when he is there. Madame Gertrud keeps a bottle in a cupboard, though under lock and key.

An epidemic has broken out in the crew house. A handful are dead within the week. He assists at the funerals. He drags corpses from the feculent house that stinks foully of rotten flesh. The dead stick to him like tallow. It can barely be washed away. The male corpses reek abominably, a heavy and uncompromising stench. The women's smell is sour, yet rather lighter, while that of the dead children – a number of the woman have given birth since their arrival here – is acrid and pungent, tearing at the nostrils like pepper, and yet fleeting. The men are the worst. But for some reason he prefers the men. They do not bother him as much, even if their odour is unbearable.

The carpenter asks him to help with some jobs that need finishing in the governor's house, skirting boards, panels, windowsills. The jomfru is there. But it is as if she does not know him. She sits rocking in a chair, observing them with a half-baked grin on her face and looks like she has not been washed in a long time, her hair is unkempt, and stale spittle and remains of food are stuck to her lips. Infested she is too. He sees the lice crawl upon the down of her cheek. Her eyes gleam with the piercing clarity of madness. Skård sits in a corner smoking his pipe.

The Governor is satisfied with their work. He asks the carpenter to make some furniture, for several of his chairs are no longer service-able. They work from morning till eve in the stable building where also a foundry is housed and where there is shelter from the incessant rain and wind. They sit in the warmth, amid the sickly sweet smell of sheep and goats as they hammer and saw, carving intricate patterns in the wood, working with full focus like musicians practising a difficult piece of music. He likes the slow, meticulous nature of the work, and the carpenter too is a quiet and amiable man.

He feels the most dreadful urge to drink. But no one offers him anything. When the crew eat in the evenings, he reaches his glass out when the bottle is passed around, yet he is ignored.

No more for you, young sot, they say.

If a man's to drink, he must learn to drink in moderation.

The priest ought to give you a dressing down.

He should give you a good hiding.

But he won't.

You're his pet.

He wouldn't touch a hair on your head.

What is it with you and the priest, boy?

All he can do is smile. He is an enigma to them, and he likes that it is so. But they are not fond of enigmas. Enigmas make them spiteful. They say you behaved like a savage when you were drunk.

Did I? I can't remember. You behave like savages too sometimes.

There's two ways to behave like a savage, they say.

A right way and a wrong way.

They laugh at the notion.

You are a native, they say. You can't take it. You should be ashamed.

But they will not let him drink ale either. Only water.

He steals into Egede's rooms when there is no one in. He tries to prise open the cupboard where the aquavit is kept. Eventually he loses patience and breaks it open. He takes out the bottle and drinks what is in it as he stands. He staggers upstairs and collapses into his bed.

Egede will not beat him, yet declines to pray with him. It is painful to him.

///

The following Saturday, after the council, the Governor announces that there will be a display of fireworks. The weather is clear and still. The bombardier and his men have been at work all day. A couple of hours after darkness they commence the display. A crowd, a hundred and fifty strong, is gathered on the open ground in front of the colony house, Danes and natives alike. Dancing fire, Bengal lights, bangers, fire fountains, spinning Catherine wheels spitting their sparks in every direction, rockets whistling upwards, pausing, exploding silently above, their sharp reports following within the second, as they bleed their coruscations into the sky. The natives watch with polite and indulgent interest, as if they are used to the sight and have seen it many times before. The crew, considerably reduced in number these past months, stare at the colourful sparks with weary indifference.

The Governor orders a salute:

A toast and a salute to the Grand Chancellor Holstein!

!!!

To the Royal Equerry Danneskjold-Laurvig!

!!!

To Count Sponnack, Commandant of Copenhagen!

!!!

To the President of the Treasury Chamber, the Baron Gyldenkrone!

!!!

The War Secretary Revenfeld!

!!!

The Secretary Møinichen!

!!!

The Ministers of State!

The Admiralty!

The Commissariat-General of the Army and Navy!

To all our generals and admirals!

To the Royal House, Their Majesties and an endless line of royal family members by name!

And finally to the advance of the Grand Greenlandic Design!

To the Imperium Daniae!

!!! !!! !!!

The cannon boom, and to Frederik Christian's ear they say:

Døden!

Døden!

Døden!

Death, death, death.

4

Deliver Us from Evil

To-day the Trader returned from the trading excursion in the south and with the boat filled with blubber.

This same day the wife of one of the soldiers gave birth to a daughter, to be christened on the 10th.

On the 15th another of the bedridden soldiers died, and in the evening another likewise.

On the 28th yet another of the soldiers died, likewise his small child, to whom his wife gave birth the 6th of October.

On the 30th the Governor celebrated the birthday of his royal highness Crown Prince Christian, to which occasion he had invited the council and officers of the colony.

FROM HANS EGEDE'S JOURNAL, OCTOBER 1728

. . . edicamus domino what i feel is a tree something with branches perhaps a birch something sprouting and growing the tiny seedcorn put inside me with a stick the seed-man put it inside me gently and with love and a bit careless that it found root latching on straight away with its claws digging in sucking my blood like a leech and growing in this treeless land there grows a tree inside a person and this person is me little titia ave maria gratia plena thus the nuns did teach me to pray but can a tree really grow inside a person

yes no?

domine jesu dimitte nobis debita nostra it is a good prayer it renders me calm it maketh soft the heart and doth tire the eye and cool the burning flesh i say it when i go to bed but a man it was who stuck the seed-stick in my soil-hole my earth-hole my cunt-hole my cock-hole my hole-hole flaming with lust i flamed bayed barked yelped growled with desire this is how we women are he quite cold and calm i remember so very well and calm and with kindness and caution and very slowly did he put it in and placed it well so that it might grow and grow it did tis growing now we women are like that we eat up what they give us lick their hands as grateful dogs it takes on a life of its own and wriggles out of us i saw it at the apothecary's when one of the servants a young girl birthed a child how she bled the poor girl yet she lived and the child lived but they came and put her in irons and off they took her to the spinning house on account of fornication it was not a tree she bore but a bastard child and the apothecary was the lecher but was never put in irons he dribbled his tinctures and mixed his decoctions and weighed his coffee the same as before i don't think it's common to birth a tree but men can do so too i heard of a man who died of the consumption or so they thought but when he was dead they saw foliage protruding from his mouth and were given permission to cut him up and i think it was in france because such things are forbidden in denmark and there was a whole tree taken root inside him with leaves and branches the lot the roots had pierced his lungs and suckled his blood like an infant child or a baby lamb and they took it out and put it in the ground and put the man in the ground too until he rotted and became mould but the tree took nourishment from that same soil and grew to become a splendid tree though at first it was yellow and pale from lacking sun but then it turned green and i think it to be there still in a garden somewhere where it is watered and no doubt growing as yet how strange it is i know not if the tree inside me is the same i think it to be a birch perhaps the man lived on as a tree i hope my tree is green and fresh as the spring at home in köln ave maria gratia plene will i birth the tree or will they cut it out of me and plant it in the soil will i myself become a tree will god have me when i die?

up down?

yes no?

i will end in the ground no matter it is quite certain but who knows the answer to that other matter my falling sickness is nearly gone the tree has made me well or differently ill perhaps more fatefully so

but i no longer froth at the mouth at least or bite my tongue gloria
patri et filio et spiritui sancto as the nuns would sing between the
singing lashes of the whip they say that lash i smile and lash i do
they say that lash i am beautiful and so lash i am so lash lash happy
i am in happy circumstances i bear a tree into a treeless world and
that is at least something and happiness is delightful they say and
the folk they say so too even though their faces are the faces of bleating
goats

baa-aa-aa!
tis the goats
baa-aa-aa!
tis the old sheep
baa-aa-aa!

tis the lambs that shiver as if with fear though all have the faces
of men i care not to look at them yet i cannot help myself i pull the
door of the stable ajar and sure enough there they are i knew it sheep
and goats standing there staring at me with stupid human faces
someone must have swapped them around maybe it was master
kieding he does so many strange things creeping about and examining
sticking his finger in decent folk can it really be necessary to stick
one's fingers in a person's every hole sniffs at their every opening he
does and is amused by everything even death amuses the master
kieding or perhaps the lieutenant it was he who did it first put on a
goat's mask and since then they've all had such woolly faces the
officers the crew the clergymen in fact i find them appealing with
sheep and goat faces woolly-haired skulls their sheepish grins they
have no hooves for feet that would be someone else entirely but we
shall not name him no we shall not speak of him libera nos a malo
he can hear us you see he has long ears with hairs sticking out and
piercing eyes and pupils in the vertical and then he comes all smarmy
you called my friend? a smell of something burnt

forked tongue
goat-green eyes
billy-goat legs

the tree grows and grows i can feel it mr pors does not like it he
scowls at me what are you standing there gaping for girl? i think

perhaps he can see it? see what? you demented child do you think a person can stare down your throat and see it? maybe the other hole not the throat i can see it myself i look in the mirror i open my mouth a thin branch pokes up and green foliage i put my fingers down my throat and try to nip off a leaf only it draws back it is alive and aware of itself and of me and afraid but he cannot see it will not see it he thinks only about matters of his own he wants to be cut he lies in his bed come here dear his voice is thin as a thread his eyes as frightened as a sick hound i am so scant today it is the rheumatism he says perhaps the consumption i say consumption of the lungs and his eyes grow wide and afraid as a child's do you think so? my father died of it i tell him it went to his bones he thought it was the rheumatism too but it was consumption of the bone and bad it was too he lay and would not leave the bed complaining all the time of rheumatism like you perhaps it is just rheumatism he tells himself to comfort his mind I need to be bled right away titia before it gets worse and i fetch the knife the doctor has shown me how make the incision here says mr pors and points to his arm at the elbow and skård enters from out of the shadows where he lurks all day and holds him from behind never says a word skård dear skård i cut through the skin the fat the flesh that swells about the blade the blood leaking forth quite black it is too and smells rotten i place the cup upon the wound I do as the doctor has shown me i warm the little cupping-glass over the lamp and place it on his arm it grips the skin it sucks the blood and is slowly filled and i cut myself so very slightly too for it makes me so delightfully still and calm inside

blood red red blood

oh he groans and turns his head to the side he closes his eyes clever girl now the other arm and i cut into that one too at the elbow and place the cup upon the wound oh yes he says yes oh yes now it will be better you'll see and skård lays him down and mr pors he sleeps

kyrie eleison

i remove the cups when they are filled before they've gone cold and fallen off

christe eleison

i toss the blood onto the fire it crackles and spits and becomes as honey as syrup as tar a dark and charred lump of meat melting in on itself burning and carbonizing

kyrie eleison

mr pors is a sick man but skård is the sicker his insides are dry as parchment his flesh is tainted his eyes are as boiled egg-whites his blood as stringy as slime his guts but a mash of substance his head a goat's head skård mr pors is simply mr pors but it is enough i will cut into skård but he wishes it not he backs around the table i after him with the knife he hits out at me get away from me with that knife girl it is a game we play for a person has only the fun they make themselves as they say i'll do it when you sleep i tell him it's for your own good you old fool

agnus dei

you stick your knife in me too i say he says that's not a knife you silly girl if you stick me i shall stick you too and so we chase each other around the table get away from me girl he says and lashes out at me miserere nobis he lashes out again from below this time and strikes my arm and knocks the knife out of my hand it buries itself in the wall he pulls it out and puts it in his pocket quitollis peccata mundis i have enough in my pipe he says the best medicine there is i will have none of your cutting and slicing good old skård

man goat?

master kieding comes and prods at my abdomen he feels inside me can it really be necessary long fingers he has the master kieding expert fingers gentle hands indeed he says a child in the spring perhaps an easter child can you see it? i ask him and open my mouth no but i can feel it he says the child is thriving thrives well you must make sure to get some food inside you so to make it healthy and strong he gives me some herbs he has picked eat this and the child will be of sound health and go out and take in the fresh air i can go with you if you want he wants to marry me too have you ever heard the like but i will not be wed i hope he forgets all about it or else becomes sufficiently repulsed by me to dismiss the thought from his mind i will not be wed to such a finger-fucker it is a tree i tell him ah he says blessed are the fools beati pauperes spiritu for they shall inherit the land yes i shall plant a tree in a treeless land in a hundred years it will stand here yet and the men in the crew house have lost their minds their eyes shine red like chinese lanterns but when they die the light goes out at first it flickers then it is extinguished miserere nobis they chased one of the women and her child into the fjord dona nobis pacem she had stolen a loaf they stoned her and she ran down to the shore and drowned herself with the child they did not surface again the nokken did take them libera nos a malo johan bretel ended in the stocks for drunkenness and fornication and threats to the governor they pissed on him and kicked him and spat on him and now his eyes have no gleam in them his wife is left to spit blood and curses on the floor she too will die benedicamus domino the natives are strange i am afraid of them they are burning red one of them came to me in the other house deo gratias he lay with me he burned himself into me like a branding iron in snow fidelium animae misericordiam dei requiescant in pace he did not harm me it did not hurt or anything kyrie eleison it was he who put the seed-corn inside me christe eleison i have seen nothing of him since kyrie eleison though he would be welcome to come back and say hello i think christe eleison but the tree grows it grows and i become smaller and smaller and soon i will be gone completely and there will stand a tree to the memory of little titia kyrie eleison amen

///

Sise 'Petticoat' Hansdatter and her spouse, Johan Hartman, have moved into a dwelling hut in the style of the savages a quarter of a Danish mile north of the colony on land that slopes towards the shore. Sise is pregnant. Johan is concerned. He is afraid to touch her. She has crossed the sea with him. Now there is a sea inside her, with a ship and a little seaman on board standing quite alone on the deck and gazing towards a distant coast. No sea voyage is more perilous than this. The vessel may go down with mice and men at any moment. The brave little seaman may be washed overboard. Johan carries water and firewood to the house and scolds her if he sees her lift as much as a soup pot.

I'm not ill, she says with a laugh. I'm pregnant, that's all.

I know what you are. All I want is to make sure it stays that way.

Once the bugger's got a grip he won't fall out, she says.

You never know. My mother lost three.

He is not sure whose child it is, though he knows it is not his. He has not been with her since they were married. And before that it was as her whoremonger, which is not enough to make any woman. At least as far as he knows. He thinks the father is most likely Pors. Pors it was who claimed the privilege of 'the first night'. It doesn't bother him. Quite the opposite. He considers it will give them some advantage to bring up the Governor's child. As long as he's willing to acknowledge it, of course. And anyway, a child is a child. Now, for example, they have been permitted to move into this dwelling. But he is saddened by Sise not allowing him near her in the bed. He has no desire to be with any other of the rotten wenches, though certainly he could. It is Sise he is married to.

He has obtained some of the coffin planks which he has used to clad the earthen inner walls, and he has lain his hands on a cracked window pane complete with frame which he has tightened with putty and put into the wall in place of the window of gut casing that was there before. The place is their home. It is dark, though well insulated by its thick peat walls. He has experimented with peat as a source of fuel, but it is impossible to make it dry in this weather. He has tried to prise some coal from Fleischer, though without luck. Fleischer would rather have the crew freeze to death than part with so much as a lump of coal. But now he has found that the shores are strewn with driftwood if only one travels far enough away. Great, heavy logs, and dry too, at least those which have lain long enough on the land. Their savage's hut is small, no more than a hole in which to creep, but better by far than the unhealthy crew house where folk succumb by the day.

///

The Governor has announced that he will ride over the ice to the eastern side of the country and the people who are said to be living there. Time is of the essence, it is October. While there may not be snow for the moment, much has already fallen which has melted again, and according to Egede a lot more will undoubtedly come. But

Pors will not be moved. Snow or not. We cannot let those Norsemen wait a moment longer. Egede is not happy at the prospect, yet agrees to go with him, together with his son Niels and his foster-son Frederik Christian. Moreover he invites Johan to join them. All are armed with muskets holstered in front of the saddle so that they may quickly be drawn if the Norsemen should resist being reformed. Egede's own purpose is to visit some native settlements said to be frequented by the shaman Aappaluttoq.

That devil has been on the loose for too long, he says. It's high time he were put in irons. If necessary, I shall shoot him down where he stands.

The morning dawns. They plod away over the island, each on his own mount, through the little pass and down the stony slope to the great harbour where the *West-Vlieland* lies anchored for the winter. Johan sees her from above. Quite still she lies, held on four sides by taut mooring ropes. The rigging rises up from the deck like a withered copse, the barrel of the crow's nest high upon the mast. A shed stands huddled on the land, a dinghy drawn up on the shore. Not a person is to be seen. The world is darkened hues of grey: the sky grey as wet cotton, the sea grey as a knife's blade, the rocks grey as shards of coal. But there, the little merchant flag flutters red and white atop a mast. Denmark. Egede, who leads the way, breaks into voice. Kingo. *Morning Song.*

On the other side of the valley is a steep ridge of rock, impassable to the horses. They veer left, following the valley bottom. Two horses have come along with them, without harness, and thus every horse of those left living is with them. The two are allowed to run as they please, the exercise will do them good, the Governor believes. One is the mare gifted to him by the King. Pompadour. He wishes it spared the exertions of carrying rider and pack. It deserves to be pampered. The two horses trot across the wetlands, clearly in high spirits, with fluttering manes and raised heads, together at the front as if leading a team. Pors is a good horseman, his seat is supple and erect, and yet relaxed, following the movements of his mount. Egede and his son are plainly unused to riding. They hump about in the saddle, by turns sitting and standing stiff-legged in the stirrups.

Johan is more accustomed. He rode in the regiment and at home on the farm at Altona.

The loose horses have begun to wander. When they catch up with them they are standing grazing. Pors's mare whinnies a greeting and tosses its head, the younger horses and their riders come charging along with the bog water splashing about their fetlocks. Pors digs his spurs in and gallops off. The others follow suit.

The land is either rock or wetland, an uneven ride. Everywhere, the matt, tin-grey sheen of ponds and lakes and soggy bogs. They ride in a line, Pors at the head now. The landscape is mute and vast, sinister. A raven follows them from above, angling great arcs in the sky, effortlessly airborne, with but the slightest quiver of its wings.

I am happy, Johan thinks to himself. He has wandered these plains several times before, but until now he has found them alien and inhospitable. Now, for the first time, he feels the land, for all its grey and sodden deadness, accepts him with some form of familiarity.

They come to a river and stride into its waters, the horses unhesitant. They cross and clamber onto the opposite shore with dripping coat tails. Further downstream the river narrows, yet is plainly deeper and with the pull of a strong current. They forge through an area of dense vegetation that reaches to the horses' flanks.

Niels Egede rides at Johan's side. They have allowed the other three riders to draw ahead.

Have you heard our governor is to be a father? says Niels.

Who with? Johan asks guardedly.

The mad housekeeper girl. She's several months gone already.

I didn't know.

He's married as it is, I believe, Niels goes on. I wonder what his wife thinks of it.

Johan is indifferent to the Governor and his dallyings. He has enough on his mind with his own fertility, and Sise's too, and with the consequences it will have for them both. A number of the women in the crew house are pregnant, and some have already given birth. But in each case they have been still-births, grey, reptilian creatures that poked their barely human heads into the world and then immediately changed their minds. His own mother died in labour and with much suffering when he was still a small child, though not small enough for him to have forgotten. Sise's giving birth looms like a column of nameless horror in front of him, as yet blurred and ill-defined, though more distinct with every day that passes. A spring child. They must soon decide whether to remain in this land or return home with the ship in summer, an option already sanctioned by Pors. He will even be of assistance in finding them a place to live.

This country is another world, Johan says. The life here bears no relation to life at home.

God sees otherwise, says Niels. To Him there is no difference. It is the same world.

How is the jomfru at present? Johan asks. Is she as strange as before?

It seems to be up and down, though mostly down, says Niels. My father says it is quite normal for them to change with the phases of the moon.

Who?

The women.

Ah, them.

The mad ones, I mean.

I understand.

She is not so unattractive, the jomfru, Niels continues. And she is young. I am sure we can find a man who would want her.

Is the young lad there not her sweetheart?

Who? Frederik Christian? Well, he might not be bad.

Even if he does drink, says Johan.

Indeed. A madwoman and a drunkard, what could possibly go wrong. Though at the moment she is not mad.

But will the madness return after she has given birth?

My father believes her possessed. As you know, he sees the Devil wherever he looks. He believes her to have been poisoned by the false doctrine of the Antichrist.

What's that?

The Pope in Rome. She grew up in a Catholic nunnery. But now that she is among Lutherans, my father believes she will correct herself in time.

How old are you? Johan asks.

Seventeen, says Niels.

Betrothed?

Me? Niels laughs. Betrothal's not for me. I've known a couple of girls, of course. Native girls. But they are heathens. My father would kill me if he ever found out.

I won't let on, says Johan. But tell me something. What is the story about that native boy and your father?

The story? He is adopted, I suppose you could say. My father uses him in his missionary work. There is nothing unnatural about it.

No, says Johan. But people talk about it.

People should mind their own business and refrain from poking their noses into matters that do not concern them, Niels replies, and spurs his horse into a gallop to catch up with his father.

They ascend a long slope and find in front of them a new valley with rounded sides, like a drainpipe in cross-section. A river runs through it. They can see how it widens into a delta on the plain. On top of the ridge where they stand are several small tarns. They dismount to allow the horses to drink and to drink themselves. The water is cold as ice and tastes of the bogland. He is quite sated by it.

A cold breeze causes the men to shiver. They pick their way down the other side. The descent is steep and perilous, with sharp rocks and slippery moss. They must dismount again and lead the horses by the bit, though still occasionally the beasts loose their footing, snorting nervously and continuing only with reluctance. The two loose horses refuse to follow and they are forced to leave them by the tarn and hope they can find their own way home. They reach the bottom without mishap and the five men mount once more and ride side by side across a stony plain in the direction of a bay where they have seen the outline of some peat dwellings. Presently they smell the stench of soapstone lamps which hangs thickly over the settlement. Egede rides flanked by his son and foster-son. They speak together. Egede is plainly instructing them. Pors quickens his horse and brings himself to the fore. His seat is as light as before.

At the settlement they are met by a handful of skin-clad men armed with bows. They are not especially friendly. Egede dismounts and with Niels and Frederik Christian at his sides approaches and begins to speak to them.

What are they talking about? Pors wants to know.

Johan can only partially follow what is said. Mr Egede is asking if they know of a shaman, whether he comes here.

What does he want with him? says Pors.

I think he wants to arrest him, Johan replies.

Arrests are my business, says Pors. And why on earth does he want to arrest a heathen?

He believes him to be putting people against the colony.

Against the Mission, more like, Pors mutters. Let them keep their faith, if that's what they want. They're happier in their natural state. I've never understood this urge to drag people to the church.

Egede's conversation with the men seems mostly to consist of a number of questions and brief, dismissive replies. Egede becomes angry. He lunges at one of the men, managing to clutch the man's ear and twisting it in his fist. The man emits a shriek. He falls to his knees in front of the priest and peers up at him pleadingly. Egede stands over him and speaks now quite kindly and paternalistically. He ignores completely the four armed men who stand scowling at his rear.

I don't care to see this, Pors intervenes. What do you think you're doing, Egede?

I'm doing my work, Egede snaps over his shoulder.

I hope you don't force us to use the muskets. I want no bloodshed here.

Egede ignores him. Do not lie to me, he says to the man who kneels before him. I know he's here.

A man comes towards them quite calmly, unarmed, naked from the waist up, an assured smile on his lips. He greets Egede.

Peace of God, priest.

So there you are, says Egede. I thought this would be where you were hiding. We've come to take you back to the colony.

The man's smile is unruffled. He turns to Frederik Christian and says something to him in a low voice. It sounds almost like a reproach. The young man lowers his gaze and looks ashamed. He shakes his head several times. Johan cannot make out what is said between them.

As you see, I have brought him with me, says Egede.

You shouldn't have done, says the man.

Do you not wish to see him, speak to him, be with him? If you come with us to the colony, you can do all of these things.

He must come alone to me, says the man. Then we will see what he chooses.

No, I cannot allow it. I don't trust you.

Are you afraid, priest? Is your god not a strong god? Are you afraid that I am the stronger? That is a sorry god, priest.

It's not too late, says Egede, his voice now surprisingly mild. It's never too late. You are filled with hatred and bitterness. But hatred is your weakness. I wipe it from me as I wipe away the rain. God is love. It's not too late to receive his love.

The man shakes his head. He seems to wince at the priest's words. If God is love, then why has He taken my son from me?

In love He has taken him unto Himself, says Egede.

What are they talking about? Pors asks impatiently.

I don't know, says Johan. I can only grasp the half of it.

Let the man in peace, Pors says to Egede. He's not done you any harm. This isn't the way I want to approach the natives, with such harshness. The King wishes us to show the people of his land kindness.

You mind your own business, Egede spits. You don't know these people. Show them kindness and they'll show you an arrow in your back. Treat them harshly, though, and they will come to heel. They are indeed a cowardly and wretched lot.

Cowardly and wretched, perhaps, Pors says, glancing at the four men with their bows. Though probably very good shots too.

The bare-chested man mutters some words, then leans quickly forward and blows into Egede's face. Egede is enraged and loops a punch into the air in front of him, which his opponent evades skilfully, twisting his body to the side while standing firm with his feet planted on the ground. The four men are at once enlivened, they disperse and make themselves scarce.

Pors curses. The devil take that priest and all the world's blackcoats. I ride out to find our Norse friends, and he goes and starts a war with some natives.

An odd silence descends. Niels smells the air. *Apilerpoq*, he says. Snow is on its way.

At the same moment, a wind comes down from the fell. The bare-chested one stands some few paces away from Egede and stares unflinchingly, not at Egede, but at Frederik Christian. Then he turns his head to face the wind and the flakes of snow that come swirling. Again, he mutters some words and the snow falls thicker and thicker. Within minutes they are in the midst of a snowstorm.

They seek shelter in the peat-hut, which is full of women and children and the old, perhaps thirty people in all, who receive their guests politely, make room for them on the benches and offer them boiled meat and fresh blubber. It is swelteringly hot and they must remove the greater part of their clothing. Pors and Egede hang their wigs under the roof, where they become sooted by the lamps. Native women massage their legs. Their smiling faces glisten with fat. Children crawl upon them. There is a ceaseless bustle of chatter and laughter, a chomping of jaws as they chew their food, a squealing and trumpeting of farts and a splashing of piss into night pots. Johan lies in the dark and stares at the mattly gleaming square of gut casing that is the window. He thinks of Sise back at the colony. He prays for her. He is certain she senses it.

They remain in the dwelling for three days. The armed men are nowhere to be seen, their shaman neither, though how he may have survived without clothing on his body would be a puzzle.

Dead he is most certainly not, says Egede gruffly. We shan't be rid of him that easily. I ought to have shot him while I had the chance.

One of the woman complains to him of childlessness. She asks him for help.

What am I to do about your barrenness, woman? he says. Go to your husband, not to me.

The woman exposes herself to him. The light of the lamp flickers about her sex. Blow on it, she says.

Oh, blow off, you silly woman, Egede splutters.

But the woman begins to moan and to grind her hips. God blows on dead things and makes them living, she says.

Who told you that?

Aappaluttoq has spoken of it. He knows your stories. He has told us about Jesus as well.

Then he is worse than I thought, says Egede. The man is condemned to the torment of Hell.

Blow on it now, *palasi*, the woman insists. Look, here it is, blow on it now so that I may be given a child.

Cover yourself up, woman, Egede replies, his tone lighter now, if not a sign that he is about to laugh. I cannot blow and make you fertile. And even if I could, I would not. Ask rather that the Lord redeem you from this ungodliness, then perhaps I will hear you.

The storm howls outside, but the peat walls of the dwelling mean that they hear nothing. The horses, however, are out in it. They go in turn to see to them. But there is nothing they can do. The entrance is too small for them to be brought inside, and anyway there would hardly be room for five horses. They cover them with skins, but to no avail. When the storm is over, the five animals stand like pillars of salt, rigid with ice, stone dead. They trudge home with what they can carry from their packs. What took them half a day on horseback takes three days on foot. At long last they spy the ship, the *West-Vlieland*, its red and white merchant flag. Denmark. Some people of the colony come out to receive them. They were sure they had perished in the storm. The two horses they left behind, including the King's mare, have returned to the stable.

///

. . . a malo the tree grows bigger and bigger with every day that passes i can feel the way my arms my neck my legs become treelike with bark ave maria gratia plena i thought i was going to birth the tree that it would twist its way out of me as a bloodsmeared child so that i might take it by the root and plant it in a place outside and watch it grow gladdened by my child as it dug its roots into this treeless land a triumph over the wilderness but the truth is the tree is me benedicta tu and i am the tree i shall never leave here for trees cannot go their own way or sail with ships what are you standing there gaping for? says mr pors he looks in my mouth is there anything in there hello! i see nothing why do you hold your arms out thus you've been standing there like a scarecrow this past hour say something girl he circles me and stares at me from all sides he slaps my face o maria sine laba concepta the nuns would sing when they whipped themselves no i can move again now i can speak but it comes back to me it always does i stiffen and become as a tree soon i am tree from top to toe come and cut me says pors

beati pauperes

i have caught a cold on my trip he says could you see anything in there? i ask we came to some savages he says a settlement we stayed there several days during a storm but the horses died my lovely horses now they are food for the savages did you see a man? i ask a red man? yes he was hardly red but i know what you mean he was there i saw him there were others there too proud heathens i rather liked them but the priest that idiot chased them away he looks at me with his big fearful eyes i must be cut he says it can wait no more nip it in the bud that i may escape the lung disease the consumption that i may escape death i don't want to die in this land and i cut him and place the cups and watch the blood as it trickles

sanguis christis

a delight indeed he says more cups cup me about my whole body and so i place all the cups we have on him sancta maria he goes about the room clicking and clattering as the cups fill slowly with blood he looks a sorry sight afraid of death i don't know i don't think we're all meant to die that we're meant to stay up here

mater dei

he calls for skård i must be emptied skård and skård empties him and the cups they chink ora pro nobis oh oh he moans and skård shakes his thing his stick and spills his seed on the floor like onan you must not do so for it is a sin

libera me

skård wipes his hand on his trousers he sits down with his pipe mr pors retires to bed whimpering and moaning and coughing

libera me

release me i wish to be here no more i am hot he says i am burning i have the fever feel my brow his brow is cold you are ice-cold i say coldly you are cold as a corpse there is nothing the matter with you certainly you have no fever no i am sick i am dying he says i shall die without ever again to see my king my dearest denmark cut me titia what again? there's no more cups then leeches he says fetch the leeches from kieding leeches are what is required and i go to the priest's house and find the master kieding's leeches and borrow them i put the brown molluscs on his chest they attach themselves and suck his sickly blood and swell with it ora pro nobis yes that's better he says thank goodness for leeches i have placed a couple on my own forehead I have put them to suck the poison from my sickly mind and i have always been the same ever since the first time i bled and the nuns whipped me the first time blood-back blood-cunt cunt-blood back-blood i stick a leech up my cunt sancta maria mater dei she beat me the prioress herself with the birch with the whip and then she lashed herself and we wept together and prayed for satan to depart us libera nos a malo but it only got worse i frothed and foamed i arched my spine i pissed in my bed and the prioress birched and whipped first me then herself howling and crying she was but what good was it she should have used leeches i feel my thoughts begin to collect themselves and become clearer to me i feel the child move inside me most likely it is the leech which is sucking it out

agnus dei

a kick below my ribs it turns a somersault it is a child a real child not a tree! and soon it will be out why does no one tell me these things? mr pors is concerned now he calls for skård again and skård must do his job again libera me wipes his hand on his trousers that's better says mr pors i think i may pull through only later he climbs out of bed and walks restlessly about the floor sighing and whimpering finding no peace he lies down again moans and groans i'm dying he wails fetch the master kieding and so i fetch the master kieding from the priest's house the governor is ill i tell him what are these marks on your brow? he says air vents i tell him to let out the poisonous fumes and the third one is in my cunt he shakes his head dear jomfru titia what on earth am i to do with you and mr pors comes staggering towards us covered from head to foot with clattering blood-filled cups and writhing, squirming leeches cuts and wounds all over him he reaches his hands out to kieding and kieding emits a cry of dismay libera nos a malo what has the mad girl done to you? but mr pors recovers and becomes quite well again so do not come and say i did something wrong and now my thoughts become clearer and clearer to me as water from the purest spring as aquavit ora pro nobis i think it was the leeches that did it but the one inside my cunt i never found again or else it was the prayers which did their job libera me libera me libera me a malo libera me a malo libera me amen

5

Nothing Human is Alien to Me

To-day the Governor's engineer has passed away, having long been sick and confined to bed. Many of the folk began also to feel illness, for both the wet summer, in which they were compelled to camp in tents which could not exclude the rain, and the damp and unhealthy dwellings in which they now were lodged had contributed much to the feebleness of these sorry folk, which day by day grew only worse, and nearly all suffered from the scurvy.

FROM HANS EGEDE'S JOURNAL, NOVEMBER 1728

Scurvy and consumption are the cause of most of our deaths. As well as the poor living conditions and the miserable provisioning of the crew. Building materials were brought only for the main house and a couple of annexes, and much was ruined during the voyage or by having been left in frost and damp after our arrival here. For this reason accommodation has been knocked up for the crew in the shape of a large peat-dwelling, though regrettably placed where water from the wetlands above collects, turning the floor into a mud pool, the walls made soaking wet. It is a dwelling which attracts the elements rather than offering protection against them. Moreover, no thought was given to providing them with bedding, they have but a few thin covers graciously provided by His Majesty. Therefore they hardly ever remove their clothing at all, meaning that it becomes worn out that much quicker until quite threadbare. Wood fuel is rationed to cooking use once a day. The only way they have of keeping warm is to work, though they lack the strength for it, fatigued by the above-mentioned afflictions and the poor nutrition.

When I am required to attend to them in the crew house I must wade through water and mud and unmentionable effluvium which reaches to my bootlegs in order to get to the beds in which they lie tormented by sickness and cold. The stench of their human humiliation mingles with the chill air from outside.

How can you live in such filth? I say.

Where else are we to live, Master?

You might at least keep things decent and tidy around you.

The women who are to give birth, of whom there are quite a few, made pregnant back home by virtue of their profession, are given room in the main house where they are attended by the missionary's wife, Gertrud Rasch, the colony's nun and kindest spirit. But the newborn die, one and all, and many of the women too, in the same endeavour.

The land is in many ways splendid and magnificent, and with the passage of time the natives have come to terms with the trying conditions here and manage to keep themselves alive into their adult years, though without hope of a long and happy life into old age. Only seldom do I see a grandfather or grandmother among them, and only in such cases where the women among them breed when barely having left childhood, the generations thereby being as close to each other in age as the eldest and youngest of brothers and sisters. But the Danish crew, and in particular the former inmates of Bremerholm and the women's Spinning House – tarts, fornicators and procurers – who have been sent here forcibly, do not understand why they are here, nor do they wish to know. It would have been better for them to have remained in their gaols.

Not that I feel any sympathy for them in the everyday run of things. They are convicts, dregs, dishonest with their superiors, disgusting towards each other, and mindlessly negligent unto themselves. The short respite that is accorded them from their time of arriving here, until weakness and fever send them to their sickbeds, is spent drinking and fornicating and committing the basest and most unmentionable foulnesses. I am not the one to bewail their fate, it is to a large extent their own doing.

The sight that meets my eyes every day when I descend to the crew house is like a vision from Hell. The sick lie on their beds, sometimes several to a bunk, men and women in a single heap. Many are senseless. Barely a day goes by without someone expiring. The only movement detectable in those who are poorliest is the strained rising of the chest whenever the body demands a breath. Their mouths hang open, they are limp and feeble, gall and slime dribble from their lips, and now and then the body convulses when the bile comes up in them, and the vomit they do not swallow or else breathe back into their lungs ends on the earthen floor that is no longer a floor but a putrid and feculent pond. When at last they expire – and it is by no means uncommon for death to take several weeks, for they are young people with strong hearts – and their comrades wipe the filth from them and lay them out with their hands folded, a certain dignity comes over them which they have never possessed in life. The dead are wrapped in the blankets so graciously provided to them by His Majesty and carried up to the boggy moor, the only place anywhere around where the earth is more than a few handbreadths in depth, and are buried there. However such practice soon must be ceased. The folk say they can smell the stench of the corpse fluids in the water which seeps down from the bog, and the whole colony is at risk of contamination. A new cemetery is being established now north of the colony, where the bodies are enclosed by rocks rather than being buried in the ground, this being the way of the Greenlanders with their own dead. But these graves are opened and plundered by the natives, who put on the clothing of the deceased instead of their own. A watch is posted to prevent such robbery. However, the watchmen allow themselves to be bribed, accepting various services and payments from the natives and turning a blind eye when they desecrate the graves. This is an example of the co-existence that is being established between Danes and natives to mutual exploitation and gain. I choose not to intervene in what happens to the dead. But when it comes to the living, and the conditions they must endure, I endeavour to improve matters as best I can.

I complain to the sergeant Kinck about the living conditions for the folk. There is no latrine, I tell him.

Is there no latrine? he says. Why is there no latrine?

Because nobody has thought to dig one, I say.

There's the communal latrine, Kinck replies.

It's too far away, I point out. They are too weak to go there, and besides they are suffering from dysentery. There would be an unceasing traffic.

Where do they shit then?

In the house.

The filthy swine.

Exactly.

I suggest at the very least that a ditch be dug to drain away the effluvium so the house needn't be awash with their swill.

Can't they do it themselves? he says.

Perhaps, but they have not done so.

Then it's their own doing, Master Kieding.

They didn't decide where their house was to be. That was the council's decision.

Kinck gives a shrug. What am I supposed to do about it? The house is where it is.

They've hardly any bed covers, I tell him. There's no heating, and the frost will be here soon. What do you think will happen to them then?

At least we'll be rid of the stench, he says.

The women who are as yet on their feet use wide rakes with shovel blades instead of teeth to push the swill towards the door. They are barefoot, their skirts pinned up, their movements slow and measured, graceful almost. When I have time, I find myself watching them. Their hair hangs down over their shoulders, matted and tied in half-hearted plaits that dangle like thickly wound rope from their scabby scalps. They seem to enjoy this work, though the swill is ice-cold and they cannot avoid becoming sick from it. Jaundiced and coughing, sweating hot and cold they go about with their rakes, balanced as it were on the very precipice of life and death, yet quite as imperturbable as if they were raking hay in a meadow of grass. Before, they were loud and filthy-mouthed. Now they are still and patient.

I go to the Commandant Landorph.

Commandant, I request a temporary lift of the ban on fire-lighting in the common house. The folk are freezing to death.

He must go to the Governor. The civil crew is nothing to do with me.

But there are soldiers in the crew house too.

Then speak to my officers about it.

I already have.

And what did they say? he asks with a smile.

Nothing of any use.

No, they're a useless lot, he says.

I go to the Governor Pors.

We need wood for fuel, Mr Pors.

Then speak to the Paymaster Fleischer. He's the one who's hoarding it. I fight a daily battle with him myself for coal to heat up the residence. It'll soon be life or death. I very nearly got myself into a duel with him only the other day.

The crew are dying, Governor.

I know. I've been down there to see. Atrocious.

The Governor is the supreme authority here. Can he not exert his influence and ensure that conditions are made more tolerable?

I can relax the aquavit rationing, he says with a snap of his fingers. That usually helps.

It's fuel they need, Governor, not aquavit.

We have only the wood fuel we have. The winter may be long and cold. Where would you get the extra fuel?

The native huts are always warm. Sweltering, in fact.

They burn blubber.

And?

Blubber-burning for heat is forbidden in the colony. All blubber procured is to be turned into train oil. That's actually what we're here for. Burning it to keep warm would be tantamount to stealing from the King himself. And no one ever called me a thief.

But the crew are dropping like flies, Governor. Does he not think the King to be interested in keeping his people alive? They too are his property, in a way.

I cannot go against the regulation.

But whose regulation is it? Who made it out?

We did, he says with a grin.

We?

We, he replies, straightening his shoulders, grinning still.

I go around the main house to the other side where the Egede family lives and where I myself lodge in a room on the first floor. In the passage I hear the voices of Madame Gertrud and her two girls. I go inside and clear my throat politely. The Madame rises from her chair and comes towards me, smiling.

Monsieur Kieding, come and keep us company.

She leads me into the parlour and indicates a chair next to her.

The girls look up from their sewing, then look down again just as quickly. The parlour also contains a handful of native children partly clad in European clothes, hand-me-downs, I shouldn't wonder, from the Egede children. They sit in a circle on the floor, playing a game with a stick. A small child lies sleeping on the bench.

I get to my feet again and step over to the stove to warm myself.

Is it cold outside? the Madame enquires.

So-so. More raw than cold. But snow has fallen on the fell.

Yes, I've seen it. Come and sit down, Master Kieding. Would you not care to light your pipe? She smiles again.

Indeed, if I may?

I adore the smell of tobacco, she says. It reminds me of my childhood home, the lensmand's manor at Kvæfjord.

I fill the pipe and light the tobacco.

Madame Gertrud has lived here some years now, I say. Does winter come early to the land?

Often it comes later than at home in Lofoten. Sometimes it does not come until Christmas, not properly. But when it does, it is harsher and more obstinate and is not inclined to let go of us again once it has taken its grip.

I see. Both good and bad, then.

Are you concerned about the crew, Mr Kieding?

I've just come from the crew house, I reply.

She lowers her sewing to her lap and studies me. I can tell from her expression that I must have sounded solemn.

I have been there myself, she says. Such misery. Is nothing to be done?

Much can be done. But for a lack of intent on all sides. I've run from pillar to post seeking permission for the stove to be lit, but to no avail. The Governor was willing only to relax the rationing on aquavit.

It is his own medicine. And those who are given to it seem always to wish so singularly that others be so too.

Indeed, it is strange.

Pors is not a bad man, though, she says. He wishes well.

I'm sure he does.

We must not judge our fellow men. Such matters are up to the Lord.

I judge no one. But to offer only aquavit to those who are dying of the cold is to mock them.

She fidgets absently with a corner of her daughter's skirt. The girl is distracted by it and looks up at her, bringing her back from her thoughts. She gets to her feet and steps over to the window to look out.

Some people are more favoured than others, she says. We who live in this great isolated house have all the conveniences a person could wish for. We live a life that is in every sense normal, barely any different from the way we live at home. Whereas those who must live over there, well, it hardly bears thinking about.

The Madame and her family have surely had their fair shares of difficulties here in this land, I say.

Not as many as one might have thought, nor even as many as one's family back home predicted. Naturally I have been anxious on many occasions when Hans or the boys have been away and the weather has been bad. But I have placed such concerns in the hands of God. I have left it to Him to worry, or whatever it is He does, and it has given peace to my heart. I was more anxious at home in Vågan than I have been here. It was a difficult parish, so many quarrels and disputes, and Hans is never a one to yield if he knows he is right. He was happy enough with his parishioners, and they with him, but there was forever such a dreadful to-do with the sognepræst and the bishop and the officer of the parish, an eternal bother which spoiled the peace. Here we have only ourselves to look after, and it has been good, until now. All four children have come unharmed from the perils of childhood and we have hardly been sick ourselves. The scurvy has left us alone.

What of the natives? I ask. Have there not been problems with them?

Only the odd savage wishing harm on Hans. But he understands how to subdue them. Besides, the natives are so very good at heart. All they want is to live in harmony with each other and with the Danes. I do not think there is a more peaceful people under the sun.

I have heard rumours of a shaman who has sworn to kill him?

Oh, he's quite harmless. An unhappy man burdened by grief. Such is the nature of grief. It can paralyse a person, but it can also fill a person with malice.

What is the cause of his grief?

His son.

What does Egede have to do with it? Does the man blame him for his death?

He is not dead. He is very much alive, and here with us. It is the boy, Frederik Christian. No doubt you have seen him.

Aha, I say. The lad in the funny hat. He seems to have lost his footing.

Yes, he is weak.

He should stay with Mr Egede, who is clearly fond of him and wishes to look after him.

Indeed, says the Madame. The folk amuse themselves tempting him from the straight and narrow.

They give drink to the natives too, I've seen.

Yes, the depraved like nothing better than to coax the innocent into depravity with them. I believe much unpleasantness will await them on the day of reckoning for spoiling the Greenlanders who know of no such things from earlier days.

She falls silent, perhaps feeling she has said too much. I think she is reminding herself not to judge anyone, as she said to me just before.

Does Mr Egede not speak to them about it and rebuke them?

The natives? Oh, but they vex him, the savages. Sometimes he is driven from his senses by their perpetual questioning and teasing. For they are not stupid, far from it.

No, I believe they are artful, I say.

Yes, artful is the very word. They know where his tender points are and find much hilarity in pressing them until he loses his patience and becomes unrestrained. And then he will punish them. They do not care to be punished. It makes them cowed and afraid. A Greenlander, be he adult or child, will never resort to striking another, not even their wives know of being beaten. They cannot suffer it, it is quite as bad as the whip or the stocks. And yet they provoke him to it so easily, as if they cannot resist. It is a game they play with each other.

The child on the bench is waking. One of the girls steps across and lifts it up, placing it on her hip and walking about the room with it.

Indeed, we Danes are so very different in that respect, I say. We are used to disciplining those we love and consider a lack of discipline to be indifference.

Yes, but you can see for yourself by looking at these children, Monsieur Kieding. The most well-behaved and unobtrusive children one might find, and yet they have never been subjected to even the slightest discipline.

Interesting, I say. They seem gentle indeed. I would have thought it to be the result of Madame Gertrud's influence.

Not at all. The little angels here are with us for such a short time. Their parents deliver them to us when they are sick, but as soon as they recover and are well again they come and take them back. It is rather a shame.

Are they baptized before returning to their families?

Hans is very reticent when it comes to the baptism. It is not a thing to be dealt out like bills of exchange and lottery tickets, he says. Were they to be baptized, they would have to remain with us, naturally. For who else would keep them to the faith and ensure they observed the baptismal vows? They would fall by the wayside again and be doubly lost, and the responsibility would be the priest's.

But this young Greenlander, Frederik Christian, was he not baptized rather promptly? Why he and no other?

I remember when he came with him, she says. He had been with the boys on a tour of inspection and had encountered this man whose son was very sick. And so he brought him home with him, without much hope of the boy becoming well again. And yet he livened up. Hans himself looked after him. Usually they are given over to me for care. But there was something about this particular child that made him rather fond. It has been that way ever since.

She sends me a glance, enigmatic and secretive. An unmentionable relationship? One has heard of such things, especially in the case of the clergy. But I cannot see Egede in such a constellation. Indeed, I cannot see Egede as anything else but morally upstanding, if not undeviating, a servant of God impassive to urges of the flesh.

Outside, an almighty boom wrenches me from my thoughts. The Greenlandic children jump. The two girls rush to the window and look out.

Sit down, their mother says. It's nothing to get excited about.

Another explosion causes the house to tremble.

Is it that time again? I say. Cannonades the rest of the day, and most likely into the night as well. How annoying.

Yes, it is rather tiresome, she concedes. But sooner or later I suppose they will run out of gunpowder.

I fear it is the only thing of which there is no shortage here in the colony.

It will cease, she says. Like everything else.

It must be strange for you, who have lived in such peace and harmony these seven years, to have this turmoil of the colony forced upon you.

Yes, the times have changed, she says with a sigh. It is as must. I have no insight into the matter.

At once she rises and puts down her sewing. Let us go and attend to the sick.

The sick? What sick?

The sick in the crew house.

She puts on a black bonnet in the passage and ties it under her chin, steps into a pair of high-legged leather galoshes and slings a cape over her shoulders.

It is not a place for respectable people, I protest. But she is already gone. I bow to the two young ladies and follow after her.

The crew house is situated on the other side of the little inlet, a half-hundred steps from the residence, at the foot of a low rise of rock. Its positioning there was down partly to the haste of putting a roof over the heads of the crew, partly to one place seeming to be as good as the next, or quite as poor, for the structure seems now to have been erected in the midst of the muddiest quagmire.

The Madame strides firmly and with purpose. I must exert myself to keep up with her.

I must warn Madame Gertrud that the conditions are somewhat unpleasant, I say.

I have seen hardship, she replies, striding on. Her head is held high, her eyes fixed firmly ahead. She holds up her skirts and nods briefly to those we meet.

And then we are standing in the doorway of the large crew house. I peer quickly into the dimness inside, like a master of the house who has brought home a guest, to make sure at least that no indecency is going on. A few lamps hang from the ceiling and cast the faintest of light upon the bunks and the sick that lie in them. The women sweeping the filth with their rake-like implements pause as our shadows fall upon the floor. They greet the Madame with curtsies. I glance at her. Her face shows no indication that she regrets having come.

How many are confined to bed at the moment?

A score, I'd say.

She steps inside the room. I follow. Someone must have taken note of my complaint earlier in the day, for now some planks have been laid out, allowing a person to proceed between the beds without getting their feet quite as soaked as before. I lead the Madame from bunk to bunk and explain to her the symptoms of each patient in turn – fever, scurvy, consumption, general weakness, diarrhoea and vomiting – my words, however, being rather superfluous, as these signs of sickness are plain to see at a glance, and accompanied by the familiar stench that is so abrasive to the nostrils.

What can you do for them as a physician?

Not much, Madame Rasch. I can cup and bleed them, but whether it makes a difference or not I cannot hazard a guess.

At her behest I let the blood of two of the sick, a woman and a man. She sits with them during the procedure and holds them by the hand.

I have never understood the meaning of bleeding the sick, she says. Why is it done?

The blood maintains the body's liquid balance, I explain. Perhaps the Madame has seen a spirit level used by builders to ensure that an object is level or plumb?

Yes, I know such an instrument.

It is the same with the blood. It wishes only to be level. But sometimes it shifts to the left or right, meaning that we have an imbalance in the fluids. This may be counteracted by bleeding.

We sit and watch as the blood runs from the patient's arm into a bowl.

As the Madame can see, this blood is impure, I say.

It looks almost like oil.

Those are globules of fat, I explain.

Where does this fat come from, she wants to know.

From the glands. They excrete a fatty secretion when the body is in a state of fever. With other patients you will see the blood to display a greenish tinge and be rather malodorous on account of gall. That would indicate a sick liver. If the blood is pale and translucent as thin wine, then it is anaemia, as seen in advanced stages of the scurvy.

But is the state of the blood a symptom of the sickness or its cause? she asks.

That would be akin to asking if the chicken or the egg came first, I reply. It is an ancient practice to bleed the afflicted.

But one cannot remove all the sick blood from a person?

One could, but then naturally the patient would die.

What if blood could be infused from a healthy person?

Yes, it has been tried. Blood has been taken from sheep and dogs and introduced into the human body. As far as I know, such experiments have always failed and the patients have died. Of course, they may have died anyway.

They say the soul resides in the blood, the Madame says. The blood of an animal and that of a human being would surely be incompatible.

Undoubtedly, Madame Rasch. Besides, such practice has been forbidden by law, most surely due to that very notion of the inviolability of the blood. I believe the experiments have been discontinued accordingly.

What these poor souls need is a good and nourishing broth, she says. Wood fuel cannot be had, and the house is built where it lies. But broth we can manage.

We walk back to the residence. In the passage I bid the Madame good day and go upstairs to my room. I am very tired.

///

Some days later I encounter Madame Gertrud again. She has now her daily turn in the crew house, where she hands out hot broth, usually boiled from stockfish or from freshly caught fish from the fjord. Moreover, she has initiated that the sick be gathered at one end of the house, furthest from the door and the cold draughts that come from it, and has installed two soapstone lamps and engaged some native women to attend to them, a matter that demands much practice and vigilance and which the Danes have neither the skill nor the patience for. The house has become rather less chilly because of it, and the effect on the dwellers is noticeable. Fewer have fallen ill, and more have become well. I praise the Madame for what she has done.

Following my rounds I accompany the Madame back to the house and am invited again into the parlour. The girls sit reading Luther, as their father expects. They sit hunched over their books, their long, thin plaits coiling neatly like rope on the table in front of them. I see their lips moving as they read, and hear the mumbled German text that cannot be so very meaningful to them yet.

I ask the Madame about the mark she has on her cheek. Has she taken a fall?

No, no fall.

And no one has struck you? One of the convicts, perhaps? I wouldn't put it past them to show their gratitude in such a way.

No, the convicts are certainly coarse and boorish, but quite compliant.

You have been struck, I say, taking her chin between my hands and examining her closer. She winces slightly. Definitely a blow of some sort. How did it happen, Madame Gertrud?

I become aware that the girls have paused in their Lutheran mumblings and are listening with ears pricked. And then the penny drops.

Aha, the one you love is the one you chastise. Egede seems not to approve of his wife's enterprise in the crew house.

I let the matter lie and leave marital conflict to the jurisdiction of the marriage, it being no business of any outsider to involve himself in such matters. I change the subject:

Is the Madame not concerned as to what these scoundrels might expose her children to?

Not at all. They are accustomed to looking after themselves.

And you place your faith in God?

We do.

It must be a comfort. To be able to do so. I am not so strong in faith.

Pray, she says. Pray, and the Lord will hear you.

'Nihil humani'
Christian Kieding
The Colony of Godthåb
Autumn, 1728

6

The Son

On this day I journeyed with my beloved Frederik Christian to visit the Greenlanders who were settled a good Danish mile from us up the Baal's River. We remained there for two days in order to instruct them and their children.

FROM HANS EGEDE'S JOURNAL, DECEMBER 1728

By God, it is winter again already. The summer was cold and rainy, but the autumn was mild. Snow fell in October, though it did not settle. Now we are well into December and the snow is thin on the ground, but holy mother of God the weather is raw and we shiver to the bone. Yet my father's word is law and if he is set on sailing, then we sail. The winter's darkness is upon us, the coast is sombre and forbidding, the sea a sour and inky milk. But I love the darkness, one collects oneself in a way that is quite inconceivable when the sun flits about the sky from morn to eve, wreaking its havoc on the mind.

I grew up with darkness, first at Vågan in the Lofoten isles and now here, to where we came when I was ten years old. But I know the light too. Darkness or light, according to the season. Now I am eighteen.

I am his son, the youngest. My elder brother is Poul. He is departed to Copenhagen, to the seminary to earn his ruff and a powdered wig for his lice. My father has instructed me to write about our trip so that I might become more practised in using the quill. It was Mr Top who taught me to write, a priest who assisted him the first few years, though now returned. But it seems I am better suited to handling a musket than quill and ink, for my efforts are so many smudges and smears and my sisters laugh and tell me I am quite black about the mouth from licking the nib.

Now I shall endeavour to tell of the recent excursion into the fjord. Not that it was in any way unusual. As so often before, it was an outing without purpose, but so it goes. Life is as meaningful as we wish it to be, as someone said – I think in fact it was Mr Top. No matter, I think my father would kill me if he heard me say such a thing. And so I have put it in writing instead. I give my thanks to the Master Kieding for having taken on the task of mentoring me in the art of writing now that Mr Top is gone. Mind, good master, that my father does not read this. In writing, Mr Top told me, a person may pour out their heart and confide to the paper their innermost thoughts and secrets. It is almost like confessing one's sins to the priest. No doubt he will read this anyway, my father, and I shall be compelled to suffer his beating. One is never too old for a slap in the face. Not even my mother . . . But now I will tell of the excursion.

If only the boat had been watertight. Yet it was lacking several ribs and the wood was quite mouldering and rotten. We had constantly to bail. It was a *chalup*, as they are called, a rowing boat with a sail. One is quite mobile in such a vessel, and it may be drawn up onto the land. The best, however, are the natives' skin boats. Their capacity for carrying cargo is so very great and they are exceedingly seaworthy. They have their women row them, so they are not stupid. The women can suckle their infants whilst rowing, drawing their drooping breasts back over their shoulders where the infant, suspended in a pouch on their backs, latches on and will not release until the last drop has been wrung, and in this way they need not waste time on it. Long and dangling breasts are therefore considered an ideal for the beauty of their women, as is a good set of teeth, useful in the tanning of hides, and moreover small noses and inward-pointing feet, though the advantages of these latter properties are unclear to me. But what I meant to say was that the largest of these skin boats, called the *umiak*, is the best craft of all for the transport of people and equipment about this land.

We sat together on the stern thwart, my father and I, bobbing in unison. I held the rudder and the sheet of the little jib, and had thus plenty to do. He was not wearing his cassock, both of us clad in ordinary linen clothing and coats, sturdy boots and skin hats whose ear flaps were tied under our chins, and by the living God, with his great beak of a nose he looked most of all like a falcon with its leather hood pulled down over the eyes. And yet through and through he is a cleric, even when submerged in the tub at home, as naked as Adam, with Mother scrubbing his back. I imagine the time he came out of his mother's womb, the midwife holding him aloft to exclaim, and here we have the Pastor Egede!

My dear brother Poul departed with the ship this August. If only it had been me. He would have preferred to become a sea captain than prepare for the priesthood, but our father would say to him that in such case he would build him a gallows and hang him on it, for which reason his dreams have come to naught. A happy journey to you, brother! Now my ears are doubly boxed, for he lays not a hand on Frederik Christian and is so tender towards him as if he were the very Christ child in his own high person. Still, as my father says, I am thick-headed. Priest you will never be, he says, but a merchant. And thank God for it. Rather a shopkeeper than a prelate, any day. Of course, I say nothing of it. One must be careful as to what passes one's lips, for though a person may be thick-headed, a clip round the ear hurts all the same. In any case, my neck is not right for the ruff. I have tried on my father's and it was as tight as hell, nor is it my way to force things upon people that they would prefer to be without. Surely it is for themselves to decide if they wish to become Christian. For my sake they can believe in that fellow Tornaarsuk as much as they want. My father though thinks him to be the Devil, an old man convinced him of it. Tornaarsuk is a volatile spirit with whom one is advised to deal with the utmost caution, but he is also good, perhaps the strongest of all their spirits. Sila is milder, gentler, an altogether brighter spirit, whereas Tornaarsuk is dark and rambunctious. I like Tornaarsuk, and if I were a native shaman I would endeavour to make him my helping spirit, though again my father would kill me for saying so. So yes, I am only glad that my brother is to be a man of the Lord and not me. A dress belongs on a woman, and the cross is a murderous weapon. I think it wrong to go about with such a thing around one's neck. And now no doubt I will be boxed about the ear again when he reads this, but be that as it may. I am to be a merchant, my father and brother are men of the cloth, and as such this colony place will remain a family business much as a roadside inn.

Often I sail on my own. I have my own kayak, built by my own hand. I cannot fit into a native kayak, being fuller about the arse than them. I have much pleasure in my kayak and enjoy getting away from the colony, out into the good and quiet wilderness. I've been all sorts of places. I think that of all the white men here I know the fjord system the best. It is called Baal's River and was named by some Englishmen. Now, however, they have begun to call it the Godthåbsfjord. There are many foreign place names along the coast, especially Dutch, for the Dutchmen and the Englishmen have sailed here for more than a hundred years. It was the Dutch who set fire to our houses up north at Nipisane, a trading station founded by my father, and they trade illegally still with the natives. My father is enraged by them. Often I will sail with my foster-brother Frederik Christian too. He is a couple of years younger than me, although he is unsure as to exactly how old he is. Nonetheless, he is both baptized and confirmed, and my father seems to have plans for him and will train him as a catechist. There is something particular about the two of them which is impenetrable. I think he is the only one of the family my father really loves. He came to us some years ago. My father and mother took him in, for he was sick, and wrenched him from the claws of death, from the heathen darkness and certain damnation. But when he became well again his father wanted him back and my father for his part would not return him, so they were forced to hide him away whenever his father came sniffing about the Hope Isle where we were settled at the time. And thus there is bad blood between them, his father and mine. He is the one they call Aappaluttoq, the Red One. They say he is a murderer.

I suspect there is not a missionary in any colony on earth who is less inclined to baptize than my father. Were he a merchant and Christianity the ware he wished to sell, he would surely be compelled to go with a beggar's staff. He has baptized barely two score natives in all, and they are now dead nearly to a man. At the same time, he is ruthless when it comes to shamans and witches and all such native diableries. I have seen him raze to the ground an entire skin-tent full of natives in the business of lantern games. He pulled the whole dwelling down, kicked away the blubber lamps and cooking pots and thrashed his walking staff about, causing the poor people to run away half-naked and screaming to hide from him in the wilderness.

But now back to our excursion. Frederik Christian sat on the floor of the boat at my father's feet. His head see-sawed with every pull of the oars. By God, how comical a person can look when they are falling asleep. The sail was up, though with barely a wind to fill it but the slightest breeze from the south-west. I strove to slacken and tauten, but it flapped so limply and to little use at all. The four oarsmen had their work cut out to bring us to our intended haven before darkness. My father wished to visit some settlements inside the fjord, some fifteen Danish miles from the colony, where there lived some natives. Although the air is considerably colder there in winter, the weather is much calmer than on the sea and there is always a plenitude of hare and reindeer, the river teeming with fish waiting to be stabbed by anyone who wades into its waters. There it was that the ancient Norsemen settled in the olden days. They had the right idea. I would much rather have lived then than now if I could choose, for I think the old Norsemen had a more enjoyable time of it than we and were that much more relaxed in life. In summer one may find traces of their settlements, foundation walls and stone circles. There are many delightful places there. Valleys of the lushest grass, bushes and vege-tation so tall as to reach above one's head, small waters milling with trout, and a mildness to the air that is quite astonishing if one only knows the land from its coast and the skerries where the colony lies. My father has often said it would be a more suitable place for a Danish colony, tucked inside the bottom of the fjord, and knowing him as I do he has likely not abandoned the thought, for when first an idea comes to him it will stick and not be removed. That's the way he is, the old man. Otherwise we would not be here in Greenland at all, but back home in Lofoten. One might even cultivate cereals and beet and cabbage there. However, living there would mean seeing barely the shadow of a native. One can journey for days without passing a single inhabited hut, so it is best to know where they are settled before embarking on any excursion. We are here for the

Mission, my father says, not for creature comforts, nor to revive the Norsemen's agriculture. But still I know he yearns for the gentle valleys and green swathes inside the land, as I myself likewise. It is a longing that resides in every Norwegian, I suppose, but for the Greenlanders the interior is but a temporary refuge. The skerries are their own earthly paradise, to where they forever yearn.

How marvellous it was to get away from the filthy colony, the drinking and whoring and all the misery that has come upon this otherwise so pure and splendid land. When we Danish subjects shake our heads at what is happening here, we must ask ourselves what thoughts the natives must have of these new colonists whose behaviour is more outrageous than that of any savage. Certainly it is no positive testimony to whatever it is the Danish crown might have to offer them.

My father sat there on the thwart and said nothing. He had been silent ever since sailing from the colony. He sat writing in a book, reading his Luther, the one with the table talk from which he always reads aloud to us and which he carries with him everywhere, for which reason barely two pages remain joined. When my father is silent, and especially when he is reading Luther at the same time, it generally means that he is angry or discontented about something. But when he screams and scolds and shouts it is most often because he is glad and contented. It is his way of having a laugh, though genuine heartfelt laughter is something I cannot recall ever having issued from his mouth. Has the sun ever shone inside his mind? It has been my mother who has been the source of the lighter moments in our lives, though she is no humorist exactly, and so much older than him to boot.

I knew what was irking him, having seen the mark left on her cheek by his most recent display of affection, by the looks of it a rather savage blow with the back of his hand. He had been brooding over her wilfulness for days and opined that women were rich in shite though impoverished in thought, for which reason their arses were broad and their shoulders narrow. I have no idea what she might have said to him, but clearly it was sufficient for him to erupt and strike her. It happens not nearly as frequently as with us children, whom he will beat about the ears at the slightest provocation, for he knows that such a blow is his own shame, not hers, and I think too that when one is a woman and is beaten by one's husband, the pain of it is dulled by the awareness that in a way one has got the better of him. Christ, a palaver it must be to be married. I shall keep well out of it. Such constellations are not for me, for I would be bound to compare any woman with my mother, which would hardly redound to the former's benefit, though if I did happen to find one to match her, then I would surely find myself unworthy.

But now he sat there, absorbed in Luther. I found myself thinking how little it would help him in his torment, and how more likely it would only make things worse.

The wind had dropped. We took down the sail, it seemed more a hindrance than a help, and continued by the oars alone. We realized by then that we would not arrive before dark. Yet there are always points from which one may take one's bearing in Greenland, even when the night is at his darkest, for the darkness is never as dense as at home. Always there is snow and ice, absorbing even the faintest light from the stars and moon and reflecting it back even when the sky is cloudy and one cannot see a single one of those heavenly bodies with the naked eye. The profiles of the fells are never quite obscured, but remain visible like cut-outs in front of a fire. It is a phenomenon I know from back home, but which is not seen further south where the night can be pitch-dark, as in Bergen where we resided until leaving for Greenland. I was fond of Bergen. Good coffee they had there. Moreover, one's travels were by land, for the town lies not on an island, but on the mainland.

As the darkness descended about us, we became gripped by a sense of unease. All we could hear was the creaking of the oars in the rowlocks, the blades scooping the water, the low-voiced chatter of the rowers. My father was compelled to close his book, and I sensed his disquiet. We left the lanterns unlit, for they seem only to shine inwards, producing a sphere of light that renders the surrounding darkness quite impenetrable.

It was Frederik Christian who first sighted the gleam, despite him having fallen asleep. Abruptly, he sat up as if stirred by a loud

noise and peered out to his right before pointing and exclaiming
– *aajikkua!*

The rowers paused on their oars and turned, and all of us stared
into the darkness.

Can you see it, Niels? my father asked.

Yes, I see it, I replied. The faintest of gleams I could only make
out if I looked at it askew, for it is as if the edges of one's visual field
are more sensitive to light than the middle.

Dwelling or open fire? my father asked.

A peat house. I can at any time distinguish between open fire and
the warm glow of a blubber lamp seen through a window of gut-skin.

The boat scraped against the sand. We jumped ashore and moored.
The dwelling lay half dug into the slope that faced the bay, and the
air was thick with smoke and the smells of simmering meat which
always make my father drool so, for he is an insatiable meat-eater.

We crawled through the entrance and emerged into a large room
containing perhaps a score of them, naked to a man and glistening
with sweat in the great heat. We removed our outer layers and our
boots so as not to suffocate immediately on coming in from the cold
fjord. They showed us a place to sit on the side bench beneath the
glughole. The oldermand gave us meat and boiled fish, of which there
was plenty, and we ate greedily, for there is nothing like the cold to
build up a hunger, and my father in particular devoured as much as
he could shovel inside him. He says his stomach is a cavernous hole
that can never be filled. In this he is like the natives, for they too can
put away enormous amounts of meat, causing them to bloat and be
dormant for days afterwards, as if they had drunk themselves into
oblivion.

I had noticed their angakkok, who stared at us sullenly from a
corner. It was Aappaluttoq, father of Frederik Christian. No doubt he
had been up to his tricks when we came and interrupted them in
their entertainment. I sensed only too well that we were unwelcome,
yet hospitality is more important than anything for the natives, it is
a kind of boasting to them, and demonstrative of their wealth, so they
said nothing. Still, I could tell that Frederik Christian was rather
uncomfortable with the situation. He ate his meal quickly, then said

to me that he would go down to the boat and sleep with the rowers.

No, stay here, my boy, my father said to him, ominously mild in voice. I know their sorcerer is making eyes at us. But let us teach him a thing or two.

And so my foster-brother was compelled to seat himself again, though he was far from happy with it. His eyes kept glancing towards the angry angakkok, and I watched him.

I wish to tell you about our saviour, the Lord Jesus Christ, my father said.

I translated his words. Several of the natives nodded appreciatively. One said, we know your angakkok. He was indeed a great angakkok. But did he not kick the bucket a very long time ago?

He died for our sakes. Now he is in Heaven, at his father the Lord God's side.

When I translated this they looked astonished.

Naalagaq? they said. This is the word for 'lord and master' in their language, but they could make neither head nor tail of the notion.

Now Frederik Christian had to intervene, much against his will. He whispered to my father, they think you mean the Governor, for he too they refer to as *naalagaq*.

Ah, I see, said my father, two lords by the same name. That will not do. We must find some other name for our Lord. No, tell them there is a Lord in Heaven who is God and of whom there is but one, and then there are earthly lords, of which there are many, including Pors in the colony and King Frederik who is blessed by God, and other kings in other countries. But can you not find a good word for it, my boy, so that they may distinguish one from the other?

Must I? Frederik Christian replied. He seemed indeed reticent. Am I to name God? Would that not be blasphemy?

My dear boy, said my father, do not concern yourself unnecessarily. I stand between you and the Lord and will shoulder the blame if needs be.

Well, said Frederik Christian, when I teach them I tend to call him *Guuti*. Then they know we are speaking about a heavenly lord rather than an earthly one.

Excellent, said my father. A simple derivation from the Danish. I knew you'd come up with something, and of course these deranged people need a name for the Lord in their own tongue. The name is hereby in force and will be used henceforth. I shall notify Lange and Miltzov so that they may circulate it. Thank you, my boy. And now we shall talk about the Devil. Do they know who he is?

I call him *Tiaavulu*, Frederik Christian replied. But they know nothing about him from before.

To conquer him is to know him, my father said. These sorry people have been easy prey for the Devil. That is why they live in such squalor and filth. But we shall help them from the gutter of ungodliness. Tell them, my boy.

They want to know what a gutter is, Frederik Christian said after a brief exchange. I'm not sure I know either.

The gutter is that part of a street in which a person expels his urine and excrement, my father said.

They wash their hair in their urine, said Frederik Christian.

Indeed, they are the Devil's children, my father replied, and I could tell he was becoming impatient and that he for his part could tell that Frederik Christian was reluctant to translate for him for fear of annoying his countrymen and, more especially, his father. So my father began to preach to them in his homespun blend of northern Norwegian and Greenlandic in which, unhappily, he came to confuse the doer with the done-to. Christ, how ridiculous it sounded to a person who knew both languages well, and how singular he looked as he stood there in the middle of the dwelling, his long shadow a hunched and crooked figure enlarged upon the wall by the flickering blubber lamps. And all the time I could see Frederik Christian become increasingly uncomfortable, while their angakkok at the same time smiled maliciously from his corner. The latter knew well that my father before long would lose his temper, that he would make a fool of himself, and that he, the angakkok, would then stand as the wiser man in the eyes of his own. My father began now to rail against their house god, Tornaarsuk, only then to proceed to the sea-woman Arnaqquasaaq and thereafter to inveigh further against Ilisiitsut and angakkoks, witches and sorcerers, and Inua and Sila, jumbling all into a single hotchpotch he then condemned to the eternal flames of Hell. This tirade did not please the natives at all. Increasingly they became dejected and scowling to look at, whereas their angakkok's grin only widened, for he knew my father was divesting himself completely of his believability, and quite without his help or incitement.

But who is God? a native ventured to ask.

God is God, replied my father. He hath built us.

Built?

Created, Frederik Christian translated.

God hath built us, my father went on. He is our property.

We belong to him, Frederik Christian translated.

We may do with him as we please.

He can do with us as he pleases.

We may strike him!

He can punish us.

We may kill him!

He can kill us.

God is God, and all are above him.

No one is above God.

Even you, said my father, pointing now directly at the angakkok, well knowing that the natives loathe to be pointed at, that they take it to be a challenge and a threat upon their lives. Yes, I have seen you, and yet I tell you, you too are above God.

God decides over you too, Frederik Christian translated, his voice now a barely audible croak, for the man was his own father by blood.

At first Aappaluttoq said nothing. He sat and considered his son with an oddly sorrowful gaze. But then he did something that was far stronger than any word. He spat on the floor right in front of where my father stood, and then he said, I spit on your God.

My father had not expected such a reply and was rendered quite speechless for a moment. But presently he spoke: Sneer you not at God, you Satan. If you were alone I would put you in chains and drag you to the colony and place you in the stocks we have made for people such as you.

I cannot be enchained by you, said Aappaluttoq.

Oh, that's right, I'd forgotten, my father replied mockingly. For you can fly and conceal yourself behind the moon. But I say to you that the King's irons are stronger than any sorcerer's trick, and the flames of Hell await to consume your flesh, you wretched individual, for you are condemned. I would have met you halfway before, but you wished it not, for you are irreconcilable. I can do no more for you.

You stole my son, Aappaluttoq then said, and a great silence descended. All ears were on this exchange between my father and the angakkok, for surely they feared them both and were unable to make up their minds with whom to side.

You remember, I take it, that he was ill, my father said. The boy was at death's door, and I took him unto me in order to give him care and comfort, and indeed he became well again. Should I have left him to die?

When I came to take him back, you would not let him come to me, Aappaluttoq replied. You chased me from the settlement and forbade me to come anywhere near my own son.

He wished to stay with us, it was his own decision. He was brought up a Christian. Such a child cannot be given over to a heathen, and certainly not to any sorcerer.

But now you are grown, said Aappaluttoq to his son. How fine and strong you are.

Frederik Christian gave no reply to this.

Look at me, said Aappaluttoq, but Frederik Christian would not look at him, and then, not without gloating, my father said: He is yours no longer. He belongs to the Lord. I have plans for him. Together with my son Poul he is to carry on the missions here in this land when I am gone from it.

Aappaluttoq whispered some words to his son, unintelligible to the rest of us. He reached out and touched his arm as if to caress him, and straight away my father shouted: Touch him not, you devil, I know what you're playing at, you will blow on him, but you shall see it has no force, for it is heathen theatre and mummery and I have only laughter for such things! And with that he laughed loud and rattlingly, and several of the children in the dwelling began to cry. But Aappaluttoq seemed not to hear him and continued to speak whisperingly to his son, while he, Frederik Christian, sat between the two and looked so very shameful and dejected.

When later we lay down to sleep, tempers had abated. The oldermand had spoken conciliatory words to my father, and Aappaluttoq had withdrawn to his corner where he sat carving a figure from a piece of driftwood. But we all of us slept uneasily that night and were visited by nightmares and unpleasant dreams. I myself dreamt I had got lost somewhere in the interior. I found myself in a great, open flatland where no fells or lakes could be seen, nor anything else that might indicate to me where I was. Quite undifferentiated was the land, and the sun was hidden behind the cloud. I wandered and wandered, not knowing if I was getting anywhere or merely walking in circles. Such a dream.

We rose early. The natives were still asleep when we crawled out through the passage. The house had grown cold, for the women who looked after the lamps had fallen asleep too. We pulled on our clothes and went down to the shore where we clambered into the boat, shaking the rowers awake, and then began the long excursion further into the fjord. My father praised Frederik Christian for having resisted the onslaught of his heathen father. But when light came, he took his Luther from his bag and settled himself to read, and I'll be damned if I know what the idea of that excursion was, for all we achieved by it was to make fools of ourselves in front of some natives, though of course the fact of this never occurred to my father at all.

Now I shall close this account, my good Master Kieding. Perhaps you will look at my wrist for it feels now like it is broken. The pen is harder to command than the paddle.

Niels Egede
The Colony of Godthåb
December, 1728

7

A Prayer for Jomfru Titius

Besides the misery I saw in these poor, enfeebled individuals,
which I concede did travel to my heart, though without any aid
which I could offer them, I sensed moreover to my considerable
annoyance and displeasure that a great misunderstanding and
discordance had arisen between certain persons, which ought not
to have been the case. I shall not speak of the ungodliness which
was practised by many of these common and libidinous folk, and
which to my chagrin I could neither alter nor prevent.

FROM HANS EGEDE'S JOURNAL, DECEMBER 1728

In the evening, when the Governor is out, comes Harlequin, face powdered with flour, half-hidden behind the mask, an insistent, clinging smile and a piercing gaze.

Peek-a-boo, Columbina.

Oh, you frightened me, says Titia.

He glides sideways through the door and is then standing in the room.

I'll call for the Governor.

The Governor, as you well know, has gone north.

Then I'll call for Skård. He'll tear your bollocks off.

Ha, ha! Landorph laughs. Be nice, Columbina. Play with me.

She is darning socks. She puts them down and looks at him. It is not the usual black mask he is wearing, but something woollen. What can it be? Ah, now she sees.

Have you disfigured one of the sheep? she says.

A goat, actually, he replies. Slaughtered yesterday.

He has cut the skin from the face of a goat and uses it now for a mask. Blood and fibres of flesh still stick to its edge.

Baa-aaa, says Landorph.

You're drunk, Jørgen.

Funny you should mention that, he says, and sits down at the table. You wouldn't have any of the Governor's good aquavit handy by any chance?

She fetches him a bottle and a glass and puts them down in front of him. He pours himself a dram and drinks.

Ah, that's better.

It's best you leave.

I'll leave when I want. It's not for you to decide, little Titia. There are two kinds of people in this world: those who come and go as they please, and then, well, the rest.

I'll tell Pors you drink his schnapps.

Oh, be nice to me, Titia. Why can't we have a bit of fun? I thought we were sweethearts?

Will you marry me then?

Of course I will. I shall speak to Egede and ask him to do the honours.

Do it now.

He's out on his visitation today.

Then go to Miltzov or Lange.

I imagine we'll need the King's permission first, you being so young, my little Columbina. He fills the glass again.

That won't arrive for at least a year.

Two years. If I'm not much mistaken, there and back is twice as long, and the postal service in this country is somewhat tardy.

We'll all be dead by then.

Yes. He stares at the liquid in his glass. It wouldn't surprise me in the least, if a person can at all be surprised when dead. He looks at her and smiles behind his goat-mask. Anyway, why wait for something good when it can be done right away?

I'm pregnant.

That doesn't bother me. I'm no prude. But tell me, who is it that has made you pregnant? I think I might be rather jealous, if truth be told.

The Devil, she says. He came and stuck his long finger up my cunt and squirted his juice inside me.

I see. He sits for some time and stares at her vacantly, his gaze piercing through the holes where the eyes of the goat used to be. He is not wearing any wig. His hair is lank and sticks to his scalp, and he is in need of a shave. I must have you, he sighs. I'm afraid there's no two ways about it.

Then let's go upstairs. But take that mask off.

Baa-aaa, he bleats, and jumps to his feet.

The house is empty apart from Skård, wherever he might be lurking. Most likely he's asleep as usual in his bed. The man has slept constantly ever since they came to this land, as if he intends to enter the eternal life from sleep. She follows the Commandant up the steep staircase. They step inside his room, where there is a bed and a table on which a pile of papers has been placed, and an ink pot from which protrudes a well-chewed quill pen. She sits down on the edge of the bed.

Take off your clothes then, he says impatiently, and with perhaps a hint of annoyance.

She obeys and pulls her dress up over her head, then the shift, then loosens her stockings and rolls them down her legs. She lies down and waits for him, a hand held protectively over her swollen abdomen, her other arm flopped over her sore breasts.

He stands a moment and looks at her, his face still hidden behind the goat-mask, smelling firstly of goat, then of aquavit, tobacco and arousal. His eyes pass over her body. He leans forward slightly and removes her arm from her breasts.

That's it, he says softly. Now I can see you. He tilts his head a touch, reinforcing his goat-like impression, or at least the sense of something bestial. His breathing is heavy. Slowly, his gaze remaining upon her, he removes his shirt and trousers, though not the mask. She wishes he would take it off, but she knows too that he is obstinate, that he prefers to hide his face, to conceal himself whilst doing the unlawful.

He curls, dips down and kisses her crotch, slobbering between her legs as he moans and sighs. She must control herself so as not to kick out with her legs and perhaps kick him in the face. She lies staring at the ceiling, her body bracing itself for half an hour of pain, shame and unpleasantness. Why am I doing this, she wonders. There are two kinds of people in the world, those who must endure such things and then the rest.

Landorph's/Harlequin's/Billy Goat Gruff's face appears between her thighs. He looks at her. I love your cunt. I don't know why. A few folds of skin. Why is that? It's only skin. What makes it so fantastic? I could fight a duel, wager my life, renounce everything for the sake of these fleshy folds. How can that be, can you tell me, little Titia?

It's one of life's mysteries, she says, examining her dirty fingernails.

He is still wearing the shaggy mask as he takes her. His dark, penetrating eyes gaze at her unyieldingly through the holes in the skin, mouth drawn together into an uneven crack, he arches his back on top of her, holding her tight around the ankles and pressing her legs back, but he is not rough with her, sliding more than thrusting inside her, slobbering with pleasure, and when he comes he bleats, or perhaps sobs, and she mumbles some words in prayer: *Magnificat anima mea Dominum.*

Lying there, with all his weight upon her, she thinks: I shall never get away from this place.

///

The Devil himself must have made you, Jomfru Titius, Landorph says. Look what you make me do. I know it is wrong. But I cannot help myself.

She has suffered a seizure and lies exhausted in the bed with a damp cloth, wrung by Skård, upon her forehead. The Commandant sits drinking the Governor's schnapps. The goat-mask is gone. It had begun to smell, and so he has thrown it away.

No one forces you, she says in the frailest voice. I'd rather you didn't.

But I cannot help myself, he says again. It's the Devil's work. I'd like to leave you alone, but I cannot. You have bewitched me.

Don't call me a witch.

It's not me. It's the crew.

If I'm a witch, then they are devils.

Perhaps. If so, they are many. They wish to put you on trial. They believe you to be the cause of all these deaths. They've spoken to Egede.

Egede knows full well I'm not a witch.

Egede believes you are a papist. Witch or Catholic, it's all the same to him.

I'm a good Christian.

You'd be shrewd to let him baptize you.

I'm already baptized.

Then be so again. It would put a stop to all their talk.

Has he spoken of it? Egede?

I can have a word with him and speak your case. I will help you, little Titia. But you must help me too.

I'm weak today.

You women and all your weaknesses, he sneers. You, who have it all so easy. You inhabit a land of milk and honey. We men have the hard life. A man cannot allow himself to lie in bed with a wet cloth on his brow.

What am I supposed to help you with?

It's Pors. He accuses me of being father to your child.

You're not the father.

I know that, and you know that, but he does not. Tell him. He has written a report. He wants me dismissed from my position.

You can marry me like you promised.

We've talked about that. It would require a special licence. It could take years.

We could be betrothed to start with?

We can't. I'm already betrothed. And anyway, it would be admitting my paternity.

She sits up in the bed, only to become dizzy and be forced to lie down again. You are betrothed? You didn't say. Who to?

Her name is Julie. Julie Holck. I apologize. Oh, don't start crying. I can't abide women weeping.

I'll never get away from here, she snivels.

You should never have come in the first place. It was your own wish, so I've heard. Once a person has made the voyage to the colonies, returning home is the hardest thing. Many go out, few come back. It's a one-way journey.

It wasn't my decision to come here with Pors. It was my father's brother, the Apothecary.

In that case, I pity you. It does seem like a sorry situation, I can see that. I'm not entirely callous. But speak to him anyway. I cannot live with such suspicion upon me.

I'll tell him you're the father.

Do that and you will no longer enjoy my protection from the crew. You'll end up being lynched, you witch.

Who cares. I'll never get way from here anyway.

You silly little girl. It will end badly for you. Landorph empties his glass, rises and leaves.

Skård! she calls. Skård!

The Icelander comes shuffling. He removes the cloth from her brow, soaks it in the water barrel, dips it in vinegar and places it on her brow again.

Thank you, dearest Skård.

And Skård returns to his observation post by the window.

///

Both Pors and Egede have returned from their excursions in the district. She catches sight of Frederik Christian and calls out to him. She sees him stiffen. But then he goes, pretending not to have heard her. My only friend, she thinks to herself. Why will he not acknowledge me?

Winter comes, with frost and snow and storms. The jomfru Titius is encaged in her few square alens of the governor's residence. She moves from window to window, trembling with anxiety, seldom going out, and then only when she must use the privy or when she cannot employ Skård to fetch meat and grain for the food. Skård must suffer from some particular Icelandic melancholy that compels him to sit all day long staring out of the window as he smokes his pipe, or to lie in his bed and snore, his bast-shoed feet sticking out over the bed-end. A sorry lot of servants the Governor has found to keep his house, she thinks. I shall never get away from here.

Pors takes on one of the Spinning-House women, Sise, to help Titia with the housekeeping. It seems she too is pregnant, they are both as far gone. Sise is an engaging wife of nineteen, healthy, cheerful and somewhat frivolous. She is married to one of the former inmates, Johan, and lives with him in a peat-hut they have established to the north of the colony. But until Christmas she is staying here in the governor's house and sleeping together with Titia, though first after having changed the bedding straw. Your bed stinks worse than a stable, she says with a laugh. I don't think you're quite house-trained yet, girl.

It's my seizures, she says. They make me let go.

Poor Titia, Sise says. She washes her and rubs ointments into her dry and scabby skin, and sings for her when she lies down to sleep.

Do you think we shall ever get away from this place? Titia asks.

The important gentlemen will, I'm sure, Sise replies. The rest of us will no doubt have to stay. It's such a very long voyage, and do you know the Earth is curved between us and home? When we sailed up here, one of the seamen in the *Morian* told me about the Earth's curvature and how our old land is gone once you've sailed far enough away. I began to cry. Is it gone for always? I asked. Yes, forever and ever, he said, but only to tease me, I knew that. But still it was like everything at home was gone for all time, Øster Kvarter, Sankt Nikolaj, the Dragoon, Karen Busse's brothel-house and the square of Amager Torv, my entire home turf, you understand.

Are your parents still alive? Titia asks.

Dead both. They too are sailed to the other side. We're all of us dead, or as good as, Sise says, throwing a laundered tablecloth over the table. It hangs suspended in the air for a moment, then settles to be smoothed.

I shall never get away from here, Titia says darkly.

Poor little Titia, says Sise and places a jug filled with paper flowers on the table.

They dress up together when left alone. They pull the Governor's clothes from the chest, parade uniforms with twirlings of braid and cord and passementerie, three-cornered hats, wigs, knee-length stockings, silver-buttoned waistcoats, shoes with shiny buckles, and adorned in this abundance of oversized apparel they stagger about and fall on the floor in great heaps of fabric, roaring with laughter as native children stand with noses pressed to the window panes to stare in at them in bewilderment. How good it is to laugh. With laughter, anxiety dissolves, at least for a time.

One morning when they are seated drinking fresh goat's milk, Titia smashes her cup and gashes a long shard into her crotch, the blood oozing from her immediately. Sise screams and leaps to her feet to find a cloth she presses against the wound.

Why did you do this?

I wanted to, says Titia, her voice dull. I'm like that sometimes. It makes me calm.

You're not of sound mind.

No.

Sise kneels with her head in Titia's lap, her arms around her hips. Titia strokes her hair.

You've got such lovely hair, she says. Thick and so very fair. So lovely you are. I wish I could be you. She gazes down at her. Why are you crying?

Because I'm sad, Sise replies, her tears streaming down into Titia's lap. You make me sad doing such a thing.

I'm sorry. I won't do it again.

Why can't you just be happy?

I don't know. I try all the time, but I'm not like you, Sise. I'm more like Frederik Christian.

The native boy?

We're both mongrels of a kind. We can't really ever be happy.

I don't understand that. A person can just be happy. What's so difficult about it?

I shall never get away from here, says Titia. I shall never get away from here. I shall never get away from here.

Sise drags her outside to get some fresh air. They walk arm in arm through the colony to the soggy moorland.

Why are those people asleep there in the snow? Titia asks.

They're not asleep. They're dead.

Dead? Is that what it's like? She prods at a corpse with the toe of her boot.

Sise pulls her on. There's an epidemic, she explains. Nearly everyone is sick. People are too weak to bury the dead, so for the time being they leave them lying here.

Are they not cold in the snow?

They don't feel anything any more.

So that's what it's like. Being dead. Not feeling anything.

I think so. Come here. I'm sorry I took you out now.

But can a person feel that they can't feel anything? Titia wants to know.

Perhaps not.

Then it doesn't matter. Why be dead if you don't know you're dead? She opens her mouth wide and puts a finger down her throat.

What's the matter? Sise says. Do you feel sick?

I'm just feeling for something, that's all.

Feeling for what?

The child, of course. Can you see anything? She turns her gaping mouth to Sise.

Come on, let's go home, Sise says and tugs at her arm. I should never have taken you out.

Do you think we'll all die? Titia asks once they're home.

Yes, Titia, sooner or later we will.

I'll look forward to it. Do you know where we go when we die? Us women, I mean.

To Heaven or Hell, I suppose.

Titia laughs. No, that's only what the priests say. Perhaps the men will, but not us women. We go to a boarding house somewhere in the countryside, in Jutland maybe, near the sea, I think. You can hear the sea from the house, a gentle rush, not the thunderous sound it makes here. Apart from that it's all quiet. Of course, there aren't any men. Only Frederik Christian, or no, I'm not sure. But there are children, lots of children, for the children go there too. There's a big garden, looked after by some old women, nuns, I think, or angels, with flowers and shrubs and green trees. And we lie in beds of soft, clean linen and can sleep as long as we want and get up whenever it pleases us. And we've all got musical instruments we play on.

It sounds like a lovely place.

But you've got to wait before going until it happens by itself, because you know what happens if you shoot yourself, what happens to suicides?

What happens?

Then you're condemned. You have to join the men then, and must slave and toil for them and keep them satisfied. And you can never get away.

Sise wants to know who the father of her child is. It's the Commandant, she says. It seems like the most convenient lie. She knows it's the Devil who got her pregnant, and that she even enjoyed it, that it was like bursting open, splitting down the sides like a pea-pod in the most wonderful way, but she is unable to say so, for then she would most certainly be thrown on the fire.

Such a fine gentleman, Sise says, impressed. You struck lucky there, girl.

He doesn't want me. I've told him he's got to marry me, but he says he's betrothed back home.

Sise is appalled. She goes to Egede, and speaks to him about it. Egede speaks to his wife Gertrud about it. Their conversation is overheard by the couple's daughters, who pass it on to the young Miltzov, who then speaks about it with his colleague, Ole Lange. Somewhere along the line, a misunderstanding arises; by which it becomes the Governor and not the Commandant who is the father of the child. Therefore, Lange goes directly to Pors, presenting the accusation to him and inviting him to confess his sins.

Indeed I am a sinner, Pors says, and have often departed from the straight and narrow, I shall readily admit the fact, Magister Lange. But I never laid a finger on the jomfru. I only recently found out she was carrying a child. What devil could have done it?

You, so it is said, Governor.

Pors flies into a rage and ejects the cleric on his ear. Bloody black-coat!

He goes to Titia. He sits by her bed and takes her hand. My dear child. You know I promised your father's brother that I would take care of you, and now this. Who did it to you? Tell me, and I shall personally remove his cock with my sword.

Titia has had another attack. She is muddled and doesn't know quite what she is saying, or else she knows exactly what she is saying, but exploits her state as an excuse to be malicious. It was the Commandant, she says.

I knew it, says the Governor, jumping to his feet and overturning the chair in the process. I'll keelhaul the swine!

But Landorph denies having been anywhere near the jomfru. The girl is quite mad, he says, she is unbalanced, as well you know, Governor.

You swear? says Pors.

I swear.

By the Holy Bible?

Certainly, if I had one I would.

Egede has a Bible.

They go from the Governor's rooms to the priest's and put the matter to Egede. He presents them with a Bible, Luther's German translation, and Landorph places his hand upon it.

I swear, says Egede.

I swear.

By this holy book, and in the Lord's name.

By this holy book, and in the Lord's name.

That I did not violate the jomfru Titia by enjoying physical intercourse with her.

Er, says Landorph. I thought I was to swear I wasn't the father of her child?

Despicable swine! Pors exclaims. I'll have you sent to the colonies.

But I'm already in the colonies.

So you've had intercourse with the girl, then? says Egede.

I didn't say that.

Then why will you not swear to it?

I'll swear to not being the father of her child is what I'll swear to. He places his hand on the Bible once more and repeats the oath with Pors glaring at him, enraged.

Then she must be lying, says Egede. I shall speak to her.

///

Egede has long wished to confront this suspicious jomfru who grew up in a Catholic nunnery and who doubtless is severely infected with the false doctrine of the papists. But another suspicion, even worse, has at the same time preyed on him, one that he has been unable to release from his mind. He resolves to ask her about it before moving on to the other matter. He goes to her alone, without Frederik Christian.

Do you belong to the people of Judea? he asks.

What?

You heard me, he barks. Trying to worm your way out will not lessen the suspicion against you. On the contrary.

I don't understand, she says.

Are you Jewish?

Not as far as I know.

You must know if you are Jewish, surely? You seem rather swarthy to me. And that nose of yours cannot be of Danish lineage.

You should be careful talking about people's noses with the hooter you've got, she says.

Who was your mother?

My mother's name was Kristiane.

Was she Jewish?

Not that I know of.

Jews are surely aware that they are Jews, whether they have been told or not. It is innate knowledge.

But then I can't be Jewish, can I?

I hope not, for your sake. You are aware of what Luther said about the Jewish people?

No, what did he say?

That they are cheap and filthy debauchers. Are you a true Christian, my child?

Yes.

Do you believe in the Lord Jesus Christ?

Yes.

Do you renounce the Devil?

She hesitates and he thinks, aha, interpreting her indecision to be significant. The Devil's usual hesitancy when pressed into a corner. He has seen it before. And now he has forgotten all about what it was he came here for, her pregnancy and the issue of the paternity. Now it is of the utmost importance to him to investigate whether she is a true Christian, whether she is familiar with the Augsburg Confession, and whether she is at all at home in the Lutheran faith. He challenges her about various tenets and articles of faith. Naturally, it transpires that she knows nothing. And so he is forced to begin at the beginning.

Do you renounce the Devil? he says again.

Who? she says, confused.

You heard me. Tell me now, without further ado, do you renounce the Devil? Answer me!

She feels her muscles quiver with tension. A new seizure is on its way. They have come and gone these past several days. Sometimes she can keep them at bay by concentrating with all her might, drinking cold water, breathing deeply and praying. She mutters an *Ave Maria, gratia plena*. Immediately she feels herself relax, only now the priest begins to roar.

Desist with this devilry! I will not hear it. It is the Antichrist speaking through your mouth, you ill-omened child. Say after me: I renounce the Devil.

Dominus tecum.

I renounce. Say it!

Benedicta tu.

The Devil!

Sancta Maria.

I believe in God the Father!

Ora pro nobis.

No, no, no!

He stands at the bed and bellows at the top of his lungs, only to leap back in alarm as she turns her head to the side, her eyes rolling, her face contorting hideously. He knows she suffers from these attacks, but this is the first time he has been witness to it. He stands pale and stiff, clutching his Bible as the seizure unfolds. It seems more to be the bed shaking than her body. On its legs it shuffles back and forth across the floor, creaking at the joints, so loudly that he is afraid the whole construction will fall apart. He rattles through the Lord's Prayer, kneeling cautiously at the bedside with hands folded, thumbs pressed against his forehead, Our Father who art in heaven.

But now her body arches, cresting upwards like a wave curling towards a shore, the covers fall from her frame and her thin white body with its visibly swollen abdomen is quite naked and bare. He crawls from the bed on all fours and sits down on the floor and stares at her. She is an arc, supported by her shoulders and heels, the rest of her quivering like the tautest bow.

Hallowed be thy name, he continues, but can proceed no further. The sight of this violent attack has him mesmerized. The Devil, he thinks to himself. The Devil is here. He wonders for a moment if she might be in mortal danger, whether he should call for Kieding. But he cannot wrench himself from the sight of the skinny girl's body in the grip of such powerful forces. Surely it is the Devil tormenting her, summoned by her Latin prayers.

Thy kingdom come, he squeaks, only to stall once more, for now she passes water, a long, arching emission that splashes against the stove with a hissing and a spitting, and in the steam that rises from the hot iron he sees, clear as day, the grinning likeness of the Satan himself.

And when Titia, exhausted, at last collapses and the seizure subsides, Egede is gone.

///

Two days later. Now it is the Governor who lies in his bed. Sise has returned home to spend some time with her husband.

Are you ill, Claus? Titia asks him.

My blood is boiling with the fever, he whimpers.

Do you want me to cup you?

No, no cups today. What I need are leeches. Go to Kieding and ask if you might borrow his leeches. Hurry.

She tramps around the side of the house and knocks on the Egedes' door. It is opened by one of the girls, Kirstine. She stares at her without a word.

I'm to speak to the Master Kieding, she says. Is he in?

Kirstine calls up the stairs. Kieding! It's the jomfru to see you.

He appears on the landing. My dear little Titia, he says, descending a couple of steps. What can I do for you?

It's not me, it's the Governor. He's under the weather. I'm to ask if we can borrow some leeches. The Governor says it's an emergency.

He beseeches for leeches, eh? the physician says jokingly, and disappears back into his room, returning again a moment later and descending the stairs with a box in his hands. He lifts the lid and shows her the leeches that lie in a bed of hay.

Pay the Governor my regards and wish him a speedy recovery, Kieding says.

She reaches out to take the box, but Kieding keeps hold of it and will not let go. He gives her a long and peculiar look before handing it to her, whereupon she goes back round the side of the house. The Governor is waiting for her with fear in his eyes. Tentatively she places a pair of the leeches on his chest. Immediately they latch to his skin. She places others on his legs, and then a pair on his neck. He sighs contentedly. Whatever would we do without these creatures, he says into the air. Skård! Where are you, Skård!

And Skård appears from his corner. He knows what he is to do. He rolls up his sleeves. Titia sits and watches. She is grateful it is not her job. Skård stands, his smoking pipe fixed in the corner of his mouth, massaging the Governor's member with a look of intense concentration. The leeches wriggle and swell, Pors stands in the doorway and clutches the door frame like a man crucified. He moans, oh God, dear God! Skård, shrouded in tobacco smoke, speeds the process. Pors whimpers and ejaculates with a sigh. It is done. Afterwards she harvests the leeches, returns around the side of the house and delivers them back to Kieding.

Thank you for your help. He feels better now.

Yes, I heard as much, Kieding says. You're a good girl, Titia.

She descends to the latrine where she sits and savours the cold air as it wafts her behind. Outside rain falls, drumming against the roof. It is a cosy, comforting sound. But then she gives a start. What was that? A fart that changed its mind? She feels with her fingers.

Again, a spasm ripples through her abdomen, and then another, and she realizes that it is indeed real, that which until now has seemed so unbelievable to her that she has barely considered the matter, that she has been made pregnant with a child, and that it has grown and grown until, at some point in her suddenly conceivable future, it will no longer be able to remain inside her and must instead seek to be expelled. There is a human being inside me, she says to herself. Only now, at this moment, does she realize the momentous nature of it.

///

That evening she speaks to Pors. I want the priest to baptize me.

But you're baptized already.

Yes, but I want it done again, so that I may confirm my faith.

You'll find that's what they call confirmation. You're mixing things up. And to the best of my knowledge, you've already been confirmed too.

Can't you speak to Egede about it, or one of the other priests? Preferably Egede.

He promises.

They say I'm a witch, she tells him.

Don't let it bother you. I'll look after you. I pledged my word to your father's brother. Nothing bad will happen to you, Titia.

It is dark outside. She hears cries and laughter from the crew house. She hears the Commandant Landorph's footsteps on the floor of his room above. But when she lies back and stares up, she sees straight through the beams and rafters and planks and into the eternal darkness that hangs over the colony, and she thinks: I shall never get away from this place.

Libera me.

Stop that, says Pors. Sleep, little Titia.

I shall never get away from here.

Quiet!

The Governor gets up and splashes his urine into the night pot. He fills his ears with cotton wool and returns to bed.

I'm to be here forever.

The Governor groans.

And never get away.

Never.

And then the jomfru Titius sleeps, to dream of her boarding house in Jutland. And she dreams too of Frederik Christian, of lying with him. He is the only man she can bear to think about. But the Governor is awake and dreaming of Imperium Daniae and its glorious future.

8

Diableries

To-day the council was assembled to examine a diatribe, uttered by a sergeant in the presence of many others, the nature of which arguably was encouraging of mutiny among the soldiers. Other such utterances had previously been heard, though without then giving rise to action, it being said apparently of the Governor and myself that we were to be the first to be done away with. The greatest malice seemed to issue from the slaves who have been brought here, whose words excited the others too, though from such common folk one can expect little else, and if the good Lord had not consigned the majority of them to their sick-beds, they would without a doubt have carried out their wicked design. Therefore, to our precaution and safety, we were compelled to equip our lodgings with muskets. It was indeed regrettable that we, who on our excursions far outside the district may safely lie down to sleep among wild savages and heathens, could not be sure of our lives when being among our own.

FROM HANS EGEDE'S JOURNAL, JANUARY 1729

Stop that, Pors says to Titia. I cannot abide to see it.

She is seated at the window eating flies, snatching them in flight with the swiftest swipe of her hand and consigning them to her mouth, smiling secretively as she swallows. She seems not to hear him, but follows one of the buzzing insects with her eyes. It bumps heavily, lazily against the pane. Her hand darts out and grabs it. Pors winces. He knows there are no flies. It is the middle of winter. But he sees them nonetheless. Her madness is apparently catching.

I don't know if you're mad or just pretending, he says. Are you mad?

No reply.

Is it because you wish to be sent home with the ship? Is that why you pretend to be mad?

Mad people do not exist. Or rather, there is always an element of play-acting in those who are mad. If only one could stop them from acting like madmen, they would be normal. He is certain of it. But the jomfru insists on her madness. He is up to here with her and feels he must soon marry her off. But who would wed such a lunatic? Egede's native lad would seem the only candidate. He for his part would only benefit from stepping away from his mentor. How nauseating it is to see the way they can barely be parted, as if they were a pair of sweethearts. If Egede knew what is said about them, he would surely get rid of the boy like a shot. But now he will think no more about these matters. Now he will go out, he will ride and feel himself free.

He engages Skård to assist him with his boots and spurs. He removes his wig and hands it to the manservant, and Skård shakes it vigorously with abrupt and repeated snaps of his wrist. Clouds of lice-infested powder puff into the air and descend slowly towards the floor. He tosses the wig onto the bed and helps Pors be combed, his pigtail tightened. This done, he shuffles back to his chair at the window again and lights his pipe. At one window the lunatic Titia, at the other the geriatric Skård. Has he even uttered a word since we arrived in this land? Pors wonders. Why can't people just be normal?

He steps outside, stands on the rock and gazes out over the colony. My realm, he thinks to himself. Imperium Daniae's furthest province. Boglands of the stiffest sedge, dark rock, inky sea, fog, the salty air, a few scattered peat-huts of the natives, with smoke spiralling up into the dampness. He wonders if the Roman generals felt quite as lost as he at their outposts, for example Britannia? Hardly. They knew what had to be done. He imagines England as it must have been back then. A foggy Albion. They drove the fog away with the sword and established a Roman civilization there that has held to this day. And then they went home and were appointed to the Senate to live a sumptuous, toga-clad life steeping in hot baths. It is in reach for me yet, he tells himself. Privy counsellor, perhaps. I am not yet old. But senator sounds better. I was born fifteen hundred years too late.

From the shore comes a malodorous whiff of kelp, like rotten meat. Everywhere is still. Ominously still.

He descends to the stable and saddles Pompadour, the white mare given to him by the King, patting and scratching her, talking to her gently. Pompadour stamps the floor and whinnies. She seems almost to be laughing.

Yes, I know, he says, scratching the soft spot under her muzzle. You know what's happening, don't you girl?

The King seems to have a penchant for mares, he thinks, and smiles to himself, for His Majesty is fond of the womenfolk too. A man should never ride a stallion. It is against nature.

Emerging from the stable, leading the horse, he finds Landorph to be standing there.

What now? His foot is in the stirrup already, his hand on the saddle horn.

The crew are grumbling, Governor.

You don't say. As long as a dog is growling it won't bite.

They're threatening mutiny, Your Excellency.

What are they dissatisfied about, the swine?

Landorph hesitates. He looks at Pors as if he were not right in the head. The living conditions, Governor. They're dropping like flies.

Flies, Pors mutters, reminded unpleasantly of Titia. Which of them growls the loudest?

Peter Hageman, one of the convicts. He has threatened to shoot both the Governor and the Pastor. He has broken into the stores and stolen a musket. Took some spirits with him too.

And he is not in irons yet?

He has gone off somewhere. My men are out looking for him. Maybe he's hiding out with some of the natives, in one of their dwellings. But the Governor should be alert riding about up there. He should take a firearm with him.

I shall.

Glitker! the Commandant barks at a man who happens to be passing. Bring the Governor a musket!

He straps it to the saddle.

Shoot him down if you see him, Landorph says. We could do with weeding out amongst those bandits.

Thank you, Lieutenant Landorph. Dismissed!

The latter utterance is a barb. As the colony's highest ranking military man Landorph is of rank with the Governor, who is the principal civilian. He responds with a grimace of offence and a casual, unmilitary wave of his hand.

Goat, Pors mutters to himself.

He jabs his spurs into Pompadour's flanks and proceeds through the colony, spattering mud and slush. As he comes to the priest's residence, Egede abruptly steps out in front of him. The native lad is with him as usual, like the shadow he casts on the ground. The horse rears up in fright at the sudden sight of the black-coated man and his attendant, and Pors must cling to her so as not to be thrown from the saddle.

What the hell's the matter with you, man! he shrieks. You frightened the life out of the horse.

I wish to speak with the Governor, Egede says, regardless.

I haven't the time.

It will only take a moment.

Pompadour is agitated. She turns about on her own axis, whinnying and snorting, Pors working the reins to keep her in check.

Then say what it is.

It's about the jomfru.

Yes?

It has come to my ear, says Egede in the stiff and methodical way he has of proceeding through his sentences when speaking with Danish officers, that she has expressed a desire to be baptized.

As far as I know she's already baptized.

Indeed, but as a Catholic. And, as the Governor well knows, Catholicism is false doctrine and worship of the Antichrist in Rome. His temper increasing, his language departs more and more into the Norwegian. The Devil wipes his arse with papist certificates of baptism.

Pors glances from Egede to Frederik Christian, then back at Egede again.

All right. So you will baptize her then, Egede?

Most certainly not.

Pors looks down on the priest with incredulity. Egede looks up at him in anger. The boy is silent and expressionless at his rear. And I thought you were friends with Titia, Pors thinks to himself. Sweethearts even. You should defend her against this lunatic priest. But then I suppose he has the power over you.

Such is the matter, Egede continues. Let her come to me and I will tie a millstone about her neck and throw her in the fjord before I will declare her baptized in the name of the Father, the Son and the Holy Ghost. Egede cackles at his declaration, though without sign of amusement. The girl is possessed, he goes on. Positively reeks of papal gut gas. It is a disgrace. We cannot have such a person to go about the colony. She unsettles the parishioners.

Parishioners?

The crew, the public. They believe her to be a witch and want her to the pyre.

She may be rather peculiar, the Governor admits. But possessed by the Devil? A witch? What was Egede thinking of doing with her, apart from drowning her in the fjord?

We must perform an exorcism, Egede replies. The sooner the better.

An exorcism, of papism or diablery? Pors enquires, amused by the priest's profanity and wondering if he can propel him into some more.

It's all shite from the same arse, Egede obliges.

Well, the Governor says ponderingly, I don't suppose it can do any harm. Perhaps it will help. Tonight at six, he says. The mission-house parlour.

The priest and his young assistant remain standing and watch him as he rides up the hill. Pors senses their stares in his neck even when they have vanished from his sight.

Now, my love, he says to the horse. Now perhaps we may go for a ride, you and me.

Outside the smithy a man sits staring dully into space. Pors brings Pompadour to a halt.

Who are you?

Hans Wiencke, says the man, looking up at him with wide black eyes, and in each of his vacant pupils Pors sees the image of himself and his mare.

Why are you sitting about doing nothing?

Ik bin kraank.

Has the surgeon seen to you?

He shakes his head.

Then go to the Master Kieding and get something to make you well.

Daanke, Herr Gouverneur, the man says. His head lolls onto his chest as if he has fallen asleep.

From the crest of the hill he notices a piled-up structure of discarded building materials, driftwood, a broken wheelbarrow and other such things. He sees some men come dragging what remains of a rowing boat.

What are you doing with that boat here? he barks. Who has given permission for it?

They let go of their burden and draw themselves upright, wretched, meagre and hollow-faced, a darkness hanging about their brows in a manner that reminds him of the sleepwalker.

The boat's rotten, Governor, one of them says without looking at him.

I can see that. But I'm asking who gave you permission to drag it up here? And what on earth are you building here, a Babel's tower?

A bonfire.

For what purpose?

For burning.

Who gave you permission to burn the colony's building materials?

It's only some rotten planks and the like.

Was it Landorph?

They shrug.

I will not see any bonfire here. Carry it back immediately to where you found it.

All right, Governor.

Now!

They grip the boat and begin dragging it back to the colony again.

As of tonight, I am relaxing the alcohol ration, he shouts after them, though they stagger on without looking back.

Now, surely, there will be no further impediment to his ride? He feels a near-painful urge to jab the spurs that the horse may extend itself and he feel the wind in his face. But now, predictably, a man comes running from the crew house.

Governor, Governor!

He recognizes him. It is one of the sergeants, a Norwegian by the name of Kinck. His face is a grin.

Come, and the Governor will see something hilarious.

I haven't the time. Can't you see I'm out riding?

But it's a sight for sore eyes, Governor, I can tell you. Kinck doubles up and can barely stand for mirth. Pors's curiosity is awakened.

What is it?

It's terrible, the sergeant says with a splutter. I promise, the Governor has never seen the like.

Then show me.

Kinck leads him to the crew house. An increasing commotion reaches his ears from inside. A fight. Are they at each other's throats in there? he asks.

I'll say, Kinck replies.

He dismounts from Pompadour and steps to the door. Momentarily blinded by the sudden dimness of the light, he at first sees nothing but animated shadows. He narrows his eyes, blinks. The noise is infernal. He hears laughter and whooping cries, shrieks and curses, the crack of splintering wood, bodies thrashing about in the sewage that lies several inches thick on the floor. The stench is abominable, he can barely breathe, so intense and material, so despicably human a smell as to be almost delicate. He steps further inside and sees now that the figures he saw were women, all naked and covered in filth. They look like they're playing a game of tag, swinging each other about, pulling each other by the hair, falling onto their backs with their legs splayed in the air, the slop and swill of human discharge spraying to all sides. Beds have been tossed about, most of them appear to be broken. Armed with lengths of wood, the women lay into each other, ducking and turning, hitting out, losing their footing, slithering about the floor, scrabbling blindly, leaping to their feet, shaking the filth from their frames and launching into new, screaming attacks.

Good heavens, he blurts. Are they murdering each other?

It's a game of longball, says Kinck.

Longball?

Lavatory longball. They use the planks of their beds as bats.

And what do they use for a ball?

Erm, says Kinck.

Something foul slaps against the wall above his head. He ducks and steps back towards the door. Ah, I see, he says.

Some people have all the fun, Kinck sniggers.

He goes back outside and fetches the musket, returning to fire a shot into the ceiling. The deafening report prompts the women to halt in mid-movement. They gape and blink at him with wide eyes in their filthy faces. Their bare breasts are dripping with swill. Their faces are beaming, insane smiles.

Order! he roars. Get this filth washed away at once. And put some clothes on!

One of the women steps towards him, unrecognizable behind her dirty mask. Immediately, others follow suit. He takes aim at them with the musket, but already fired it is of no use. The women come closer, still armed with their lengths of wood, their broken planks, the sewage sloshing about their bare feet. He senses the stench undulating towards him and steps backwards, retreating out through the door, Kinck likewise, slamming it shut and bolting it behind him. The women inside protest screechingly and pound their fists on the door.

Turning, he sees a small crowd has gathered at the residence. He groans and rides over, dismounting once more, still with the musket in his hand. No one notices him. They are gathered around one of the men, he recalls the name to be Johan Bretel, another of the former inmates, now standing shouting on the steps of the house. Like the others, he too is emaciated, his face grey as ash, lips tinged with blue, eyes radiant with the fever, he punches the air feebly to lend force to his words.

We want food! he shouts.

Yes! the crowd shouts back.

We want fuel!

Yes!

We want better living conditions!

Yes!

Down with the masters! the crowd shouts.

Down with the priest!

Down with the Governor!

No! Bretel shouts, holding up his hands to stop them. We want no mutiny, no rebellion. Governor? He turns to Pors, whom he has now seen. We are good working people and good soldiers too who are loyal in service to the King. We wish to carry out the work we have been asked to do in this cold land. But we are hungry, Governor. We are dying from cold and sickness. Our women have lost their minds. We live worse than the rats that scuttle in the hovels of Copenhagen. Even the savages have it better than us. Is this reasonable, Governor? What use are we to you if we all kick the bucket?

Pors hands the horse's reins to Kinck and climbs the step slowly, turning to survey the score of men who have gathered there. He sees how shabby and wretched they look, and cannot decide whether to laugh at such a woeful assembly or to sigh in empathy.

He clears his throat. Good Danish men! I will give you what you ask me for.

Liar! one of them shouts.

Paper admiral!

Your mother's a whore and your father a lecher!

When? someone else shouts. When will you give it to us, Pors?

Today, he improvises, feeling himself perspire. Immediately. Go to Fleischer and tell him I have given you permission to fetch the coal and food you need.

We'll get nothing from Fleischer, says Bretel. Not an ounce. He'd sooner see the lot of us dead than give up a pound of flour.

I will increase the spirit ration, he says. I will double it. And tonight we shall put on a celebration with fireworks.

We don't want your fireworks and salutes. We want better living conditions.

We want the witch! a voice shouts out.

Give us the witch!

On the fire with her!

He manages to duck the first stone. The second strikes him in the chest. It is a small stone, he can barely feel it. What impacts on him is the realization that they are turning on him.

I'll have you all hung! he bellows, but his words are drowned out.

The witch! The witch! The witch!

Suddenly the air is thick with missiles, with stones and peat. A number of the men are armed with spades and hoes. They congregate upon the step, and now they are joined by others who come running. As if in a dream, he sees that the newcomers are women, naked women with eyes glaring wildly in their filth-caked faces. He sees them come spilling from the broken windows of the crew house, slitheringly birthed through the small opening to land howling in the shards of glass which lie strewn upon the ground, scrabbling to their feet and now running towards the residence with sewage and blood spattering from their flailing hair, their flapping breasts as flat as flatfish, squalling their oaths at him. At once, a gusting wind sweeps through the colony, and moments later it is followed by rain, small, stabbing droplets which nonetheless can do nothing to dampen the tempers of the angry crowd, rather the opposite in fact. He no longer hears what they are shouting, and sees only the pale and smeared faces as they come closer, brandishing their spades and hoes, and he backs away, step by step, until he finds himself with his back pressed against the door.

A cry goes up: There she is! The witch!

He glances to the window and is horrified to see Titia's face, elevated above him, in a halo of raindrops.

Get away from the window, Titia, he shouts, waving her away with his hand. Get back, you silly girl!

She seems not to hear him, but stands motionless, expressionless, as if she were an image let into the pane.

Stones and sods of earth hurtle through the air, and now someone swings a burning torch. It is one of the women. She looks like a heathen deity, naked and covered in slime, the torch raised above her head. I'm burning the whole bloody colony down, she shrieks. I'm going to tramp through the ashes in my bare feet!

Johan Bretel, the agitator and speech-maker, steps towards her, he speaks to her, seemingly come to his senses, endeavouring now to calm the incensed throng, and in particular the mad, torch-brandishing woman. But she will not be placated, the sparks spit from her waving torch and Bertel must duck so as not to be set alight. Pors remembers the musket to which he has clung this entire time. He raises it now and aims it at the madwoman.

Get back! he shouts. Get back, or I will shoot you down, woman!

His words merely incite her further and she is before him in two strides, cloaked in her nauseating haze of burning pitch and human effluvium. Her mouth opens to reveal her swollen gums, and to expel a most diabolical cackle.

Shoot me! she bawls. Shoot me now. Don't think I'm afraid of your bullets!

At the very moment her words are uttered, her throat is torn open, blood, gristle and filaments of flesh fan to her chest, her mouth gaping as if to splutter some final round of invective while still able, yet not a sound is emitted, and she sinks to the ground. Deftly, Pors swipes the torch from her hand. Shots ring out, and barked commands. The crowd is dispersed, its members scattering in all directions, pursued by soldiers with bayonets lowered. Within seconds the area is emptied, only the Commandant Landorph remains, ascending the steps now to Pors. He removes the torch from his hand.

Is the Governor unharmed?

You took your time.

Better late than never.

Where is my horse? Kinck, where are you? I want my horse!

///

At last. He is away from the colony. He rides over the moor at a gallop. It is raining, but he doesn't care. He feels the enormous power of the horse between his legs, the heavy hooves thudding over the rock and the boglands, in their slipstream a cloud of atomized water. He stands in the stirrups with knees gently bent as they cut through the weather that seems so increasingly cold, its rain now lashing, and yet he relishes the feeling of washing everything away: Titia, Landorph, the crew house and its filthy women, the uprising. Crags loom out of the mist and vanish again. He lets the horse choose its way and gives himself up to their wild and rolling flight through no man's land.

He has been riding a couple of hours when he pulls Pompadour up and dismounts. He gasps for breath. The horse trembles, steamed up and excited. Its teeth snatch at the grass, keen, scrunching tugs. Pors surveys the landscape. They are flanked by dark, wet faces of rock. He has no idea where they are, whether he has ridden in a circle or a straight line. It matters not. Nature is good and quiet.

He hears the sound of trickling water and leads the horse towards it. A stony shore. No tide line. He dips a finger in and tastes. Fresh water. He kneels and slurps up some mouthfuls. He feels the horse tug on the rein, and when he draws himself upright a man is standing there with a musket aimed at him.

Governor. What a surprise.

Who are you?

Don't you know your own people?

Ah, yes. Peter Hageman. I recognize you now. So this is where you're hiding. Are you intending to shoot me?

I don't know, says Hageman. Now that I'm able, it doesn't seem to matter any more.

My life has already been threatened more than once today, Pors replies wearily. I'm beginning to tire of it.

Hageman slings the firearm onto his shoulder. Has the Governor anything edible on him?

I've a bottle of aquavit and some bread.

I don't suppose he would mind sharing some of it with me?

Why should I share with you?

I'm starving to death. I've not eaten in several days.

All right, he says. The world has already come apart. Come and sit down here. But give me that musket first.

Hageman hands him the gun. Pors fastens it to the saddle and takes out the bag of bread and the bottle of spirits. They seat themselves on a flat rock. Pors breaks the bread and hands one half to Hageman, who attacks it greedily. They drink some swigs from the hip flask. Hageman soaks his bread with aquavit and stuffs himself. For a while they sit in the driving rain and gaze out across the water.

Where does the Governor come from? Hageman asks.

The area of Thisted, says Pors. The name of the village is Sennels.

A farmer?

My father owned a farm but fell into debt and was forced to sell. I have another farm up there now, with a tenant.

A gambler, was he? Your father? Hageman says with a smile.

I have no idea what was the matter with him. Something must have been wrong for him to lose the place. I myself entered the military at an early age, though I never did well. I could never agree with anyone. And then I was called to the governor's position here.

So it goes, says Hageman with a laugh. Have you any kids, Governor?

I am the last of my family. And you?

I fathered a whoreson that died. Apart from that the same as you, Governor. Last of the family.

Sad, says Pors.

The hip flask passes between them. Pors listens to the fine patter of rain on the water.

Snow in July and rain in January, he says. Everything is back-to-front.

What would the Governor have done with his life if he'd been able to choose? Hageman asks.

I should like to have bred horses, he replies pensively. Horses are the most beautiful thing I know. He knocks back a swig and hands Hageman the flask. And what about you? What would you have been had you lived in a world of choice, a world in which everything was back-to-front?

Then I'd have had myself a postal station. With food and drink to serve to travellers. Out in the country somewhere. A nice little house with an upstairs and downstairs, a good stone house, no timber frame.

I'd brew my own beer and my wife would be cook. There'd be a little field on the south side of the place where we could grow vegetables and keep some animals, and my wife would be beautiful and curvy, and her name would be Jensigne.

Such detail, says Pors.

When I get home I'm going to go to Hamburg and start again, says Hageman.

Let's drink to it, says Pors. Skål, for a future of fine dreams come true.

They empty the bottle. Afterwards they return to the colony together, Pors on horseback, Hageman loping at his side. They are soaked to the skin by the time they get back.

///

Down at the blubber house he catches sight of Landorph and some soldiers who are keeping guard. He dismounts.

Have tempers settled?

It's all forgotten now, says Landorph with a sly grin. He points to the door of the blubber house. Pors steps forward. He hears voices from inside, perhaps even song? He pushes the door ajar. Landorph stands behind him.

A sight for sore eyes, don't you think? says the Commandant.

The great copper has been filled with water and the air is boiling hot. The women are washing themselves, half-obscured by steam. Pors looks as they scrub each other, seated naked on the bench, doused with bucketfuls of steaming water, rubbing under their arms, their breasts and crotches, combing each other's hair with their fingers, squashing the lice between their nails. Several are indeed singing. They turn their heads towards him in the doorway and smile at him dreamily.

What have you done with the men? he asks.

I've got them mucking out in the crew house, the Commandant replies. That should be punishment enough. And I've ordered them to fetch the wood they've collected for their witch's pyre and use it in the stove instead. The place might even be habitable by the time they've finished.

///

At six o'clock he appears in the mission parlour with Titia as agreed. Egede is there already, alone, in black cassock and ruff. He glares at the jomfru harshly, lips tight about his mouth, and begins immediately to interrogate her with Bible and catechism. She answers him sensibly. Pors has instructed her not to take refuge in any Catholic mumblings, and indeed she is able to suppress all Latinisms and papisms. Egede fixes her in his rigorous gaze, though otherwise would seem to be appeased. Then his hand dips into his coat and like an illusionist he produces a large crucifix and hands it to her. She takes it without hesitation.

Do you renounce the Devil and all his deeds, my child? Egede asks.

I renounce the Devil and all his deeds.

Do you believe in God the Father almighty?

I believe in God the Father almighty.

They proceed through the Creed, questions and replies. Egede wanders about the small parlour. Now and then he glances gaugingly at Titia from the corner of his eye. She sits staring straight ahead, her gaze like glass. Pors senses it is a matter of minutes before she breaks down and begins to rattle some madness from her, and then they will be back to square one.

Where were you baptized? Egede asks.

In the Skt. Laurentii kirke in Herlev, says Pors.

What was the priest's name?

Tived, says Titia. His name was Tived.

But you were not confirmed until the age of seventeen?

No.

Why not?

I don't know. I don't suppose it was up to me.

With rising anxiety, Pors sees that she has stiffened and holds her head immovably while tightening her jaw. Signs, as a rule, that an attack is on its way.

Perhaps poor Titia has been through enough today, he says. Can we not continue on another occasion?

If the Devil appeared to you, Egede says, unperturbed by the inter-ruption, what would you then do?

I would tell him to be gone in the name of Jesus, Titia replies.

Would you indeed? Egede retorts mistrustfully.

A tremble appears in the corner of her mouth. Pors halts Egede in his wanderings about the floor.

Titia and I thank him for his patience, but I'm afraid we must now retire.

Why the hurry all of a sudden? Egede wants to know, and stares at him.

There has been trouble in the crew house, an uprising amongst the folk, a witch-hunt if you like, and my own person has been phys-ically assaulted. I have ridden about the wilderness half the day, I am soaked, exhausted and hungry. Let us now agree, my good friend, to break off these investigations and perhaps resume in the course of the next few days.

Very well, but there shall be no baptism, Egede replies. I cannot allow it. It is a matter of conscience. Conceivably it might be granted at some later time, much later, though only after a course of the most thorough instruction. That, or else it must be attested with the proper documents that she is indeed baptized already. These must be written off for to her family, a matter which of course may take a while indeed, years in fact, and in the meantime, well, who knows what can happen?

Pors has gripped the young Titia by the arm, he lifts her now into the upright and leads her to the door. The priest watches them as they go, but says no more.

He drapes the jomfru over his shoulder and scurries around the side of the house with her, flings open the door and flops her down onto the bed. It is just in time. Her eyes roll like billiard balls and a thick froth wells from her mouth. Skård comes shuffling. He mutters some words and bends over the girl, holding her arms tight until the seizure is past. Pors takes off his still wet clothes and drops them in a pile on the floor. Where's Sise? he says. Who is to attend to my clothes? But Sise Petticoat is there no more. She has moved back to her peat-hut where she lives with her man. Now he must make do with Skård and Titia, the one more useless than the other.

At last she is pacified and Skård may attend to him. He drags the great washtub out onto the floor and fetches water from the blubber house, twenty paces from the residence. When eventually the tub is filled, Pors immerses himself, sinking into the water, sensing himself become embraced by a great warmth, and immediately he falls asleep.

9

A Theatre of Death

*Today I sent Frederik Christian to the Raven isles, a good
Danish mile from the colony, to catechize for the Greenlanders'
children there, since I myself, for want of crew, was unable to
go anywhere, much to my regret that my time thus be passed
in idleness, for the very purpose of the Design consists in these
people's Christian enlightenment. While the summer was still
with us, I would often take the little dinghy with my son and
my Greenlander boy and sail out to the nearest natives, though
now the winter weather will not permit it.*

FROM HANS EGEDE'S DIARY, JANUARY 1729

I enter the crew house. An icy, miasmatic stench of dead bodies and
the rot of the as-yet living assails my nostrils. Nearly half the crew
who inhabited this damp structure have perished. The remainder are
half living, half dead, unable to decide whether to be one or the other.

January 1729.

I saw my share of death and dismemberment in the garrison at
Bergen. It was during the Great Northern War. But war does not
merely leave holes in people. It brings with it too the strangest of
sicknesses, enough to fill an entire compendium. Yet this is worse.

As a young man I studied to become a physician, attending lectures
at the Frue Plads in Copenhagen, though I could not come to terms
with professorial abstractions of what at bottom is a very practical
discipline, and so I dropped out and became a garrison's surgeon
instead. However, I have read widely, and add to such knowledge my
own observations. The colony has it all: consumption, dropsy, sepsis,
bilious fever, gall fever, nervous fever, putrid fever, childbed fever,
starvation fever, cold fever, catarrhal fever, camp fever, also known as

ship fever, dysentery, scurvy, all suffer from the scurvy now, and we have even seen several instances of French pox. There are sores that will not heal, spontaneous leg fractures, hair loss, the falling out of teeth, diarrhoea *ex ano*, from the anus, but also *ex ora*, from the mouth. This latter I did not see at Bergen. The folk think it is because the afflicted person has consumed faeces, desperate, from hunger, for some variation in the unchanging diet. But I make my observations, I listen to their squealing intestines, the sounds of which are indicative of torsion, a twisting of the passage which accordingly becomes blocked. And out it must, of course, their filth, and will always find a way, upwards being then the only possibility. There is madness, quite common in fact. Raging, destructive madness, and listless, helpless madness. Of course, there are suicides, danglers hanging in the mornings with blessed grins on their faces.

I visit Titia each day. Her madness is a puzzle I have set myself to solve. Briefly, I intend to make the jomfru well. I am certain it can be done. I read in the books, but the books provide me with no answer, apart from the usual concerning gall and blood and demonic possession. It can be done, I am sure. There is something inside her that is out of order. I will find it and put it right.

I prepare a bath for her with herbs from the wilderness. Come, little Titia, the tub is ready. When she sits immersed in the hot, fragrant water and is on the verge of nodding off, I pour without warning several bucketfuls of crushed ice into the tub. She shrieks and tries to get up, but I am ready with rolled-up sleeves and press her down into the icy water by force.

I'm doing it to help you! I insist.

Her thin, bloodless body with its swelling abdomen writhes and thrashes. She scratches and bites. I call for Skård and together we lift her out of the bath, lay her down on the bed and towel her dry.

I will give you this treatment until the madness is gone, I tell her. Why are you vile towards me, Master Kieding? she asks. It is not you I am vile towards, I say, but your insanity. Your mind is split in two, a mad part and a reasoning part. I seek to chase the mad part away.

I speak with Pors about her treatment and ask him to keep an eye on any change in her person. And indeed, there seems to be an improvement. She appears rather more gathered, Pors informs me. She has told me of her time with the nuns. It was rather sensible, her telling that is. The nuns themselves were of course quite insane. I think it is from there her madness stems. They lashed her with willow twigs every morning for years.

But I do not believe in metaphysical explanations or sentimental tales of tribulations in childhood. I adhere to the new philosophy that says the body is a machine. And a machine can break down. If it does, it must be mended. Unfortunately, unlike a machine, a clockwork for instance, the jomfru cannot be taken apart, cogs and screws cleaned, and put together again. So we must proceed by trial and error.

I have read an interesting book about Louis XIV's physician-in-ordinary who had the idea that all illness springs from the oral cavity. He asked for the king's permission to extract the teeth of all at the court, including the royal family itself. And the Sun King lived to a ripe old age, so something of it must have been right. I speak to the Governor about it, and he tells me: Do as you please, Master Kieding. But why do you think the folk are dying?

I quote him Hippocrates. All sickness arises due to gall and slime. When there is too much moisture, dryness, warmth or coldness, sickness will occur.

And what is there to be done about it?

One must restore the balance, Governor.

Then do so. The sooner, the better.

Hippocrates also says the physician's most important duty is to do as little as possible. *Primum non nocere.* First to do no harm, sometimes to heal, often to relieve, always to comfort.

When did this Hippocrates live?

Two thousand years ago.

Has the art of medicine not progressed since?

The human body is the same as it was in Ancient Greece. Therefore, its treatment must be the same too.

But the folk are dying. I will not have it. We need the labour. Do what you can, Master Kieding.

Indeed, Governor.

The teeth are always the first to be stricken by the scurvy. They loosen and fall out. Nearly the whole colony suffers from looseness of the tooth. And the thought appeals to me to turn cause and effect about – in this instance scurvy and teeth – to deprive the cause of its effect, to attack the effect as it were in order thereby to eradicate the cause. Which is to say: The teeth must out!

Jens Smith helps me in the matter. He extracts every tooth left in the crew house, apart from in cases where a person resists and demands to keep their rotten stumps in their mouths. It is a painful procedure, they wail and whimper. Jens Smith is hardly cautious or sensitive in his method. He breaks more teeth with his heavy pliers than he succeeds in pulling out by the root. I prescribe slops and aquavit. And yet the folk continue to die at the same rate, perhaps even more frequently than before.

And what about the jomfru? says Jens Smith. Am I to remove her choppers too?

Yes, the jomfru too must relinquish her teeth. There is no other way. But Titia, it transpires, is very sensitive about her dentition. She pales as I enter the room, Jens Smith hovering behind me in his blood-spattered apron, snapping his pliers together.

No, she says. I've had enough of your antics, Master Kieding.

Jens grabs hold of her, but she resists, and she is crafty. One minute she pretends to have given up, the next she wrestles free and stands triumphant with the smith's pliers in her hand. She lashes out at him, and Jens, heavy and ungainly when not at work in his smithy, is struck on the chin and sinks to his knees. Titia tosses the pliers into the stove, where quickly they are glowing hot.

I said no, she says. And no means no.

But what use are teeth to you? I protest. Everyone else has had theirs pulled out.

To bite your dicks with, she says.

I must support Jens Smith as we retreat and leave her to her own devices.

Numerous complaints of ailing eyesight. Their eyes run like egg yolks. Several have gone blind or are becoming so. The reason in my own opinion is the low-hanging winter sun, which, when eventually it deems to shine, etches the lens of the eye. Together with the colony's barber-surgeon, Thomas Tode, an experienced remover of cataracts, at least in his own estimation, I conduct a series of oculistic procedures on the poor of sight. Tode inserts a needle into the eye and dislodges the opaque liquid from the pupil. In Denmark it is an operation performed by itinerant quacks and market entertainers, but it is nevertheless known to have good effect on cataracts. Those who before saw fog, see now only darkness.

Increasing numbers of the blind and toothless fumble their way about the colony, unable to work or do anything of use. One by one they succumb. The Governor is not content with his physician. I did not ask you to kill them, he says.

They would have died anyway, I contest to my defence.

Tode, known by the folk here as the Knife-man, is already busy when this morning I enter the crew house. Three men and a woman are being bled. Each lies with an arm dangling from the side of their bunk, blood dripping into a bowl. Wearily, they lift their heads and squint in my direction with a mixture of fear and hope as my figure appears in the doorway.

I step between the bunks, the slurry squelching under my boots. I hold my hands professorially behind my back and nod before moving on. Tode follows on my heels. Three dead this morning, he tells me.

Good. Carry them to the blubber house for dissection.

Dissection? That won't please them.

But they are dead.

The others, the ones who aren't dead yet. If they get to know they are to be cut into pieces, they shall die of fright.

Order of the Governor, I tell him.

One of the convict women, Cellar-Katrine as she is known, comes to me. She bares her breast. It is discoloured and swollen. I palpate it. A tumour.

Do your bleedings continue? I ask her.

Not since last summer.

A number of the women have ceased to menstruate, some because of malnutrition, some on account of pregnancy. I give them a potion I have prepared from herbs, juniper, hawkweed, wild thyme and swine bristles, mixed with resin and extract of hare-testicles. It has settled into a thick, dark syrup with a pungent odour not unlike asafoetida. I stir a spoonful of this slimy substance into boiling water and instruct the woman to squat over the pot with her genitals bare, and explain to her that the steam will be absorbed into her lower parts and make her well. Obediently, she does as I say.

Unfortunately, the remedy has no effect. Katrine continues to complain of pains. Her breast is still swollen and discoloured, and now rather misshapen because of the tumour that is growing inside. I palpate it. It is hot as fire to the touch.

In his book, *De Cruce Christi*, which I have read with a mixture of scepticism and interest, the professor Thomas Bartholin puts forward a theory that animals may absorb disease if placed on the affected site. I consider it must be tried and instruct Tode to fetch one of the goats from the stables. When he returns with the bleating beast, I press it down onto the sick woman's chest, Tode having first placated it with a nip of chewing tobacco on which it happily munches. They're devils for the stuff, he says.

A singular calm comes over both patient and beast.

I can feel its beating heart, Katrine says, and looks tenderly upon the animal as if she were breastfeeding it. It feels nice and warm against my bosom.

The treatment has no effect. The goat does not ail, the woman does not become well. The tumour breaks the skin and forms an irregular, weeping sore that looks like a contorted, slobbering mouth. Her pain has at least subsided now that the pressure inside her has been alleviated.

I have heard and read about the famous necropsies performed in Copenhagen at the University's anatomy house next to the Church of Our Lady on Frue Plads. When I studied there, they had already been prohibited. I have a German book, outrageously expensive, which is illustrated with coloured plates throughout showing how the physicians proceed through the corpse, peeling back layer upon layer, removing the organ block, splitting muscles and tendons along their length, exposing the nerve paths, folding skin and fat aside like a theatrical curtain, opening up the human body as if inviting the beholder to look upon a stage and wonder at what he sees upon it.

Before declaring a person deceased and giving him over to the coffin-maker, it is important to ensure that the person is in actual fact dead. Several methods are described in the literature. The simplest is to place a glass of water on the chest of the person in question. Even the slightest pulse will cause the water's surface to tremble. One may also tickle the nostrils with a feather, or apply some irritating powder to them, for example gunpowder. To be completely certain, one may put a burning dip to the gunpowder. The latter is a most efficient method, and entertaining to any audience when flames leap from the nose without the person as much as batting an eyelid. Another way is to knead the ribs of the lifeless individual with the knuckles of one's fist, a procedure more painful than anyone would care to believe.

All of us fear death. But more than death we fear being taken for dead when we are not, and thereafter being buried alive. Terrible stories abound of the apparently dead who have woken up seven feet under the soil and have scratched at the lids of their coffins until their fingers have bled. Therefore it is imperative that as a physician one has at one's disposal a certain repertoire in the art of reassuring friends and family of the deceased and assuaging their fears of being put in the ground alive themselves.

So there is always an element of comedy about declaring a crewhouse corpse to be dead. I shout loudly into the ears, pummel and knead, set fire and burn, prod the nostrils with sticks, insert hot needles under the fingernails, slash the soles with razors. The spouses and friends who stand and watch these performances gasp and groan. I blow tobacco smoke into the anus through a tube and listen to the stillness of the colon, or else I am more brutal and pour boiling wax over the deceased or prod red-hot irons into the flesh. Always a woman will faint at such a procedure and its attendant stench of caramelized mucosa, but always they are convinced in the end. Sometimes I conclude by slitting the person's throat, whereafter no doubt remains.

Unfortunately, Titia has suffered a relapse and has begun to pull her hair from her scalp. Pors comes to me and tells me he has been unable to get a sensible word out of her all day.

I give her the bath, scalding hot at first, the steaming water aromatic, then buckets of ice. She utters the fiercest curses in Latin. Not even when towelled will she be placated, but kicks and screams. We are compelled to hold her down, myself, Pors and Skård, and when we release her she leaps to her feet and strides hectically about the room with hands flapping at the air, mumbling furiously to herself.

The world is based on reason. It may indeed occasionally seem like a place of madness, as in the colony here, yet it works according to rational laws. I mention this to Pors.

What are you trying to say? he asks.

If one were to change the nature of the world and make it such a place of madness, perhaps it would restore the balance in those who are now mad. A form of paradoxical treatment, if you like.

Some number of sheep and goats have been slaughtered here of late. I have the skin of their heads removed and make masks of them. All who pay visit to the governor's residence must wear them, I decree. Even the Governor himself must wear such a mask, and Skård too.

I consider it will frighten the life out of Titia. Yet my hope is that the shock she receives when all around her suddenly resemble sheep and goats will shake up her mind and restore it to its rightful, reasonable state. To my great distress and disappointment, however, she fails to react at all when I, as the very first, pay visit on her wearing the face of a goat and proceed to carry out my usual examinations concerning her pregnancy. On the contrary, she seems to think it the most natural thing in the world that I address her as a goat, and she responds quite coherently to all my questions.

I instruct Skård to wake her at intervals during the night by appearing at her bedside to rattle on a cooking pot whilst bellowing at the top of his lungs, preferably in Icelandic. Remarkably, she barely stirs, and the only person to be wakened by the commotion is Pors, who now suggests it is I who am mad.

Tode commandeers some men to collect the corpse I have selected for my necroscopy and carry it to the blubber house. I follow on some paces behind, my mind wearied by ponderous thoughts of Titia, who recoils from my every endeavour to make her well. The frost is severe, the air as cold as ice, and yet one is near-blinded by the rays of the sun. The pitch darkness of the blubber house is cut apart by the light from the doorway.

The men dump the body on the bench and hurry away.

I stand and consider the corpse. It is Peter Hageman, one of the freed men from Bremerholm, wedded to Cellar-Katrine, the woman with the tumour in her breast. He makes a long corpse, perhaps five and a half feet from head to toe. The glaring sunlight that shafts in through the as-yet open doorway bathes the body's marbled blue limbs. After a moment, Tode closes the door and lights the lamps which hang from the rafters.

He took to his bed a couple of days ago after returning from his disappearance, Tode says. He never got up again. Most likely he caught a chill, though he had complained of fatigue for some time.

Any other signs of illness?

The usual. Coughing, blood in his spit, nosebleeds, swollen joints, bruising. Yesterday his eyes bled. He asked then for the priest, who came and gave him the sacrament.

The symptoms accord with the scurvy. But what is scurvy apart from a word? Perhaps the necroscopy will reveal it.

God will punish those who sin, says Tode with solemn conceit, puts on his apron and unfolds his sharpened blades from the cloth. He picks one out and perforates the skin of the corpse approximately at the middle of the belly. A sickly smell issues from the little hole and the swollen mound of the gut subsides. Thereupon he proceeds with something akin to rage. I stand at the other side of the bench and watch. The lamps cast a warm light upon Tode's stooping figure and the soon yawning innards of the deceased.

The belly is opened along its length. The blue worm-pit of the guts glistens. Tode selects a short, broad-bladed knife. His arms are stained to the elbows with thick, dark blood. His probing, sensitive fingers feel their way to the gristly joints between breastbone and ribs, severing them with a number of quick and expert cuts. The sound of the separating sections fills me with satisfaction, perhaps even joy. The chest begins to gape. Once Tode has loosened all the ribs, he pulls apart the ribcage. A crisp, cracking sound breaks the air, like twigs snapping underfoot. Tode steps back, turns his head slightly to one side and wipes his dripping nose on his sleeve.

All yours, Master Kieding.

At that moment, the door opens and in marches the Governor accompanied by the Paymaster Fleischer, the Trader Kopper and a pair of officers. They gather around the bench, proffering small witticisms about the corpse. Death has a way of jollying people up, unless it makes them weep.

Who's your specimen? Pors enquires.

Hageman, says Tode.

I see, says Pors cordially. Good old Hageman, eh? Not much postal station for you now, my friend.

A scoundrel if ever there was one, Fleischer adds, peering from vulpine eyes. He threatened both Egede and Pors, said he was going to shoot them.

By rights we should put his head on a stake, Kopper chimes in.

The door opens again and once more a glaring light falls upon the body, whose insides gleam like tallow. Miltzov the priest enters, fragrant with the wind and fumes of alcohol. He looks like he staggered in from a rather bibulous luncheon.

Ah, our theological authority, Fleischer says. It seems we are complete.

Why does man become ill? Kopper muses philosophically. Why does he die? Are we not made in God's image? Why then does He allow us to die?

Are you asking me or the surgeon? Miltzov replies.

Does it make a difference?

Of course.

Then I am asking you first, Magister Miltzov.

We've all got to die, Miltzov slurs. The fall of man robbed him of his immortality.

Are you drunk, Magister?

Me, drunk? You know I never touch the aquavit.

What thinks Master Kieding? Pors enquires.

That we all must die is irrefutable, I say. Though of course there are many ways in which we may go.

Is there a right way and a wrong way, perhaps?

I should prefer to die surrounded by my great-great grandchildren, says Fleischer with a wink.

As long as I am free of pain, I shall be reasonably content, Kopper declares.

Certainly, I would consider there to be right and wrong ways to die, I respond. If the cause of one's death is a disease for which a treatment is found, or one that might have been avoided by prophylactic means, then one may naturally consider such a death to be wrong in the sense of unnecessary.

Yet the medical profession would seem unable to do much about what ails us here in the colony, neither prophylactically nor in terms of treating the symptoms. Am I not right? Pors stares at me.

If conditions here were better, the folk would not be dying, Governor Pors.

I see, says Pors. So now I have the power to rid us of death? I thank Master Kieding for the honour.

Not to rid us of death, but to postpone it, Governor. To keep it under control. We could bring down the death rate considerably if we so wished.

One should strive to die at p-peace with oneself and one's God, Miltzov hiccups. Many die without finding peace. Such a death must be considered inap-propriate.

Hageman here must be a restless soul indeed, says Fleischer. I suppose now we shall have his spirit to contend with.

Not at all, Miltzov protests. I was with him last night to give him the sacrament. He asked sincerely for forgiveness for the error of his ways. I gave him absolution and am certain Ch-rist will vouch for him.

For goodness' sake, you drunkard, Fleischer grunts. The man was an incorrigible scoundrel as everyone knows.

But dismembered like this, I don't suppose he would be amenable to salvation? Kopper suggests.

The salvation of the soul has nothing to do with the state of the body, says Miltzov. That's superstition. Soldiers blown to pieces on the b-attleground may also go to heaven.

I have read some of this new philosophy, Fleischer says, and pats the corpse on the shoulder. It tells us man is a machine.

Quiet now with your heresy, says Pors. A man of God is present. Albeit a rather intoxicated one.

As long as one recognizes that such a machine was cre-ated by God, then it cannot be h-eresy, Miltzov rejoins.

Descartes, I say.

A machine that becomes sick and dies, repents its sins, prays to God? Kopper says. What about the spirit? What does Descartes say about that?

He says he doesn't know, I reply. And whereof we know nothing, thereof we cannot speak.

And so we are back at the beginning again, says Fleischer. Philosophical nonsense. Round and round in circles.

Is he a Christian, this Descartes? Pors asks.

He is a Frenchman, I reply.

Ah, a papist, there we have it. A good thing Egede is not here. But let us now get on with our corpse.

The attendants gather in a semicircle around the bench, slightly removed so as not to be splashed with blood and bodily fluid. They crane their necks, sour alcoholic exhalations mingling with the stench of the corpse. I issue my instructions to Tode and he removes the dripping organ block in its entirety, holding it momentarily aloft before manoeuvring its squelching mass onto a side table.

This, I am sure, is where we may find the reason for all this death that has been going on, I declare, and begin at once to dissect the lungs. I hold up a pulmonary slice in front of Pors, like a butcher offering a cutlet. It oozes yellow slime and a white lint-like substance. The lung is rotten, I say. It is why they cough and spit the whole time.

I proceed to dissect the liver in the same manner, squeezing a piece of it in my hand and causing the blood to trickle between my fingers. As the Governor may see, the blood is quite pale, as thin as redcurrant juice. This is the second major cause of our troubles. Anaemia.

All very well, says Pors. But I cannot see that what you are showing us are the reasons, Master Kieding. Surely they are the effects?

It can all be traced back to poor diet and damp habitation.

On the bench lies Peter Hageman's empty frame, innards scooped out before us. I select a small and very sharp blade, holding it between my fingers like a quill and making a single incision along the length of the left forearm, then a number of transverse incisions, drawing the cutis and subcutis aside to expose the muscles, tendons and nerves. I summarize the mechanics of the muscles for my audience as I prod at the flesh with a pair of forceps. I then instruct Tode to cut off the arm at the shoulder. I place the severed limb on the side table and demonstrate how one may cause the fingers to move by pulling on the tendons. For this I receive congratulations.

But what about thought, says Kopper. Where does thought come from? Is it the same as the soul, and may it be exposed by the Master's blade? Perhaps even one may tug on some tendons and cause the deceased to think?

Descartes believes thought to have seat in the brain, I answer. In what he calls the pineal body. A gland that forms the bridge between flesh and spirit.

If we are to find Hageman's spirit, I would suggest we look lower down, Fleischer says. The man was a fornicator.

Where is this pineal body? Pors asks. I should like to see it.

Somewhere in the base of the brain, I tell him. But I have never opened a skull. I glance at Tode.

We'd have to saw it, the Knife-man says.

Then let us do so, says Pors.

Tode begins with a fine razor. We hold our breath. Removing the scalp from the bone is a meticulous process, Tode folding it aside as he proceeds, severing veins and membranes. When done he removes the facial skin but allows the muscles to remain along with the eyes, whose lids have been cut away, the orbs seeming enormous and quite alive now that they are no longer surrounded by the perished dermis.

How shall I open the skull? Tode asks.

A chisel? I suggest.

He rummages a moment and finds one, and a hammer too, beginning then to chip a rut along the natural sutures of the cranium before wrenching loose first the great parietal bone, then the frontal bone, and placing them both on the side table. They look like potsherds.

I ask the two officers to turn the corpse on its side, allowing me to reach between the vertebrae with a sharp knife and sever the prolongation of the spinal cord. With that, the brain slips by itself from its casing onto the bench, a grey and slimy lump.

Is that it? Pors exclaims. Is this what has given us two thousand years of philosophy? It looks like a cowpat.

The Paymaster and the Trader each take a lamp from the rafter and hold it to the brain. I make a couple of incisions and thin slices of cerebral substance fall away. I arrange them in a row much as a delicate dish of sweetbreads. I instruct Tode to pour some water over the slices so as to rinse away the blood.

Here is a gland, I say, picking loose a red knob of matter and holding it up in the light with the forceps.

It looks like a boy's scrotum, says Pors. And that is what housed Peter Hageman's spirit. I would have thought as much.

///

Once I have wiped my blood-smeared, foul-smelling hands with a cloth, I proceed to the colony house to attend to Hageman's wife, now widow, Cellar-Katrine. She complains of her sore oozing malodorous pus and that even the slightest touch causes her the most shooting pains. I decide on removal.

Why are you drawing on me? she asks.

It is time we cut away the infected breast, I inform her.

She starts to cry. I can't, she says. I haven't the courage.

Do you wish to die, woman?

Now that Peter's gone, I might as well follow. Most likely he's feeling lonely.

I think Peter would have wanted you to get well, I say.

Will the pain go away?

It will remove the cause of the pain and thereby the pain itself.

But it'll hurt when you cut into me?

Plenty of aquavit and you won't feel a thing.

Then I'll do it, and may the Lord God save me, she sighs.

I allow Tode to perform the surgery. We are compelled to call for the aid of several soldiers to hold her arms and legs, and one to keep a firm grip on her head to stop her trying to bite the barber-surgeon's hand with her toothless gums. The breath from her mouth is foul and demonic. No sooner has Tode made a circular incision around the outline of the breast than it oozes thick yellow pus. He pulls the breast away as he works, short, quick slashes of his blade, and when it is loose he tosses it aside without further ado. I call for Jens Smith and have him scorch the blood vessels with a hot iron which he presses to the wound. Our nostrils are assailed by the suffocating smell of burning flesh and sizzling human fat. The patient screams curses so foul they could have her punished at the whipping post. She is given more aquavit, guzzled between cries.

With the breast removed, I see that the tumour has grown into the breastbone and cannot be removed in its entirety. It resembles a wet amphibian parasite as it clings to the bone. Tode sews up the wound with saddlery thread and dresses it with rags. Katrine is more or less unconscious and lies sighing and occasionally hiccupping. In a moment of clarity she reaches for my hand and speaks of the tribulations of life as I stand at her bed and listen. Clearly, she thinks me to be the priest.

All my life, I have known nothing but wretched times, Father, she says. I long for another life. None can be worse than this.

I feel her pulse. It is fierce and racing. I administer a vomitive. Its effect is immediate. What comes up is as dark as tar. She feels it to be a relief, thanks me and sleeps for some hours. In the evening, she is assailed by traumatic fever. She dies some few days later, and like her husband, Peter Hageman, she is able to speak to Miltzov and be given the sacrament before passing.

///

I call in on Titia. I press her stomach and enquire as to her state. She seems to be in one of her lucid moments. I speak to her about nothing in particular and she answers in her usual plain manner in sentences that are short and blunt. I sigh, feeling that I am up against a force greater than myself, greater even than the art of medicine.

Perhaps it is true what they say after all, that madness is possession by the Devil. It cannot be right, I tell myself. Surely something can be done for the poor girl?

Of course, it is the old story from Bergen come to roost, I realize it now. The jomfru Hall, my former fiancée whom I deserted. And now I seek to make good by attending her substitute, Titia. I wonder what became of little Sørine with her buck teeth and bad breath? I presume her long since to be dead.

Dear Titia, how are you today?

Fine.

Can you feel the baby?

Yes, it kicks.

What thoughts are on your mind, dear Titia, as to what is to be done with the child when it is born?

I think it will be a boy.

Yes, but what provisions are to be made for the boy, if indeed a boy it is? Will you keep him?

Yes, it's my child.

But you are unmarried, Titia. A child must have a father. Surely you know that?

It's got a father.

Who, Titia?

I know him.

Yes, but will he marry you?

No, he made the baby, that's all. He gave it to me.

Suppose another man in the colony here offered to marry you and take the child as his own, what would you say to that? I hold her hand in mine. My head is rather empty after the exertions of recent days. Perhaps I too am not entirely of sound mind.

I don't want to be married. No one would have me anyway.

Oh, come now. I know someone who might.

Who?

Think.

I won't marry you, she says. You smell of dead bodies.

I was not referring to myself, you silly girl, but to someone else. A young man of your acquaintance.

Who?

The young man who is Egede's young assistant.

The priest would never agree. Besides, we'd need special licence, she adds with the sudden good sense that occasionally comes over the mad. I'm not old enough yet. And neither is he.

Allow me to take care of the matter. I shall have a word with Egede and the Governor, and with all concerned.

Do you know whose son the lad is? she says.

I know the father to be a savage. But the boy himself is a good Christian.

All right, I'll take him, if you can arrange the matter. Rather him than one of you.

Some of us men here in the colony know what is best for you, I tell her.

Then do what you want, she says. You will anyway.

Dear Titia, I say. Let me kiss you.

She turns her face away. My lips brush her cheek, but I press her mouth to mine and gobble at her lips and tongue before releasing.

This kiss is my promise to you that I shall relieve you of these tribulations.

A Judas kiss, she says, and her upper lip, reddened by my ardour, curls in a sneer.

I am still holding her hand in mine. Farewell, I say. Think on what I have told you.

She considers me solemnly as I leave. I think to myself that now it is I who am mad. I have absorbed her madness, and now I take it away with me into the fells. Some distance from the colony I vomit. I wipe my mouth. There it is, the madness. It looks like pease porridge and pork-meat.

10

Correspondence

Mr Miltzov conducted the sermon this Sunday. Mr Ole Lange administered the communion to two of the bed-ridden soldiers.

The weather this month had been rather good, yet the infirmity of the colony folk has been merely compounded, a case of the longer, the worse. The colony surgeon has sickened likewise in these days.

FROM HANS EGEDE'S JOURNAL, FEBRUARY 1729

Mr Søren Fuchs, Apothecary
The Apothecary House, Køge

Dearest Uncle Søren

This is your little niece Titia writing to you, daughter of your brother, driven by the misery and wretchedness that has befallen her and which now must flow through her pen. From this far-flung colony I write in the hope that my letter may reach your hand at the Apothecary House, so that you may read of my tribulations these past six months, and of the prison in which I am confined, that you might remember your little Titia and with her weep at her fear and need and most heartfelt grief.

Thanks be to the almighty God and to the grace of Mary, without whom in my distress and misery I would find not a shred of comfort, moral force nor help, for never did God place a burden on me that did bow me down without Him bestowing on me the strength to withstand it with the blessed Mary at my side, to Thee, God, be honour and praise for ever! The Almighty has allowed the strangest things to befall me, His ways are indeed inscrutable, but Mary has been beside me in it all, her name be for ever blessed, how else would I have resisted so many great and unexpected calamities had she not been here to soothe me, blessed Virgin, she gives me her hand and strives for me in this prison; indeed, it is quite unfathomable that I have endured it with reason and senses intact. How remarkable it is that I am not now witless, that my eyes have not receded into blindness for all that I have wept, that my body has not rotted away in this cold and muggy weather, for though now and then I am breathless and cloudy of mind I am as yet of this world.

The second impelling reason for me writing to you is that I have been made pregnant. I assure you, dear Uncle Søren, and indeed you too, Aunt Karen, in case you happen to be reading this, that I am quite without blame in the matter, though the folk of the colony here call me a whore and a witch, believing me to have conjugated with heathens and Christian men alike, and indeed with the Devil himself, and for this they wish to cast me on the fire like any sorceress, without process for the shameless acts of which they accuse me. But you, dear Uncle and Aunt, will know me to be a good and Christian girl who attended church and received her communion and is knowing of the grace of the Lord Jesus Christ by which mankind shall be released. Now I must beg you, Uncle Søren, with this knowledge to write to Egede, who is priest here, so that he may at last understand that I am not Catholic, but a person christened in the Lutheran faith, nor a Jew, which also he suspects. They had built a pyre for me outside the colony and came to the governor's house to drag me outside and throw me upon the flames; the Devil curse them, but my principal, the Governor, stood at the door and repelled the mob, thereby saving me before they took hold of my person. Let this be a comfort, my dearest family, that I am protected by a merciful God and a good principal, for it is thankworthy, as the apostle St Peter says, if a person for conscience toward God endure grief and suffer wrongfully. I am now so far gone in my pregnancy that I sway through the rooms here like a ship in distress; you would scarcely recognize your little Titia, so ponderous she has become, and the colony master tells me it will be a spring child.

But who is this man, I hear you ask, who has put you in such shame and need? My reply is that I do not know, I swear it is true by the blessed Mary and her son Jesus Christ. One minute I was the slender jomfru Titia, the next a gestating hag. Yet fear not, my dearest ones, for the Governor, as good and protective a gentleman as one could wish, has hatched a design by which to save me. To this end, however, I have need, Søren, of your . . .

Titius! Jomfru Titius! Whatever's keeping you? We're dying of starvation here.

She has been bent over her letter. Now she sits up with a start.

Coming!

She lifts the pot out of the oven and carries it into the parlour, where they are seated around the table. The Paymaster Fleischer rises, takes the pot from her hands and puts it down in their midst.

She ought not to be carrying such heavy things in her condition, he says. Before we know it she'll be giving birth in the midst of our dinner.

An old wives' tale, says Kieding, peering up at the jomfru with a weary look in his eyes. Once a child has implanted itself properly it will not come out before it wants to.

But who put it there in the first place? says Fleischer, his eyes darting up and down the length of the table. Does anyone know? Is there anyone here at this table who will admit paternity?

A silence descends in the Governor's parlour. The clock ticks on the wall. Each and every man present is keenly aware that any denial will immediately cast suspicion on him.

Perhaps you are the one responsible, since you enquire so, says the Governor.

Not at all, I have no interest in such things, says the Paymaster.

A more important question is what is to be done with the child once it's here? Kieding says, and sighs heavily. The Governor and I have spoken about it. I think we've found a good solution.

Let Madame Gertrud have it, says Fleischer. No doubt she'll take it anyway, her being so eager to help children of doubtful heritage. He looks sideways at Egede, who says nothing.

No, Titia is to marry, says Pors.

Marry whom? says Landorph.

That is a secret for the time being, Pors replies. But the skies will clear soon enough.

I'll wager it's the native lad, Frederik Christian, says Fleischer. He flashes a grin at Landorph. Which means you won't be having her after all, Jørgen.

Frederik Christian, says Kopper. That'll never work out.

Never mind for now, you'll see soon enough, Pors says.

I'll be intrigued to see what kind of a runt comes out of her, says Fleischer. Some pale and misshapen creature, I shouldn't wonder, being bred outside the law and that?

Another wives' tale, Kieding snaps in annoyance. An illegitimate child can be at least as healthy as any born in wedlock. I'm more concerned about the mother. He glances at the jomfru again. She is narrow-hipped. I predict a difficult birth.

Maybe it would be for the best if neither survived, says Fleischer. Harlots and their bastard kids have a hard time of it.

I believe she is without blame in the matter, the physician replies. The poor girl barely knows how it might have happened.

She must be simple then, Landorph mutters, knowing full well that he is a main suspect.

I suppose it will have to be adopted into a foster-family, says Kieding. The jomfru herself is certainly unable to bring up a child.

Unless she's married off, says Landorph.

Our priest here believes her to be a Jew, says Fleischer with a laugh.

I thought she was meant to be Catholic? says Kopper. Wasn't she brought up by nuns?

Catholic or Jew, what's the difference? Egede growls. It's all shite from the same arse.

Even a Jew can be converted, surely, Mr Egede? says Miltzov as if to conciliate. A Christian deed would be to turn her towards the Lutheran faith.

Egede scowls but says nothing.

Is it not the case, says Fleischer, the fox who delights in prodding at Egede's peculiarities, that the offspring of Jews are more frequently deformed than those of any others?

Absolutely, it is a well-known fact, says Egede, lighting up in a smile. Their fruit is rotten indeed.

Was it not the Devil who begat them? Fleischer goes on.

It is said, Egede responds, encouraged now, that every time the Devil shits his pants a Jew or a papist is born. They belong among the very lowest orders of Hell, with only each other for company.

She'll have to be married though, says Kieding. We'll make sure she is.

That will require licence from the King, says Egede. And whoever performs the ceremony it will not be me.

Then I shall do it, says Miltzov. With Egede's permission. And the King's, of course.

We must all act according to our conscience, says Egede. If there's a written licence, then far be it from me to oppose it.

Enough of the jomfru, says Pors. We'll deal with it all when the time comes.

The other one's pregnant too, says Kieding. Sise Petticoat.

A good piece of womanhood she is too, says Landorph. Healthy as the ripest apple.

A harlot, too, says Fleischer. They all are. All the way down the line from Eve. In the Spinning House for being on the game, she was.

It doesn't show, says Landorph. She looks so pretty and spry.

Then perhaps she was only slightly on the game, Fleischer replies, his eyes narrowing. As one may be only slightly dead.

Desist with such talk, says Pors. We've had more than enough witticisms for one day, my head is spinning. Anyway, Sise's a good girl.

How many dead this month? Landorph asks.

Fifteen, says Kieding wearily.

Good gracious, as many as that? Both men and women?

Four of them women. The men are more inclined to succumb. Their constitution seems to be the weaker.

Yes, the stiffer the stem the easier it snaps, whereas the softer one bends in the wind and remains standing, says Kopper.

The women snaffle all the good food, says Fleischer. They know how to bargain with a man.

We've lost Dines Marsvin too, says Kieding. The carpenter.

Another carpenter, Kopper sighs. Soon we shall have no craftsmen left.

What would we need them for? says Fleischer. All our building materials are either rotten or else have been used for firewood.

Surely new supplies will come with the ship? Egede interjects.

You can never be too sure, Fleischer replies. Maybe the King's forgotten about us.

Why do they burn the timber? Miltzov enquires. Wouldn't they be better off building a good house out of it?

They're perishing from cold and damp. They've got no choice but to burn it for fuel, says Landorph.

How many dead has he cut up, Master? Pors asks.

Five, Kieding replies, staring blankly ahead.

Has he arrived at any cause of these rampant deaths?

I'm afraid not, the physician says. I really haven't a clue.

Consumption, Egede says. The same as Hageman. And then there is the scurvy, which most suffer. Though not I. Eight years here and eight years free of the scurvy.

Wine! says Pors. Let us bring a toast for Prince Karl.

Who? several of the others reply at once.

The King's youngest, says Pors. One year old today, he is. Titia, my wonky-eyed wench, bring us some bottles, we are in need of aquavit. And let us bring a salute. Bombardier! Will someone tell the bombardier to fire the cannon?

Titia fetches three bottles of the Governor's schnapps and places them in front of Pors, who proceeds to open them.

But what is the matter with our Master? says Fleischer.

Everyone turns to Kieding. They see the Master Kieding's shoulders tremble.

Good God, the man's blubbering in his glass! Fleischer exclaims, laughing incredulously. Skål, Master Kieding! Cheer up!

He's been like this for some weeks, Pors whispers. He's like a broken man.

Back in the saddle, Kieding, says Fleischer, and slaps him on the back as if to comfort him. Don't be so glum. Cut up some more cadavers, that should do the trick. Skål, Master Kieding!

Let's have that salute! Pors shouts.

The cannon pound, and Titia sits down in her corner to continue her letter:

To this end, however, I have need, Uncle Søren, of your help as my guardian and trustee.

Alas, dearest Søren and Karen, I cannot fully tell of the scorn and persecution I have been made to suffer, and if the blessed Mary had not given me courage and Mr Pors had not defended my life and limbs by placing his own person between me and my assailants, I would now be lain in my grave, and indeed it would be a mercy to suffer such indignation if only to be rewarded with His blessedness, for the worldly life here is harsh and gives me little happiness. So many perils and discomforts I endured on the voyage here, and yet in this land I must undergo hardships even greater than on board a ship in howling storms, and one misfortune follows on from another, for crew and gentlemen alike treat me with the utmost disdain, even the servants of the Lord accuse me of witchcraft and devilry. How heartbroken and devastated I have become by it I cannot write with any pen, nor can I believe that I shall withstand it much longer unless by some chance I am saved, thus briefly the Governor's design.

A young man, his name is Frederik Christian, born of this land and its native people, born in fact of a savage woman, yet baptized in the name of the Holy Trinity, now confirmed and living as a good and pious Christian and servant of the Lord and of the Pastor Egede who has included him in the mission, wishes on Pors's recommendation to be married to me so that we may live together as man and wife and that I may wash the shame and disgrace from my person. He is unsure of his birthdate, having been born into the house of a savage, whose people do not keep tally of the years as we do, only with the passing of the seasons, yet he himself considers that he must have come into this world in the year of our Lord 1714, making him younger than me by three years. Although we have not yet had any inclination towards each other besides friendship and sympathy, we are nonetheless devoted to each other. He is, moreover, a catechist of the Mission, as well as a proficient hunter and kayaker able to provide for a wife and child, a right-minded man who has no hesitation in plunging into this scheme which Pors has devised, whereby to be my wedded husband and rescue me from this torment, in so doing also finding advantage in the matter.

I would ask you, dear Søren, to go to the King and secure an audience whereby to give us, two loyal subjects of his colony in Greenland, his written licence in order that we may join and remain together until death do us part, I swear it on the blessed Mary's name who art the holiest to me of everything in this world, so that you may believe me on my word and thereby, as you may also tell the King, the two countries, Denmark and Greenland, will likewise be joined with each other, I believe it to be a thought of which the King will approve, so please tell him, and remember to mention also that the recipient of his licence is to be Egede, for he knows the Pastor well.

Now, though, I must say you farewell, my dear father's-brother Søren, and also you, Aunt Karen, with my deepest and most heartfelt devotion. Please do not think badly of your little Titia, for she suffers here a harsher fate than when she lived with the nuns from whom she fled in the darkness of night to seek haven in the Apothecary House. But this land cannot be fled, she who tried would be drowned, otherwise I would long since be gone from it. May the Lord bless and keep you. In the name of the sacred Mother, most precious of all, yours forever faithful and grateful,

   Anna Dorothea Titius
     Written in the Colony of Godthåb
      Anno 1729, the 16th of February
       in the 18th year of my age.

///

In the spring of '29 I make the voyage north again, a sheer delight on this occasion, no horses, no women, no convicts, no Pors, though the weather is rather stormy and the good ship, the *Jomfru Cornelia* this time, a pink, is slung this way and that, like a worthless wood shaving on the great sea, and yet she reaches harbour safe and well, mail is distributed, reports written, and then a drinking party is held, salutes fired, and there is much fornicating and everything else that goes on when a ship has been long underway and the men have been a long time wanting, but much has happened here, a whole colony has gone up on the bare rock and nearly all the convicts I brought here in the *Morian* last year have been swept away by an epidemic, yet the Major Pors, or the Governor, as one must remember to call him, for otherwise he will become sullen and cross, looks to be in good fettle, and it seems he has even made the young jomfru pregnant, a terrible tale if ever there was one, but a lot happens while a ship is away on the sea, and she hands me a letter asking me to deliver it to the Apothecary Fuchs in Køge, and so I sail back home again with a good stiff wind to whisk us along, and I write this in my log: 'Arr. Hafnia Aug. 10, safe after voyage marked by calamities attendant to men's stubborn challenging of the hostile element, the sea, on which they in essence do not belong, as they belong neither in the blue and empty air. All cargo preserved. Seven men dead.'

I send Titia's letter immediately from Copenhagen with my own address for return and receive only a week later a sealed reply from the Apothecary, though by this time the last ship to Greenland has sailed.

This autumn, I betroth myself, daft old bugger that I am, to Caroline Dahl, and have plenty matters to be getting on with of the kind that accompany any such drastic a step, but I am to sail again, I hear the church bells peal over the Copenhagen rooftops, they sound like the plague bells, but this time once more with the *Morian*, I leave all behind me, arrive at the colony and hand the Apothecary's letter to the jomfru.

What has happened to your child, I ask, and where is your betrothed? For I knew she was to be married to a native boy and that this was the subject of the correspondence, but she withdraws immediately to her room without answering me so as to read the letter on her own.

///

Anna Dorothea Titius
The Colony of Godthåb

I shall now tell you what we, your aunt and I, have resolved after your letter confiding to us your deeds and sins, which plunged us, and in particular, as I am sure you can imagine, your aunt, into a state of consternation and distress, my dear wife being so assailed by anguish and grief, and so hand-wringingly distraught, that I felt myself compelled to stir a spoonful of sleeping medicine into her wine before bedtime in order that she might become calm again, for never before has such a calamity befallen us in the Apothecary House. I fear now that she in her weakness and already failing constitution will decline yet further, and I must concur entirely with her when she refers to you as a filthy girl who never ought to have been admitted over our threshold thus to poison us with debauchery and the Klatsch und Gerede of our townsfolk who come here to us in the dispensary and on whose goodwill we are reliant, our livelihood stemming so directly from their purses, whose strings would instantly be drawn together if any one of them should get wind of this Schmach und Schande.

That you add insult to our shame by so unabashedly declaring your intention to take a native as your lawful wedded husband, making you thereby a savage's whore, is a sin not only against your relatives who took you in and housed you in your time of need following your untimely Ausbruch und Flucht from the nunnery, but also against the Lord God Himself. What on earth has possessed you, girl, that impels you to give yourself to such an ape? And yet we cannot blame you alone, poor child, for this despicable offence, but also the nuns who fed you their papist Wahnsinn when you still but ein kleines Kind war and knew no better.

My aged heart wavers as I read your letter again, between sympathy and horror at your plight, which will tarnish us all, your relatives and our name. Go to the Governor, unhappy child, speak with him on this matter, which no doubt, by the time this letter reaches you, will already be decided, but which must be done in such a way that we do not all suffer under this Saurerei, the consequence of a libidinous young girl's escapades the minute she is away from the moral Christian atmosphere of her home.

I shall do you the good service of quite forgetting your unverschämte request for me to go to the King and thereby sully his name with this unmentionable business by which our good Name und Verruf would be altogether zerstört werden.

Pray to the Lord, that He may dir helfen, and speak to the Governor.

Søren Fuchs
    Apothecary

Immediately, she pens a reply:

Distinguished Uncle!

How are things with you and Aunt Karen? Is she now risen from her bed? I have had a cold but am now healthy again. I have coughed throughout the winter, which has been dark and cold and damp, with a number of the colony folk perished, though not me. I live on, as an unwanted weed.

You must go to the King and ask for his licence. Your name and that of the family is at stake, you say. And indeed it is, as well you know, Pharisee. I wished not to do this the hard way, but amicably. I could write a letter to my aunt, do you think then she would rise from her bed?

Men are beasts, and yet they will never admit to it, for they are Pharisees. And as it is women to whom they are beastly, so it is women who hold the key to their salvation or ruin.

Give my regards to Aunt Karen if she should awaken from her sleep.

Your brother's daughter, Anna Dorothea.

///

I arrive at Bergen carrying the letter, it is October and we have endured the usual hardships along the way, among them a fire that destroyed one of the sails and much else with it. Oh how I despise the sea, never more the sea, now I intend to cast anchor in the calm waters of marriage, and so I sail from Bergen to Copenhagen as a passenger on a packet ship. There stands my Caroline. She takes me with her to my new home in Christianshavn. A fine home, is it not? Indeed, I say, and yet a week later I am with the postal carriage to Køge in order to hand over the letter in person and make sure it is delivered to the rightful recipient, it is the beginning of the Christmas month when I arrive at Køge's postal station, our king has died a month before, the country is in mourning and his son, Christian the Sixth, is now Denmark's sovereign. It snows.

The Apothecary House is situated on the town square, a two-storey building with no less than eight windows, a fine home for fine folk. I have written to the Apothecary and informed him of my arrival but have received no reply. Nonetheless, the letter is to be delivered and I will do so myself, or else I will be thinking of the matter in years to come. I knock on the door.

A young girl comes to answer and curtsies nicely, I step inside into a hall from where a door leads off into the dispensary on the left, another into the private residence straight ahead, and a stairway leads to the first floor. I say my name and business. Is Mr Fuchs at home? Indeed, he's in the dispensary, the girl says, and so I go in.

There's a sharp aroma of spices and coffee, three men in long coats stand with their backs turned, looking as if they're sorting some items, I clear my throat and the eldest of them turns, Søren Fuchs? I enquire, Didrik Mühlenfort, ship's captain, a pleasure to meet you. I bow. Has the Apothecary received my letter? The man says nothing, but stares at me with bulging eyes. I come from the colony at Godthåb, I venture, where the Apothecary has a relative, and then he glares at me like I dropped a sack of money on the counter and told him I wanted to buy the Apothecary House with all its inventory, cash in hand. Anna Dorothea Titia? The housekeeper of the Governor Pors? But still he says nothing.

I've a letter, I tell him, and produce it from my inside pocket, it's travelled a long way, and I wished to make sure it found its destination, it being of some importance. I see, he says, and snatches it from my hand, casts his eye over it and tucks it away inside his coat. Gone from sight it is. Has the Captain come far?

From Copenhagen, I say, relieved that the man has at last decided to speak. With the postal carriage. Was there much snow on the way? he wants to know. A fair amount after Karlstrup, it forced us to stop several times, and the driver had to climb down with his shovel. He'll be cold, then? Indeed, I say, feeling uncomfortable now at the Apothecary's reservation, but I've been colder and it seems the winter will be long. Yes, I dare say, he says, there were rings around the moon just recently, always a sign of a long and harsh winter. Not too harsh, I hope. Would he care for a hot drink? A cup of tea, or coffee perhaps? We're weighing out a new consignment as it happens. A cup of tea would do wonders, thank you, I say, coffee gives me palpitations.

I'd hoped the Apothecary would invite me inside into the residence, maybe even offer me a bed for the night until I could get home again with the postal carriage, but nothing would seem to indicate he has any such intention. He leads me into a side room where I'm shown a chair between tall bookshelves filled with thick folios, and there I sit and sip my tea amid the pungent smells of camphor oil and dusty books, and I wonder if there will be room for me at the local inn.

///

Why doesn't he go? Why does he remain seated as if he were contemplating staying here forever? I did not invite him here. I am not obliged to house people who turn up from all corners and inflict upon me letters I would prefer never to receive. When he has drunk his tea he ought to have the decency to take his leave. But seamen, as everyone knows, are quite without manners.

Now he rises at last and comes back into the dispensary with his cup.

I thank you for the tea, Mr Fuchs.

He's welcome. Will he be lodging at the Swan?

Would that be the local inn?

The best, certainly. Right on the square here, all but twenty paces away.

Then I shall enquire there. Goodbye, Mr Fuchs, and thank you again.

He puts the fine porcelain down on the counter, where the cup rattles on its saucer. Clearly, the man is offended.

Pleasant journey back to Copenhagen, I say.

I go into the side room, which smells as yet of the aromatic tea I served the captain, and take the letter from my coat. I notice my fingers tremble as I insert a fingernail and tear open the envelope. I hold the letter to the window and allow the white light of December to fall upon it.

That evening I inform my wife: I must journey to Copenhagen and will be gone briefly.

As always in the evenings she is drowsy from the opium tincture I give her, as well as from the sanctimonious publications that so tickle the fancies of their women readers with details of the libidinous behaviours they warn against. They are in fact but the sleaziest literature wrapped up in pious mottos, hymn verses and biblical quotes, moreover illustrated with coloured pictures of men having their way with women, and women submitting themselves. My wife is absorbed. She looks up at me listlessly.

Copenhagen?

Business.

Christmas is coming, she reminds me.

I know. That's why I must leave in the morning.

I take the postal carriage. I have not been far-sighted enough to anticipate that I would be crammed in with the very captain who visited me the day before and with whom I am now obliged to share the long journey to the royal city. I pull my collar up to my ears and pretend to sleep. It is a strenuous endeavour, for the journey, which normally takes less than four hours, today lasts from early morning until mid-afternoon. Exhausted from my pretence, stiff-legged and freezing cold, I take a room at a Christianshavn inn, only to find that I barely close an eye all night due to noise from the street and because my body thinks it has already slept some eight hours. By the time morning comes I have a cough and a slight temperature, but nevertheless I make my way to the palace in order to seek audience with the King.

But I am informed there that the King is inclined to be rather less accessible than his father. A letter of application must be written. I comply and deliver it the next day. The courtier skims its contents, hands it back to me between the tips of his index and middle fingers, and without looking at me says: What does the matter concern?

A dispensation to marry, I reply.

Then he must go to the bishop. The King does not run a marriage bureau.

I apply to the bishop's office, which after the great bishop's palace burned down a couple of years ago is now housed in the Nikolaj Kirke. But Bishop Worm is busy. It is the bicentennial of the Augsburg Confession, and moreover he is to deliver the eulogy for the recently deceased King Frederik. I am however permitted to deliver my application, now rewritten and addressed to the bishop. I ought to go home, for I am not well. Yet, for the same reason, I am disinclined to embark on the long journey and moreover may be called in to the bishop's office at any time. I remain therefore in my noisy lodgings where I become steadily woozier and venture out only seldom. After some days, a woman calls after me in the street. I recognize her as one of my former servant girls. I pull my hat down over my ears and hurry on.

I write to my wife: I am occupied by business and am uncertain as to when I can return home. I lie in the bed in the tiny room in the days up to Christmas and sense the walls closing in on me from all sides, the way I waste away by the hour, death creeping towards me like an old friend I didn't know I missed.

///

In mid-January the King's licence arrives at the Apothecary House in Køge. The Apothecary's wife, who is in mourning, reads it, grasps the situation and places it along with some other letters she has not had the strength to read in an envelope she sends to the Missionskollegium in Copenhagen, though directed to Mühlenfort whose address she does not know. The principal, who receives all mail to the college, remembers Mühlenfort taking care of some correspondence between the Godthåb colony and the Apothecary in Køge, and duly sends the letter on to the captain's home in Christianshavn.

Mühlenfort receives it there and takes it with him the following summer when, for the fourth time, he embarks for Greenland.

///

'Letter of Royal Dispensation

That We, Christianus VI, upon the humblest application and request, most graciously grant and approve the joining together in holy matrimony of Frederik Christian, native of the Greeenlandic people and catechist of the Mission, baptized in the colony of Godthâb, and Anna Dorothea Titius, christened in the church of Skt. Laurentii, regardless that she by carnal knowledge outside the institution of marriage has become with child, under such condition that by family they are unrelated in any sense other than as stated here, which matter they must first duly prove. Moreover, We most graciously grant that they may, without preceding betrothal and publishing of the banns, be wed in private by Mr Hans Egede, Missionary, or by any other available priest, in the presence as witness of His Excellency Governor Claus Enevold Pors.

Hafnia, 10th January 1731
    Chr. VI Rex'

///

Who would have believed that the miserable Apothecary would pass away shortly after my visit? Found dead in a lodging house but steps away from my own new house in Christianshavn, but his widow sends me the letter from the bishop so that I may take it with me on my next journey to Greenland.

Now it is the good ship *Hope* of which I am captain, but alack, hope does not spring eternal, for she is wrecked in a storm, a hole torn in her hull by rocks off the Norwegian coast. We manage to reach the shore in a ship's boat along with some portion of the cargo, whereafter we proceed to Bergen and then on to Copenhagen where the salvaged goods are sorted, boxed, archived, etc. among them the letter to Titia, which I deliver to the Missionskollegium, though it will not be going anywhere soon, neither this year nor next, for the colony's future is uncertain, it is said both the Governor and the crew are to be sent home, so all matters pertaining to the *Hope* are consigned to various attic rooms where they languish in dust and damp.

Not until the summer of 1733 do I leave for Greenland again, this time with the galliot the *Eyland Schilling*, carrying as a passenger the renowned merchant Jacob Severin who has been given monopoly on the Greenland trade and who wishes therefore to journey there and inspect the place. I can scarcely wait for the open sea, to leave behind me the marital doldrums of the house in Christianshavn. I have collected together most everything I could lay my hands on from the *Hope*, including a large envelope inside which, among other documents, is the letter sealed with the Bishop Worm's own wax seal, reminding me thereby of that old matter. The Major Pors is returned home, this I know, but no one can tell me what has become of his young housekeeper, and so I carry the letter among my own personal effects, reasoning that it should be delivered no matter, and indeed delivered it is, and opened and read, but of course it is all too late.

///

The envelope containing the King's dispensation, opened now by Egede, contains moreover a folded sheet of paper that slips out as he is about to crumple the envelope in his hands. The document is a short note, undated and unfinished:

> I hereby wish to declare some past actions which may already have been rumoured and therefore by some be considered known, that they shall not be concealed from those who follow us. I have resolved to proclaim my sins to the Lord God and to my relatives and offspring, that my future family shall know of them. And those children who are to be born shall proclaim them to their children, and so on, that they may place their hope in God and not forget His deeds, that a sin conceived is a sin committed, and a sin committed shall be punished, though shall first be confessed by the sinner himself, for therein lies his salvation from the fires of Hell.

Thus: I, Søren Fuchs, Apothecary of the market town of Køge, who am in full possession of all my faculties, though now at death's door, confess that I have sinned.

And there it stops. Egede, who has decided to open the letter in the absence of anyone else of authority, turns this sheet of paper, which for some reason has come with the royal licence, this way and that in his hands. He can make neither head nor tail of it. And such an antiquated matter. Most probably sent here in error. Anyway, I have better things to do with my time than attend to such balderdash. He crumples the document in his hand and tosses it onto the fire along with the King's now useless letter of dispensation.

11

The Art of Producing Gold

After the sermon I travelled from the colony to the Kook Isles for, as is my custom, to instruct the Greenlanders who have established their summer settlement there. I asked after Apaluttork and where he might be at this time, for he makes me more uncomfortable by his absence than if I know his whereabouts, but they denied even the slightest knowledge of him.

FROM HANS EGEDE'S JOURNAL, MARCH 1729

In the spring Egede, accompanied by Niels and Frederik Christian, journeys up the fjord to collect ore for his experiments in alchemy.

Ever since his time in Bergen he has studied the literature. He has read the publications of Tycho Brahe and Paracelsus, Johann Becher's *Chymischer Rosengarten*, Bernard of Treves' *De chemico miraculo*, as well as the works of other writers who by mixing horse dung, blood, semen, quicksilver, vitriol, alum, saltpetre etc. discovered, or produced, arsenic, antimony, bismuth and the cure for syphilis, but never gold, and he has spelled his way through the *Tabula Smaragdina* in the German, though without gleaning even the slightest idea of what it sought to tell him, or rather hide from him. He is certain, however, that someone must have solved the puzzle. But why would they then write it down to share with others? He most certainly would not. Thus, surely, they employ code, ensuring thereby that only the initiated may glean the secret. Is he an initiated? Not yet. But soon, perhaps. It is a matter of great delicacy, which cannot be confided to just anyone. He is certain that some form of divine intervention is required if he is to succeed. Therefore, to the physical ingredients he adds a metaphysical: prayer.

In the fireplace in the parlour at home, where Gertrud boils her porridge and stews, simmers the whole winter a pot of alloys and malodorous substances of whose composition and origin he is somewhat ashamed. Their disgusting and shameful nature, however, is but part and parcel of achieving the desired result. In order to rise, one must first stoop. His prayers are full of ambiguous allusions to the pot. He does not ask directly for gold in these prayers, for he lacks the inclination to display such unveiled avarice. God would surely disapprove. And besides, the Lord knows his innermost thoughts, for which reason it would be superfluous. The power of prayer resides in the intention and in genuine sincerity. Gertrud and the girls complain of the stench. It gives them headaches and makes them nauseous, at times they are quite dizzied by it. He assures them of the benefits that will come to them all once he succeeds.

Gold, Gertrud. The purest gold. Unimaginable wealth. We would be free of the Trade and the Chancellery and the uncertainties of their funding, and not least we would be free of the Governor Pors and his infernal circus. We could finance the colony from this single pot!

Gertrud fixes his gaze, that look of hers he so despises. She is thirteen years older than he and sometimes she acts like she is his mother or guardian.

The children are becoming ill from it, she says.

In her lap is a small, brown-eyed native girl whom she has recently taken in. Her father is drowned and her mother, who already has a large flock of offspring on her hands, has threatened to send the little girl the same way, for on her own she is unable to feed so many mouths. Gertrud saved her at the very last. She sits and bounces her on her knee.

But if you discover how to bring forth gold in a pot, will it not quickly lose its value?

That is why it must be kept a secret, he says with a sly grin. I stand before a breakthrough, lacking but a single substance, a feldspar the natives inform me may be found on a fellside inside the fjord.

I see, says Gertrud, but I take it you know the saying, Alchemist, all is lost? She lifts an eyebrow and again he feels like a small boy come running to his mother to tell her he has seen a unicorn grazing outside the house.

Silver, too, he persists doggedly. Silver comes with it, as a by-product, like the fat that rises to the surface when you boil a blood-sausage. Have we any more blood-sausage, by the way?

There may be some left, yes. Shall I bring it to you?

I'll find it myself. He disappears into the pantry and devours what he can find, salted pork, blood-sausage, herring, a hunk of bread. I have seen it with my own eyes be formed on the surface, he shouts with his mouth full.

What, blood-sausage? says Gertrud.

No, silver! Silver! Separated out onto the surface. He comes back into the parlour again, munching something indeterminable, a cup of ale in his hand, which he guzzles in great mouthfuls. I tried to skim it with a ladle, but it was too elusive. It needs a stabilizing ingredient which can capture the alloy before it disintegrates into base particles. Anyway, expect us to be away for a few days. Come, Frederik Christian. And Niels. You shall be my ore master.

Before she can say anything he is already out through the door and striding to the shore, the young men on his heels. He climbs into the boat, hoists the sail and puts away. Niels and his foster-brother are nearly left behind.

On their way up the fjord they gather firewood and pile it onto the floor of the boat. The other boat went down in a storm a couple of weeks before and one of the oarsmen perished. This is the only vessel at their disposal for the time being. And crew are in short supply because of the rampaging sickness, for which reason they are alone.

The shores of the fjord are littered with timber, which they saw up into manageable lengths and carry to the boat. Niels asks his father where the timber comes from. Egede believes it to have come drifting from the other side of the land, for the currents seem to follow the coast all the way until veering off to the west in the waters off the colony. But where it might originally be from he has no idea. Perhaps the great forests they say may be found on the eastern side. Perhaps it comes from the old Norsemen, perhaps they felled the trees to provide timber for their ships and then lost some of it while floating it down a river. It is plain that the logs have been sawn rather than broken off or torn up by the root, and there are marks from the axes that have been used to debranch them.

In which case they must be many, he says. Thousands, perhaps.

But if they build ships, why do we never see them? Niels asks, knowing his father's obsession with the legendary Norsemen.

A good question, his father replies, to which I have no reply.

Perhaps they are building a navy to conquer all the lands of the North? Frederik Christian ventures.

Indeed, it would not surprise me, my boy. Perhaps they have ensconced themselves beyond the ice and are waiting for the right moment to attack us.

The timber, which appears to be fine oak, makes good firewood. However, it is becoming scarcer the more it is harvested by the folk of the colony. On a whole excursion one can be lucky to come across two logs. Today they find two by the afternoon.

A good sign, Egede says. I think fortune is on our side this time. He glances sideways at Niels, who so often displays the same sceptical expression as his mother. Yet he knows full well what to expect if he should be impudent. He smiles and sends his father a nod.

They put in at a settlement on the north side of the fjord. Only old people and children are there, the others are off hunting the reindeer, they say. A great herd has been observed. Egede decides to find them and join them for a while, partly to missionize, partly to acquire fresh meat. As ever, the mere thought makes him ravenous.

They wander over the low fells of the Northland, which are no taller than a couple of hundred fathoms, with soggy boglands in between, countless pools and tarns, and everywhere the gurgling of running water. There is still some snow, but they are able to proceed dry-footed by following the south-facing slopes. The vegetation is vigorous, a bed of verdant shrubs and colourful blooms. So as not to become snowblind they wear their snow goggles, a kind of mask made out of skin with small slits through which they peer. The wilderness here is unchanging, with no other fixpoint than the sun. After a couple of hours they scrabble up a peak and look back towards the fjord and the high fells on the other side. They speak about which direction to go, pointing and listening to each other's views. Egede is attentive to the boys' opinions, for they are more at home here than he, and for this reason he lets them decide. Shortly afterwards they hear voices and smell the pungent odour of burning firewood.

How splendid it will be to eat some food, he says.

The camp is some half-score of tents and perhaps ten times as many people: women, men and older children. The natives receive them warmly. As ever, he feels divided by such hospitality. He knows it to be partly genuine, partly false. Much as their piety when he tells them about redemption, as feigned as it is heartfelt. He is certain that not even the King's court can compete with the Greenlanders when it comes to their equivocalness. Yet he senses they are more relaxed than usual today. He supposes it must be the hunt, which sweeps aside all else in importance. Moreover, his old adversary the shaman is not here. Otherwise, as always, he would surely sense his presence.

They sit down beside a fire and take off their skin boots, hanging them to dry on sticks they twist into the ground. They stretch their bare feet towards the warmth. A woman comes with boiled char and seaweed. They get their knives out and eat greedily.

How many of the savages here do you think have heard about Jesus? he asks Frederik Christian.

All of them, his foster-son replies. Or as good as.

Do you really think so?

Word spreads, says the lad. Jesus is actually quite popular. The stories about him have circulated for some years.

Most likely it's entertainment to them.

Perhaps, says Frederik Christian. But it's a start, surely?

Who can say? Their sniggering detachment is hardly the most favourable starting point for a true understanding of the Gospel, Egede says. They are easiest to approach in times of adversity, then they will listen in order to find comfort. But after a few days they've forgotten all about it again. Sometimes I think the blood of serpents runs through them.

Some men have gathered around the fire. They lie relaxed on their sides, resting on their elbows. They ask Egede to tell them a story from the Bible. He tells them about Jesus in the garden of Gethsemane, how he was betrayed, imprisoned and crucified, about his prolonged suffering, the wounds, the pain, the blood, the way he was scorned.

It is a strange god you have, one of the men says. He is so weak.

He is a man, Egede says. He descends from heaven in the shape of a man, with the weaknesses of a man.

But he doesn't die, does he? He is a god, after all.

He dies in his human form, but is resurrected in his divine form to return to his father in heaven.

His father will have been glad?

Indeed, God loves his son.

How then can he send him to Earth to suffer and die? Only a harsh father would do such a thing.

Egede shakes his head. God is love. And he and his son are the same flesh. God suffers just as much as Jesus.

Then why did he bother sending him here?

God has compassion for all men, he says. He shows them his mercy by sending them his son to atone for their sins. Because of the sufferings of Christ you may find salvation.

Does that mean we have to be like you first? another man asks.

Yes, you must receive instruction, then you must be baptized, and later confirmed. Then you will be Christian.

Must we also drink aquavit?

You may drink aquavit if you wish, though in moderation. Drinking too much alcohol is not Christian.

Are there bad Christians as well as good?

Certainly. Many of the colony people are bad Christians.

Perhaps we Greenlanders will also be bad Christians. Would it not be better for us to be good Greenlanders than bad Christians, priest?

Yes, it would, he says. Christianization must occur slowly. It cannot be forced, for then you will only bring shame on the Lord's name.

Like the natives in the colony. They drink and whore like the Danes.

Indeed, they are neither good Christians nor good Greenlanders. They ought to be chased away.

They can't come back to us either. We don't want them. What would we do with them?

I don't know. They are lost, and so they must perish.

Is the King our father? a man says.

Yes, in a way he is. He is our earthly father, whereas God is our heavenly father.

I hope the King does not sacrifice us Greenlanders the way God sacrificed his son.

The King loves us. He loves all his subjects.

But he doesn't know us. He's never seen us.

God loves us all, and feels solicitude for us.

Can we keep our helping spirits if we become Christian?

No, most certainly not. Jesus will be your helping spirit. He is stronger than all of your spirits put together.

He can't be stronger than Sila. No one is stronger than Sila.

Oh, but he is much stronger, Egede says. Stronger by far. Sila is but a fart on a winter's day compared to the Saviour.

But Jesus is weak, they protest. How can he be both strong and weak?

He is ascended to heaven and sits at his father's side. Therefore he is stronger than all others.

If a man has two wives, can he keep them both when becomes a Christian?

No, he must part from the one he married last and keep the first.

Aah, they say around the fire. What will happen then with so many women loose?

They must find themselves other men.

But there are far too many women. There aren't enough husbands to go round.

God does not allow polygamy. He thinks it quite as repugnant as fornication.

One of the men steps up, dragging his two wives with him. Incensed, he says: Tell me, priest, which one am I to part with?

The one you married last is not your lawful wedded wife. You must part with her if you are to be Christian.

So this one here must starve to death? The man shakes the unfortunate woman by the collar. Is that a Christian thing to do? God sacrifices his own son and then tells man to sacrifice his wives. This Christianity is not for us.

Perhaps not for you, but for your children, he replies. That is why we proceed gently and slowly with our Christianization.

When we become Christian, will you then go home again?

No, this land belongs to the kingdom. It has done for hundreds of years.

Does that mean you'll be here for ever? They look astonished, and Egede cannot help but laugh.

Indeed, we're going nowhere.

But it's not your land.

Oh, but it is. It is the King's land. But it will remain the Greenlanders' too.

You Danes are strange, says the man with the two wives. Your god is both weak and strong, and the other god, his father, is both cruel and kind, the Christians are both good and bad, and our land is ours and not ours at the same time. Everything is two-sided with you Danes. It gives us the kayak sickness just to speak with you. He gets to his feet again and leaves.

They stay with the hunters for two days. Niels spends much time with the natives. They teach him to use a bow and arrow, shooting at a target of stretched hide, then killing some hare and grouse. Egede sits mostly outside the tent, wrapped up in a reindeer skin, reading Luther's *The Bondage of the Will*, on whose pages he encounters the following sentence: 'For my own part, I frankly confess that even if it were possible, I should not wish to have free choice given to me, or to have anything left in my own hands by which I might strive toward salvation.'

Interesting, he mutters. No free choice. The notion of free will is human hubris. It is a sin against the will of the Lord.

Thus he decides he has had enough of this dossing around, and orders the young men to pack their things together. They find their way back to the settlement and sail on up the fjord.

///

I am Aappaluttoq. I pay my calls while the priest is away. First I visit the girl with whom I lay last summer after the ships had come. I sit with her in the night, sit in the dark and listen to my son's beating heart; I lay my hand on her abdomen and feel him turn lazily inside the dark well of his mother's womb. She does not wake. She mumbles in her sleep, Latin prayers, *Libera nos a malo, ave Maria gratia plena*, and I pray with her. We are almost family now. She is to marry my son, and my son is to be my son's father, and his foster-father, the priest, is to be my family too in a way. What a mess. It will not be long now before we all are bound up in each other, tied together in an un-unravellable knot. That is where we are heading. We are all of us part of the cosmic dramaturgy. I do not even think it is God who is doing this. Praying to him is certainly of no help. I don't know if I want it. I am gripped by doubt. And doubt makes a man weak, the way it made Peter weak when he walked on the water. You sink, and drown. If my son is to marry her, and thereby make my second son my grandchild, I muse, it will mean a bringing together of Danes and Greenlanders, a marriage and a depraved mixing of blood between two peoples who are vastly foreign to each other, and thus we will be stuck with each other for ever, bound to each other by chains stronger than both the colony and the mission, and who is then to say if we will be each other's blessing or curse? Probably both. I don't know what's right here. I place it in the hands of the Lord and whisper *fiat voluntas tua* as my child's mother whispers the same words in sleep.

I go next door. I find the priest's bed chamber in the darkness, I lie down beside Gertrud and half asleep she turns and embraces me. Are you back already, she whispers. Yes, I am here, I say, and mount her. I have her, and it is what she wants, for although she moans and grips me tight and breathes, oh Hans! she knows full well it is me, for we have done it so many times together and she knows my smell by now, my ways of doing things, my unhurriedness, my patience and my strength, and I too am fond of it, for the older a woman is the purer her enjoyment, knowing as she does that it is perhaps the last time. A mature woman has much more to give than a young girl who is scarcely grown, and besides, it is pitch dark in the priest's bed chamber, and what's more I need not worry about making her pregnant, this is a sterile copulation, as any intercourse between Danes and Greenlanders rightly should be.

///

The next evening, Egede returns with the two lads to the settlement close to the ice, from where can be seen the vertical azure-blue wall of the glacier standing some thirty fathoms high, a deep thunder rumbling as it calves. As always on seeing the ice he thinks of what might be on the other side, the fabled Eastern Settlement perhaps, teeming with Norsemen, or perhaps centaurs, unicorns and fire-spitting dragons. Who knows what lies beyond the ice? It could be anything at all, or it could be nothing, a great limbo. There must be a reason for God having established such a barrier. Is it to protect us from the other, or to protect the other from us? He imagines all sorts of things that might be concealed there. An entrance to some underworld. Forests. Ancient farmlands. He yearns to go there, yet knows it will never happen. God wishes it not.

Before breaking up to wander south, he reads for the people of the settlement. He has been here many times during the past seven years and by now they are familiar with a number of tales from the Gospel. Some of them can even read. It is not he who taught them, but the missionary Albert Top, who returned home a couple of years ago. Egede himself cannot abide these half-schooled sciolists. He can tell they have discussed the matters in which they have been taught. They delight in asking difficult questions he is not always able to answer. There are many things to which no reasonable answer may be found. That is why we call it faith. Luther despised reason, a cousin of free will, and believed it to be poisonous to faith. But these filthy heathens approach the Gospel with logic and common sense, as if they were students of law. Smirking, they sit there and ask who is the greater, God or Jesus?

God the Father is greatest.

But Top has told us they are one flesh.

They are one in the Holy Trinity, but God is the head, where Jesus and the Holy Spirit are the limbs.

What part of the body is Jesus exactly?

How come Christian people are so cruel?

It happened with the Fall of Man.

Why did God allow Eve to eat the forbidden fruit?

If God knows everything, then surely he knew she would eat it?

Why didn't he just kill the serpent?

Why does God get angry with man if he already knows what they're going to do?

How many animals are there on Earth?

Many thousands. He cannot keep up with all their questions, and answers only selectively.

How did Noah find room for all the animals on his boat?

What did they eat during all the days of the Flood?

How could Noah and his family build such an enormous boat all on their own?

Were they boatbuilders?

How could there be room for all their provisions?

What if one of the animals died?

How many people were on board Noah's Ark?

Noah, his wife, their three sons and their wives.

How could eight people get all those animals on board in only a few days?

And so on.

When he can provide no satisfactory answer, they pretend to be disappointed. The reality of the matter is that they are gloating. He liked them better in the beginning, seven years ago, when their questions were physical threats and his reply was to box their ears or bloody their noses. He has no counter to this sly interrogation. Frederik Christian handles them better: he tells them he doesn't know, and that he must ask the priest. If truth be told, he ought to leave the missionizing entirely to his foster-son.

A man of the settlement is in grief at the loss of a family member. They bring him forward and present him to the priest so that he might be comforted.

Why are you sorrowful?

His son has drowned, one of the others replies.

Are you aware that you may find solace and comfort in Jesus?

He has already prayed to Jesus, they say. And Jesus has answered him.

Indeed? Immediately he is on his guard. And what did Jesus say to him?

He said his son could not be given salvation because he died a heathen. Can this really be so, priest?

He has not spoken with the Saviour. The Saviour would never speak as such.

He whispered in my ear while I was lying on the sleeping-bench, the grieving man says. Egede can see that he is broken down with grief and that he believes without a doubt that he has spoken to Jesus.

The Lord Jesus does not go about whispering in people's ears. It is something you have dreamt.

I don't know, says the man inconsolably. I heard a voice. I prayed to Jesus and then I heard a voice. Do you think it was because I wanted to hear him, priest?

Undoubtedly. He is restless now, positively itching to get into the fells and search for the feldspar.

Is it really the case that his son cannot be given salvation? the men want to know.

Yes, that is correct. If a person has not been baptized, he cannot be saved. That is the long and short of it. It's very simple.

But didn't Jesus raise the dead, and didn't he say to the thief, you will be with me in Paradise?

That's different.

Was the thief a Christian?

No, I suppose he was Jewish, if not a Babylonian or something.

Indeed, because they couldn't have been Christian while Christ was still alive, could they?

No, of course not.

And yet he said, you will be with me in Paradise, to a Jew and a criminal. But Aqqaluk, who did nothing wrong but be struck by the kayak sickness and drown, cannot go there?

That is correct, yes. He can scarcely contain his impatience.

So he is gone for ever? the dead boy's father asks.

Yes, but there is nothing new in that here. You people are used to the dead simply being gone when they die. Therefore you cannot feign dissatisfaction. Your son ought to have been more careful while out in his kayak, then I might have instructed him.

But we've heard the Christian message now, they reply. That makes it hard for us to think of all our dead who cannot gain from it.

The message is for the living, not the dead.

Can the priest not pray for him? the father asks. My grief is so great.

You can come to the colony and receive instruction, then we'll see about it. Now, if you don't mind, we must be making tracks.

As they go through the valley, he speaks with Niels and Frederik Christian about the Greenlanders' even-temperedness and inveteracy. They really are astoundingly obtuse sometimes, he says. But as soon as they are stricken with some grief that presses down on the heart they are more amenable. Take now that father who had lost his son. I think we shall see him in the colony soon. Perhaps his hardened savage's heart will mature and soften enough to receive the divine message. But when fortune is with them and the hunting is good, and no one has kicked the bucket, they are utterly implacable and will neither be led nor driven. One must go to them in their grief, that is when we will find our candidates.

They wander south with their ropes and packs, following the river up to the tarn and crossing into the Austmannadalen where the Norsemen of old had several farms. They ascend to the melting snow. The ground is sand and gravel which yields underfoot. They stumble often and must pull each other up and help each other along.

Here, he says. It must be here somewhere.

They put up the tent in a dry spot and lie under the reindeer skin like three spoons in a drawer, Egede first, in front of him Frederik Christian, then Niels. He holds his free arm over them both, and can feel them breathing.

The next day they come to the place. Niels smooths his hand over the rock, testing to see if he can climb it. The cliff is almost vertical, an area of the face displaying a faint red tinge. Niels removes the coiled rope from his shoulder and ties an end around his waist. He steps up to the cliff, pats a hand against the rock once more and begins to climb. Egede stands with Frederik Christian at his side, watching him intently. He delights in seeing his son climb. The lad makes it seem so easy. He knows that he could never do it himself. Niels climbs diagonally upwards to the right, where the sheer face drops several hundreds of fathoms. He wonders what use the rope is. If he falls, it will be of little help. I could give the slightest tug, he thinks. And he would fall. No one would know. Apart from one, of course. He happens to glance at Frederik Christian at the same moment and realizes his foster-son has read his thoughts. The slightest smile curls the corner of the boy's mouth as if to say: If you do it, I will not tell. He dispels the thought from his mind and shouts a word of encouragement to Niels, directing him towards the reddish discolouring. Now and then, rocks dislodge from under the lad's boots and tumble into the abyss.

Don't fall now! Egede shouts. A little further to the right and you're almost there.

He is indeed. It is admirable work. He hangs from the sheer face like a fly. He takes the hammer from his belt and strikes at the rock, working loose a few shards and placing them in the bag he carries at his waist.

A little further to the right! Egede shouts. It looks a bit better there.

His son edges to the right. He can almost hear the grunts of his exertions and can see the way he must continually adjust his footing, the soles of his boots slipping on the narrow ledge.

That's the way! You can come down now.

In a few short moments the lad is again standing before him, feet firmly planted on the solid ground.

Egede digs a chummy elbow into his side and tells him what a fine job he has done: Well done, my boy, I wasn't worried for a moment! What a fine pair of lads I have! He hugs them both, slaps them on the back and must contain himself so as not to become too soft-hearted.

Unfortunately, when they return to the settlement the grieving father has taken his own life. The news makes Egede angry. Suicide is to spit in the face of God, he rages. Life is a divine gift, and to take one's own is to trample on that gift.

They sail home to the colony. He embarks on more of his chemical experiments. The two young clergymen, Lange and Miltzov, come to him seeking advice and guidance, but he dismisses them abruptly. His mind is on metallurgy. It is now or never.

There are some small barrels in the parlour, containing poisonous chemicals. He has strictly forbidden his family to even lift their lids. But children will be children, of course, and if one says to them there is something they must not do, one can be certain only that they will do it at the first opportunity. The little native girl is particularly inquisitive, forever rummaging in drawers and cupboards in her own quiet way. One day she lifts the lid of one of the barrels. A foul and suffocating odour fills the room. Everyone flees from the house with handkerchiefs to their mouths. But they forget the child. A while passes before Frederik Christian suddenly emits a cry and runs back inside to get her. He finds her unconscious.

In the days that follow, they feel wheezy and suffer the most dreadful headaches, nausea and diarrhoea. Kieding prescribes theriac, a cure-all which Egede and all those who have breathed in the fumes are to imbibe several times a day. But the little girl, who has now woken up, is forgotten again and receives none. After a couple of days she falls ill. Gertrud summons Kieding.

She's breathing normally, the physician says. I don't think she's been harmed.

But in the night she takes poorly. She groans, twists and turns in her bed, and vomits too. Her eyes are bloodshot and bulge like those of a fish from the deepest sea. Gertrud and the girls sit with her. Egede keeps his distance and looks on despairingly. The next day she is passed away.

You can at least read over her? Gertrud says when he refuses to give her a Christian burial.

Am I to alter the liturgy? he snaps angrily. Am I to change the dogmas? The girl was a heathen. What do you want me to do?

You are not without guilt in her death, says Gertrud.

I know my guilt, thank you. It is a matter between me and the Lord.

I suspect the Lord will let you off lightly, Gertrud hisses.

He raises his hand to strike her, but she is standing with the dead child in her arms, as if she were intending to give her to him, and stares at him without blinking. It is sufficient to stop him.

I suppose I could read a couple of passages, he mumbles.

The surviving carpenter puts together a small coffin. Niels carries it to the grave on his shoulder. Gertrud and the girls, and Frederik Christian, follow on behind. They toss dried flowers on the casket. Then they cover it with rocks.

He makes a note in his diary about this event, quite open-heartedly and not without admitting his guilt. I thank you, God, he writes, for keeping me and my family from this calamity and sparing us injury to our lives and health.

A week later he actually succeeds in producing not gold but silver. He has now moved his paraphernalia down to the blubber house where he stands stirring the pot for some hours each day. And one day he comes home and triumphantly presents a dull grey lump to Gertrud.

What did I tell you, he says. I have weighed it. There is no doubt. It is genuine silver.

She considers him for a long time without speaking. Then returns to her sewing.

12

Thy Children So Fair

The Governor assembled the council in order to deliberate with them some matters concerning the affairs of the colony, among them the question of how the reconnaissance expedition most graciously commanded by His Majesty over the ice to the Eastern Settlement could and would be carried out.

From Hans Egede's journal, March 1729

Now plainly the spring is on its way. I breathe in the air and peer up at the sky which is patched with blue and white. I stroll in the colony harbour with my hands behind my back while humming an indeterminable melody that has come fluttering to me in the night. The tails of my coat wave in the damp flurries and I shiver. Yet in the lull between gusts, and when the sun peeps down upon me, as cautiously as I squint upwards at it, the weather feels almost warm. I am inspecting the buildings, part of the surveying work I am to perform for the Chancellery. I oversaw their construction what feels like years ago now, though barely more than six months have passed, issuing instructions as to length, breadth and height, how the space inside was to be divided, where the stoves were to be placed, and so on. I feel they are my buildings. I feel tenderness for them, more than for the people who inhabit them. They are constructed of peat and timber and stone. There is an animal shed where the goats and sheep and the two surviving horses dwell. There is a blubber house we have still to make ready for production, though for the time being it is used as a bath house and for storage. It is the colony's smallest structure, only eleven alens in length. It stands at the top of my list of jobs to be started now that the winter has begun to loosen its grip and those whose time it was to die now seem to have done so. Death keeps its own ledger. If the colony is to have any reason for being, we must soon be productive. Next to the blubber house is the bakery, twenty alens. Then a timber house, twelve alens, for storage. A small village, in every respect, and it is mine.

They call me Fox. I suppose it is because of my slanting eyes, inherited from my mother's family, and my red hair, from my father's side. I think there was Finnish blood in her veins, my mother. Or perhaps it is because I am sly. My name is Johan Seckman Fleischer, and I am Paymaster of the colony.

I am twenty-eight years old and deaf in my right ear. It happened in a skirmish in Moss when a cannon recoiled and knocked me out. Presently, the hearing returned to my left ear, though I am still tormented by bells that ring and hymnal tones, some days loud, others barely audible. Occasionally I will hear the sound of what I take to be musket balls flying through the air, which makes me cower even after all these years. When people address me I turn my good ear to them, though sometimes the poor one, depending on whether I can be bothered with them, and then they think I'm having them on. They say I mock them with the way I peer at them. But it's all because of this bad ear. Well, perhaps there is something of the mocking bird about me, but only because of that bloody cannon that has made me half deaf.

I was born on 15 September at the manor house Dragsholm on Sjælland. The manor lies near the bay of Nekselø. My father was Captain Herman Reinholdt Fleischer. He took part in the battle of Gadebusch, or the Gadebusch slaughter as some people call it. A ridiculous war if ever there was one. The Swedes won. My father died. He took a Swedish bullet and it did away with him. I was ten years old. The path that led me here has been long and winding. I prefer not to talk about it, though I will say that something happened in the early spring of 1728. It happened, of course, because I wanted it to happen, or wanted something to happen, whatever it might be. At a dinner party held at his home by the assessor Baltzer Seckman, my foster-father, I ran into an old friend of mine, Jørgen Landorph, a lieutenant with whom I had previously attended the naval college. He told me of Greenland, of the new colony where he was to be

Commandant, and that they were looking to appoint a merchant. I knew nothing about Greenland, had already dabbled unsuccessfully in trade, and to take on a position as colonial Trader would moreover clearly be a step backwards in my career, so I asked him directly: When do we leave?

Two days later we met at a drinking house in Vestergade with two other friends from the naval college, Jesper Reichardt, who was to be first officer of one of the ships that was to make the journey up, and Ole Lange, who had abandoned the military and become a priest, of all things. We drank ourselves senseless and enjoyed a splendid evening with women and music, and polsk dancing. And thus do men make merry, rolling themselves in the dirt, when they know they have frittered away their lives, and I who was never even a one for the ladies.

I was admitted to the King. I had seen him once before, ten years earlier. He had become elderly, though remained quite spritely and with all his faculties, friendly and hospitable, albeit with the peculiar bashfulness for which he is known, even before ordinary citizens, peasants even, and humble folk, which causes his speech to race away with him, reducing him often to stutters and giggles. The King informed me that I was not to be Trader, but Paymaster. Another step down the ladder. Still, I accepted the position. The King himself was offering it to me, and I'd already lain awake several nights in succession imagining a life in Greenland, so I could hardly decline. Indeed, Your Majesty. Thank you, Your Majesty. And I bowed and touched my forelocks as I withdrew backwards out through the door.

The Assessor, my guardian, was of course horrified. He didn't shout, but spoke sternly, though in the thinnest, most wizened of voices: Have you, without my knowledge and permission, taken on a subordinate position, in the colonies? Do you realize that you are consigning a career in law to the midden? What would your dear deceased father . . . etc.

And so it was that I left it all behind. Farewell.

The colony in which I arrived was moreover not a proper colony at all, the land barely land at all but a strip of rugged coast between

the sea and the ice, with a garrison that was not a garrison, and
no fortification either, though such had been planned, a governor
who was governor in name only, for what was he supposed to
govern? And with friends who were friends no longer, for the closer
we were lumped together the more we drifted apart. Reichardt
returned home. Lange went about in his black cassock and
immersed himself in his missionary work along with the other
young priest, Miltzov, who however spends more time drinking
than he does on the Scriptures. Landorph seemed mostly intent
on making life difficult for the governor, though Pors was as much
to blame himself.

Life is strange. So why should I not cock my head and play the
mocking bird? Or should I weep instead? Is laughter not but tears
that change their mind at the last minute? Sometimes, at least, it can
be hard to tell the difference.

I think about a person's personality and character. Is it, I wonder,
the case that such things are attached to place, by which I mean
geographical location? And can a person then be shipped out from
one personality, transported away from it in the direction of another
and thereby, in short, become a different person? I see it in my old
friends. They are scarcely recognizable after they came here to this
land. Has the same thing happened to me? Have I become another?
And would it be a good thing, I wonder?

It could be said that death was on my side this winter. For as
resources and materials for the construction of the buildings meant
for storage and production dwindled, the need for them too dimin-
ished as the numbers of the living fell. Death worked its way up from
the bottom, as always. First it raged in the crew house, where the
great majority, forty-five in all, succumbed, the former convicts, then
the enlisted men and the non-commissioned officers, then the
tradesmen, the servants and domestics, the attendants. Some two
score remain, counting everyone, a suitable number for a colony this
size. A good thing we began with so many, or else there would be
no one left. We are but fodder for Death. How it had been supposed
we could feed five score full-grown adults in a wilderness such as this
is more than I can fathom. Even now with our numbers decimated,

we have only just enough to scrape by. However, things have a way of levelling out. My inspection duties include keeping a record of the crew's daily consumption. I myself have set the weekly menu. It looks like this:

Weekly Menu, Colony of Godthåb:

	Mid-day	Evening
Sunday:	Pork-meat and pease porridge	Pork-meat and pease porridge
Monday:	Grain porridge and herring	Flour porridge
Tuesday:	Pease porridge and salmon	Pease porridge and salmon
Wednesday:	Grain porridge and herring	Flour porridge
Thursday:	Pease porridge and dried fish	Pease porridge and stockfish
Friday:	Grain porridge and cheese	Flour porridge
Saturday:	Grain porridge and herring	Flour porridge

Moreover per person: 3 jugs of ale per day and one fifth of a pot of aquavit per week.

The warehouse. Something smells rotten, puh! I rummage in the dark to find out what it is. A foodstuff gone bad can contaminate all else around it. I may be half deaf, but my sense of smell is keen. There. I pick up a sack and my hand feels something wet and slimy. What can it be? Urgh, how vile! The corpse of a child. One of the old tarts in the crew house must have given birth on the sly and got rid of it here in the winter. With the thaw these past days, decomposition has quickly set in. Now I suppose there will be proceedings, a hanging perhaps. But then the unfortunate child-murderer is most likely already dead.

I open the door wide to let the light and then cut open the sack. Who knows how long it's been lying here frozen. But that which once housed a human soul, a crying, blabbering child, can scarcely be discerned in these skin-covered bones. I prod it with the toe of my boot. The lump still sticks to the sacking, which comes with it when I turn it on its side. The stench assails me. I bend forward while holding my nose. Clear signs of strangling. I feel a rage well inside me at such a despicable deed and hope the woman will still be alive, that I might have the pleasure of seeing her dangle from the gallows.

I go outside and call two men to me who are sitting on a rock in the sunshine. A job for you in the warehouse!

They look up at me, dull and listless. Their cheeks are sunken after the physician extracted their teeth.

Do you hear me?

Without enquiry, they stand up laboriously, holding onto each other for support like a pair of old men, before trudging over to the warehouse.

Take this to Lieutenant Landorph, I tell them. And give him my best regards, I shout after them as they go.

The melody returns to me. I listen to my humming. What is it now? Something my mother once sang to me? Detached words and rhymes, the faintest of echoes, *Agnes, O Agnes, dear daughter of mine.* Yes, that rings a bell. But how does it go then? *Where e'er hast thou been in all this long time?* Splendid, I remember! It's coming back to me now, the whole song, so many verses, but I remember them nearly all. To think, there they've lain, coiled inside my mind, and all it takes is to pull on one end, like a cord, and the whole song unravels. *On Højelands Bridge maid Agnes did stand . . . up came a Merman and reached out his hand* – ha ha!

How amusing, that old nursery ballad. It must be at least twenty years since I heard it last. *Agnes, O Agnes, to the sea come with me, thy children so fair await us with glee . . .*

A peculiar song indeed, on reflection. But of course I never thought about it like that at the time. I was afraid of the Merman though, forever afraid, whenever it was time to sleep, whenever I was at the sea, or wandering by the stream. I would think he was going to pop up and reach out for me, and pull me down into the water with him.

I am the one they call Fox, and I think about my life as I walk up the muddy bank, past the crew house that seems almost on the verge of collapse after the ravages of winter, on to the squelchy peatland where I stand a while and feel the wind and the sun on my face. I remind myself that I must not cross the peatland but walk around it. To cross it would be a poor idea indeed. A man will sink into his knees, then to his waist, and I am in no doubt that he could also drown and be for ever consigned to the bog if he should venture so far. Sooner or later we shall have to drain it. It would give us new land in one fell swoop. We could build a whole town. What should we call it? Something including Fleischer, perhaps? But no, more like something royal, I imagine. Fleischer the Fox is not destined to be commemorated in the name of any town.

I sit down on the rocks between the moor and the colony, take my pipe from my pocket and puff some tobacco. Again, reminiscences of childhood, nursery songs. I rarely think of my childhood, more of my time in the army, and the time I spent in Copenhagen. But childhood, why should a person think of it at all? Why now? Is it because I am to die? I have heard it said that those early years return to a person when death is on its way.

Someone must have seen me, for I can hear my name be called. The Lieutenant, of course. There he is. Forever dashing about like he has a firework up his arse. Can a man not sit in peace for a minute in the sunshine? He calls again, and I can see him quite clearly, Landorph, standing there gazing up towards me. Too late, then, to hide. How annoying! Nothing for it now but to climb down again. Most likely it's nothing that couldn't wait either. The Lieutenant likes to keep people busy.

He calls again, and I acquiesce. I put the pipe back into my pocket and climb down the steep, though rather low, rocks which are wet and slippery with meltwater. At the governor's residence Landorph stands waiting with his hands at his sides.

Was it you who found the child?

The body, yes. It was the smell that led me to it. I touch the side of my nose with my finger. Will there be an investigation, Jørgen?

There is no body, says Landorph and studies me to gauge my reaction.

But there is, I saw it with my own eyes.

No, there is no body. The child is alive.

I am startled. It was dead when I found it.

Not any more. It's a boy.

For a moment I feel quite dizzy. It was a corpse, it was a festering mess.

Yes, he was certainly rather filthy. But apart from that he seems to be all right.

Well, I'll be . . .

The strangest things can happen, says Landorph.

Do you know who the mother is?

We'll find out soon enough.

There can't be that many left who are even capable of childbirth.

A couple at most. Although it could be one of the women who died last week.

How many were there?

Two, no more.

And what about the Governor's housekeeper? She strikes me as the type who could throttle her offspring.

The jomfru Titia is still as abundant as a fully laden schooner. Unfortunately. There's Sise Petticoat as well, but she's still pregnant too.

What are we supposed to do with a foundling?

The child has been taken to Madame Egede. She has only just lost one of her foster-children, poisoned by the old man's chemicals. I don't doubt she'll be glad of another to take care of.

Yes, our Gertrud is a good person, I say, and sincerely too.

Perhaps the only one in this whole land, Landorph concurs.

I will go and see the child, I tell him. I can hardly believe it was alive.

Indeed, I am quite unable to grasp that the filthy rotten corpse I discovered could possibly have been living. I must see it with my own eyes.

I go around the side of the governor's residence, to where the priest lives. I knock on the door and go inside. The place is quiet apart from a clock that ticks. The Egede family are gathered at the other end of the parlour, Egede himself and his son and foster-son standing with their backs towards me, the two girls kneeling on the floor. The Madame is seated in a chair. It is she to whom their attention is directed, or rather the bundle she holds in her arms.

Peace of God, I say, stepping closer over the creaking floorboards.

Egede glances at me over his shoulder and waves me on. Come and see, he whispers. A veritable wonder of the Lord.

Now I can see. The child has been washed and swathed in clean linen. The Madame is feeding it with milk from a bottle whose neck she has plugged with a switch of fabric. The child is very pale and its eyes are closed. But I can see the way it trembles as the Madame brushes its cheek with the bottle, its mouth searching for the teat. The nursery song appears in my mind again, yet now it seems wicked and taunting. *He covered her mouth, that she could not speak, took her to the bed of the sea so deep.* I clear my throat.

Ah, there he is, I say as if the child were my own and I have been looking for him.

Yes, he lives, says Egede. He wished not to die.

Großartig, I say.

The first viable child to be born here, Egede says. A little nourishment and he will be fine, I'm sure.

Yes, he'll need some, to be sure, I say. And we still don't know who the mother is? One of the natives, perhaps?

No, the boy is a Dane. No doubt the mother is already among the dead. I have spoken to Kieding. He thinks he knows who it might be, one of the women from the Spinning House gaol.

The son of a whore, I think to myself, but say instead: Presumably there is a father too?

He has departed this life long since.

I leave the Egede family to themselves, they look like a tableau, a nativity scene, and walk up to the moor again, though this time I continue in a southerly direction. I want to go to the inlet where the ship lies anchored for the winter. I have walked here many times before, but this is the first time since the snow has gone from the ground. It is wonderful to walk again, to stretch the limbs and feel oneself to be free in the wilds of this land and beneath such a great infinity of blue. There are sparrows everywhere. They must have arrived here only recently. They flit about and busy themselves with their sparrowy pursuits. How old can a sparrow be, I wonder? Hardly more than five or six years. Born on the very thresholds of death. They have much to do, and all at once, and are obviously keenly aware of the fact, though it does not seem to worry them. Migratory birds. So much time they spend flying back and forth. Like a ship's voyage of ten years or more. Gulls and ravens and grouse, sedentary birds, are idler altogether. They live longer too, so I imagine. More time to pass. What is best? I will soon be thirty. How many more years can I expect? *Hear me, O Agnes, I say to thee now.* Wings beat in the air that surrounds me, I place my feet tentatively on the sods before transferring my entire weight, sensing myself to be slightly sinking, the bogwater gurgling up, and then I lift my foot once more with a squelch before my sock is soaked. One has to keep moving, or else one will be sucked down.

Parallel ridges of rock run towards the fjord. Between them lies a flat, open bed a couple of hundred alens in width. My eye sees peat-huts and skin tents at the shore below. Thin spirals of smoke rise from the holes in the roofs. These people too are migratory, for never do they stay in one place for any length of time. But now they are here. Might I pay them a visit? I have never spoken to a native apart from those who are naturalized and work in the colony, pitiful, pipe-smoking individuals in threadbare woollens, breeches of linen and worn-down military boots passed on from the dead.

At once a man stands before me, a native, as if risen out of the ground. He gives me a fright. The shock of finding the dead child, who nevertheless was alive, is in me still. Or perhaps it is that dreadful song. But the man smiles kindly and speaks to me. He turns and makes his way down towards one of the tents, glancing back at me as he goes.

Inside the tent, where perhaps a score of half-naked natives sit, mostly women and children, someone places a tin plate of meat in front of me. I eat heartily.

I look across at the man who invited me in. Where are you all from? I ask.

The man leans forward and studies me.

From the north? I point in the direction.

Now he understands. *Kujalleq*, he says, and points too.

From the south, I understand.

He jabs a finger at me.

Copenhagen, I say.

He nods. He has understood. *Kunngi*, he says.

Indeed. The King's city.

Guuti? he says. *Palasi?*

No, no. I laugh and shake my head. I am not a priest. Paymaster. A kind of merchant. Trade. I rub my fingers together.

Niiverneq, says the man.

In the summer, you and I, *nivernek*, I say.

Puisi, he says. Seal? *Orsoq*. Blubber, yes?

A pleasure, I tell him. Narwhal tusk. Whale. I try to illustrate.

The native shakes his head. He makes wave movements with his hand, angling his other hand against it. *Schip*.

Ship, I say.

He nods. *Vaalfis*.

I don't understand. What ship?

Vaalfis. He gestures towards the sea, then splays his fingers, counting them one by one.

Many ships? I say. Ah, I see. Whalers?

He twists his face into a grimace, puts his hands to his temples and furrows his brow. *Qallunaat!* Laughter ripples through the tent.

Europeans? Dutchmen? Ah, Dutch whalers. Now I see. The man has been speaking Dutch to me. Do you trade with the Dutchmen? Has Mr Egede not forbidden it?

The man smiles and produces a knife. I study it. It is from Europe, a cheap sailor's knife, though probably of value to the natives. Then he finds a box and opens it. Inside are a number of sewing needles of various sizes.

I understand, I tell him. Money. But our king has now taken over the trade in your country. He does not wish for you to deal with the Dutchmen. The man considers me intently. I draw a sweeping gesture. Dutchmen no more, *kradlunat?*

The savage raises his eyebrows, whatever it may mean. He looks rather sceptical. I point at myself, then at him. *Nivernek*, I say. I put my hand out and he takes it. We shake hands at length.

Jørgen, I say, pointing at myself with my free hand.

Miteq.

Friend, I say.

Peqatik, says the man.

He will not release me. His handshake is excruciatingly firm. Eventually, I see no other option than to extricate myself from his grip.

///

I walk back to the colony along the shore, a rather perilous expedition, as it turns out. Treacherous rocks drop away to the seething, swelling sea whose foam-drenched tongues flick at me, fall back and assail me once more. I find safety on a beach of sand and pebbles, kelp strewn upon it like a woman's hair released from its ties. I wander along. Merchant. Yes, that is what I am. The Trader Kopper has no aptitude for it, with his sour horselike face and his moping about, complaining of all his ailments. When he returns home, or when it transpires that one of his imaginary illnesses is not imaginary at all, but actually does away with him, I shall take over the Trade. My mind busies itself with sums: the Greenlanders in the south are well supplied with blubber, but are in need of more reindeer skins. They pay one barrel of blubber for one skin. A regular Danish smock is valued at 5 marks . . . The natives will pay two skins for a smock . . . da-dum da-dum . . . two reindeer skins bring 16 marks when purchased in Bergen. But two barrels of blubber give 8 rigsdaler, sometimes more . . . that's, what, per barrel . . . about 27 marks, which is 4½ rigsdaler . . . da-dum . . . da-dum da-dum . . . there's that melody again now . . . *hear me, O Agnes, I say to thee now, be thou my sweetheart, this must thou avow* . . . I feel myself drenched by figures, a downpour of numbers, falling in columns all around me. If now I purchase reindeer skins for smocks, then after conversion I will be paying 2 rigsdaler, 8 shillings per skin . . . I then sell on the reindeer skins to the Greenlanders in the south and take a barrel of blubber per skin in payment, then ship the blubber to Bergen . . . that means I rake in, let me see . . . the figures shower down on me . . . a profit of 2 rigsdaler, 4 marks and 8 shillings, a tidy sum! *O yes, but of course, I gladly will so, to the deep of the sea with thee I'll go* . . . But then there is the sea passage and the uncertainty of that

... *he covered* ... How many ships go down? Probably no more than one in twenty, but still ... *he covered her mouth*, oh, go away, silly song ... that will have to be factored in ... which means, in total ... da-dum da-dum ... 264 shillings divided by 20, let me see ... yes, a loss of about 13 shillings per skin ... *he covered her mouth, that she could not speak, took her to the bed of the sea so deep*, oh, how annoying ... my brain creaks ... let's say I have 2,000 skins, that would make a dizzying sum! Fortunately, the shipping trade has become much safer these past years, and our captains are so much more competent. I shall trust in my good fortune and strike off the 13 shilling loss. A merchant has to be something of a gambler. Kopper has no conception of it. Therefore he will never amount to more than a simple grocer.

These reflections have returned me unwittingly to the colony. All of a sudden I find myself between the warehouse and the blubber house. I pause to collect myself. I realize I am smiling like a fool at Landorph who is telling me something.

Who is dead? I say.

The child.

What child?

The foundling.

Now dead again?

No, you imbecile. The child. The one that was alive and was taken in by Madame Egede.

Oh, that one, I say, confused. It didn't look much alive. So the Egedes have done in another one. *Hear me, O Agnes, I say to thee now* ...

Are you now deaf in both ears, Fleischer?

No, there's nothing wrong with my hearing. I hear as well with my left ear as you do with both of yours.

I said, it's Sise Petticoat.

What is? ... *thy children so fair await us with glee* ...

The child's mother. Sise Petticoat is the mother.

The child?

The foundling! Landorph yells. For crying out loud, man!

I come to my senses. Sise? I thought you said she was as abundant as a fully laden schooner?

She's been wearing a pillow.

Good lord. So she concealed the birth?

It seems so.

Then there will be proceedings against her?

Pors is against it. He says because the child was alive there's no reason to pursue the matter. What's your opinion, Fleischer? Do you think Pors is in a scrape? Landorph smiles shiftily.

But the child is dead, you say?

It is now, yes. It wasn't before, though. It died in between times.

What says the woman herself?

Very little. Refuses to say a word about it. They held the boy out to her, but she turned away.

The dead child?

No, the living one. The dead one while it was still alive.

I feel like I've been drinking. I shake my head in the hope that everything will fall into place. I can hardly sort out who's alive and who's dead, I say.

I know, it's all a bit of a muddle. But the child that was alive is now dead, that's the long and short of it.

I suppose the matter will be taken up by the colony council?

Yes, we're bringing it forward to tomorrow. I just wanted to hear your opinion, Fleischer.

But the Governor is against proceedings, you say? Perhaps he doesn't care to see a woman dangle from his gallows?

No, Landorph sighs. And he's not alone either.

///

The colony council convenes on the Thursday, the same day the dead child is laid to rest. I give evidence. I was certain it was dead, I say. It's so very strange. I mean, it's not the first time I've seen a corpse. That's as may be, Pors interjects, but what you discovered was not a corpse. No, I'm not contesting it, I reply. It is now, though. Indeed, though before it was not, and that's the crux here. The child was not dead, and therefore there has been no crime. Or at least no murder.

But why would Sise give up a living child? says Landorph. She is married, after all.

Derangement, says Kieding. I have spoken to her. She cannot recall the birth. She has become very melancholy.

I think I'll be deranged soon, I say.

Another madwoman, says Landorph. As if we hadn't enough with the jomfru. But what says her husband, Hartman?

He says nothing, says Pors.

He's not looking especially downhearted at the moment, says Landorph, fixing the Governor's gaze. In fact, I'd say he's looking rather chirpy.

Who knows what goes on inside these people's minds, says Pors. They are ravaged by drink and gambling.

I don't believe Sise and Johan are that way inclined, I say. They're decent folk. That's probably why they're still among the living.

I find it odd, says the Commandant. There is something fishy about this. He glances sideways at the Governor, though without having the nerve to confront him further.

The council decides, with the full backing of its members, not to begin proceedings against Sise, since the boy, who in the intervening period has perished, at the time of his discovery did not appear to have suffered injury, and because Sise, in the opinion of Kieding, cannot be considered to be of sound mind, for which reason it is deemed that she had not fully comprehended her action.

///

That same day something else happens: the body of a child is discovered in the warehouse. This time there is no doubt. I hurry down to see it with my own eyes. Signs of strangulation.

There you are, I say. I was right all along. I tour the colony to inform Pors, Landorph, Kopper, the Egedes, declaiming to whoever will listen: The child was dead. I was not mistaken. It was not alive! I thought I was going mad. But now everything has fallen into place.

The problem is that we now again have a dead child on our hands. Kieding examines Titia, though finds her still to be incontrovertibly pregnant, no pillow down her skirt. It must be one of the dead women who is mother to this second child. Or perhaps it is Sise. It is decided that no investigation will get to the bottom of the matter, and I, to be frank, am relieved. I am a fox, deaf in one ear, though possessing the most sensitive nose in all the colony. I think I have sniffed out an explanation of what has occurred. But I tell no one.

13

Wanderings

To-day those who had been away with the purpose of trade arrived home with the boat well laden with blubber. They had encountered a Dutch ship in the south where they were, which brought to them rather sorrowful news from Copenhagen, that in a very unfortunate conflagration the city had been for the most part reduced to ashes, which since, regrettably, has been confirmed to be true.

FROM HANS EGEDE'S JOURNAL, MARCH 1729

Late evening, sunshine, stillness. The Governor has sailed north on the pilot galliot together with a large number of the surviving crew in order to oversee the establishment of a new colony at a place called Nipisane. He has also taken one of the priests with him, Ole Lange, leaving Miltzov alone with Egede, of whom he is rather afraid, as well as with the two girls, about whom his feelings are mixed.

The weather has become mild, an unusually early spring, almost summer-like, and the days are longer now. The sun sets, the earth darkens, but the sky remains light, and just as darkness seems to take the upper hand and night is becoming night, light again pools in the sky and the sun appears once more. Carpets of anemones, dandelions, rosebay and orchids cover the ground, appearing out of nothing, almost from the bare rock, an insistent flourish of life, opening out and absorbing the sunlight, the pale-yellow grass becomes green and lush, and the sheep and goats, as well as the single cow which as yet has managed to avoid the cooking pots, stalk stiff-legged to the moor in order to graze. During the course of the winter, some fifty people, half the crew, have perished. The stillness of the colony is reminiscent of a churchyard.

All this he sees from his perch on a rock a short distance from the colony. He has wangled a bottle of aquavit from one of the Trade constables and sips at its contents. He must make sure to leave some for tomorrow, and the day after that. There is much peace of mind in such a bottle. And much warmth. Though the weather is not cold, he has wrapped himself in a sheepskin and wound a rug around his legs. These evenings are his survival here. Previously he never drank at all, nothing stronger than ale. But now he has become an inebriate. He is fully aware of it. A person can be a drunkard and still be a good priest. And a good person too. Probably it is impossible to be good without aquavit. Only women can manage such a feat.

He is preparing one of the Egede daughters for her confirmation and predictably, though much against his will, has become attached to her, if not to say chained. It is due to his weakness in general and with respect to Egede in particular, and also for the simple reason that she is there. For Kirstine Egede so much resembles her father that he cannot avoid but think of him whenever he is with her. She has the same agreeable, rather equine features, the Egede nose, a near phallic feature in the face of a young girl, the Egede mouth with its knowing smile, as if she has discovered something about you and finds amusement in it, the moist gleam of the Egede eyes, the big hands. Her cheerfulness is sinister, her melancholy sarcastic, and her jocularity has a tendency to become malicious and to descend merci-lessly on whoever happens to be closest to her, which for the time being is Henrik Miltzov. Her temperament is direct and confronta-tional, she never speaks ill of anyone behind their back, yet will readily insult the person who is standing in front of her. He excuses her on account of her harsh upbringing with poor weather, an unchanging diet and her father's frequent boxing of her ears, all of which has made her as dry and as salty as stockfish. Sometimes, however, a gleam comes over her, a door is pushed ajar and a narrow ribbon of light streams out, and then he will forget her caustic jibes, her cold-ness. This rather rickety infatuation has now continued for a month or so as he has been instructing her.

No doubt it is Egede's own doing. Schemingly, he has served her to him on a plate, wafting her in front of his nose like a piece of pork. He wishes a priest for a son-in-law. His grand design is to make Greenland a family business. He is coming to terms with the thought that he, Henrik Balthasar Miltzov, will take Kirstine Egede, with her puzzling, codlike smile and her cold fish-blood, to be his lawful wedded wife, then to beget a flock of gloomy Egedes gradually to spread along the coast. Fortunately she is not old enough yet. They can first be married in three years at the earliest. And a lot can happen in such a time, especially if one thinks about all that has happened in the year that has passed.

For the time being, then, he is in love with her, albeit somewhat bitterly and riddled with doubt. He wishes he could be in love with a girl who was less complicated, warmer, more sincere, more adoring, fleshier, more beautiful or simply plainer. Her younger sister, Petronelle, is likewise the spitting image of Egede, though milder and more playful than Kirstine, coy as a little girl, and flirtatious to boot; she follows them everywhere as if she were her sister's chaperone, and they must constantly endure her silly giggles and frivolous questions and comments. When are they getting married? How many children are they going to have? If you kiss her, Magister Miltzov, I shall tell my father. She is a pest. Her nose is in everything and her eyes never miss a trick. He could easily imagine falling in love with her. But she is far too young, only thirteen years old.

Madame Rasch, Gertrud, is the one he gets along best with in the family. He would be quite happy to have her as his mother-in-law, providing she lives that long. She is approaching her three score years, a kind wife forever seated with her handicraft. She says little, and when she does she speaks in a voice that is softly resonant, like a gentle echo among the fells of Lofoten. He is also able to speak with her about serious matters, about faith and the Mission, about Luther, of whom her husband is so fond. If the Egede family were a wind orchestra, she would be the oboe, Egede the trumpet, his son the French horn, and the girls would be two chattering shawms. And then of course there is the foster-son, Frederik Christian. What instrument would he be, I wonder? I find it hard to say. He seems not to fit in, though Egede is seldom seen without the native lad in his three-cornered hat traipsing along at his heel.

The Madame has taken in a number of native children. One could ask oneself, if one were so inclined, what kind of unsatisfied needs these children fulfil. Miltzov knows how much she is opposed to giving them up again once they have come into her home, but their native parents have discovered that by placing them in her care the children will soon be fattened up, whereafter they, the parents, will show up on her doorstep again to claim them back. Presumably she has brought down the infant death rate among the native population quite considerably. Miltzov often sits with her.

The Madame does not often go out, and when she does she moves with difficulty, with a marked sway in her gait on account of rheumatism in her hips. Her husband is fleet-footed and supple, he will rather run than walk, rather walk than stand still, and rather stand than sit. One might reasonably wonder if he ever lies down? In her case the opposite is true, and for that reason they seem such an odd couple.

Niels Egede, Miltzov's prospective brother-in-law, resembles his mother, though has also inherited the family curse: the nose. Miltzov is fond of him. He is somewhat evasive and cautious in the company of the Danes, yet free and lively with the natives. He speaks the language fluently, better than anyone in the family with the exception of his brother Poul, who is now in Denmark preparing for the priesthood.

Henrik lies in his bunk upstairs, nursing his daily hangover, when he hears the girls, or one of them – their voices can be hard to distinguish – calling for him up the stairs.

Magister! Are you to sleep all day?

Kirstine. He sighs, swings his feet out of bed and rises.

She is standing at the foot of the staircase looking up at him with a smile on her face. Holier than thou.

Have you slept badly, Magister? You look tired.

No, not at all, he mutters.

Put your boots on, we're going for a walk.

Yes, dearest.

He descends cautiously, step by step.

Where are we going?

Out in the fine weather, she says. Petronelle, are you coming?

They go up to the graves, a half-hundred piles of stone with higgledy-piggledy crosses. The names of the dead are etched into the wood along with the year of the person's birth, if known, and the year of their death, which is to say 1728 or 1729.

Does the Magister know the word for dead? Kirstine asks.

No, I can't remember.

Toqu. I've told you before. Remember it now. Isn't that what you priests tell us all the time: Remember death?

Prepare for death, more like it. But I suppose it's the same thing.

When are we meant to prepare for life? Petronelle asks. Why do priests always have to talk about death?

It's our job, to prepare people for the afterlife.

Do you think they're all rotten down there? Kirstine asks.

Miltzov swallows a suddenly ascending mouthful of acid reflux.

They're frozen stiff, says Petronelle. Preserved.

Black and blue, I imagine, says Kirstine. They turn that way after a while. Look, who's this? She bends down to read: Ane Antoniusdatter. I remember her. They called her Ane Woollen-sock.

She was a tart, says Petronelle, scratching herself hectically under her armpits.

They all were, Kirstine replies, seemingly catching her sister's itch, for she too begins to scratch under her arms.

Do you think she is in heaven or hell, Henrik?

I don't know.

Can tarts go to heaven?

Certainly. Maria Magdalene is believed to have been one. She was the first to whom Jesus appeared after his death. She is even described as the disciple Jesus loved.

This gives them something to think about. They sit and contemplate, scratching and twitching, obviously pestered by lice. He himself barely notices them, most likely a blessing of the aquavit. His evening leisure hour on the rocks strikes him to be a religious image, tinted by the radiance of the night sky reflected in his schnapps bottle.

Did Jesus really love a tart? Kirstine asks.

Yes, after she changed her ways. Jesus feels particular tenderness for sinners who have repented and found the one true way.

I don't think he loved Ane Woollen-sock. She was dreadful. She lay with a great many men and took money for it.

Shall we go somewhere else? he says.

Why do we actually have to die, Magister? Petronelle asks. What's the point if we're going to be resurrected anyway, whether we're sent to heaven or hell?

Because the Lord wishes to test us, he says. We must prove to him that we are worthy of his salvation.

But doesn't God know that already? I thought he knew everything.

He has given us a choice. The same choice he gave to the first two people on Earth.

That didn't work out too well, did it? says Kirstine. Why do you think Eve ate the forbidden fruit?

Because she could not resist the serpent.

Why didn't God kill the serpent?

He punished it. But the serpent, and evil, is part of life, unfortunately. On the judgement day he will crush the serpent's skull under his heel.

What is your serpent, Magister? asks Petronelle, who is even more talkative than usual today.

Oh, he says, embarrassed. There's always something, I suppose.

Aquavit, Petronelle says. I've seen you drunk lots of times.

Do shut up, says Kirstine.

No, I don't drink any more, he lies. It is true that I suffered a weakness last winter. But now I partake for medicinal purposes only. Apart from that I drink only ale.

Fibber, says Kirstine with a smile.

Ale can make a person drunk too, says Petronelle. Especially the strong ale the baker brews.

What splendid weather today, he says, and turns his face to the sun.

I still don't understand why we have to die, Kirstine continues solemnly. Her finger moves absently over Ane Woollen-sock's cross. Several times her arms twitch as if in spasm, and her hand darts inside her blouse. He hears her nails as they scratch at her skin. Or why we are even alive, for that matter, she adds. Why must we be dragged through such suffering and degradation? Do you know what all these crosses ought to say, Magister?

No, what?

They should say, 'Why?'

A good question, says Miltzov. He feels more affinity with Kirstine when she is in sombre mood, as clearly she is today, much more so than when she is mean and scornful. That is what we might call the 'bone of contention'. But come, let us walk a while. The girls rise from the graveside at which they have knelt and follow him over the rocks in a southerly direction across the peninsula. He continues: The serpent of course is Satan, you know that, I'm sure? And Satan was a son of God.

Some son, says Petronelle. If my father had been his father, he would have thrashed the daylights out of him and then we wouldn't have had such a pickle of a life.

Put a sock in it, says Kirstine. Let the Magister speak.

Satan of course knew that God is almighty, that He is all-knowing and governs everything, that not a leaf falls to the ground without His will. But what he did was to doubt, not the almighty nature of God, but rather His right to be so. Do you see the distinction?

The girls make affirmative noises.

So what happened was that they squabbled. God and one of his sons, or cherubs, Lucifer as some call him. And Lucifer scorned his father and said that if man were given free will he would no longer worship Him. So God said to him, very well, then test him, I shall give you five thousand years. And thus Lucifer descended to Earth and with him several more of God's sons, whom we refer to as fallen angels. Now it is they who rule our world. But on Judgement Day a final battle will be fought between God and his heavenly hosts, led by Jesus, and the rebels, Lucifer's proselytes.

So we're no more than pawns in a family quarrel, says Kirstine. It is as if we are trapped in a game.

But you are more than a mere pawn, he replies. You are blessed with your own free will. You may decide for yourself which path to take. Therein lies God's kindness and love.

I see, she says. My father would probably disagree with you on that. He hates the idea of man's free will. Luther did too. Let us say I have a knife, here in my hand. And now I say, Magister Miltzov I give you a choice: Shall I cut your throat or shall I not?

Yes, hm, he says. I'm not sure if your analogy holds. In this case it is you, with the knife in your hand, whose will is free. Will you cut my throat or will you not?

That's just it, she says. Even if I wanted to, I would never cut your throat. The very idea would be out of the question.

Thank you, says Miltzov, I'm glad to hear it.

Abruptly, Petronelle begins to run. First one to the top! she shouts.

Kirstine sets off after her at a gallop. He sees their flowing skirts zigzag over the rocks. Butterflies, he thinks to himself. Or rather moths. No, mountain goats. He catches up with them and wipes the sweat from his brow, seating himself on a rock.

How old is the Magister? Petronelle enquires.

Thirty-one.

That old?

Well, none of us is getting younger.

You're twice as old as Kirstine. Aren't you ashamed, Magister?

Yes, I am.

A view of the fjord, the skerries. Twittering birds and the cries of gulls. Blankets of tiny flowers among the rocks, quivering in the faint breeze. The colony is out of sight.

I have promised your father to go through the Augsburg Confession with you. We might as well do so now.

They groan. Oh, not the Augsburg Confession. It's so boring!

Article Eight, he says mercilessly. Am I to tell your father that you refuse to learn it?

They slump in resignation. Their fishlike eyes swim in their sockets. They are seated close together on the flat rock, hands together in a confusion of interlaced fingers. Their thin plaits hang down over their lowered backs. He feels sorry for them.

The sooner we get started, the sooner we'll be finished. Have you done your homework, Kirstine? 'What the Church is.'

'Although the Christian church, properly speaking, is nothing else than the assembly of all believers and saints . . .'

She rattles off the entire article, a monotonous landslide of words. He is always astonished at how quick they are to learn, beneath their dark and sulky exteriors. Kirstine sits broodily, her upper body rocking.

Is there something the matter with you? he asks with concern.

Some pains. It's nothing.

It's her time of the month, says Petronelle with obvious pride. Mine too. It's not that bad. The worst thing is the lice get so blood-thirsty.

He senses his lips retract in disgust. He wishes to get to his feet and leave them, but does not wish to make them feel rejected, nor even that they should think he knows what they are talking about. And so he remains there seated on the rock. Kirstine curls up, holding her head in her hands and lifting her shoulders. Petronelle lays her cheek against her sister's back and puts her arms around her. She whispers something he doesn't catch. He realizes she is crying. And now he is assailed by a wave of sympathy for his unlovely fiancée.

Is it the Augsburg Confession that has upset you? he asks.

Petronelle shakes her head angrily.

Is it the pains?

No.

It's the pains as well, says Kirstine, her voice thick with sobs. It's everything. I hate him, I hate him.

Who? he says stupidly. Satan?

Oh, shut up, you twit! Petronelle bursts out, her enraged eyes glaring at him from her horselike face.

Her aggression abates. Kirstine lies now with her head in her sister's lap, Petronelle gently stroking her hair. After some moments she sits up.

///

Now they play hide and seek. The girls have concealed themselves somewhere among the rocks and he is supposed to find them. He wanders about, calling their names, hears their girlish whispers, their whinnying and snorting, but cannot for the life of him discover where they are coming from. He stands below on the moor which unfolds around him like a vast light-filled void. Kirstine? Petronelle?

At last he finds them. They have hidden beneath an overhang of rock. The first thing he sees is a brown boot. He creeps up close, then leaps forward with a roar. Found you! They stare at him with expressionless faces, and he feels like a clown no one thinks funny.

Kirstine wants you to kiss her, says Petronelle.

He doesn't know what to say. Certainly, he feels no desire to kiss her, a menstruating woman. It cannot be healthy, surely?

She wants to know what it's like, says Petronelle. She smiles, albeit, he finds, rather unpleasantly.

I see, he says, and clears his throat. I think perhaps it would be inappropriate.

If you want her, you must kiss her. Otherwise you shall have to find someone else.

He flaps his arms theatrically in a gesture of resignation. Then you give me no choice.

Come in here. The man must come to the woman.

He crouches down and crawls on all fours into their den. Kirstine looks at him strangely. Her upper lip is retracted, making visible her teeth. It is a childlike smile, though with a lot of other things in it too, astonishment, revulsion, curiosity. He shuffles further inside and sits up against the crumbling rock. He feels her menstrual breath in his face. Now I shall kiss you, he warns, then leans forward and presses his mouth against hers. She screams, a shudder runs through her, and she stares at him with wide eyes.

Was it that bad? he says.

No, it wasn't bad. It gave me a fright, that's all.

I want a kiss too, says Petronelle. May I?

Kiss him, kiss him! Kirstine says.

He kisses her as one would kiss a child.

Now you must choose, says Petronelle, scratching her scalp and armpits like a person possessed.

Choose?

You've tried us both, now which of us do you want?

I want you both, of course, he says. Why should I make do with one when I can have you both?

///

Later that day he speaks with Egede. Egede wishes to walk too. Anyone would think it were a family of peripatetics he is to marry into. It will be a marriage requiring solid walking boots. The priest strides briskly, and Miltzov has difficulty keeping up. On a spit of land Egede at last pauses, puts his telescope to his eye and sweeps the horizon in search of sails.

Nothing yet, he says, collapses the instrument and returns it to his pocket.

There was a ship a few weeks ago, with timber and some mail for the colony. Thus they learned of the great conflagration that has lain much of Copenhagen in ruins. Strange, he thinks, to live so far away from everything that one must hear of events such a long time after they have occurred. Now Copenhagen has in a way burned twice in a space of months.

Is she making progress? Egede enquires.

Who? he asks, confused.

Kirstine.

Ah, Kirstine, yes. Yes she is, a good deal in fact. I think she knows the entire Confession by heart.

Splendid. The Augsburg Confession is the very foundation of our faith, Magister. It is our bulwark against papism and other false doctrines. If a person takes care to learn it, I cannot see how there might be any way back.

Indeed, he replies, hearing how false he sounds, and Egede turns his head to look at him.

She is a good girl, Egede says.

Yes, she is. Very good.

She will be a pillar to her husband, especially if he is a priest.

Indeed. She could be a priest herself, she has the aptitude.

Gertrud has been a stalwart to me. I don't know what I would have done without her.

We are all very fond of Madame Gertrud.

Sometimes, however, she is rather too clever for her own good. It is not the place of women to lecture their men. One must be alert.

You must think on. They will assume control. Egede fixes him in his gaze.

Indeed, he says tamely.

You know what Luther says, I take it? She is much filth and little wisdom. That's why her arse is broad and her shoulders narrow. In the man's case the opposite holds.

I shall make a note of it, Mr Egede.

Luther says too that what goes in through a woman's ear comes out again through her mouth. Therefore a secret is to be entrusted only to a dead woman, ha ha!

Miltzov says nothing.

She is not getting too clever in her written work, our little Kirstine?

No, we stick to learning by heart.

She takes after her mother. Thinks she knows better. One must nip it in the bud, make sure they know their place.

Indeed.

And punish them when necessary.

I see.

If you are to marry her, you must listen to what I say.

I'm listening.

Perhaps you would rather have Petronelle?

No, not at all.

No, she is very young yet. You probably can't wait that long. A priest is a man too, of sorts. He erupts with laughter.

They have come to the shore. Egede places a hand on his shoulder. Miltzov immediately loses his footing on the slippery rocks, and if it were not for Egede he would have fallen. The man blabbers on in his clipped north-Norwegian dialect. Miltzov would like to talk to him about Titia and Frederik Christian, about the plans to have them marry. No doubt it will be he, Miltzov, who will join them, and first publish the banns for them, but he will not care to do so without Egede's blessing. But it is as if somehow Egede senses that he wishes to approach some precarious matter and therefore continues to follow his own trains of thought.

Had it been up to my wife she would have become a procurator. Her father was the lensmand at Kvæfjord. He had his own approach to matters and allowed her and her sisters to be instructed by the deacon. It gave them ideas.

Urgh! Miltzov groans, not in response to what Egede is saying, but because he has inadvertently put his foot in the sea, soaking his boot and sock with icy water.

Exactly, says Egede.

But surely some measure of wisdom is not undesirable? Miltzov ventures.

That's what I thought too, when I was young and newly wed. I thought she was the cleverest person I'd met. But it becomes rampant, bookish knowledge makes them arrogant and soon they wish to debate, and will argue until the Devil himself pisses his breeches. Perhaps I am old-fashioned. You, however, are young, Magister Miltzov. You must go your own way, and we old fuddy-duddies step back and stand with hat in hand.

They stand on the rocks above the wide natural harbour on the eastern side of the peninsula. The ship that has lain there all winter is gone, sailed north with Pors and his men. It is a dark and gloomy place which for some reason always seems to lie in shadow, the vegetation spare, a meagre scattering of white flowers shivering in the wind.

A good harbour could be made here, Egede muses. The water is of sufficient depth, and there is little current to speak of. And in winter the only ice here stays innermost at the shore.

The colony will grow in time, says Miltzov. There will be need of a harbour.

Do you think? Egede sounds sceptical. The question is whether the Lord wishes it.

I am certain He does, Mr Egede.

Not much would suggest He applauds our efforts thus far. I came here with such grand designs. I saw a fine and enterprising mission, I saw a trading station and ships laden with barrels in their thousands, full of train oil. I saw a church, and happy Christian folk. I saw a prosperous town rise up out of the rock. But now? He shakes his head with a sigh.

All these things will happen, says Miltzov. But such matters require time and patience.

Yes, perhaps. A long time indeed, if it is to happen at all. I have seen the future, Mr Miltzov. And I was not a part of it.

///

Tuttut. Repeat after me, Magister.

Tut tut?

No, no, no, *Tuttut!*

Tutut.

Better, but not good. We'll come back to it later. Now: *aappaluttut.* Isn't that the name of that shaman?

Yes, that's what he calls himself. Paapa's native father. Say the word.

It's far too long, I can't.

Say *aa.*

Aa.

Paa.

Pa.

No, *pa-a.*

Pa-ha.

Hopeless. *Paa!*

Paaa, paaa, paaa.

That's better. And now the last bit: *luttut.*

Lut-tut.

She slaps him on the cheek, not hard, but hard enough.

Ow!

Luttut. Say it.

Luttut.

You see, you can if you must.

But it's so difficult, Kirstine. Can't we take a break?

No, it's a trade-off. If I'm to learn the Augsburg Confession then you can learn my rhyme.

I don't even know what it means.

We'll get to that, she says with a playful smile. Now: *nuluttut.*

Nulu-tut.

She slaps him again, this time rather harder. *Nuluttut.*

Yes! *Oqaluttut.* Go on!

He has taken her hands in his. Let me say it without you boxing my ear. What was it again?

Oqaluttut.

Okralu-tut. Dear me.

Tuttut aappaluttut nulutut oqaluttut, she says, the words rattling off her tongue.

It sounds funny, he says. Like a poem. But what does it mean?

I won't tell you until you've learnt it by heart.

Half an hour later he has managed to string the sounds together after a fashion: *Tu-tut apalu-tut nulu-tut okralu-tut.*

Hm, she says. I'm not satisfied with you, Magister. I ought to give you a good spanking. But I shall let you off this once.

So what does it mean then?

It means, 'The red reindeer talk through their arse'.

Ha ha ha!

///

Oddly, the sky becomes paler in the evenings as the earth darkens. There is a separation of earth and sky for a few short hours. He sits on a rock, philosophizing drunkenly upon life in heaven. What is it like? He does not believe in the idea of angels and harps, though he does consider that the heavenly existence ought to involve music of some kind. He has a good singing voice, one of the few among his attributes of which he is proud. He hopes it will stand him in good stead in the afterlife. He could join a choir, stand with a candle in his hand, eyes turned to the heavens, and simply sing his way through eternity. His heaven is also bright and pleasant in temperature, an endless summer's day, not too hot and not too cold, and no wind to make one's head reel. But what of that other place? I have no wish to descend to it. Besides, I am not that bad, surely. Yet every time I drink myself senseless I am edging closer to a place in hell. The Egede girls are well on their way there too, the way they carry on. If only Egede knew. He would gladly kick them downstairs himself, if only he knew them well enough. He imagines the punishment: to wander upon an endless moor with the two girls chattering ceaselessly at his heel. Not being able to get away from them. Hell. I have no wish to go there. I have promised myself. But then I must soon stop drinking. He lifts the bottle and slurps a couple of mouthfuls. I must become a good priest, a good shepherd for the Christian flock here, and a good missionary for the savages. If only I could convert one or two, save a couple of souls, surely then there would be a place for me in heaven and I would escape that other place. But Egede stands in the way of it. The greatest hindrance to the conversion of the natives is the Pastor himself. Now the bottle is empty, and he is sated. Tomorrow will be hard. He gets to his feet and staggers home to the colony.

///

Kiss me, she whispers.

Oh, Kirstine, what is it with all this kissing? I feel it to be inappropriate. We're not married yet, not even betrothed.

Don't you want to marry me then?

I feel myself unworthy of you. This is what he has decided to say after pondering the matter at length. It sounds better, he thinks, than telling her she is repulsive and that he feels only loathing for her.

Let me be the judge of that.

Their exchange is whispered. She has come upstairs with a tray for him of bread and tea. She sits on the edge of the bed.

I'm not feeling well, he says.

I'll go, she tells him. But you must kiss me first.

Your mother will hear us.

No, she won't. A kiss makes no noise. Don't you like kissing me?

Of course I do. But here, directly above your mother's head?

Life is short, she says. All of a sudden we are dead. If I die without you having kissed me, I shall come back and haunt you.

But I've kissed you lots of times.

And now you're going to kiss me again. If you don't, I'll let Thomas Tode instead.

Tode? That desecrator of corpses? You're welcome, is all I can say.

He has fondled my breasts. I allowed him to do it. Horny as a stallion he was. She smooths her hands over her chest.

You shouldn't be doing such things, he says. It displeases me to hear you tell of it.

Tode wants to have me. He told me so.

Tell that to your father, he replies with sarcasm.

Perhaps you could challenge him to a duel?

I'm no good with a sword. I think I shall wait until I'm dead for Tode to cut me up.

So kiss me then, for goodness' sake. I won't bite.

He leans forward to give her a peck on the cheek, but is assailed by nausea.

She looks at him. What's the matter with you. Is it because I'm ugly?

Oh, Kirstine. He feels sorry for her all of a sudden. You're not at all ugly.

I know I'm not pretty. I can tell by looking at Petronelle. She's ugly too, and she looks like me.

You are sweet and lovely girls, both of you. Your future husbands will be fortunate indeed.

But I want you, Magister. Can't you understand? She picks up the tea cup and lifts it to his mouth. He sips dutifully, and in the same instant the contents of his stomach rise up in his mouth. He manages just in time to drape himself over the edge of the bed and vomit on the floor. Kirstine picks up her feet and sits now in the bed beside him.

Is it the alcohol sickness, Magister?

He hopes now that she in the least will have lost the desire for him to kiss her. But she has not, and will not yield until he has done so. Eventually, however, she gives up and goes downstairs. He hears her speak to her mother: The Magister is ill, he's puked up on the floor.

///

He drinks again. The aquavit may indeed send him to hell, but it may also save him from the clutches of the Egede girl. Now he drinks openly, staggering about the colony and showing himself up in a variety of ways. Oddly, he becomes more popular for it among the crew. They pause to speak to him and ask his advice on personal matters, a sweetheart, a conflict among the men, a matter of faith, and he stands there with his wig askew, slurring his senseless replies. Egede issues a reprimand, not unkindly, more in a fatherly way, though without boxing his ears. He promises to improve himself, and returns to the drink. One morning he wakes up outside with Jens Smith shaking him. He staggers to his feet and looks around him in a daze. I cannot continue like this, he tells himself. He coughs and feels a shiver run through him. Now I am properly sick.

And indeed he is. He is compelled to stay in bed for several days with a fever, trembling, and begging for aquavit. Kirstine nurses him, but will give him nothing but water and bread soaked in sweetened tea.

A week later he is up and about again. He eats porridge with the Egedes, recovered, albeit still rather weak. Kirstine attends to him, spoons more porridge into his bowl, sprinkles the sugar on, her hand touching him lightly every time she goes past. He has never seen her so mild and gentle before. He wonders if he should start drinking again, properly this time, but cannot endure the thought of imbibing even a drop of aquavit ever again.

///

A ship comes early. New people arrive. They bring with them fresh supplies, mail, news from home. For a couple of weeks, Denmark–Norway seems that much closer. And then the ship departs again. Pors and his men are still in the north. There is a stillness. There is light.

14

A Virgin Birth

Another of the soldiers died to-day. The others had been restored to some tolerable degree of health. Since their treatment with the splendid scurvy grass, we had now, God be praised! no more than four patients confined to bed.

From Hans Egede's journal, April 1729

Spring, almost summer, buzzing flies, the mildest of breezes, stillness. Oh, such a blessed stillness. The Governor remains in the north, and Titia is on her own with Skård, which is the same as being on her own, for although Skård casts a shadow, it is a shadow that is increasingly lonely. Most of the time he sits at the window, the dusty sun falling on his ashen face.

Or rather, she is not entirely on her own, for there is something that flaps and flutters inside her, something which feels trapped and wants out. The jomfru Titius is a pregnant nun who has come adrift, and soon she must give birth to a new shadow who shall wander among men for a number of years.

And then there is Madame Egede, who comes to see her daily. Kieding comes too. He presses her stomach with cold and trembling fingers, places his ear to her and listens, and then with a melancholy smile says: a delightful sound, little Titia.

What can you hear?

I hear two hearts beating, one quickly, the other slowly. Everything is fine.

He feels inside her too, with his fingers, as she lies there with her legs apart, staring at the sodden army of lice in the band of perspiration that trims his wig.

Half an inch, he says softly. The child has positioned itself well, the head points downwards, thank goodness. Let us hope all goes well. He sits down on the edge of the bed. Are you in good spirit, my friend?

I'm fine.

Does it kick much?

Night and day. It keeps me awake in the night. I don't mind, though.

And you will still not say who made you pregnant?

I don't know.

Don't know who did it, or don't know if you'll say?

I don't know.

But now you are betrothed, at least, says Kieding with a sigh. And your general state of health seems to have improved. Still no attacks?

No, it's been a while now.

Good. He smiles and takes her hand. I will not praise myself, but I do believe the treatment I gave you in the winter has been beneficial, in terms of your convulsions and your state of mind.

Maybe.

A physician can be wrong, certainly. And indeed, I've lost a good number of folk over the winter. The blame is mine alone. But if one may save just a single human being from the clutches of death, then one may justifiably feel satisfied.

He is interrupted by Madame Rasch entering the room. You must not torment the girl any more today, Master Kieding. She puts a bowl of porridge in front of her. Eat now, my child.

Kieding withdraws. Skård's shadow shuffles by in his slippers, the smoke from his pipe spiralling in the air in his wake, but Skård himself is not there, or hardly so. The Madame studies him thoughtfully.

That man is becoming stranger all the time, she says. He doesn't bother you, does he?

Skård would never hurt a soul, says Titia. He scarcely exists.

He's not the child's father, is he?

I don't know.

Well, it is a blessed time, regardless of circumstances. The Madame sighs and smiles. I remember what it was like with my own two. One feels like a princess. But once the child is out, it becomes a different matter altogether.

I know.

Have you looked after small children before?

No, I grew up in a nunnery. There weren't any children, only nuns.

We shall all be lending a hand. And your breasts are full, so I think the milk will run freely enough. If not, we can always find a wet-nurse for you.

I don't want it to have milk from a whore. I don't want that.

Why not, my child?

They're not like us, are they? Their milk is sour.

They are human beings just like us, the Madame says reprovingly. There is no difference. Only on the outside might it seem so.

I'll feed it myself.

Yes, of course, but we must take one day at a time. First you must have the child, then we shall deal with any problems as and when they arise.

Can't the Madame just mind her own business? says Titia.

I'm only trying to help, Gertrud replies offendedly.

The children you take in all end up dying.

What a thing to say! Some have died, certainly, but most do very well indeed, thank you very much.

I don't want God-botherers in here. You're all accursed.

Madame Egede pales. Slowly she gets to her feet. You malicious little beast, she says quietly, and then leaves.

Skård! Titia calls out. Skård! Come and lie down with me.

And Skård, the old man, comes shuffling to lie down beside her, sinking into the mattress and simply lying there without a word, and without wish to interfere with her in her highly pregnant state. Last year he came to her when she lay in her stuporous state following an attack, as did several of the men, Fleischer, Landorph, Kopper, even one of the priests, whoever it might have been, but once her belly began to swell they made themselves scarce. Now she lies here and is untouchable. And Skård lies at her side. One can be with him without having to have anything to do with him. All people should be like that.

///

Gertrud feels physically unwell after her visit with Titia. She enters the parlour unsteadily and flops down on a chair. It takes some time for her to settle. She begins at the shock of what the spiteful young girl said to her, then travels backwards through anger, indignation, despair, more indignation, and sorrow, eventually ending up back at the feeling with which she embraces the rest of the world: sympathy. I must not take it personally, she tells herself. Her words were not directed at me, at us, but at something inside herself. Things are not easy for her. She is ill, possessed even. She has need of someone to talk to, someone who will guide her. Should I send Hans? No, no good would come of it. They would simply argue. Miltzov, then? He is mild and gentle, certainly, if rather yielding, and he too has his problems. She cannot for the life of her under-stand why Hans should wish so strongly to have him for a son-in-law. But he is a priest, and the priest in the man is greater than the man himself. She calls for him.

Magister Miltzov?

He comes down the stairs with heavy, uncertain steps. He is wearing neither cassock nor wig and is instead shabbily dressed in work breeches and a coat that is too short for him. His hair hangs down his neck, a limp and greasy pigtail. He smiles sheepishly.

Madame Egede?

There is something I wish to speak to you about, she says.

///

He sits down and glances smilingly at the native children who are playing quietly in a corner. He finds it astonishing how well behaved they are. The Egede girls are there too, sitting on the floor with the children. They take no notice of him. Kirstine reads out loud from a book. One of the children lies with its head in her lap, sleeping. At the table, Egede's foster-son, Frederik Christian, sits hunched over a book.

Mother Gertrud has quite the little children's home here, he says. It is a conversation they have had many times before.

She removes her bonnet and smooths a hand over her flat grey hair, raking it with her yellow fingernails. Yes, there is a great need for care and solicitude. There will be others soon.

Indeed. I suppose it never stops.

I don't know what will become of them when I am no longer here. Are they all orphans?

No, most have families now. But they need fattening. The youngest are given milk by native wet-nurses whom we feed for their trouble. After a while they are generally claimed again.

And Mr Egede will not christen them, I imagine?

No, for what would happen to such Christian souls when returned to their heathen families? He would never allow it.

You are an angel, he says with conviction.

Not yet, she says, and smiles.

I'm sorry. I didn't mean it like that.

I wished to speak to you about the poor jomfru, Magister.

He looks at the flies which are buzzing in the window. Is she not due soon? he enquires cautiously.

It can be any time now. And who knows how it will proceed, as small and frail as she is.

A good thing we have the Master Kieding.

Yes, but that wasn't what I wished to speak with you about. I am concerned for her soul, Magister. Let me be frank with you. If she does not survive the birth, she will be lost. I have no idea when she last received the Communion. As you know, my husband, Hans, wishes nothing to do with her. Have you or Lange received her?

No, he says. At least, she has not come to me. I think she is dangling in suspense, as it were. It would not surprise me if she had no knowledge of the Communion.

Then speak to her, Henrik. You know the girl. Go and see her. She's unhappy, and I think afraid too, even if she does try to conceal it with her bad language and poisonous utterances. She sent me packing just before. I think she is afraid of us, the family here. It's my husband's fault, I shouldn't wonder. I can't bear to think of her on her own in there, contending against the most demented thoughts and ideas. Read to her, Henrik, read from the Gospels, or the psalms of David. Say the Lord's Prayer with her.

He looks down at the girls, who are pretending not to be all ears, and he does what he can to make his voice sound normal. I will visit her, indeed.

Crossing to the governor's residence a short time later, he is in the full vestments, cassock, ruff, wig. A priest must look like a priest, not a seaman on a drinking spree.

Who are you? says Titia when she comes to the door.

He feels a tremendous relief. She does not recognize me.

You know who I am, surely, Titia?

She never seems to be looking at a person directly, but at something beyond them, on account of her squint. It gives him a creepy feeling that someone is standing at his shoulder.

It'll be the witch downstairs who sent you?

Witch? The jomfru is not mad today, only mean, he thinks to himself. He would prefer to turn and leave, but finds himself asking if he might come in? Or we can speak here in the doorway, if you prefer?

She moves aside and he steps past her into the house. He glances around the parlour. He was drunk here many times this last winter. This is where he learned to drink. Where he became the person he is now. A priest in need of guidance. Titia stands in the middle of the room, heavy and pear-shaped, scowling.

Would you allow me to pray for you, Jomfru Titia? he asks, rather more to the point than he had anticipated.

I know more prayers than you, priest.

Indeed, though perhaps of a different kind, even if they may be quite as good, for it is the heart that matters. But praying together is a very special thing, to come together, erm, to unite in prayer. He could have bitten off his tongue.

The priest can pray all he likes.

Relief. Nothing bad is going to happen, he tells himself.

Shall we not sit down together?

I know what he's here for, and it's not for prayer.

Oh no, he thinks. Here it comes. What for then, little Titia? he croaks.

He wants to take my child.

Oh. He stiffens. Then laughs. Why would you think such a thing?

The witch sent you. She collects children, all sorts. That other one, the one they found down in the warehouse, died on her. Now she's looking for a replacement.

He must concede, if he is to be quite honest, that she may well be right. He has never thought of it before, but now that he does he finds it rather probable. Madame Egede lives and breathes for her foster-children. And there is no doubting that Titia's child would fare much better with her than with its mother.

She would never think such a thing!

Well, she won't be getting it either, so you might as well tell her so she can get it out of her head. I'd rather strangle the child at birth than give it up to that witch.

Mind what you say, he warns. You know what happens to child-murderers?

You can't send me to the gallows. I'm protected.

By Pors, you mean? Not even Pors would be able to help you in that situation.

No, not by him. By the other one.

Who would that be?

I mustn't say.

You're making this up, Titia.

He's here now.

Skård, you mean?

No, another one. The one they call Red.

The shaman. Have you now taken up with him?

He looks after me. He's to have the child.

But he is a heathen, Titia.

No, he's a Christian. It's just the priest who won't baptize him.

That's as may be. But why would you wish to give your child to a native you barely know?

It's his child.

How on earth did that happen?

How do you think? Her venomous smirk makes him squirm.

What I mean is when, where? I think you're making things up again. Much of what you think has taken place is, I'm sure, figments

of the imagination come to you during your fits. He instructs himself
to keep going along these lines. To convince her that she cannot rely
on her own thoughts, even if it will send him directly to the Inferno.

You can think what you want, she says. I know what happened. I
may be mad, but I'm not stupid. And you and the witch aren't getting
my child.

No one wants to take your child, Titia, I promise you. Look at me,
I give you my word. Besides, you're getting married, aren't you? To
Frederik Christian?

The witch does as she pleases. You've no say over her.

He shakes his head. Yes, mad she is indeed.

Will you not pray with me?

If you insist. But I've got my own prayers.

Sit down here with me. He pulls up a chair. I shall sit down here
facing you, like this. Fold your hands together, as I fold mine. He
can hear how screamingly false he sounds. Do you know the Lord's
Prayer?

Of course I do.

Then let us pray. Our Father, who art in heaven . . .

Pater noster qui es in caelis . . . She sniggers impishly.

Very good, he says. Latin is quite all right. God knows Latin too.
Hallowed by thy name . . .

Sanctificetur nomen tuum . . .

Thy kingdom come . . .

Adveniat regnum tuum . . .

Thy will be done . . .

Fiat voluntas tua . . .

On earth as it is in heaven . . .

Sicut in caelo et in terra . . .

Give us this day our daily bread . . .

Panem nostrum quotidianum da nobis hodie . . .

And forgive us our trespasses . . .

Et dimitte nobis debita nostra . . .

As we forgive those who trespass against us . . .

Sicut et nos dimittimus debitoribus nostris . . .

And lead us not into temptation . . .

Et ne nos inducas in tentationem . . .

But deliver us from evil . . .

Libera nos a malo, ave Maria, gratia plena, dominus tecum, benedicta tu in mulieribus . . .

She babbles away, and he must stop her with an abrupt: Amen! He hastens through the Communion, then springs to his feet.

He staggers from the residence with Latin prayer echoing in his ears. Sacrilege, he thinks to himself. Sacrilege! A papist prayer, and I gave her the benediction, I placed the wafer in her mouth, laid my hand on her head and blessed her. I am a liar, a blasphemer, a drunk, a fornicator, the most wretched person I know. And he can confess to no one, for Egede would certainly beat the daylights out of him if he were to hear only half of what he had to confess, and Lange, who would surely be more understanding, is in the north all summer. I am going to hell with the jomfru Titia, he tells himself.

The Egede girls look up as he enters. Madame Gertrud rises and steps forward towards him before he can ascend the stairs.

How did it go, Magister?

We prayed together.

She scrutinizes him. Is there something the matter, Henrik?

I'm tired. I think I'm catching a cold.

I shall send Kirstine up with some tea.

No. For God's sake. Let me be in peace!

At last he is on his own in his chamber. There is a half bottle under the mattress. He twists off the cork and gulps it down in one. *Libera me a malo*, he says to himself. He goes out like a lamp.

///

In the night he is awakened by noise and tumult. Loud voices speaking all at once. Someone runs over the floor, a door slams, a woman wails, porcelain clatters, and moreover a wind seems to have picked up outside. He gets out of bed and is about to put his clothes, then realizes he is still in his cassock.

Downstairs in the Egede family parlour, Niels and the young children are sleeping peacefully, moreover a native woman and Frederik Christian on the bench. The door of the bed chamber is open. He sees Egede lying on his back with his hands folded on his abdomen. He sleeps like a corpse, his nose poking into the air. The Madame and the girls are nowhere to be seen.

He guesses the time to be around three. The sun is behind the Northland plain, but the jagged ridge of the Saddle Fell glows in the low rays of morning. The wind blows, a warm foehn wind, without a cloud in the sky, a phenomenon, like hail and rainbows, which has always frightened him, for he senses in it the presence of God. From the tents in the bay, smoke curls upwards and his nostrils detect the smell of burning blubber and boiled meat. The natives have an easy life, he thinks.

Kirstine opens the door. Her cheeks are flaming. So there you are, she says.

Is it the birth?

Yes, it's underway now. We'll need a priest, I shouldn't wonder.

They have pulled the bed away from the wall and stand gathered around it. Gertrud, Petronelle, Kieding, an officer's wife and a pair of native women. From the ceiling hang several smoking oil lamps, and at least twenty candles have been lit. The room is boiling hot and smells of raw flesh.

The Madame sees him enter. A woman is giving birth here, she says.

So I see. He cranes his neck and peers among the figures which are hunched over the bed. A pale and naked body, arms and legs stretched out, held down by multiple hands, almost as if they were tearing her apart. Is there anything I can do?

We could use some help. Gertrud's face and the front of her dress are splashed with blood. She is radiant. The little Titia is as strong as a woodsman and is all but tearing our hair out. Not to mention her biting. And her waters have not yet even gone.

Kieding, who seems to have crawled halfway up the bed, says: If you wouldn't mind holding her arms, Magister, it would be of much assistance. But mind she doesn't scratch your eyes out or bite off your nose.

He sits down on a stool behind the bedhead and grips Titia's wrists tightly. She is a frightened animal, her mouth is wide open and she snaps at the women's hands in rage. He pulls her wrists towards him, drawing her arms up over her head.

Excellent, says Kieding. Just keep her like that so that we may work.

The officer's wife comes with a glass of aquavit. Titia drinks gratefully. Only then she screams, a vaporous cloud of schnapps sprays from her mouth. She twists her head to the side and upwards, her eyes as black as tar, though she appears to be fully conscious. Her abdomen tightens in a contraction. He sees something move under the surface of her skin, a struggling arm or leg, a creature trapped and wanting out. This will not end well, he says to himself, at the same time acknowledging a rather selfish element of wishful thinking in the scenario.

Has the Magister attended a birth before? the officer's wife asks, as if to pleasantly converse.

I have seen cows calve, he replies stupidly. And I am familiar with the basics from my studies at the university.

It's not as bad as it seems, she says reassuringly. It's how all of us have come to the world. Life is often more brutal at its beginning than at its end.

Kieding is brandishing a knife. He looks like a wildman in the midst of a heathen sacrifice, his eyes blinking, face smeared with blood as he fixes his gaze on Titia's vulva and brings the knife closer. For a moment Miltzov thinks he is about to murder her, this heretical young, that Kieding wishes to cut the child from her womb in order to save what can be saved, but instead he makes a quick incision between her legs and shrinks back as a deluge of murky yellow fluid gushes from her, accompanied by the fetid smell of genitals and slimy foetal membranes he suddenly recalls from the calvings.

There we are, says Kieding. Something should be happening soon now.

Titia screams again. She struggles to come free, but Miltzov holds her wrists tightly as in a vice, as the native women hold her legs. The Madame speaks warmly to her, telling her now to push, and Titia pushes until her face is blue with exertion. She gasps and moans and pushes again as the Madame and her daughters knead her abdomen, pressing their hands down at the top and smoothing them down the length of her womb.

Kieding dips down again with his knife. Hold her tight now, he instructs, and a moment later her body jerks violently, followed by an ear-splitting shriek, and Miltzov can only wonder what on earth the man is doing. He sees blood, streaming down Titia's thighs. The officer's wife wipes it away with towels she tosses on the floor when they can absorb no more.

I can see the head now, says Kieding. Push, my girl!

Again, a prolonged shriek. The mound of her abdomen is misshapen now, the child inside her kicking visibly. The two Egede girls knead and smooth, sweat pouring from their brows, while Kieding and the Madame toil between the girl's legs, it looks like they're trying to work something loose that's got stuck.

It's coming, Kieding announces. Keep pushing!

Titia's screams become hoarser now, she tosses her head back and forth, the two native women chatter excitedly, the Madame urges, push! push! The officer's wife pours jugfuls of warm water over Titia's bleeding genitals as the blood keeps coming in repeated, rhythmic waves; he hears the blood and water splash to the floor, he struggles to keep tight hold of Titia's wrists, she is almost pulling him over the headboard into the bed with her; she arches her body upwards, roaring like an animal struck by a musket shot, but the Madame is calm, hold her down, she says, it will soon be over, and she and Kieding tug on what Miltzov as yet cannot see, but which he considers must be enormous, it seems almost as if between them they will tear the child to pieces, yet they appear to be not in the least bit perturbed, quite cheerful in fact, rather like a pair of happy butchers, ceaselessly splattered with tiny squirts of blood and foetal fluid which they endeavour to evade with quick, sudden movements of their heads, and Miltzov clings to Titia's hands, the stool has slipped away beneath him and, unable to keep his balance, he must rise to his feet and leans over the headboard where his ears are immediately filled with screams. Nonetheless, he feels an increasing tempo in all that is happening, the kicking of her legs on top of which the native women have placed all their body weight, Kieding's rocking movements, the Madame's calm instructions, the girls' kneading and smoothing, all of it comes together in a climax of screaming, kicking and rocking, and now, as he struggles to stay upright, he sees a long, plump and blood-smeared child be pulled from between the jomfru's thighs, and clearly she feels it herself, for now her screams are triumphant, and Kieding straightens up holding in one hand a blue, lizard-like creature, which dangles head-down from his clenched fist, a grotesque-looking beast with an enormous head and a furrowed face, spitting and hissing, then instantly reacting to the hard smack Keiding delivers to its buttocks by breaking out into a high-pitched wail. Miltzov succumbs to Titia's frenzied scrabbling, he flops exhausted over the headboard, half on top of her, then feels a frantic pain and begins, he too, to wail; in chorus they wail, he releases the jomfru's hands and drops to the floor, where he lies rolling, moaning, screaming, he tries to slither away on his back, his eyes staring up at the bed in which the jomfru Titia has now pulled herself up onto her elbows, moving her jaw as if chewing on something, screaming no longer, and then her cheeks bulge and she spits Henrik Miltzov's ear onto the floor beside him where it lands with a faint and feeble slap. Everything goes quiet.

///

Kirstine sits with the priest's head in her lap and gazes lovingly at his sleeping face, the now blood-soaked bandage she has wound about his head. He has told her everything, much of it in delirium, yet she has heard and understood, and her love for him is pure, purer than ever before, for now it is tinged with forgiveness, and the tenderness she feels for him is unconditional, unrequiring of being evened out with sarcasm and pointed remarks. Now you are with me for ever, she whispers. He opens his eyes.

Poor Magister Miltzov. Does it hurt terribly?

He shakes his head and looks up at her in bewilderment.

I have bandaged the wound. I could not put your ear back on, although I tried. But at least it wasn't your nose she bit off.

He moves his lips, but utters nothing but a hoarse croak.

She laughs. Oh Henrik, how sweet you are! Poor, poor Magister. I feel an urge to kiss you.

She raises his head slightly and kisses him on the mouth.

Have I slept long? he croaks.

The whole day.

And the child?

The child is well. A boy.

The jomfru?

Sleeping. Kieding has given her something.

Is the child with her? And where is Frederik Christian? After all, he is the father in one sense. They must . . . I must . . . right away . . . He tries to sit up, only to fall back with a groan.

Kirstine shakes her head. Relax, she says. It's all been taken care of. You don't have to worry about a thing. Lie still, my dearest.

But the child? The child?

She can't look after a child. My mother has taken it. It is with her in the bed chamber.

Oh no, he sighs.

But yes, dearest. It is for the best.

Does she know?

We took it away immediately. We have told her it was dead. It's for her own sake. She wept and wept, and kept asking, Where's my child? Is something wrong with it? Why can't I see my child? Kirstine mimics Titia's voice. We found a stillborn infant with the savages and showed it to her. It calmed her down. It was almost as if she was glad. I can see he is mine, she said. The native women washed her and changed the linen. She has lost a lot of blood. Perhaps she will die. But for the time being she is asleep.

You lied to her, he says quietly.

It was a good lie, says Kirstine.

Where am I exactly? he wants to know, lifting his head.

You're with me, says Kirstine. You're home now. I am looking after you.

He groans. The full weight of his heavy head falls back into her lap.

Sleep now, she says. I am with you.

I am condemned, he says. I am going to hell.

She laughs. Oh, Henrik. You're not going to hell. There is forgiveness for everything once a person confesses. I love you. Sleep now, my dearest.

She sits cross-legged on the floor in the priest's house, stroking the hair of her betrothed, quite filled with love and solicitude. Outside it is evening. Sunlight falls in through the windows, onto the head of the wounded priest. Now he sleeps again. This is what it's like, she thinks. Love. Such a sense of empowerment. No one ever told me. She has never felt like this before, never felt as happy as this. She could sit here for ever, she thinks.

///

Spring, a buzzing of flies, stillness. Titia walks up to the grave. She places flowers, says a couple of Hail Marys, caresses the cross. She is quite shrouded in sorrow, and sorrow is good, it resembles happiness. Something inside her turned half a revolution and fell into place when she saw the dead child. There is a clarity in her mind now which has been absent for many months. Perhaps it was her madness she expelled and which now has been put to rest in the grave.

I shall not leave you, she says. I shall be here for you for ever and ever. And you will be with me.

She sits in the winter-pale grass by the grave and sings a song, a German hymn she believes, taught to her by the nuns, simple words put to a melody.

She remembers something that happened in the nunnery. It was early in the morning, shortly after matins. She went out to the hens. Sister Rose had let them out and they were busy pecking about in the earth. They thought she was coming with food, and gathered around her legs. She picked them up one by one and bit off their heads. Her mouth filled with blood and feathers, their wings beat against her face. She spat out the heads and tossed the dead hens aside onto the ground, where they twitched and flapped and writhed. The other hens milled at her feet, as if to say, take me! take me! She bit the heads off them all, twenty-four hens and a cockerel she had to chase around the run, for it knew what was going to happen. That clever cockerel. But it too lost its head eventually, and its fragile skull crunched delightfully between her teeth. After all this carnage, the run was full of fluttering, headless hens and it was the funniest thing she had ever seen, so of course she laughed. The nuns were not pleased to discover her crouched on all fours in the hen run in a cloud of feathers among the dead, though still occasionally flapping, fowl. She recalls how tired she felt. They carried her in and punished her, the way they punished themselves and each other. Imagine biting the heads off a whole run of hens. She smiles at the thought. It's not the sort of thing a person is supposed to do.

She wonders if it happened because she was insane, or because her life in the nunnery was insane and she in some way had to do something completely insane in order for the insanity to stop. In any case, stop it did. She managed to run away. Had it not been for the hens, she thinks she would be there still. So in actual fact, what she did was not insane at all, but a very astute and cunning move.

Titia gets to her feet at the graveside. The world is mostly sky, with a frieze of fells at the bottom. She stands for a moment in the sunlight. I'll come and see you again tomorrow, she says. Goodnight, little savage.

She returns to the house, to Skård, who is silent as always. She eats some bread and makes a cup of tea with sugar in it. It's so quiet everywhere. She wonders how the Governor and the other colony folk are making out? They have been gone a month now. What is she meant to do? She doesn't read and can't be bothered to darn any more socks. Being mad is so boring, one must find something interesting to do.

Skård?

Shall we play a game of cards, Skård?

No, he doesn't reply. He just stands there like a pillar.

She goes outside again and walks around the house, and knocks on the door of the Egede residence.

Is Frederik Christian in?

She hears her voice as if for the first time, thin and girlish.

What do you want with him? Petronelle asks.

To go for a walk. We are betrothed, after all.

Frederik Christian is busy. Shall I go with you?

No, thanks. Thanks all the same, Petronelle. She curtsies.

Around the colony she wanders, up and down, to and fro. The baker is baking bread, the smith repairing muskets, the carpenter renewing the planks of the colony boat. They greet her. Hello, Jomfru Titia. Everything all right?

Can I help with something? she asks in the same thin voice she has never heard before.

It's no work for a young girl, I'm afraid. But kind of you to ask.

And so she must return home again. Home to boring old Skård.

///

I go inside
   Skård is still stood in the corner
   Completely silent
   Floating almost
   Like one of the angels that dangled from the ceiling of the cloister church
   The way it turned in the air every time the door opened
   He doesn't say much Skård
   Drip, that's all
   Drip, drip, says Skård
   Never been the chatty sort
   He turns in the air
   He looks around
   But sees nothing
   He is silent
   He is blind
   Hello Skård!
   And deaf he is too
   Deaf as a post
   Why are you dangling from the ceiling?
   You've dropped your pipe on the floor
   I pick it up, and right the overturned chair
   I step up to put the pipe back in his mouth
   I open his mouth and press it together again
   The stem rattles against his teeth

But now he's got his pipe at least
I put my arms around him and lay my cheek against his stomach
I close my eyes
Good old Skård
Dear old Skård

///

There are ships again. The colony is deluged with strangers. Everyone is busy. Barrels full of foodstuffs are rolled up from the harbour, men shuttle backwards and forwards with building materials and goods, officers stroll and take in the scene, speaking occasionally with Egede and the crew. On the rocks behind the crew house, men sit smoking and chatting, food is prepared under the open sky, and the Egedes' house is full to the brim. No one wants to stay in the governor's residence, where it appears someone has hanged themselves and moreover a madwoman resides.

In the open expanse between the warehouse, the blubber house and the bakery down in the colony harbour, a couple promenades arm in arm. It is the savaged, earless priest, Miltzov, a bandage around his head, and his betrothed, Kirstine Egede. They are a picture of premarital bliss.

15

A Night-time Conversation

To-day, Sunday, Mr Miltzov gave the sermon.

On the 16th of this month I allowed my dear and precious Frederik Christian to depart to the Greenlanders of the Kook Isles in order to instruct and read to them. He carries a musket with him always for his protection and has given me his word that he will shoot the sorcerer on sight if he should see him. Yet there are still no signs of this Apaluttork who wishes us all so ill. My son believes him to be dead, though I fear it to be wishful thinking.

FROM HANS EGEDE'S JOURNAL, MAY 1729

It was January, the door to the new year, and a large number died. Then came February, and that was no better. After that March, the mulching month, and indeed the colony soil was mulched, but I don't think anything will come of it but the bones that were laid to rest in it. Then it was April, the grazing month, when the livestock were put out to grass up on the moor whose bog water stinks of corpses. And now it is the month of flowers, May. Flowers, laid on the graves, catchfly, rosebay and camomile. And all the time, new graves appear with crosses poking in the air and flowers that wither and blow away. But still, the year has months aplenty.

Sise, are you awake?

Hm.

I was telling you about the Governor's expedition to the ice. Do you want to hear?

Yes, yes, I'm awake.

Your eyes were closed.

I like to lie with my eyes closed when you tell me stories.

What did I just say, then?

Something about the dead, Sise mumbles. Can't you tell me about your expedition? Or the time you dined with the King in the Deer Park.

That's a long time ago. It feels like it was a dream. Maybe it's because of that cutlet of veal that I'm alive today. Maybe I'm only here by royal privilege?

I'm alive too, says Sise. And they gave me slops to eat in the Spinning House while you enjoyed your cutlet of veal and wine in the company of the fine gentlemen.

It's because you were housekeeper for the Governor this winter that you're alive. The Governor's place is nice and warm, not like this peat-hut here.

I'm glad of our little house, she says. It's better than the crew house. It's the first house I've lived in that I can call my own.

I sing Sise a song that comes into my mind. It goes like this: *It helps not to say no, with death we must go, our path through the world is known by none, we walk it together as one.* It's a kind of drinking song, I tell her. Death and drinking belong together, don't they? I suppose that's why it's called dead drunk. Sise, Sise? Now you're sleeping again.

Hm.

Then sleep. She won't admit she falls asleep, she gets grumpy if I say so.

I was at the great ice-cap this spring. The Governor said he wanted me with him. He seems to have got the idea I'm his best friend, and so he wants me to accompany him whenever he pokes his nose out of the colony. Cavorting with my wife, some men do that kind of thing, making a cuckold of a man, then thinking he's his best friend.

We were away together last autumn too, for the same reason, only we didn't get far then. The horses died. We had to return on foot through thick, heavy snow. But then he wanted to try again. There's something not right about that man. There was about half a dozen of us who went with him. The Governor wanted to cross to the eastern part of the country where they say descendants of the Norsemen are living. Østerbygden, they call it, the Eastern Settlement. The idea is for it to be reincorporated into the Danish realm now that the King's got himself a colony here. For the time being though they needn't worry, because we never got there.

Did you see the ice? Sise asks.

Oh, so you're pretend-sleeping, are you? Yes, we came to the ice and climbed it too.

What, with horses and everything?

No, the horses we left in the valley, silly. We had to climb, and the ice was steep and wet here in the spring. It's a wonder we didn't fall and kill ourselves.

What were you wanting up there anyway?

Like I said. Pors wanted to cross over to the Norsemen on the other side and tell them he was their governor from now on.

Couldn't they come over to him? They must know the way.

How stupid you are.

Who are these Norsemen anyway that everyone goes on about?

Old forebears of ours. They came here to the country from Iceland and settled in the fjords. Some of them even lived here in the district. That's what they called Vesterbygden, the Western Settlement. But the biggest place was Østerbygden, where there was a monastery, a church with a bishop and a fine bishop's residence and a whole hive of people. Farmers they were, they grew crops and kept sheep and horses, same as the Icelanders.

And they live there all on their own?

Yes, the ice has cut them off from developments in the rest of the world. They probably haven't even heard of Luther and his reformation, and most likely they still hunt with the bow and arrow.

Who's Luther?

A German. The one who wrote our Catechism.

I thought that was Moses?

Now you're being stupid on purpose. Sometimes I don't know you at all.

Did you meet these Norsemen, then?

No, we never got that far, did we. Besides, there's been no sign of them for hundreds of years. The Master Kieding doesn't think there's any of them left. They're all dead, he says. It's what happens to people in this land, they die.

What can't live must die, Sise mutters.

I suppose. Like the little boy, you mean?

She says nothing, but pretends to be asleep.

Did you throttle him, or was he the one they found alive down in the warehouse?

Sise sleeps.

Or was it the Governor?

Hm, she grunts. Tell me more about the expedition.

We sailed for a long time. In through the Ameralik Fjord, which Pors insists on calling the Admiral's Fjord. It's a very long fjord. The innermost waters are shallow and the bed is of clay, making it difficult to get close to the shore. But we found a river mouth where it was deeper, and put in there. We packed the horses and then wandered up into a valley. It was green and lovely, and warm, almost like in Denmark. But it was very wet. The fellsides were streaming with water and then there was this wide, rushing river coming from the ice further up, like emerald it was with meltwater. We reached the foot of the ice on the third day in the afternoon. The edge was as tall as a church. We camped and waited there until we'd got our strength back. The next day we climbed it.

I pause now in my story. I bite off a piece of chewing tobacco and chew on it for a while, then tuck it under my top lip. I listen to Sise's breathing. You never know if she's asleep or lying there listening.

I went and fetched Pors when your time came. Do you remember that? He'd told me that was what I had to do. Come as soon as she feels the child is on its way, he said. I went there and knocked on the door and called for him, Your Grace, I called, now's the time. Try shouting a bit louder so the whole colony wakes, he said. Anyway, I've never seen the Governor run as quick. Slammed the door in my face, he did, when we got back here. Wouldn't let me in. What were the two of you doing?

Having a baby, Sise mumbles. Tell me more about the expedition.

Will you then tell me what's what about that child?

Hm.

Anyway, we came up onto a ledge in the ice, maybe a half-hundred fathoms above the land. In places the ice was jagged and sharp, elsewhere it was rough like the underside of a sieve, and if you fell you cut yourself. Mostly it was slippery as soap, and half the time we didn't know whether to walk or crawl. We had to use our hacks so as not to fall down, and the one who went first would have to feel his way forward with his testing pole, for there were hidden clefts in the ice all around and we went in single file, tied together with a rope, the clefts were deep and at the bottom of them ran underground, or under-ice, I suppose you'd call it, rivers and rushing streams that rumbled and echoed in a way that suggested there were great caverns down there. It was frightening. But then at one point we couldn't get any further because all we could see was hundreds of alens of rotten slushy ice with great big, dark crevasses and pools of meltwater, and if we'd carried on we'd have been goners for certain. Grubby it was too, the ice, not shiny or white at all, but dirty and sad-looking. But beyond the broken-up bit that looked like a sea in a storm, only frozen, the ice was quite white and wound in and out and off into the distance for what seemed like forever, merging with the sky, the way the sea does too, and we stood there, seven men, and just stared at it, and it was cold and still, apart from the deep rumbles that came from the underground rivers, and one of the men said it could just as well be the other side of the moon or somewhere in hell, and I think that was how all of us felt. There were huge rocks and boulders too, strewn all about the surface of the ice like wreckage, only it was rocks, many of them were the size of a house. Pors thought there must be a fell somewhere beyond, maybe a volcano, from where these rocks had fallen into the ice and then been carried along. For we could tell the ice was moving, slower than the eye could see, maybe only a foot a year, because at the point where it met the land it looked almost in places like the baker's custard, you know the way it splats out between the layers of a cake, and there were also great chunks of ice that came away and came crashing down all around us. The men wanted to go back down again as quick as possible, for they were afraid the ice would come apart completely and cut off our way back, but Pors insisted on bringing a toast first to the King, and he got out a flask of aquavit, for he never goes ten paces without, and we toasted the King, I even had a mouthful too, and then we fired off our muskets, nine shots straight into the air, and Pors said the ice-mountain had almost certainly never been shown such an honour before, more than likely it was the first time anyone had ever set foot there. Like I said, the man's not right in the head.

It sounds like a terrible place, Sise mumbles.

Yes, in a way it was. I stood there just waiting for the signal for us to go down again, I didn't feel like I was on solid ground at all. But then when we came down again I looked back and felt like I'd been to a very special place, a fabulous world, and immediately I felt a longing for it. And that's how I've felt ever since. It's not a place you forget once you've seen it, I don't think there's anything quite like it on all of God's earth. I want to go there again. Perhaps you'll go with me?

Me?

I'd like to move out there. Tend a piece of land, like those Norsemen did. We could buy some sheep. I'm sure Pors would help and support us in it. He owes us. Are you still not going to tell me what happened?

She has turned onto her side and lies with eyes closed, her hands folded under her cheek.

You had the baby, I say, and Governor Pors was the midwife. A funny arrangement if ever there was one. And when at last I was allowed in, the child was dead. I saw the marks on its neck in case you want to know. Of course, I said nothing when it was found. I'll keep my mouth shut. Anyway, it wasn't my child, was it. What the Governor does with his offspring is his own business. He said we'd be compensated. What do you think he meant by that?

She doesn't answer. She knows the Governor gave me fifty rigsdaler. There's not a lot a man can spend that kind of money on in this country. Apart from paying his wife for copulation. Five marks a go.

Were there wild animals there? Sise asks. They say there are white bears, ten alens tall when they stand on their hind legs?

That's right, change the subject, I think to myself. I know she's sorry for what happened. But what did happen? She won't say. It's driving me round the bend. She doesn't think about that.

Those bears, I never saw a sign of them. The only animals we saw were hares and foxes. Not even a sorry reindeer did we see. But it was a lovely place. I wish you could have seen it, then we could have remembered it together. Things feel realer when you remember them together.

I'm not going anywhere, says Sise. I'm all right where I am.

You'll want to be where he is, I suppose. I know he comes here when I'm away.

So what? says Sise. It's what I do. You knew that when you took me.

So he pays you as well, does he?

Five marks, she says. Fixed rate. You know that.

Five marks. The same as I pay her to sleep with me. She can't do it unless she gets her five marks, she says. Now I've got the fifty rigsdaler the Governor gave me. And money's a fine thing. Not that it's any good to me, for if I ever splashed it about people would think I'd been stealing. And what need does anyone have of money in this land? To go to the playhouse? At least I've got enough to be shagging Sise a good few years.

Once a tart, always a tart, Sise says. You can't teach a cow to bleat like a goat. Tell me what happened when you came down from the ice.

We went down by another route, then collected the horses and continued further north. There we came to a very beautiful valley where the sun was shining and it was warm. This is where I was thinking a person could settle down with a little farm with sheep and cereal and beet. There were streams and rivers. Some we could jump across, others were so wide we had to wade across. In some places there was ice on the bottom of these rivers, and if you went through it would tear your boots to ribbons. Cold it was too, this water from the glacier, it made your teeth hurt to drink it, but refreshing and tasty it was. When evening came we made a fire and sat around the flames, talking about people from the colony while we ate the fish we'd caught in a stream and having a very pleasant time of it.

We stayed there a few days. It was like no one felt like going home. The weather there is a different thing altogether compared to here,

I tell you. The summer must be a couple of months longer, at least. I wish you'd let me take you there. It might give you back your good humour.

There were pastures with tall grass, and places that looked like they'd been cultivated. We found rocks from what must have been field boundaries, and foundation stones too. Their farms must have been situated with fine views over the land and the fjord, and with the fells on all sides. It must have been a paradise. I can't for the life of me understand why they placed the colony out here when there's such a lovely place only a couple of days' journey away, and where you can even grow things too.

We shot hare and grouse and roasted them on wooden skewers. We slept on the ground next to each other and didn't freeze. The vegetation was thick, heather and moss, it insulates from the cold of the ground, you see. There wasn't a breath of wind. I lay awake all night and couldn't sleep. Just lay there gazing up at the night sky. There were stars, the sky was quite clear, and then the moon came up, round and shadowy, and you could see the whole land in its light. They were good days.

I lie on my back and look up at the peat ceiling. Sise has turned towards me. I can feel her breath on my cheek.

The best days of my life, I say.

My father farmed the land at a place north of Hamburg. That's where I'm from. Good German soil it was, fat and sticky when you picked up a handful. The cereal stood thick and golden. We had a good life. I love the earth. It's where we're from, the priest says when he lays us down in it again. That was what I came to remember up the fjord, that it was where I belonged, not here in this clammy colony where the fog wraps itself around us like a shroud around a corpse.

Pors asked me to reconnoitre the prospects for agriculture there. I dug up a patch of ground, barely a few feet on each side, and showed it him and said you could grow all sorts there. He's kind of a farmer himself, he told me so, from a farm over in Jutland, and feels the same longing for the soil as me, though he's been a military man now the most of his life, same as me, even if I'm much younger.

I sat with the Governor and looked at that little patch of ground, like we were waiting for something to sprout. Like the rest of the men we were both of us rather long-bearded by then.

I thank the Lord for letting me come here, said the Governor as we sat. A place in the world without fear, he said. I don't think I've ever felt such peace in all my life. Why did you not stay on your father's farm? he asked.

I was the thirteenth child, I said. My brother was to take on the farm. So I had no choice but to join up, the Fynske Land Regiment.

I don't suppose anyone wants to be the thirteenth in a flock, he said with a chuckle. I was the first-born. Not that it's any better.

Why didn't you stay on the farm? I asked.

My father lost it, he said. He was unfortunate and fell into debt. I inherited his debt. That's what came of being the first-born.

But you've another farm in Jutland now? I said.

Yes, indeed. But the King then called upon me and I was compelled to leave.

I thought about you all the time we were up the fjord, Sise. How you might be faring. You weren't yourself after the birth. Wouldn't talk to me, wouldn't eat your food. You were distraught about the child, I realize that. I tried to be distraught too. But I couldn't, not properly. I was more relieved than anything. A child like that has a hard time of it, an illegitimate child, I mean. I didn't know if I'd be able to love it like it was my own. A father like that's no good to anyone. It tormented me, though. Who strangled the child? Can you not tell me?

What can't live must die, Sise says again. Tell me about the horses.

The horses, yes. The most peculiar thing. Eventually we broke up from the camp where we'd done nothing but enjoy the good life, men under the stars. But at some point you've got to be making tracks. So we packed the horses and walked back to the place where the boat lay. It was a long hike, over the same rushing rivers and boggy plains, and the horses grew more and more contrary, thrashing under the rein, rearing up and kicking out at us. I think one of them at least was getting lame. Both were limping, anyway, and eventually they refused to go on. The mare hoofed the Governor and he was so mad he drew his sword and laid into the beast. He was already in a bad mood about going home, and I think there were other things weighing him down too, and he just lost his head and was thrashing the daylights out of his horse, shrieking and yelling like a lunatic. He'd had a fair bit to drink and wasn't quite in possession of his senses. We tried to hold him back, but he just kept flailing away at the mare until it dropped to the ground with blood pouring from great gashes in its flesh. One of the men had to shoot it. Of course, the other horse was terrified by all this, wrenched itself free and ran itself into a ravine. It had to be put down too. The Governor himself went out like a light once he'd calmed himself down. He slept for several hours and when he woke up he couldn't remember a thing and asked where the horses were. We had no choice but to tell him, and when we did he wept like a child. My splendid mare! he wailed. What am I now to tell the King? He was like a madman, completely out of his senses. Mad as a German, as they say.

He killed the one he loved, Sise says quietly. The poor Governor.

16

Sunlight Streaming

To-day came to us the married couple among the as-yet living former inmates, Johan Hartman and Sise Hansdatter, with their foster-boy whom they have adopted from the Governor's unfortunate housekeeper, and requested that I baptize the child, saying to me: We thought he would die and therefore did not come to you before, but since they wished that he might join the realm of God, they requested he now be baptized. After I impressed upon them the imperative of upright intentions regarding the child's christening, and of not departing from the good virtues they have shown until now, the boy was baptized in the name of the Holy Trinity and given the Christian name of Lauritz.

FROM HAN EGEDE'S JOURNAL, SEPTEMBER 1729

Now there's a fist-fight outside the governor's house. Blood, sweat, spit, the rubbery smack of lunging blows, muffled groans, urgh, urgh, shouts and cries of the crew folk who have gathered in a ring around the combatants. The buildings, the rocks, the fjord, the fells as grey as the shadings of a lead pencil in the rain. September 1729.

It is one of the seamen from the *Morian*, which has arrived late this year, and the colony cooper who are embroiled in a boxing match. They have wound rags around their knuckles and are bare-chested. They circle each other, sideways on, their guards raised, and now the cooper lunges forward, twisting his body in an attempt to land a blow to his opponent's kidneys, but the seaman, who is younger, bigger and less afflicted by the scurvy, evades and plants a simple and effective fist in the cooper's face. There is a crunching sound, a very satisfactory sound for a boxing audience, or indeed a seaman, though less so for the cooper or anyone who has put their money on him. It seems the cooper is in for a leathering. The crowd whoops. The cooper staggers and blinks as his blood spouts from his nose onto his bare and hairy chest. A gentle prod would be enough and he would undoubtedly go down. But the seamen slackens, he stands back with a foolish grin and crows over what he has done to the haemorrhaging cooper, and the older man has time to collect himself, he doubles up, bobbing and ducking behind his guard, edges a few wobbly steps forward and lets fly at his opponent's chin, missing the mark completely but demonstrating thereby that he is far from finished.

The cooper is a meagre, hollow-cheeked man of thirty. He only just survived the last winter and does not anticipate making it through the next. He has nothing to lose, but a bottle of the Governor's cognac to win. He economizes with his punches, which more times than not land crisply when at long last he strikes, and moreover possesses a keen, intelligent gaze beneath his flaxen fringe. He goes for the liver, kidneys and chin. But he is tiring.

The seaman is young, large and fleshy, strong but laborious, a giant waiting to be slain. His eyes are brown and peer lazily, revealing unfeeling amusement at his ageing, rickety opponent. Most have put their money on him. He and those who have wagered in his favour have yet to grasp that he is proceeding towards defeat.

The Governor is the referee. He circles around the boxers, clad in full uniform. He has asked for a fair fight and ordered the two men to remove the knives they have concealed in the shafts of their boots. The contest will be decided when one of the men lies flat in the mud and cannot get up again. A bottle of cognac stands ready for the winner. The pot is almost five rigsdaler, and the odds, calculated by the Governor's own book-keeper, are three to one in favour of the seaman.

Now the cooper bobs and weaves again and gets in a punch to the seaman's ribs. Winded, he doubles up in pain and when he ventures to raise his head and look up the cooper butts him. The seaman's eyes roll in his head and the cooper lunges quickly, a haymaker to the younger man's chin which seems almost to be stuck to the cooper's fist as it follows through. Nonetheless, the giant seaman remains on his feet. His arms tremble as if in spasm. The cooper realizes he has finished him off. He stands back and watches as the man falls on his face without so much as putting his hands out to break his fall. The onlookers groan their disappointment. Weakling! Milksop! Old woman!

The seaman lies on his side in the mud. His eyes are closed, but it seems he is awake. He is ashamed of himself. The cooper looks down on him benevolently. He rolls his shoulders and performs a lap of honour around the ring while the crowd, even those among them who have lost money on him, cheer enthusiastically. Age conquers youth. This is something they can relate to. And it is easily worth a few miserable marks that cannot be spent on anything here anyway.

Pors declares the winner to be the cooper, whereafter someone empties a bucket of water over the seaman, who gets to his feet unsteadily. The crowd whoops and derides him. He laughs and shakes his head apologetically. He and the cooper shake hands.

Get away from the window.

It is her mother calling. She is darning socks in her chair.

Petronelle, Egede's youngest, now fourteen years of age, has been watching the bout through the filter of the lace curtain.

Now there are two more, she says. How long are they going to keep it up?

Until not a man is left standing, winners and losers alike, her mother replies. Come here and sit down with me, dear. Draw the drape.

She sits down on the floor beside her mother, tucking her feet underneath her. The figures of the people outside project as dancing shadows on the ceiling.

Such things are not for a young girl to see, her mother says.

Petronelle sighs aggrievedly and is bored. Where's Kirstine?

Out walking with Henrik, I think.

I'd like to have gone with them.

You know they prefer to walk on their own now that they're betrothed.

They kiss each other.

Yes, and they're allowed to as well.

Imagine having someone else's spit in your mouth. It's disgusting.

Is that what you think, little Petronelle? Her mother smiles.

Restless, she gets to her feet again. I think I'll go and find them.

Not on your own, you won't. It's not safe for you with all these strange men going about from the ship.

She goes to the foot of the stairs and calls for Frederik Christian. Paapa!

Busy footsteps cross the floorboards.

Will you go for a walk with me?

He beams. I'll be right there.

Oh, he's such a puppy dog, she tells herself. And yet she is smiling.

Wrap up warm, says her mother. It's not summer any more. And don't go out there. She nods towards the window, the renewed clamour of fist-fighting outside.

///

Upon the moor the air is still. Petronelle and Paapa walk side by side. They veer to the right and follow the edge of the bog in the direction of the inlet where the ship lies anchored, on the eastern side of the peninsula, half a fjerdingmil from the colony. A visible path has been tramped between the colony and this harbour by men going back and forth with goods, bent under the weight of rucksacks, yokes and enormous bundles held in place by means of headstraps. They meet several on their way, decent and meek toilers staggering along with their burdens. On the flat land of the moor, on the tongues and islets of the bog, goats and sheep graze with the colony's only surviving cow. Somewhere, from where they cannot tell, they hear a voice, a series of interrupted sounds, as if someone were calling to them.

He's out again, I hear, says Frederik Christian. He always sings when he's out walking.

I'm not sure I'd call it singing, says Petronelle. He sounds more like a bleating goat.

No, I think he sings well, says Frederik Christian. He wanders here in the wilds for hours every day with the Danish hymns.

They stop and look around to see if they can see him, but all they have is the voice, the man himself eludes them, an ethereal, omnipresent song mingled with the gentle clanging of bells from the livestock.

Let's go this way, says Petronelle, disinclined to meet her father. She picks up her skirts and strides off, stepping over the pointed rocks and squelching through the puddles of the bog. Frederik Christian scurries to keep up with her.

He catches up and slaps her on the back. Got you!

She wheels around like a fury and sees the way he shrinks back in fright. It makes her laugh. Oh, so that's what you think!

He cottons on immediately, turns and runs, glancing back over his shoulder in giggles, and she sets after him, all flapping skirts and flying hair, her feet inside her *kamik* boots gripping the rocks with confidence, launching her forward again without her even needing to take care and watch where she is going. She knows the rocks, it is as if her feet themselves know where to tread, only on the level ground does she stumble, but now she is flying, her dress unfolds behind her in a rustle of fabric, he escaping her clutches with a sharp change of direction, before hurtling down a slope, she pursuing him still, fearless, and at once they tumble, grit and earth kicking up in their wake and tumbling with them; at the bottom they spring to their feet and run down the gentler slope towards the fjord, she the quicker, and he must zigzag in order to shake her off, though she knows of course that he wants her to catch him, for it is the whole point of this game of tag, an erotic frolic, to stand panting and sweating in close embrace, and she foresees his evasive movements, she cuts him off and closes in on him, though not too fast, for the hunt itself is so very delightful, and now she grabs hold of his coat, she clutches it tight, and he tries to wriggle free, only then she is literally on his back, riding him, tightening her legs around his chest, and he staggers on, though at last he must sink to the ground, she on top of him, locking his arms tightly and digging her knees into his ribs until he groans with pain and she bends over him, feels his sweet breath in her face, her hair sweeping over his cheeks, and she exclaims in triumph: Got you!

They roll onto their backs and gulp in air. He looks at her sideways. Her hair. It is untied, and flows all down her shoulders. He sees beads of perspiration at her hairline. Like silver. A butterfly of freckles across her nose and cheeks.

Why are you staring at me? Is there something wrong?

I love you, he thinks. He sits up with his arms around his knees and looks out over the fjord, smiling quietly.

You're my best friend, she says. You're my brother.

He replies with Greenlandic silence, lifting his eyebrows. She often does the same when her father speaks to her, which annoys the priest intensely: Say something, girl, instead of pulling such a devilish face at me!

When was the last time you saw your father? she asks.

I see him often when I'm out in the skerries.

Does he still want you back?

I don't know.

Don't you want to be with him?

No. Egede is my father, and your mother is my mother. He is a heathen and a sorcerer.

But he is your flesh. I wonder if you ought to meet with him and talk to him. You could persuade him to become a Christian. He has already received instruction from Top.

He shakes his head. He won't have it. Your father, I mean. He will not baptize someone like him.

No, he's odd like that. Sometimes it seems the biggest obstacle to the natives becoming Christian is the man who is meant to christen them.

We must tread softly, says Frederik Christian. We can only baptize those who understand the articles and who genuinely feel themselves to be Christian. Otherwise we'd be desecrating the sacraments.

Now you sound like my father.

He has taught me everything.

They get to their feet and walk along the shore, a series of inlets, one after another. After a while they veer away from the water's edge and climb up onto a rocky ridge. The voice of her father comes drifting from some indeterminable direction. Kingo's 'Morning Song', she thinks. *From eastern skies I now see sunlight streaming.*

They settle in a hollow where there is shelter from the chilly gusts coming in from the fjord.

I love that hymn, says Frederik Christian.

Yes, it's beautiful.

They sit and listen to the voice as it floats and drifts on the air.

It gilds the rockface brow, sets hillsides gleaming.

The words are so fine, he says.

It's poetry, she says.

She feels herself observed by him again, though says nothing. Let him look, if that's what he wants. Perhaps he finds her pretty.

Her hair, he thinks to himself. Dark and tumbling, the occasional hint of auburn, like long strands of tobacco. And the nape of her neck, where her perspiration beads like silver – he would give anything to be allowed to kiss her there.

Rejoice, my soul . . .

And let your praise be ringing, he joins in, then laughs embarrassedly. *From earthly home set free . . .*

Now they both sing along: *Through thanks and faith now be to heaven winging.*

Abruptly, her father's voice falls silent.

So, this is where you hide, my children.

He is standing on the rock above them, leaning on his staff.

Father! they exclaim at once, leaping to their feet.

I thought I could hear you.

We could hear you too, she says.

Yes, the 'Morning Song'. A very long hymn, it takes a morning to sing. And what are you two up to?

Frederik Christian is testing me in the Catechism, she lies.

Is he indeed? He gauges them quizzically. Well, it's good to see you out in the fresh air, he says after a moment, with kindness in his voice. God likes us to appreciate his Creation.

Yes, Father.

Mind you don't get cold. The summer is gone.

He jumps down effortlessly from the rock and strides away with the lightest of steps, his boots crunching the sandy earth.

Be good, children, he says, and descends to the shore.

They watch him as he goes. Eventually they look at each other, and each sees their own fright reflected in the face of the other.

///

In front of the colony house, two combatants are engaged in a new contest, a tradesman from the *Morian* and one of the colony's native *kiffaqs*, a helper at the Trade. They are poorly matched, yet the contest appears to be even, the tradesman is a tall, lanky type, the *kiffaq* compact and muscular. They have been fighting for some time and their bodies are glistening with sweat. The bottle of cognac won by the cooper earlier is passed among the onlookers, and the two contestants swig from it too.

Fight! says Pors, who is still the referee. The cannon pounds.

The two boxers step towards each other, rolling the sweat from their shoulders, glaring into each other's eyes. The Dane throws a punch but strikes only the *kiffaq*'s arm, his opponent quickly sidestepping to his right and at the same time launching a left uppercut that catches the Dane in the ribs, causing him to emit a hollow groan. The onlookers cheer. They are a crowd divided. The Greenlander represents the colony, but as a native he is quite as much a stranger as the ship's carpenter, who on the other hand is Danish. The odds are in the latter's favour, four to three, making him a slight favourite.

They fight with legs firmly apart, pummelling each other from all angles. The punches rain, yet neither of the men will yield. The shouts of the crowd escalate into rage. Now the native falls, only to spring to his feet again instantly and jump up and down on the spot to collect himself. He grins and spits blood. Someone hands him the cognac, he sweeps the bottle to his mouth and gulps down its contents in a single swig, the crowd cheering him on. He stands still for a moment and considers the empty bottle with a look that suggests he is already regretting it.

The cannon pounds again, and Pors barks: Fight!

The carpenter comes charging, but the native dodges him deftly. He turns, meets the Dane with his guard up, and after a couple of cautious jabs unleashes himself onto his opponent like a madman, the Dane seeing no option but to put his arms around his head, backing off until reaching the crowd. Brutally, they shove him back into the ring again, directly into a hail of ferocious punches, and after a moment he drops to his knees, then to all fours, though without Pors yet seeing reason to stop the fight. Now he lies with his face in the mud, gasping for breath. The native kicks him repeatedly, shouting in his incomprehensible tongue. The carpenter clambers to his feet, blindly, feebly punching the air, only to double up once more when the Greenlander delivers a well-aimed blow to the side of his head. He staggers and is jostled this way and that by the crowd who roar their scorn at him, but he will not fall and stands jabbing the air with a senseless grin, the Greenlander observing him with a proud smile. Then, after a second, he steps forward and punches his opponent hard in the chest and the Dane falls silently to the ground. The crowd kicks him and tries to haul him to his feet, but he remains lying in the mud, where he sighs happily. Two men take him by the legs and drag him away.

Salute! the Governor roars, and the cannon pounds.

///

Petronelle has been standing watching from the corner of the house. Now she steps inside the parlour. Frederik Christian goes upstairs. Her mother sits darning. Kirstine has returned from her walk with Miltzov.

I saw you with your native slave, Kirstine says teasingly.

I saw you with your priest, she replies quickly.

I suppose you know he's in love with you?

Petronelle says nothing.

You must be careful, Kirstine continues. He is a man, after all.

Come and sit here with me, their mother says. There's plenty of work for you to be getting on with.

They sit down on the floor on either side of their mother's chair. She hands them each a sock, a darning needle and wool. Shadows dance on the ceiling. Cries and laughter resound from the arena.

///

The following day she is out walking with him again. This time they veer left and go up to the rocks at the peninsula's highest point. They sit down. The wind is blowing. Snow has fallen on the fell and she can smell the frost. He wishes to take her hands to warm in his, but she pulls away. He resigns and stares down at the colony, smiling faintly. Your father isn't out today, he says after a while. I can't hear him singing.

No, I think he's gone up the fjord.

It feels almost empty without him.

Yes, thank goodness.

I like your father. I'm very fond of him.

He's fond of you too. More than of the rest of us.

She senses there is something he wants to say but feels he can't. But then he does: Tell me, Nelle, can a native from the colonies become Danish?

It happens, she replies after thinking for a moment. There are slaves who have been bought free and have entered a Danish family and public office.

Oh, he says. Have you met any of these people?

There were a couple in Bergen. It's said that the King's best friend is one, a blackamoor.

And they live like ordinary people?

Certainly.

And are considered to be Danish in every respect?

I think so. I even think they are held in esteem. To be bought free is a royal privilege.

Do they have Danish wives?

Yes.

What do they look like?

They're black, of course.

Black in what way?

Their skin is very dark, bluish almost.

I've seen pictures of such people, he says. But I can hardly imagine it. Black in the face, like someone hanging from the gallows?

No, they are beautiful people. Many women find them attractive. She blushes.

But what about their children, are they black too?

More brown than black.

Does the King really permit black and white to mingle?

It's taken to be right and proper, even if they do differ in appearance.

But I'm not like that, says Frederik Christian. I'm not black, and I'm not a slave. Do you think I could be accorded such a privilege?

I don't know. Is that what you want?

Yes, of course. I'm not a Greenlander any more.

What are you then?

I don't know. Perhaps I'm more Danish than Greenlander now. Sometimes I wish I were a slave too.

You fool, she says and laughs. What on earth for?

Because then I could be bought free. The way things are, I am neither free nor a slave. I don't know what I am.

But you're Paapa, I mean Frederik Christian.

There, you see.

To me you're Paapa.

The baptism ought to make a person forget their old life, and their old name, so they can be born anew.

To us, to Father and Mother and Kirstine and me, you're a part of the family.

An Egede?

Not quite, but sort of.

There you are, you see. Do you think he would give us permission to marry?

She has been waiting for him to say something like this, and yet is quite unprepared for the question. She is annoyed, not so much by him as the situation itself, though it is him who bears the brunt.

Don't say that, she tells him. You shouldn't say such things.

Why not?

It's not allowed.

I don't understand. If I'm a Christian, and a free man, why mustn't I speak to a girl about marrying her?

Speak to my father, she says. He will explain.

I wanted to ask you first.

Ask? She gets to her feet. You make it sound like you'll be proposing to me next.

Yes, why not? He looks up at her with puppy-dog eyes.

Oh, I don't want to hear this, I don't want to hear it at all.

He smiles distraughtly. His lips move, soundlessly forming the words, I love you, I love you.

Shut up!

I didn't say anything.

Can't you understand it's not possible? You're already betrothed.

That's just something they made up.

Who?

Kieding and Pors.

You mean you're not going to marry her?

I don't know. I'd prefer not to. But if I have to, I suppose I must. I don't love her. And she doesn't love me.

She's not right in the head.

No. Sometimes she scares me.

Then I suppose it's best you don't marry her then. You must find someone else instead.

No. It's you I love. And I thought you at least liked me.

Don't talk to me like that. She sets off and begins to descend the rocky slope.

He gets to his feet and follows after her, some paces behind.

I knew it, he says. I knew you were leading me on.

She pretends not to hear. She feels turmoil, rage and sadness. What a fool, she thinks to herself. Where would he get such a stupid idea? I've been too nice to him, and now he thinks he can get away with whatever he likes. How can he put me in such a spot? She marches on over the sodden moor, crossing the bogland instead of circumventing it, her boots sinking into the mire, her feet soaked. She hears him following on behind, without catching up.

///

Go away from that window. It's not for young girls to see.

But she stays put, unable to tear herself away. There are so many worlds, so many spaces. There is the priest's residence, there are the moors and the fells further inland, there is the church, even if there is no church here, only a mission room, but the church as a concept; and then there is home in Lofoten, where she lived for the first six

years of her life, and the house in Bergen where they also lived; and
in all these spaces she feels at home. There is also the world of the
natives. She is reasonably familiar with it. She has been friends with
a number of their children and has slept in their homes. But nevertheless it is a very foreign world. Then there is the world of the
Governor, his parlour next door into which she has scarcely set foot,
the world of the jomfru Titia, a world of madness, papism, fornication
and confusion which is quite unknown to her, frightening and titil-
lating at the same time; and then there is the crew house, a pigsty
in which so many have perished, and the world of the ships, likewise
unfamiliar; these male spaces, in fact, filled with things she does not
understand and which are unpleasant for her to think about, their
violence and toil, their drunkenness and barbarity, for instance what
is going on out there now, the boxing match, two men fist-fighting,
their brutal exchanges, the blood and spit that flies in the air. Her
own spaces are enclosed rooms with thin walls in between, and doors
through which she may pass in and out, and where she feels more
or less at home. But sometimes, such as now, she senses a longing
for other worlds, a yearning to mix together their different spaces.
But it is not allowed. If you do, your entire reality will be torn asunder,
with no knowing where it will end. This was what he did not understand. Paapa. And I cannot understand it either, she thinks.

Go away from the window. How many times do I have to tell you?
Sit here with me and help me darn these socks.

///

He stands bare-chested and swaying in the ring. Someone has put a
bottle in his hand. He tosses his head back and drinks, and the crowd
whoops and cheers. He tosses the bottle into the mud. The crowd
urges him on, they shove him in the back and roar, and he raises his
arms above his head, certain he can beat anyone at all, for he knows
that she is standing watching him, and the knowledge of it makes
him strong and invincible.

But the man he is to fight, the boatswain from the *Morian*, looks
at him and says, I don't fight children, I'm no child-beater.

But Pors will hear none of it. It's just an innocent bout. Money has changed hands, the pot is more than five rigsdaler. You've a responsibility now, boatswain.

The boatswain steps reluctantly forward and the lively featherweight goes at him like a windmill, an occasional punch even hitting home, but the boatswain barely feels a thing, he barges him about a bit, growls at him angrily, and when the boy comes at him again, arms flailing, he delivers to his chin an uppercut rather more forceful than intended, and the boy is sent flying, a spiralling, backward-twisting arc, to end in a sorry heap in the mud.

The crowd falls silent. The boy is lifeless on the ground. A man steps forward and pokes him with the toe of his boot.

Is he dead? Is there life in him?

They turn him over and upend a bucket of water in his face. He coughs and splutters, and the crowd erupts.

Salute! Pors barks. A triple salute for Two-Kings!

And the cannon pounds three times for Paapa, baptized Frederik Christian.

17

The Final Palace

*To-day came two Greenlanders from the Raven isles and related
that they had heard our King to be passed away. When I asked
them who had told them this news, they would not answer
me. But I think it to be their sorcerer, Apaluttork, who again
is at large and practising his hocus-pocus and lies.*

FROM HANS EGEDE'S JOURNAL, FEBRUARY 1731

In the autumn of 1730, King Frederik the Fourth together with his
entourage and his queen, Anna Sophie, arrives at Odense Palace
following a tour of inspection to Holstein, curtailed due to the King's
fatigue. He has come to the end. He is burdened by dropsy, breathless
and bloated, an elderly Don Juan shivering with cold; he is, frankly
put, at death's door. As ever, one hopes for the best, a period of
remission, another spring. But the spring is too distant by far and in
his heart he knows he is at his final station, his final palace. In fact
it is fitting. It was here that his half-brother, Christian Gyldenløve,
passed away some thirty years ago, he himself kept the vigil at his
bedside. But apart from having to die, he is in good spirit. The Queen
is next to him in the carriage. She has dozed a while, her head upon
his shoulder, and now she wakes. He squeezes her hand. It is burning
hot. Or else it is he who is cold as ice.

Here we are, he says as the carriage curves up in front of the white
building, its wheels crunching the gravel. The Queen yawns behind
her fan, it sounds like she is about to sing, but she says only *verzeihen
Sie*, I'm sorry, and he lifts her hand to his lips.

In a rustle of tulle and damask the Queen steps from the carriage.
He shuffles sideways to the door. The Count Plessen comes fussing,
wig and coat tails flapping. Dog-like, he endeavours to kiss the Queen's

hand, which she quickly retracts, then bows deeply and begins desperately to tug on the King's arm as if the sovereign were a calf only halfway delivered.

I can manage on my own, Plessen, he says, and cannot help but emit a chuckle.

But he has spoken too soon, for manage he cannot. Not quite. He must support himself on Plessen's arm as they dodder towards the door. Fortunately there are no steps to climb. He tries to straighten up and maintain some element of dignity, but it is clear that Plessen, the sycophantic puppet, is in his element with His Majesty's helplessness.

Did His Majesty enjoy a pleasant journey? he enquires.

No.

His Majesty's rooms are made ready.

Have they been heated?

Yes, Your Majesty. His Majesty will find them nice and warm.

Thank you, Plessen, my friend. He has recalled that he must treat the Count kindly, perhaps even accord him some privileges, so that he might speak favourably of the Queen to Crown Prince Christian when she becomes dowager queen and must look after herself. Christian despises his stepmother, whom Frederik made his queen consort several years before the late Louise breathed her last. Little Christian, so full of spite and bitter piety, the only person of whom he is truly afraid. And his dreadful Saxon wife, Sophie Magdalene, as ill-tempered as a German schnauzer. He is worried about what sanctions might be devised against 'the whore' once he is dead. Confinement to the Blue Tower, perhaps, that despicable structure which ought to have been pulled down long ago after the release of his great-aunt Leonora Christina. Plessen is the only one who can deflect this fanatic hatred of the Queen. Whether he will or not is another matter. There is so much over which one loses control when one happens to be dying. Everything comes apart like a mouldering wine-skin from which sour old wine and dregs seep like pus from a boil. One cannot even allow oneself to reveal one's natural disdain for arse-lickers of Plessen's ilk. And what use is it then to be king?

Her dignified figure accompanies him on his right. She does not support him. It would look like he was being dragged along between two carers. They come inside and a footman helps him upstairs where immediately he climbs into bed. His queen sits at his side. He gulps air with difficulty and perspires from his exertion.

Withdraw, by all means, he says. I need to get my breath back.

She bends down and he turns his cheek so that she may kiss him.

Sleep well, dearly beloved.

Her breasts dangle before his face. He senses her heavy odour of perspiration and lavender water and contrives to send her a dirty look. She stiffens slightly, looks at him enquiringly, only for him to turn away with a sigh. Lovemaking is the body's laughter, sometimes the body's tears. In any case, it is an outlet for all that is pent up inside. But he can laugh and weep no more.

Sleep well, my angel heart. Until our supper table.

She withdraws, leaving him alone. His fingers find the little Greenlandic bone figure, his household god, and he places it on the bedside table. It crouches there, staring at him, exuding an immense power which calms him.

///

I am Aappaluttoq, and I am flying. I can be in all places. I am bound by hand and feet, and the tighter the straps that constrain me, the more effortlessly I fly. It hurts. But the pain is a good pain. It focuses the mind and sets me free.

The sea is black, the sky white; the sea rises, the sky falls, and on the horizon they come together in a grey line. This is what I see when I look to the west. In the north and east stand the fells, they too white and black, though now scintillating in the sunshine of spring. There is Kingittorsuaq, the Deer Antler, rising up menacingly like an admonishing finger. It is on fire. A long plume pours seemingly from its peak. It is of course snow, not fire, not smoke, for the wind blows on Kingittorsuaq even when there is not a breath in the colony. The fell to the north-east is Sermitsiaq, the Saddle, two sharp and jagged ridges, one throwing its blue-tinted shadow on the other, like two men walking in single file. It is a beautiful and frightening fell. No one from the colony has felt inclined to climb it. I, of course, have been there many times. And between these sharp-toothed peaks stand the Malene fells, Quassussuaq, the lesser, and Ukussisaat, the greater, their sweeping lines gentle as a woman's breasts, yet quite as dangerous as their neighbours, precisely because of their innocent and captivating appearance.

A man from the colony ascends there, for the sole reason of never having done so before. He reaches the top and is struck by the sun, and it is as if his whole skull lights up, an entire fairground of merry-go-rounds and lanterns and crackling fireworks inside his head, only stronger and without sound. He sighs deeply with delight. Of this I may tell my grandchildren. But the occasion never comes, this we know, not even to tell those of the colony this same evening. For he cannot find his way down again. The wind, or whatever it is, has erased his tracks and he wanders blindly among a system of ledges, one after another, until he comes to a point where both ascent and descent are quite impossible. Backwards and forwards he goes on his ledge, cautiously, for the rock is treacherous, he leans out and looks for a way down. But there is none, only a sheer face of ice and rock. He tries to clamber up the fellside down which he slid. What a mistake I have made, he thinks to himself with a mixture of amusement, fear and annoyance, but his feet find no foothold. And so he must attempt to climb down instead. Down he will come, by whatever means. The only question is how. But his courage fails him.

Peering over the edge again it is as if someone nudges him in the back, and with a shriek he plunges, no more than thirty fathoms, somersaulting on his way, thinking fleetingly that he sees a figure leaning over the ledge above him, a hideous face with a hideous smile, and then he lands in deep snow and discovers that he has survived the fall. He has plunged into a chimney of ice and is wedged tight. He struggles to come up, but sinks only further, feeling the walls press against his chest, the snow packing around him. He shouts and screams, but to whom? The snow fills his mouth, it fills his nostrils, as if driven by a form of human malevolence. The life seeping from him, he succumbs and floats dreamily away, as meltwater, deriving from his bodily warmth, trickles between his clothes and skin, the blood thickens in his arteries and veins, his muscles stiffen and the water becomes ice again as light glints inside his mind, tiny flashes as if from a passing thunderstorm, and thus he dies, upright like a sentry at his post, at the bottom of an ice-shaft he becomes ice himself, and no one will ever find him, and almost no one miss him at supper, for he was but one of the colony's nameless who was to die anyway.

///

Days pass, weeks, in which nothing happens, neither deterioration nor improvement. He feels too fatigued to travel home to Copenhagen, and to die with young Christian and his sour wife at the foot of his bed is no alluring proposition. He resigns to staying put for the rest of the winter. If he lasts that long. He walks a little each day, supported by Plessen, and he is invariably present at dinner, the Queen at his side.

His old fear of the Inferno returns to him. He has enjoyed many women in his life and disappointed as many again, with the possible exception of the present queen whom he still loves. But God has punished him through her. Six children has he begotten with her, and all have perished. It is his earthly punishment. The heavenly one will be worse still. And his dread of hell is worse than ever before.

He seeks the guidance of his priest, Hersleb, whose words provide him with some measure of relief even though the man himself is an idiot. He speaks in a gentle voice and with a slightly apologetic smile on his lips which irritates Frederik, who instantly recognizes the false humility of all priests. However, he feels he is in no position to put the man in his place. The priest's fleshy chin wobbles as he speaks, his small mouth uttering his words through pursed red lips jammed between baggy cheeks. He is in the habit of dabbing his mouth with his handkerchief as if they were at dinner, yet continuing to talk, his eyes darting uncertainly this way and that, and always he seems on the verge of stopping short, but whenever Frederik is about to say something he picks up the thread again, forestalling him with some banality or other, laughing at himself in embarrassment, plainly aware that he must soon wind things up and come to a conclusion, but droning on regardless, as if he simply cannot stop, meandering off into theological diversions utterly irrelevant to the matter at hand, backtracking, repeating something he has already said once or more, leaping onward to something else, summing up, recapitulating, reiterating, adding something new on which he feels compelled to expound, noting the King's obvious relief at some approaching conclusion, only then to say, *which incidentally, Your Majesty, reminds me of,* then to be away on some new digression, increasingly ill at ease and perspiring, his eyes flickering desperately as he racks his brain for something firm which may extricate him from the confounded torrent of claptrap on which he has embarked, and the King sighs and clears his throat, he reaches out his hand and clutches the sleeve of the priest's cassock, giving him a start, and precipitating yet another landslide of jittery theological drivel, but then eventually, as if by some miracle, he returns to something the King said to him at the beginning of their talk, about the nature of death, and feels himself measurably liberated when, as if having discovered a doorway leading out of this labyrinth, he declares one's death-day to be of greater significance than one's birth-day, Your Majesty, for it is verily the entrance into the heavenly life. And with that he shuts up.

But one has become so attached to this world, says Frederik rather pitifully.

When the time comes, God will release His Majesty from all that is earthly, Hersleb says. Be not afraid, Your Majesty. The Lord will receive him with open arms like his own lost son. That same evening, His Majesty will be seated at the table with all who have gone before him.

Which of course sounds promising indeed. He resolves, by a sheer act of will, to believe in it, retaining the image of the heavenly table that is being made ready for him, cheerful preparations, a light-filled hall, good food and wine, music, laughter and the joys of reunion.

Will Queen Louise be there? he asks.

She will be there too.

But I think she hates me.

In heaven there is no hatred, only love and forgiveness.

Count Plessen waits on him. Frederik can barely put up with the worm, but retains his poker-face nonetheless and continues to be civil with him. He cannot make an enemy of Plessen, who holds in his hands the fate of Anna Sophie. To fill out their time together he invites him to play cards with him in the afternoon, after their walk, before supper. That way he avoids having to talk to him. He even lets him win at ombre, and the shameless nincompoop rejoices gleefully at having beaten his dying king in a game. And so pass his days.

///

Autumn comes, and with it storms. It is an old wife who comes with the autumn. On her back she carries a sack full of wind, and she rushes about the land, as fast as an old wife can rush, her legs moving so quickly they cannot be seen, her hair fanning behind her, and then she will open her sack and let out the wind for there to be storms. The quicker the old wife has run, the stronger the wind. The spirit of the air is called Sila. Sila is not among my own spirits. But I do know her. Sila comes with the darkness, the wind and the cold. She brings the air together, compressing it, making it dense and compact. This is the darkness of winter. In darkness is pain, and pain is still-ness and contemplation. But the storm, which is another aspect of Sila, released from the old wife's wind-sack, will try to shake away the darkness with all its bluster. As if the darkness were a fog that could be dispersed by the wind. But the darkness is not a fog, and cannot be blown to the sea. The darkness is firm, it sticks to the land and cloaks its people, descending from the north, sweeping the sun below the horizon and pressing its head down into the sea until it is drowned. And when the sun is gone, Sila settles and finds peace with herself, and then comes the cold. In the cold is the final stillness and calm. This is the true winter.

///

He adores mirrors. Mirrors expand the world, doubling it, multiplying it, if several mirrors are placed at a certain angle to each other, revealing in their depths an entire litany of repetitions of this earthly life. Yet one cannot properly get to the bottom of such consecutive reflections, for the beholder obstructs his own view. Always there is a head and body in the way.

A mirror is also a portrait, though plastic as its model. Moreover, it never embellishes, never glorifies, never adorns its subject with superfluous attributes of symbolic nature. His is a face knotted with scars from the pox he suffered as a child. It looks like a lump of minced meat. It is an honest face, and true. The mirror is a portrait in which the subject grows up, grows old and dies. But the odd thing about this portrait is that the only person who can properly see it is the person whose portrait it is. This solitude, or intimacy, of picture and beholder, fascinates him. As long as I see a man in the mirror, I am here yet. For the picture is mortal. When the beholder is gone, the picture too is gone. He sometimes fears there will be emptiness. Nothing left but chairs, tables, chests of drawers, papered walls. This is the terror of the dead, to step in front of a mirror and see in it nothing but a *nature morte*, a still life devoid of human presence. But of course there will always be someone in the mirror. His successor in this mirror-world is called Christian. The mirror is thereby death, he thinks to himself, gazing at his reflection, and contains death's abstract chaos.

He stands up in the salon, looking at himself between two mirrors, straight-backed and yet at ease, the sun coming in from the rear, two kings considering each other, and a hundred thousand with their backs turned. But in the mirror behind him, which reflects the mirror in front of him, they all stand staring at him over each other's shoulders, while he himself stands between these two endless friezes of kings. His shadow is thrown onto the floor in front of him. The figure in the mirror possesses a shadow too. In fact, this shadow interests him more than the person he sees. A reflection of a shadow, ambivalence again. Like the figure of the King himself, his shadow is multiplied, projected infinitely into the mirrors' bewildering cylinder! He finds it dizzying.

Suddenly he kicks out, an impulsive action whose reason is unknown to him, for he is not in any way enraged, and the mirror cracks from corner to corner. Yet, even though it is old and blotched with quicksilver, it does not shatter. And now, strangely and remarkably, as he steps backwards and the figure in the mirror, distorted by the crack in the glass, divided in two at the waist, likewise steps back and away from him, his reflected shadow remains stuck to the same place on the floor. And while he knows this to be an impossibility, an optical illusion caused by the sun or by the mirror's quicksilver, he nonetheless sees his shadow quite clearly abandoned by the body from which it was cast, and with a small flutter of sunlight shining upon it, making it partially diffuse, albeit not enough to make it disappear completely.

///

The moon is in love with the sun. The moon is the man, the restless suitor. He hurtles back and forth across the sky. The sun is the woman, big and warm and lazy, the paths she wanders barely changing from day to day. In the winter she hides away, while the moon continues to tear about looking for her. Very occasionally, and there can be years in between, they meet and merge together in love, or what the Danes call an eclipse, lasting only the briefest of moments, less than an hour, and in the few minutes in which the sun at last yields to the courtship of the moon, in which his love for her is consummated, the earth narrows its eyes as if in modesty, and darkness descends.

///

The palace barber, who is also the surgeon, comes to cup him. The physician looms above him, peering over the surgeon's shoulder to make sure everything goes by the book, literally so, for he is reading aloud from a German handbook of medical surgery. The barbersurgeon, a waggish sort, winks at his king and smiles, and Frederik smiles back conspiratorially. Let the man enjoy his work.

He has suffered an attack in the night, with fever and feebleness, pains in his chest, coughing and congestions of thick mucus. It is the damp weather that has gone to his lungs, the surgeon says. His Majesty ought to travel south and be warmed up.

Yes, if only I could, he says.

The Queen is with him. She holds his hand and is quite calm.

Her serenity settles his mind. But then it is day now too. It is the nights which are bad. Their dreadful fantasies, their wispy, wandering figures, scarlet imps and perished queens.

We should properly draw off some blood as well, wouldn't you say? the surgeon enquires, turning his head to the physician.

Cupping and bleeding on the same day? The physician seems sceptical. I've never known it before. Let the cups do their work.

It helps too, though perhaps it is more the hand of the Queen which helps. He fears the night and all its diableries. He fears hell while still alive.

And hell will come, even for an absolute monarch. It comes for the rascal and the scavenger, like filth and lice and consumption. Often it comes in the night. It must be the darkness itself carrying with it a poisonous vapour which seeps in through the closed windows and wraps itself clammily around the human body which lies and waits. He is assailed by choking fits after midnight and the Queen summons both the physician and the priest. The priest summons the Lord, and the physician summons the surgeon who lives inside the city. He arrives as the priest is administering the sacrament. Plessen too comes shuffling in his dressing gown and nightcap and stands by the window looking out through the curtains as if waiting for some nocturnal visit.

The surgeon measures the King's pulse, empties the contents of his chamber pot into a round-bottomed flask which he then holds up to the light, and looks into his eyes.

No, he says. Not yet. The time has not yet come. We must let some blood.

Then do so, snaps the physician. What are you waiting for?

The surgeon takes out his needles and syringes, taps the King on the chest, presses his hand down into his abdomen and releases, causing the royal belly to wobble a moment. He prods and probes. If His Majesty will permit? he says, and lays his ear to his chest and listens. He inserts a long needle into the King's midriff and a clear fluid begins to run into a bowl. Frederik lies listening to it gurgle and feels his strenuous breathing to be relieved somewhat. The Queen wipes his brow with a cloth she dips in lavender water. It cools him pleasantly. She looks upon him without sorrow, unpained, and with a strength in which he finds comfort.

The surgeon taps his fingers against the King's chest and listens once more. He says there is quite an amount of pleural fluid. With His Majesty's permission I should like to draw some of it off. He indicates with his finger.

Do whatever you find necessary, my good man, Frederik tells him.

Another needle, considerably thicker this time, is inserted into the chest, and again fluid trickles and gurgles.

It seems to be quite clear, not at all cloudy, says the surgeon. He sniffs at the fluid, dabs a finger into the bowl in which it has collected and tastes it. Good, he declares appreciatively. Very good indeed.

Frederik falls asleep and on waking the next day he feels well. He even gets out of bed, aided by two servants who help him into the great chair where he nibbles at a plate of boiled pears.

A very good day to you, says the Queen. How is my king today?

Much better, thank you. Where is the surgeon?

Downstairs in the salon, sleeping.

Send him up. I wish to reward him. Call for Plessen too. I've something for him as well.

A short time later, Denmark has a new baron, and Plessen is given the Order of the Elephant, the King speaking to him in private, sending even the Queen outside. And Plessen smiles graciously, his new order nestled in his pocket.

///

The snow falls thickly this autumn, first wet, later dry. All edges become rounded and soft. The colony dwellings sink into the accumulating mounds and blow their curls of grey smoke into the air where they mingle with the grey blanket of cloud which drops lower and lower, again to compound itself into the densest snow which then precipitates once more onto the roofs. The fjord is black. It consumes the snow which falls upon it, remaining unchanged in its blackness, insatiably absorbing the descending white. Along the shore the snow settles and collects into a thick porridge bobbing with the swell and forming a greyish crust that is oddly elastic, but which

nonetheless can bear a person's weight if anyone should have need
to walk upon it. Now the bays are filled with ice, particularly those
which face away from the open sea. When the wind is up, the waves
wash into a frozen embankment which grows with every storm. And
when the wind is in the north, which happens once or twice in every
month, the swell is powered through the fjord, breaking up these icy
banks, the rocks become black and slimy, and the waves surge well
onto the land, raging and wreaking their havoc, crashing and exploding
in vertical spuming columns which drop as quickly again, to be sucked
back into the next assailment.

A flash of light in the night, followed by a dull thud. A salute for
the King on his fifty-ninth birthday. Long live King Frederik! A toast
to the King!

But I am not in the colony. I am with the King. And the King has
but hours left on earth.

///

Here I am. Here I lie. It is all I can do.

The Pastor Hersleb prays and sings for me, and I hum along to show
my good will. I confess my sins, which are many, receive the sacraments
and the holy oil, and lie and count the minutes. The clock moves so
slowly. It is quite unfathomable. Days pass, weeks, months between
every movement of its hand. One could live forever like this. I doze off,
and when I awake more than four hours have passed. What a relief.

I have no pain. The body has succumbed. It no longer tells me of
its suffering. What's the use? I am now separated from my own body.
It has given me much pleasure, albeit also much trouble. I have
always enjoyed riding, horses especially, but also the ladies. Will I
ever see a cunt again, a cunt that breathes its warmth in my face and
kisses me softly on the mouth? Only my mind is horny now. The
body cares not. It used to be the body that ran ahead of me like a
dog. It could bring most everything into jeopardy. A king ought not
to have a body. Now, though, it has abandoned me. Where did it go?
Ah, there it is. It lies here in the bed, quite limp and on its back.

They are all here. Plessen and his fat wife, Hersleb with his
blubbery chin, the physician, the surgeon, the servants, my valet

Torm. And my queen of course. She wipes my brow and cheeks with her damp lavender cloth and looks upon me with a patient expression, quite without pathos. I am grateful to her. The Greenlandic talisman is on my bedside table. It stares at me knowingly. I would like to reach out for it, to feel the smoothness of the bone between my fingers, but I cannot. Someone ought to get rid of it, or put it away in a drawer. It is pagan, I suppose. Yet I feel comforted by it. It wishes me no harm. It knows me, it knows who I am. And yet it likes me.

After midnight time passes more slowly. My lungs wheeze and struggle on, breath by breath, like the strokes of an oar, but still I watch the long hand of the clock. It has stood still for a long time now. How incredibly slow that clock is.

///

Long live Christian the Sixth, says Plessen quietly. He is standing by the curtain. His Majesty has just now arrived.

The King is dead, declares the physician.

But the King is alive. He has at this very moment pulled up in front of the palace, the gravel flying about the wheels, and Plessen sees him jump from the carriage and run to the main door. They hear his footsteps on the stair, and a moment later the door is flung open and Christian marches into the chamber, his cheeks blooming with exertion.

Where is he? Am I too late?

His Majesty is just in time, says Plessen, bowing low and kissing his hand.

///

November was windy. December was a deluge of sludge and rain, interspersed with sleet and glaze ice. Now it is January. Hard frost and still weather. The ground is slippery underfoot. Nuuk, or the cape on which the colony is situated, is girded by a thick belt of ice that makes putting a boat in the water a perilous affair. The native hunters climb into their kayaks on land then slide down over the icy embankment to all but vanish into the water, then bobbing up into view again like a cork, flapping their hands to brush the ice flakes from their gut-skin waterproofs. They paddle out across the ice-cold, silent sea, armed with harpoon, hunting float, arrows and a resolve to kill.

The native dwellings are well heated with their blubber lamps which never seem to go out, and their pots of boiling meat which seem always to be filled to the brim. The women wash their hair in the urine pots and help each other with their grooming, picking out the lice and crushing them between their nails with a small and satisfying snap; they tan and scrape hides, sew and mend, and chew the skins so as to make them soft; they lie with their men, whisper stories sniggeringly into each other's ears, rock their children and are busy the whole winter. The men have little to do apart from when they venture out into the cold to hunt. When they are home they sit and recline on the benches, naked, glistening with sweat, and lazily allow themselves to be groomed by their women and children. Or else they tell stories, frightening the lives out of each other with tales of evil spirits crawling inside the bodily orifices of people while they are sleeping.

I am Aappaluttoq, the Red One. I am a man condemned to solitude. Some few short years ago I took a new wife, Isigannguaq, or Sara, for she was baptized, but now she too is dead. She gave birth to a child with three heads, one had blue eyes and fair hair, another brown eyes and black hair, and the third had blue eyes and black hair. Such a monstrosity cannot live of course. Nor indeed can the woman who gives birth to it. Now I am alone again. So it is to be a shaman. A shaman is the dregs, held everywhere in contempt. But they cannot do without me either.

Now they have bound me with leather straps, and off I fly. Far, far away.

Where have you been? they ask. To the far side of the moon? To the Pope in Rome? They laugh until they nearly split their sides.

I've been with their king, I tell them. I'm exhausted. Give me some meat.

They give me meat and fresh water. And when I have eaten I tell them. The King is dead.

Sunaaffa! they exclaim in dismay. Can the King die? What will happen to us now?

And of course the women begin to cry. A shrill wail, piercing and persistent. And this is how we Greenlanders mourn King Frederik the Fourth, long before the Danes have any idea that he is dead.

18

A Duel

From a Dutch ship to-day the very sorrowful news that our most gracious and noble Majesty, King Frederik the Fourth, has passed away, which news saddens my heart. The lamented gentleman, who has conducted a laudable and exemplary government, shall in our minds be as the memory of Josiah, immortal and fragrant through generations to come. But I am reminded now that some Greenlanders as early as some months ago believed to have heard that our King was dead. I have borne the truth of this death in my heart ever since, albeit concealed and suppressed. For how can they have known of it and received such a message in the midst of winter? This question poisons my days and confounds my sleep at night.

FROM HANS EGEDE'S JOURNAL, MAY 1731

What time is it? Landorph wants to know.

Just gone ten, says Fleischer. Nearly time.

Oh, plenty of time, he replies with a forced, unnatural laugh. They can't start without me. Skål, Fleischer!

Skål, my friend. May God be with you.

God or the Devil, he mutters. As long as I stick a hole in that scoundrel's stomach, I don't care.

Lieutenant Jørgen Landorph is Commandant of the military personnel attached to the colony, but no man can command his own fear. Therefore, aquavit is required. Landorph is not scared, he is petrified. He has muddled himself into a duel with the Governor Pors. Things have accumulated into a confrontation in the three years that have gone since they came here. There have been small provocations and conflicts, mutual accusations and suspicions, smouldering

anger, slander, and the crew have been obliged to step between them
on several occasions in order to prevent a shameful fist-fight.

This antagonism became particularly pronounced when they both
were in the north to inspect the small whaling station at Nipisane
where the Dutch had once again been at work and had set fire to a
house. He tried to sit down with Pors and work out a plan with him
as to what they should do. Pors wished to set up a new colony there
with a permanent crew, while he, Landorph, believed a year-round
military presence to be a more expedient step, allowing the King to
establish a colony there at some later date should he so wish. It was,
of course, a clash of leadership and rank, governor or commandant,
and this organizational conflict trickled down like poison and caused
their personal animosities towards each other to flare up. Pors called
Landorph a billy-goat, which hurt him more than he cared to admit,
while he on his part retaliated by referring to the Governor as a comic
admiral, which anyone can see is what he is, so what was he so
incensed about? Pors demanded he retract, but Landorph was unable
to find any reason to do so. To call him, Commandant of the
Greenlandic colonies, a goat was in his own estimation a different
matter altogether and much graver.

Look forward to an official reprimand for this, he threatened. The
Governor must understand that he cannot under any circumstances
call me a goat.

You don't say, said Pors. And who do you imagine might issue
such a reprimand, goat?

I've already written to the Chancellery.

This was a cheap trick, if ever there was one. For one thing, the
Chancellery had much more important matters to deal with, and for
another it would undoubtedly, if and when it even replied, instruct
the parties involved to resolve the matter amicably. Moreover, he had,
in fact, not written to them at all.

Skål, Fleischer!

Skål, my friend, skål, says the Paymaster.

What time is it?

Nearly half-past ten by now, I shouldn't wonder.

Still plenty of time, then. They can't start without me.

The eleventh hour, he thinks to himself. Quite appropriate, as it happens.

Matters grew only worse. Pors realized of course that Landorph neither could nor would lodge a complaint with anyone. This was their own business. Thus, the Governor would bleat like a goat every time the Commandant was compelled to approach him in the performance of his duties. Indeed, Landorph was unable to get any answer at all out of the Governor but a series of bleats and eventually saw no other option but that all communication between them take place in writing, even though they were camped in tents only a few steps away from each other.

Landorph hit back by initiating a rumour among the officers that the Governor had cultivated a taste for young native girls and that he was in the habit now of creeping into their dwellings at night and having his way with them. There was no substance to this, of course. Yet the rumour spread, and after a short time he even began to believe it himself.

When the Governor heard this he was enraged. He went to Landorph's tent while its occupant was asleep and tore up the stakes by the guy ropes, slashing the canvas to ribbons with his sword while yelling that he was going to haul him before the colony council and bring proceedings against him with the demand that he be sent back home by the very first ship.

Landorph denied any involvement in the rumour. But of course I have heard the talk, he said. And is there ever smoke without a fire?

This he said to the Governor's face in the presence of several others, which of course was rather foolish. As a military man he ought to have known better, that a strategic advance is preferable to a frontal attack, a prolonged siege involving spies and informers and long-range artillery, ambushes etc. He was forced onto the defensive. The Governor glared at him with ice-cold eyes and said, When I refer to you as a goat, Lieutenant, I am not resorting in the least bit to conjecture. And he told him he knew of Landorph's visit to the housekeeper when he had covered his face with the skin of a slaughtered kid. I have it from the poor Titia herself, he said. The men realized this was true. He did not bleat at him this time, for it was unnecessary.

So then they were returned to the subject of Titia, for which he was not happy. Titia was his weakness.

Although this was the most serious of their conflicts until this point, it was in essence not much different from their usual bickerings, which had now been going on for three years. Both of them knew it would all fizzle out at some point. And yet here they were.

Is it time, Fleischer?

It's just before eleven, Jørgen.

How it drags, he thinks to himself. I wish it would go even more slowly, or much faster. This is unbearable.

Shortly after they had returned from the north, Titia hanged herself. It was the Governor who found her. She had been alone with her madness for weeks, but when finally there were people around her again, and summer came with all its light, she had taken her life. It was hard to comprehend, though in one sense, he had to concede, it was a relief. Many felt the same way, men who had compromised themselves with the little Titia, the colony's secret pleasure girl. Why Pors should be so angry with him, of all the girl's suitors, he failed to understand. It was hardly his fault that she was suddenly to be found dangling from a hook in the ceiling of the governor's residence. The old matter of her pregnancy was now resurrected. Pors was gathering witnesses to the effect that he, Landorph, had committed offences against her and that he moreover was father to her child.

Landorph countered by levelling the same accusation against Pors. He too gathered witnesses. A number signed an indictment he drew up.

So there they were. Claims and counterclaims. To dismiss the entire matter and forget all about it was in the interests of both men. But neither could see how it might be done.

Then an idea came to him as to how it all should be resolved. Immediately he scribbled down the following letter to the Governor: 'Honourable Governor Pors! He knows me. He has inflicted damage upon my honour, which only a duel with weapons of his choice and at his specified time and place may restore. His humble servant, Jørgen Landorph, Commandant.'

He was confident the Governor would be too cowardly to take up this challenge and that the threat of a duel would thus be sufficient to put the matter to rest.

Skål, my friend!

Skål, my good Lieutenant!

And what does the clock say now?

Now it strikes eleven, Jørgen!

Time enough, time enough. They can't start without me.

It felt good to have written that little note with its challenge to Pors. It felt less than good to receive the Governor's reply. Barely an hour later he stood with it in his hand and read: 'Most honourable Jørgen Landorph, Commandant over sheep and goats, his challenge hereby accepted, gauntlet taken up, that we shall meet with swords outside the colony house this first of August. Bonam fortunam! C.E. Pors, Royal Governor.'

Which was to say a whole month later. That was some relief, at least. A long time yet. Unfortunately, time has the regrettable property of passing. Now it has run out and he sits at the eleventh hour priming himself with Dutch courage. The duel is imminent.

He downs another glass, seated upstairs in the governor's residence playing a game of piquet with the colony paymaster. He is losing.

Of course, he has duelled before. Settling insults and quarrels by means of the sword is part and parcel of the military life. But always it was but foolery, a lark that perhaps would result in a torn shirt or the slightest of flesh wounds, nothing even remotely perilous. This time he is properly frightened. Either he will become a murderer or else he will be murdered himself. He may very well have seen his final sunset.

He ought to write a letter. A last will and testament. A last goodbye to his family. Both his parents live still, and several of his siblings. Indeed, he has endeavoured to do so, but the quill trembled so violently in his hand that it was impossible for him to commit anything legible onto the paper, which quickly disintegrated into a pulp of inky blotches, snot and insufferable self-pity. So humiliating is fear. Especially for a soldier. And Pors is moreover an old man, nearly twenty years his senior.

He has been dealt *carte blanche*, but forgets in his distraction to declare it and loses heavily. Fleischer scrapes the pot towards him, a number of wooden counters in the place of money. A whole pile of them now resides on his opponent's side of the table.

Still he persists. And loses. Four rigsdaler, five, six. He pretends not to be bothered by it. And anyway, what good is money to him? Even if he does manage to avoid death in the duel, he may just easily kick the bucket on his way home to Denmark. And if he should manage to return home having killed the Governor in a duel, everything he owns would be confiscated and he would be demoted to the rank of junior officer, *fændrik* or sergeant. Or else be put in irons and consigned to a very dark hole.

Skål, Fleischer!

Skål, my friend! Soon time now.

They can't start without me.

He has aged with these three years of tribulations, among them the scurvy. Four teeth have fallen out, his cheeks are lined with long, vertical furrows that make the face he sees in the mirror unfamiliar to him, and he has lost half his hair. He tires quicker than before and his hands tremble slightly when for example he lifts the aquavit to his lips or eats with a knife and fork. Also, he has completely lost the desire to fornicate. Not that there is anyone left to fornicate with. Perhaps it will return to him once he gets home.

He places his final card, and loses again.

To hell with it, he says with a laugh. Luck is not with me today. Make me an IOU to sign.

Fleischer counts his winnings. Seven rigsdaler and six marks he consigns to a money-bag.

That sounds about right. Write it down.

The Paymaster finds a pen and scribbles down a note. Landorph takes it and scratches his name, a careless squiggle.

Time for you to get ready, then?

All right, there's no hurry.

He fills their glasses.

The Paymaster peers out through the window. There's a whole crowd out there, he says.

You don't say. Are they betting on the outcome?

I would think so.

And you? he says. Who are you putting your money on?

I shall put my winnings on you, my friend, the vulpine Fleischer replies, rattling the counters in his money-bag.

Liar, he mutters. A fine second you are.

Fleischer shrugs.

Then drink with me. It's the least you can do after emptying my pockets. There's time yet. They can't start without me.

They down two drams in swift succession. Now the bottle is empty. It was full just before, and he is drunk. Much too drunk for any sword-fight. He is not even sure he can stand up. Can a man shy away from his duel because he is feeling unwell?

Fleischer is a sorry second to be wagering on his opponent. He sits there with his slanting, dishonest eyes and a grin on his face. Still, there's nothing to be done about it. He has always been friends with Fleischer, whom he has known since before they came here. But Fleischer has changed, like everyone else. No longer the joker in the colony, he has become quieter and will often retreat into his thoughts. Kieding, long of beard now and weakened in spirit and health, resembles a rag-and-bone man. Kopper, who for the briefest time was married, only to become a widower before a month had passed, has not uttered a word since the spring. And Pors, well, Pors is Pors, though a shadow of resignation has fallen upon his formerly so wrathful gaze and he looks as if his forehead is now sliding down his face to cover his eyes. Egede, who has never before wished to baptize anyone, is now making Christians of the natives in a flurry. And then, of course, there are the many dead. What is this forsaken land doing to us? he wonders. It is turning us into something else. Will my family even recognize me when I return home? Will I recognize them?

Pors's second is Thomas Tode, colloquially the Knife-man. No doubt they have been fencing with blunted rapiers all morning to get the Governor warmed up for the contest. Landorph himself is elevated above such nonsense. A duel is a serious matter, and moreover forbidden by Christian the Fifth's Danish Law, even if the soldier's code decrees that it be taken lightly, as a prank or a game of cards.

On the other hand, one may drink and perhaps even preferably be drunk on appearance, thereby displaying one's scorn for an opponent. In this, at least, he seems to have succeeded.

Cries go up outside.

Who are they shouting for?

They are impatient, Fleischer says solemnly. They are calling for the duellists. He feels his bones grow cold. I am to die, he thinks. Lord, make my death an easy one. Let me not suffer. Let me not show how cowardly I am. And now I come to think of it, let me not go to hell for what I did with the jomfru Titia.

There is a knock on the door. Lange, the priest, pokes his head inside.

Lieutenant, I think it's time.

Let them wait. They can't start without me. He laughs at his own joke, though senses he has repeated himself.

Would you like to say the Lord's Prayer with me, Jørgen?

In fact he would, certainly, yet he feels he must follow the customs of the military, for which reason he declines: I shall save my Lord's Prayer for this evening when I retire to bed. Fleischer would have howled with laughter at this once, but his audience is now depleted. The Paymaster merely sits and stares absently out of the window. Lange does not laugh either. He too used to be a cheerful sort.

Would you like to confess your sins before the duel?

I think you know my sins, he says. You have committed many of them yourself in my company.

He feels his body to be in the grip of a great ice. He senses what feels like a great fist take him by the scruff of the neck, causing his skin to contract all the way down his spine, the hairs at the nape of his neck to rise as if he were a hedgehog, and yet he persists in his humorous vein and adds, I shall raise the matter of my sins with God when I retire to bed this night.

He glances from one man to the other. Lange displays not a smile. Fleischer is silent. Here he stands, about to meet his death, though making fun of it like a man, and yet not a smile can they muster. Landorph feels most like thrusting his rapier into both the Paymaster and the priest. And then himself.

Instead he brings a toast with the remaining drops of aquavit, and he realizes how dreadfully drunk he is. He is ready in his mind, but his legs are like water as he staggers to his feet. The room spins in front of him, but still he manages to pull himself together for a moment. And it occurs to him that the sly Fleischer, now pretending to be utterly uninterested, has doubtless got him drunk on purpose in order that he lose, thereby securing himself a nice little windfall. As if his pockets weren't already full of his money. Is it even permitted for a man's second to have money at stake in a duel to which he himself is party? He would not be at all surprised to find it written down in some statute from times past when hardly a day went by without a man being killed in a duel. He thinks it must be the case, but concedes that it now matters not a jot.

Where is my good friend, the Governor?

Getting ready, says Lange.

Then let's go. Fleischer, my sword.

He staggers down the steep staircase, his trailing rapier clattering against every step. Reaching the downstairs passage he hears a clamour from within the residence, and Pors's blustering voice. He opens the door on the right and tumbles out onto the open area where the gun carriages stand. The Paymaster supports him. He stands there swaying, waiting for the Governor to appear.

It is the middle of summer, June. The weather has been warm and stable for several weeks, but now there is a chill in the air. New snow has settled on a couple of the peaks. Et memento mori. The darkness is out there somewhere, always in wait. He looks at the crew, who are gathered in a semicircle, some half-hundred men. Just as many have perished these last years, and more will die before they return home. They know it too. And yet they look glad and excited. They want to see blood. They want to see others die. They want to see one of the fine gentlemen be run through and fall. And that gentleman is perhaps me, Landorph thinks sadly. No doubt it would suit them well. I am not popular, I know. A commanding officer is never popular in peacetime. In war, of course, it is another matter. But he knows the Governor enjoys more support than him. It feels so desperately unfair, for if anyone is to blame for the calamities of this past year it must surely be Pors. Still, the common men will always prefer the gentleman who acts like a clown, as they will despise a leader who strives to be responsible and conscientious.

Now a roar of enthusiasm goes up. Pors appears on the step in a full-bottomed wig that would make even the King of France envious, a splendid form-fitting three-cornered hat and his finest uniform. Thomas Tode grips him tightly by the upper arm, steering him like a deathly hospital patient: One more step, Your Grace, and we'll be there. That's it, just a bit more to the right. No, that's left, sir. To the right, that's it. Now, straight ahead and mind the step.

What's the matter with the man? Landorph asks himself. Ah, he's paralytic, of course. The Governor has a wild, bloodthirsty look on his face, and it seems like all the clouds in the sky, and all its blue and empty air, have congregated in his eyes. He staggers about with Tode in tow, apparently trying to shake him off, and has already drawn his rapier and swipes the air with it madly, a brisk swishing sound. The crowd cheers and Pors seems to wake up for a moment and stands unsteadily, tall as a tower, peering at those who have gathered round. The wide and foolish-looking, slobbering grin of the drunk spreads across his face as he realizes himself to be the object of their cheers, and he feels prompted to take a couple of unsteady steps forward unaided, though Tode must come to his rescue when he stumbles and is about to fall.

Landorph feels relief. He will not die. The Governor is much the drunker of them and would be unable to walk through a barn door even if he were standing in front of it. A gentle prod of his shoulder and it will be over, he thinks. He glances at Fleischer. The Paymaster stands peering philosophically into the air as if he were somewhere else entirely, which probably he is.

How fortunate you put your money on me, Landorph says sarcastically. Otherwise your stakes would be lost.

The two seconds step forward. They bow to each other and proceed with the initial formalities. In the meantime, Pors has disappeared. He has barged his way through the crowd and stands now passing his water against the wall of the residence while supporting himself on his rapier as if it were a walking stick. The crowd howls with laughter and breaks out in applause.

Landorph stands with arms folded, a smirk on his face. He breathes in deeply, drawing the air into his lungs. It is a splendid day. It is the first day of the rest of his life and not, after all, its final minutes.

Governor! he cries. Be finished with his pissing or I shall come and slice off his dick!

But before he knows what is happening, and without the referee having given the signal, the Governor storms forward, his wig-wings flapping as he roars, brandishing his rapier wildly, and strikes him on the cheek, elegantly springing backwards to stand *en garde*, swaying, though not nearly as unsteadily as a minute ago, and before Landorph has fumbled his weapon from its scabbard, Pors thrusts forward again and runs him through to the hilt. The crowd gasps. Landorph looks down at himself. There is no blood, no pain. He genuinely saw the rapier enter his body and be withdrawn again. And he could hear from the crowd that he had been struck. I must be dead, he thinks, and therefore I feel nothing. Thank you, Lord!

Halte! shouts Kieding, the referee.

No, no, I am not hit, he protests. Am I?

Kieding steps forward and conducts a brief examination. No, you are clearly unharmed. It looked quite clean. *Touché*, do you concede?

No, certainly not. It was a miss. He snaps for breath.

A *passé*, Kieding announces. I must ask the Governor to adhere to the rules. He should at least wait until his opponent has produced his weapon.

The Governor has no time for words. He is vomiting. He spews his guts, coughing and hacking, then returns to the arena. Landorph sees that his gaze has become clearer now and braces himself for another onslaught. But Pors stands *en garde*, with Tode at his side, ready to hold him back or make sure he remains upright in the next gust of wind.

Prêts! says Kieding. *Attaque!*

Landorph has unsheathed his rapier now. He is the first to advance. Pors stands stonelike in the same spot, stiff as a statue, watching him with his beady little eyes. Landorph advances again and puts his blade to Pors's, a slither of metal against metal. Pors does not move but stares at him attentively. Landorph has the feeling he is like a coiled spring waiting to be released, and hesitates to attack.

Now Pors takes advantage of his dawdling and lunges forward, thrusting his sword upwards, pressing Landorph's back, whereby he, Landorph, avoids being struck in the face. He steps diagonally backwards to his right, then lunges forward, he too, ducking an attack and sweeping his rapier upwards across the Governor's chest, removing thereby a button.

Plaqué, Kieding shrieks, but the two men duel on. Pors parries a strike, lunges forward, legs bent lightly at the knee, and thrusts the length of his sword upwards into the flesh of his opponent.

Touché!

No, I'm not hit, I'm not hit! He walks away, arms raised to show that he is unharmed.

The crowd have fallen silent. This time it was a clear strike. Everyone could see. They wait for him to fall over dead. But he does not fall. There is no pain, no blood. I am invincible, he thinks. Or dead. But surely one cannot die twice?

Fearless now, he launches himself at Pors without thought of protecting himself. He strikes the Governor fiercely, in the face, on the arms and several places on the body, and with each hit Kieding barks a *touché*, the duellists, however, fighting on regardless, the Governor retaliating in kind and likewise striking his opponent in more than one successful foray. Landorph feels a searing pain in his side and looks down to see blood seeping through his shirt.

Touché, touché!

He replies immediately, striking Pors's free hand, which rather than being held behind his back bats at the air in order that he may keep his balance, and his rapier runs through the flesh.

Ow! Pors shrieks, and comes at him with a feint, or else he is merely staggering. Landorph parries, circling left, Pors right, the crowd circled around them, and then they turn and clash, suddenly the Governor is behind him, but where is he now, ah, there, and again he lunges forward and they fence. Their swords clatter. The crowd roars them on, closing in on them the whole time, the arena growing ever smaller, but Pors swipes out at them and like a single organism they back off, and he feints again, strangely, or perhaps he is about drop, a peculiar pirouette that baffles Landorph completely, and the Governor runs him through for the third time, piercing him this time in the side, below the heart.

Halte!

Landorph jumps away, unharmed but for all his minor flesh wounds, and ignores Kieding's call. Pors too continues undeterred. The two men fence. They feint and thrust, lunging and parrying. They strike and are struck, but indecisively, both bleeding from wounds, but he, Landorph, feels nothing, nor seemingly does Pors, for they are in the heat of combat where neither hate nor fear exists, only a circle in which the fixed choreography of fencing is performed, a dance whose participants are relieved of the problems of the world, a place in which one is happy and wishes to remain, never to leave again.

But now they are so exhausted they cannot remain upright. They crawl and scrabble in the mud, groaning and laughing, mustering the odd half-hearted lunge, eventually to flop down flat and depleted.

Thus, Jørgen Landorph lies on his back and looks up at a cloudless blue sky. He sees a gull squirt out some excrement. He sees houses. He sees faces bent over him.

Is he alive?

I saw the sword go right through him.

More than once, in fact.

He looks more dead than alive.

And he sees the Governor who has scrambled to his feet. He looms over him, a giant in a full-bottomed wig, smeared with mud and blood. He holds his rapier in his hand, pointed at Landorph's chest, and smiles. Landorph tries to speak, to acknowledge his defeat, to tell Pors he can go to hell, but is unable to utter a word.

Kieding enters his field of vision. He places a preventive hand on the Governor's shoulder. *Indeterminé*, he says. Neither of you would follow the rules of fencing, and so neither of you has won.

Pors shakes him off. I've been wanting to do this for a long time, he says.

He puts the point of his sword to Landorph's chest.

The jomfru Titia sends you her greetings, Lieutenant.

Mercy, Landorph breathes.

But Pors drives the rapier in to the hilt.

Is this what it's like? he wonders. No pain, no fear, but blue sky and excreting gulls?

19

A Final Salute

While I still was away in the north, Captain Mühlenfort arrived with the good ship the Caritas *and not only did he confirm previous sad news of the King's passing last autumn, he also informed us that it is the will of our most blessed King Christian the Sixth that all Danes be called home from Greenland and the colonies abandoned on account of their great expense, which until now seems to have been incurred here in vain. This news grieves me immensely and pains my heart as nothing else in the world when I think of the efforts and hardships I have exerted and endured, and of the enlightenment moreover of the ignorant people of this land, which now will be wasted and of no avail. And though His Majesty allows me the grace to decide for myself whether I wish to leave or remain in Greenland, and will allow some small number of the colony folk to remain with me should they so wish, the circumstances are such that no reasonable person could resolve to stay, for we should be granted but one year's provisions, and no additional assistance might we expect from the King. This sets my mind in the greatest confusion, not least since I discern that none of the folk will be persuaded into staying here with me.*

FROM HANS EGEDE'S JOURNAL, JUNE 1731

Claus Pors has taken a chair outside and sits in pouring rain in front of the governor's residence enjoying his cognac without the intermediate instrument of a glass to retard the passing of alcohol from bottle to mouth. He peers out over the fjord and the skerries which lie partially obscured behind curtains of rain or mist, whatever it might be. Somewhere out there lies the *Morian* too, which brought him here in the first place and which now is to take him home again. The ship has been anchored here all winter. The *Caritas*, recently arrived from Bergen, is being loaded. He cannot see the ships, but hears them creak and sigh on the swell. The boats sail in and out of the mist, laden with goods to be taken back home, and realized for the sake of stakeholders who have already lost fortunes on account of the grand Greenlandic design. An economic disaster, no less. This is what he must explain on his return.

It is a strange mist. Quite dense, like tulle or cotton wool. And yet above the ground is a clear horizontal band, a couple of alens in height perhaps, in which wander the legs of men, backwards and forwards, bodyless. He has seen many meteorological phenomena in this land, but never this. Where he sits there is no mist, only gently pouring rain. I shall catch a cold, he thinks. But no matter. I am not to die in Greenland, but somewhere else, and soon. I shall take a proper bath when back in Copenhagen. And I will eat an apple. I must have a woman too. I will go to the comedy house, and I will pay my respects to His Majesty, and ride in a carriage. I will drink ale at the Dyrehavsbakken and wander beneath the tall crowns of the oak there. How splendid it will be, however short my time. And I will return home to my farm. I wonder what state it is in? Most likely it is quite as neglected as my father's farm eventually became.

And of course I must find myself a new manservant, he tells himself dejectedly. Perhaps also a new housekeeper.

He thinks of his duel with the Commandant Landorph and laughs to himself. At least he has chalked up a victory to tell of back home. The man thought he was dead. How many fencing matches have I won with that rapier? They think they are run through, when in fact the blade is retractable. But the Commandant's was genuine enough and he wished to kill me with it. My wounds were rather deep. A wonder they did not become infected.

Salute! he barks hoarsely. A salute, Bombardier, can't you hear me? But the bombardier is sheltering somewhere from the rain. Pors himself remains obstinately seated, sensing his clothing become sodden by the minute. He puts the bottle to his mouth and drinks.

The land is impenetrable. It has proved impossible to conquer. It does not fight openly, but exerts its passive resistance. It is the most infuriating of tactics. In fencing, such defensive opponents are impossible to beat. No matter how hard one tries, one swipes the air, and eventually one becomes exhausted and enraged. So it is with this country here. Cannonballs and brute force are no match for mist, it simply moves aside and comes together again. Men perish quietly, they sink into the ground. He scrutinizes the bottle and sees in it a little man descending slowly to the bottom with eyes closed. He drinks a swig. The man is gone. It is the same with the natives. Smiling and friendly, seemingly obliging and subservient, but one can never get a hold on them. Fog people. They will never be good Danish subjects. The whole project has been a waste of time and money, and he will say the same to King Christian. Perhaps the King will reward him for his honesty. Or else he will punish him. It no longer matters.

All the legions of Rome would not be able to conquer this Albion and all its fog. There will be no new *Imperium Daniae*. No triumphal procession. He will be no senator, nor even a counsellor of the Chancellery. He will return to his farm in Jutland in a bumpy cart, just like his father before him when he sold the cow and the goats and returned home to the village. I am my father, he thinks to himself. Greenland was a mirror held up before me, and not only did it show me my father, it also turned me into him.

And who were you, Father? I had never an inkling of the person you were. All I knew was that you did not care for me. Why not? What had I done to you?

Do you remember the time you took me to the market at Thisted? Pors asks his father, the cavalry master. We drove with a pair of goats and a cow tied to the cart. The cow lumbered along and tugged on its rope. The goats bleated so pitifully. They didn't want to go. Perhaps they understood what was going to happen. Listening to them was driving me to distraction. I shuffled restlessly on the box and your listless voice said, Sit still, boy. Eventually we came to the town and drove into the narrow streets there, and I saw the way people looked at us and said here comes the penniless cavalry master Pors with his poor lad, he made his bed and now he must lie in it. We could have found each other in the face of their scorn and pity. But you did not wish it. You stared out ahead as if I was not even at your side. I saw the way you rolled your eyes, and they were wide with resentment. We bumped along and passed the red-brick town hall, and the white stone church in which I was christened and confirmed, and where you were married to Mother, and it took an age to enter the market square, but when finally we did you climbed down and said, You take the cow, lad. And you yourself took the goats. We led them to the meat merchant and sold them for a song. When it was done we set off home again, that long and endless way, and the townspeople's eyes followed us as we went. Roadside trees and fenceposts filed slowly by, and we were so irreversibly and separately alone. Back home only a single cow and a couple of pigs were left, but they too were soon gone. You never struck me, never punished me, never said a harsh word to me. And yet I was terrified of you.

Bombardier! Where are you?

But the bombardier is gone, and Pors is alone. The falling rain instils in him the oddly inverted feeling of rising up, as if the rain were standing still and he himself floating towards the heavens from some dark depth.

Egede hasn't had much luck either, he thinks to himself. All right, he may have started baptizing a few natives here and there, but they seem to have decided to die at the same rate as they are christened. No sooner are they welcomed into the church than they are off to heaven. He sees them standing in their skin clothing outside the pearly gates. I suppose he'll be off home again too, the priest, and to some cushy benefice, I shouldn't wonder. I hope never to see his miserable face again.

This is a kind of status. A balancing of the books. He will be called to account before the Chancellery, the King, merchants and the Commission, so he must think things through. On the ship he intends to write down his considerations as to why everything has failed. He knows full well the reason. The officers have been against him. In particular that goat Landorph. The priests have put the Mission before the Trade. The Trader was plain incompetent. And the common crew, among them the former inmates of Bremerholm and the Spinning House, were utterly unfitted to the climate and harshness of the land. They are dead now, apart from a single enlisted man, Glitker, and the couple, Johan and Sise, who were sensible enough to move from the crew house to their own peat-hut. She gave birth to my son, he thinks to himself. Begat *jus primae noctis*, dead by my hand. I was forced to throttle him. There was no choice. They received a good sum of money in compensation. He it was too who made sure the other boy, Titia's child, was given over to their care. But who the father of that child might be remains a mystery most likely never to be solved now that Titia is no longer here.

More than seventy people have died these past three years. Their corpses lay strewn across the peninsula, covered up by rocks, their frayed wooden crosses angling up into the air. Poor, wretched asses, dunces and rabble! These were not fog people, but people of the earth, and therefore they perished. Tragically they will not become soil now that they are dead, only corpses mummified by frost and bog water and the wind that rattles through the stones of their graves.

How much blubber and train oil have we actually procured? he wonders. Not much. The washed-up whale we found up north yielded a few barrels of rancid oil, about enough to light up an alley in some market town for a week. There remains a widespread illegal trade between Dutch ships and the natives. The little whaling station up north, Nipisane, came to naught.

And so on. The reasons are plenty. The explanations he must deliver to the Chancellery should be quite as numerous. But whether they will match up is a different matter. The truth is certainly of no use, not the whole truth, regardless of how much they make him swear on the Holy Bible.

The natives know something we don't, he muses. They elude the storms and the cold, the hunger and the scurvy, slipping in and out of the fjord, following their own leisurely rhythm, being born and dying like us, but equipped with their own strategies for survival, like the moss that clings to the rocks. They would not teach us their art. Or perhaps we wished not to know.

He drinks again, emptying the bottle, tossing it away and opening another.

Salute! he cries. Let's have that salute, Bombardier!

Ah, there he is at last. The gunpowder is wet, Governor Pors.

Wet? All of it?

The dry stuff's on the *Morian* now.

Can't you at least try? If not a bang, we might at least go out with a whimper.

I can give it a go, says the bombardier. He wanders down to the warehouse and comes back with a barrel which is weeping wet gunpowder.

Pors sits and watches him load the cannon with the ramrod. He peers down the length of its barrel and sniffs inside, picks up a pinch of the powder and rubs it between his fingers.

Mind you don't blow your head off, says Pors.

Not much danger of that, Governor, the bombardier replies.

He strikes the steel, lights the tinder, catches the flame with a tarry rag and holds it to the fuse. The cannon coughs like a cow with a bad chest and spits out some smoke, licking its lips briefly with a blue-tinged flame.

A splutter, albeit not much of one, says Pors.

Wet powder, Governor.

Try again, Pors instructs. Wedge it full. Blow the place to smithereens. I want a proper salute before I go.

///

I am Aappaluttoq, the Red One, and I sit in a peat house inside the fjord, moaning and groaning. They have tied me with straps of leather. They have kicked and beaten me, at my own request. Pain and humiliation are what is required. I tremble, and sweat pours from me. I try to levitate from the earthen floor, but cannot.

Damp out the lights, I say, making my voice weak and pitiful.

They damp out the lights. The air chills, an invisible river of dampness and cold streaming in from the entrance passage, and the people wrap themselves in skins and blankets. But I am boiling hot. Soon it will happen. I can sense it. I focus on the drum that lies in front of me, the beater resting on its skin. Somehow I manage to pick it up and begin to beat an irregular rhythm while keening plaintively. The irregular beats have a calming effect on me. I breathe in deeply. I collect myself. And then I begin to speak in a voice that is alien to me.

I run. I am outside now, running around in the colony.

The Greenlanders on their benches, cloaked in their reindeer skins, gasp. What do you see, Red?

I am running around many times, and very quickly. My running is a strap of leather I wind around the colony, around and around. And now I am tightening it. I am strangling the colony.

Oh yes, they breathe. Go on, Red.

Now they are packing up. The ships are almost ready to sail. The King has called them home. The old king sent them here, his son calls them home again. But who is it who whispers in the King's ear when he lies sleepless and unsettled in the night and thinks he is alone with himself and his thoughts?

You do, Red! the audience says with a laugh.

Who makes everything happen?

You do, Red!

No, I say. It is God. It is God who makes things happen.

What god?

Their god. He is a good god. He is our god too.

The drum beats harder and more rhythmically. Its rhythm makes me strong.

But what about our spirits? they ask. What will happen to them?

They are still here. They are God's children too, they are his angels, and they will be with us always and help us. But God is above them all.

How are we to speak with this new god? they want to know.

You must learn the prayer, I tell them, beating rhythmically on the drum without knowing how I am able.

What prayer?

Our Father, who art in heaven. Repeat after me.

And they repeat the prayer, the drum beating as they speak.

Now you are strong, I tell them. Now you can do anything. Who makes you strong?

God, God!

The ships will soon set sail, taking the Danes and all their clutter with them. I could ask God to sink the ships with every man on board. What do you say, friends? Shall I sink the Danes' ships?

Yes, yes!

I laugh. No, this is not God's will. God can be cruel, but he is not cruel without reason. There must always be reason in any wickedness in the world, no matter how hard we find it to understand, even if we lose the person we hold dearest on earth there is meaning in it.

Yes, yes!

For we are reunited with the dead when we ourselves die. Do not believe the priest when he says the unbaptized are gone for ever. The Lord has spoken to me and told me they shall rise again, the innocent in flesh shall rise again in flesh, for blessed are the innocent, and He shall wipe the tears from the cheeks of the grieving, and those who believe shall enter Paradise where the wolf and the lamb shall feed together, and there will be no harm or destruction on my holy mount, says the Lord, for so saith His book, and I have read it myself.

You are our priest, they say. You, you!

Yes, I am your priest. I am the first. Now it is I who am the Black Man. But there will be other priests after me, priests who are not Danes, but also priests who are Danes, good priests, unlike the nincompoop we at present must suffer.

But what about the nincompoop? they say. What is to happen to him?

The priest, my old adversary, will not be let off the hook. We shall keep him. The priest and his family. We are not finished with them yet.

But is the priest not God's man in spite of everything?

Indeed he is, but I too am God's man. God has many men here on Earth, both good and bad. His plan for the world is grander than we are allowed to comprehend. Repeat now the Lord's Prayer with me, so that you may learn it by heart. Our Father.

And from their cocoons of darkness they repeat the prayer.

Now the drum begins to dance before me. The drumstick beats against the skin, a hollow thud whose echo is hundreds of times greater than the little dwelling in which we sit, and I vary its rhythm by tapping the drumstick against the wooden frame on which the skin is stretched taut, then beating again on the skin itself, and the sound it makes is wild and unworldly, at once transforming the foul-smelling space into a great hall, a cathedral, the Uffizi, St Peter's Basilica, St Paul's Cathedral, places I have visited this past winter after the death of my friend, the King, and I whimper with pain, for the leather straps are tight around my wrists and ankles, but I must clench my teeth and continue, rocking back and forth, and suddenly I have endured, I have entered the pain instead of fleeing from it, and the people on the benches are silent now apart from the occasional wailing of a child, they are listening to the drum whose beat seems to swirl beneath the ceiling, coming now from this side, now from that, rising in volume into an ear-splitting noise, its beat descending then into the gentlest tapping, the smallest patter, until the drum drops to the floor with a clatter and is silent. The drumskin is in shreds. They untie my bonds and drag me half-conscious across the floor and dump me on a bench. They light the blubber lamps again.

///

Egede makes his usual round of the colony, past the blubber house, the warehouse, the smithy. He pauses to say hello to the surviving smith who is busy dismantling a pile of flintlocks.

The peace of God to you, Jens Smith.

The peace of God. The smith looks up. Is Egede leaving with the ship?

Yes. I am going home.

So no one will be left here then?

That's it.

Such a shame, says Jens. To give up on something that's barely been started.

The King's orders, says Egede. He leans over the smith's work.
What are you doing with these firearms?

Taking them apart, cleansing them with oil, filing here and there,
putting them back together again. Cheap rubbish they are. Seconds,
as they say. Mostly it's just to pass the time. But I think some of them
will be serviceable again.

One should have been a smith, says Egede, and repair things that
have broken.

Well, says the smith, glancing up at him again. It's not always as
easy as that.

No, I know.

Egede has done good work here, Jens says. No one else could have
done such a job. It makes me exhausted just to think of all he's done.

I did what had to be done.

And now that's it?

The King's orders, he says.

If Egede stayed behind, I'd volunteer to stay. I understand the
King's given us the chance?

Yes, with a year's provisions. No ship until next summer. Do you
want to die here in this country, Jens? Are your bones to lie and rattle
in a grave of stones?

Rather here than so many other places I know. There's meaning
to what a person does here. Your Niels could be colony manager.

And you? What would you be? His assistant?

I would be smith, that's all. It's what I am. Smith, stick to your
forge, as my father used to say.

Indeed, a smith is indispensable, says Egede. No colony without
one. Have a pleasant afternoon, Jens Smith.

You too, Hans Priest, says the smith, and chuckles good-naturedly.

In the open space between the buildings he meets Fleischer sitting
on a rock outside the bakery, mending his wig with a needle and
thread. His red hair dangles in front of his face. He looks up, his
slanting eyes peering out from behind the strands.

Good morning, Fleischer.

Good morning, Egede.

And what might you be doing?

A game of tag with my lice, Fleischer replies, crushing a louse between his nails at the same moment.

Egede leans on his staff and looks out over the smooth rocks at the shore.

I hear Egede will be going home with us?

Yes.

He'll be missed.

By whom? Everyone's leaving.

The natives. Those baptized and those not. They hold him in great esteem.

Oh, I should take that with a pinch of salt. More likely they will dance with joy.

Not at all, says Fleischer. It will be a day of mourning for this country. And we, the crew and officers alike, feel the same way.

Well, he says, we shan't be missing each other for a while yet. We've each other's company to look forward to on the voyage.

It's sad, though, Fleischer goes on. That everything should end this way.

The King's orders.

The priest will be given some good words from us all on his way, though. He's been well-liked, as opposed to certain others, mention no names.

How beloved one has become all of a sudden, says Egede. And you, Fleischer, have become so mellow of late.

Yes, says the Paymaster. Greenland is our downfall and our resurrection, at least for those of us who are not dead.

And here comes the Commandant. Egede hurries away before Landorph too begins to speak of how fond he is of him.

He walks along the shore and comes to a camp of tents filled with natives making ready to move out into the skerries. He sits down with them, picks up a child and puts it down in his lap to bounce it distractedly.

Are you leaving us now, priest?

Oh, don't you start as well, he sighs. Yes, I'm going home with the ship.

But we'll miss you, *palasi*.

You've not done much to show it while I've been here.

But it's true. You're our *palasi*, not the other two, and we're fond of you. You've taught us a lot. Why are you leaving us?

Our king has decided it.

Why?

Because you're so cold-hearted and callous, he says, or would like to say if only he could. Instead, his poor grasp of the language allows him only to say that they are 'bad'. He should have brought Niels with him, or Frederik Christian, to interpret. He would have been able then to deliver a parting shot on which they could have pondered after his departure. On the other hand, he's told them often enough what he thinks of them, so an interpreter would in fact be superfluous.

Because you don't appreciate my teaching.

They react offendedly. It's not true, they say, and touch his cassock fondly. You must not say this to the King, *palasi*. He will think we Greenlanders are bad people and that we do not love him. But we do, we love the King, the new one too, and we wish to learn more about Jesus and Moses.

It's too late now, he tells them. He can scarcely allow himself not to savour this little twist of the knife. Now I am going home. There I shall preach the good word for people who appreciate it. But if any of you should wish to take heed of the Lord, then remember at least the prayer I have taught you, and pray together each evening.

We know the prayer, they assure him. We say it all the time.

Perhaps one day another priest will come, he says amenably. He will tell you about Jesus. And by then you may be ready to accept His word.

We will remember everything that *palasi* has told us, they say.

So you say, he says. But as soon as I've turned my back you'll have forgotten all about me. I've wasted ten years of my life on you.

He walks home. Sunlight shafts down narrowly through the blanket of cloud, a milky haze casting diffuse shadows on the ground. The rain has stopped. He enters the parlour and takes off his wig, slapping the moisture from it against the back of a chair.

Ah, there you are, he says. As if nothing has changed.

Gertrud sits with her sewing. Yes, why shouldn't I be?

Aren't you going to pack the kitchen utensils? And what about the furniture? Shouldn't the men have been here by now to carry it away?

They've been.

Oh? But then why is the furniture still here?

I told them to go away. She continues to sew without looking up.

Why would you tell them that? The ship will be sailing in a couple of days.

Let it sail.

He sits down, quite nonplussed. My dear Käthe, whatever has got into you? Do you not wish to go home?

Stop calling me that. My name is Gertrud, and we're not going anywhere.

He stares at her in astonishment. And the decision is yours to make?

I've spoken to the girls and to Niels. We've decided what we want, you can do as you wish.

I see, he says curtly. Without discussing the matter with me?

That's right, Hansie.

He leans back in his chair and lights his pipe. The tall clock ticks. It makes him think of a lame man he once knew, one heavy step, one light, one heavy, one light. He glances at the time. Half-past ten.

The fog will be lifting soon, he says.

Gertrud looks at him and smiles. Yes, the fog will soon be gone from the fjord. I think it will be a fine day.

He sits brooding for a while, and she begins to speak to him. Her words are considered, with occasional pauses to look down at her sewing. A job begun is a job to be finished, she says. If not, it will live on inside a person, crippled and deformed. I know it's true, I've seen it in others, and I think of what it would be like to be somewhere else, in a parish. It would not be good for any of us, and certainly not for you. There's so much we've begun her which we are nowhere near finishing. Our living is here.

But what of your own living, Gertrud?

I've committed myself to the savages.

Hm, he says, still dumbfounded. What lot do you have in their fate that you don't have in mine? You are my wife, after all.

I am your wife. But I am also Gertrud Rasch. I have a say as well.

Indeed. Quite a large one, it seems.

Oh, Hansie, in all these ten years you've never shown even the remotest interest in what I have at heart, that the welfare of the Greenlanders is something I feel as strongly about as you. You men are like the ancient Ptolemaics, who placed the earth, which is to say the man, at the centre, and the sun, which is to say the woman, in his periphery. Yes, you allow us to shine, but you do not appreciate us. We women are not blameless either, for we too position the man at the centre, but you should know that we do so with our fingers crossed behind our backs, as Galileo did when they forced him to say that the sun revolves around the earth rather than the opposite, even though he knew better.

Where on earth did you learn such things?

Do you think all I've done these ten years is darn socks? I have read. I have spoken to people. I have observed. I have thought. I have written. I know you say women think with their arses and that's why we're broad below and narrow above. But in that case my arse may be quite as intelligent as what lies under any wig.

He is stunned. He is unable even to puff on his pipe, whose bowl grows cold between his fingers.

Do you not care for my language, Hansie? It's how you speak yourself. Let me show you something.

She gets to her feet, crosses to the dresser and takes out a pile of papers from the bottom drawer. She hands them to him. He flicks through them. The handwriting is hers, neat and legible.

This is a whole book.

Yes, it's become that way.

He reads at random from one of the pages: 'The relationship between man and woman is founded, and must necessarily be founded, upon a lie, albeit a useful one. Where would I be had I not made his lies my truth? In Vågan on the Lofoten Isles!' He snorts in astonishment and turns the pages: 'The colony is in these days as if imagined by the bard of Florence.' He looks up. The bard of Florence? You mean you've read that papist ink-slinger? But we've never had him in the house.

I read his work as a young girl at home at Kvæfjord. It was before you were born, Hans. It troubled my dreams, but there was grandeur and goodness in it. I still know long passages of it by heart.

He sits the whole day and reads her manuscript. He is absorbed. He thinks: Why did I not write this?

///

Christian Kieding attends to an ailing soldier in the crew house. The man lies on his bunk and gasps for air. His chest rattles and he is burning hot. Kieding cups him routinely, though he no longer believes in the treatment. He offers a glass of aquavit and the patient gulps it down. His cheeks are grey and sunken, his chin pointed as that of an old man and peppered with white stubble, teeth long since gone, yet his eyes are a young man's, filled with guileless terror.

Am I to die, Master Kieding? he whispers.

Of course not. You'll soon be right as rain, Kieding tells him. In two days you'll be on your way home with the *Caritas*.

The man smiles, the credulous smile of a youth. His eyes are glazed with fever and joy. It'll be good to come home, he says.

What will you do when you get back? Kieding asks to take the man's mind off sickness and death.

Go back to my regiment, I suppose. The Sjællandske. I'll see my old friends again. We'll drink, visit a whorehouse and be merry. Some sounds emanate from his throat. Is he crying? Kieding wonders. No, he is singing. *I had me a girl down Shitehouse Lane, her cunt was as big as a hall, oh, her lice they did laugh as they crawled.*

Charmant, says Kieding and pats him on the shoulder.

In the night he is called over again. The man has fallen out of his bunk and lies unconscious on the floor with his head twisted back at an angle, gasping spasmodically for breath. Kieding orders him lifted back onto the bed. He makes a round in the light-drenched night and on his return the poor soul has passed away. He makes a note in his journal: 'Franz Glitker, German, enlisted Geworbener, formerly an inmate of Bremerholm on account of absence from duty, latterly released and adjoined to the common crew of the colony of Godthåb, deceased this night of June the eleventh 1731, of consumption and scurvy. Twenty-two of originally twenty-four inmates now perished.'

Christian Kieding has been forced to concede that the art of medicine is a worthless one. Everything he has done these past three years has at best been without effect. No, if he is to be completely honest about it, he has done more harm than good. Basically, he has been killing people in cold blood. An executioner is what he has been, and Thomas Tode, the Knife-man, has been his assistant. Not even Titia was he able to help. He did what he could for her, cold baths, cuppings, leeches, blood-letting, herbs and medicine, he even endeavoured to marry her off. But all to no avail. Medicine and common sense, these two things were what he arrived here with, and both have been useless. He has himself suffered sickness and managed only just to shiver his way through this last winter. Death breathed directly into his face and in the jaws of death he saw a truth. That everything is meaningless, and in particular that he, Christian Kieding, can do not a thing about it. If Egede should decide to stay on in this land, he would volunteer to remain here too. He cannot abide the thought of the voyage. But now he is going home to drag out an existence in some garrison or other, to cut open boils and carry out cuppings. He hopes he will die before he gets there. He ought properly to follow Titia's example. He is not afraid of the Inferno. But death by his own hand seems to him no less ridiculous than life.

///

Henrik Miltzov boarded the ship some time ago. For several days he has suffered from agitation in expectation of the journey ahead, and moreover from nightmares in which he finds himself left behind, marooned, hideous dreams in which he stands on top of a rock and sees ships vanish into the horizon, leaving him utterly on his own here. This is one reason for his early embarkment. The second is the Egedes. They are leaving with the *Morian*, he is on board the *Caritas*, a smaller and less comfortable vessel, but without the Egedes.

He has been living with a Greenlandic woman these past couple of months and it has almost done him in. It began as an adventure and ended as a nightmare. Nevertheless, he is glad to have had the experience. She rid him of at least some measure of his guilt with respect to Kirstine.

He stopped drinking after a bout of delirium up at Nipisane. She it was who looked after him, washed him, fed him, and later loved him back to life. She came back with him to the colony and they moved into a peat dwelling at the shore. They were in love, or so he felt, and made love without circumlocution. For the first time in his life he felt like a man. His flirtations with the Egede girls now seemed absurd and indecent, whereas his daily rounds of coitus with Tummalaat appeared pure and innocent. Naturally, his engagement to Kirstine was broken off, and to his huge relief.

Tummalaat. He never did discover what it meant, if it even meant anything at all. He read with her and prepared her for the baptism, an endeavour which came to naught on account of his rudimentary Greenlandic and her non-existent Danish. For the time being they communicated with caresses. Still, she managed to make him understand that when she became baptized she wished to be called Ane. He had already begun to address her as such, even if she didn't seem much like an Ane at all.

It had not occurred to him that by living with her he had made her an outcast. Nor, it seemed, had it occurred to her. But at once her family wanted nothing more to do with her. She was allowed to visit them, but no one would speak to her. They pretended not to see her, and thus it was as if she no longer existed. She tried to speak to him about it, but he was unable to comprehend what she was trying to tell him. He taught her to say the Lord's Prayer, and she would lie there and rattle it off until realizing it was neither help nor hindrance. After a while, she turned nasty on him, hissing like a cat whenever he tried to kiss her, beating him about the head with a ladle, pinching his member between her nails as he lay sleeping, spitting in his face. He threw her out and was then alone in the peat house, but she was now homeless and begged to come back to him, whereupon she carried on as before. On hearing that he would be leaving on the ship, she pleaded to go with him. She would be unable to look after herself in this country, that much was clear to them both. He promised to take her with him and cautiously approached the captain of the *Caritas* with the matter, only to be turned down point blank. The natives stay where they belong, the man said. This isn't Noah's Ark.

And now he has stolen on board without her, though through a gun port he has glimpsed her a few times on the shore. He has heard her call for him too, and has found it harrowing. He knows her voice will haunt him all the way across the sea. But still he cannot see what else he can do. Apart, of course, from marrying her and remaining here, a solution he nonetheless considers rather unrealistic.

He knows what he can look forward to on his return to Denmark: a half-decent parish, ploughed fields, peasants to tend his land, a run-down rectory and the grateful, dried-up widow of his predecessor. It will be akin to going to heaven.

The atmosphere on board is characteristically Danish: noxious and muggy. In a way he finds himself already there, detached from this strangest of dreams that is Greenland. A dream that turned him into someone else. He hopes this other person will be able to manage his life in Denmark.

He lies down with a book he has borrowed from the captain's quarters. As the waves glug under the keel and send shimmers of reflected light across the ceiling, he reads the following sentence: 'Having been condemned, by nature and fortune, to active and rest-less life, in two months after my return, I again left my native country, and took shipping in the Downs, on the 20th day of June, 1702, in the Adventure, Captain John Nicholas, a Cornish man, commander, bound for Surat.'

///

Jürgen Kopper, Trader, sits into the night with long lists of provisions and materials to be returned with the ship. He is winding up a losing concern, and it is his duty to make sure the loss is as small as possible. He has sought the advice of the assistant, the Paymaster and the Governor, but in the final end the agonizing responsibility is no one's but his own. Such accounts require a very delicate form of ingenuity. He has a row of very tangible figures with which he cannot fiddle, resources supplied to the colony. But then there is the matter of consumption and shrinkage, which gives him some considerable room for manoeuvre. Useful variables here are weather conditions, fair wear and tear, theft (committed, of course, by natives), inappropriate storage, vandalism, damp, fire, and so on. Such factors must be weighed and weighed again on the financial scales until they find a balance. Which is impossible. The books will never balance, the figures never tally. But nearly, and perhaps well enough. The problem is that he has no way of knowing if this 'well enough' will be sufficient to satisfy the Commissariat-General or whether he risks having to make up the loss himself by deductions in his monies owed.

Eventually, having decided that he has finished and the accounts completed, he makes a final inspection of the colony, and now, on this final day, a man says to him: Did you remember to include that consignment of timber that's stacked up over where the ships lie anchored?

What consignment of timber?

It's been there three years now.

Good Lord, no! Show me.

They cross the peninsula and come down to the harbour. Concealed, to all intents and purposes, under an outcrop of rock lies an enormous stack of timber. He remembers now. It was he who gave the order to put it there, sheltered from the rain. He had forgotten all about it. There is enough to build a house. Human lives might have been spared if only he had remembered this timber. The crew could have escaped that filthy earthen construction, a death-trap if ever there was one. He feels he has personally caused the death of some seventy human beings.

What am I to do? he asks himself. How can I make this great pile of timber disappear? He can't set fire to it. It's far too damp to burn. He can't dump it in the sea, because he'd need to involve others then, and people tell tales. In fact, he can do nothing about it. It lies there like a great, stinking turd, and he is the culprit who has laid it there. They'll put me in gaol, he thinks. My life is destroyed.

Do many people know of this timber? he cautiously enquires of the man who directed his attention to it.

Most likely it's been forgotten about, the man says. I'd forgotten myself, only then I happened upon it just the other day.

And have you spoken to anyone about it?

Only you, Kopper, the man says with a sly smile. Stupid, but canny nonetheless. He knows what's coming.

Do you agree it would be best to keep it that way? Kopper asks.

Maybe. I suppose. The man is clearly enjoying the situation. It'd be against the law, of course.

No one can possibly benefit from this being made known.

On the contrary.

So we understand each other?

Well, I'm not sure I do, Mr Kopper, says the man, now straining himself so hard in order to look canny that he mostly resembles an idiot, which is to say himself. Unfortunately, however, the idiot has the upper hand and needn't care less about what he looks like.

Have we an agreement?

Agreement?

A contract, let's call it that. A very valuable contract, of course.

Ah, now the penny's starting to drop, the man says, and taps the side of his head with a bony finger.

Excellent. Shall we say ten rigsdaler?

What? Sorry, could Mr Kopper speak a bit louder? My hearing's not that good.

Very well, twenty then. That's as much as someone like you earns in a year.

Perhaps, but someone like you earns more, Mr Kopper. What do you make in a year? Two hundred?

Oh, nothing like it, he lies. The fact of the matter is that he earns three hundred. I'll pay you fifty for your silence.

I wonder what that timber's worth in ready money?

Absolutely nothing. It's been ruined by the weather.

As new, I mean.

Well, that's another matter. But it's not new. Or perhaps you'd like to buy it?

I thought you wanted to buy it? So I was thinking of what it would cost. Five hundred?

Are you completely mad? I'll give you fifty, not a mark more.

One hundred.

Sixty.

One hundred and ten.

Stop, stop! That's not the way to do business. To reach a deal the parties must approach each other and meet somewhere in the middle.

This isn't business, the man says unflappably. I can go higher if you want. You know I can, Mr Kopper.

Oh, all right, all right. One hundred.

And ten.

I'll make you out a bond. You'll receive the money once we're back in Denmark. But don't show it to anyone, otherwise you won't get a pfennig.

If I die during the voyage, the money's to go to my family. The bond's got to say so.

Yes, all right. Now shake on it. My goodness, you're not an easy man to do business with.

My father was a pedlar, says the man, beaming. I suppose it's in the blood.

Come with me, says Kopper, and we'll drink a toast to our contract.

He does not sleep well that night. In fact he has suffered from sleeplessness since the winter his wife died. Her name was Karen, called Jewish Karen, widow of Christian Peyn, the German, who passed away in '28. Kopper was married to her for no more than a couple of months before she died following a stillbirth. Now he spends his sleepless hours thinking of the timber stack at the harbour, there for whoever cares to look. On the other hand, if it has lain there undiscovered for three years he supposes it can lie there another day yet. But it won't be going anywhere. In a hundred years it will still be there. Sooner or later someone will find it. The timber follows him into his dreams. It haunts him, as Jewish Karen haunts him, and his stillborn child, Christian Peyn and all the rest of the flotsam and jetsam that will be left here in this land. It will all continue to haunt him many years after he has returned home.

///

The final meeting of the colony council is held on 11 June, the day before the ships are to depart for Bergen and Copenhagen respectively. At the table in the almost empty governor's residence are, apart from the Governor himself, whom the others playfully refer to as 'the former Governor Pors', the Commandant Landorph, the Trader Kopper, the priest Ole Lange, the captains of the two ships, and Hans Egede.

Pors calls for a minute's silence for the jomfru Titius. Poor Titia, he says. There she dangled with her broken neck and bulging eyes, her blue tongue hanging from her mouth. With the dress she had on she looked like a bunch of flowers hung to dry from the ceiling. He glances up at the hook. And poor Skård too. It was the same hook she used. I cut her down and dropped her in a casket, and carried her on my shoulders halfway to hell, if I may say so, past the black-coat there. That's right, you, you bloody Pharisee. You wouldn't have her within sight of the colony, and out there I stood on my own and sang a hymn for her.

Yes, suicides are indeed shunned, says Kopper to his neighbour, Fleischer. I certainly would not wish to follow one to the final resting place.

At least the Governor's heart is in the right place, says Fleischer.

We can always send a prayer to the poor girl, says Lange, and then appeals to the Lord, asking that the jomfru's unsettled soul may find peace and that God may look upon her with kindness. Egede fumes, but says nothing. However, once the little ceremony is concluded he speaks immediately, announcing briefly that after consulting his family he has decided to remain here in the country. Ten men have promised to stay behind with him, among them the surgeon and the smith. The colony will thus merely tick over with a minimum of activity, and it is his hope that the King will in time change his mind and continue his support. He asks that the Governor pass this on to His Majesty in person, along with a lengthy account he has written concerning his decision.

A safe journey home to you all, he wishes the stunned assembly. Farewell! And with that he rises and leaves.

What a release! Now the land is mine again. He wanders inland over the island. He sings a hymn. He hops across the grassy mounds of the bog. He walks along the shore. He meets some natives and tells them he is staying, and they even seem glad to hear it. Life is good!

He thinks about Gertrud's book. He read it in one sitting during the night just gone. It is a complete account, partly in the form of a journal, of their life in this country since they arrived here in '21. He has relived it all, the joys and sorrows, the fears and sufferings, the inhuman strains. Indeed, he is rather impressed with himself having now read of all his achievements here. The second part of the book is a description of the natural environment here, though goodness knows how she gathered the material for it. In his conception, she sits bent over her needlework or attends to the sick in the colony. As far as he knows she has never ventured further than a fjerdingvej from the colony, apart from one or two short trips with him in one of the boats. Yet he gets the impression she has seen considerably more of the country than he has. He wrote something himself in a similar vein, publishing some years ago his rather well-received 'Perlustration'. Now, however, he feels only shame at his book, which compared to Gertrud's manuscript is poor indeed. He resolves to revise it, to rewrite the whole thing from start to finish. But how can he do so without copying her own work? It feels unfair that she, who received only a modicum of instruction from a deacon at home, and who has only ever read for pleasure, should be able to write so much better than he can. If truth be told he feels rather angry about it, as if he had been betrayed.

He trudges home, and there lies the 'book' with her name on the title page. A thick stack of papers. He picks it up and weighs it in his hand. 'Greenlandic Relations. Gertrud Rasch.' Who would have thought the woman could have produced such a thing. The idea is beyond him. Lucky for her she had not lived in the previous century. They would have thrown her on the pyre.

The house is empty. He assumes everyone to have gone to the harbour to say their goodbyes and watch the last of the cargo be loaded on board. He is alone. Is it a sign, Lord? He stands alone in the parlour with the manuscript in his hand. What saith the Lord?

He tilts his head. Is He saying what I think He is saying? Indeed. Thank you, Lord!

Quickly he opens the drawer of the writing desk. He removes the title page from the manuscript, crumples it in his hand and tosses it into the stove. He then takes a new sheet of paper and writes on it his own name along with the title 'The Old Greenland's New Perlustration, or Natural History'.

He locks the manuscript away in his private drawer and drops the key into his pocket. There. Now it is done. That's the way to milk a cow. Now it is there in the drawer. Mine. I have taken it. It is my right. After all, we are but one flesh. Later I will edit the work, and cleanse it of its womanly weakness.

His heart is pounding. The palms of his hands are sticky. He takes out his tobacco pouch and fills his pipe, and smokes to calm himself down. He is still seated there with the pipe when Gertrud and the children come home.

The afternoon passes, and the evening and night, and then it is morning. She has not mentioned the manuscript. But she has given him a look. It is a fearsome look.

///

Everything is packed. Pors stands in front of the governor's residence. He is wearing his finest uniform. Now is the time for him to descend to the boat and be sailed out to the *Morian*. But he cannot bring himself to go. The moment he stands on the deck of the departing ship he will no longer be governor but simply Major Pors. Then, truly, he will be 'the former Governor Pors'.

A final salute, Bombardier?

We can always give it a try, sir.

Stuff it full, that ought to do the trick.

The bombardier obliges. The entire barrel of gunpowder is stuffed into the cannon.

We'll not get any more in there now.

Then give the salute, says Pors. Let me go out with a bang.

The torch is lit and put to the fuse. Immediately it begins to fizz, only to go out again before reaching the gunpowder.

Bugger, the Governor says. Can't you even give me a salute before I go home?

The bombardier shrugs apologetically.

Pors takes the still burning torch from the man's hand, walks around the big gun and peers down its barrel.

If she won't have it up the arse, we'll try the other end instead, he says.

He puts the flame to the mouth of the cannon, which seems then almost to take in a breath. He stands for a moment, wavering in a gust of wind that sweeps across the colony. From the corner of his eye he sees the bombardier doubled up and fleeing towards the shore. But before he manages to react, the cannon goes off with an almighty bang, spewing from its mouth a cascade of fire that plumes over the rooftops. At the same time, the recoil wrenches the gun loose from its carriage, causing it to spin around, spitting fire in all directions. The bombardier, now a half-hundred paces away, throws himself to the ground and rolls down the bank. In the roadstead too they feel the force of the detonation, a warm and sudden wind in their faces.

Afterwards everything is silent. And then everyone at the shore runs back up to the colony house which is completely shrouded in gunpowder smoke. Tatters of clothing and flakes of soot descend from the sky like the blackest snow.

Governor! they shout. Governor Pors?

Yes, I'm all right, says the Governor, a soot-smeared figure appearing out of the smoke. His smouldering uniform hangs in shreds, and his wig has been blown to who knows where. He staggers towards the shore. His eyes gleam unhumanly in his blackened face.

Thank you, thank you, he says, nodding and smiling right and left. I'm fine, never felt better. Thank you. A slight ringing in the ears, that's all. Nothing to worry about.

He stumbles, though avoids falling, then reels away in the wrong direction, smiling and nodding still. I'm fine, yes, thank you. His uniform still smoulders, and a tail of smoke follows him as he goes.

If the Governor will have me excused, a hurrying seaman says at last, and douses him with a bucket of sea water.

He shakes it off like a dog and stands unsteadily for a moment.

Thank you, thank you, he says. Very kind of you, my friend. You shall receive a rigsdaler.

Two of the men catch him as he drops, haul him to his feet again and help him to the boat, which sails him out to the *Morian*.

PART THREE

Fathers and Sons

1

Nielsus Egidius Groenlandicus

To-day my son departed with both merchant boats on a trading mission, compelled by lack of assistance to serve in the Trade, since previously I have employed Frederik Christian as catechist and helper in the instruction of the Greenlanders but was now incapable, wherefore Niels was obliged to undertake both trade and instruction with them.

FROM HANS EGEDE'S JOURNAL, SEPTEMBER 1731

God, what an idiot my father is. He said this: I will not punish you. You have already received your punishment. Your punishment is to be you!

Now, again! The same thing happened last year, and the year before that. He's getting worse, my bloody father. Am I any the wiser? Nope. Thinking I was to escape his beating, having already received my punishment as he so pointedly said, I allowed my shoulders to drop, and whereas normally I keep a keen eye on his hands, I was now inattentive for the briefest moment. I looked at him scornfully, thinking myself to be on the safe side, and yet he struck me such a blow as to rattle the teeth in my jaw, and sun and stars came raining down on me like it was the Apocalypse and I John of Patmos.

You lied! I said, wiping a smear of snot from my face with my sleeve. You said you weren't going to punish me!

And he laughed and replied: A lie in the name of Jesus is a good lie, but a truth in the name of the Devil is a poor truth. Therefore I punish you so that you may learn your lesson.

A beast, that's what he is. The beast itself from the Book of Revelation. That's all I can say. I hate him.

Goodbye! I said.

Where do you think you're going? he replied.

None of your business! I said.

You're staying here!

Kiss my arse!

The Devil take you! he screamed at me, and the windows nearly rattled in their frames.

The Devil? The Devil is you! I told him.

He fell silent at that. Mother wept. Kirstine wept. Petronelle wept. I wept. Frederik Christian was as pale as a corpse. Rain was falling outside.

Goodbye, I said again, though quieter now. We won't be seeing each other again.

Wrap up warmly! my mother called out after me, for I think she knew where I was intending to go, it not being the first time I had gone off and slammed the door behind me following an argument with the old man.

I carried my kayak down to the shore and then I paddled away into the fjord, away through curtain upon curtain of densely falling rain, and so furious with indignation I think I must have been going at a speed of some seven knots, because before I knew it I was well up the fjord, and then eventually I rested on the paddle, gliding slowly on as I listened to the heavy beating of my heart and the pouring rain. At last, I went ashore at a delightful looking place that seemed so very peaceful, and I sat down there on the ground and thought about what to do then and what on earth was going to become of me.

I am writing this back in the colony after my excursion, which nonetheless lasted a good couple of months this time. It was good for me to get away from it all and not have to look at my father's sour face for a while. Master Kieding, please be kind and read this account of mine, and weed out the mistakes for me, for the written language is still a slippery eel in my hand, for which reason your help will be invaluable. Thank goodness you remained here in the colony with us and like us chose to place your fate in God's hand when the King would no longer have to do with his deceased father King Frederik's Greenlandic design, for even in the royal household there may be disagreement. I wonder if anywhere in the world there might be a father and son who honour and respect each other without squabbling and bickering and hating each other? I hardly think there is. I don't know if you, Kieding, have a father still alive? Perhaps he died, since you have never spoken of him? I could almost think you to be a lucky man if that were the case. For it is as if the blood despises itself and wishes only for foreign blood by which to renew itself. Perhaps that's why we Danish men are so fond of the native women.

I shall never learn, I say to the Master Kieding after having broken my third nib that same morning.

Oh, but you are improving, he says. It merely needs some correction here and there. You write as the wind blows, my boy, but still there is much good in it. It has life and soul and heart. So yes, carry on. Write the way you speak, and don't bother about whether it is right or wrong for the time being, we shall go through it later with the pen. I will teach you to use the comma. No, I don't care for commas. They're like nails knocked squintly into a wall, while the full stops are hammered all the way in. I like them the best.

I think Kieding has become a kind of philosopher. He was rather hard-bitten when first he came here some years ago, always out and about with his helper, Thomas Tode, the one they called Knife-man, who went home on the ship. Now Kieding has grown a long beard and looks like a prophet, and in his blue eyes there is fjord and fell and sky, and a serene smile on his lips. A person can go to the Master Kieding with all his worries. He never judges you, and doesn't say much, but he will listen. Often he sits in the house talking with my mother, though only when my father is out, for Father cannot abide that she speaks to him. I think he's afraid she might say something unflattering about him that will not be to his advantage and thereby put a stopper to him being canonized. I don't think they talk much about him, but more about philosophical matters in which I know my mother to be interested. Sometimes they will read a book together, and it will be neither the Bible nor Luther. My mother writes a lot too. Her fingers itch to hold the pen. She shows Kieding what she has written, and then they talk about it. But as soon as my father comes back she puts her writings away.

Now Pors and his men have gone home, and all the clamour of the colony with them. Such peace and quiet we could enjoy if not for my father, that devil. I tease him about it, knowing full well he dislikes to hear it. The Devil is you! Ha! At last I found his weak spot and will not relent from antagonizing him!

Nuuk, as we Greenlanders call the Godthåb peninsula, has always been a postal station for the natives between summer and winter, though never a place to settle permanently. Most of the year, even in the coldest time, they live in the skerries where they exist on their catches from the sea: whales, seals, birds. But during the reindeer hunt and the trout season and other seasonal hunts they live spread out over the land.

It was the time of the autumn hunt now, I realized, and I decided to go into the country to see if I could find a hunting party to join, and hunt like them with the harpoon and bow. I get along much better with them than with the Danish crew, not to mention my father, that Satan, Lucifer, Beelzebub.

I hope he reads this. It will do him good.

The reindeer gather in great herds when the bulls are rutting and the cows are on heat, and then one may get close enough to shoot, much better than in the summer when they are more wary, or, one could say, sensible. So it is with us males. Once we catch a female rump in our sights, we think not to look after ourselves, but run panting after the lovely arse as it wobbles before us. The rutting males can be bad-tempered beasts if they think you will come between them and a female they're lusting after. They can gore a man to death and cause great calamity if one isn't careful. The best thing is to come up behind them, and if you succeed in getting close enough they will be easy prey, for they have nothing on their minds but to stick their cock inside a cunt.

Another way to hunt them is by baiting them and encouraging them to attack, and if you're standing on the edge of a drop they will often fall into it and injure themselves, whereafter they may easily be finished off with the harpoon.

Another form of hunting, and this is the most common, is by driving them and rounding them up. Here the women and children will approach a herd from the sides and behind, driving them on by shrieking and striking rocks against each other, for then they think there is a rockslide and will set off on the move. The hunters then drive them towards a stone wall they have erected, with small openings through which the animals squeeze until almost standing on each other's backs. On the other side of these openings, of course, stand the men, armed to the teeth, shooting their arrows into the beasts or else slashing their throats with a quick incision so that they will bleed to death within a short time. Then the men will go about and collect the dead reindeer. They may be spread over a very large area, meaning it can take days before they're finished. It is a very productive form of hunting. I have seen the men cull a half-hundred reindeer in one go, and afterwards they are smeared with blood from head to toe, and such a bloodbath is pure joy.

But anyway I came to this secluded place where I went ashore and sat down on the ground and composed myself somewhat. My father's words still rang in my ears: Your punishment is being you! What kind of a father would say such a thing to his own son? He would never speak like that to Frederik Christian, who is his pet. He always appeases him even if sometimes he is a complete cock and known to fornicate with men as well as women, and to indulge in drinking bouts with the Danish crew, who poke fun at him and call him Two-Kings. And well, he never did get Titia as you had planned for him, you and the Governor, Kieding. I thought it a shame, for it might have saved them both from damnation. But it suited my father well seeing as how, to all intents and purposes, it would have made her his daughter-in-law. She was a real thorn in his flesh, he was certain she was a Jew or a papist or both. A papist Jew. Even the thought of her made him see red, and so of course he refused to marry them, the King's dispensation or no. Had he done so, married them, how would it all have turned out, I wonder? It's impossible to say, but wholly innocent in the jomfru's sorry fate, her now lying under the rocks with only bog water to drink, he is most certainly not, which he also well knows.

I have been thinking about another matter which I find to be rather sad. The natives have increasingly taken to using flintlocks when hunting. It was the Governor who introduced the practice of using these second-rate firearms as a means of payment. And now the natives are almost bound to their guns, and thereby to the Danes. Many barely know any more how to handle their former weapons, the harpoon and the bow and arrow. It is a shame. For what will they do now that Pors and his circus have gone and they no longer are able to lay their hands on new muskets, the old ones broken and their gunpowder run out, with no one to cast lead bullets for them? They will be forced to return to their old weapons, albeit they perhaps have forgotten how to use them.

I love my bow. I made it myself from the rib-bones of a whale, planing them into thin slivers no more than a couple of skrupler in width and binding them together with a thong of skin. For arrows I use barrel staves. They are firm and possess a certain weight, which is good for the flight of the arrow and its stability in the air, as well as for the force whereby it buries itself into the prey. For arrowheads I use shards of bone which I file down into shape. For fletchings I use the raven's feathers, for they are easily had. Eagle feathers are better, but near-impossible to find. Now that Pors has left with all the equipment, we Danes will do well to learn how to hunt with the old weapons, for who knows when we might see a ship from the home-land again, bringing with it Danish wares. Perhaps King Christian will forget all about Greenland and us who live here, leaving us on our own for all time like the old Norsemen my father believes to inhabit the other side of the land, and then like them we will descend into heathen ignorance and worship Sila and Tornaarsuk and go about clad in skins talking gibberish to each other, until in a couple of hundred years a new Hans Egede arrives in the country to thrash the daylights out of my great-great-grandchildren, for thus does history repeat itself for ever and ever. But let tomorrow look after itself, and let every day be like the last, that's my motto. I don't think much about the future. I find the present to be a big enough mouthful on its own.

I trudged into the land with my bow slung over my shoulder and my sheath of arrows dangling at my side. I had sewn my trousers myself out of fox skin, a good and warm material, and moreover very soft and unrestricting. My cap was of lemming skin, for last year was a lemming year, as we know them from back home in Lofoten, and you could hardly put a foot forward without treading on one of the vicious little beasts. My vest was of sheep's wool and on top of it I wore a sheepskin coat with the wool on the inside. I wore mittens of ox-skin too, though only in the night when I slept, for the weather in the daytime was fair and mild as the nights were bitterly cold. I had no tent with me, there being a limit to how much weight a kayak can bear before sinking to the bottom, but I did have with me a sleeping bag of reindeer skin. And so, with my sleeping bag on my back, I went off inland to see if I could find any native people, and of course I did.

I came to a settlement of two tents. Some women were there, and children, and a few old folk whose legs no longer allowed them to follow the hunt. I stayed with them for a couple of days, eating and sleeping with them. I went out hunting and bagged grouse and hare to pay for my keep. They praised me and said I was a true *inuk*, which means human being, and no greater accolade could be bestowed upon a Dane by any Greenlander.

I lay with one of their girls, whom I knew from before. She was very nice, and very enamoured too. I said I would marry her and take her back to the colony with me once my father had kicked the bucket or elsewise betaken himself to some other place. But she wouldn't, she said, as they always do. They must always play unwilling and hard to get, it's their way of showing how virtuous they are and not just available to anyone, but still I sensed that she would accept me taking her with me by force as is their custom. In their eyes a man must demonstrate that he means his courtship seriously, otherwise nothing will ever come of it. Usually they take the girl of their choice and drag her away by the hair. This gives rise to much shrieking and weeping, on the part not only of the girl herself but also of her family. But once they arrive home at his place all is well again.

I sat with her in the tent and listened as she told me the most frightful stories of killings and other gruesome deeds, probably something she was making up to frighten me away, for this is how they test a suitor, to see if he will put up or shut up, as my mother says. And so I was not deterred by these horrible tales, but merely laughed at them, and when I lay with her in the night she was tender and gentle, and gave herself up to me with soft lips and sweet words.

On the third day I broke up from the settlement to see if I could find those who had gone on the hunt further inland to the north. I kissed my betrothed goodbye and she cried the saltiest tears and told me she loved me and did not want me to leave, for as she said, when a man goes hunting he forgets all else, and of course there is something of a truth in it. Nevertheless, I had to go, and so it was goodbye, my dear, see you again when the hunt is over!

I had time to think as I walked, the landscape of the Northland being monotonous and allowing one's thoughts to wander. Perhaps, I thought to myself, I have chosen a native girl for my wife in order to antagonize my father, for I knew that he would be apoplectic if he ever found out. I found myself wishing I had taken her because I was fond of her rather than to get my father's back up, for as it stood I was in a way acting according to his mind rather than mine. Oh, if only he could go somewhere and die like a good father so that his sons might live as they wished instead of being either with him or against him.

And yet I do not wish him dead, because I love him.

Can a man be both an Egede and a savage?

Can he love as well as hate?

Can he be happy as well as distraught?

Can he be a Greenlander as well as a Dane?

Etc.

I walked over the land and was quite alone with myself and my thoughts. But then again, not entirely alone. For my father came creeping after me and I argued with him. He scorned me for one thing after another: I was cowardly, I was of poor character, I was a fornicator, the head on my shoulders was useless and ought more properly to hang between my legs and yield its place to my arse, I was a bad Christian, and so on. But I strode on to keep him at a distance. Clouds swept in from the sea and were dispersed by the Northland's blue air. It was autumn, but the weather was mild. I shot a hare and roasted it over an open flame, the heather I used for tinder crackled so pleasantly and gave off such lovely smells. I drank water from the becks and picked mushrooms and herbs and gathered roots I found on my way, munching and chewing as I went. It would all have been so agreeable had it not been for the shadow of my father following me the whole time. I did not find the hunters, perhaps because I did not wish to find them, and so I returned to the settlement. My betrothed was quite bewildered to see me again so soon and could barely contain her joy. I sang a magic song, she said, so that you would get lost and fail to find the hunters. I was slightly annoyed by this, but also touched by it since it told me that she loved me, and I loved her too and wished that our love could be pure and unimpeded by my father's shadow. It is only when one must part from one's beloved that the extent of one's feelings for her become clear, and we spent a long and happy night together, and the others in the tent were happy too on our behalf. But a man should not say to such girls that he loves them, nor should he be too tender and loving, for they do not care for it. It will then be to them as with lice and fleas, they will itch terribly and be as sulky as a horse in rain.

There was an old woman in the settlement, a widow who had fallen out with the other women because of some dispute. They had thrown her out of the tent in which she lived at the mercy of the group, always a perilous existence, and she had moved into the other tent only to find that they too would have nothing to do with her, nor even give her any of their food. It was the oldermand of the settlement who told me this.

The woman is a witch, he said. She cast a spell over one of the young women who was pregnant and caused her to give birth to a dead child which moreover was deformed.

I felt obliged to step forward with the voice of reason and say to him that he should tell them to think better of it. What you describe to me here is superstition, I said. I know the woman. She is not a witch.

I know, he said then, immediately standing down. It's not me who says so, it's the others. They've got it into their heads that she is a witch. They're frightened of her.

Regrettably I had to take on my father's role and try to talk them to their senses, even using the Bible's words about loving thy neighbour and caring for the weak. Thus immediately I felt my father's clammy hand upon me like a wet overcoat, and I looked upon them with his eyes and was quite able to see and feel what he so often had complained about, that they are falsely forthcoming when one speaks to them man to man, and act only according to their own minds as soon as one turns one's back. And I said to them what my father would have said, it was as if he were speaking the words through my mouth: Leave the poor old biddy in peace, she has done nothing, and if I ever hear that you have harmed her in any way, I shall personally see to it that you are punished severely, for I was afraid they would kill her.

Yes, I completely agree with you, the oldermand jabbered wheedlingly, and then even called me *palasi*, which normally they will only call my father. I shall tell them what you have told me, *palasi*, and make sure they do her no harm.

Remember the commandment that says you must love your neighbour, I said again, and, as my father always says, if anyone should smite you on your cheek, then turn to him your arse and let him smite you there too.

The oldermand laughed at this and told me he would pass it on to the women and that he would personally make sure to give them one from behind if needs be. But perhaps you should tell them yourself, *palasi*, for they take no notice of me, they don't respect me, and what are we to do and think if the old bird ups and dies all of a sudden, or if something else happens to her? After all, things do happen without our having any say in them.

I'll speak to them, I promised him. Therefore, that same evening I spoke up in the tent in which all were gathered, for it had been rumoured that *palasi* would read and speak to them. I stood up in the midst of these people and spoke admonishingly to them, though I would rather have not, for as I have said I felt I had taken on the figure of my father and addressed the people I felt to be my friends and countrymen, or even my family, with my father's voice, and thus had suddenly removed myself from them. Still, they listened kindly to what I had to say, albeit with the usual interjections, which always so enrage my father, and replied as follows: But you Danes also have the custom of killing your witches. You even burn them at the stake. Why should we not kill a witch?

Because she is not a witch, I told them.

Why is she not a witch? How can you be sure, *palasi?*

Because I know her, and she is not a witch.

But she sang about us and blew on the pregnant girl so that her child was born with a great big head and died. If she is not a witch, what is she then?

She is just a poor old hag, I said. All the rest is merely superstition, silliness and nonsense.

They smiled at me and I could tell they weren't swallowing it and were intending only to do with the woman as they wished. I felt sorry for her. I wished so dearly to save her from the clutches of these ignorant people, but there was nothing I could do, I realized it as I looked at them, and I saw it too in the woman herself, who was sitting in a corner with her head bowed, listening to all that was said about her. I could tell that she had prepared herself for her final hour, and the very next day they indeed killed her.

I woke up to tumult and commotion outside the tent and knew immediately what was going on, and so I jumped up and ran out in order to intervene. What I saw then was a group of women running across the rocks armed with their men's spears and knives. I shouted after them, Stop, in the name of the Lord! But they were in a blood frenzy and could not be halted. I don't think they even heard my shouts. Then I saw the woman herself hurrying away with her loose hair flying behind her, naked and with flapping breasts, and I could see that she was out of her mind with fear, knowing full well that her fate could not be avoided, and yet she was unable to simply accept it. She turned several times and shouted something to her pursuers, angry and challenging at the same time, which only made the other women even madder and prompted them to start hurling their spears at her, though all of them missed. The woman shouted at them again, taunting them now, and the whole scene was like children playing a game of tag at school, and indeed I remembered how afraid I was that one of the boys, the smith's son, would catch me and then of what he would do to me if he did, but this naturally was a different matter altogether. I was about to run after them and try to talk them into giving up their witch-hunt when I felt a hand on my shoulder. It was the oldermand with whom I had spoken so sensibly the day before and with whom I thought I had come to an agreement, but he said nothing, only smiled and gripped my shoulder firmly.

What are they doing to the poor woman? I asked him.

Oh, they're only playing, he said. Let them have their fun. Silly women. It's nothing for us men to watch. Come into my tent and eat with me.

But I wrenched myself from his grip and stood helplessly and watched as the women pursued the poor widow, and there was nothing I could do about it. My father would have known what to do.

The hunted woman had now reached a steep rock face and had begun to clamber up it. She quickly ascended several alens, remarkably adroitly, for she was driven by fear, clutching at the narrow ledges, her feet scrabbling for purchase, and before long it seemed almost as if she would escape her tormentors, who clearly were disinclined to risk climbing after her. But then, all of a sudden, she came to a halt and could reach no further. She clung to a small outcrop, dangling and taunting the other women, while they in turn shouted back quite as scornfully, knowing now that she was stuck and would either have to find her way down of her own accord or else fall, meaning that all they had to do was wait. Thus they settled at the foot of the cliff and began singing in piercing voices that went straight to the bone. The old woman was perhaps ten fathoms up, and I saw that she was struggling to keep hold, her eyes searching the rock face for some way to continue upwards, though what she might have done if she reached the top I do not know, naked as she was. Now again she moved her foot up to a small projection, but her hands could find no hold, her foot slipped and she fell with a scream into the midst of the waiting women below, who now descended on her like hideous crows upon a carcass and dragged her away. Some seconds passed before I caught sight of her again, but by then she was already dead and covered in blood, so they must have driven their knives into her too, to make sure.

They dragged the body to the shore where they cut her up and tossed an arm into the fjord, another onto the land. Another hag ran off with her head, though I don't know where she took it, and thus they scattered her limbs and parts to the four winds, for much as Christian people they believe that man has a soul, or rather several souls, and that these souls will try to come together when a person dies. But if the body is cut up into pieces, the souls cannot find each other and the dead person will be unable to rise again. After this iniquity they washed the blood from themselves in the beck.

In the evening a kind of solemnity had descended over the people who gathered in the main tent. I ate with them, though without appetite I mostly just stared at the hunk of flesh I had been given, paralysed by the thought that it had once been part of a living creature. But then a man came up and sat next to me and comforted me. He spoke to me and said such events were simply their way. It was important to offer sacrifice and thereby atone for guilt and sins or else a native would go to the dogs with all his sorrows and hardships, which are so numerous in this harsh land. You Danes do the same, he said.

I told him that in Denmark we no longer burn witches or even believe in witchcraft. It is but old superstition, I said.

But you punish those who break your laws by separating the head from the body, by burning them at the stake, by whipping them in public and by pulling out their tongues. I have seen it myself, the man said.

Then I saw who he was. It was their sorcerer, Aappaluttoq, whom they call the Red One, and Frederik Christian's father. I had not seen him for a long time and had thought him to be dead, for the last time I saw him he looked like a man condemned, but there he was next to me, lecturing me in his mild voice.

You've been to Denmark? I blurted.

Yes, many times, he replied.

When?

This winter, he said.

But you were not with any ship of ours?

He said nothing, but smiled and then began to tell me of an event that had taken place on a public square in Copenhagen where he had seen a woman have her head chopped off with a sword, after which the executioner had displayed it on a stake. She had given birth to a child in secret, he said, and had strangled it and got rid of it in a heap of horse-dung.

From the many details of his story I realized the event he was talking about had taken place at the scaffold by the City Hall. I asked him, who had told him about it?

I was there myself, he said with a smile. I saw it with my own eyes, and he pointed at his eyes with his index and middle fingers.

I understood that what he said was true, yet I could not for the life of me comprehend that he, a wildman, had been there, nor how he might have travelled to Copenhagen without passage on any ship and then come all the way home again to tell of it.

I have been to many places in the world, he said. It is something we do, we shamans. He did not say this to be boastful, but quite humbly, the way a priest might speak about God. Indeed, he was most kind and spoke not a hard word to me, even though he knew me to be my father's son and despite the two men being the bitterest of enemies and my father repeatedly having striven to put him in chains.

The next day I went on an excursion with Aappaluttoq. He took me to a great herd of migrating reindeer and we spent the whole day from morning until evening following them on their wanderings, a veritable river of beautiful beasts. We did not shoot a single one of them, though we could easily have done so. I felt an enormous joy and delight at watching these animals without harming them. Aappaluttoq said we have plenty to eat, so why should we kill them?

Thus we wandered about the land for several weeks. We slept in old peat-huts or beneath the open sky, we caught fish in the streams and rivers, and in the evenings we lay talking about all manner of subjects, and I spoke a lot about my father in particular. These were probably the best weeks of my life and the most instructive, for I now had a good friend much older than myself, perhaps as old as my father, and it is good, I believe, for a young man to have an older friend who is more experienced than he. He told me too about his son and the pain of having lost him, how it felt as if he were dead without being dead, and how terrible it was to see him going about the colony in Danish clothing and that silly three-cornered hat. But it was not with bitterness he spoke of this. We talked a lot about faith as well, about the Christianity of the Danes and the beliefs of the natives, and in this he surprised me, for he said:

Jesus is the wisest man who ever lived. I know he loves us people, and us Greenlanders too.

Do you believe in him? I asked. Do you worship him? Have you read the Scriptures?

Yes, he said. I have a Bible I bought from a seaman, and have read it from beginning to end, for Albert Top – do you remember him, the missionary who was here some years ago? – taught me to read and write, and I was meant to be baptized too, but your father would hear nothing of it, and so it came to naught.

I believe that, I said. He was like that then. It was harder for a native to be brought before my father's baptismal font than for a camel to pass through the eye of a needle.

Jesus is the greatest, he went on with warmth in his voice. I feel his love and I believe he will guide us Greenlanders and help us become a united people who can live in peace and harmony with the Danes.

But then you will have to discard your shaman ways, I said, for I do not think they will find God's favour.

Not to mention your father's, he said with a laugh. They are heathen ways, I know, but I am loath to part with them, for a shaman is what I am, it is what I am able to do. Without them I am nothing to my countrymen, for they keep a firm grasp on the old customs and ways of living, but our children may become good Christians. We will teach them to believe in God and Jesus and the good works of love.

How many children have you got? I asked him.

Oh, a couple of boys, he said. But both mothers are dead now. I am alone and free. And the boys are beyond me. Can you tell me how Paapa is doing?

As far as I know he is doing well. He seems to be a good help to my father in his missionary work, and I think they are working together on the translation of some passages of the Bible.

His face lit up in a quiet smile. The Bible? he said. That's something at least. I'm sure he can teach your father a thing or two there.

Yes, sometimes I think he's the only person my father listens to properly, I said. The rest of us haven't much standing with him.

Why is that? he asked. A native boy like him, son of a shaman. I don't get it.

I think they keep a secret between them, I replied, not realizing what I was saying until the words were out. It's as if they are in some alliance together. I don't get it either.

He became pensive and did not speak for a while. Then he said, to be separated from one's flesh and blood is painful indeed, and the other boy is not with me either, for which reason the pain is doubled. But I know not to be self-centred and to think only of what is best for them. I have sacrificed them, yet have done so for their own sakes. This is how it is. A father must offer his children as Abraham offered his son Isaac.

This conversation gave me much to think about. But otherwise our talks were mostly light-hearted, banter and tales, stories from the hunt, and he gave me much good hunting advice.

When at last we parted after such a long time in each other's company in the wilderness, I found I had a good Christian friend in Aappaluttoq. Who would have thought it! I returned alone to the settlement, and my betrothed was glad to see me, it felt like I had come home. One day I went out hunting with her, her name was Arnannguaq, which means little woman. We killed a reindeer cow and its calf, and Arnannguaq taught me how to cut open the calf and remove the stomach, knot the intestine and drink the milk it had suckled from its mother. We drank this curdled milk directly through the open tap of the gullet, lifting the stomach and emptying it into our mouths, and very fortifying and nourishing it was. We ate what was in the stomach of the cow too, a warm and fermented mush whose slightly bitter taste I found refreshing, though one must make sure to eat it as soon as the animal is killed, for if one waits too long it takes on an insipid taste and becomes rather slimy in its consistency. We wandered about in the wilds together, Arnannguaq and I, smeared with blood from our catch, but we bathed in the streams and in the pools of still water that had become warmed by the sun, for the weather remained balmy and mild as never before in the years I have been in this land. I discarded what was left of my Danish clothing and wore skins from head to toe, which Arnannguaq sewed for me, and I considered her in every way to be my wife.

But what of our future together? I wondered. I could hardly stay there the rest of my life, or could I? What did I not have there, which I could find in the filthy confines of the colony? Nothing. And yet I was in two minds as to what to do with myself and my life. I had already sensed a boredom come over me when in the evenings I lay in the tent and listened to the talk and tales of my Greenlandic companions, which I found far too wearying and fantastic to hold my interest. These were but endless variations of the same horror stories, of ghosts with their heads under their arms and all sorts of terrible creatures who came to haunt the humans, and after a while one becomes tired of it. I found their hunting tales to be more entertaining, but there is a limit to how much a person can endure listening to such things.

The custom, previously mentioned, of scapegoating women as witches and evicting widows and old hags with the instruction to go to the fells and perish was still very much practised and was something I had difficulty coming to terms with. There was an old toothless wife who knew which way the wind had begun to blow. She could contribute nothing to the household and was unable even to tan hide, for she had not a tooth left in her mouth. And therefore she had to go.

One day she went around sadly, saying goodbye to the people with whom she had lived for a great many years, and I saw that her eyes were moist with tears and her lips trembled, yet her friends pretended not to care less and hardly looked up at her when she came to say farewell, for this is their way, not because they are without compassion, but because it makes parting that much easier. It was a heavy path to walk for such an old and worn-out woman.

I could not tolerate it. No, I said to myself, this has gone far enough! And so I went after her and, catching up with her, pulled her sleeve and said: Come back, dear woman, I shall not allow that you go away to die. I will help you with food and clothing.

She was so glad that she wept, and she followed me back to the settlement. We went inside the tent she had only just left behind her and sat down on my bench, smiling right and left, and the Greenlanders looked at her and said, What are you doing here, why have you come back?

It was *qallunaaq*, she said. He came and fetched me back. He will give me food and shelter.

Arnannguaq was not pleased with what to my own mind was this good Christian deed of mine. For the first time, she became angry with me and would not sleep with me any more, but said I could sleep with the old hag I had picked up in the fells instead, for obviously I was more fond of her, and she laughed out loud and mockingly, for the old woman was but skin and bone and as wrinkled as Methuselah's grandmother. I tried talking sense to her, but by then she had already moved to another bench where another man had his pleasure with her. I was both saddened and in uproar, but what was I to do about it? I wished not to give up on the old woman whose life I had retrieved from the clutches of death. I think in a way she had taken the place for me of the widow they had killed before, and I refused to let her go. However it was far from pleasant to lie on the bench with her wrapped around me, wanting to perform certain services in gratitude, and I had to keep shoving her away all the time, telling her to keep her hands to herself, and this made her crabby and sulky and she told me she would rather have gone off into the fells, that it was my fault that she now lay there not knowing if she were fowl or fish, and hated by everyone.

A mood of ill-feeling arose in the winter-dwelling in which I had set myself up in the manner of some *pater familias* and I could feel it was directed towards me. Yet it was the old woman who had to bear the brunt, she on whom they took out their frustrations. Soon they were at it again, with nonsense about her blowing on their children in order to cause them harm, and then it was the old witch-business all over again. I knew full well that as soon as I left the settlement they would cast themselves upon the poor hag and drive her into the fjord, or in some other way cause her death, and so she clung to me and was quite from her senses with fear and anguish. Either I would have to bundle her onto my kayak and paddle her to the colony or I would have to accept that she be sacrificed like the widow before her.

It was December then, without firm snow on the ground, but windy and cold. A journey down the fjord in a kayak was a poorly attractive prospect, certainly so with a passenger on the deck. The Greenlandic men will often ferry their wives on their kayaks, where the women will sit on the rear, back-to-back with their men, but the extra weight presses such a small vessel down until it is more under the water than above it. I had only tried this twice with my sisters, and on each occasion the vessel had capsized and sunk, but that was inside the colony harbour where the water is shallow, so the only catastrophe was that we were soaked. But to paddle on a storm-lashed fjord in cold and darkness and with heavy waves coming in from the sea would be the certain death of both me and my passenger. And so I had little choice but to remain and await the relentless passage of events.

Now at once my friend Aappaluttoq appeared in the settlement, as if he had been called. I spoke to him of the problem, how they had got it into their heads that the old woman was a witch and now wished to kill her.

Let them kill her, he said. Her life is no longer of any worth. She is but an old hag.

I became angry with him and spoke to him harshly. I thought you were my friend, who believed in Jesus and the mercy of the Lord. But he shook his head and looking straight at me said: Who are you?

I was appalled that he was now so dismissive. After all our experiences together. Do you deny me? I said. It is as if you have become another. Do you not remember our time in the wilderness? The conversations we had? But he would have nothing to do with me and turned his back to continue carving his figures, speaking neither to me nor to anyone else, and then I understood that I had lost a friend, though without having any idea as to why.

And then my saviour came: my father.

One day a cry went up that a boat was approaching, and I ran out and saw right away that it was him, for it was obvious from his black coat and the staff he always carries with him, as if he were a bishop. What was I to do? Should I run into the fells and hide from him, or should I stay and receive him, and save the old woman? And what about Aappaluttoq?

I told Aappaluttoq to run to the fells, for they are coming to get you and take you back to the colony. But he was as sullen and bad-tempered as before, and completely unperturbed by what I said. So I stood on the shore and watched the boat as it came closer, and then my father jumped ashore and with him Frederik Christian, and my father came to me and looked at me and said, Look at the state of you, you look like a savage! And he kissed me and laughed, and said that I smelled like a savage too, and I walked with him up to the settlement where my father preached to them and Frederik Christian translated, and Aappaluttoq was there too, though they pretended not to know each other.

I told my father about the old woman, that she was in great peril, for they wished to kill her.

That's their business, he said. It's beyond our jurisdiction. Now, let's go inside and get something to eat. I could devour a whole hind-quarter.

We were to leave again the next day, only something happened. I knew what was going on, but it passed over my father's head. He gloated in the presence of Aappaluttoq for having his son with him, as if almost he held him up under his nose and said, Look, here he is, he is mine and there is nothing you can do about it. The people in the dwelling were not pleased to have him amongst them, for there was the matter of the old woman, whom they wished him not to see. But as is their way they were polite and fed him with great piles of meat, and I think perhaps his appetite and the way he could dispatch such enormous quantities endeared him to them, for in that way he resembled them. Indeed, his spirits grew higher as the evening wore on and he prattled on about the Creation and Moses and the burning bush, and dealt too with the story of Abraham and Isaac, a subject to which he always returns, for it is there that his own shoe pinches, the subject of fathers and sons. The usual discussion ensued between him and the natives. Why did the Lord tell him to sacrifice his son, and why did Abraham obey him? Such a thing is wrong, they said. He ought not to have agreed to it. He ought to have refused outright. You will not take my son. Anything else, but not him. And yet he agreed, my father told them, and the Lord rewarded him for his obedience. Better to be condemned by the Lord, they retorted. Nothing is more important than our children. And thus they kept on at him. I was translating, since Frederik Christian had gone outside, and I noticed that Aappaluttoq had crept out too. I could hear the murmur of their voices and knew then what was happening. But I said nothing. I thought it would do my father good to learn a lesson.

Not until it was time to sleep did he ask where Frederik Christian might have got to.

A silence descended, for everyone in the dwelling except my father had cottoned on, and in those seconds of total silence I could see that something occurred in my father. It was almost as when two people are fighting and one feels himself to be much stronger than the other, only then to be punched to the ground, where he sits on his arse for a moment unable to fathom how such a thing might have happened. But then he gave a cry and dashed out of the door, I following him.

I could see them on top of a crag. They stood side by side looking down at us, and then they were gone from sight. My father ran to the boat and fetched two flintlocks, handed me one and said, Now I shall put a bullet in that devil once and for all! This time he will not escape.

We climbed up to the place where we had seen them, but they were nowhere to be found. My father seemed to sniff the air, his nose twitching like a rabbit's. And then he pointed. There they are!

Now the hunt was on, into the Northland. It is a difficult terrain in which to find one's way, for the fells are low and look the same, and the land is dotted with small pools and bogs. Before long a person has become completely lost, with only the sun to keep his bearings. We clambered up onto the craggy tops and scanned the surrounding land, and on each occasion we caught a glimpse of the two fugitives.

I think Aappaluttoq wanted us to see them, for that was his nature, he liked to tease people even if it carried with it a certain risk to his own person.

Night fell and we took shelter in a small cave where the ground was reasonably dry. There we lay and shivered with cold, hugging each other tightly until it became light again. My father loves warmth and good food, but he can be very enduring when needs be and can go without eating for several days if there is something he deems to be more important. We walked many hours that day, without food and with only water from the pools and becks to drink, and all the time we came upon small signs that revealed to us where Aappaluttoq and Frederik Christian had gone before us, a scrap of fabric, a small cairn on top of a ridge, the remains of a fire, an arrow drawn on the face of a rock with the coal of whatever they had burned. It was as if they were only just ahead of us the whole time, and my father hastened to reduce their lead, and yet it felt like we were hunting shadows and ghosts. I knew that Aappaluttoq would reveal himself to us when he felt it to be time and would himself choose the place where this would happen.

It was the following night. I stood on a high rock and saw the faint glow from a fire. My father clambered up to me and I pointed it out to him. Immediately he became incensed and began to run towards the place.

We reached the fire an hour later. It was now but smouldering embers, but on the ground next to it lay five grilled trout, as if served for our delectation and delight.

Don't touch them, my father said. We shall not fall for his tricks.

But I was too hungry and could not resist their delicious aroma. I sat down and began to fill myself, and then my father did likewise.

He's here, he said. I can feel it.

My father had eaten three of the fish, I the remaining two, and now we circled about, though keeping ourselves within distance of the fire. My father shouted into the darkness: Will you fight with me? Is that what you want? Then come and fight!

Suddenly there was a movement in the darkness to our right, down by the fire, a crouched figure approached it and sat down heavily on the ground. It was Frederik Christian. My father ran down to him, but something whistled through the air and skidded over the ground beside him. An arrow.

My boy, he called out. Has he harmed you?

But Frederik Christian said nothing. My father had loaded his musket now and raised it to his shoulder, sweeping the barrel through the air in front of him.

Come forth, spineless Satan!

Aappaluttoq responded with another arrow, this one penetrating the ground where my father stood. My father fired his gun, a blinding light flashing from the barrel, a thundering detonation which echoed among the crags. In that briefest illumination I saw Aappaluttoq. He was standing some short distance away, bare-chested, his bow raised at the ready. My father removed himself quickly from the light of the camp-fire.

Shoot, then! he shouted out. Shoot, for I am not afraid of your arrows.

Another arrow whistled in the air. It struck my father's coat tail, and he leapt back in fright. The darkness would not allow him to reload his musket and he could not return to the light of the fire where he would be an easy target for Aappaluttoq's arrows.

Can you see him? he asked me. If you see him, shoot on sight!

I could indeed see him, for my night-sight has always been good, and moreover the sky seemed also to be lighter now, albeit only slightly. But I did not shoot. I cannot remember what I felt. I was not afraid. More than anything, I felt a kind of composure.

My father began then to walk forward in the direction in which he believed the last arrow to have come. He had abandoned his musket and inched towards the shadow that was Aappaluttoq, though without being able to see him. But as he approached I think perhaps he picked out his shape, for his steps became at once more hesitant. And then I heard them wrestle. They grunted and groaned, and suddenly my father let out a roar and fell to the ground.

At last I wrenched myself from my paralysis and ran towards him. He was lying flat out on the ground. I called out to him: Father! Father!

Yes, I'm all right, he replied with no small measure of annoyance. No harm done. See if you can catch up with the beast. I think he ran that way.

As if to demonstrate to him my good intent, I ran this way and that, searching for Aappaluttoq. But he was gone. I helped my father to the fire. His nose was bloodied, but otherwise he was unharmed. Frederik Christian was still sitting there as if he were made of stone. My father hugged him and made a fuss of him. My boy, my boy, he said. I thought I had lost you. What on earth could have made you go with him? Tell me why you did so.

He told me to, said Frederik Christian.

And you wanted to? You wanted to be with him?

No. Yes. I don't know. I went with him.

I could tell he was shaken by what had happened. He went into a kind of stupor and said no more.

We headed back to the settlement. It took two days before we found it. We saw nothing more of Aappaluttoq. When on the first night of the journey we bedded down in a hollow among the rocks my father told of the time he had received Frederik Christian, or Paapa as his name was then. You hung limply in your father's arms, he said, and were pale and feeble. You looked like the Saviour himself taken down from the cross. For weeks you hovered between life and death and I felt the Lord himself had entrusted you to me, that you were a gift of grace from Him, but also a gift from this land, Greenland, and a sign to me that I must remain here and lead the savages to Jesus, and that you were to help me in this. To my mind you were a pact I concluded with the Lord. That's why you are so precious to me, and it is why I shall never give you up, and no matter what happens to you I shall always be your earthly father, for this responsibility is given to me by the Lord.

It was the first time I had heard my father speak in such a way, so heartfelt it seemed he would burst into tears at any moment. It made me feel strange. It was as if my father had become someone else entirely, a human being of flesh and blood, it could almost be said.

I wonder, my good Master Kieding, now that this account of mine with the disclosures it contains has reached its conclusion, whether you might leave it somewhere so that my father might find it and read it. I should like to know what he thinks of it. I am not sure what to make of it myself. But now at least he will be able to see that I, his poorly talented son, have become more adept in the use of pen and ink, and also see himself as I see him, for I think it will do him good.

Nielsus Egidius Groenlandicus
Christmas 1731

2

A Minor Perlustration

Today, the Lord gladdened us with the happy arrival at the colony of the ship from the homeland. With it arrived a man by the name of Matthias Jochumsen, accompanied by his brother and son, most mercifully sent to us, who is to reconnoitre the passage to the Eastern Settlement, if such passage is at all possible, and furthermore to investigate if there are minerals in the land, a matter of which he claimed to be knowledgeable.

FROM HANS EGEDE'S JOURNAL, MAY 1732

Stillness. The fjord is like a sheet of silk. I propel myself forward, stroke by stroke, the paddle blade scooping up the water, splashing it back against the side of the kayak; the little twist of my torso as I plunge the opposite blade into the water then draw it back to complete the cycle, feeling the element's resistance in the trembling tendons of my hands; the slight, lurching thrust of the vessel at every stroke, the water pressed against the thin membrane of the kayak skin, parting at the bow, cleaved aside to fall away in maelstroms and scintillating spray, the wind buffeting my face. Swish, swish, swish, like a mill the paddle twirls its small, flattened circles, above me the eternity of the heavens, below me the seventy thousand fathoms of the sea. The kayak is a knife, its passage upon the calm surface an incision which opens and heals at once. I am Frederik Christian, the one they call Two-Kings. The breath of the sea lifts me up and sets me down, and I am a part of it, this great respiring world.

But notwithstanding that all these superstitions are authorized by, and grounded upon the notion they have of him they call Torngarsuk, whom their lying angekuts or prophets hold for their oracle, whom they consult on all occasions, yet the commonality know little or nothing of him, except the name only: nay, even the angekuts themselves are divided in the whimsical ideas they have formed of his being.

I have a toothache. A cheek-tooth. It is quite rotten. The smith will not pull it out. It will come out on its own, he says. Yet it hurts me so much! Drink aquavit, he says. But I do, I tell him. Then drink some more, he says. The aquavit dulls the pain in the tooth, but removes it to the soul. Now the tooth throbs again, but my soul is as calm as the sea, as quiet as the great murmuring expanse I slit with the blade of my paddle. Soul and flesh each in different states. One cannot have it all.

The soul is as the sea. When the wind blows it is unsettled. When it is cold it falls into torpor. And when one is suffering from inappropriate desires it throbs like a rotten tooth. To kill a child in its cradle would be better than to nourish such wrongful lust. To drown would be preferable by far. To vanish into the blue. To die.

The natives are fearful of the kayak dizziness. One understands them well on a day such as this. The crisp, impermanent boundary between sky and sea becomes almost erased, the firmament all-engulfing, and up could just as well be down. I keep my eye on the islets, the fells, reference points that help me maintain the distinction.

My hunting bow is at my shoulder, arrows splayed out in a fan held in place by the deck lines of the foredeck, along with the harpoon and darts. On the foredeck too is the rack which holds the hunting line. Behind me is the hunting float, an inflated, depilated seal-skin finely stitched and sealed with blubber. I have made all the equipment myself, to the smallest detail. I have shaped the wood, filed and honed the arrowheads, softened the skin, inserted the rivets. No woman has laid a hand on any of it, nor on me. I have no love of women. I was fond of Titia. She was a good friend. We were supposed to have been married. I had no objections. But she belonged to another, so it transpired, and he came and took her and strung her up, and all that was left was her small and withered body, which the Governor carried onto the fell alone and placed in its grave. I loved the priest's daughter. Yet it was a false love, it turned into fear and loathing, and then it died. Love is like paddling a kayak. The thin and delicate boundary between the light of the firmament and the darkness of the deep is almost invisible and may cause a man to dizzy and drown. Or to begin to hate himself. For if he looks down, he sees only himself, and then he is lost for ever.

I paddle. I could paddle for days without sleep, without food, without a thought in my head, the blades twirling their endless ovals, sprinkling their spray into the air around me. Beyond the islets the swell rises. It lifts me and pulls me down. It feels wonderful. A seal appears before me, upright in the water, looking at me, trustful and unsuspicious. *Natsiaq.* A small ringed seal. I paddle closer. It submerges, but I can see where it swims and pursue it cautiously, rest the paddle across the deck, pick up the harpoon and thrust it forward as the seal appears again exactly where I anticipated. Such a thing must be in the blood. Passed down from heathen to heathen, and now to me. I do not hunt very often. And my body is stiff after hours in the mission room with Egede each day, working on his Description. Not a word about that. It is not a matter that may be spoken about. It is a secret. He has already written a stack of pages, a manuscript locked inside a drawer. I am not to breathe a word to anyone and must not disturb him when he writes. Instead I sit quietly, hardly daring even to swallow my spit, so quietly I can hear the lice as they chew the powder of his wig. Presently he will read aloud what he has written and ask if it is good enough in such a wording. What do you think, Frederik Christian? And at that juncture I am permitted to speak, but I must say only that it is good, I must praise him, for he dislikes being spoken against, and therefore I have no idea why I must sit there hour upon hour and listen to his lice grow fat.

If one aspires to the office of an angekkok, and has a mind to be initiated into these mysteries, he must retire from the rest of mankind, into some remote place, from all commerce; there he must look for a large stone, near which he must sit down and invoke Torngarsuk, who, without delay, presents himself before him. This presence so terrifies the new candidate of angekutism that he immediately sickens, swoons away, and dies; and in this condition he lies for three whole days; and then he comes to life again, arises in a newness of life, and betakes himself to his home again.

The harpoon has embedded itself in the shoulder of the seal. The animal emits bleats of pain, arches backwards into the water and submerges itself in its blood. It twists, writhes and thrashes. The line sings, and when there is no more I tug on it to see if the harpoon head is embedded firmly. Then I release the float. It dips beneath the surface twice, after which I draw it back and forth repeatedly, playfully almost, and in high spirits. I watch the seal as it struggles to come free. But it cannot come free. It is doomed. A living creature in the throes of death.

It surfaces again, snorting and coughing, eyes filled with fear, pain, resignation, but not rage. It is a fine little creature, quite without anger or malice. There is no anger in small seals. Small seals are soulful. I think God blew his breath into them, and when they die I sense something inside me die too, that must be given up so that something else may be born and take its place, a hardness, an insensitivity. I am not suited to living in this land. Why did God have me born here? What sense is there in it? Can He not see that I am a stranger here?

The seal adopts a new strategy. It swims away, dragging the hunting float with it. But it has not the strength to swim from me. I paddle gently after it. There is no need to hurry. It needs no more help to die. It turns its pale belly upwards and capitulates. As yet it breathes, and squirms slightly, eyes rolling in its head. But then, before I can extract the harpoon head, a shadow darts forward from my right, the line is cut with an audible reverberation, and the seal is gone.

I almost capsize. My seal!

The thief pretends not to hear me. He paddles away at furious speed, churning the surface, the seal laid across his deck.

Thief! I shout after him.

He hears me well enough. I can tell from his neck and shoulders that he is laughing.

I retrieve the float and attach it to the rear deck, wind the line around the rack. The kayak rolls in the swell. It is not the seal which is important. I can always catch another. It is the humiliation. If I were a savage, I would paddle after him and kill him. But I am not a savage. I am Frederik Christian, not Paapa. I am a Christian. Am I not?

I plunge the blade into the water and begin to paddle. The thief is heading south. He paddles quickly, torso thrusting forcefully. Behind him he draws a trail of blood, and the blood connects us to each other. Probably he is a better kayak man than I, and stronger too. But the seal will slow him down.

I pick up speed. We round an islet, and the sea becomes choppy, low waves breaking over the deck. I plough through them. The water flies from the paddle blades as they snatch at the crests, I catch the air, and then the sea again, the spray consumes the bow and I am flying, skating across the surface.

The Greenlanders' ignorance of a Creator would make one believe they were atheists, or rather naturalists. For, when they have been asked from whence they thought that Heaven and Earth had their origin, they have answered nothing, but that it had always been so.

He realizes he is being pursued. He glances over his shoulder, then lunges forward once more, paddle attacking the waves, heaving himself onwards at speed. But I too am quick. His strength is gathered in the name of fear and guilt, mine in vengeance and rage. They are well matched. The distance between us is undiminishing, unincreasing. But I will catch him. I have killed once today. I can kill twice. Or die myself.

We enter the open sea. The swell is lazy, the waves tall and long. I adjust my rhythm, deep and steady strokes, riding a crest, slipping down behind it, reversing my strokes to keep the vessel upright. I see him in glimpses, when we mount a wave simultaneously. I am closer now. I know why, and it is not because he is weary. He is dropping back to fight me. Combat at sea? Then let it be so. I am ready to kill or be killed.

But suddenly he is gone. I rest on my paddle and glance to all sides. All I see is the ocean, the rolling sea, but no man anywhere. Yet there are no hiding places here. How could he disappear? I paddle further, narrowing my eyes to see what cannot be seen. Who is he? I know who he is.

A figure rises up out of the water and hurls something at me. In his upturned kayak he has lingered, his body upside down, suspended, though bent double, his face breaking the surface for air, and thus he has kept me in his sights, waiting for the moment to right his vessel and strike. The harpoon hurtles past me to lodge itself in the foreside of the stem. The skin rips open with a sigh. He hauls back his harpoon. I snatch the hunting bow from my shoulder, load an arrow and fire seamlessly. But the angle is wrong, and his position now means I have the sun in my eyes. The arrow whistles above his head and cuts into the sea. Yet he is frightened. Had he not expected me to defend myself? He ducks, turns and paddles away. He has no bow of his own.

My feet are drenched. I realize what is going to happen. Soon my legs are wet to the thigh. My kayak is drinking the sea. And it is thirsty. My opponent has turned again and paused some distance away, beyond the range of my arrows. He rests on his paddle. He is laughing, and watches me with interest.

The angekuts, as before observed, are kept in great honour and esteem, and beloved and cherished as a wise and useful set of men; they are also well rewarded for their service, when it is wanted.

I am lost. What will he do with me when I am drowned? Will he simply turn and paddle away, boil his seal and devour it with good appetite? Or will he fish me up and put me in a grave, sing over my body and give me a heathen burial? Will he weep over me? What is he thinking?

I try to paddle, but like a wounded bird I get nowhere and sink only deeper. If he wished, he could harpoon me and put me out of my misery. Yet he does nothing. He sits and watches, his mouth curled in an inquisitive, roguish smile. It is considered an impoliteness among the savages to reveal oneself to one's victim. A harpoon in the back and quickly away is a preferred method. But he is no ordinary savage. He does not abide by their rules. The seal hangs draped over the foredeck of his kayak and bleeds into the sea. Calmly, he puts his weapon away under the deck lines, picks up his paddle, turns his vessel and sends me a final look before sedately paddling away.

God will punish you!

May you burn in Hell!

I hate you!

Now I am alone. Alone with my death. The sea is sucking me in. I am sinking and will descend slowly through its seventy thousand fathoms. I blink. No, I am afloat. Balancing. The kayak is under the surface, I am in water to my chest. But I am not sinking. A pocket of air must be keeping me up. I try to paddle, but cannot. The kayak points its nose to the sea-bed and threatens to sink once and for all. I size up the islets that lie but a musket shot away to my left. If I am lucky, I will drift towards them. But no, it seems I am drifting away, to the north. I must find some way to manoeuvre.

I undo the spraydeck that is fastened around the coaming of the cockpit, tighten it again around my waist and wriggle free. Now I am lying flat on my stomach on top of the kayak. It remains buoyant, though beneath the surface. Most of my body too is below water, only my shoulders and head are above. My watertight tunic, my *tuilik*, keeps me afloat for the moment. But the sea is freezing cold. My feet and legs are numb. Like an eel, I slither forward to the tear in the bow, pull off my mitten and feel the damage with my fingers. It is a clean tear, an incision. It gurgles and spits like a dying seal as the kayak rises and falls. I try to cover it with my hand. I feel the air stream in and out between my fingers.

A fog moves in, thick as whipped cream, sucked into the fjord. Soon it will be evening. I lie prone on the drowning kayak, half-drowned myself, dead and yet alive, but the balance between death and life is shifting in the wrong direction. I have given up holding my hand over the tear. I can do no good, only wait. I say the Lord's Prayer. The sky around me changes colour. Evening falls. Darkness. Good night.

I am woken by a cry. It startles me. I tumble into the water, claw at the kayak, but succeed only in pushing it away from me. My arms and legs flail desperately, my mouth fills with water, water fills my clothing, water rises above my head. Silvery bubbles effervesce around me, and I collide with an object. I make a grab for it, but it is slippery like soap, smooth and cold. And then the respiration of the sea lifts me up and gently puts me down again on a stony beach.

I lie gasping for air. Breakers rush through the pebbles. It is the most wonderful sound.

It was a raven that cried. It sits on a rock, hopping about, cocking its head, watching me. Further ashore, in a grassy nook among the rocks, sits the man who stole my seal.

He casts a glance at me as if I had merely happened by. I stagger up the beach towards him and fall down in the grass.

You're soaked, he says. You must be freezing, you fool. Look, I've boiled meat for us.

The seal lies butchered and bloody beside him. The raven descends from its rock in a series of hops, directly to the entrails thrown to it by the thief. Its beak pulls at them, scarlet filaments.

Eat now before it gets cold, he says.

My teeth chatter. I pull off my clothing, my trousers, my kamik boots. And then I am naked. I sit down at the fire. The heat settles my breathing. He tosses me a piece of rib. I tear the meat from it with my teeth and swallow it. He pours a mugful of the stock and hands it to me. I drink the salty liquid, scalding my mouth, but drinking. I shudder and tremble as the cold releases my muscles, teeth as yet clacking. The man sits and stares at me through the flames.

What's the matter with you?

Nothing. I'm cold.

Why do you hold your hand to your cheek like that?

A tooth. It's driving me mad.

He nods. I could tell right away. A little red devil in the corner of your mouth. He's the cause of the toothache. Do you want me to send him away?

You know very well I don't believe in your heathen ways.

Please yourself. Look at me.

I lift my gaze, I look at him. The flames flicker between us.

What do you see? he says.

I see you. Your face. Your eyes.

Good. Eat now. Soon your clothes will be dry.

The rib I have gnawed falls on the ground. I sigh. My eyelids droop. I yawn.

Don't sleep, he says. Not yet. Sleep must wait.

He leans across the fire and the flames wrap themselves around him, he is quite engulfed, and yet unburned. He embraces me, and now we are both enveloped by flame, though I feel nothing. All I feel is tired, I can think only of sleep. I sense something warm and moist against my face, like slime running down my cheeks, but I have no idea what it is. He mumbles some words, heathen rigmarole, it puts me at ease, makes me feel safe and secure, even though I resist. I feel like a child being rocked by his mother. And then I vomit, emptying my stomach completely, my body convulsing, and he grips me tightly, holds me to his chest and mumbles. Mumbles me to sleep.

I am still naked when I awake. But I am not cold. I am lying on a reindeer skin next to the fire. I must have slept for some time. It feels like Sunday, when the sun slants in through the window and one needn't get up but can stay in bed all morning and watch the shifting light. I am limp as a rag. My eyes, the only part of me I can be bothered to move, scan the surroundings. There are my skin clothes, draped on the rock to dry. There is the butchered seal. There is the raven, tugging at the bloody entrails, flapping its wings in annoyance to attack its meal from a different angle. Clouds drift slowly across the sky. And there is my killer, my saviour. He sits bare-chested and stares into the fire.

Have I been asleep for long?

You were far away. You threw up a lot of sea water. Sit up and eat. There's still plenty of meat.

I eat.

Have you performed sorcery?

It's not sorcery.

What is it then?

It's hard to explain. It's secret. Something one is allowed to share only with those who wish to learn it. Do you wish to learn it? Do you wish to be like me?

No.

I pick up a piece of meat and chew. My head feels light after sleeping.

You stole my seal. Why did you do that?

I'm a poor hunter. I can admit that. I'm a good shaman, but a poor hunter. I have to steal my food.

You almost killed me.

I missed. I'm useless with a harpoon.

You could just as easily have got me. I could have drowned.

I was trying to get you. That was the idea. Only I missed as usual. Maybe God put a swerve on it. He sighs. You didn't have to chase after me. It was stupid of you.

I was angry.

Anger is a dangerous thing. It gets people killed. You should have paddled home to your people.

I say nothing. I put my hand to my cheek and rub it.

Still got that toothache?

Yes.

Get the smith to pull it out.

He won't.

Then get Master Kieding to do it.

You know Kieding?

I know everyone in the colony. I know your father too.

He's not my father. He's my teacher.

Are you going to be a priest?

Perhaps. He says I will. If I stick in.

I'm a priest as well, you could say.

You're an angakkok.

But I know Jesus too.

Do you believe in him?

Yes, I believe in him.

Are you prepared to put your old ways behind you and become a Christian?

No, not yet. Maybe in a few years. When your father's gone.

He's not my father.

He's made you his son. I think he loves you.

What makes you think that?

Someone whispered in my ear.

I hope to become a catechist. The first Greenlandic catechist.

Indeed, that would be something. I'm sure you'll make a good catechist. You could baptize me.

The priest does that. You'd have to go to him.

Fair enough, but not until there's another priest. Once there's another priest I'll let myself be baptized. But tell me something. Tell me what salvation is.

Salvation is forgiveness and the heavenly life.

But what are you supposed to do up there? Isn't it better down here? I mean, God made the world, and he made it a paradise for people.

I'm not sure. But all of us hope to go to Heaven. Life on earth is merely a rehearsal to separate the sheep from the goats. In heaven we shall be reunited with all those who are dead, and join again with our loved ones.

Can a goat become a sheep? Would you know that?

Yes, it can. God forgives him who in honesty asks for absolution.

So there's still hope.

Yes, I think so often.

You know your father's a thief?

A thief? What did he steal?

He stole what was most valuable to me.

You mean me?

You said it.

He looked after me when I was ill.

And kept you when you got well. I call that stealing.

Egede is no thief. I cannot help but think of the pile of papers he has locked in his drawer, the secret I must reveal to no one. He is a good man, I say.

Don't you ever miss the old life? Wandering in pursuit of the animals, living in the tents in summer, the peat-huts in winter? Being with your people?

I can't remember it. I was only small.

You could come back. You could wander with me. We could be together for all time.

A person can never go back. It can't be done. I belong with them now.

But you're not one of them. They treat you poorly. What is it they call you?

Two-Kings. It's because of my name. Frederik Christian. King's names both.

There you are then. They make fun of you. They make you drink aquavit and lie down with their women. I happen to know you lie down with men too.

I look away, fearful of his gaze. I'm weak, I mumble. But Jesus forgives. He forgives seventy times seven times.

You'll not have many left, he says.

That's where you're wrong! I reply. One can keep on repenting. It never stops. Always there is forgiveness, if only one asks for it in honesty. That's the difference between you heathens and us Christians.

How sad, he says. Our rules are different entirely. You'd be a lot happier if you came with me.

No, I belong to him now.

Black Man, he says. He's taken you from me, and that's worse than dying seventy times seven times. If you don't come with me, I'll come and get you.

Where will you take me?

I won't take you anywhere. You'll go yourself. He stares at me.

I remember I always used to be afraid, I say. Before Egede gathered me up.

Afraid of what?

The monsters the elders always used to talk about. And people dying. People died all the time. My mother died. I remember it. And there was no hope. Egede says God gave hope to man to balance out his misery.

I understand, he says. It's no joke being a heathen. I wanted to be Christian once as well. But your mother wouldn't let me. It was her fault everything went wrong.

When the land has become Christian, it'll be better for everyone, I say.

It's possible, I suppose. But they'll have lost something too.

What will they have lost?

The same as you have lost. The same as I have lost. And dear to us is but that which we have lost.

Who said that?

I did, he says, and looks at me with a sad smile.

The time has come for me to go home. I feel my clothes. They are still damp, though warm from the fire. I put them on.

Where are we?

A small island in the sea. How are you thinking of getting home? Your kayak's no good.

I don't know. Are there other people on this island?

No, just you and me. It's more an islet, very small.

Then I suppose I'll have to wait until someone comes by and picks me up.

No one comes by here. It's off the shipping route, if any ship ever comes. Maybe a native boat, if you're lucky. But I'd prepare myself for a long wait if I were you.

He goes down to the beach, launches his kayak and gets in.

I saved your bow and arrows, and your harpoon too. They're up there.

You're going to leave me?

Keep the seal, he says.

You can at least tell someone I'm here, so they can come and get me.

I don't know where we are myself, he says. And with that he paddles away and is gone.

///

Stillness. The fog is as silk. It is not to say if it is night or day. The sea breathes heavily in and out, clacks the pebbles at the shore. The raven is here yet. It hops about with entrails bloody in its beak, then vanishes above the rocks. I follow after it. At once I am above the fog. The weather is clear, the sun ablaze. I am surrounded by an ocean of mist that reaches to my knees. And there is the colony, beyond the bay. This is not an island in the sea at all. I gather my belongings together and follow the curve of the shore.

When I arrive, the sun has burnt the fog away. The flag flutters on its pole. And there are the Egede girls, walking arm in arm at the harbour. They glance in my direction without waving. There is the carpenter, repairing a roof, and Egede looking up at him, instructing him. And there is Jens Smith in his smithy. He sees me, puts down his hammer and comes out into the doorway, from fiery darkness into sunlight.

Let's sort that tooth out, shall we? Pull the bugger out.

My toothache's gone, I tell him. The tooth is well.

3

As Long as I Breathe, I Hope

*With such fine weather as ended the old year, so began also
the new, which continued until the 18th day of this month.
But from then such a sharp frost has set in that even the beasts
in the stables are near perished with cold, and a calf almost
a year old was found dead in the stall.*

FROM HANS EGEDE'S JOURNAL, JANUARY 1733

I am Aappaluttoq. I am in the colony. I wait for winter. In the winter
it will happen. It is neither fate nor God who has decided it will be
so. I have decided. I am Aappaluttoq.

///

Matthias Jochumsen is my name. In the good year of our Lord 1680,
when a great comet appeared to a terrified rabble in Rotterdam and
then until the following spring allowed its ominous flaming body and
tail to be seen in the sky, foreboding all kinds of calamity, though in
the final end merely leaving in its wake the usual wars, sicknesses
and other ills which have always descended upon the lands of Europe,
I was born in the town of Frederikshald. My father, Jochum Matthiasen,
whose name was the inversion of his father's, as mine is of his, in
the way that has been the custom through many generations, a chain-
dance of Matthiases and Jochums back to the darkest times of the
plague, was a merchant, one of the wealthiest men of the town, held
in esteem by high and low alike, confident that, as he himself was
the son of a merchant, he too would beget generations of merchants,
among them me, destined to follow in his father's footsteps and add
to the family's wealth, but this was not to be the case. Declining times,
war and strife befell us. Such is war, some rise up, others sink. It

drove him into death and me to the furthest corners of the realm, the Danish king's poorest provinces.

At first I embarked upon writing and published a small monograph, a pamphlet entitled *De Longitudine* in which seafarers might find instruction in the art of plotting a given position west or east of a meridian line. I knew nothing about navigation. I had heard about, though never seen or held in my hands, Professor Newton's octant, to say nothing of more modern instruments such as the sextant or the chronometer, but among my father's many books I had fallen upon a very old manuscript in Latin which must have been several centuries old, written by the hand of a Catholic monk and bearing the title *Registrum secretum domini abbatis*. It concerned the art of navigating at sea and I proceeded to translate it into Danish, embellishing here and there along the way, adding my own common-sense considerations and eventually having it printed by a printer at Frederikshald, a process which cost me the remainder of my meagre means and would yield me nothing in money since only twenty-three copies were sold.

Yet His Majesty had somehow taken a shine to me and when it came to his ear that I had dedicated my small publication to him, he showed me the grace of sending me to Iceland to conduct studies of an economic nature in order that the poor, mad Icelanders might get the better of their poverty and falling numbers. I remained there for three years, travelling far and wide over the great island on horseback and visiting even the smallest fishing communities along the coast as well as the inland farms where the population primarily supported themselves by means of sheep-keeping, though also from a small amount of agriculture as practised since the times of the old Norsemen. To the scattered harbours of this island came but seldom a ship, however once when I was in the eastern part of the country a royal frigate came by the name of the *Morian*, on its way to the new colony in Greenland and calling at Iceland to replenish its stocks of fresh drinking water, fuel and hay for the livestock on board. The captain of this ship told me of the King's new enterprise of which there were high hopes indeed. I asked him if the name Greenland was not to be considered a witticism or perhaps an embellishment with the purpose of attracting Danes to its shores, much like a sign outside a shop, for I had heard that the land was covered by ice, yet he replied that while there indeed was ice in abundance in the country's interior there was also a broad belt at the coasts which was without, in some places more than fifteen Danish miles in width, with deeply cut fjords, lush and of great natural beauty, and where also various relics could be found after the Icelanders and Norsemen who had once lived there. With his descriptions he ignited a fantasy in my mind of a virginal land with good prospects and opportunity for enterprising and industrious men.

On completion of my duties in Iceland I returned to Denmark and compiled there a report of my observations, including suggestions as to what could be done for the poor Icelandic people, adjoining to my report a prospectus as to how such initiatives might beneficially to the royal household be coordinated with the new colony in the west – the throne held now, following the death of King Frederik, by his son Christian the Sixth. In this I took the liberty of proposing that a number of Icelandic families be selected to comprise the core of a new population of settlers. Moreover, I drew up a plan for the traversing of the great ice-cap which divides the western tracts of the country from the eastern, a feat which both the missionary Egede and the country's governor Pors had previously endeavoured without success, though my own proposal involved the use of skis and sledges drawn by captured and tamed reindeer. The young king saw no less kindly upon me than his father, and no sooner than in the spring of 1732, in my fifty-first year, I boarded the good ship the *Jomfru Cornelia* together with my younger brother Just and my son Knud, then twenty-five years of age and yet unmarried. Though my flesh was weak, my spirit was more willing than ever before. I thought of Greenland as the land of the future, the land of opportunity, a new world which would allow the King to resurrect the ailing finances of the realm and I my family's name and honour.

///

Matthias Jochumsen endures the many hardships of the voyage, the heaving deck, the mouldy legumes and the green-tainted meat, the indecencies of the crew, their bodily stenches and their altercations, and arrives at the colony of Godthåb on 21 June. Egede receives him kindly and puts him up with his brother and son on the first floor of the colony house. He sleeps for a long time. Two days later, when he has recovered, they slaughter one of the sheep in order to celebrate a successful journey. The three newcomers spend their evenings downstairs in the priest's parlour, a fire crackling in the stove as rain lashes the panes. They talk at length with Egede about the country, asking him this and that. They find him to be a friendly sort, rather quiet though with an occasional harshness to his gaze, particularly when the subject turns to the Mission, which it seems is not as successful as one might have hoped. The words of the Gospel fall like rain into the sea here, he says with bitterness.

The men puff on clay pipes. Matthias has brought a plentiful supply of tobacco with him from Denmark, a good, moist and syrupy tobacco whose aroma seems to them like a concentrate of long tropical summers dispersing into the low-ceilinged parlour, and the women as well as the men are all but swooning over it. The two Egede girls sit reading Luther's sermons at their father's behest. Matthias listens to their brittle voices as they read through the German text, which in parts is highly vulgar in its language, with words such as piss and shit and arse, though which the girls read without pause. The great wall-clock ticks haltingly and strikes, and outside they hear the fire-watch shout out the hour. The smoke from the stove and the pipes collects densely beneath the beams.

The priest tells of his expeditions into the district and of the attempts made, firstly by himself and later by the newly departed Governor Pors, to cross over to the eastern side of the land where it is thought there still must live descendants of the Norsemen either in papist infidelity or else regressed into the heathenism of old, which perhaps would be preferable, for as he says, heathenism is but superstition, whereas Catholicism is the very shite that sprays from the arse of the Devil. Egede puffs vigorously on his pipe and gazes up at the ceiling. He sits with his legs stretched out in front of him, the red glow of his tobacco pulsating. No, the heathens are by no means the worst, he says. They are like demented children. It is the false Christians who damage the Christian message the most.

Matthias asks him about the three years of the colony. Was it as bad a time as he has heard?

Worse, says Madame Egede from her chair in the corner, waving her needle and thread dismissively. Best not to speak of it.

Yes, it was a strain, Egede says with a smile. But one should not be envious of the godless who live a life of pleasure, for they are as swine fattening for the slaughter.

He tells them of the disastrous winter of 1728–29 when half the crew perished, of the Dutchmen and their regular plunderings along the coast, their destruction of the northern colony station at Nipisane, all matters leading to the abandonment of the colony project and the calling home of the Governor along with most of those who were still left.

Now only a small handful of us remain, says the priest. It can scarcely be called a colony at all any more. But we have started afresh and hope for His Majesty's continued favour and kindness. He is clearly disappointed that the ship has brought with it no word from the King as to what his plans might be for the colony, yet is relieved nonetheless to receive substantial provisions, which would seem to indicate that the King wishes to wait and see and has not forgotten them completely.

Matthias tells of his idea to have some Icelandic families settle in tracts of the country where it is possible to cultivate the land, and of the King having expressed interest in the matter. Egede becomes animated. He relates his experiences sowing grain and vegetables, endeavours which to a certain extent have shown to be promising. And there is good pasture land, he says. Like Iceland, the country is mostly suited to grazing. Agriculture must come second, but with systematic cultivation and conscientious tending of the crops, there would be every chance of becoming self-sufficient.

Matthias listens attentively, making mental notes for the reports he is to write. His son Knud is good company for the two young Egede girls, who remove themselves from Luther and walk with him on the peninsula, returning home with ruddy cheeks. The priest's son, Niels, teaches him to paddle a kayak. Just, Matthias's brother, spends most of his time with the natives, conducting his studies. Matthias barely sees him.

In early July they embark on a preliminary expedition into the Ameralik Fjord, the young native man with the impressively royal name of Frederik Christian accompanying them as pilot. The land, the high fells edging the fjord in silence, bears down on them. They are alone.

They paddle up the tributary fjords and inlets, put up their tents and wander in the wide valleys. Matthias gathers rock samples. He notes the horizontally grooved rock high up on the fellsides and asks himself if the sea has sunk or the land risen, and wonders what forces might make such a thing possible. If it is God's work, he thinks to himself, then he must have some plan for the world which extends far beyond man's six-thousand-year existence. He compiles tables detailing the deviations of the compass, he directs his son and brother to their different peaks so that he may triangulate, and draws up maps with precise topographical indications of height; he makes lists of tidal variations in the various phases of the moon, he collects, dries and registers countless plants that will become part of the great work he will publish on his return to Denmark, and he investigates the different manifestations of the ice – fjord-ice, glacier-ice, icebergs, black ice, white ice – its viscosity, colour, smoothness and porosity, and he observes the animal species of the sea and land, even capturing specimens he then freezes for the later purpose of taxidermy. Just is an excellent illustrator. He produces sketches of everything living and dead. Matthias's son sits and gazes dreamily across the fjord. He seems strangely content. The native lad, Frederik Christian, sits beside him. They appear to have become friends.

Matthias keeps an eye on his son. For several years now he has suffered from increasing apathy, has always been introverted and indolent, and now moreover dishonest. He lies inexplicably about matters of no concern, as if he simply is fond of the lie itself. Matthias had previously attributed it to a lively imagination carried over from childhood and assumed he would grow out of it. But he has not. On the contrary, his lies have become ever more serious, and he has begun also to steal. On the occasions they have discovered him lying or thieving and have confronted him with the matter, he has in each case become so enraged as to make his mother afraid of him, and for that reason they have let it drop. He ought to take him to task, Matthias thinks, shake him up a bit. But he feels a strange awkwardness in the face of such shameless duplicity. It paralyses him. His son exploits this, of course. He has been like a dead weight this past time. He does what is asked of him, indeed, though in a half-hearted, slovenly fashion which can only prompt admonishment, in which instance he will hunch his back and mumble incoherently or else flare up in anger and slam the door. His mother has despaired of him. Yet now it seems as if he has emerged from his shell. Perhaps it is the presence of the two girls, Matthias thinks to himself. Perhaps he will begin courting at long last. Perhaps it is the country here and the adventure into which he has been thrown. He prays for this improvement to last.

The summer and autumn are one long expedition with short stopovers in the colony. They go out into the skerries and visit settlements where without exception the natives receive them warmly. Just is becoming quite naturalized, and Matthias's son clearly seems to be emulating him. They practise with their bows and arrows, they paddle their kayaks and speak together in the native language. Matthias wonders if his son might remain here. Perhaps he might be taken on as an assistant by the trading company and then work his way up. Naturally it would in all likelihood mean never seeing him again, and his mother too would be quite distraught. Yet he cannot help but feel drawn by the thought of being able to leave the lad here in Greenland with good conscience.

Knud himself spends increasing time with Frederik Christian. Matthias sees them walking together engrossed in conversation. They are more or less the same age. Often they do not come home in the evenings, but return only the next day, and when Matthias asks where he has been he says out in the fells.

With your Greenlandic friend?

Knud nods. Is there anything wrong in that?

No, there is nothing wrong in it, my boy.

And yet there is. Egede comes to see him. I don't know who's leading who astray, he says, but they drink and carouse with the crew.

I see, Matthias says. But surely they are allowed a measure of fun?

The crew are filthy swine, the priest replies. I have previously forbidden him to drink with them. But now he's with your own son and no doubt he feels beyond reproach.

He brings the matter up tentatively.

We weren't drinking, Knud tells him, though he reeks of alcohol and is bleary-eyed the morning after. Anyway, it's got nothing to do with me what's between Egede and his foster-son.

What do the men get up to when they drink? he asks.

Oh, all sorts, Knud says, and can scarcely conceal a smile. It's quite astonishing the things they can think of. They drag native women into the house and fornicate with them while everyone watches.

And you find it amusing?

It's not something I take part in.

But watching what they do to those poor women makes you a part of it.

It's only what I've heard, says Knud. It doesn't interest me.

He lets the matter drop. He knows from experience that he will not get to the bottom of things by speaking to the lad. Lies, concealment of the truth, evasion, is all a part of his constitution, and perhaps he is even unaware that he is lying at all.

One evening he goes over to the crew house. The carpenter has invited him to join a game of cards. He enters the room. The floor is new and the walls partially clad with timber planks. Previously the floor was stamped earth and the peat walls were bare, but now the place is being fixed. He has heard much about this house. Here it was that so many of them perished that first year. Young people became old, wasted away and were gone within months. The few who survived returned home. None of the present crew were here then. But all are familiar with the harrowing tales that are told of 'the Death House' and all know it to be haunted. It is the dead women in particular who show themselves. Several of the men say they have seen them in the night with long wooden poles as if they were raking hay, their white shifts tucked up, their hair hanging loose in front of their faces. The whores of the Spinning House. But they are friendly ghosts, they say with a smile. The poor wenches, they would surely have preferred their bones to be laid to rest in Danish soil.

The house is quite cosy now, well lit by lamps which hang from the ceiling and a great fireplace which heats the entire room in which there is both sleeping space and a communal area furnished with a long table. Matthias sits down with them and is given a cup of ale. As far as he can see there is neither drunkenness nor the slightest approach to indecency, and he remains there until into the night, losing a few marks in the card game but enjoying himself nevertheless. Most of the men are his countrymen, which is to say Norwegians. He feels at home. And to his relief Knud is elsewhere.

Walking back to the colony house he notices a light in the stable. He peers in through the window, pressing his face to the pane and cupping his hands around his eyes, but at the same moment the light is extinguished. There is a rustling from within, a scuttle of goats, and he calls out, receiving what seems to him an oddly good-humoured bleat in reply. Knud? he calls again. Again the same peculiar bleat. He feels certain Knud is there. But what is he doing?

The bed chamber upstairs in the Egede house is indeed empty. Knud's bunk is still made. He retires to bed and sleeps immediately. When he wakes the next morning, Knud has returned.

Where were you last night? he asks.

We were out walking, that's all, the lad replies.

We?

Me and Frederik Christian.

Were you in the stable? I saw a light there.

The stable? No. What would we be doing in the stable?

Indeed, that's what I wondered.

But we weren't in the stable.

Indeed not, so you've said.

Unsurprisingly, the lad is annoyed by this exchange. He does not speak to his father the whole day and turns away whenever he approaches. Damn the surly boy, Matthias thinks.

When winter comes, they hibernate in the colony. The weather becomes windy and cold, and darkness shrouds the peninsula and the colony's scattered structures. As the days grow shorter, the circles in which they move grow smaller. Eventually they come to a standstill. Matthias reads the priest's books, mostly religious works, but also some philosophy, and of course Egede's own Perlustration, published some years ago, but which the author himself now contends is full of errors, and a new and much revised version is apparently on its way. Moreover, Matthias works on his grand description of the country, his own Greenlandic relation, and the systematisation of his investigations during the summer and autumn. All is well. Apart from the forever gnawing anxiety he feels when he thinks of his son.

///

I am Aappaluttoq. Call me Abraham.

I wrench the boy's chin upwards and to the side with one hand and brandish the knife with the other, and he whimpers, he wriggles and squirms and tries to come free. I whisper to him, easy now, it will be done in a second, and my hand describes a flattened arc with the blade as I slice a smile into his throat and release him slowly. He kicks a bit, only then to become heavy and still and sink into the snow which at once absorbs his blood, and he is dead.

Dear to us is but that which we have lost.

No, no, what have I done!

But now he rises, the snow is sucked up into the sky, the river runs into the fells, the clocks tick backwards and I embrace him, I hold him tightly to my chest, the knife springs into my hand, I brandish the blade, though in the other direction, making what is done undone, and the blade closes the wound in his throat as a painting brush rectifies a mistake on a canvas, and the blood is drawn back into him, and he glides from my grasp.

Now he goes between shimmering clouds in the scribbled blur of the snowstorm, away from me. He has sheathed the knife in his belt. I see my own shadow break into an angle against the outside wall and vanish, and he knows I am there, but he does not know it is me, and now he calls for me:

Father?

He stands obliquely, a supporting arm against the wall in front of him, pissing against the warehouse building, the jet of his urine spraying in the wind. A sheep brays in the stable. He has called out his name, but only a sheep replies. His breeches are filled with excrement. Even in the whipping snow which launders the whole world clean, which consigns all human detritus to darkness, I sense the smell. My poor, miserable, humiliated and shamed boy.

I am Aappaluttoq. Murderer and father, I believe in Jesus Christ the Lord. Dear to us is but that which we have lost.

He could not open the stable door to go inside. That was what he wanted. To go inside to the animals. Inside to his loved one. But his loved one was not there, or at least did not reply when he called. He battered on the door and called out again:

Knud!

Before this he came staggering from the crew house, its windows beaming yellow with the warmth of what binds the Danes together when outside are darkness and storms. He struggled with the door, the gusting winds tugged it this way and that in his hands, and they shouted after him:

Close that door, you fell-monkey, before the weather gets in!

He only went out to piss, but shat himself instead and thus could not go back inside. He fought to close the door behind him, but the wind was too strong, until at last a heavy gust, violent as a sudden kick, slammed it shut for him.

Since the new year the colony has been locked in an ice-cold, silent exchange of light and darkness. But this morning, the day of Epiphany, the ropes which are stretched tight across the rooftops began to whistle, a quiet yet shrill melody, and the flag in front of the colony house began as if to shiver with cold, and above the Saddle Fell appeared a legume-shaped cloud which seemed almost to stare from the heavens so ominously, and then the storm was upon us and filled the air with prickling snow of the kind that sweeps straight through a person and out the other side. The snow in itself is light, and white as paper, though illuminates nothing but itself. God roars and staggers about like a giant who is drunk or gone mad, most seemingly both. And with him staggers the boy. I follow him like a shadow.

Close that door, you fell-monkey, before the weather gets in!

He dropped down on all fours and vomited, the snow accepting it all, the salt-cured pork-meat and pease porridge of his dinner, the aquavit with which they had plied him, the woman they had coaxed him into lying with. And now it all came back the other way. He had lost control of his body, his body had usurped him and its will was not his. Groaning with loathing and grief, he stared at the mash of food and alcohol as it was consumed by the snow. Moreover he had now soiled himself. He could not go back inside. He turned his face to the storm which lashed his skin.

Lord Jesus, save me!

Yes, my boy. I am here. Come to me.

And he rose unsteadily to his feet, he pulled the three-cornered hat down over his ears and stood teetering, supporting himself against the iron six-pounder gun which was bolted fast to its carriage, staring back with eyes filled with both abhorrence and longing towards the illuminated windows behind which were laughter and human warmth, music, the card game, aquavit and oblivion. Outside, where he was now, were only darkness and cold, and God's deafening silence, amid the stench of his human excrement. But I was there too.

A hesitation told me his thoughts: I must go home. But where is home? 'Home is where Jesus is', as Mother Gertrud always said. But no, he could not go home to them and step inside the priest's righteous parlour stinking like a pigsty.

He reeled his way down to the colony harbour, buffeted this way and that by the wind, stumbling to the ground several times, cursing, muttering to himself, spitting out the words of the Apostles' Creed: *I renounce the Devil and all his works and all his ways.*

Perhaps I can go to the savages? he thinks. They will not turn me away. They are my own people, after all. I could read for the children as I normally do, tell them about the Saviour, they like that. But the savages too are averse to the smell of human excrement, even though they wash themselves in the contents of their own night pots.

I believe in God, the Father almighty, creator of heaven and earth.

He wears the clothing of an officer now dead, a worn-out coat with buttons of bone, woollen breeches with patches at the knees, white knee-stockings, high-leg boots and a cocked hat long since wearied to hang limply at each of its three corners, though now fluttering madly in the wind. And these fine clothes of which he is so proud, and which have distinguished him so obviously from the savages, are now soiled by his own filth.

He wants into the stable. To the animals who lie and breathe so warmly, to their comfort and forgiveness. They care not if he smells of dung. And in the stable it is that he frolics with his loved one. Now he wants only to sleep in a bed of living wool. If only he could open the door.

Born of the Virgin Mary, suffered under Pontius Pilate, was crucified, died and was buried, he descended to the dead.

The Apostles' Creed is like an annoying song he cannot banish from his mind. It was Egede, his foster-father, who ground it into his head, yielding not until he knew it by heart. And now it is stuck.

He pushes and pulls at the stable door, and kicks it repeatedly. It too is stuck.

Knud! Are you there?

A sheep brays a reply. The coming together of warmth from the animals inside and the cold outside has caused the door to perspire an impeding bank of ice. If only he had an axe or a crowbar. The only thing he has is a small flensing knife. He begins to hack and scrape at the ice. But his efforts are to no avail. His bare hands are stiff with cold. He blows on them. He feels the wetness of his breeches freezing into ice. Abruptly he wheels around. A gust of wind removes his hat and sends it tumbling away into the darkness.

Who's there?

Dear to us is but that which we have lost.

I am standing looking at him. He ought to see me. But he does not.

He pisses against the warehouse wall. The wind howls, whistling around the buildings. It is dark, though not completely.

Is anyone there?

He stands unsteadily with his breeches around his ankles and glimpses a fleeting shadow break into an angle against a wall and hasten away. A lamp somewhere. But he cannot see it, only the shadow it casts.

Who's there? Come out!

He is not alone. Of this he is certain, the boy, though whoever would be lurking about in such a storm he cannot imagine. Perhaps just the fire-watch. Nothing to be afraid of, he tells himself.

On the third day he rose again; he ascended into heaven, he is seated at the right hand of the Father.

He shakes his member before pulling up his breeches, sensing again the unpleasantness of his involuntary evacuation.

And he will come to judge the living and the dead.

Oh! he blurts in fright. Was that my own voice? Or someone else's?

Now again he sees a shadow, it passes quickly over the snow, flutters against the end wall, lengthening and then shortening again before vanishing from sight, and he narrows his eyes and peers.

Hello?

He staggers, fingers fumbling with his buttons, mouth still murmuring the Apostles' Creed as if to chase away all things bad, whoever or whatever is tramping about here in the darkness now, as well as the badness inside his mind.

I believe in the Holy Spirit.

In the storm he stands, stiff-legged, clutching the flap of his breeches, listening like an animal.

I know you're there! Come out. Make yourself known!

And when he hears the voice which replies he is startled: *The holy catholic church, the communion of saints.*

Father? he says hesitantly, and turns.

Dear to us is but that which we have lost.

But then comes the hand. It covers his mouth and twists his head to the side, wrenching the chin upwards, exposing the throat, and he loses his footing, his legs kicking in thin air, arms thrashing, gasping, shrieking, his cries break up and disperse in the air like scraps of paper in the gale; he struggles for breath and fumbles for his knife, but the knife is gone, someone has taken it, and now he sees its glinting steel, we see it both, for we are together in this, terrified we see the blade describe its flat and lunging arc, and the boy clutches at the air to repel the attack, no, my knife, no, please, what, is it you? But I am too quick for him, I slice a smile into his throat and he drops limply into the snow and is dead.

No! Tell me it isn't so! What have I done?

Now he rises up again, as if by the aid of an invisible hand, everything runs backwards, or else time is run into a stagnant pool, whirling its little vortex, and he comes to life, trembling anew, whimpering in terror, his living, warm stench of excrement; I hear the wound slobber the blood into its mouth and see the blade repeat its arc, though in the opposite direction, closing the wound as if by a stroke of a painting brush, and not so much as a drop of sanguine red remains; I release him and he staggers backwards into the alabaster-white darkness, to the colony house and over the threshold, only then to appear before me once more, struggling with the door in the wind.

Close that door, you fell-monkey, before the weather gets in!

But each time he returns. Dear to us is but that which we have lost. And each time it ends up the same. For this is how it must be. He ends in my embrace, and I hold him tightly to my chest, O heaven, will this curse never stop! The blade glints in the dark and a slobbering laughter issues from the smile I have sliced into his throat. I put him down carefully in the snow, or I let him drop like a rag doll, for there is room for variation in this eternal treadmill, and I toss the knife, I run away, into my own damnation, to guilt and anger and hatred; now I bend over him and he is lifted up, sucked into my arms, he pulls away, staggers backwards, his strides feeble and precarious from drink; he emerges from the colony house – Close that door, you fell-monkey, before the weather gets in – he lurches about in the gale, an eternal pendulum swinging between life and death; he batters and kicks at the stable door, the sheep brays, the blade glints, again and again, and there he lies, a blood-red flourish in the snow, the great seeping gash in his throat, and I bend down, to my sacrificial lamb, I kiss him and whisper in his ear: Dear to us is but that which we have lost.

///

6 January. A storm has lasted all day. Matthias sits downstairs in the Egede house, puffing on his pipe and conversing with Madame Rasch. Just has gone up the fjord with Egede's son Niels. Doubtless

they are biding their time in some savage's dwelling until the weather improves, wishing they had never left home, says the Madame. Matthias is oddly fond of the occasional storm, finding they allow him a very particular kind of peace in which to work. He has plenty to occupy him here at home with his studies and his notes. He has sent Knud down to the little shed they have built, in which they keep their collection of specimens from their summer and autumn expeditions. There is some considerable value there, several thousands of rigsdaler according to Egede's assessment, and he has impressed upon his son how to secure the shed with ropes and make sure there is nothing for the wind to take hold of. He knows he ought to supervise Knud and satisfy himself that the lad does as he is instructed, but at the same time he wishes to demonstrate to him that he trusts him.

The two girls sit immersed in their reading at the high table, the usual Luther he assumes. The murmur of their voices, the warmth from the stove and the creaking of the floorboards above the ceiling, the physician, Kieding, pacing restlessly about upstairs, tormented by his demons, have a soporific effect on him.

The gale makes the house groan in its joints and causes the shutters to rattle. Now and then, a gust whistles down the chimney and black clouds of smoke fill the parlour. A native girl wafts them away with a towel. The Egede couple's foster-children, presently four small ones and two older girls being prepared for baptism and confirmation respectively, live their quiet and undemanding lives at the far end of the parlour where they play with some wooden blocks previously belonging to the Egede children proper. They draw little attention to themselves apart from suffering from disconcertingly chesty coughs and constant sniffling colds.

Abruptly Knud comes in and is on his way upstairs when Matthias stops him.

Where have you been?

The crew house. Knud ascends the first pair of steps.

Are they carousing there?

They are drinking, yes.

What have you done with your friend?

Who?

Your friend, Frederik Christian?

I don't know where he is.

Did you see anything of Hans? the Madame enquires.

No, I haven't seen him.

Have you done as I told you and secured the shed in the storm? Matthias asks.

I checked a short while ago and tightened the ropes. They can withstand anything now.

Good boy. Upstairs with you, by all means.

He sits listening to the gale as it gathers force, the way it sings, rising and falling in tone as it rounds the corners of the house, the way it makes the fire in the stove flare up and roar.

Madame Egede is highly knowledgeable about the country and in particular the natives. She tells him about their faith. In her opinion it is not a proper religion, merely a way in which they relate themselves to the severeness of nature here and the rigours of an unpredictable climate.

I imagine, she says, that they would easily be able to acquire the Christian faith without giving up their own. After all, they have survived here for centuries. And they show a natural fondness for Jesus. They are always interested to hear about Him.

But these shamans, Madame Egede, says Matthias. They seem to have the upper hand on the savages. Are they not a hindrance to the spread of Christianity?

She is darning a sock. Her hand bobs a rhythm. Certainly there are hindrances, she replies. But they too must be cautiously approached. It's no use being heavy-handed about it.

Some would perhaps not quite be in agreement, he says with a smile.

No, Hans can be rather stubborn. He becomes fiery if someone should go against him. It has always been his way, even at home in Vågan. It makes enemies for him of people who ought properly to be his allies.

I've heard of an angakkok they call the Red One. The crew say he has cast a curse upon the colony?

From the corner of his eye he notices the Egede girls halt in their reading, lift their heads and exchange glances.

The Madame puts down her darning and looks up. Her hands settle in her lap. The first winter was bad. More than half the crew perished. Certainly it was a curse, but a curse precipitated by poor planning and even poorer implementation. Sorcery was not required. She turns to her daughters and tells them to continue their reading. When your father gets home you need to have learned it by heart. You know how despondent he becomes otherwise. They hunch over their books once more.

Sometimes I don't know who is worse when it comes to letting their imaginations run away with them, the Greenlanders or the Danes. Superstition is in us all.

Madame Egede would no doubt make a fine missionary, he says. Perhaps even she could convert a die-hard shaman.

She holds him in her grey, matronly gaze. Indeed I could.

Heavy footsteps sound in the passage, the door is flung open and the smith enters. He has removed his cap, not for the sake of politeness, but to wipe away the snow from his face. The warehouse, he blurts breathlessly. The gale's got a hold of it. We need help.

Matthias shouts up the stairs for Knud, but his son does not reply. Let him sleep, he tells himself. Kieding, however, has heard him and comes hurrying.

They put on overcoats and follow the smith outside. The air is thick with great globs of snow. Matthias sees objects hurled by the wind and recognizes parts of his collection. By the time they reach the warehouse they are too late. The building is flattened, its contents dispersed or destroyed. My collection, he exclaims. But the smith grips him and he is forced to go with him and help secure the other structures, nailing the shutters tight and drawing the ropes taut over the roofs. The men appear from the crew house. Several are reeling drunk, but do what they can to assist. Afterwards they go up to the colony house and the smith even climbs onto the roof to nail down some planks he finds to be in danger of being torn away.

They sit down in Egede's parlour over an aquavit and feel the warmth return to their bodies. Neither Egede nor Frederik Christian is anywhere to be seen. The men last saw them earlier in the evening, though cannot say where they went. Madame Gertrud is worried as to what might have happened to them. But then almost at once Egede appears, clad in his cassock. They stare at him in disbelief. Where have you been in this weather? his wife asks. And in your vestments too!

In the mission room, he says. I have been immersed in prayer and only realized a few moments ago there was a storm.

He has not seen his foster-son.

Matthias goes upstairs. He stands for a while watching his son who seems to be sleeping. The lad reeks of alcohol. Matthias feels an urge to strike him, no, to beat and torment him. But he goes to bed and lies there for a long time, shaking with rage before falling asleep.

The next day the weather is still. He goes about salvaging whatever items of his collection he can find in the snow. Hardly any of it seems to be of use to him any more and he ends up discarding everything, bitter and enraged. He imagines beating his son, shaking the daylights out of him, screaming into his face. But then he is overcome by pangs of guilt and his anger is superseded by sympathy. Now I must start again, he thinks resignedly. Fortunately, his rock specimens and geodetic sketch maps, along with his brother's drawings and his own notes, are safely stored in his room. That's something, at least.

Later in the day the body of Frederik Christian is discovered by the carpenter. He almost falls over him down by the blubber house where he lies half-buried in the snow with his throat cut and his breeches around his ankles. Kieding examines him and notes that the incision to the throat is clean and deep, almost to the cervical vertebrae. He can say nothing of what kind of knife might have been used.

The crew are interrogated. The boy's movements are charted hour by hour. He was drinking in the crew house, but then he left and after that no one saw him. Every man in the colony is made to declare solemnly on his honour and in the presence of sworn witnesses his movements throughout the evening and night. Egede himself conducts these interviews and writes down the answers he is given. No evidence is forthcoming as to who might have killed the boy.

The funeral takes place five days later. Egede speaks at the grave. He takes as his point of departure Genesis chapter twenty-two, the story of Abraham and Isaac. His voice trembles with grief. Madame Gertrud weeps loudly. Matthias's son Knud is absent. He has descended into a state of torpor and lies in his bed from morning till night.

///

January, February, March. The days become lighter, but also colder. Because of the tidal currents the fjord does not freeze over, and on particularly cold days an icy mist rises from the sea to settle as white fur on all surfaces, ripping at every human lung. The days are spent in Egede's parlour with legs outstretched to the warming stove, bootsocks steaming. Reading and needlework.

Renewed hope. Egede has taken Knud under his wing. Matthias sees them going about the colony immersed in conversation. He wonders what the priest might have to talk to his son about, yet feels a faint guilt-tinged joy at the prospect of the Egede family taking the lad off his hands and perhaps getting him started in a position with the Trade in this furthest corner of the realm. Knud has been mute and withdrawn following the murder of his friend. But during the spring he comes rather more to life. When Matthias speaks with him he hears echoes of his talks with Egede. The priest has now offered him a place as assistant in the Trade and Knud tentatively enquires with his father as to what his mother will say if he should accept. She will be proud of you, Matthias tells him, knowing full well that his wife will be enraged and heartbroken if he should return home without him.

Then I will do it, says the lad. I like it here. It feels as if this land has simply been waiting for me.

The light returns, dazzling and relentless. The weather becomes milder.

///

20 April 1733.

The weather is gentle and sunny. Matthias, Just and Knud embark on a great expedition to the south, in two boats manned by a nine-man crew and rigged with spritsail and jib. They make swift progress, sailing in the sheltered waters of the skerries, punting through the narrow sounds, sleeping under the open sky when the weather permits, or else in the tents, boiling legumes and meat, freshly caught fish and birds over fires kindled with heather. The breeze is light, though it comes from the sea and blows gently into the sails, tilting the boats into a speed of some five knots. Once a day they put into an inlet and replenish their water from a stream or river. Matthias makes notes and is reconstructing his collection of specimens. Just sketches the profiles of the land and draws up the beginnings of maps he compares with those already completed the year before. Knud often goes off into the fells, returning ruddy-cheeked and with a bashful smile on his face. The further south and the further away from the colony they travel, the lighter their mood becomes. They make no mention of any event of the winter past. The blue sky, the fells and the pure air make all that has happened disappear.

After two weeks they cross the sixty-first latitude. Here they find a fjord which spits out so much ice that they must drag the boats onto an ice-floe, take down the rigging and bide their time. The current sucks them up the fjord. Great frozen sheets break apart with loud reports, buffeting and mounting each other. They labour to haul the boats over the ice and bring them ashore, but it is an impossible task and they must submit themselves to fate as the land glides slowly by.

Matthias cannot bear this idleness and incapacity on the drifting ice. To make use of his time he decides he will attempt to reach the land, taking with him a flintlock and a rucksack. His son accompanies him. For the better part of the day they skip and leap from floe to floe, icy islets that wobble underfoot, and several times come perilously close to falling in, though eventually they manage to step ashore onto a spit of land. Here they erect a cairn so that the crew might find them again once the fjord-ice disintegrates into slush and the waters become open. They spend the night in sleeping bags under a starry firmament, and the next day proceed into the luxuriant valley.

There is snow where the sun has yet to penetrate, in dales and gorges, but the ridges and spits are covered in dry mosses and grass with small flourishing eruptions of rosebay, orchids and bluebells. The flora is far richer here than up at the colony only three degrees further north. Moreover there is creeping willow, which he has also seen in the Godthåbsfjord, though somewhat taller here, in places almost like woodland, and great clusters of dwarf birch and worm-wood, as well as whole hillsides of crowberry. He picks a handful of berries and chews on them. They have lain under the snow all winter and have lost their sweetness, but he can sense how filled with nutri-tion they still are.

This fjord is so full of sunshine and life, so far from the dismal colony and all its bleakness. They talk about it. His son says: Why did they not set up the colony down here? This place is far better.

I'm sure people will settle here one day, says Matthias. I think only accident decided the colony should be where it is today.

The Danes ruin everything, says Knud. If they placed a colony here, it would be just as abominable as the other in a couple of years.

But you are a Dane yourself, my lad.

Am I? We are Norwegian.

Like Egede. We are all of us of the same sour-dough.

I don't feel Danish, his son says.

What do you feel, then?

The lad shrugs.

You're young, says Matthias. You're still developing. There will be many changes in your life. I found out on my journey through Europe when I was young. I wasn't the same when I came home.

Do people not change when they get old? Knud asks, smiling at his father. An unusually genuine smile.

It gets harder the older you get. It's as if we stiffen. We old people prepare ourselves for death, you understand, as the priests keep reminding us we must. I suppose the reality of the matter is that we are simply afraid.

What is there to be afraid of?

To lose oneself, perhaps. The older you get the more cautious you become. Most likely it's a sign of fear.

I don't regret what happened, the lad says all of a sudden.

What do you mean?

In the winter.

But what happened? Matthias asks.

He was my best friend, and then he died. In a way it was only right.

They sit and eat in silence.

Knud says: I'm going for a walk. Can I take the musket with me?

He gets to his feet and trudges off with the firearm over his shoulder.

Goodbye, Father.

Matthias watches him as he goes, the figure of his son gradually diminishing, consumed into the landscape's canvas of rising fells, sky, snow and lush hillsides, until at last he is an invisible element in a picture. When evening comes he has failed to return, and does not come back the next day either. Matthias lets go of him. He has known all along it would happen. And he has wished it.

One of the two boats appears in the bay, and the crew embark into the valley, as far inland as they can without being consumed themselves. One of them finds bootprints in the snow, but on the stretches of heather they are lost.

Where is the other boat? Matthias asks.

Crushed by ice, they tell him. The men only just saved themselves.

And my specimens?

At the bottom of the fjord.

On 6 June they return to the colony, where the good ship the *Caritas* is already arrived from Denmark laden with heavy timber and provisions and bearing with it the glad tidings that King Christian has resolved that the Greenlandic colony be consolidated and expanded. Matthias Jochumsen writes in his journal:

'Having realized now that I can do nothing of use in my service to the King, I hereby conclude my Greenlandic adventure.

Dum spiro, spero!

Matthias Jochumsen

Aboard the good ship the *Caritas*,

This twentieth day of June, 1733.'

///

I feel so light. The land inclines slightly upwards, but it is as if I have been given wings. I follow a river and come to a lake, then follow its shore, ascend a scree-covered slope still shadowed by the fell and then reach the sunlight to stand on top of the ridge. Behind me is the past, in front of me the future. An eagle circles high above. My eyes follow it. I shout out – hey! I feel joyful and free. I look down on a moor with intermittent rock, pools and lakes, water courses and bogs. This land is vast. The wind is gentle and brings with it a fragrance of ice and wild herbs. The sea to the right, empty and calm, swelling upwards to meet the sky, two arching vaults, a giant mouth, and here am I.

I notice the man at the shore of the tarn below. He sits looking up at me. He is waiting for me. Yes. His chest is bare. Now he waves to me. I wave back.

I begin my descent, lose my footing, fall, recover again. I have nothing, no provisions, no equipment, only the flintlock, a pouch of gunpowder and a handful of lead bullets. It is enough.

When I reach the tarn he gives me food. Trout roasted over an open flame. We eat. The fish is succulent, it tastes of heather and smoke. He has only a knife. It is his only weapon. His long hair hangs down his back, kept from his face by a band of colourful beads. The trout lie fanned out in front of him. I ask him how he catches them. His hand snatches the air. Like that. He laughs. They are plentiful. Plentiful enough for the two of us, my lad.

4

Mene, Tekel

To-day the ship's captain hoisted the sails for the voyage home.
With him embarked also Matthias Jochumsen and his brother
Just, there being nothing in this land for them to do.

FROM HANS EGEDE'S JOURNAL, JUNE 1733

The moon is in the way of the sun. A three-quarter eclipse sends a
shaft of darkness sweeping over the land. At two in the afternoon it
is evening, and morning again within the hour.

Egede observes the phenomenon with his telescope. He has
smeared soot on the lens. Now he sees the moon glide like a sickle
over the platter of the sun, and together they form a single copper-red
disc. A blood moon. Is it an omen? He makes a note in his journal,
his hand trembling slightly. It is but a simple phenomenon of nature,
he tells himself. It is included in the almanac. Nothing to tremble
about. And yet he trembles. He can hardly hold a knife, much less
the quill he uses to note down his observations. But this is how it
has been for some months now.

His apprehension is by no means assuaged when a native woman,
one of the baptized, comes to him the next day and speaks babblingly
of an ill omen. Naturally, this has been brought on by the same
eclipse, but the coincidence merely increases his anxiety. I dreamt
about my sister's son Carl, she says. The one who went with your
ship to Denmark. He came back to kill all the people in this country.

Do not go about with such talk, Egede tells her, ill at ease. Events
of the future do not make themselves known to people in the form
of dreams. That is superstition.

Will you say the Lord's Prayer for us? the woman asks.

He prays with her, and blesses her. When she is gone, he feels relieved. Yet he is more burdened by anxiety and fear than ever before. Something is wrong. I can feel it. Is God punishing me? No, it is only the usual restlessness of spring.

The good ship the *Caritas* – 'charity' – arrives only a week later, carrying with her a cargo of building materials, greetings from King Christian and his gracious undertaking to support the colony with two thousand rigsdaler per annum. With her also are three German lay brothers, Moravian missionaries dispatched by the Count von Zinzendorf. It is the King who has been infected by this pietistic fervour. Egede understands it is largely for this reason that the colony has been allowed to continue. Rightly, then, he should be glad of these new foreigners. Moreover, a Greenlandic boy, Carl, has arrived too.

It seems the new king has taken up the baton and wishes to carry the Greenlandic design further. All is well. But is he happy on that account? No, he is not. Or perhaps in principle he is. In practice, however, in the depths of his innermost Lutheran soul, he is a storm of opposing emotions, among them anxiety and guilt. He hears the sound of jangling chains. He hears the pillory slam shut about his neck and wrists. He hears the crunch of his cervical vertebrae as the rope halts his body's fall. I am a criminal, he thinks. I am condemned. God's wrath is consuming me.

The boy Carl is the only survivor of the Greenlandic children who went with the *Morian* in '31. A girl died only a few days ago on board the ship. The crew say her illness proceeded with astonishing speed. She began to bleed from her eyes and nose, swelled up and lost consciousness, then lay gasping for some few hours before passing away, all in the space of a single day and night. Scurvy, Egede thinks to himself. Consumption, cold. They are so frail, these natives. They cannot withstand the voyage to Denmark. And when first they are there they cannot withstand coming back.

He asks Kieding, who mumbles something about the pox.

What indications are there for the pox? he wants to know.

The acute course of the illness, the bleedings, the physician says with a sigh.

And what speaks against it?

That no others are ill. The pox never occurs on its own. It is an epidemic disease.

If it is the pox, what would be the consequences?

Disastrous, says Kieding, and smiles into his long and tangled beard.

Fortunately the boy Carl seems to be well enough. In fact he is in the highest of spirits, parading about in his new Danish clothes, speaking like a lord and pretending to have forgotten his own mother tongue, apart from when he is boasting to the natives of everything he has seen. Houses as tall as cliffs, he says in a strident voice, painting a picture with sweeping gestures. Halls illuminated by lamps in their thousands. Rooms with holes down which to shit, and servants at the ready to wipe your arse with tissue paper. Crowds of people like great shoals of fish. Jets of water spouting from the ground with golden apples balanced on top. Women who lie with you for money. No one believes him, or else they choose not to. They find him annoying, he is too full of himself, and moreover neither fish nor fowl, neither Dane nor Greenlander, a native boy who has lost his mind. They are ashamed of him, and laugh at him behind his back. The Danes poke fun at him. They ply him with drink and place a paper hat on his head. You can be our new Two-Kings, they say. Long live King Carl! He cannot grasp that they are making fun of him. He believes he is the King of Greenland. He bosses his siblings and his mother, the only ones who will put up with him. He is unreasonable towards them, and shouts and screams. Eventually they throw him out. He reels about in the colony at night with his paper crown on his head, singing sea shanties and hymns, until the fire-watch takes him by the collar, bundles him into the blubber house and bolts the door.

Natives come streaming to the colony from the entire district. Others, who have seen the ship on its way north, come from the south. All wish to trade. Their boats are laden with fox-skins, bear-skins, blubber and the fine, spiralling narwhal tusks which they know find favour with well-to-do Europeans who think they stem from some fabled creature with a horn projecting from its forehead. Egede and the traders of course know where these tusks are from, but somewhere on the route between Greenland and Denmark the simple narwhal became the mythical unicorn, which has proved to be very good business indeed, for any Greenland trader worth his salt knows that he is dealing in dreams more than prosaic goods.

The natives also come to listen to Egede tell his stories about Jesus. It seems that word of the good Christian message has spread. He has himself made trips to the south, and also some way north, but these were tours of inspection, not missionary work. In the main he has kept himself to the surrounding fjord systems of Godthåb, inhabited by perhaps two thousand natives. He has harboured no wish to spread, and thereby dilute, the message, but rather to concentrate it upon a small flock of genuinely believing natives who might then, little by little, pass on their faith to others in more outlying areas. Such a process cannot be hastened. It has been his conviction and his method in all the years he has been in the land. But now he discovers he has more than enough to do preaching for natives who seem to him to be sincere in their interest in what he has to say. He finds this odd. Where does this interest come from all of a sudden? He is mystified by it, though also happy for the diversion it brings from his darker thoughts.

The colony is filled with drunken Danes fornicating with native women, and with each other, vandalizing the buildings and spreading their muck and obscenity. The shore is packed with native tents, and still they keep coming. Smoke and the smells of cooking meat rise up all around. The permanent colony crew, normally so well behaved, are whirled into the general mood of abandon and the officers are compelled to introduce the harshest military discipline. Floggings and other forms of corporal punishment are a daily occurrence. People lie about outside, sleeping it off. The blubber house has been turned into a house of detention and is crammed with inmates. It reminds him of the summer of 1728 when the colony was first established and the place was milling with seamen and military. Unlike then, however, the weather is good this year. The earth is like a slowly turning disc, gently oscillating, the sun circling in waves above the horizon.

It is strange how the weather affects him. Always he longs for good weather, sunshine, a gentle air, stillness, all that was missing in

Lofoten and now here in Greenland. But when for once the weather is good, he is miserable. Then he will yearn for fog, wind, the pouring rain and cold. There is peace in poor weather. It provides room for spiritual absorption, for prayer and studies of the Scriptures, for writing and contemplation. The summer now allows neither reading nor writing. It is hustle and bustle, and shallowness. Yet beneath this buzzing activity dwells his great and all-consuming pain. He feels alone and abandoned.

But it is good for him to be busy. The summer months are always hectic, but this year they are livelier than ever. His gloomiest thoughts are kept at bay. He writes a large number of letters, to the Missionskollegium, to the Chancellery, to the King in person, to his family in Norway; he sends lists and reports, an appraisal of the state of the colony buildings, and draws up a trade forecast for the year to come, less optimistically, more realistically, and perhaps more resignedly than in previous years. At the same time he is of course the priest, the only source of spiritual guidance for natives and Danes alike now that the two young clergymen have returned home. He attends the sick and dying, he comforts, admonishes and punishes, he listens to confessions which cloud his soul and heighten his sense of guilt. But who is to comfort the one who comforts? Where is a priest to go with his guilt? To God, of course. Yet he feels the need for an intermediary, for he has fallen into doubt as to whether God wishes him well.

The boy Carl comes to him. He is rather the worse for wear, having been drunk for several weeks. Now he wishes to repent. He weeps and begs forgiveness for his sins. Egede grants him absolution. They kneel and pray together.

I am ill, says Carl. He holds out his hands. They are red and skinless.

This is the scabies, Egede tells him. Stay away from the bottle and from the Danish crew, and doubtless it will heal of its own accord.

He cannot help but see something of Frederik Christian in the boy. The same bastardly division between Danish and Greenlandic. The same corrupted mildness. The same useless intelligence. Like a mark on the forehead. He will die, he thinks. Of course he will die. And it is we who will kill him.

The three Germans of the Moravian brethren are a headache to him. His spoken German is not good, though he writes the language reasonably well and reads it without issue. The men are Christian David, a yellow-toothed carpenter in his early forties with a flat, pentagonal face, and two younger wool-spinners, doleful-looking cousins, Matthäus and Christian Stach. All three have something of the craftsman's solidity about them and seem perpetually to be aglow in their faith. Lay preachers. Egede despises them from day one, particularly their leader, David, who combines arrogance with ignorance, and self-assurance with utter helplessness in practical matters.

David delivers to him a letter from King Christian in which the King asks him to receive the three lay brethren well and to help them settle in every way possible.

He has invited them into his home. Gertrud and the girls serve them a meal. They converse. Gertrud turns out to be far more proficient in German than he is. It surprises him. No matter how long he has known her, she continues to reveal new aspects of herself, he thinks. It would not surprise him in the least if suddenly she broke into fluent Hebrew. Several times he must ask her to translate a word or expression, and in each instance she does so effortlessly. Casually he mentions Luther. No reaction. How is it now with these pietists, he asks himself, do they even acknowledge the Reformation? He has not investigated the matter and is unwilling to show his ignorance by asking stupid questions. So to begin with they merely chat about one thing and another. He talks about the difficulties a missionary encounters here, about his constant battles with wily natives, with the shamans, with the beliefs of old, the customs and habits which all accord so poorly with a Christian life. And during their whole conversation he receives the same refrain in reply: the Lord Jesus Christ will help us.

I hope then that I may be His valuable instrument, he says.

They reply more vaguely than unreservedly and accommodatingly. Insolent prigs, he thinks.

How many years has Mr Egede been in the country? David asks.

Twelve years this summer.

And how many followers has Mr Egede assembled in those many years? David's tone is sarcastic. He knows full well the nature of his baptismal practice.

I have been reticent with the holy sacrament of the baptism, he replies, brushing some fluff from his sleeve. However, this past year or two I have baptized more children than before. He looks up and sees David's smirking flat face. He breathes deeply and endeavours to explain himself. To baptize heathens indiscriminately would be hazardous indeed. Many would simply fall back into their ignorant ways as soon as they left the colony.

We Moravian brethren practise mass baptism, as John the Baptist did himself.

He did? Egede intervenes, but David continues unperturbed.

We place our trust in Jesus Christ. Once a person is baptized, he or she is with the Saviour.

Yes, exactly, that's my point, Egede says, and wishes to go on, only to be interrupted again.

We are not miserly with the baptism. Baptism is a gift to mankind, not something to be kept and hoarded. Baptism is not a stash of money with which to line one's coffin. It does not diminish by being spent. On the contrary, the more who receive salvation, the more there becomes of it.

Baptism is a serious matter, Egede interjects. It is lifelong devotion to the Lord, and requires thorough preparation.

David laughs impertinently, and the two Stach cousins snigger an echo.

Baptism is not a game for the masses, Egede insists.

To us, baptism is a celebration, says the German in a schoolmaster-ly tone, the two cousins nodding their agreement, faces frowned in abrupt earnestness. The more who take part, the better.

What about the Augsburg Confession? Egede ventures. Do you refer to it?

We adhere only to Jesus Christ and His love.

He senses they are moving in circles and changes tack: What will you live on here? Have you brought materials with you to build a house?

We will cultivate the soil and build with the land's own timber. We shall not come begging to the colony.

The land is very difficult to cultivate. We have conducted trials with beet inside the fjord, though with meagre results. Out here by the sea the climate is too harsh and cold.

Then we will live on fish and wild herbs.

And as for timber, Egede goes on, there is no woodland here to provide building materials.

Then we will dig holes in the ground and live there. David's stoicism is as heroic as it is stupid. And in Egede's experience, stupidity is as impenetrable as granite.

Well, I wish you luck, he says in a tone meant to be foreboding, but which comes across as prickly instead. But now I must return to my work.

The Germans take their leave. He hears David in the passage whisper theatrically to his acolytes: Is there anything more repugnant than an unreformed Lutheran?

Yes, he thinks. Yes, there is.

The *Caritas* departs. The colony is quiet again. He makes some visitations and a couple of small reconnaissance trips. Nothing is the same as in the old days, those first pioneering times when every day was an expedition and he travelled the land with the certain feeling that the Lord's hand was guiding and blessing him. Now it is a miserable chore. Still, it feels good to be away from the colony and all it reminds him of. He takes Niels with him. They sail together, sleeping in the same tent, or, if the weather allows, beneath the open sky. He endeavours to get to know his son, but finds it far from easy. Niels humours him to make their conversations as brief as possible. An exchange might proceed as follows.

Egede: How splendid to be out and about.

Niels: Indeed.

Egede: And I sense the savages are warming to our message.

Niels: Yes, I think perhaps they are.

Egede: I think their sorcerers are losing their grip on them.

Niels: Yes, I'm sure.

Egede: Take this Apralutork. (He intentionally mispronounces the name so that his son might correct him, but Niels pays no heed to the error.) Have you seen anything of him recently?

Niels: No, he hasn't shown himself for some time.

Egede: He's hiding out. He knows he has lost, I shouldn't wonder.

Niels: Yes, I shouldn't wonder.

Egede: And you, are you content with your work in the Trade?

Niels: Yes, I am. Thank you.

Egede: I was thinking that when we return home in a year or two you might take a formal apprenticeship with a merchant. What would you say to that?

Niels: I think it sounds good, Father. I'd like that.

Egede: It would only be natural if in some way you remained with the Greenland trade. Or have you other plans?

Niels: No. That sounds fine, Father.

Egede: It pleases me very much to think that one of my sons is a priest and the other a merchant. No more is needed to push our civilization on.

Niels: Yes. No. That's right, I'm sure.

Egede: Anyway. Goodnight, my boy.

Niels: Goodnight, Father.

He wishes the lad would oppose him more, perhaps even contradict him. Previously they would quarrel until they spat with rage. No one could make him angrier than Niels. Well, perhaps Gertrud could. But they are two of a kind. Often he would end up boxing the boy's ears in sheer fury and frustration. And always it helped. The mood would about-face immediately and Niels would be good-heartedness itself. Or at least sometimes he would. Now he is a young man. His cheeks are rough with stubble and he smells like a man too, as Egede has ample opportunity to note when they are off on their trips together.

Lying sleepless in the muggy tent with Niels snoring and farting beside him, he thinks, as he has done so many times before, of Abraham and Isaac. God's command to Abraham, that he offer up his son, may certainly seem unreasonable. What kind of a God would demand such a thing? But in fact God is merely demonstrating to him what is necessary and unavoidable. All fathers must give up their sons, in the sense that they must let them go so that they may discover their own ways. They must let them go out into the world, the perilous world, let them make their own mistakes and bring their lives into jeopardy. We might just as well be told to put a knife to their throats. For that is what we do, we fathers.

For Gertrud, as for all mothers, it is a different matter. They can have the children with them and at the same time let them be free. He has no idea how they manage it. It must be to do with the motherly feeling and attachment. It is God who has made us as such. The man must kill his sons, metaphorically speaking, while the mother is allowed to remain a loving anchorage point throughout the boy's life. Abraham and Sarah. It is a harsh acknowledgement. For who can a man feel attached to if not his sons? No one.

Frederik Christian in the mission room that night, kneeling, weeping in his drunkenness, and what did I do? I sent him away. Unforgivable.

He recalls a conversation:

Egede: When I leave, you shall carry on my work.

Frederik Christian: I'd rather go with you to Denmark.

Egede: What will you do in Denmark, my boy?

Frederik Christian: I could prepare for the priesthood. Is it not possible for a Greenlander?

Egede: Yes, I suppose it is, though it has never happened before. First you would have to go to Latin school, then graduate from the university. The question is what the professors would say about it. I don't know. It would take a long time at any rate.

Frederik Christian: That doesn't matter.

Egede: Is it what you want, my boy?

Frederik Christian: I think so.

Egede: We shall talk about it when the time comes. But you must not make the passage on your own. Look what happens to the natives who go to Denmark. It destroys them, even if they survive.

Frederik Christian: It would not be like that for me. If I could study for the priesthood everything would be all right. I would make a good priest, I'm sure of it. I have been well taught.

Egede (chuckling): You little rascal. You know how to ingratiate yourself.

And thus their conversation went on. Frederik Christian spoke his mind, for he was always forthright. Never an ambiguity was muttered from the corner of his mouth, unlike the majority of Danes. Sometimes they discussed theological matters. The boy far from agreed with him in everything concerning the manner of his practice, for instance the way he would put down dissenting voices by means of brute force, and then the eternal bone of contention concerning the deceased kin of baptized heathens, whether they were saved or lost. These conversations could be lengthy and heated. And in fact he learned from them, altering his practice and baptizing rather less selectively than before. It was Frederik Christian who changed his mind. Without him everything would still be like it was. And he never felt the urge to beat the lad. Strange. Apparently, thrashings are only for one's flesh and blood.

These thoughts direct him to the mission room, to kneel and pray. Lord, forgive me. Or punish me immediately.

///

The first sign of disaster comes in August. A skin disease runs rampant, tormenting both Danes and Greenlanders. The afflicted scratch themselves until they bleed and are all but driven out of their minds by their itching. Kieding prescribes frequent washing in salt water and the application of fat. He applies leeches and cups, he lets blood. He places moist cloths on seeping, eczematous sores, only for the patients to swipe them away in order to scratch themselves. The wounds become infected. Arms become oedematous, glands swell in armpits, break through the skin, bleed and weep, veins become infected and to the eye seem to meander upwards through the arms, red and pronounced, advancing ever closer to the heart. Kieding knows then. Sepsis, as Hippocrates called it. It spreads through the blood vessels like a tree spreads its branches, sooner or later reaching the heart, from there to be slung in all directions. After that the end comes swiftly: spiking fever, death.

Smallpox, Kieding says to himself. And not a thing I can do about it.

///

A common cold, Egede thinks. It can strike hard at the natives.

The first to die is a Christian Greenlandic girl. She is ill for three days. Egede anoints her and they say the Lord's Prayer together. She passes away with a happy smile on her mouth.

More become ill. He visits them in their peat-huts and tents. Often he meets the doctor on his way in or out. They discuss what the matter can be, for now it is clear to them that something malicious has come to the colony and is spreading.

It must be something brought with the ship, says Kieding cautiously. He knows Egede will be angry if he speaks of the pox.

My thoughts exactly, says Egede. But what?

An epidemic catarrh, influenza perhaps.

You mean something infectious?

Clearly. And with the numbers who have come streaming to the colony during the summer we can brace ourselves for a dismal autumn.

But the primary source, says Egede. Who can it be?

No one in the *Caritas* showed any particular signs of epidemic disease, says Kieding. Apart from the girl who died on board.

Then how can it be that this . . . epidemic . . . should break out so suddenly now?

The girl most likely passed it on to someone who took it ashore as a dormant passenger, not making itself known until the second or third party removed.

Is that possible?

It is often seen – in certain diseases. But the intermediate links in the chain of infection will themselves become ill sooner or later. And in the meantime they infect others. We can do nothing but wait and see.

And pray to the Lord, says Egede.

Yes, let us do so, Kieding replies, and strokes his long beard philosophically.

At the beginning of September the death toll increases dramatically. Many have contracted the rash and their skin is a mess of red blisters which ooze after only a few hours. Soon the afflicted will display bloodshot eyes, spontaneous bleeding from eyes, nose, mouth and genitals, blisters will spread to cover the body, whereafter internal haemorrhaging occurs, manifesting itself in swollen bellies, pallor, loss of consciousness and death. Egede will still hear nothing of smallpox. He flies into a fury if he even hears the whisper of it.

There is no pox here! he barks.

The next day he says to Kieding in private: What if it does turn out to be the pox?

And the next day again: Who do you think might have brought this pox to the colony, Kieding?

I am in no doubt, the physician replies. It is the boy, Carl. He has most likely been carrying it since Denmark, where the girl too was smitten.

But he has not been ill?

He has been rolling drunk the whole time, says Kieding. I imagine it has camouflaged the disease somewhat in his case.

He has been all over the colony, Egede says pensively.

Yes, he has been the perfect carrier, says Kieding, and smiles.

///

4 September sees the death of Greenland's king, the boy Carl. His body is dumped in a mass grave. There is no one to cry over him, for his family are all deathly ill.

Egede goes to see the Moravian brethren. He needs to get away. The Germans are erecting a house at the southern end of the peninsula, half a fjerdingmil from the colony. They say they have found a great stack of old timber down by the ship harbour, obviously left behind from the early colony days. Egede says nothing of it. He ought to speak up. Strictly speaking it is theft of the King's property. But he remains silent on the matter. The three men are clearly in high spirits and filled with the joy of life, quite untouched by the ongoing calamity on the other side of the fell. Is there anything I can help you with? he asks. They hand him a hammer.

For a whole day he labours with the Germans. He knocks in nails, saws timber, levels the ground for the foundation wall, digs holes for the uprights. They exchange barely a word, but sweat together in the sun, drinking water from the beck and frying fish over a fire. Can it be true? he wonders. That they are blessed by the Lord?

Late in the evening he returns home and goes directly to bed, quite exhausted from flexing muscles sorely unused to being flexed. Gertrud is up, attending a sick mother and her several children who have moved in. He is once more in the thick of it.

The epidemic is now a frenzy. Kieding and Egede endeavour to contain it by forbidding all movement about the district. One might just as well forbid birds to fly or fish to swim. People are scared. Rumours run rife among Danes and Greenlanders alike, rumours of a curse, of a naked man going about blowing on all the houses. The natives flee in all directions. The fjord teems with kayaks and umiaks, laden to the brims with sick people whose only thought is to get away. News arrives of sickness and death in the skerries too. The epidemic crosses the waters. Terror spreads like a wildfire, and in its wake follows the epidemic. And soon they see a counter-movement, natives fleeing to the colony to seek protection there. The numbers of sick and dead rise by the day.

The central room of the colony house, the mission room which is also Egede's study, now doubles as a hospital. Gertrud attends the afflicted, she gives the children goat's milk, she boils broth and gruel and brings it to the sick, she holds the dying by the hand, prays with them and comforts the bereaved. The girls, Petronelle and Kirstine, help her. They work around the clock, allowing themselves not a minute's rest and forgetting completely to look after themselves, to eat and sleep, if only for the briefest time. In the mornings, men come and remove the bodies of those who have died in the night and toss them in the mass grave.

Egede makes a tour of inspection in the district, wading through the dead who have been left to lie where they fell, many with the pulp of chewed hide still in their mouths, for with the men too weak to hunt, the coverings of the kayaks have been their only food. Corpses float in the fjord, bobbing on the swell. The worst thing is to arrive at a settlement and crawl inside the dwelling, not because of the dead who await him inside, but because of the one or more children still half-alive, alone and gasping among stiffened corpses. He gathers them up and brings them back with him, delivering them into the hands of Gertrud. But they too perish. He carries them out of the house and dumps them in the grave as if they were kitchen waste.

Panic spreads. This is a threat from which there is no hiding. In fact, hiding only makes it worse. The colony is teeming, a constant influx and outflux of natives seeking help or hastening away. Almost all fall sick regardless. Nine out of ten perish. Those who remain unaffected are picked out as sorcerers and are murdered or else elect to drown themselves. A boy points the finger at his own mother's sister. He tells his father he saw her standing at the foot of the bed gesticulating peculiarly and pulling faces at him. Resolutely, the father cuts her throat, though to no avail: the following night both father and son succumb. In the skerries, children stagger about, wailing in grief and despair, alone. They clutch their mother's corpses, suck in desperation on their breasts. Tents containing the bodies of whole families are torched and burnt to the ground. The natives strike out to the south, to the north, away from the district, as far away as possible. And with them travels their infectious disease.

///

1 November. The dead outnumber the living. Strewn about the landscape they lie, as if in the aftermath of some clash of militaries, the victors long since departed. In the sea they float like flotsam after a naval dispute. The natives turn to Egede. Who is doing this to us? Is it God or the Devil?

God's wrath is upon you, he tells them, seizing the opportunity to put the fear of the Lord into them that they might at last be imbued with the requisite solemnity to become good Christians. He is angry with you for not listening to and living by His message. You engage in fornication and adultery and indulge in sinful relationships. You live in polygamy even though I have told you it is an abomination to the Lord.

But why is he first angry with us now? they ask. We have always lived that way.

Because you have heard the message and are now free to choose the path of righteousness or the path of evil. And you have chosen the path of evil. Therefore God is angry.

They are crushed to hear him say this. They weep heart-rendingly and beg him for mercy.

Help us, *palasi*! Plead for us!

Then come to me, he says. Follow me and I shall redeem you. But you must abandon your old ways, renounce your faith in the shamans and the beliefs of old.

Yes, they reply. Whatever you say.

But it is too late. These people too perish. And Egede is on his knees in the mission room, his folded hands raised towards the cross on the wall.

Thank you, Lord!

5

Messenger

To-day came a man and two women with a small child from the house where the child pox has become rife and where five people in this week have passed away, and implored that they might stay with us; for the poor souls did not know where else they should go. Four others, a man and three women with two small children of the same house, departed to some other place. And was this not the saddest of things, that by such escape they made unfortunate others wherever they came, which I would have prevented, though could not.

FROM HANS EGEDE'S JOURNAL, OCTOBER 1733

Backwards and forwards every single day, sometimes several times a day. Johan Hartman has become a messenger. He runs theological messages between Egede and the Moravian brethren at Neu Herrnhut. They have established their mission station in the long, flat valley at the southern end of the peninsula. The distance between the two communities is no more than half a fjerdingvej, a musket shot perhaps, and yet Johan pendulates as if between separate worlds. The colony is gripped by the blackest mood. At least eight of every ten Greenlanders has succumbed to the pox. It is as if time has been set back six years. The bodies are everywhere. No one has the strength to put them to their graves and the natives will not touch them. The Danish crew pile them up and cut the skin clothing from them, and there they lie, dappled by the frost, twisted and naked, with gaping mouths and exhausted eyes.

The settlements in the skerries and far up the fjord, teeming with people in the summer, are now deserted and abandoned. The peat-huts and tents are crammed with corpses, and the dead lie strewn about in the open air too. The ravens have a field day, stalking about with their stomachs full, barely able to take flight. Glutted foxes slink about with guilty expressions and swollen bellies.

The colony house too is packed with the sick. The dogged Egede family do what they can to assuage their sufferings. Madame Gertrud works tirelessly in their attendance with her two daughters. Yet no matter how many sick drag themselves to the house, as many dead are carried away.

Johan still lives with Sise in their little peat-hut north of the colony. They are alone and childless. The boy, Lauritz, Titia's child who lived with them for a couple of years, travelled to Denmark three years ago and lives there now with foster-parents in whose care, according to a letter they have received in his own hand, he thrives: 'Dear Father and Mother. This is your son Lauritz writing to you in good health and sending his best wishes from Denmark. It rains a lot here, and is cold and dark. I attend school and have learnt to write words on paper. My foster-father, the provost, says that I am to become a priest. Forever your faithful son, Lauritz Johanssøn.' Johan has read the letter aloud for Sise many times, and each time she must grip her hand-kerchief and wipe the tears from her eyes.

No other child has been forthcoming. Johan has spoken to his wife about returning home, but Sise will hear none of it.

You can go, if you want.

And what will you do then?

Stay here.

Alone?

. . .

Do you wish to live all your days here in this land?

That's my plan.

I miss home sometimes.

Your memory embellishes it. Copenhagen is one big gutter.

Yes, but cities are like that. There are lots of other delightful places in the country.

Is it a farm you're wanting? Where would you get the money?

I've got family down near Hamburg. They would surely take us in.

I don't want to live by the grace of your family. We've our own house here and are free.

Our own house is a hole in the ground. And free to do what?

Just free, that's all, she says.

Free to grow old and die, he replies.

Yes, she says. What's wrong with that?

He receives twenty rigsdaler per annum, enough by far to meet their needs, and the work is easy. Sometimes it pays to survive, to simply make sure not to die, and it is Sise he can thank for still being alive. But his salary is of course insufficient to allow for any savings. The winter brings paucities of one thing and another, grain and oats and treacle in particular, but they own a boat and catch birds and fish and hares, as well as gathering eggs. They have not gone hungry a single day since they arrived in the land, apart from that first chaotic winter.

She is good at preparing food and making the best of what they have. He has absolutely no reason to complain. Moreover, they are good enough friends and live a quiet life without saying much to each other. All there is to say has either been said already or else is unsayable. Sometimes he tries it on in the evenings, but always she stiffens or will dig an elbow in his chest.

Haven't you forgotten something?

And then he must get up and fetch the five marks and drop the coins into the bowl with a clatter. Only then may he slide his erection in from behind and deliver his load.

Once a tart, always a tart, Sise says. It cannot be changed. And the money at least stays in the family.

Thus, their physical intercourse costs him some twenty to twenty-five marks a month. It could be worse, he thinks. She could put up the price to ten a go.

How he longs for Copenhagen, for the smell of horse muck in the streets, the teeming crowds, the noise, the very particular golden light which drenches the city in the spring, the flickering street lamps of winter, the watchmen singing the good old verses as the clock strikes the hour. To live here, in the world's smallest and most northerly colony, for the rest of his life? He might just as well have died back

in '28. If only there had been children between them, at least then
life would have had some measure of meaning. A little Hartman to
play with and later take fishing. But the only child they had was
stillborn, their foster-child is far across the sea, and now it seems that
Sise is barren, most likely because of the birth. If she had died in
labour, he thinks to himself, what would he have done then? Such
freedom he would have enjoyed. Freedom to travel wherever he
wished. To join a ship and sail away. But he pushes the thought from
his mind. We have a good enough life here, he tells himself.

He comes to the valley at Neu Herrnhut. The build is to all intents
and purposes finished and the Germans have moved in. He comes
from wailing anguish to the industrious sound of hammers and
rhythmically rasping saws. Moreover, they sing as they work, the
Germans, belting out a kind of round, keeping the rhythm with their
hammers as they intone the praises of the Lord, singing cheerily of
his sufferings. But there are no sufferings here in the Moravians'
valley, only the joys of work and hymns, a vaulting blue sky and great
vistas of the sea. Johan sits down and watches them. They call out
to him, needing help to lug some rocks up from the shore, foundation
stones for the goat shed they have begun to build. He forgets all about
the letter he has with him from Egede and instead labours for them,
fetching rocks, levelling the ground and laying the foundation. They
use a kind of spirit level and spend much time making adjustments
in order for the structure to be as straight and as stable as possible.
They are good craftsmen, Johan thinks to himself. Germans.
Compatriots. They do things properly.

They lay the first four timbers, a good day's work. The next day
he returns there again, and each day after that during the whole
week, always with letters from Egede. The work progresses swiftly
now. The structure is erected, a solid half-timbered building with
fillings of unhewn stone, with a door and a window-opening, a roof
covered by a layer of peat, and even a chimney and a fireplace inside.
And when the goat shed is finished their leader, Christian David,
leads them in a prayer of thanks, whereupon they kiss each other
and weep. Johan too breaks down and weeps. It is a marvellous
feeling. When finally he returns home he is full of jubilation,

swinging Sise in the air and laughing until she turns sour and hits out at him with her ladle.

At the same time as the Germans erect their buildings, the old colony seems to sink back into the ground. The houses there, only a few years old, are already in decline and let in the weather. Undoubtedly it is the matter of a foundation, Johan thinks. If only there had been sufficient time to prepare good foundations, the rest of the structures would have been that much more stable. The crew house, in which more than fifty people died during the first year, has collapsed at one end, though remains in use, inhabited at the other, which as yet is intact. A floor has been laid too, and the house is otherwise a decent enough dwelling, albeit gloomy and damp.

The colony house by contrast remains splendid with all its many windows, the two fine wings and its battery of cannon. The cannon, of which two have been allowed to remain, have become silent and rust now in the rain, without a bombardier to fire them or even keep them in working order. The house itself is cold and draughty. Always there is some tradesmen crawling about on its roof, hammering nails in and making repairs with lengths of wood, sealing the window frames with putty, slapping mortar into the joints, but their tinkerings are but stop-gap measures of little lasting effect. And now the house, and the mission room within it, is full of sick natives who groan and wail. The folk have therefore retreated to the inferior crew house where they can be on their own.

He goes over the rocks, over the moor and descends to the colony. He finds Egede upstairs in the priest's residence. It is impossible for him to be downstairs. The stench of the sick is excruciating even with the windows thrown open, and then there is the draught. And so he sits at his desk, his bare head supported in his hands, his pigtail at rest on his hunched back. He lifts his head as Johan comes up the stairs, and looks at him with strangely vacant eyes.

There's a letter. From Mr David.

Egede grimaces and takes the folded sheet of paper Johan hands him, reading the letter immediately. He expels various sounds as he reads – ha! hmpf! tut, tut, no! – and shakes his head several times.

Mr David asks for his prompt reply. Am I to go with it right away?

Yes. Wait a minute. Sit down while I write.

He seats himself on the edge of a bed. Egede dips his pen and scratches down some words. The quill flutters across the page. He folds the letter and hands it to Johan.

Tell him it's the last from me. I want no more of his blather.

All right, says Johan. I told him that yesterday too.

Let us hope he will soon desist with his nonsense.

Nonsense?

Pietistic *Quatsch*.

Is that what you want me to tell him?

No, say nothing. Just give him the letter. It's all in there.

He opens it and reads it on the moor. It is written in German, his native tongue, but the writing is partly blotched and Egede's spelling is a poor aid to understanding. He makes little of it, though sees that it begins with 'Lieber Christian David. Gott sei mit Euch!' He skims backwards and forwards. Three closely written pages in less than half an hour, full of references to the Scriptures, to Romans, the Acts of the Apostles, the Epistle to the Galatians, the Epistle to the Ephesians. His gaze stops at the words *Augsburger Bekenntnis*. He knows it well, and knows too how Egede harps on about it in his sermons and forces the poor natives to learn it by heart when they are to be baptized, and again when they are to be confirmed. He spells his way through a few sentences, his lips moving as he reads. Seemingly there is nothing about him. And why would there be? Yet he has always been inclined to believe that whenever anyone whispered to each other or wrote each other letters, they were conspiring against him. For the same reason, he reads Egede's letter. But as usual it concerns nothing but theology, specifically some particular details of the Augsburg Confession. Nor is there anything about the catastrophe which has befallen the colony, not a word about the sick and the dead, which in spite of everything is even stranger than Egede not mentioning him. He jumps to the conclusion: 'Since happily I know to spend my time more wisely than debating with someone so ignorant in the points of theology, I hereby conclude our correspondence. Your most faithful etc. Hans Egede.'

David receives him with a beaming smile and a heartfelt embrace in his warm parlour whose air smells of armpits and sweaty genitals. The fug of men. The two cousins come and kiss him on the cheek. They seem genuinely pleased to have him back. What do they see in me? he wonders, though he cannot help but be gladdened by his reception. David takes the letter, but puts it aside. He asks him how he is, how his wife is doing, and whether they remember to pray together and with fervour.

We say the Lord's Prayer every evening and at every meal, he says.

The Lord's Prayer is the essential prayer as given to us by the Saviour, the German says. It is our reminder to thank Him and praise Him and pray for our daily needs, demonstrating to Him thereby that we know that everything comes from Him. But it is not His intention for us to merely rattle it off. A prayer is a personal plea to the Lord. We stand before Him and speak to Him directly in His presence.

Oh, says Johan. I wouldn't know what to say if I had to think it up myself.

You must say whatever occurs to you. You must be honest. Prayer is a space from which all lies and pretences are excluded.

Yes, indeed.

You can tell Him everything of which you are ashamed. Everything you have kept secret, your sorrows and concerns, your most malicious thoughts, everything, everything.

But doesn't He know my thoughts already?

Of course! Therefore there is no reason to hide anything.

But why must I say such things if He already knows everything?

Because the power of prayer is great indeed. In prayer we stand before the Lord and empty our hearts. There is nothing better in this life, no greater liberation.

Can a person pray for any reason?

Naturally. There is nothing we cannot pray for. But our prayers must be genuine, we must humble ourselves before the Lord in prayer. Now, return home and pray to Him in the way I have described, and let the priest and the other Pharisees rattle off their Lord's Prayer.

He returns home. He tries to pray the way the German has

instructed. But he finds it difficult. It is as if his words become empty, as if somehow they beget their own lies and pretences. Dear God, he prays. I am a sinner. Please let Sise be kinder to me. Make her turn towards me in the evenings.

He tries it on with her when they go to bed that night. But she shoves him away in annoyance with her elbow. He gets the money and drops the coins in the bowl. She sticks her behind out, allowing him at least to relieve his desire.

Teach me to pray, he asks David the next day. The correspondence between Egede and the German continues in spite of what Egede put in his last letter.

All right, says David. I will teach you.

I find it difficult, Johan says.

Indeed. But you have tried. And you must not believe that the Lord has not heard you. For indeed He has.

It just feels like words.

Yes, we must shorten the distance between words and emotions, so that they become one and the same.

How is that done?

Sit down here with us, says David. Let us speak together. Do you love Jesus?

Well, I suppose so. I can't really say I know Him that well.

Good, my child. That was an honest answer. The Lord loves you for such an answer. Do you believe He suffered for our sakes?

I suppose so. I mean, that's what it says, isn't it?

Oh, how reserved you are! You are in serious need of conversion, my child. Think of Jesus hanging there on the cross. His hands are penetrated by nails, and these nails bear the entire weight of His body. Imagine that! The spike tearing at your flesh, the merciless baking sun, the mob taunting you. You know you are going to die, but it takes such a very long time, for they wish to torment you first. You are thirsty and they give you vinegar. In your agony you call for your father, my God, why hast thou forsaken me? And they jab you with their spears until your blood flows. That was what it was like. Do you believe He endured it all for our sakes?

The German's voice is a tremble, and Johan senses his own jaw tighten, a lump appearing in his throat. He emits a tiny sob and clears his throat.

Yes, he says in a thick voice. I believe so.

And do you believe that the only way to salvation is through suffering?

The two cousins are now quietly weeping. It sounds like they are humming. Their faces are contorted and they lean forwards, their tears falling to the floor.

Yes, I believe it, he sniffles. I think about what's happening over in the colony. All that sickness and death. So much suffering. They must be very close to salvation.

They are suffering, but not in the right way, says David.

Are they not?

Proper suffering is to suffer with the Lord. The heathens who are dying, they who flock around the priest's house and are tended by the Madame, have been led astray. That is why they suffer. They are herded into the abyss like ignorant sheep. Their sufferings are but preparation for the anguish they will encounter when they die. I am sure you know what I am talking about?

Hell?

Yes, the Inferno. David beams a smile. There they will burn, yet they will never burn up. Imagine that. To burn for ever! And who will be there with them, do you think?

I don't know. The former governor? He was a sinner if ever there was one.

David shakes his head. The governor may repent his sins. But there is one who cannot. He bears a black cassock. The priest!

Will Egede go to Hell? Johan blurts in astonishment.

Indeed he will. Together with his rabble of a family. They are unconverted, cold-blooded teachers of false doctrine, hypocrites. Every time they say the Lord's Prayer is a stab of pain in the heart of the Saviour. The Inferno is but the mildest of punishments for their sort. Their suffering will be eternal. But the other suffering, with Jesus Christ the Lord, will lead to salvation. Look at him, hanging there on the cross, bleeding, dying. Can you see him? The German points at a picture on the wall. Do you see the way he suffers?

Yes, says Johan, his voice small and trembling. But he was God's son, wasn't he? Could he not endure it?

He was born of man, with a man's weaknesses, his doubts and pains and fears, and therefore he suffered as a man. Look at this.

The German rolls up his sleeve. He is clearly worked up. His lower arm is criss-crossed with scars. He holds out his upturned hand. In the centre of his palm is a star-shaped white scar.

What is this? Johan asks. Did you injure yourself?

It is the wound of Christ. My mark. This is what we do, some of us. It is voluntary, without coercion, but the Count looks kindly upon those who inflict pain upon themselves in gratitude to the Lord.

What count?

Our good and loving leader, Count von Zinzendorf. I bade some of my brethren do this to me, he says proudly. They tied my hand tightly and hammered through it a nail. Look. He turns his hand over and displays the scar on the other side where the nail went clean through.

Jesus, Johan blurts. Did it not hurt?

Yes, of course. The wound became infected. The hand is still stiff.

But why did you do it?

So as to suffer with Him. But this is not the way of the priest. He knows nothing of suffering, nor does he wish to. Therefore he cannot be saved. Tell me, how old are you, my child?

Thirty, Johan replies.

Oh, you are young indeed. You are not lost. I sense you are a seeker. I feel a sorrow in you too, a pain. Am I right? the German asks with a smile.

Well, yes . . . I suppose. Life has its . . . is a person ever free . . . oh!

He breaks down sobbing. The German embraces him. He hears the two cousins come closer.

Tell me everything, David instructs.

What shall I tell?

How did you come to this land?

Well, he sniffles. I'm not quite sure to be honest. Someone decided it. I was an inmate of the gaol at Bremerholm. Deserted from duty.

But then lots were drawn that meant I got married to Sise, my wife. We were sweethearts already, so I suppose it was a stroke of luck. Only then they sent us up here.

A lottery! The German lights up in a smile. I too came here because my lot was drawn. It is our way whenever missionaries are to be sent out from Herrnhut. This is a sign from the Lord, my child. A lot with your name on it is akin to being appointed by the Lord. The German kisses him on the cheek and brow.

Do you know that Jesus loves you? Now it is one of the cousins who speaks.

Do you know that Jesus suffered and died for your sake? the other one asks.

Think about it, dear child, says David. Think about the sufferings of the Lord.

Think about His wounds.

His bleeding wounds.

Those seeping wounds.

Kiss His seeping wounds!

Kiss them!

Lick them!

Lick the blood!

Lick the pus that seeps from the wound.

Feel His pain.

Hear His screams.

But what does He do? Does He curse his tormentors?

Does He command them to Hell?

No, He does not. What does He do?

He says, Father, forgive them, for they know not what they do.

And He says, verily I say unto you, today you shall be with me in Paradise!

Who does He say this to?

To the trespasser!

The offender!

The murderer!

He promised the murderer eternal life.

Is it not unfathomable!

Is it not wonderful!

You too are a trespasser, my child.

You are a sinner.

You are an offender.

Yes, he squeaks.

But not only you. You must not think as such.

We are all of us offenders.

We are swine.

We are worms who crawl upon the earth and deserve to be crushed under His heel.

But what does Christ do?

He lifts us up.

He forgives us and blesses us and takes us by the hand and leads us into heavenly bliss.

But do you think He does the same for the priest?

No, the priest He ignores.

The priest is left behind with his hat in his hand.

The priest is condemned.

He feels the flames of Hell already.

He hears the Devil call.

Komm, Pfarrer Egede, komm zu mir, is what he says.

But you He takes by the hand.

For he who lifts himself up shall be put down, and he who makes himself humble shall be lifted up, as the Scripture says.

That other one, the priest, he shall be thrown into the snake pit.

To the serpents.

And the snakes will twist and writhe and sate themselves on all the wretched priests He has cast down to them.

Snake-fodder!

That is what he is. Snake-fodder!

But they will not eat him up.

For in Hell one cannot die.

Hell is the eternal life of which the priest he speaks.

But he knows it not himself.

He thinks he is going to Heaven.

What a surprise he has in store!

David is standing right up close to him now, slobbering and gripping him tightly by the shoulders, shrieking into his face, showering him with spittle. Johan feels paralysed, yet pleasantly so. He finds this vociferous assault oddly liberating, the sobs and weeping, this raw reek of genitals and steaming armpits. The German's face is flaming and wettened by sweat and tears. He seems like a person on the brink of losing control of himself, though strangely it is a loss of control which in itself appears controlled. What will happen now? Johan wonders. What will he do? Is it but theatre? He looks askance at the two cousins, who flank him and the German and have now put away their pipes, as if in readiness to catch the two men should they fall, or else to step between them if fists should fly. Perhaps they will assault me, he thinks. Perhaps they will be violent with me, violate me and do unmentionable things. Perhaps it is what I want?

I ask you now, David then says, seemingly pulling himself together, I ask you now to confess your sins.

I've confessed my sins to the priest, he replies.

Have you indeed? David's voice oozes sarcasm. Then I suppose everything is in the finest order. Did the priest confess his own sins to you?

No, I can't say he did. It doesn't interest me what the priest gets up to.

Indeed, such are the ways of your kind. You care not what the other man does. You are complacent. Each to his own. But this is not our way. We lower ourselves for each other, we humble ourselves in each other's gaze, we kneel down that we may be kicked in the arse, but would your priest ever do such a thing, do you think?

I shouldn't think so.

Then confess your sins, my child, and brace yourself for what happens next!

He hesitates. Where to begin? Well, I have indulged in fornication.

Hallelujah, he has indulged in fornication!

The two cousins chorus: Hallelujah!

What else. Come on, out with it. The worst you've got.

I took the Lord's name in vain? he ventures unimaginatively.

Urgh, that's priests' talk. We won't hear of it. We want the shameful stuff. True guilt. We wish to revel in filth. Come on, my child.

He racks his brains. What on earth can he say to satisfy the man? I have sold my wife to lecherous men for a pittance, he then puts forward.

Hallelujah! What else?

I have paid her myself in order for her to lie with me, for otherwise she will not.

The Germans are jubilant. Praise be the name of the Lord! David roars with laughter now. We'll drag a lot more filth out of you later, he says. But now it is my turn. I have lusted for my mother's breasts. I have kissed them and even liked it.

More rejoicings from the cousins.

Was it when you were a small boy? Johan asks.

No, I was a full-grown man. I tore the neck of her dress aside and licked her nipples. I lured her into fornicating with her own son. Oh, I remember it like it was yesterday. They were very dark, and wrinkled as prunes. And she pulled me to her bosom and moaned with delight and ground her hips against mine.

Transports of delight, deafening hallelujahs.

But wait, says David, and holds up his hand. There's more. I'm not finished yet. I have fornicated with my own sister whilst our father watched us!

He looks at Johan and the two Germans with a proud and boyish smile, and the cousins respond with howls of enthusiasm.

Well, I must say, says Johan. That certainly is what I'd call filth. Worse than making a whore of one's own wife, I think.

Oh, much worse. Much, much worse! I've never told anyone that before. In fact, I only remembered it now. But such is the act of confession, if only one is genuine of heart.

Abruptly, the German bursts out sobbing, causing Johan to jump. He has a strange way of crying. It sounds like he is forcing it out with all his might. His eyes bulge and the muscles of his face look like they have taken on a life of their own. He stamps on the floor with one foot. Eventually he gets down on all fours, weeping and sobbing still, his backside jutting into the air. He looks over his shoulder and his eyes find the two cousins. I am ready for my punishment, he sobs. Spare me not!

The two men step forward heavily. It seems they know what to do. One takes off his belt and begins to lash the wretched David, roaring at the top of his voice: Sinner! Sinner! The other proceeds to kick his behind with the toe of his boot. It is no sham, David's cries of pain no comedy act. He farts loudly and begs for mercy. Eventually they stop and David staggers to his feet, his face wet with tears, his crying unabated. He sits down at the table, buries his face in his hands and weeps heart-wrenchingly. The cousins sit down and re-light their pipes as if nothing had happened.

Am I to be punished too? Johan asks.

The cousins shake their heads. Not today, one of them says. Today we want only to show you what happens. We'll punish you hard next time, the other one says, and both of them smile. But punishment must of course be voluntary. One must love one's punishment, and yearn for it.

David shows him out. I give you no letter to take back this time, he says. I fear Egede and I have exhausted each other. He will not be converted. I do not judge him for it. Send him my regards and wish him well.

I will.

And bring your wife next time.

Ah, he says. I'm not sure if she'd care for it.

Bring her anyway.

He walks back to the colony in darkness. A gentle snow descends, and the air is still. Snow falling in a straight line, a rare sight.

Egede sits where he left him several hours before, at his desk upstairs.

Have you no letter for me? he asks with a look of disappointment.

I am to give you David's regards and wish you well.

Egede grimaces with annoyance. Do not let those deranged brethren muddle your thoughts. They are not in possession of their full faculties.

In the evening he prays: Lord Jesus Christ, my Saviour, you who knows my heart, listen to me now. I am not a good man. I do not love Sise the way I'm supposed to, my desire is purely selfish, for it thinks only of its own satisfaction. Show me how I can love my wife, dear Jesus, for I wish to be a better person, and I wish to begin with Sise, because I owe her, and then I can be good to others later. Amen.

Sise turns to him in the bed. What's that you're muttering about?

I'm praying to Jesus.

What for?

That he might make me a better person. The Germans taught me how to pray. The Lord's Prayer is no good. It's only a template to show what a prayer might contain.

You're over there a lot these days.

Yes. I've been talking to them all day today. They want you to come with me next time.

Sise accompanies him to Neu Herrnhut a couple of days later. The parlour has been aired and cleaned. They eat a meal of fish. There is no confession, no punishment, but David tells them about their mission and their pietist faith. He says that von Zinzendorf believes all men to be equal before Christ, rich and poor alike, nobility and rabble, free men and inmates, native Greenlanders and the blackest savages of Africa, women as well as men, and that everyone has the same right to hear the good word. He tells them of something he saw in a dream, that the whole valley of Neu Herrnhut was filled with tents and Greenlanders by the hundreds who had come to be baptized. If we believe in Jesus and are upstanding in our faith, he will bless our work, he says.

Sise is susceptible to the pietistic message. She weeps with the brethren, and laughs with them too. David offers to teach her to read and write, and after only a few weeks she is able to pen a whole letter to her family in Denmark. She is happier than Johan remembers her ever having been before. And most importantly: she has begun to turn towards him in their bed, and when for the first time he is allowed to fondle and kiss her breasts without prior payment, it is him who weeps and laughs.

When spring comes, Sise and Johan move in with the Germans, and are the first to join the Moravians in their faith. They build a new house, half peat, half timber, and with the help of the skilled

Germans their new home is infinitely better than the old one. They are nervous as to what Egede will say, whether he will become incensed and punish them by withholding Johan's salary. But Egede says and does nothing. Egede has other matters to which he must attend. It is by no means certain he has even noticed they are gone.

6

Get Thee Behind Me, Satan!

To-day I journeyed to the Greenlanders out in the Kook Isles and on the cape of the former colony. The condition of those on the Kook Isles was quite wretched, the poor souls there were become quite despondent of fear and despair in that they should witness most every day some or other among them be taken from their midst such that one saw dead bodies lie all about, some in the houses where they had lain, some dragged out onto the ground for the dogs and ravens. In two dwellings the people were yet healthy. I enjoined them all to solemn penitence, making clear to them that the wrath of God had come upon them for they had not with proper devotion heeded His word and endeavoured to live by it. They seemed to take this depiction to heart, showing great eagerness to be instructed in how they should pray to God for mercy and be saved if they should die.

FROM HANS EGEDE'S JOURNAL, DECEMBER 1733

Egede has taken the boat with Niels and has sailed up the fjord to assess the extent of the catastrophe. The oars slurp through the inches-thick, porridge-like lid of slush that lies on the water. They make slow and laborious progress, the boat edging forwards and sighing at every stroke. The oarsmen stare glumly over the heads of the two passengers in the stern. The fells are dark and moist. The wind is still. Forever calm in the land of the dead, thinks Niels. Clouds billow about the peaks. The icy fog draws ribbons of wet, glistening tulle across the fjord.

He sits beside his father, eyes peeled, watching the shore, watching for signs of human life, but also for reindeer. He is wearing native garb, the only clothing that can withstand the raw cold and still allow some freedom of movement. His father is well wrapped up in his reindeer-skin sleeping bag, sheepskin tunic, thick woollen mittens and fox-skin hat, barely visible in all his furs. But when Niels looks askance at him he can see his eyes in the dark, moving from side to side, following the lines of the book he is reading.

Egede, cocooned, is quite comfortable. His belly is full of barley porridge and goat's milk butter. He is oblivious to the cold, is away from the unpleasantness and obligations of the colony, and engrossed in his reading matter. The comforting weight of his book rests between his hands. His student days at Copenhagen University taught him a reading technique he has employed ever since. The reader must not pause, but drive his gaze onward in the text, devouring its words and sentences in a single uninterrupted flow. It almost feels like sleeping. The book is a selection of Luther's sermons. The Reformer's style is highly colloquial, intense in its presence, especially when he is writing in German, though even the translated Latin texts possess this same immediacy. It is as if the man comes to life before him in flesh and blood by virtue of his style alone. It is perhaps this aspect of the Reformer he likes best, his urgent, physical presence. He is a strong and dependable friend. A shame he died almost two hundred years ago. He writes often of man as a rational animal, *Animal rationale*. Luther has a fondness for writing about animals, both as metaphor and more literally, and about the difference between animals and men. Do animals feel fear? Do they display empathy? Grief? In brief, do animals have a soul, and is having human-like emotions the same as having a soul? Highly interesting. Egede himself has never felt attachment to any animal. Luther had mostly dogs, which he clearly loved and even, in this particular sermon, promised would enjoy a life after death. No, surely he cannot have meant such a thing? He is pulling the reader's leg. The incorrigible old fox. He cannot for a moment imagine that the great Wittenberger wished to be falling over all manner of dogs and pigs and poultry in heaven. But had he still been alive he would have asked him personally, as a colleague and as a fellow human.

He is shaken abruptly from his thoughts when a cry goes up from Niels.

There! Niels points.

The oarsmen change their course. They enter an inlet and drag the boat ashore. Some short distance behind a tall bluff is a peat house. They can see a woman, hunched on her knees in front of the entrance, as if in prayer. She is quite motionless.

Go up there and see if she is alive, Egede instructs.

He watches as Niels approaches tentatively, bending over the woman and speaking to her. Seemingly she is alive. He clambers up the bluff to join them.

Is she ill?

I don't think so, Niels replies. But she won't speak.

He bends down and takes her arm to pull her up, but the woman gets to her feet unaided. Her hair is uncombed and matted, her smell nauseating. Her eyes swivel in their sockets without latching on to anything, as if she cannot see the two men standing in front of her.

What's the matter with you, woman? Egede shakes her.

Niels repeats the question in Greenlandic.

No reply.

They breathe in deeply and crawl inside the dwelling, prepared for the worst. It is much as expected. On a bench lie two dead men, one young, one older. On a side-bench two other figures facing in opposite directions. Both lie gasping for breath. Niels makes to step forward, but Egede grabs his arm and holds him back.

Wait. We must find out if they are Christian. We don't want to expose ourselves to sickness for the sake of a couple of heathens.

They crawl out again. The woman has fallen to her knees again, scraping snow into her mouth, or perhaps washing her face. She vomits slightly, thin filaments of bile dribbling from her mouth. She groans and is gripped by spasms.

Egede shakes his head. Is she not one of my own from last year?

I think so, says Niels. I've definitely seen her and her sons in the colony. As far as I know, they're all baptized, apart from the husband inside. But if she's gone mad, it will be all the same.

The woman sits up in the snow with her legs splayed out in front of her like a child. Her face is wet with snow and slaver, but her gaze has become clear. She looks at the two Egede men, and utters something inaudible. Egede nudges his son towards her.

Speak to her. Hear what she has to say.

Niels crouches down in front of the woman. *Ajoravit?* Are you ill?

He keeps his mouth closed so as not to breathe in her unpleasant smell.

The woman shakes her head vigorously, as if he has accused her of something. Her eyes dart between madness and reason. Yet he senses she is there somewhere. A person he can talk to. The strings of coloured beads with which she has decorated her hair have come apart and dangle senselessly about her shoulders. Her skin clothing is torn open at the front. She must have done it herself in despair. One of her breasts is exposed.

Cover yourself up. My father wishes to speak to you. Do you know who my father is?

Yes. I know who both of you are.

Are you baptized?

Last year.

And the ones inside, are they baptized too?

My boys are.

Niels turns and sends his father a look.

Ask her what has happened here, Egede says.

I prayed to God, says the woman. And still he punishes me. Why?

Niels translates.

Do not argue with the Lord, woman, Egede barks. It won't help you.

Suddenly she spits at him, a thick gob landing on his boot. I spit on you, she hisses in Danish. I spit on the priests, I spit on God.

Egede steps backwards. He rubs the toe of his boot clean in the snow. You are condemned, woman. Let us go inside and see to the sick. Perhaps they can be saved.

When they enter the house again they are met by a gurgling, rasping sound. It puzzles them as their eyes adjust to the dim light of the blubber lamp. The sound is coming from the side-bench. Egede steps forward, then expels an angry cry.

He has cut his throat! You wretched man, what have you done? Here you are at the gates of heaven, and now look!

The suicide is still alive. Spluttering, he draws his breath through the gash in his throat. His blood streams onto the bench and from there onto the earthen floor. His body rises and falls, racked with convulsions, and it sounds like he is trying to groan, or perhaps even to say something in his final moments.

Don't touch him. He is already in Hell. See how he writhes!

Egede must concede that his feelings are not untainted by schadenfreude as he watches the dying man in his agony. What a fool, he thinks to himself. He must have sensed I was here. He knew all he had to do was stay alive until I administered the sacrament. Before evening he could have been in Heaven. It is almost funny how foolish people can be.

They have not heard the woman enter. But now she emits an ear-splitting shriek, throws herself upon her son and wails his name. After some moments the gurgle of his breathing ceases, the spasms die away, and the sounds in the dark room are of the woman's sobs and the wheezing chest of the man who remains.

Egede sighs. And what have we here, I wonder? He leans forward to the other end of the bench and snatches away the skin covering. A child is lying there, a young boy, curled up and without doubt terrified. Egede places a hand on his brow and the boy shrinks back in fright.

I'm not going to hurt you, he says, annoyed. And then, quietly: The Lord bless you and keep you. He pulls the skin up to cover the boy again and draws himself upright.

The child is also sick. Strange how the pox will often attack the men of a household and leave the women alone.

Is he dying? Niels asks.

I don't know. Probably.

Egede sits down on the edge of the main bench, cautiously, so as not to come into contact with the two bodies. Sit down with me here, he says to Niels. Let us pray.

He says the Lord's Prayer. The words, simple and uttered so many millions of times before that they ought long since to have lost their meaning. Yet their power is abundant, and always they bring comfort and calm. He feels himself drawn down into a whirling black vortex, carried away in the good darkness of the prayer. He emits a small sigh after his amen and opens his heavy eyelids. The woman's sobs have ebbed away. Niels sits looking at the boy under the cover. His eyes are trusting and enquiring. The pure gaze of childhood.

Stand up, woman, Egede says gently. Come here to me.

At first she does not react. But after a moment she gets to her feet and approaches them like a sleepwalker. A calmness has come over her features.

I sense another to be present here, says Egede. I think you know who I mean, Niels?

A shiver runs down Niels's spine. Who is it? he whispers.

Oh, I shall not mention his name, his father says. I would not wish to accord him the pleasure.

Niels swallows his spit. He feels now that the house has grown colder. A sure sign. The evil one will always draw warmth towards him. The cold prince of hell.

He has taken these men to him now, Egede says. But there are still two souls here who might be saved. We can't have all these baptized natives dying all over the place without receiving the sacrament. Every soul matters. Do you wish the soul of your last son to be saved? he asks.

The woman nods stiffly.

Do you wish to be saved yourself, so that you may be with him in the afterlife?

Yes.

Then go and wash yourself, he barks. You are soiled with the blood of your lost son. If you have other clothing besides the torn rags you have on, then put it on. You must be decent before the Lord and make yourself presentable.

Obediently she pulls the urine tub from under the bench and splashes her face, removes her skin clothing and washes her whole body in urine. When she is done she combs her hair and ties it up, finds another set of clothing and puts it on. The rank smell of ammonia fills the air.

Disgusting, Egede mutters. Washing in one's own fluids. I shall never understand it. And with such an abundance of delightful clean water right outside the house.

I think it's cleansing, says Niels. They use it to tan their skins with too. They say it removes germs. Perhaps that's why more women than men avoid being smitten by the pox. They wash more frequently.

Really? says Egede. How interesting. Remind me to write it down.

They step outside and call to the oarsmen, who are reluctant to approach a dwelling full of sick savages. But Egede orders them to drag out the bodies and cover them up with rocks so that they cannot be eaten by roaming foxes.

The mother is sitting with her sick son when they go back inside.

Let me look at him, Egede says. The woman makes room for him. She attends to the seal-oil lamp which is nearly extinguished, places some lumps of blubber in it and prods them about with the poking stick so that the oil collects in the hollow. The circular flame licks lazily upwards from the soapstone and casts flickering shadows against the walls.

Are you baptized, my boy? Egede asks.

Yes, says the boy. A priest baptized me. His name was Ole.

Excellent, says Egede. And are you prepared for death and the heavenly afterlife, my child?

I know I'm dying. I'm looking forward to it, I'd rather go to God in Heaven than be down here with nothing to do.

Egede smiles. I can hear that Lange has taught you well. Did he tell you about the Augsburg Confession?

I don't know, the boy replies, uncertain.

You must know it, Egede tells him with a laugh. Listen now and tell me, what is God?

God is our Father, says the boy. That's what we say when we pray to him.

Indeed, this is true. But he is more than that, don't you think?

Yes.

Niels? he says, turning his head to face him. You tell him.

Tell him what?

The Confession. The article about the nature of God.

I've forgotten it.

What? You indolent blockhead, I'll give you forgotten it. Listen here, God is eternal, without body, without parts, of infinite power. He slaps out a rhythm on the boy's chest as he recites.

Wisdom and goodness, the boy chips in, apparently remembering now the rhyme Lange taught him several years before.

Yes, that's it! Egede exclaims. Continue, my child.

The Maker and Preserver of all things, the boy goes on, visible and invisible, and yet there are three Persons, of the same essence and power, who also are coeternal, the Father, the Son and the Holy Ghost.

Why, this is excellent! Egede splutters and seems almost on the verge of tears. Here, in this wilderness, one is granted the privilege of hearing an unblemished recital of the first article, whilst one's own son can only bleat that he has forgotten it. Such a clever boy you are. A shame that you are so unwell. I could have made use of you in the Mission. My own son is good only for shopkeeping.

Do you think Jesus will want me? the boy asks.

Jesus loves you, Egede tells him. In that you must not doubt. Can you remember the story about Jesus walking on the water?

Yes, in the storm.

That's right. The wind was contrary. But what happened when Peter went to walk on the water?

He started to doubt and began to sink.

Correct! What a splendid child! Who would have thought it. But remember now, you must not doubt the way Peter did. You must have faith, for faith will liberate you from your mortal frame.

But do I have to confess my sins first? the boy asks.

Oh, I don't think that will be necessary. You are only a child.

But I have sinned, the boy insists.

All right, confess, Egede replies.

I have listened to my father's stories about the ancient ancestors and the spirits of the heathens.

Yes, that is indeed heresy, as a clever boy like you knows.

But they are here. You have to give them something or else they'll hurt you. There was a man here, an angakkok. He lay writhing on the floor and called upon the spirits. I saw them.

Did you call for Jesus, my child?

No, I was too afraid. I fell into doubt. I prayed to Him afterwards. Only I fear it was too late. We fell sick. Is God punishing us?

Yes, perhaps He is. I shall not lie to you, my boy. God's punishment to those who worship false gods is without mercy. He spares no one. God loves all men, but He makes himself blind when He must punish us.

Can I not be saved then?

Yes, indeed you can. You have committed no deathly sin.

I'm afraid of Hell, I've seen the Devil. He's been here several times. He said he was going to come and get me.

Do you repent your sins, my child?

Yes. I don't want to go to Hell.

But you must repent because it is right to do so, not because you are afraid of the punishment.

Perhaps I'm not good enough to go to Heaven. If I hadn't been baptized, I wouldn't go to Hell, then I'd just go to the place where the unbaptized children go when they die.

You should not wish for such a thing. It is a wicked place, wicked indeed.

But it must be better than Hell?

The boy's voice trembles with anxiety. He bursts into tears.

Egede rolls his eyes despairingly and shakes his head. He grips the boy's shoulders, looks him in the eye and says, Renounce Satan, my child!

The boy sobs. I don't want to die, I'm not ready. I don't want to go to Hell.

Shut up, boy! Egede snaps, releasing him. Instantly the boy falls silent.

Niels, fetch the blood-letting instruments from the boat. Bring the sacrament with you too. It's in a skin pouch.

Niels crawls out of the house and goes down to the shore. The air has become colder and crisper. It is dark, but the sky is clear, and when he looks up he sees the wheelbarrow of the Great Bear trundling across the firmament. The two oarsmen have covered themselves with skins and lie close together to keep warm.

Are we off? one of them mumbles.

Not yet. I think you can prepare to stay here for the night.

He rummages through his father's things and finds what he has been asked for. Returning to the house, he finds Egede in discussion with the woman. She sits cross-legged on the sleeping-bench where her eldest son and her husband lay before. Her voice is shrill, but when Niels enters she becomes silent. Egede takes out his instruments, the fine, sharp knife. Niels helps him hold the boy's arm while his father makes the incision at the elbow. The boy lets out a groan. His mother fetches a bowl.

Egede sniffs at the blood and makes a satisfied sound. It runs well, he says. And looks quite fresh.

When the bowl is filled he closes the wound with a cloth. The boy settles in his bed and after a short while he sleeps. His mother lies down beside him, her arm draped across his chest. Egede and Niels retire on the other bench.

They wake to the sound of quiet, unyielding weeping. Egede jumps up and goes to the boy. The mother clings to her son.

Is he dead? Egede asks.

He is still alive, the mother sniffs. But he is close to the end.

Egede listens to the boy's chest, his wheezing, irregular breaths.

Indeed, it seems to be near.

He kneels down at the bench and says the Lord's Prayer. He takes a wafer and presses it between the boy's teeth, moistening his lips with a couple of drops of wine. He places a crucifix on the boy's chest and says, Lord, take this innocent child to your arms. An hour later the boy is dead.

The mother now becomes enraged. She laces into Egede, pummelling him with her fists. He puts his arms up in front of him to defend himself.

You killed my child! she rages. You took away his blood.

She leaps into the air and darts about the cramped room as if searching for something. Before he knows it she is at him with a harpoon. She hurls it at him, though jars her throwing arm against the wall as she launches the weapon, weakening its force considerably. Egede ducks and catches the shaft deftly in one hand, thrusts forward and strikes the woman on the jaw with the other. She drops to the floor and knocks over the lamp, which bursts into flame. Her clothing is alight, she screams and tries desperately to swat away the flames. Niels is quickly on hand and douses the fire with a bed skin.

She lies on the floor, sizzling, with serious burns. She whimpers. The room is pitch black, but Niels manages to light the lamp again. He and his father pull off her clothing. In several places it has burned into her own skin, making it impossible for them to tell what is her and what is the bed cover. She comes round and screams in pain. Egede takes the urine tub and dabs her burns with the pungent liquid. She wails.

You've only yourself to blame, Egede admonishes her. I've never met such idiocy in my life. Still, the boy will go to Heaven.

They lift her onto the sleeping-bench next to the boy's body. But she refuses to lie down. Stark naked she leaps to her feet and lurches madly about the room. Egede and Niels watch her keenly in case she assails them again. She stumbles and falls full-length onto the floor, scrambles groaning to her feet and stares dementedly into space.

I'm at a loss with her, says Egede. Perhaps we should give her some aquavit.

Niels gives her some schnapps from the flask. She swallows it in a single mouthful, coughs and splutters, and asks for more. Niels gives her the bottle and she downs its contents in one. She sits down on the bench, settled now, though still whimpering, her upper body rocking to and fro, her breathing seemingly impeded and accompanied by groans.

I should have listened to my husband, she wheezes. He said we should go away, to the south where there is no sickness. The whole district is cursed. All are cursed, Danes and Greenlanders. He said so, Aappaluttoq said so, I heard him myself. All the Danes will die, he said, and all the Greenlanders who follow them will die too. But not the blackcoat, he said, for God will keep him and punish him with a fate worse than death. We're all going to die, priest. Except you. And she breaks into coarse laughter.

Egede stands stiffly in the middle of the room. The lamp throws the shadow of his hunched figure onto the ceiling. Niels sits on the bench, staring wearily at the woman. Misfortune makes people cruel, he thinks with sympathy.

The crucifix, Egede says quietly. Give me the crucifix. It's over there.

Niels takes it from the chest of the dead boy and hands it to him. Egede clutches it tightly and holds it up in front of the woman. She spits at it, but Egede is prepared, he steps aside as her gob flies through the air and lands on the floor.

Ah, so there you are, Egede says, his voice oddly changed. Niels scrutinizes him.

Greetings, his father goes on, staring towards a corner of the room. Do you recognize me?

Father, what's the matter? Niels asks.

His father seems not to hear him, but continues to stare into the dark corner.

The woman gazes at the priest wildly. Her hair has fallen loose again and hangs in front of her face. Her eyes glisten darkly among the strands. She blinks several times quickly in succession, then glances towards Niels.

What's wrong with your father? she whispers.

Egede approaches her. His face widens in a great and malicious-looking grin. He looks as if he will consume her and suck the madness from her marrow.

Both she and Niels jump when suddenly he roars: Satan, I command you in the name of Jesus Christ to leave this woman!

He swipes the air with the crucifix and roars again: In the name of the Father, the Son and the Holy Ghost, I command you to leave her. O, Lord Jesus, he roars, his voice guttural and trembling, release this poor woman from her demonic possession!

The woman emits a scream, leaps onto the bench and crouches down in the corner behind the body of her son, cowering against the peat wall. She glares hatefully in turn at Egede and the crucifix. The priest approaches her cautiously, holding the crucifix up in front of him. He places a knee on the bench, extends the crucifix towards her and repeats his exhortation as loudly and as forcefully as before. Spittle flies from his lips, and with each barrage of spray that falls on the woman's face she shrinks back.

Who are you? Egede roars. Say your name!

The woman whimpers. Egede repeats: Say your name, say your name!

Tornaarsuk, she stammers. I am Tornaarsuk.

Ha! Egede exclaims. You think you can trick me! He continues to wave the crucifix in front of her. Cowering still, she lifts up the boy's head and upper body and clutches him to her chest, as if he were a shield against the furious priest. Her feet scrabble in the straw of the bed, but she can withdraw no further than to the wall at which she is already crouched.

Satan! Egede yells at the top of his lungs. I greet you. Do you know who I am? Look at me. Tell me who I am! He snatches the boy's body, wrestling it from the woman's clutches, and slings it to the other end of the bench, allowing him to edge closer towards her.

I don't know, she pleads. What am I supposed to say? What's wrong with him? What does he want with me? Is he going to kill me? Who are you?

I am God's holy apostle! I am the Master of Wittenberg. Do you know me?

And the voice of Satan grunts back at him: Go away, priest. You're annoying me.

Egede says: You are Satan. Speak to me!

Luther, is that you? Satan replies. Long time no see. A couple of hundred years at least. A Sunday, I recall.

I kicked your arse that time, Luther/Egede says. Remember?

Yes, I remember. It hurt like hell.

I can kick you again. I'm not frightened of you.

Yes, you are. You're afraid of me. I know you. Remember that. I know your weaknesses. I know what you've done.

Luther/Egede bellows back: Beside the point! I shall beat you from this poor woman, just you wait.

She's mine. A wretched savage. Surely you can let me keep her? You've got the boy.

Beelzebub, get thee away! And he swipes the air with the crucifix.

How rude he is, Satan retorts sarcastically. But then he always did spout shite. Stop waving that crucifix at me, you nearly put my eye out.

Lord Jesus, Luther/Egede prays, almighty Father, deliver us from evil!

Stop, stop, stop. Let's talk about this. Can't we make a deal like the last time?

No talking, no deal. Get thee away, in the name of Jesus!

You're going to have to make a deal with me whether you want to or not.

I can't hear you, Luther/Egede says. Get thee away, in the name of Jesus! He thrusts a finger towards the exit.

You know I know your secrets, Satan hisses. I know what you did to the boy.

Be silent, Satan!

I know exactly what you did. I could put it about. Is that what you want?

Our Father, who art in Heaven . . .

Prayers won't help you, priest. My father won't listen to you. He knows what you did too. He's letting me take care of this.

Egede, for now plainly it is he, falters. Is that what He said?

Indeed. Go to Egede, He said. Punish him for what he did to the boy. I'll let you have him. He's all yours.

Oh! Egede groans. I am lost. I am lost. Lord, have mercy on me, this miserable sinner. Forgive me, forgive me. He drops to his knees and weeps as if his heart were broken.

There, there, Satan says comfortingly. It's not that bad, surely? Some get saved, some are lost. The books have got to balance. That's the deal I made with my father long ago. But you, priest, you think yourself too good to strike a deal with me? Who are you to elevate yourself like that? Who do you think you are?

What do you want from me?

Not a lot. Hardly anything in fact. You know what I want.

The woman?

There, you said it. You can't take it back now.

Then take her, take her. But the boy is mine.

Yes, the boy is yours. God help you!

Get thee behind me, Satan. In the name of Jesus.

So long, priest. See you again.

Egede screams. Red and blue scintillations flash before his eyes. A great darkness opens up before him. He proceeds down a long and winding staircase of stone and senses the abyss below him. He continues to call for Jesus, his cries echoing all around, gradually diminishing into a whimper.

///

Niels has remained stuck to the bench, watching it all with a mixture of terror and fascination. His father shook the woman violently, he beat her with the crucifix until she lay curled in a ball with her arms covering her head for protection. He sat on top of her with all his weight, and rode her as if he were copulating with her. His hand, clutching the crucifix, is stained with blood.

He rolls away from her onto his side. He lies and stares at the ceiling. The dead boy slides to the floor. The woman lies beside him, whimpering and moaning. Blood runs from her nose, one eye is swollen. She is shaking.

Abruptly, Egede gets to his feet. We must go, he says. There is nothing more for us to do here.

Are we to leave her like this? Niels asks. Should we not take her with us?

No! She is lost. I couldn't save her. But her son is ours. We must put him in the ground.

Egede staggers out. Niels follows him. Light has come. The whole night must have passed. Egede goes down to the river and submerges his head in the water. He drinks. Niels stands watching as his father's gulping motions ripple through his body. Egede stands. He casts a foggy glance at his son.

Were you fighting the Devil in there? Niels asks.

Yes, my boy. It was him.

Did you win?

Sort of. One can never truly win over the evil one. That is a matter for God. The moment one thinks to have won, victory is his.

But why then fight with him, if one cannot win?

We must fight him. It is a daily struggle. If one can do so without fear, while looking in his green and goaty eyes, one shall have prevailed over the self. Oh, I am hungry now.

They go down to the boat and wake the two oarsmen. Niels finds some ship's biscuits for them to eat. His father devours them greedily. They go up to the house again, all four, and drag the body outside and lay it to rest. Egede recites some verses and says the Lord's Prayer.

I'm still hungry, he says. Did we not have a ham somewhere?

He finds it among their provisions, cuts off some slices and fills his mouth.

Such an appetite the outdoors can give a man, he comments.

He settles into his usual place, wraps himself well in his skins and takes out his Luther. After only a few strokes of the oars he sleeps, snoring loudly as he is transported further and further up the fjord.

7

Katarina's Hymns

To-day I travelled up to the Greenlanders in the Baal's River. When we came to the nearest dwelling, some from the old colony had arrived there, among whom two were sick, wherefore the inhabitants there, for fear of being smitten by them, in all haste removed themselves from the dwelling and departed further up the fjord. The sick died the next morning. News came to me also that at the inner reaches of the fjord, to where people had come from the aforementioned dwelling, they too had fallen sick and were dying.

FROM HANS EGEDE'S JOURNAL, JANUARY 1734

I am Katarina. It is the Christian name given to me in baptism by the priest called Henrik three years ago. I know, because he told me so, that he was once betrothed to a girl by the same name, in his homeland, and therefore he thought I should be called the same. It puzzled me, because I was brought up to believe that the soul is in the name, and did it mean he wanted me for his sweetheart? But of course this is heathen talk, as Henrik said, for my soul is my own, the Lord God has given it to me. I asked him where the soul resides. I was brought up to believe that a person has many souls, one in the ear, one in the hand, one in the eye, and then, as I said, one in the name, but the Christians have only one soul, and where might it be? The soul is *incorporeal*, he said. It is not in any particular place, though is constrained by and associated with your body for as long as you are alive. When you die it leaves your mortal frame and goes to wherever God has decided it is to go. God passes judgement on your soul, not your body, for the body is mortal. But what about the Inferno, I asked him. If the soul is no more than air, then surely it cannot burn or feel suffering?

Most certainly it can feel suffering, he said, but it cannot burn up, for it is incorporeal, and therefore the torments of Hell shall endure for ever, for the soul is immortal. How can God allow people to burn for ever? I asked. Does he hate people that much? No, God loves man, and he wishes for him only salvation. Therefore he warns us of the cruellest punishment in order that we be obedient to him and ascend to him when we die. He looked at me. Even the most ignorant native girl it seems can pose questions a priest must ponder before he is able to answer, he said and smiled, though it was a solemn smile. If you are to be baptized, you must obey the word of God and be less inquisitive. And so obediently I was baptized, and then I left the colony and its poisonous air and returned to my settlement up the fjord.

I am nineteen years old, I think. Henrik helped me work out how old I might be. I was born a few summers before Egede came to our land, in the dark times when years were not counted in the same way as the Christians count them, and when the shamans were our priests and the fjord, edged by the fells, was our church. But God created nature, as too he created man. He created the sheer face of blue ice which rises at the bottom of the fjord, he created the heather on the moors, the flowers, the birds in the air and the trout in the streams. I go up there whenever I wish to pray. I have a prayer-stone, flat and white. It lies up at the falls. Whenever I feel uneasy in my heart, or if I bear a sorrow, I go there and kneel, and my ears fill with the rush of the water, which consumes all else, and there I say my Lord's Prayer and a peace comes to my soul.

My settlement is only sparsely inhabited. Two handfuls and two fingers more are all who remain. This is how we count. But I know it is called twelve, or a dozen. I have two languages and have also two kinds of soul, one Christian and some others which are heathen. Perhaps God thinks me unclean with my heathen souls. Perhaps he thinks I smell. Heaven is such a clean and tidy place. I don't know if they will ever let me in.

My brother died some few days ago. He had been in the colony when the sickness was raging there. He fled in terror but took the sickness with him like an invisible veil trailing behind him all the way here. He was baptized and could therefore die in peace. I helped him. It was in the night. I crept under his bed cover, pinched his nostrils together and placed my hand over his mouth. He squirmed a bit, but not much. He died with a smile on his lips. We sang a Danish hymn when we carried him to the grave, and we praised the Lord. My mother was sad. But then she is not baptized and has no hope of any heavenly afterlife.

But where is he now? she asks.

He is with God, Mother.

Yes, but where?

I point to the sky where the moon is shining like the blade of a knife. Up there.

Can he see us?

Yes, he sees everything, for it is so high up, higher than any fell.

She smiles. I don't understand it. But I believe it. It makes me happy. And then she cries. Afterwards, she waddles from the grave and back to the house.

At night especially, when I wake for no reason and lie staring out into the darkness, I see things which are far away, and I know that if I wanted, or had the courage, I could follow my gaze and my thoughts and travel anywhere I liked. I know it is a heathen thought. But then I take the little crucifix given to me by Henrik, the priest, and clutch it in my hand as I say the Lord's Prayer, and then it all passes. The Lord is my shepherd. He leadeth me.

Others are sick, my two young brothers, my cousins and uncles, and a sister. Not all have taken to their beds, some still manage to do their work, catching trout in the river, mending boots and clothing, preparing food. But it is hard for them. They drag their feet and shuffle about. My sister has broken out in blisters all over. They bubble up on her skin and she scratches them until she bleeds. But she laughs about it. I'm not afraid to die, she says. She was baptized with me. We talk about how much we look forward to going to Heaven.

Now and then someone collapses. One of the men fell in the river and was unable to get out again. It may have been me who pushed him, struck him with a rock or tripped him up, whatever, but no one saw, so in a way it never happened. He was dying anyway. I have nothing against seeing people die, but I cannot abide to see them dying. So I shouted and made a fuss, and they came running and waded out into the ice-cold water and dragged him ashore. His face was blue and there was a large swelling on the back of his head. He must have hit a rock when he fell, I said. In the river I could see the fish as they darted nervously about, snapping up the filaments of blood as they ran downstream and collected in the pool. We buried him under rocks, sang hymns, laughed and praised the Lord.

Not many are left now, only a handful and one finger. Which is to say six. Besides the children. I haven't counted the children. They are quite a number. They too die, though it is hard to keep up with how many. So little it takes. Everyone is glad. We sing one of the songs taught to us by Egede, a lovely hymn: 'Let the earth conceal, erase me, worms my very juice devour, fire and water me consume, I lie trusting in my tomb, that to life I shall be taken, in death's realm not lie forsaken.' And so on. I think it is the loveliest song I know.

Afterwards we sit into the night and talk about Egede and about Jesus and the time we were baptized, how it felt.

I remember how excited I was, says my cousin. He is much older than me. It was in the old house by the sea, where the priest and his family lived before the colony days. Egede called my name out, and he took me lovingly by the hand as if he were my own mother, and then he asked me to kneel. I was trembling, and I think perhaps I felt I was not quite ready for the baptism then, that I was not good enough or had not understood things sufficiently, but when I felt the water run down my neck everything became bathed in light and illuminated. It was the sun. The sun shone in through the parlour window at that very moment and made everything radiant. That was when I knew it was true, that He loves us all and wants us to find salvation and avoid the flames of Hell and ascend to Him.

I felt the splendour of it immediately, says his brother, my second and younger cousin, his voice gentle as a smile and filled with quiet reminiscence. It was out in the skerries one summer. Egede was out missionizing and he and the two other priests had been there several times that summer and instructed me. Then one day he said it was time, now I was to be anointed, and I was so glad, for I had not thought I would ever succeed. It was raining that day, a slight drizzle, but the priest wanted it done outside regardless. It took place on a grassy plain a short distance from the settlement. He looked at me and winked and said, Come here, my child, as the priests say even when they are speaking to a grown man. I approached him and he placed his hand on my shoulder. His hand was so heavy that I sank to my knees. I put my hands together and looked up at him. He said, I baptize you in the name of the Father, and of the Son, and of the Holy Spirit, and as he poured the water over me it immediately stopped raining and a rainbow appeared over the skerries. I was so moved by it I started to cry. Since then I have not been afraid to die.

I managed to bite the priest's finger, says a girl. But I was only little then. Ow, you little Satan! the priest blurted. First he asked if I renounced the devil and all his works and ways, and someone from the crew of a ship which lay at anchor that summer held me and answered on my behalf and said yes, I did. Do you believe in God the Father Almighty? Yes, said the seaman. Do you believe in Jesus Christ? Yes! And so on. I remember it all. And then he moved his hand towards me and I put his finger in my mouth and bit as hard as I could, causing him to cry out and swear. Ow, you little Satan! But I was christened anyway.

We laugh at her story. We are all so happy.

They continue to tell of their baptisms and their first days as Christians, the blessings, the happiness and joy. One of them says that when a person is baptized they stop being afraid. Before, when he was still a heathen, he says, he was always so afraid, afraid of the spirits, which were everywhere, afraid of starvation or of freezing to death, afraid that his parents or sisters would die. To be Christian is to be glad, he says. The others tell him they feel the same. They tell him of the time before their own baptisms, dreadful tales of ghosts and of death appearing in the form of a raging evil spirit. I like to listen to the old stories, about the dark times before the Christians came to this land, but I am frightened by them too. For I think that perhaps the old spirits might be awakened if we speak of them too often, and then they will surely harm us in some way, perhaps by luring us into some heathen practice, the wearing of amulets, for instance, or playing the lamp game, and thereby we shall be lost and never get to Heaven.

The small children are rather afraid. It is only understandable. My older sister calls her children to her on the sleeping-bench that she may say farewell to them. She is deathly ill and can barely speak a word. The children, a girl and a boy, begin to cry, and the boy becomes angry, he hits her and tells her to get up. But all she does is smile, and her eyes are narrow slits filled with moisture. We shall meet again in that other place, she whispers. You must not be sad, and you must not be afraid. Death is easy, it is like a cold river across which one must wade. Your feet are cold for a moment, but then you are on the other side in a delightful place. Do as your mother's sister tells you. She will look after you.

Her mother's sister is me.

I begin to sing, a hymn everyone knows, and those who are still able join in: 'Now let us sing in our pity, for Jesus Christ the Lord, God's son who was born in Bethlehem's city, and joy to us restored.'

I gather all the children around me. They sit in a semicircle at my feet. I tell them about Jesus, everything I remember Henrik telling me about his life, about salvation and the heavenly afterlife. Jesus loved all children, I tell them. He wants all children to come to him.

How can we get to Heaven? they ask.

We can turn ourselves into ravens when we die, one of them says. And then we will fly there.

There is a hole, another one says. You have to go up onto the fell and somewhere there is a hole leading to Heaven. But you can only find it when you're dead.

God's angels will carry us in their arms and take us there, I tell them.

Will our mother be there too?

Yes, your mother will be there and you will be united with her again. She will come running towards you and give you kisses.

Can a person not die in Heaven?

No, never, I say.

Are people always happy there?

Always, I say.

I say the Lord's Prayer with them and they snuggle up to me and fall asleep.

My sister dies in the night. Death often comes at night. I don't know why. Perhaps because sleep and death are so closely related, and God gave us sleep so that we will always be reminded that we are to die, as he gave us the bright new dawn to remind us of the resurrection and the eternal life in Heaven. I love sleeping. I go to bed at night and imagine I am preparing for death and that when I awake I will be in Heaven. But I do not die. I live on as those around me perish. I don't know why God does not call me to him. Does he not like me?

The last thing the sick do before they take to their deathbeds is to sew a reindeer skin in which to be wrapped when they are put to rest. I help them. I am still well. We have been keeping a great pile of skins from the hunt last autumn, when everyone was still well, to take to the colony and sell to the Trader there. But now only a few skins are left, and barely a handful of people. The children perish. They pass in their sleep while I hold their small, cold hands and sing for them. Children are good at dying. I hardly need to help them, only a bit, pinching their nostrils together and placing my hand over their mouths. It is allowed, to curtail their suffering. I cannot bear their suffering. And only a small skin is required in which to wrap the corpse of a child. Adults will often lament and ask if it is really true that they are going to Heaven, and I have even found that some have scorned the Lord while on their very deathbed. But in each case I have spoken with them and prayed with them, until eventually they settled and were ready. The children's faith is so strong and untainted when it comes to their own passing. They are so trustful when I snuggle beside them in the night. The children are never any trouble.

Now my mother is sick and I am sad because she is not baptized, and when she dies I know I will never see her again. Goodnight, Mother, I whisper, and feel her tremble in my hands, until at last she is quite still.

My mother's death troubles me. For in a way I shepherded her into damnation, that which Henrik called the other death from which we never return. Perhaps she could have been saved. Perhaps a priest might have come and baptized her at the last. But Henrik is gone. And the other one, Egede, will not baptize indiscriminately, as he says, which I quite understand. Anyway, it is too late now for my mother. There is nothing to be done about it.

It feels lonely here. The place is silent and empty. No one is left. All are dead. I wrap my mother in the skin she has sewn, and then I drag her from the house to the place where she wished to rest. It is hard work. People are so heavy when they are dead. I say the Lord's Prayer at the grave. I pray for her soul, even though it is a heathen soul. Forgive me, Lord, but this is my mother. What else am I to do?

I sit at my mother's grave and sing: 'Lord Jesus Christ, my Saviour blest, my Hope and my Salvation, I trust in Thee, deliver me, from misery, Thy word is my consolation.'

I wait for the sickness to smite me. But it does not come. Strange. I feel quite well. I go up onto the fell. Perhaps, I tell myself, perhaps there is a hole somewhere, perhaps the gates of Heaven are here. But I find nothing, only snow and fog and cold. I sit down on my backside and slide down the slopes. It is fun. I love to do it. But on one's own it is rather dull. Still, I go up and do it again. Perhaps I will fall into the abyss. Perhaps I will kill myself. Then I would be with the others. If it were not forbidden and led to damnation and the other death, I would stick a knife in my stomach. I come close to doing so on a couple of occasions. But I know it is not allowed. It would be so very easy. A quick thrust to the abdomen and a great leap towards God and my family in Heaven.

I take my bow and go inland. It is very cold and the snow is deep. I sink in to my hips with every stride. But on the other side of the pass the land slopes gently down towards the fjord where most often the wind has swept much of the snow away. Up in the air I see a raven. It watches me, sailing above my head on its broad wings. I will not shoot it. It is not good to shoot a raven. Besides, their taste leaves much to be desired.

Of course, I could lie on the bench back at the house and wait for death to come. But that would be a sin, almost the same as suicide. There would be no salvation then. One must strive to live, to show gratitude for the life God has given to one, and yet go calmly into death when it calls. Death comes to us all. But when? Perhaps I will die here in the wilderness. I might have an accident, or freeze to death. I am rather afraid of falling. I am afraid of the pain. Forgive me, Lord. But I am not afraid of freezing to death.

Dear Lord, I whisper in prayer. If you wish for me to come to you, then let me freeze to death.

On the plain below I see a herd of reindeer, their hooves scraping away the snow for them to nibble the winter grass. The wind is in my face, so they cannot smell me. I approach them using the rocks for cover. When I am close enough I pick out a calf and shoot, and the herd stampedes away like thunder. It is the first reindeer I have killed. God must have guided the arrow. He wants me to live.

I make an incision in the calf's abdomen, opening an artery and lying down to drink the warm blood. Afterwards I eat the contents of the stomach, a warm and steaming porridge which makes me dizzily sated. God does not want me to die. I have understood that now. I drag the calf back with me to the settlement. Darkness comes, and then it is light again before I have even returned. In front of the house I skin the animal and cut it up into smaller pieces. I heat up the dwelling and boil some of the meat in a pot we have taken from the colony. I say the Lord's Prayer before eating.

I remain in the empty settlement until the calf is eaten. I eat it all, the meat, the guts, the tongue, the brain, the tallow. It takes several weeks. I see no humans, no animals. God wanted me to kill this calf and eat it, thereby to live. But why? I cannot fathom it.

And then there is no more meat. I begin to feel hunger. It feels good. I cannot imagine a better way to die. But then one day someone comes. I see one of the colony boats come sailing with four men on board. I go down to the shore and wait for them. It is the priest, Egede, his son and two oarsmen. They come ashore and follow me up to the dwelling. I have no more food, I tell them.

We have some with us, my child, Egede says.

We eat pease porridge and salt-cured meat, and barley porridge fried into patties. My word, such food makes a person fart. I tell them all that has happened, how all those christened have died in belief of salvation. They look at me as if they cannot quite believe their own ears. But they can see the stone graves. They stay with me for three days and the priest says the Lord's Prayer over the graves. He performs the Holy Communion, preaches and reads from the Book of Genesis, the wanderings in the wilderness.

It is soon Easter, he says. Return with us to the colony, my child.

On Palm Sunday I am seated in the colony boat. I watch as my home disappears behind me, the graves of my mother, my siblings, my fellows, small snow-tipped mounds of rocks gradually dissolving into the surroundings. A promontory comes between us, and they are gone. I turn and look ahead. If I am lucky, death awaits me in the colony.

8

Saint Gertrud

To-day some Greenlanders visited us who had come from north of Disko Bay where they had been settled since this last winter. They could tell us that those of our folk who lived there in the colony were well. Among these Greenlanders was a woman who claimed to have been got with child by one of our men at the northern colony. Now she had given birth and called the child after its father. When I said to her that he was wrong who had done this, and that she also was wrong, she answered on the contrary that he was shrewd, for she could not have children by her own husband. The husband, who was standing with her, confirmed this to be true and believed that the person who had impregnated his wife had done to him a great service, for which reason he was indebted to him.

At this time my own dear wife was becoming increasingly feeble and would often be compelled to remain in her bed, which fact foreboded to me the most unfavourable outcome.

FROM HANS EGEDE'S JOURNAL, AUGUST 1735

So here I am, his wife, at the bitter end. For surely I too have something to say? My name is Gertrud Nielsdatter Rasch. I am a wicked person. Do not believe those who portray me as the Virgin Mary or any other of those holy women. I am Lilith, demon of the darkened desert. Wicked through and through. In what does my malice consist? Oh, in so many things. Avarice. Pride. Self-righteousness. Pharisaism. False piety. Hypocrisy. I take the weak to me, women and children, and consume their sufferings. I gorge myself with death and ill fortune. I am insatiable. I live on human flesh. See for yourself how many have come to me alive to leave again only in death. I, Gertrud, have devoured them. And everyone thinks me to be a good person, a saint. It almost makes me laugh.

Now I am dying.

Perhaps then I shall find peace.

Being the wife of a holy man is far from easy.

It can turn a person bad.

One has so little choice.

Things must balance.

My father was the lensmand at Kvæfjord on the Lofoten Islands. My wickedness became apparent to me when I saw a witch burned at the stake. I was twenty-two. I think she was the last witch to be burned in Norway. Her name was Johanne Nielsdatter. Her very name was enough! I wished to see it. My father would not permit me, but I sneaked out and went there on my own. The witch was more dead than alive when they put her on the fire. They had filled her with aquavit in order to sedate her. But she certainly screamed, I can tell you that. Hans was there too, but a little boy at the time, not yet ten years old. He was terrified. He cried. I took him to me, hiding him under my skirts, where he remained for quite some time. I felt nothing to begin with, no horror, no sympathy, but then, little by little, a certain excitement at the screams, or perhaps it was the boy snuggling between my thighs which made me feel so exalted. I heard the screams and they were the screams of a witch, but I too screamed, and as I did the boy came tumbling out from under my skirts, and at the same moment I saw the witch's hair flare like a torch, and a second later she was engulfed by flame as I too was engulfed, and we screamed in unison, the witch and I. People now noticed Hans, staggering about as if he were drunk. Why are you so wet? they asked. But he did not reply. He ran off, back to his mother's skirts, and I did not see him again until several years later.

Now witches are no longer burned. It is a thing of the past. The times move on and old customs are left behind. Lucky for me. Perhaps the practice ought to be taken up again, if only for the sake of this single hag.

Wickedness is warm and dark like a sleeping-alcove. Wickedness is not hard, as people think, but soft as a velvet cushion. Goodness is hard, goodness is cold and callous. Look at my husband, the priest. Look at my children. There is not much wickedness there. Niels, however, resembles me a lot, Kirstine to an extent. But they are good. Poul and Petronelle are the spit of their father, and not only because they have inherited his beak of a nose.

We were married in the summer of 1707. There were flowers, veils and tulle. Meat and wine, and drunken guests. The clanging of church bells. There were tears – my father's. And kisses – my mother's. There was sunshine and the smell of the sea, and salty stockfish that hung like piss-coloured lace on the drying-racks up on the rocks. I became the wife of a priest, a small parish in Vågan populated by fishers who yearned for Heaven yet were more disposed to the bottom of the sea. Funerals in absentia were more common than the usual kind. We eked out a living on a poor income. Eternal strife with the incumbent Parelius, endless quarrels which whenever they were brought to tribunal would always be settled to our disadvantage, resulting in penalties and debt and quarrels anew. Hans was stiff-necked and unbending then as now. He closed his door and immersed himself in his dreams of Greenland, of which he had heard such a lot from seamen who had been there, tales of the old Norsemen stuck in the mire of papism, waiting only for someone to come and liberate them. I was not much for it. We had four children, how could we plunge into such uncertainty? You must have lost your mind, man! But so it turned out. He forced his will on us and now we are here. I do not think we are any worse off than we would have been in Lofoten had we stayed. But I miss Kvæfjord. I miss the pissy smell of the stockfish, the flowers upon the hillside, so delicate and full of hope. I miss the chance of again becoming the person I once was, a girl picking flowers to put in her hair.

I shall never see it again. It is no more than deserved. I am a wicked woman, so filled with hatred. And hatred is a sin. One should love everything which is created by God. And yet I cannot. It is impossible. The door of love is closed. Hatred is the only thing stronger than pain, and capable of driving it away. And then there is dying. Oh, how good it will be to find peace.

It was I who seduced him. He had no idea, of course. He was so young, barely of age. I was already a middle-aged wife of thirty-four.

He was to have had another old hag, the widow of the former pastor at Vågan. But I turned his head, I lured him and he took the bait. Naturally, she was displeased, Dorothea de Fine, and conspired with Parelius against him. But I it was who won him. That was that. With what did I lure him? With piety, hymns and knowledge of the Bible, for I had been taught well by the deacon. I seduced him with other things too. I was not exactly young. I knew a thing or two. Hans may well say a woman thinks with her arse, which is why she is broad below and narrow above, but I know very well the way to a man's mind. As such I was perhaps more man than woman. I had self-abused since the age of twelve. I was a warm-blooded whore, cool and rational on the outside. I'd had a sweetheart before when I was young, but he went away to Copenhagen. I masturbated furiously in those years, my hand would find my cunt at the slightest opportunity. I taught myself. I don't know if others do the same. It is meant to be such a shameful thing. God condemns it. And yet it is delightful. It is like rubbing on a seaweed pod. One rubs and rubs until the pod opens and a slimy substance oozes out, and a splendid feeling of release washes through one's being, both mentally and physically. It is certainly better than the Lord's Prayer. But later Hans took over and I loved it. I loved to feel him inside me, it felt like I would collapse upon his hardness and break ever so slightly into pieces. Oh! the joyous feeling of being filled up inside by something from without. We had four children in seven years before that part of our life together dried up. We came to Greenland. An hour passed, thirteen years. Life is an express carriage, it hurtles on without pause. And now I lie here on my deathbed. I have tried to resume my practice of before, a digit for a lover, if only to while away the boredom of dying. But there is nothing left. I have dried up. I have called for the other one, who has visited me several times when Hans has been away, but I have not seen him in a long time.

Now the sun shines in through the window. Its light falls upon my bed, inching upwards to shine on my face.

///

In August she said to me: I feel poorly. I think I shall go to bed.

I was somewhat vexed with her: What's the matter with you. Is it the monthly occurrence?

But she only laughed. Oh, Hansie, that stopped years ago.

How am I to know? I am not charged with washing your underwear.

You may thank God for it, she said.

Since then she has not risen. She lies there in spite, triumphantly ill, bathed in the sun of autumn which the house so greedily absorbs through its windows and spreads through our little parlour. She lies as if in radiance. I think she is dying. It is what she wants. No doubt she thinks there is a seat reserved for her at the side of Mary Magdalene, Saint Bridget, Hildegard of Bingen and the other crowd of women from the papist catalogue. And no doubt there is. Man is a worm which woman crushes beneath her heel. Therefore the man must be the priest, the woman the saint. Luther was not a good man. Therefore he struggled. Therefore he thought. Therefore he wrote. Had he been good we would not have had his writings, and the Reformation would never have taken place.

I return to my Relation and endeavour to take stock of this last catastrophe to have struck our colony. Our parlour is no longer filled with sick natives. They are dead now, every one. Now only she is left, soon to follow. More than a hundred baptized natives have died this past year, which is to say nearly all who have received the sacrament from me. They have wandered on to God. Good for them. They do not weigh on my conscience. On the contrary, they are a hundred souls to my account. Only one lives here yet in the colony, the young girl Katarina whom we brought back from the fjord. She lives with us now, performing domestic work and attending to my wife.

And then there are all those who were never christened. I think eight out of ten are dead. It is quite abominable. What is the meaning behind such obliteration? Does it serve a purpose? They have been lost. And those who survived have fled the district. They too are lost. Dear God, tell me the meaning of this! Is it a sign? Is it a punishment? Is it me you are punishing? Is it because of the boy? And now Gertrud will soon be taken from me. Time is running out for us Danes. At least it is for me.

My son Poul will carry on my work. He goes about it with body and soul, I see. He has the fire inside him. He has already been up at Disko Bay where he says there are great populations, enough for several new colonies. I should have begun there instead, where the weather is better, the air purer, and the whaling prosperous. It was a great mistake to establish the colony here on this head of land which is so plagued by fog and wind. A merchant, one Jacob Severin, has been accorded the privilege of the Greenlandic trade. Poul believes him to be a man who can repair the damage done by the rest of us. But indications are that the Trade will in future take priority over the Mission. And thus the costermongers will have it their own way. Man would rather serve Mammon than God.

I'm going for a walk, I mumble to my sick wife who lies with her chin jutting towards the ceiling. I take with me my pipe, my coat and my kamik boots and wander off over the peninsula. How many times I must have wandered here, on these criss-crossing paths trampled down by my own feet. I have filled this great hall with song. I should have veered left. But my thoughts are elsewhere and I am immersed in them. Without wishing it, I find myself in the valley at Neu Herrnhut. The first person I meet is of course the excruciating Christian David with his five-sided face.

Gottes Frieden, Herrn Egede, the German says in greeting. He invites me inside.

I'm sorry, I haven't the time.

Schade, he says, the pompous codfish.

We remain standing a moment outside. I cannot wrench myself away, my assertion thereby contradicted. The place is magnificent, drenched in sunshine, sloping lazily and lushly away towards an inlet. I see vines, I see olive trees, I see an apple orchard. Then blink my eyes and see the empty land. Such room there is here, plenty enough for a whole town. More light than over on our own narrow spit with its rocky shores. Why did we not place our colony here? We could have established ourselves in any number of places far superior to where we ended up. I cannot even remember the reason for choosing the most dismal location on the peninsula.

Is it not susceptible to wind and weather? I ask, as if to find some objection to the place.

It was shown to us by the Lord.

Yes, I see. Of course.

And how are things in the colony? he asks.

Well. Thank you.

Have things settled down there?

Yes. Sort of.

One reaps as one sows, he says, and smiles.

He takes out his knife and begins to sharpen it against a strop of hide. He wipes the blade on his trousers and tests it with a fingernail before returning it to its sheath.

Two more Germans have arrived with the most recent ship. Now they are five in the little house. Besides the two who have moved here from the colony, Johan and Sise. I wonder how they pass the time. There are no natives here. The few Greenlanders who are left have been hostile to the Germans. I suppose they sing their hymns, I think to myself. To sing just one would most likely take up a whole day. A whole day of blood and oozing wounds. Working themselves into a frenzy, wallowing in their gory accounts of the Lord's sufferings. It ought to be outlawed.

Anyway, I was only passing. I turn and go up over the rocks.

Gott mit Euch! he shouts after me.

Gleicherweise!

I wander through the tin-grey heather, I leap over silvery pools, I clamber up the crumbling red slopes, I walk along the ridge where the wind comes sweeping from the north, and descend to the harbour on the eastern side of the peninsula. The merchant ship the *Caritas* lies at anchor in the roadstead. Denmark. Right before my nose. She sails in a few days. In only a few short weeks she will cast anchor in the roadsteads of Copenhagen. The wind is westerly in the autumn. The voyage home will be swift. The distance back to the homeland varies according to the seasons, sometimes it is three months away, other times three weeks, sometimes an eternity. A kingdom of dead souls is out there, in the midst of the North Atlantic. One must cross the Styx in order to return home.

I sit down and stare at the ship. They are loading her now with cargo. I could go on board, lie down in a bunk, sleep through the voyage. I could easily sleep a whole month. But what would I do with myself in Denmark? Does anyone need a missionary there? Can a person ever go back? No. Of course not. And Gertrud would not survive a sea journey. She will not survive the winter in the colony either. Death has got me in its corner. Checkmate. Or perhaps the match is drawn.

I don't know why I begin to think of the old Norsemen who lived here once. What did they do? Did they go back? There is no evidence one way or the other. Did they die out? The notion that the natives did away with them is nonsense. Only he who does not know the Greenlanders could ever think such a thing. Perhaps they waylaid a passing ship and were taken on as galley slaves. Perhaps they are here yet, invisible at our very side. The thought makes me shudder. The whole story of the Norsemen is a conundrum. And I hate conundrums. There is something diabolical about them.

/ / /

I can go anywhere I want. No door can shut me in. Now I go into the room of the priest. I sit down on the bed where his wife lies.

Peace of God, Madame Egede.

Oh, is it you? I was just thinking about you.

I heard you, and it made me want to come and see you. I hope I am not intruding?

No, come here and take my hand. Thank you for thinking of me. How are you, Gertrud? Are you in pain?

No, not really. Apart from some bed sores. They are the source of the smell, for which I apologize. And my legs feel restless. It is as if they wish to be walking all the time. But I haven't the strength for it.

Let me massage your legs. Is that good?

Oh, yes, it's wonderful. Your hands are very soft. I thought the hands of a savage were rough and calloused.

I am not a proper savage. The natives think little of me. To them

I am merely their sorcerer. They are afraid of me, and yet they have no respect for me.

Yes, so it is with you priests, she says with a smile. I'm sure you would have made a good clergyman. You know your Scriptures.

I am reading them again and have come to Job.

You know the Augsburg Confession, I take it?

Every article.

My husband would love you for that.

Yes, if he did not hate me.

It's sad. I sense a gentleness come over you since the death of your poor son.

Yes. He is dead. It was necessary.

It's been a long time since I saw you last. Where have you been?

Oh, here and there. The world is a big place, Gertrud. And I don't mean only the earth.

Tell me what you have seen. Tell me about the world. I can only lie here, an ignorant dying woman.

The planet Pluto has crossed inside Neptune's orbit. It will remain there for the next fourteen years.

How interesting. But so remote. I have no insight into such things at all.

The celestial bodies. Clever minds will learn about them when the time comes.

Tell me something else. Something more down to earth.

The Emperor of China is dying. His son Hongli stands in the wings rubbing his hands.

I see. Yes, that's very interesting too. Here we are on opposite sides of the globe, dying our deaths. But still it is almost as remote to me as the planets and stars. Tell me, who is now pope in Rome?

His name is Clement XII. His predecessor died a few years ago. I knew him.

That would be Benedict? Was he as meek as his name suggests?

Yes, if meek means old and senile. He was eighty years old.

My word, what an age. I shall never catch up. But what is happening in our own world?

Carl Linnaeus has published his work *Systema naturae*.

Who is he?

A Swede.

Has he made a system of nature? What is being said about it?

They say he is elevating himself to the level of God. That he is arrogant. That he scorns the Almighty.

Well, if he is a Swede what else can they expect? But what of Denmark and our king?

Christian holds the throne. A fidgety little weed. A pietist to his fingertips. He wishes his kingdom purged of whoring and depravity.

Does he indeed. The best of luck to him.

He has taken away everything from the former queen, his step-mother. He despises her.

Anna Sophie? Are her children alive?

All are dead. Every last one.

The poor woman.

She shifts her weight in the bed and grimaces. I can tell she has pains in her back and loins. The cushion of the mattress has become quite flattened and her backside rests directly on the wood. I lift her up. She folds her arms around my neck and laughs. Carry me away, she says. Throw me in the fjord. I put her down on a chair and turn the mattress, shaking some fullness into it before lifting her back.

Oh, she groans. How delightful. You are an angel.

I take her hand and kiss it.

In a way you are like me, she says.

Soon, I say. Not long now. We shall see each other again, Gertrud.

I kiss her hand and steal away.

///

How is she? the priest asks when he gets home.

She has been sleeping, I say. But she has been rather restless and has been talking in her sleep.

What does she say?

Nothing I can understand. Nonsense, I think.

He looks like he is concerned and steps up to place a hand on her brow.

Käthe? he says.

Käthe?

Käthe, dear?

He turns towards me.

No, she is sleeping soundly. Her breathing is good. Does she complain?

She was having some pain. It's the bed sores. I lifted her up and fluffed the mattress.

You are an angel, he says. An angel with strong arms. A good job we brought you back with us.

Yes, I say. I'm well here. And very happy.

If we hadn't you'd have been dead, he says.

Yes, I'd have been dead by now.

Like all the others, he says.

I'm very grateful.

Where are my daughters?

Out, I think. They're not here.

Go and find them. Tell them to come home. The smith and the carpenter too. And my sons, if you can find them. Tell them I am giving a service. You must attend too, my child.

I go out into the colony. The sun is shining. I am so glad I cannot help but hum to myself the hymn I love best: 'Let the earth conceal, erase me, worms my very juice devour, fire and water me consume.' I think it is the loveliest of all the hymns.

///

Upon arriving home from a trip in the north, I could see that my mother's condition had worsened. We had been hoping for recovery. But perhaps it is not her wish. She is deathly fatigued, and has been for some time. Last year's epidemic was a blow to her, but even when I returned home from Copenhagen two years ago she was weakened and enfeebled. Plainly there was only one inexorable way for it to go. We must all of us go down the same path when our time comes. I pray to God our Lord that He may make her final journey as easy as possible, not to fulfil my own wish, Lord, but yours, the Almighty's. Amen.

///

September comes and goes. Mother lies in her bed, her strengthless and rather swollen hands folded on the cover. Kirstine, the native girl Katarina and I help each other to wash her, change her bedding, give her food. She will scarcely eat a thing and is annoyed with us when we try to press the spoon between her lips. I'm not hungry, she says. Stop pestering me. You're only making things worse.

But Mother, you must eat something.

Why? she says, and glares at me with one eye.

What am I supposed to reply? Or else you will grow weak? Or else you will die? That is the case anyway. Dear Mother, what shall I do when you are gone? I will be alone with him.

Since she will not allow me to feed her, I read aloud to her. Mostly poetry and hymns, but also some tales, fables and tall stories, and other narratives too from home in Norway. She loves to hear them. Her eyes are quite alive when I read to her. She explains things to me which I find unclear, but which she plainly has grasped. She passes comment and tells stories of her own from her childhood. She asks me if I miss the place of my birth. I can barely remember it, I tell her, I was so small when we left, but I do miss it. Would you like to return there sometime? Yes, I would like to return when our work here is complete. You are sure to find yourself a good husband, she says. A fortunate man. You are a good girl. And you have a fine constitution. You shall live a long and happy life.

And she places her hand on my brow and blesses me.

We have moved her bed into the parlour so that she does not have to lie on her own in the chamber. She watches us attentively and seems quite lucid. But when she sleeps she chatters as if in a delirium, going on about popes and the constellations. She will sit up with her legs crossed and her head in her hands, and I see then how meagre she has become these past few months. Father of course no longer sleeps beside her. He lies on a mattress on the floor. I think of the winter that is approaching, the darkness that lies ahead. If only she can get through the dark time, I think to myself, then there is hope. But I know she is gone. Our mother Gertrud is dying.

Father is the same: stoic, impatient, unloving, irritable, angry. But in a way it is good that he is so. He is the rock. She is the water.

///

I can tell that Father is distraught. Dear Father. Do not be sad. You still have us. You still have me.

He does not show it. He endeavours to be an anchor to us children while everything else crumbles away. While our mother crumbles in her bed. Or rots.

October passes. The colony is sunk into snow. It is cold. The Northern Lights, cast up onto the sky, shimmer among the stars. What are they? The natives say they are the dead playing a ball game with each other. The fishermen back home said they were reflections of great herring shoals projected into the firmament. Others thought them to be old maids dancing and waving their skirts. My father says they are a kind of heavenly storm. I believe him. And yet I am rather afraid of the lights. Afraid that I will become an old maid myself, dancing in the sky to entice the young men I never had when I was young myself.

///

I kiss my mother's brow. How are you feeling, Mother?

I am fine, my boy. Everything is well. You must not worry about me.

Is there anything I can do for you?

You can sit with me a while and hold my hand. Come here, Poul.

I am not Poul. I am Niels. She can no longer tell the difference. But I say nothing.

I sit and hold her hand. A fragile bundle of dry twigs.

What makes that noise?

Her eyes are so clear. But they see something other than this world.

It is the storm, Mother.

No, it is not the storm. It is something within the storm. Can you not hear it?

I hear nothing but the storm, Mother.

What time of year is it?

It is winter, Mother. November.

Ah, November. The month of storms. I have never cared for November. I hope I am not to die in November.

It will soon be Christmas, Mother. Then the light will return.

Read to me, she says. Read to me, Poul.

What shall I read?

Read the Song of Songs.

The Song of Songs, Mother?

Yes, read it to me now.

And so I read: 'Let him kiss me with the kisses of his mouth.' It is not an easy book to read to one's own mother. But I read it from beginning to end. And she lies with her hands folded at her breast and a strange smile upon her lips.

///

In early December a storm removes a great swath of the roof. Every able man, including the new priest, whose name is Bing, me and my sons, Kieding and the officers, toils to repair the damage before the wind demolishes the entire construction. In the midst of this frenzy, the carpenter falls down and breaks his leg.

I keep mostly to the mission room in this time. I pray for the mercy of the Lord. But the Lord it seems is disinclined to show mercy at every request. In the second week of December he takes from Gertrud the power of speech. Thank you, Lord. Some days later she is no longer able to swallow the spoon-food that is pressed between her lips. I bow my head and say my thanks.

Heavy with sorrows and concerns I venture out in blustering darkness and wander the peninsula. I cross the moor, which now is frozen and mantled with snow. The wind has made great drifts of it. My tails flap about me. I let them do as they please. My coat is unbuttoned and open at the chest. And of course I arrive again in the valley of the Moravians. The window of the little house glows warmly with the light of the lamp. I can hear the Germans laughing and talking together and singing their hymns. There is music. I shudder. Hideous! I hear the waves below the house, an ice-cold, relentless thunder. The moon is askew. It tumbles its way through the darkness, casting its dull sheen upon the rocks. The skerries have become visible, secretive and menacing as sleeping whales. I go home again, over the rocks, where the gusting wind dashes me to the ground. I descend to the colony from the north, soaked to the skin.

The next day I am full of cold.

Thank you, Lord!

She is not the only one allowed to be sick. Let her not believe so.

I lie on my mattress on the floor, feeling the draught and waiting to be washed away by pneumonia and fever. But only a short time later my guts cry out for food and I must rise and go to the pantry, where I cut myself some hunks of cheese and bread which I devour ravenously.

18 December, and she begins to whimper. She kicks off the cover, her legs and arms thrashing. We must hold her down to stop her doing harm to herself. She tosses her head from side to side. Froth dribbles from her mouth. I try to force some aquavit inside her, but her attack follows its own rising, falling curve. After a couple of hours she settles and sleeps peacefully. But in the night she wakes up and is restless again.

I am lying on my mattress when suddenly she sits bolt upright like a jack-in-a-box. Her eyes are aglow.

I jump to my feet and call for the children. They gather around the bed, the native Katarina too. Gertrud gasps for breath as if she has been running. She scrutinizes each of us in turn, her eyebrows raised high as if in astonishment. What is she laughing at?

Lie down, my dear. I place my hand upon her chest and try to press her down. She resists. Slowly her eyes turn to me.

Käthe! Are you awake? Speak to me!

The girls too beseech her now with tears in their eyes.

She looks as if she is about to say something. Her mouth trembles and at last she emits some stuttering syllables, though sadly incomprehensible. Katarina places her hands gently on her shoulders, and only then will she lie down.

Distressing scenes which repeat themselves at ever-briefer intervals. She mumbles something. Yet it sounds only like a chatter of teeth. I kneel at her bedside, leaning over her. I pray. I read from the psalms of David and from the Gospels, opening the pages at random and reading to her. I doze and wake up when the book falls to the floor. She sits up again, staring, staring, staring.

Can you not for the love of God die like anyone else?

We must all go the same way.

Why make such a drama of it?

These are the thoughts of fatigue. Desperate thoughts. And when exhaustion and desperation gain the upper hand, one becomes more honest. I must bring it up with my God at some later juncture.

21 December. The darkest day of the year. It begins early in the morning. I wake up with a start at the sound of someone singing. Confused, I get to my feet. It is her. Her voice has returned to her. She sits up in the bed, her face behind the curtain of her hair, singing. Or croaking. I cannot tell what song it is, for her voice is rusty indeed and sounds oddly alien to me. But a song it is. There is no doubt. The girls and the boys gather too.

What is she singing?

Poul's glance meets my own. 'Befiel du deine Wege'.

I join in with it, and a moment later the children likewise, even the native girl Katarina. We stand at the bed and sing the German hymn to the end.

She is calmer then, and lies down again. I feel an enormous relief, though it does not last long. She begins to whimper and wail, kicks off the cover and tries to get out of bed.

What do you want, Mother? the children ask. We give her a night pot, but alas, too late. The bed is soaked. The sheets cannot be changed now, for she is restless indeed, whimpering and thrashing. Clearly she is deteriorating. We manage to lift her up and support her with pillows in her back to ease her breathing. Her head will not follow, but hangs back. Her lungs rattle. I grip her upper body, and her chin drops limply to her chest.

Open the window! I say. She is choking.

An icy wind sweeps into the parlour. I support her head. Her eyes roll in their sockets. She snaps for breath, like a child after a tantrum. Her face is white as a corpse. I feel her press back against my hand as if she wishes to lie down again, only for her spine and legs to arch upwards like a bow suddenly drawn taut.

What do you want? What is it you want?

///

This is strange. Such strength I have all of a sudden. I could do anything. I could punch a hole in the wall if I wanted. I could pull the whole house down to the ground. I think I could fly. And so I rage. It is marvellous. I should have done so before. I have raged far too little in my life. But better late than never. I call for Hans. When he comes I take him by the scruff of the neck and shake him. He staggers this way and that. I hear him shouting: What is the matter with you, dear? Release me! But I will not. I wish to rage. I wish to behave like a madwoman. If not now, then when? I am gripped by a fury. I am unruly, I scream, I piss in the bed, I lash out. But the strange thing is I can stop whenever I want.

///

Now she vomits. It is only bile, though a copious quantity. It runs down her chest. Afterwards, she is settled. We lay her down, change her night clothes and bedding, rolling her from one side to another as we work. Katarina sits down to waft air into her face with a length of linen.

I flop into a chair, trembling with emotion. When will it be over? Lord, release her.

The girls sit together on the bench and are half asleep. Poul stands at the foot of the bed, an anguished smile stuck to his face. Niels sits staring into space with watery eyes and his clay pipe unlit in his hand.

I ask Kieding to let her blood. He will not. I have taken enough already, he says. Besides, there is no point. Medicine is dead.

The calmest of us is the native girl, Katarina. There is an angelic peace about her, her imperturbable smile, her loving solicitude. It soothes me in fact to watch her. A converted heathen. I cannot even recall baptizing her. Most likely it was one of the other priests. She is Mary Magdalene. Perhaps I should marry her. The opportunity will be there. Soon.

And now Gertrud is stricken by an attack, the tremors of her body conveyed not just to the bed, but so it seems out into the entire room. She sits up abruptly like a puppet in a Punch-and-Judy show, and winks at us twice, as if she were about to entertain us with a funny story. And then she lets out a roar, not unrestrainedly, but tentatively almost, as if she wished to test her voice. Poul stands stiff with fright at the foot of the bed. Niels gets to his feet. The girls are awakened. I hold her hand.

It is a lengthy attack, the longest so far. We must hold her down. Arms, legs, torso, every part of her shakes violently, and she foams at the mouth. Katarina dabs her brow and wipes her lips. The boys lie with all their weight on top of her legs.

Let her kick, I say. But keep hold of her legs in case she hurts herself.

It helps. The boys allow her some freedom of movement, making sure she avoids the bedposts. Instead she kicks upwards into the air. The boys hold her by her skinny, mottled calves.

///

I run. It feels wonderful. It feels like flying. I run up the Reinspælen at home, all the way to the top, where I spin around and around and see the whole of Lofoten spin in the opposite direction, and then I run back down again. I run with my arms spread out at my sides, and I could fly if I wanted, but I would rather run, for it feels so very much more compelling. Now I run across the Kvæfjord, splashing as I go. Jesus could walk on the water, but I can run. I run up the bank on the other side, and I cannot stop, because if ever I stop I will not be able to start again. And so I keep moving, my legs are like a great stampeding reindeer herd, and I feel the earth about to drop away beneath my feet, I reach the peaks and run from one to another, leaving the land behind me as I run. And I will not stop, I will never stop, because if I do . . .

///

She perspires heavily, I say. We must take off her shift.

Now she is naked. She is kicking still, but her movements now are more fatigued.

Gertrud! Do not be afraid, my dear. We are with you, all of us.

She gasps for air, turns her head to the side and up, and draws back her lips, revealing her bare gums. It is as if she is opening her mouth as wide as she can, not to swallow something, but to let something out, as if her whole skeleton will wrench itself loose and emerge crawling from her gaping jaw. I shake my head. Keep a grip on yourself. Now she begins to tremble again. Her pelvis arches into the air and falls back again heavily. This repeats itself several times, and then there is an almighty crash, a startled voice cries out, and I turn to see the shelf with the fine porcelain on it has fallen down and all the porcelain lies shattered about the floor, but again my eyes meet the imperturbable gaze and smile of Katarina and I turn back to Gertrud. Now she collapses, her face becomes expressionless, her chin droops at her chest.

She is asleep, I say. For however long. Let us hold a service. Poul, will you read to us from Ecclesiastes, chapter three?

///

I find the page in the Bible and begin to read: 'To every thing there is a season, and a time to every purpose under the heaven. A time to be born, and a time to die. A time to plant, and a time to pluck up that which is planted. A time to kill, and a time to heal. A time to break down, and a time to build up. A time to weep, and a time to laugh. A time to mourn, and a time to dance. A time to cast away stones, and a time to gather stones together. A time to embrace, and a time to refrain from embracing. A time to get, and a time to lose. A time to keep, and a time to cast away. A time to rend, and a time to sew. A time to keep silence, and a time to speak. A time to love, and a time to hate. A time of war, and a time of peace.'

I close the book. We say the Lord's Prayer together, then sit about for ourselves, each to his own, dozing. An hour passes, and then another half, and there is life in the bed again. A new attack begins.

Father draws me aside and whispers: Something is wrong. Why does it persist? Where does she find the strength? And that shelf, the broken dishes?

A shudder goes through me as I realize where his thoughts are going.

He whispers again: We must perform an exorcism.

Father, for goodness' sake. I smile, barely believing he could suggest such a thing.

I mean it. I sense there is something here, perhaps not within her, but a presence. Something evil.

But that is medieval nonsense, Father.

Perhaps, perhaps not. But I feel it to be right. Are you so omniscient as to do nothing and run the risk?

///

My father and brother have stepped over to the window. They stand in a whispered exchange. He who whispers, lies. What are they up to, I wonder. Christ, they are like two peas of a pod! The outlines of their two faces together, their two beaks against the grey light from the window, form the image of a goblet.

///

But what does an exorcism involve? I ask him. It is not taught at the university.

A service, my father says. An entire service, hymns, prayer, the Communion. He shall not withstand it.

Who?

. . .

Ah, I understand. Well, I suppose it can do no harm.

We set about it. I ask Niels to ring the house bell three times and to conclude with the evening strokes. I say the introductory prayer. We sing a hymn of Kingo's, and Father turns to those gathered, which is to say us, his children and the native girl Katarina, with the words, The Lord be with you. As we join in mumbling the words of the Apostles' Creed – We renounce the Devil – Mother emits a scream.

Continue! Father commands us. Continue without pause. Continue until I tell you to stop.

I sit down with her. I splash water on her face as I mutter the baptismal ritual. Behind me the others too rattle off the Creed: We believe in God the Father almighty.

The liturgy is somewhat disorganized on account of Mother being unsettled. We sing, we say the Prayer of the Church and the Prayer of the Holy Communion. I adopt my priestly voice and chant: The crucified and risen Saviour, our Lord, Jesus Christ! I must raise my voice, and then shout as my mother's screams continue unabated. She sounds enraged, like an animal cornered, and I fall into doubt. Can there really be truth in what my father says? I see that she snaps at him and tries to bite his hand. This is indeed abnormal, I think to myself. This is not my mother.

///

I deftly avoid her attempt to bite me. But then the thought occurs to me that she has no teeth, and I allow her to do as she wants. I feel her wet gums slide over my knuckles, then clamp around my index finger, whereupon she clenches her jaw and bites down hard. I give out a howl of pain, prompting the others to halt in their proceedings. With some difficulty I force open her mouth and withdraw my digit, and she belches, emitting the foulest smell from her oral cavity.

Do not pause. Go on, in the name of the Lord!

Poul pronounces the Benediction, raising his voice to be heard: *The Lord bless you and keep you!*

I wrestle with her. Now I know she is indeed possessed. There is no longer a doubt. Such strength could never be hers alone. She screams unceasingly.

The Lord make His face shine upon you!

What forces are at work here? Her strength is beyond belief. Even the smith would be hard put to hold her down.

The Lord lift up His countenance upon you!

I must adjust my grip, and for a moment she is released. Immediately I realize I have made an error. From the corner of my eye I see her glare at me with malice.

And give you peace!

///

I see my father struck on the jaw with tremendous force. My goodness, he seems almost to be lifted from the floor, his figure describing an ungainly backwards somersault before landing in a crumpled heap on the floor.

Amen!

The voice is Poul's.

Father!

Kirstine's.

What happened?

She kicked him.

Father, are you there?

///

I hear their concern, and it is a delight. They are truly fond of me. I thought they hated me. I endeavour to speak, take care of your mother, children, I shall take care of myself. But I can utter not a word. There is something wrong with my organs of speech. And then I am consumed by darkness.

///

Such tumult. Such noise and commotion. How comical it was to see her send him flying across the floor. They all turned to see it. They cried out his name, they shook him, they wept and were quite distraught. The only one who remained with the sick woman was me. I whispered to her, whispered loving words of the Resurrection. She relished them. Her eyes became still, and she ceased to scream. I kissed her on the mouth, and she kissed me back. The kiss of death is the best of kisses, it sends ripples of warmth through my body. I help her, though it is barely required. It does not take much. Fingers pinching the nostrils. It is allowed. And I see her soul press its way out of her ear and flutter like a winged angel beneath the ceiling before finding the window and vanishing into the darkness. Farewell, my angel.

///

I come to and look up into Niels's face.

Niels? Stop shaking me like that. What's the matter with you. What are you crying for?

It's Mother, he sobs.

What is it with her?

She has passed away. Mother is dead.

Is Mother dead? It comes as a most unexpected shock. When did this happen?

A moment ago.

I scramble to my feet, gradually coming to my senses, and stagger over to the bed. Gertrud lies peacefully, her folded hands and the crucifix placed on her chest. I lean over her, not entirely without fear that she will sit up and begin to shout at me, and kiss her cheek. It feels wax-like already, as if she has been dead a day and a night. I stand for a moment and look at her. Almost thirty years. The expression with which she leaves us resembles most of all a smirk.

///

We lay the body under stone on 30 December, to be exhumed at some later date. It is a sad ceremony. I perform it myself. The prayers, the readings, the hymns, the sprinkling of the earth. This is between us, I think to myself, it is not the business of any other. I have a cloth wound around my head and have pressed my wig down to conceal it, though it extends also below my chin. The jaw is broken. I have difficulty speaking. I do not think the congregation grasp a word I utter. But you do.

9

Saint Hans

To-day it did please the all-wise God, in addition to all other misfortune and hardship accorded me in Greenland, also to sadden me with the calling to Him by her death of my dearest wife.

FROM HANS EGEDE'S JOURNAL, 21 DECEMBER 1735

He stares with hostility at what he has written. What kind of pious drivel is this? he asks himself. Why do I not write what I truly mean? God is wicked! Yes, that is the truth.

He scribbles it down and feels relief, only then to be gripped by terror on seeing the words before him. He smudges the ink with the side of his hand to obliterate them. But God saw what he did. It cannot be revoked. What am I to do? Crumple the page? Burn it? Start again. Discard everything. Eat humble pie and pray to Him. But why? He knows me already. And what I write, I write to myself, not to Him.

He kneels and prays. But all that will come to him are charges and accusations. Why her? Why not another? One of the girls? Or Niels? He could cope with Niels dying. Even Poul, for that matter. Why does He strike me where He knows I am most vulnerable? Is it my punishment?

His father, Poul Hansen Egede, was the sorenskriver at Senja, the judicial authority there. He it was who condemned the witch he saw burned at the stake from his hiding place under Gertrud's skirts. He saw it all, through the fabric of her shift, crouching between her feet, clinging to her legs and weeping inconsolably. Gertrud was more than twenty years old, he but a child. The tent-like darkness and the warmth beneath her skirts made him feel safe and protected.

His father, Poul, came from Denmark, from Vester Egede on the island of Sjælland, a clergyman's family, though he travelled to the north of Norway as a young man, where he married Hans's mother,

Kirsten Hind. Hans was their eldest son. Theirs was, to put it kindly, a modest home whose economy was dependent upon the fishing. Less kindly put, they were poor, struggled with debt and its attendant worries, constantly beleaguered by the bailiffs, all of which made him a troubled child. In some way he thought it to be his fault that the family were in such straits. His father had made it clear to him that he too had a responsibility to shoulder. He wished him to make something of himself, and plunged the family into more debt in order that his son receive an education. He came under the tutelage of a priest by the name of Peder Hind, a brother of his mother, later another, Niels Schielderup at Hamar in the south, a different world entirely, the weather oddly calm, the landscape gentle and mild, rolling hills and sun-baked valleys. He felt like a stranger. He yearned for home, to storms, sea-fog and the smell of fish. But he clenched his jaw and completed his schooling, moving on to the university from where he graduated in theology in record time, though with rather average grades. And then he returned to the north.

Had it been up to him he would have studied law and perhaps have become procurator. It would have suited his temperament so much better. But his father wanted a priest. Besides, theology was a shorter course of study, and therefore cheaper. And in all the time he was away, at first in the homes of the two clergymen, later in Copenhagen, he felt the same sense of dislocation. He discovered early on that the idea of the world and the world itself were two different things. He wished to do something about it. But apparently the world did not.

His father died not long after. On his deathbed he told his son of the guilt he felt at having sent him away. It was a heavy sacrifice, he said. But I felt it to be the Lord's will.

He married Gertrud and was assigned as pastor to a parish at Vågan. Here, he was more of a stranger than ever. He quarrelled with the sognepræst under whose authority he served, as well as with the former pastor's old widow whom he would not marry. Open conflict. Accusations. Tribunals. Penalties and reprimands. Poverty. Debt. He wished only to get away. Not just to another parish in Norway or Denmark. But to somewhere much, much further away.

They were visited by Gertrud's brother Niels from Bergen. He had been a ship's officer on some voyages to Greenland. He told them about the country. To Hans's mind, it seemed far away indeed. Sufficiently so. This is where God wants me, he thought to himself. Greenland shall be my calling!

It turned out otherwise. He came here to find the old Norsemen, and God gave him only impossible savages. Yet he took on the task with all his heart, with all his soul and physical strength. And no matter what happened, he knew that Gertrud was there with him. Sometimes when they were on their own he would crawl under her skirts and crouch there a moment. Nothing bad could happen to him there.

But even Gertrud changed. She too became a stranger. Her skirts became out of bounds. And then, at the very end, almost at her moment of death, her foot came flying out of those same skirts and crushed his jaw. It is painful to him still, the side of his face is blue and yellow and he has difficulty chewing his meat.

Someone said to him: The Devil is you!

Who was it? Was it Niels? What did he mean by it?

It is true, of course. Though with a single correction: The Devil is *in* you. The Devil is in us all. The struggle with the Devil is always an internal one. Unless one is a priest. For then one must also confront the Devil in others.

It is unfair, he thinks. That my own son should speak to me in such a way. I have always been a good father, I know I have. I am not like my own father, who in his own words sacrificed me and sent me away. The ungrateful so-and-so!

If indeed the words came from Niels? It sounds like Niels. He has always been rather contrary. The dunce. Perhaps he really does feel I have let him down? That I have sacrificed him? But in what way? Certainly not in the way of Abraham and Isaac, a story he has turned in his mind a thousand times these last months.

And God tested Abraham. He said: 'Take now thy son, thine only son Isaac, whom thou lovest, and get thee into the land of Moriah, and offer him there for a burnt offering upon one of the mountains which I will tell thee of.'

What kind of a God would demand such a thing? A loving God? He whom we call our Father? Whoever would ask us to sacrifice what is dearest to us of all, our own child? A despot. A pitiful and envious tyrant who cannot bear that we should love anyone more than we love him. And who therefore would take that person away from us.

He has never understood the story of Abraham and his son. Always he has been in doubt as to what it tells us about the nature of God, but he has never spoken to anyone on the matter, not even to Gertrud. It would have been a most uncomfortable discussion.

Nevertheless, the words are there: Take your son Isaac, take him to the land of Moriah and make a burnt offering of him there.

And Abraham obeys him. He saddles his ass. He cleaves the wood for the fire. He says to his son, we are going on a trip, as casual as you like.

Even at that point Abraham has already sacrificed him. There is no way back. The treachery has occurred. Isaac knows nothing of it yet. But Abraham knows, and God knows too. God delights. He rubs his hands in glee. God thinks: Stone me, he's actually going to do it! It seems I could get him to do just about anything. I shall make him my people's leader.

When Abraham comes to the place, he says to his servants: 'Abide ye here with the ass, and I and the lad will go yonder and worship.'

He takes the wood and gives it to Isaac to carry.

What theatre! How heartless! Isaac still knows nothing of what is to happen. He is happy to bear the wood on his shoulder. As Jesus shouldered his cross. The same story repeated. But perhaps he begins to suspect. Surely he senses how silent his father has become? Or is Abraham cold-blooded enough to remain unmoved? Whatever, Isaac says: 'Behold the fire and the wood. But where is the lamb for a burnt offering?'

You might well ask, poor boy.

But Abraham replies: 'My son, God will provide himself a lamb for a burnt offering.'

My son? Does he really say that? He is standing there with the knife at the ready and speaks to him with tenderness and love? How cold can a person be?

And they come to the place which God has told him, and Abraham builds an altar there, lays the wood in order, and binds Isaac his son and lays him on the altar upon the wood.

Father, what are you doing?

I cannot lie to you any more, my son. You are the lamb for the burnt offering. I am going to stick my knife in you and burn you on the fire to please God.

But why? the boy cries.

Because God told me to.

Is this what they said? They must have said something to each other, even if the Bible does not report it. And I cannot imagine they could have said anything else.

Abraham stretches forth his hand and takes the knife to slay his son. That's what it says. But then an angel of the Lord calls unto him out of Heaven: 'Abraham, Abraham. Lay not thine hand upon the lad, neither do thou any thing unto him, for now I know that thou fearest God, seeing thou hast not withheld thy son, thine only son from me.'

And Abraham looks up, as if in a dream, and sees a ram caught in a thicket by his horns. And he takes the ram and offers him up for a burnt offering in the stead of his son. And God blesses Abraham for his obedience and multiplies his seed as the stars of the heaven and the sand which is upon the sea shore.

But it is all too late. Abraham has already sacrificed his son. He did so days before, back in the settlement when he cleaved the wood and saddled the ass. He has already lost him.

What would have happened if he had refused? If he had said no, I will not give you my son, you can have anything else but not him? Then God would surely have punished him, his son would have been smitten with sickness or struck by some misfortune, and then what good would his defiance have done? He has no choice. He can agree to sacrifice Isaac, and Isaac will die. He can challenge God's instruction, and Isaac will die.

If the story was to have any value, it ought properly to have run as follows:

Two days later, Abraham saw the place in the distance. He shouldered the wood for the offering and went up onto the mount with his son Isaac, tied him to the altar and took out his knife without listening to the boy's sobbing and pleading for his life. The angel of the Lord then cried out to him: Stop, what the devil do you think you're doing, man! Look, there's a ram behind you! That's your offering. But Abraham ignored the angel of the Lord. He took out his knife and without a word cut the throat of Isaac and killed him, then burned his body as a sacrifice to please the Lord.

There you are, Lord! There's your sacrificial lamb.

In that way he would have taken guilt upon himself.

Yes. It is the only conceivable solution.

And Abraham saddled his ass and returned home, and everyone could see the blood on his clothing, they could see his despair, and they understood what had happened.

I wonder what Sarah said?

What did she say when Abraham came home with Isaac still alive and she realized that he had been about to make a burnt offering of him?

What would she have said when he came home alone, with Isaac's bloody tunic and the boy's blood on his knife?

I can find no way out of this labyrinth.

Out of this darkness.

What am I to do?

What am I to say?

And to whom shall I say it?

God is wicked.

Yes, it's you I'm talking to.

There is no other solution to the conundrum.

I hate you.

There, it is said.

///

His jaw hurts still. Even in February, even in March. The bone is crushed. He has difficulty eating. Mostly he ingests spoon-food accompanied by sour ale. He eats alone. He feels oddly exposed when others see him eating. He cannot read. Luther has become dust in his mouth, or a hard bone from which all the filaments of meat have been chewed. He too is gone, my old friend from Wittenberg. God, gone. Luther, gone. Gertrud, gone. And Frederik Christian is gone too. Egede is still here, or what is left of him. He who dreamed of a life far, far away.

In the fifteen years he has been in this land he has never suffered the scurvy. Now the symptoms come creeping. The bloody smile that results from the necks of the teeth bleeding, the gums then swimming in blood. Not that he is inclined to smile much. One night he wakes up coughing, with the feeling of being suffocated or drowning. He raises himself onto his elbows and coughs up an amount of mucus. He looks down at himself. His nightshirt is covered in blood. Apparently he has suffered a nosebleed and the blood has run backwards into his throat. He places a lump of ice on his nose. The bleeding stops. He lies down on his side and falls asleep again. When he wakes up the sheet too is soaked in blood.

He gets up and washes himself. The loss of blood has invigorated him in the way of a blood-letting procedure. And yet he feels miserable. He feels that life is meaningless.

How you sigh, Father, the girls say.

It is something he has begun to do increasingly. He tries not to, but it is as if something collects in him, accumulating until it must be expelled in a long and drawn-out sigh. It helps a little. But then everything accumulates again, like a bubble rising through water to burst upon reaching the surface.

He feels exhausted. He would prefer to lie in his bed and doze away these dark winter days. But he knows it to be a slippery slope, and forces himself to pursue his wanderings about the peninsula. He still gives his sermons. He preaches to the natives who are now returning after the epidemic. One day when the weather is still, Niels sails him out to the Kook Isles where a new settlement of natives has established itself. He speaks to them. The usual stories of grace and salvation. It all sounds to him like a tired repetition of things he has already said in the past and with much greater conviction.

He has lost his faith in the word, but preaches it nonetheless. It is a sin. But who cares?

The natives who know him from before have heard he has plans of returning home.

I feel I have grown old, he says frankly. As you too will grow old. This is not a land for old men. And you couldn't care less anyway about what I tell you.

He hears the bitterness in his voice. But it is not in fact directed at them. They are but simple heathens. They know not what they do. It's me there's something wrong with.

They say: But we want to believe. We want to come to Jesus.

He regards them wearily. Is there a shaman among you? he asks.

A man says: I was once an angakkok. I worshipped the false gods. But not any more. I want to worship Jesus.

I knew a shaman once, Egede says. Aappaluttoq. Do you know him?

Yes, but we don't know where he is, they say. We don't know where he's hiding. We have nothing to do with him.

If you see him, tell him I should like to talk to him.

Is he to be put in chains and taken to Denmark? they ask. Is the King going to punish him?

No, he will not be put in chains. I just want to talk to him.

He trudges down to Neu Herrnhut. Some peat-huts have been erected, and some tents. The Germans have prospered this past year, and he knows they have plans to indiscriminately baptize natives as soon as their followers are sufficient in number.

What purpose can such mass baptism serve? he asks David. They barely know the Lord's Prayer.

Lieber Pfarrer Egede, David replies. As you know, we believe in conversion. The rest will come later.

But if they know nothing about what they say they believe in, what value is there then in their faith? There will be neither head nor tail in it.

True faith comes to him who truly wishes it, David replies.

And how do you know if it is true?

Jesus sees the heart.

But it is you who performs the baptism?

Jesus commands me.

I see, he says resignedly. And how, pray, does the Saviour convey his wishes to you, David?

He speaks to me quite normally, as we are speaking now.

I see. And he knocks about these parts, does he, our good Lord?

Yes, of course.

A smile broadens the German's pentagonal face. It is a rather unpleasant smile. A smug smile. A cold smile. I know something you don't, it says, and there's nothing you can do about it. Egede has a good mind to box his ears. But he knows it would provoke only an even wider smile of the same sort. Which he, Egede, would but deserve.

May I offer my condolences to Herrn Pfarrer for his loss?

What loss?

His wife?

Ah, yes. Thank you.

She was a good woman.

Yes, her faith was true.

I do not doubt it.

You should rather have discussed these things with her than me. She would have put you straight about some of these confused ideas of yours.

I am sure, David says piously. A true believer will always be a good teacher.

Hm.

I hear it was a difficult death?

Yes, though death is never easy. Particularly for those it leaves behind.

She is with Jesus.

Indeed.

You should not be so sad, Pfarrer Egede. You should be happy.

Oh, but I am. On her behalf, of course. But the rest of us remain. And the good Mr David knows, I am sure, that to mourn is only human.

How many are left of those you christened here? the German asks.

Some. Though many were lost to the pox. They are with God now. His voice is hollow and vacant.

One would certainly hope so, David says smugly. You are aware, of course, that we Moravians consider the truest Christians to be those converted to our own faith.

Yes, it has dawned on me. I suppose we are all of us heathens in your eyes?

Oh, it is hardly that bad. Anyone may be saved. Even Catholic fathers. But I think it harder for a heathen to enter the gates of Heaven than for an unconverted priest. The natives are so true and pure at heart. When they are happy, they are happy indeed, and when they are not, they are not. There is no pretence. They are as innocent babes.

The words are Egede's own. He has uttered them so many times before. Now suddenly they seem to him to be the most dreadful drivel.

He gazes absently at the fjord as the German lectures him about the pure-hearted Greenlanders. He has no intention of arguing with him. Instead he says: You can invite this hard-hearted priest to one of your services.

David pales. I think not, he says, embarrassed.

Why not?

I am afraid that Herr Pfarrer would not come with the right intentions.

What intentions would I come with, in your opinion?

To sneer at us. As you have sneered at us all along. The German's voice trembles slightly. I know you have written to the Missionskollegium. Reported us. Cast aspersions on our integrity. Highlighted our failures, with no mention of anything good in our work.

I see. And have you not written such letters about me?

I have written to the Count von Zinzendorf. He is my spiritual adviser. Of course I have written to him.

And to King Christian?

Well, just the once.

Perhaps we have both erred, he replies with a mildness that surprises even himself.

Yes, we are imperfect, Herr Pfarrer. We make mistakes. And we Moravians are not learned people. There is much of which we are ignorant. But in our faith we are pure. We have found a new path to

salvation and it is not an easy one. It is not the well-trodden path of
the priests, the Church, the apparatus of established Christianity. We
are the new reformers. We seek a reformation of the Reformation. I
am certain Luther would look upon us kindly.

He would kick your arses, says Egede, and smiles.

You established Christians are afraid of us, says David. It makes
you angry. You understand that we are the new. We are the new
Christian faith. Nothing can stop us. You call us heretics and
preachers of false doctrine. You condemn us as the papacy condemned
Luther. This is the new age, Pfarrer Egede. And sadly you do not
belong to it.

And in that, he says to himself as he traipses back to the colony,
Christian David is absolutely right.

///

On the night of 3 March he wakes and sees a stately white figure
standing at his bedside. An elderly man with a long, prophetic beard.
He lies there for some time staring up at this figure, more paralysed
than frightened. Eventually he manages to whisper: Speak to me.
Who are you? But the ghost is of the silent kind. When he sits up
and lights the lamp, the figure melts away like steam.

In the morning he is unable to rise. Something presses him down
into the mattress, like a fat person lying on top of him with all his
weight. He gasps for breath and feels his heart race beneath his ribs.
Now I am dying, he thinks to himself. I am suffering a paroxysm, a
stroke. He tries to call for the girls, but can utter only the feeblest
croak. He can hear them downstairs. They are in the parlour chatting.
Life. The comfort of the quotidian. And here I lie, struggling against
the vastness of the universe.

His gaze moves about the ceiling. He waits for something, though
knows not what. A crisis of some kind. Perhaps sudden darkness. Or
an absence of everything, even the dark. He wonders what it will be
like. He tries to fold his hands, but cannot manage even a prayer.
Oddly, he feels very strong. Almighty, almost. I could reach up and
crush the timber beams into kindling, he thinks. I could wrench
myself from my mortal frame and fly away. I could wreak havoc

wherever I go, push people into the sea, light fires, demolish entire houses, go about the colony and kick every structure to the ground. But no, best to lie here and wait.

The girls are there. They stand at the bed.

Did Father speak?

Shh, he's asleep.

He seems restless.

He's shaking. Pull the covers over him and make him more comfortable.

I hope he's not ill now too.

He has ailed ever since Mother died.

No, leave him be.

He's not worth it.

Did you know he has begun to worship the Devil?

What? I had no idea things were that bad.

I've heard him muttering to himself, *Ave Satanas*.

Oh, that's bad.

There's not much we can do.

He is lost.

A good thing Mother is no longer here.

She would die of despair.

She knew very well what he was like.

Yes, and she said so too.

Your father is a murderer, she said.

And a thief.

He stole her book.

God has abandoned him.

That's why she kicked him like a horse.

Now you can lie there, you murderer.

Murdering scum.

They spit on him. He is startled, but cannot move.

Let's put a pillow over his face.

Let's throttle him.

No, no! he shouts out, or croaks, or thinks. Spare me, children! Mercy. I am your father. Do not make yourself murderers on my account. Let me lie here and die in peace.

It seems they cannot hear him. They are chatting in the parlour. I have been dreaming, he tells himself. It is all a dream. In a moment I shall wake up again. But can a person dream that they are dreaming? When I was a boy I suffered often from nightmares. Especially after seeing the witch burned at the stake. But I found a way out of those terrible dreams. I remember now. I had to find a certain boundary with a gate in it, and if only I climbed the gate and sat on top I would wake up. He searches his mind for a suitable location and proceeds to climb the gate with difficulty. In the dream too he is old. The old man I saw at my bedside was me, he thinks to himself. There is no doubt, this must be death now.

He remains in bed for many hours, perhaps a whole day. The children look in on him at intervals. He is rather afraid of them. But they act and speak normally, with no hint of the condemnations heaped upon him that morning. Kieding, now an ageing, bearded man, comes and measures his pulse, lifts up his eyelids, prods him here and there.

I can find nothing wrong with him, he says. His pulse is rather high, but that's all.

He swims about in a strange state of semi-consciousness. The children are there, they come and go, or else they sit in the parlour. Now and then their voices descend into conspiratorial whispers, slander, perfidiousness, rising then again into more normal volume. The clock strikes the hours, ponderous and homely. Home is where the clock strikes. As long as the clock ticks there is life. He hears sounds from outside, people talking, sheep bleating, the lowing of one of the new heifers, a creaking of floorboards upstairs, Kieding's heavy footsteps, the colony bell ringing the mealtimes. What bothers him most is the heavy beat of his heart. It feels like fear. But what is there to fear? He is not concerned about dying and couldn't care less about Hell. The bad things have already happened. Nothing can touch me now.

He endeavours to pass the time by reciting passages of the Bible. The psalms of David: 'Lord, how are they increased that trouble me! Many are they that rise up against me. Many there be which say of my soul: There is no help for him in God. Selah.' Selah? What does that word mean? He has never thought about it before. Is it Greek? Hebrew? 'But thou, O Lord, art a shield for me. My glory, and the lifter up of mine head. I cried unto the Lord with my voice, and he heard me out of his holy hill. Selah.' There it is again. What a strange word. A secret code? 'I laid me down and slept. I awaked, for the Lord sustained me. I will not be afraid of ten thousands of people, that have set themselves against me round about.'

A visitor to see you.

Petronelle.

He gives a start.

Who is it? he asks, though only a squeak passes from his throat. His eyes dart about the room. And then he sees who it is.

Ah, there you are, he says. Come here to me. His voice now is regained, albeit weak.

The man steps forward to the bed. He holds a three-cornered hat in his hand, is clad in old and worn-out clothes, like a bankrupt petty official retired to his cats and poverty. The seams are in tatters, buttons hang loose and padding peeps out of the shoulder fabric. He smiles.

Yes, here I lie. It is all I can do.

Is the priest ill?

I don't know what's wrong with me. Perhaps a minor stroke. I am not entirely young. Can you hear me when I speak?

I hear every word.

Are you real? He reaches out a tentative hand. His visitor takes it and presses it between his own.

As real as a person can be, the visitor replies.

Your hands are warm. How is the weather outside?

It rains today. But the wind is still.

Well, that's always something. And now you have come to see a poorly man?

Yes, I heard the priest was ill and wished to visit him.

I'm not sure if I remember who you are. Perhaps you can jog my memory?

That shouldn't be necessary, the man replies with a chortle.

He peers up at him uncertainly. Are you family?

I am your father, boy, the visitor replies, now somewhat put out.

Father? he says disappointed. Then I am dreaming. I thought you to be real. What do you want with me?

I wish to speak to you about a matter.

Then speak. He feels at once impatient and annoyed.

Or rather, I wish to ask you a question. Or perhaps pose a conundrum.

A conundrum, I see. I hate conundrums. But let me hear.

It's a theological matter. I am rather unsure as to whether you might be able to provide an answer.

Why should I not? I am a priest.

Here it is: If Jesus Christ is the son of God, how can he be one with him in the Holy Trinity?

That's easy. As the head and the hand are parts of the same body, the Lord and his son are parts of the same trinity.

Well, there you are. Now I see. Many thanks, Mr Egede.

You're welcome. But why do you call me Mr Egede?

What else should I call you?

Usually you call me boy or my son.

Who do you think I am?

You told me yourself, he says with increasing annoyance. You are my father.

I am not your father. You must have been dreaming.

Who are you then?

I am Bing.

Bing?

Bing.

Bing who?

Andreas Bing. The new missionary. I have been here nearly a year.

Yes, all right, I know who you are, he snaps. Have you come to give me the sacrament?

No, I hope that will not be necessary. I have come merely to—

He cannot hear what the man says. Angle the clocks?

Angle, tangle, bangle, fangle.

Now everything is a muddle again, he sighs. If only it soon were night. Tomorrow I shall either be dead or well again.

He feels a hand be placed on his arm. It startles him.

Who are you?

I am Aappaluttoq. Frederik Christian's father.

Oh. Is it you?

They said you wished to speak to me, says the shaman. And now I am here.

How did you get in?

Your son the priest let me in.

What do you want? I am not well. Everything is a muddle to me. I am having trouble distinguishing between dreams and reality.

You seem lucid enough, the other man says. I wanted to talk to you about my son, or our son, if you like.

He says nothing. He has feared this encounter and this conversation. Now he is silent.

I just wanted to say that I have found some peace after what happened, the man says.

Yes?

And I wanted to ask if the same applied to you. If you have found peace, that is.

How can one find peace after such a thing? he says.

One must accept that what happens, happens. There is no evil in the world. There is no Devil to whom we can give the blame. But life is like a great cart that is driven forward, and sometimes something falls off the back, sometimes someone gets run over.

If there is no evil, how can there then be goodness? he replies, sensing that he is drifting away into fantasy again. But no matter, he thinks.

Life is good, the man says. I believe in life.

Then perhaps evil is death?

Yes, but it is an impersonal evil. We cannot be angry with death, for death is only ourselves when we are no longer living.

To us Christians, death is good, albeit painful. Prepare ye for death, we say. For the heavenly life awaits.

Do you think he is there now?

Your son? He thinks long and hard before replying: I hope so. I administered the Holy Communion to him that night.

But he whored and drank himself into intoxication. Was he not what you call a sinner?

Many Christians are, I fear. But the thing about Christianity is that one may be forgiven.

How is one forgiven?

One must ask for forgiveness with a pure and sincere heart.

I wonder if he did before it was too late?

I don't know. I did what I could.

And what about Purgatory?

Well, he says cautiously. Purgatory is a papist construction, though I am no longer quite so sure about it. Perhaps sometimes a person must endure a time in Purgatory. In order to be cleansed. But compared to Eternity it is nothing.

He died a violent death. It must have come unexpectedly to him, if I might say. What significance does that have in the grander scheme of things?

I think the Lord will be merciful.

Perhaps he is already in Heaven?

It is not unthinkable.

Then I am ready to become Christian, says the man. Will you help me in that, priest?

No, I will not, he says politely. It would not be appropriate. Go to my successor, the Pastor Bing. He will surely instruct you and administer to you the sacrament of baptism should he find you suitable. Or else go to the Moravians. They will take you on the spot.

Farewell, priest.

Farewell, my child.

Father. Father?

What is it now?

Wake up, Father. You're delirious.

It is Poul. He stands over the bed, shaking him.

I was dreaming, that's all. Give me some cold water.

How are you feeling?

A bit peaky. Nothing serious. Let me sleep.

He gulps the water, then descends into slumber again. When he wakes up, the bed chamber is filled with the light of spring. He thinks it must be late afternoon. He hears the fire rumbling in the stove next door. There is a smell of food. But when he makes to climb out of bed he finds he is still unable to move. Such torment! How long will it last? He opens and closes his mouth like a fish. Not a sound comes out.

He is hungry. It must be two days since he ate.

Kirstine!

Petronelle!

He can hear his voice. But apparently they cannot.

He reaches out as if to find something to rattle, to make a noise and alert them to come. His hand trembles violently. He puts it under the covers and lies on top of it.

'Have mercy upon me, O Lord, for I am in trouble. Mine eye is consumed with grief, yea, my soul and my belly. For my life is spent with grief and my years with sighing. My strength faileth because of mine iniquity, and my bones are consumed. I was a reproach among all mine enemies, but especially among my neighbours, and a fear to mine acquaintance. They that did see me without, fled from me.'

Kirstine! Kirstine!

His hand has extricated itself and bats the air, feels its way across the ceiling, the walls, the window, reaches all the way into the parlour and waves desperately. But they see it not. They let me lie here and die.

'My God, my God, why hast thou forsaken me? Why art thou so far from helping me, and from the words of my roaring? O my God, I cry in the day time, but thou hearest not, and in the night season, and am not silent. But I am a worm, and no man, a reproach of men, and despised of the people. All they that see me laugh me to scorn, they shoot out the lip, they shake the head. I am poured out like water, and all my bones are out of joint. My heart is like wax, it is melted in the midst of my bowels. My strength is dried up like a potsherd, and my tongue cleaveth to my jaws, and thou hast brought me into the dust of death.'

Water! he groans.

'For dogs have compassed me, the assembly of the wicked have inclosed me, they pierced my hands and my feet. I may tell all my bones. They look and stare upon me. They part my garments among them, and cast lots upon my vesture.'

For pity's sake, help me! I am dying! Lord, why are you doing this to me? What have I done to deserve it?

'Then the Lord answered Job out of the whirlwind, and said: Who is this that darkeneth counsel by words without knowledge? Gird up now thy loins like a man, for I will demand of thee, and answer thou me. Where wast thou when I laid the foundations of the earth? Hast thou commanded the morning since thy days, and caused the dayspring to know his place? Hast thou entered into the springs of the sea? Or hast thou walked in the search of the depth? Canst thou bind the sweet influences of Pleiades, or loose the bands of Orion?'

And so on.

It is true. What am I? Nothing. Everything is of no matter. What a relief!

'O give thanks unto the Lord, for he is good, for his mercy endureth for ever . . . The Lord is on my side, I will not fear . . . Thou hast thrust sore at me that I might fall, but the Lord helped me . . . I shall not die, but live, and declare the works of the Lord . . . The Lord hath chastened me sore, but he hath not given me over unto death . . . O give thanks unto the Lord, for he is good, for his mercy endureth for ever.'

Reciting scripture is like praying, it soothes him in the same way. He feels a fever come washing through him. He shivers and trembles. Presently his breathing settles and he feels the crisis to be over. He falls asleep.

In the evening he gets up. His legs wobble beneath him. But he can walk.

I am hungry, he says. Is there anything to eat?

Niels has killed a reindeer, says Petronelle. We have roasted a hindquarter.

He sits down at the table. Poul says the prayer, but before they can say Amen he is already devouring the meat ravenously.

That was a long nap you took, says Poul. You nearly had us worried.

///

He recovers to be well again. But he is not himself, whoever that might be. He finds himself smiling mildly and indulgently at things which previously would have sent him into a rage. He near frightens the life out of Niels by embracing him lovingly and kissing his brow. He pats native children on the head and is moved to tears. The stoic and cantankerous priest of old in his black cassock seems to have wandered off into the country's inner wastelands. He weeps at the drop of a hat.

As the sunshine of spring melts the snow from the peninsula, he ascends to the moor and plucks angelica and scurvy grass which he munches with great pleasure. He goes early to bed and sleeps into the mornings. He regains his strength, but scarcely preaches, content to leave the task to the Magister Bing. The nightmares which have haunted him since boyhood are gone. The sun bakes down on the colony. It is midsummer. They make ready for departure. His books are gathered in great piles in the parlour, waiting to be packed. He picks volumes at random and flicks through the pages. At least half are Luther. The Catechism, the Augsburg Confession, the table talks, the sermons, and all the rest. Black, dusty, moulding volumes. He cannot abide to read even a single line.

///

In his farewell sermon, 29 July 1736, he reads from Isaiah: 'I have laboured in vain, I have spent my strength for nought, and in vain. Yet surely my judgement is with the Lord, and my work with my God.'

The resigned self-righteousness of the text does not accord with his mood. He is in fact glad.

The Germans are there for once. They look shabby and rather the worse for wear, bedraggled birds of passage blown astray by a storm. The winter has been hard on them too. They sit lumped together at the rear of the mission room, smiling pharisaically. He says goodbye to them with a kindness that is genuine and wishes them well.

The crisis is over. The winter is over. A new summer has begun. Never has the colony appeared more delightful. The *Caritas* lies in the harbour. Charity. He is going home.

///

Ten days later he steps on board. Niels, Petronelle and Kirstine accompany him, along with the aged and broken Master Kieding. The coffin containing the body of Gertrud is consigned to the hold. Only Poul remains behind together with the new pastor, Andreas Bing. The captain, Didrik Mühlenfort, is deathly ill. He is rowed out to the ship lying on a stretcher. Now all passengers and crew are in place. The colony folk stand on the shore and gaze out at them. Now they are divided in two: those leaving and those staying.

The sails are hoisted, the anchor lifted. The ship drifts a moment before finding its direction and gathering momentum. The colony cannon pound a salute, boom, boom, boom! A great number of natives follow the ship in their boats. The women are singing. What a fine and proud people, he thinks.

///

I am Aappaluttoq. Now the priest is gone and I am alone. I can see him out there, standing on the deck and looking back, like Lot's wife. I take off my hat and wave to him, and he raises his hand and returns my salute.

Farewell, priest. You think it is over now. You think the struggle is past. So it is for you Danes. For you, Greenland is something which has a beginning and an end, something to which you travel and later leave. But for us who belong here it is different. For us it never ends. Greenland is our land, and our life from cradle to grave. For us the struggle is not past, but barely begun.

EPILOGUE

I was born here. I am a Dane born in Greenland, the only one of us born there then who is still alive. Now I am returned. My parents are living still, two grey old people settled in the valley of the Moravians, my father Johan, a German former Geworbener of the Fynske Land Regiment, and my mother Sise, a mender of shoes in her previous life. They have a delightful little house there, with glass windows, a thatched roof, a chimney and good timberwork, a proper landworker's house. But they are free people, in the thrall of neither margrave nor bailiff. I am their only child. I think I made my mother infertile when I was born.

The first people of the colony's earliest time, the pioneers, are mostly dead now I suppose. Old Egede married again the year after his return home, though died some years ago at Stubbekøbing. I read the notice in the *Københavnske Posttidender* in which was printed a splendid epitaph. His son Poul is now Provost of Greenland, though he lives in Copenhagen where he also lectures at the university and teaches at the Missionskollegium. The youngest son Niels is here in this country where he has established several new colonies, among them the new colony of Holsteinsborg, to which I have been called as missionary. The two Egede girls are both alive and married. Governor Pors I assume to be dead, if not he will be more than eighty years old now. He continued a long military career after his return from Greenland and retired an old man to his farm in northern Jutland. I think he has no children, and is the last man of his family.

I came to Denmark as a small boy. I do not know the reason. Perhaps it was because of all the children born in the colony I was the most viable. How fortunate I was as the child of two former inmates to be given the same opportunities as a good son of the middle class. I came into the home of decent people, the sognepræst at Maarslev on Fyn, Herman Oxbøl, who took me to him and treated me as his own, since he himself was childless. When my childhood came to an end and I still was healthy in mind and body, it was decided I should pursue a life in religion. I was admitted to the Latin school at Assens, subsequently passing the *examen artium* at Copenhagen University in 1752 whereafter I commenced to read theology. After four years of study I passed the theological degree with the distinction of *laudabilis* and then gave my matriculation sermon to the bishop, Peder Hersleb. I spoke upon Luke, chapter two, on the subject of the lost and then found-again Saviour, and was awarded the second-class grade.

I knew where I was from. I wrote letters to my parents at Godthåb, though I was unable to remember them. Nor could I remember anything of my early childhood in Greenland. All I knew was that Greenland existed and it was where I was from. My foster-father, Oxbøl, who was always a true father to me, had never hidden from me that I was adopted. I returned to the rectory after passing my exam and worked there as deacon under the supervision of the sognepræst, my adoptive father. I was biding my time, waiting for a suitable living to be assigned to me. There are more priests than parishes in the Danish kingdom. Oxbøl thought I should have to wait until he himself passed away and then take on the incumbency in his place. One day, however, a man came to Maarslev rectory. This was Poul Egede, son of Hans Egede, Provost of the Greenland mission. He knew who I was, and must have spoken to the sognepræst about the matter. He remembered me from the time I was a small child living in a peat dwelling. He told me of the Mission, of the colonies up there, and about the land in general. I felt something stir inside me. I did not know quite what it was, but it felt like a longing for home. Something slotted into place in my mind. Images from my earliest childhood flared in my mind's eye: I was running in the colony, I was visiting savages in the tents, I believe even that I recalled my mother and father. Poul Egede squeezed my arms and prodded me, and asked me various questions which made me feel rather self-conscious. He asked me about my spiritual state, and whether I suffered fits of any kind. He is healthy as an ox, my foster-father said. Poul Egede was a friendly, if rather inquisitive man. His language was often strong, though not in any offensive way. The conclusion of his visit was that he told my stepfather that he found my constitution to be good and that in his opinion I was made for the Mission in Greenland. Thus, that same autumn I was enrolled in the Greenlandic seminary, where I also received instruction in the Greenlandic language.

I returned briefly to Maarslev when my adoptive father was old and sick, but in 1761, shortly after his death, I made the voyage to Greenland and was then back at Godthåb. I felt myself to be home. I have now been here almost two years.

///

One day in June I walk from the colony and cross the moor to the valley of the Moravians to pay a visit on the German brethren there and my parents. They have invited me to take part in one of their celebratory services, which are always just that: a celebration. The weather is very fine. A pale sky. Sea and fells, green pastures. There are many native boats on the fjord, laden with people and goods and belongings, all on their way out into the skerries. Small kayaks dart forwards amid whirling paddles, some carrying a passenger, the kayak man's wife seated with her back to him on the stern. The slender vessels are weighed down by it, and it looks like each couple are sitting back-to-back upon the water itself.

I enter the valley, and there lies the imposing new house with its bell-tower and two-storey wing, Greenland's largest building. After difficult beginnings, the Germans have seen *einen großen Erfolg* these past twenty years. Between the main house and the shore lies the kitchen garden where they cultivate vegetables, apparently with some success. Mostly beet and other such hardy roots, I imagine. Flanking the main house are the brethren's dwellings, among them my parents' own little half-timbered house, the food store, the timber store, stables and other structures. Moreover, some several score of native peat-huts and a large number of tents have been risen. It is a veritable town they have established here. Smoke rises from a hundred chimneys and smoke-holes. I think there must be some four hundred people living here, Danes, Germans and natives. And still they come.

Ever since the days of Egede, the Moravian tendency to such great congregations has met with opposition from the royal colony. The criticism is that it removes the natives from their natural hunting grounds and thereby inhibits the yield, which is to say the opportunities for trade. The risk of famine is also increased. But one has to say that the Germans have been proficient at bringing the natives together, much more so than we Danes. I think it is because of their principles of equality. They refer to each other as 'brother' or 'sister' regardless of standing. And the pietist liturgy, more sensitive than the Lutheran, probably appeals more to the Greenlandic nature than our own, which in comparison may seem dispassionate.

I am received heartily by the people there. Nothing remains of the old animosities between Danes and Moravians, and a number of the Danish priests have even drawn nearer to the emotions of the pietistic faith in their own practice. I am treated to freshly boiled salmon and a compote of angelica. I eat with a ravenous appetite and afterwards I join in the festivities. The men take part in wrestling matches and various other competitions, such as the tug-of-war, arm wrestling, and walking on hands. I acquit myself satisfactorily. A beauty contest is held among the women, though in quite a different form than is known in Denmark: the woman lies face-down on the ground, whereupon her husband sits with his full weight on her head and wriggles his behind to grind her face into the earth, the woman who is then able to get to her feet without displaying a nosebleed being declared the winner. After the games songs are sung, one of them in Greenlandic, for several of the baptized Greenlanders have begun to write hymns, and they are beautiful indeed. Some of the Germans play instruments: the lute, the dulcian, the flute, the fiddle. However, there is no dancing. The Moravians consider dancing to be a sin and quite diabolical.

A church service is held in the open, there being far too many people to crowd into the mission room. Twenty-five natives receive the baptism. They kneel in a row and the Moravian missionaries douse them with water, bless them and place their hands on them, whereupon they receive the kiss of peace. It is a very powerful ceremony. I cannot help but think of the very earliest age of Christianity when the first congregations grew forth in Palestine and Greece. There is something of the same pioneering spirit here. Many of those baptized swoon after the ceremony, all burst into tears, some jabber in delirium. The Moravians applaud these reactions and encourage them.

///

A day or two later I am visited by an elderly native man who says he wishes to be baptized. I invite him into the mission room. He is friendly and quiet and tells me with a smile and in good Danish of his life as a heathen. He was an angakkok, one of the sorcerers with whom Egede was forever at loggerheads, though he informs me he has long since retired. I ask him to tell me about his practice. I find it interesting, I tell him, for the angakkoks were the natives' priests before Christianity came to this country.

Oh, but this is not a thing to be talked about with any pastor, he says. It is a kind of evil. The angakkok enters into evil in order that others may be protected from it. It is his most important task. But there is much else to being an angakkok. A lot of it is theatre, he says, and sends me a sly grin.

Have you committed murder for it? I ask him. I must know if I am to baptize you.

I have occasioned some deaths, he says. And have taken life myself more than once. It is a long time ago, but I will not lie to you.

Are you sorry for your deeds? I ask him.

Yes, he says. I have been sorry every day for many years.

God will forgive you if your repentance is true.

So I can still be baptized?

Yes, my child. Of course.

He laughs. I think he finds it funny that I, who could easily be his son, refer to him as my child.

It is normal for us priests to address people in this way, I tell him, regardless of age.

Yes, I know, he says, now shuddering with laughter, eyes narrowed to slits by his mirth. Presently he composes himself and asks where I am from, and about my family. I tell him about the two old people who live with the Moravians, and about my foster-family in Denmark. He listens attentively.

I take out my pipe and my tobacco pouch. Do you smoke?

He produces his own pipe. It is carved from ivory, perhaps the tusk of the narwhal. We fill our pipes with tobacco and smoke in silence.

You look like a Greenlander, he says in his forthright manner. Has anyone ever told you?

Yes. I have heard it said many times. In Denmark I have been called both *skrælling* and blackamoor. It is my slanting eyes. I have them from my mother. And my dark hair is from my father.

You must not be ashamed of looking like a Greenlander, he says sternly.

Wishing to change the subject, I ask him what Christian name he wishes to take. You may keep your native name, but most wish to adopt a Danish one.

I want a new name, he says. But I will not say it before the baptism.

He regards me with a wry smile. How long will you be here with us, Lauritz?

Not long. I am called to the new colony in the north. Holsteinsborg. I am to go there in the autumn.

It is a beautiful place, he says.

Have you been there?

Yes, I have been everywhere.

I will prepare you for the baptism, I tell him. But later, when I am gone, you must go to my successor for your continued instruction.

Yes, I understand.

Unless you would prefer to join the Moravians?

No, I prefer to stay with your kind. It is where I belong, I think.

I am pleased to hear it.

Our conversation continues for some time, with much silence and pipe-smoking in between. But eventually he gets to his feet and I ask him to join me for instruction in the mission room the following Saturday along with the others I am preparing for the baptism.

Thank you, my child, he says, and laughs good-naturedly before shaking my hand and leaving.

///

He does not live long, the old man, but is baptized before his death. I perform the ceremony myself as the ship which is to sail me to Holsteinsborg has been delayed for a number of reasons. Throughout his instruction he shows himself eager to learn and is already able to both read and write. It is clear too that he has read the Bible and the Catechism, for he can recite great passages after having been read them only a single time. A week after I have baptized him he passes away in his sleep, presumably of old age. There seems to have been nothing else the matter with him. And thus it falls to me to bury him too. I feel the strangest sorrow as the final stone is placed upon his grave. A complete stranger whom I have known only these past couple of months. I still have his pipe. He wished me to inherit it. On his cross is written the name I gave him in the baptism: Abraham Greenlander. Of course, no date of birth is written, for he knew not even the year, though I assume it to have been in the last century sometime.

///

I have felt a great joy these past days. I know not quite where it comes from. Something of it is my excitement over the fact that I shall soon be going to the new colony and taking my place there as its first incumbent, a momentous occasion indeed. But there is something more inside me which has gradually unfurled, a quiet sense of happiness. I have been invigorated with a great feeling of industry and zest these past weeks. I have travelled in the skerries and missionized for the natives there. I have given services for the folk of the colony. I have instructed both children and adults. I have been in and out of people's homes and have been a good counsellor of souls.

Late in October the boat lies ready to take me out to the hooker the *Lovisenborg*. My parents are there to wish me farewell at the shore. Both weep uncontrollably. They have learned from the Moravians to give their emotions free rein, and I must say they are certainly not inhibited in any way. My mother Sise gives me provisions to take with me for the journey, enough for several weeks. She does not believe there to be good Christian food for a man up there. I kiss her goodbye, and then my father, before leaving my two elderly parents behind. Will I ever see them again? They stand at the edge of their graves, but stand nevertheless, hand in hand.

The weather is chilly, though clear and still. It has been a fine summer. The captain elects to sail the sheltered waters this side of the skerries, the small ship being highly manoeuvrable, and moreover we have Niels Egede aboard as pilot. At the Hope Isle we cast anchor and I go ashore with him. Little is left of their old settlement but a broken-down shed and the site of a house.

This is where it all began, Egede says. Here we lived, more than twenty people in this small house. The air was forever a raw mist. I know he speaks the truth, for it is thus still. But I remember the sunshine. Oh, good Lord, such a long time ago it is now.

And your father, the Pastor Egede, I ask, what was he like?

My father, he repeats, and stares dreamily across the grassland where we sit. He was a good and caring man. I loved him. We all did.

///

I commend myself now to God, as they say. I stand upon the deck of the *Lovisenborg* and watch the land glide south as I myself glide north. Further and further into the depths of the conundrum we call Greenland. Are my bones to find rest here? I think so, and I hope it too. Some yearn for southern climes. I have always yearned to the north. As Niels Egede said to me today as we stood together on the deck: Go north, my friend, then sooner or later you will arrive home.

Lauritz Johanssøn Oxbøl
    On his way to the colony of Holsteinsborg
        This fifteenth day of October, the year 1764 of our Salvation

List of Characters

Hans Egede, missionary (phonetically, the surname might be transcribed for an English speaker as [ˈiːjəˌðə], otherwise approximated as 'ee-uh-the', with primary stress on the first syllable).

Gertrud Rasch, his wife, affectionately referred to as Käthe (Katie) by Egede (cf. Katharina von Bora, wife of Martin Luther, whom Luther often called by the same name).

Their children: Poul, Niels, Kirstine, Petronelle.

Aappaluttoq, 'the Red One', a shaman.

Frederik Christian, also called Paapa, son of Aappaluttoq, Egede's foster-son.

Albert Top, a former missionary of the colony, now departed.

Frederik IV, King of Denmark and Norway.

Anna Sophie, his queen.

Ulrik Adolf Holstein, Count of Holsteinborg, former page to the King, now Grand Chancellor.

Henrik, an emancipated African slave, a so-called 'blackamoor'.

Johan Hartman, a deserter.

Sise 'Petticoat' Hansdatter, a sewer of shoes, sweetheart of, and later married to, Johan Hartman. Her first name might be pronounced [ˈsiːˌsə], or 'see-suh', with stress on the first syllable.

Claus Enevold Pors, Major, appointed Governor of the Colony at Godthåb.

Skård, an Icelander, Pors's valet. Pronounced to rhyme with 'sword'.

Peter Hageman, a convict.

Katrine Olofsdatter, 'Cellar-Katrine', his wife.

Jørgen Fleischer, Paymaster of the colony.

Jürgen Kopper, Trader of the colony.

Ole Lange, priest.

Henrik Balthasar Miltzov, priest.

Didrik Mühlenfort, ship's captain.

The jomfru Titia – full name Anna Dorothea Titius – Pors's housekeeper, 'jomfru' [ˈjɒmˌfruː], 'yom-fruh', being a form of address for a young, unmarried woman of undistinguished social status.

Jørgen Landorph, Commandant.

Christian Kieding, Physician-surgeon of the colony.

Thomas Tode, also referred to as 'Knife-man', barber-surgeon, Kieding's assistant.

Søren Fuchs, Apothecary at Køge, Denmark.

Jens Smith, smith of the colony.

Matthias Jochumsen, explorer.

Just, Matthias's brother.

Knud, Matthias's son.

Carl, a Greenlander boy who travels to Denmark and then returns.

Christian David, a German Moravian.

Matthäus and Christian Stach, cousins, German Moravians.

The jomfru Katarina, a young Christian woman of Greenland.

Lauritz Oxbøl, a young missionary.

Martin Luther, the Reformer.

Satan, Beelzebub, Lucifer, the Devil.

Afterword

This book is a fiction. It runs closer to actual historical events than its predecessor *The Prophets of Eternal Fjord*. But it should not be read as a reliable historical account, for it is most certainly not. Most of the characters in the novel were real people and appear under their own names. While I have made use of their biographies, of which several may be found online, I have also taken considerable liberties with them. Many of the events that take place in the novel took place in the real world too, though of course many have been fabricated to suit my own purposes. Often there is greater truth and economy in fiction than fact. I found a precise and vivid account of the period to be Louis Bobé's biography of Hans Egede. Mads Lidegaard's *Grønlændernes kristning* (The Christianization of the Greenlanders) provided a more concise review, while Finn Gad's *Grønlands historie* (The History of Greenland) was also enlightening. I made good use of all three of these books, as well as several more noted in the bibliography.

I refer with some consistency to 'the Danish colony' and to 'the Danes' who live there, though most were in fact Norwegians and a number were Germans. Since however they were subject to the Danish king, I found it convenient to refer to them accordingly as one.

Fiction writers and historians – sorcerers and scholars – do different things. We do best not to encroach into each other's domains. How many historians have written novels of literary merit? How many novelists have produced historical research good enough to pass through academic peer review? Not many, I imagine. And yet, as my list of acknowledgements attests, we depend on each other. Let historians write histories then, and let novelists write stories. I do the latter.

Kim Leine

Hafnia, this year of our Lord 2017

Bibliography

Some of the books I have consulted – for inspiration and research:

The Holy Bible. The passages cited are from the King James Version.

Roland H. Bainton: *Here I Stand. A Life of Martin Luther.*

Louis Bobé: *Diplomatarium Groenlandicum.*

Louis Bobé: *Hans Egede. Grønlands missionær og kolonisator* (English version: *Hans Egede: Colonizer and Missionary of Greenland*).

Hans Egede: *Omstændelig og udførlig Relation.* The various chapters of the novel are introduced by means of a quote from Egede's work, though with many alterations to both language and content.

Hans Egede: *Det gamle Grønlands nye Perlustration* (English version: *A Description of Greenland* https://www.gutenberg.org/files/58308/58308-h/58308-h.htm). The italicized quotes contained in the chapter 'A Minor Perlustration' are from here.

Poul & Niels Egede: *Continuation af Hans Egedes Relationer fra Grønland.*

H. M. Fenger: *Bidrag til Hans Egedes og den grøndlandske Missions Historie.*

Niels Fenger: *Palasé. Hans Egede i Grønland.*

Peter Freuchen: *Hvid mand* (English version: *White Man*).

Finn Gad: *Grønlands historie* (English version: *The History of Greenland*).

Marie Hvidt: *Frederik IV. En letsindig alvorsmand.*

Søren Kierkegaard: *Frygt og Bæven* (English version: *Fear and Trembling*).

Kathrine & Thorkild Kjærgaard: *Ny Herrnhut i Nuuk 1733–2003.*

Klaus Larsen, *Dødens teater: Lægekunsten i Danmark 1640–1840.*

Linda Lassen, *Håbets år.* With the author's kind permission I have borrowed a scene from here.

Mads Lidegaard: *Grønlændernes kristning.*

Martin Luther: *Bordtaler* (English version: *Table Talk*).

Hother Ostermann: *Nordmænd paa Grønland 1721–1814.*

Hother Ostermann: *Danske i Grønland i det 18. Aarhundrede.*

Heinz Schilling: *Martin Luther. Rebel i en opbrudstid* (English version: *Martin Luther. Rebel in an Age of Upheaval*).

Frederik Stjernfelt: *Syv myter om Martin Luther.*

Leonora Christina Ulfeldt: *Jammersminde* (English version: *Memoirs of Leonora Christina, Daughter of Christian IV of Denmark; Written During Her Imprisonment in the Blue Tower at Copenhagen 1663–1685*). Titia's letters are a paraphrase on the book's preface.

Acknowledgements

First and foremost I would like to thank historian Hans Christian Gulløv, who is especially knowledgeable about the time and place in which the events in this novel occur, for kindly having taken the time to read through the manuscript and weed out mistakes which without his invaluable help would have been all the greater and much more numerous. Any remaining misunderstandings are entirely my own doing.

Thanks are due also to the following institutions:

Danmarks Radio, DR2
The Greenland National Museum and Archives
The Danish Arts Foundation

Moreover, I am indebted to:

Anne Fløtaker
Bente Hauptmann
Bodil Kyst
Camille Blomst
Dan Aleksander Ramberg Andersen
Inge Kyst
Jesper Bonde
Linda Lassen
Mette Mortensen
Randi S. Faye
Sara Marie Røjkjær Knudsen
Signe Zacher Carlsen
Simon Pasternak
Ujammiugaq Engell

Specific to the English translation

The verses of Thomas Kingo's hymns, which appear at various points in the novel, are in John Irons's translation. H. C. Sthen's 'Lord Jesus Christ, my Saviour blest' appears in Harriet R. Spaeth's translation. Other song lyrics were translated and adapted by Martin Aitken.

The excerpts from Egede's journals by which each chapter is introduced are in Martin Aitken's translation.

And a note on units of measurement: a Danish mile was roughly the equivalent of 7.5 km. A *fjerdingvej* or *fjerdingmil* was a quarter Danish mile, or about 1.9 km. An *alen* was 0.628 metres, a *skrupel* (pl. *skrupler*) 0.00018 m.

The translator would like to thank the Danish Arts Foundation, librarian Ann Furholt at Sorø Akademis Bibliotek, and Stine Marie Mortensen.